VIKING

Odinn's Child · *Sworn Brother* · *King's Man*

TIM SEVERIN, explorer, film-maker and lecturer, has made many expeditions, from his crossing of the Atlantic in a medieval leather boat in *The Brendan Voyage* to, most recently, *In Search of Moby Dick* and *Seeking Robinson Crusoe*. He has won the Thomas Cook Travel Book Award, the Book of the Sea Award, a Christopher Prize, and the literary medal of the Académie de la Marine.

TIM SEVERIN

VIKING

Odinn's Child · Sworn Brother
King's Man

PAN BOOKS

Viking: Odinn's Child first published 2005 by Macmillan
Viking: Sworn Brother first published 2005 by Macmillan
Viking: King's Man first published 2005 by Macmillan

This omnibus first published 2008 by Pan Books
an imprint of Pan Macmillan Ltd
Pan Macmillan, 20 New Wharf Road, London N1 9RR
Basingstoke and Oxford
Associated companies throughout the world
www.panmacmillan.com

ISBN 978-0-330-50800-1

Map artwork by Raymond Turvey
Typeset by SetSystems Ltd, Saffron Walden, Essex
Printed in the UK by CPI Mackays, Chatham ME5 8TD

VIKING

Odinn's Child

MAPS

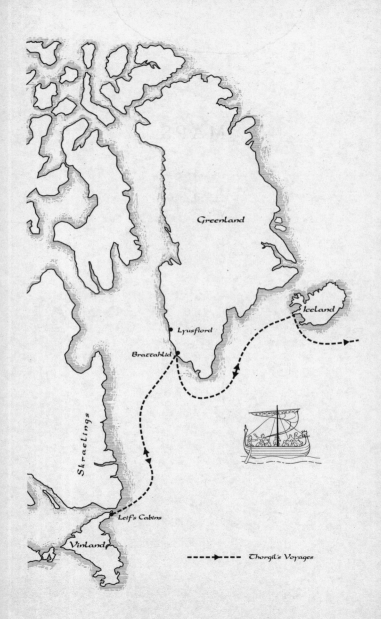

Greenland

Lyusfiord

Brattahlid

Iceland

Skraelings

Leif's Cabins

Vinland

------▶ Thorgil's Voyages

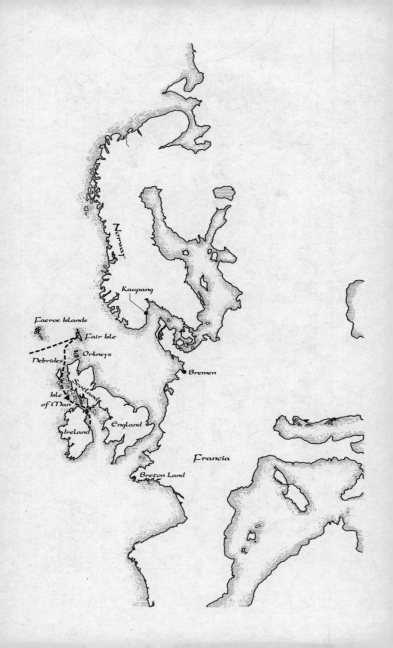

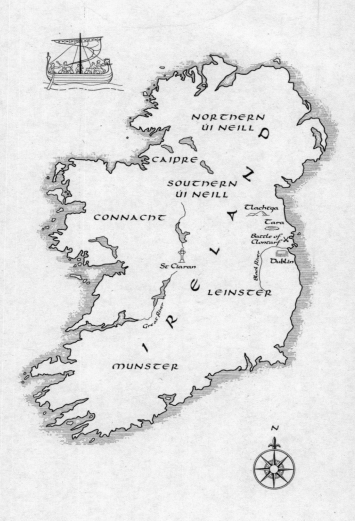

NORTHERN
ÚI NEILL

CAIPRE

SOUTHERN
ÚI NEILL

CONNACHT

Tlachtga

Tara

Battle of
Clontarf

Dublin

St Ciaran

IRELAND

LEINSTER

Great River

Black River

MUNSTER

N

To my holy and blessed master, Abbot Geraldus, it is with much doubt and self-questioning that I pen this note for your private attention, laying before you certain disturbing details which until now have been hidden, so that I may humbly seek your advice. In choosing this course I am ever mindful how the works of the devil, with their thousand sharp thorns and snares, lie in wait for the feet of the unwary, and that only His mercy will save us from error and the manifold pitfalls of wickedness. Yet, as you read the appended document, you will understand why I have been unable to consult with others of our community lest I sow among them dismay and disillusion. For it seems that a viper has been nurtured in our bosom, and our presumed brother in Christ, the supposed monk called Thangbrand, was an impostor and a fount of true wickedness.

You will recall, my revered master, that you requested of your unworthy servant a full and true inventory of all documents and writings now in our abbey's keeping. As librarian of our community, I began this task in dutiful compliance with your wishes, and during this labour discovered the above-mentioned document where it lay unremarked among the other volumes in our collection of sacred writings. It bears no identifying mark and the script is well formed, the work of a trained penman, so — may I be forgiven if I have committed the sin of presumption — I began to read, imagining to find recorded therein a life of one of those saints such as Wilfred of most blessed memory, whose shining and glorious example was so ably recorded by our most learned predecessor, the monk Eddius Stephanus.

But such is the mystery of His ways that I have found instead a tale which often substitutes hypocrisy for truth, depravity in place of abstinence, pagan doubt for true faith. Much I do not comprehend, part I can comprehend dimly and by prayer and fasting strive to expunge from my mind. Yet other – and this is what troubles me – contains notice of many distant lands where surely the seed of truth will flourish on fertile soil if it is broadcast by the faithful, trusting only in God and his sublime grace.

Of the identity of the author of the work there can be little doubt. He is remembered by several of the older members of our congregation, and by subtle enquiry I have been able to confirm that he came to us already an old man, sorely hurt and in need of succour. His learning and demeanour led all our congregation to suppose he was in holy orders. Yet this was but the skill of the arch-deceiver, for this present work reveals the unswerving error of his ways and the falsity of his heart. Truly it is said that it is difficult for a man who has fallen deeply into temptation to emerge from the wallow of his sin save with the grace of our Lord.

Also I have learned how this false Thangbrand spent long hours alone in the scriptorium in quiet and arduous labour. Writing materials were supplied, for he was a gifted copyist and possessed of many artistic skills despite advancing years and fading eyesight. Indeed, his posture, hunched close over his pages, shielded his work from others' gaze and rendered it difficult to overlook what he was writing. But Satan nerved his fingers, for instead of sacred text he was engaged in preparing this dark and secret record. Naturally I have instructed that henceforward no writing materials be provided to anyone without due justification. But whether what has now been written is a blasphemy I have neither the intellect nor learning to judge. Nor do I know whether this work should be destroyed or whether it should be retained for the strange and curious information it contains. For is it not written that 'A much travelled man knows many things, and a man of great experience will talk sound sense'?

Regrettably, two further volumes I hold in safe keeping, presuming them to be a continuation of this blasphemous and wicked memorial. Neither volume have I investigated, pending your instruction. Holy father, be reassured that no further particle of the reprobate's writing exists. I have searched the library most attentively for any other trace left by this pretended monk, who departed unexpectedly and secretly from our community, and I found nothing. Indeed, until these documents were discovered, it was presumed that this pretended monk had wandered away from us, confused in his senility, and we expected for him to be returned by the charitable or to hear that he had departed this life. But such has not happened, and it is evident from this account that this would not be the first occasion on which he has absconded like a thief in the night from the company of his trusting and devout companions. May his sins be forgiven.

On behalf of our community, beloved master, I pray for your inspired guidance and that the Almighty Lord may keep you securely in bliss. Amen.

Æthelred
Sacristan and Librarian
Written in the month of October in the Year of our Lord One Thousand and Seventy

ONE

I SMILE SECRETLY at the refectory gossip. There is a monk in Bremen across the North Sea who has been charged with collecting information for the Bishop of Bremen-Hamburg. His name is Adam, and he has been set the task of finding out everything he can about the farthest places and peoples of our world so that he may compile a complete survey of all the lands known, however dimly, to the Christian Church, perhaps with a view to converting them later. He interviews travellers and sailors, interrogates returned pilgrims and foreign diplomats, makes notes and sends out lists of questions, travels for himself and observes. If only he knew . . . right here in this monkish backwater is someone who could tell him as much about strange places and odd events as any of the witnesses whom he is cross-examining so diligently.

Had I not heard about this assiduous German, I would be content to spin out the last years of my life in the numbing calm of this place where I now find myself in my seventieth year. I would continue to copy out sacred texts and embellish the initial letters with those intricate interlacings which my colleagues believe I do for the greater glory of God, though the truth is that I take a secret delight in knowing that these curlicues and intricate patterns derive from the heathen past they condemn as idolatrous. Instead, their refectory tittle-tattle has provoked me to find a corner seat in

our quiet scriptorium and take up my pen to begin this secret
history of my life and travels. How would my colleagues react, I
wonder, if they discovered that living quietly among them is one
of that feared breed of northmen 'barbarians', whose memory still
sends shivers down their spines. If they knew that a man from the
longships wears the cowl and cassock beside them it would, I think,
give a new edge to that plea which recently I found penned in
the margin of one of their older annals – 'From the fury of the
foreigner O Lord preserve us.'

Writing down my memories will also help pass the time for an
old man, who otherwise would watch the play of sunshine and
shadow moving across the edge of the page while the other
copyists hunch over the desks behind me. And as this secret work
is to keep me from boredom, then I will begin briskly – as my
mentor the brithem, once drummed into my young head more than
half a century ago – and of course at the very beginning.

My birth was a double near-miss. First, I failed by a few
months to be born on the millennium, that cataclysmic year foretold
by those who anticipated, often with relish, the end of the world as
we knew it and the great Armageddon prophesied by the gloomy
Church Fathers of the Christians. Second, I only just missed being
the first of our far-flung race to be born in that land far distant
across the western ocean, scarcely known even now except in mists
and swirling wisps of rumour. It was, at that time, dubbed Vinland
the Good. As luck would have it, my foster brother had the
distinction to be the original and perhaps only fair-skinned child to
come into this world on those distant shores. However, I can claim
that the three years I spent there are about as long a span of time
in that place as anyone from our people can boast, and because I
was still so young they have left their mark. I still recall vividly
those huge, silent forests, the dark water of bog streams lit by the
glint of silver salmon, the odd striding pace of the wide-antlered
deer, and those strange native peoples we called the Skraelings,
with their slant eyes and striking ugliness, who ultimately drove us
away.

My own birthplace was a land on a far smaller scale: Birsay, an insignificant, dune-rippled island in the windswept archipelago off the north coast of Scotland which the monk-geographers call the Orcades. When I first drew breath there, Birsay was home to no more than a couple of hundred inhabitants, living in half a dozen longhouses and sod-walled huts randomly placed around the only large structure − a great long hall shaped like an upturned boat, a design I was to grow very familiar with in later years and in some strange settings. It was the main residence of the earls of Orkney, and the widow of the previous earl, Jarl Haakon, told me of the circumstances of my birth when I visited that same long hall some fifteen years later, seeking to trace my mother, who had disposed of me waif-like when I was barely able to take my first infant steps.

My mother, according to the earl mother, was a massive woman, big-boned, muscular and not a little fearsome. She had green-brown eyes set in narrow sockets under very dark and well-marked eyebrows, and her one glory was a cascade of beautiful brown hair. She was also running to fat. Her family was part Norse and part Irish, and I have no doubt whatever that the Celtic side predominated in her, for she was to leave behind an awesome reputation for possessing strange and uneasy gifts of the sort which trouble, yet fascinate, men and women who come in contact with them. What is more, some of her character passed on to me and has accounted for most of the unusual events of my life.

The earl mother told me that my birth was not an occasion for rejoicing because my mother had disgraced herself. I was illegitimate. Thorgunna, my mother, had suddenly appeared at Birsay in the summer of the previous year, arriving from Dublin aboard a trading ship and bringing with her an impressive quantity of personal luggage, but without parents or a husband or any explanation for her journey. Her obvious wealth and self-confident style meant she was well received by Jarl Haakon and his family, and they gave her a place in their household. The rumour soon arose that my mother was the ill-favoured offspring of one of our opportunist Norse chieftains, who had gone to try his luck in

Ireland and married the daughter of a minor Irish king. This speculation, according to the earl mother, was largely based on Thorgunna's aloof manner and the fact that Ireland abounds with kinglets and chieftains with high pretensions and few means, a situation I was to experience for myself in my slave days.

THORGUNNA LIVED WITH the earl's entourage through the autumn and winter and was treated as a member of the family, though with respect for her size and strength of character rather than with any close fondness. And then, in the early spring of the pre-millennium year, it became obvious that she was with child. This was a sensation. No one had ever considered that Thorgunna was still of child-bearing age. Like most women, she said as little as possible about her age and she was far too fearsome a woman for anyone to enquire, however discreetly. By her appearance it had been presumed that she was in her mid-fifties, barren, and had probably always been so. Indeed she was such a broadly built woman that not until the sixth month was her condition noticeable, and that made the sensation all the more spectacular. The immediate reaction after the first stunned disbelief was to confirm what the sharper tongues had been saying all winter: Thorgunna employed sorcery. How else could a woman of her age be able to carry a child inside her, and how else – and this was the crux of the matter – had she been able to seduce the father so utterly?

'There was never the least doubt who your father was,' the earl mother told me. 'Indeed there was a great deal of jealousy and spitefulness from the other women of the household on the subject. He was such a dashing and good-looking man, and so much younger than your mother. People were hard put to explain how he had fallen under her spell. They said she had brewed up a love potion and slipped it into his food, or that she had cast a foreign charm over him, or that she had him under the effect of the evil eye.' Apparently what infuriated the critics even more was that neither Thorgunna nor her lover tried to conceal their affair. They

sat together, gazed at one another, and in the evenings ostentatiously went off to their own corner of the long hall and slept
beneath the same cloak. 'What puzzled people even more was how
your father became so besotted with your mother less than a week
after he arrived. He had barely set foot in Birsay when she carried
him off. Someone remarked that he looked like a good-looking toy
being seized to comfort the giantess.'

Who was this glamorous traveller, my natural father? He was
a well-to-do farmer and fisherman whose ship had sailed into
Birsay's small anchorage in the autumn while en route from the
farthest of the Norse lands, Greenland. Indeed he was the second
son of the founder of the small and rather struggling colony in that
ice-shrouded place. His father's name was Eirik rauda or 'Erik the
Red' (I shall try to insert an translation wherever appropriate as
my wanderings have given me a smattering of many languages and
a near fluency in several) and his own was Leif, though in later
years I would find that more people had heard of him as Leif the
Lucky than as Leif Eriksson. He, like most of his family, was a
rather wilful, dour man with a marked sense of independence. Tall
and strong, he had tremendous stamina, which is a useful attribute
for any frontier colonist if combined with a capacity for hard work.
His face was rather thin (a feature which I have inherited) with a
broad forehead, pale blue eyes and a prominent nose that had been
broken at some stage and never set straight. He was, people seemed
to find, a man whom it was difficult to argue with, and I would
agree with them. Once he had made up his mind, he was almost
impossible to be persuaded, and though he was capable of retreating
behind a series of gruff, blunt refusals, his usual manner was
courteous and reserved. So he was certainly respected and, in many
ways, very popular.

Leif had not intended to stop in at Birsay. He was on his way
from Greenland to Norway, sailing on the direct run which
normally passes south of the Sheep Islands, which our Norsemen
call the Faeroes. But an unseasonal bout of fog, followed by a
couple of days of easterly headwinds, had pushed his course too

far to the south, and he had made a premature landfall in the Orkneys. He did not want to dawdle at Birsay, for he was on an important errand for his father. He had some Greenland products to sell – the usual stuff such as sealskins, walrus hides, walrus-skin ropes, a bit of homespun cloth, several barrels of whale oil and the like – but the main reason for his journey was to represent his father at the Norwegian court before King Olaf Tryggvason, who was then at the height of his mania for converting everyone to the religion whose drab uniform I now wear.

Christianity, I have noted in my seventy years of lifetime, boasts how humility and peace will overcome all obstacles and the word of the Lord is to be spread by example and suffering. Yet I have observed that in practice most of our northern people were converted to this so-called peaceful belief by the threat of the sword and our best-loved weapon, the bearded axe. Of course, there were genuine martyrs for the White Christ faith as our people first called it. A few foolhardy priests had their tonsured heads lopped off by uncouth farmers in the backlands. But that was in an excess of drunken belligerence rather than pagan zeal, and their victims were a handful compared to the martyrs of the Old Ways, who were cajoled, threatened, bullied and executed by King Olaf either because they refused to convert or were too slow to do so. For them the word of the Lord arrived in a welter of blood, so there is little wonder that the prophesied violence of the millennial cataclysm was easy to explain.

But I digress: Erik had sent his son Leif off to Norway to forestall trouble. Even in faraway Greenland the menacing rattle of King Olaf's religious zeal had been heard. The king had already sent messengers to the Icelanders demanding that they adopt the new faith, even though they were not really Norwegian subjects. The Icelanders were worried that King Olaf would next send a missionary fleet equipped with rather more persuasive weapons than croziers. With Iceland subdued, fledgling Greenland would have been a mere trifle. A couple of boatloads of royal mercenaries would have overrun the tiny colony, dispossessed Erik's family, installed a new king's man, and Greenland would have been swallowed up as a Norwegian fief under the pretext of making it a colony for the White Christ. So Leif's job was to appear suitably eager to hear details of the new religion – a complete hypocrisy on Erik's part in fact, as he was to remain staunch to the Old Ways all his life – and even to ask for a priest to be sent out to Greenland to convert the colonists. I suspect that, if a priest *had* been found for the job, Leif had secret instructions from his father to abandon the meddling creature on the nearest beach at the first opportunity.

Erik also instructed his son to raise with King Olaf the delicate matter of Erik's outlawry. Erik was a proscribed man in Iceland – a hangover from some earlier troubles when he had been prone to settling disputes with sharp-edged weapons – and he was hoping that the king's protection would mean that certain aggrieved Icelanders would think twice about pursuing their blood feud with him. So, all in all, Leif had a rather delicate task set for him. To help his son, Erik devised what he thought could be a master stroke: a gift to catch the royal eye – a genuine Greenland polar bear to be presented to the royal menagerie.

The poor creature was a youngster which some of Erik's people had found, half-starved, on a melting floe of drift ice the previous spring. The floe must have been separated from the main pack by a back eddy and carried too far out to sea for the polar bear to swim to shore. By the time the animal was rescued it was too weak to put up a struggle and the hunters – they were out looking for seals – bagged it in a net and brought it home with them. Erik saw a use for the castaway and six months later the unhappy beast was again in a net and stowed in the bilges of Leif's embassy boat. By the time Birsay was sighted, the polar bear was so sickly that the crew thought it would die. The creature provided Leif with a first-rate excuse to dally away most of the winter on Birsay, allegedly to give the bear a chance to recuperate on a steady diet of fresh herring. Unfortunately this led to unkind jests that the bear and my mother Thorgunna were alike not only in character and gait, but in appetite as well.

That next April, when a favourable west wind had set in and looked as if it would stay steady for a few days, Leif and his men were eagerly loading up their ship, thanking the earl for his hospitality, and getting ready to head on for Norway when Thorgunna took Leif on one side and suggested that she go aboard with him. It was not an idea that appealed to Leif, for he had failed to mention to Thorgunna that he already had a wife in Greenland who would not look kindly on his foreign import. 'Then perhaps the alternative is going to be even less attractive,' Thorgunna continued. 'I am due to have your baby. And the child is going to be a boy.' Leif was wondering how Thorgunna could be so sure of her baby's sex, when she went on, 'At the first opportunity I will be sending him on to you.' According to Leif, who told me of this conversation when I was in my eleventh year and living with him in Greenland, my mother made the statement about sending me away from her with no more emotion than if she were telling Leif that she had been sewing a new shirt and would deliver it to him when it was ready. But then she softened and added, 'Eventually, if I have the chance, I intend to travel on to Greenland myself and find you.'

Under the circumstances my father behaved really very decently. On the evening before he set sail, he presented his formidable mistress with a fine waterproof Greenlandic sea cloak, a quantity of cash, a thin bracelet of almost pure gold and a belt of Greenland ivory made from the teeth of walrus. It was a very handsome gesture, and another speck in the eye for those hags who were saying that Thorgunna was being left in the lurch and was no better than she deserved. Anyhow, Leif then sailed off on his interrupted journey for Norway, making both a good passage and an excellent impression. King Olaf welcomed him at the Norwegian court, listened politely to what he had to say, and after keeping him hanging around the royal household for almost the whole summer, let him sail back to Greenland on the westerly winds of early autumn. As for the wretched polar bear, it was a temporary sensation. It was admired and petted, and then sent off to the royal kennels, where it was conveniently forgotten. Soon afterwards it picked up distemper from the dogs and died.

I was born into this world at about the same time that the polar bear departed it. Later in my life, a shaman of the forest peoples in Permia, up in the frozen zones, was to tell me that the spirit of the dying bear transferred itself to me by a sort of spiritual migration at the moment of my birth. I was reluctant to believe it, of course, but the shaman affirmed it as fact and as a result treated me with respect bordering on awe because the Permians worship the bear as the most powerful spirit of all. Whatever the truth about the transmigration of souls, I was born with a minimum of fuss and commotion on a summer's day in the year my present colleagues, sitting so piously around me, would describe as the year of our Lord, 999.

TWO

SHE CALLED ME Thorgils. It is a common enough Norse name and honours their favourite red-haired God. But then so do at least forty other boy's names from plain Thor through Thorstein to Thorvald, and half that number for girls, including my mother's own, Thorgunna. Perhaps Thorgils was her father's name. I simply have no idea, though later, when I wondered why she did not pick a more Irish-sounding name to honour her mother's people, I realised she was preparing me to grow up in my father's household. To live among the Norsemen with an Irish name would have led people to think that I was slave-born because there are many in Iceland and elsewhere whose Irish names, like Kormak and Njal, indicate that they are descended from Irish captives brought back when men went a-viking.

Thorgunna gave me my Norse name in the formal manner with the sprinkling of water. It might surprise my Christian brethren here in the scriptorium to know that there is nothing new in their splashing drops of water on the infant's head at baptism. The pagan northmen do the same when they name a child and it would be interesting to ask my cleric neighbours whether this deed provides any salvation for the innocent infant soul, even when done by heathen custom.

The year following my birth was the year that the Althing, the general assembly of Icelanders, chose to adopt Christianity as their religion, a decision which led to much dissension as I shall later have reason to describe. So, having been born on the cusp of the new millennium, I was named as a pagan at a time when the tide of the White Christ was beginning its inexorable rise. Like Cnut, the king in England whom I later served as an apprentice court poet, I soon knew that a rising tide is unstoppable, but I resolved that I would try to keep my head above it.

My mother had no intention of keeping me around her a moment longer than necessary. She proceeded to carry out her plans with a massive certainty, even with a squawling baby in tow. The money that Leif had given her meant that she was able to pay for a wet nurse and, within three months of my birth, she began to look around for an opportunity to leave Birsay and move on to Iceland.

She arrived in the early winter, and the trading ship which brought her dropped anchor off Snaefellsness, the long promontory which projects from Iceland's west coast. Most of the crew were from the Orkneys and Ireland and they had no particular family links among the Icelanders to determine their final port of call, so the crew decided to wait in the anchorage until news of their arrival had spread among the farmers of the region, then shift to the ripest harbour for trading to begin. Iceland has always been a country starved of foreign luxuries. There is not a single town or decent-sized village on the whole vast island, or a proper market. Its people are stock herders who set up their homesteads around the fringes of that rugged land wherever there was pasture for their cattle. In summer they send their herds inland to the high meadows, and in winter bring them back to their byres next to the house and feed them hay. Their own food is mostly gruel, sour milk and curds, with meat or fish or bird flesh when they can get it. It is a basic life. They dress in simple homespun clothes and, though they are excellent craftsmen, they lack the raw materials to work. With no forests on the island, their ships are mostly imported ready built from Norway. Little wonder that the Icelanders tend to join viking expeditions and loot the luxuries they do not have at home. Their viking raids also provide a channel for their chronic pugnacity, which otherwise turns inward and leads to those deadly quarrels and bloody feuds which I was to find it impossible to avoid.

Here I feel that I should try to clear up a misunderstanding among outsiders over what is meant by 'viking'. I have heard it said, for example, that the description is applied to men who come from the viks, the creeks and inlets of the north country, particularly of Norway. But this is incorrect. When the Norse people call someone a vikingr because he goes viking they mean a person who goes to sea to fight or harry, perhaps as a warrior on an expedition, perhaps as an outright brigand. Victims of such raids would readily translate the word as 'pirate', and indeed some Norse do see their vikingr in this light. Most Norsemen, however, regard those who go viking in a more positive light. In their eyes a vikingr is a bold fellow who sets out to make his fortune, takes his chance as a sea raider, and hopes to come home with great wealth and the honour which he has won by his personal bravery and audacity.

The arrival of a trading ship at Snaefellsness – moored in the little anchorage at Rif – was just the sort of news which spread rapidly among these rural farmers. Many of them made plans to row out to the anchored ship, hoping to be the first to look over the cargo in her hold and make an offer to buy or barter for the choicest items. They quickly brought back word that a mysterious and apparently rich woman from Orkney was aboard the ship, though nothing was said about her babe in arms. Naturally, among the farmers' wives along the coast this was a subject of great curiosity. What was her destination? Did she dress in a new fashion? Was she related to anyone in Iceland? What were her intentions? The person who took it upon herself to answer these riddles was almost as formidable as my mother – Thurid Barkadottir, wife of a well-to-do farmer, Thorodd Skattkaupandi, and half-sister to one of the most influential and devious men in Iceland, Snorri Godi, a man so supple that he was managing to be a follower of Thor and the White Christ at the same time and who, more than once, was to shape the course of my life. Indeed it was Snorri who many years later told me of the relationship between Thurid Barkadottir and my mother, how it began with a confrontation, developed into a wary truce and ended in events that became part of local folk memory and scandal.

Thurid's extravagant taste was known to everyone in the area of Frodriver, close by Rif, where she and Thorodd ran their large farm. She was an extremely vain woman who liked to dress as showily as possible. She had a large wardrobe and an eye-catching collection of jewellery, which she did not hesitate to display to her neighbours. Under the pretence of being a good housekeeper, she was the sort of woman who likes to acquire costly furnishings for her house – the best available wall hangings, the handsomest tableware and so forth – and invite as many guests as possible to show them off. In short, she was a self-centred, ostentatious woman who considered herself a cut above her neighbours. Being half-sister to Snorri Godi was another encouragement for her to preen herself. Snorri was one of the leading men of the region, indeed in the whole of Iceland. His family were among the earliest settlers and he exercised the powers of a godi, a local chieftain-by-election, though in Snorri's case the title was hereditary in all but name. His farmlands were large and well favoured, which made him a rich man, and they contained also the site of an important temple to the God Thor. Thurid felt that, with such illustrious and powerful kin, she was not bound by normal conventions. She was notorious for her long-running affair with a neighbouring farmer – Bjorn Breidvikingakappi. Indeed it was confidently rumoured that Bjorn was father to one of Thurid's sons. But Thurid ignored the local gossip, and in this respect, as in several others, there was a marked resemblance between the two women who now met on the deck of the trading ship – Thurid and my mother.

My mother came off best. Thurid clambered aboard from the small rowing boat which had brought her out to the ship. Scrambling up the side of a vessel from a small rowing boat usually places the newcomer at a temporary disadvantage. The newcomer pauses to catch breath, straightens up, finds something to hold on to so as not to topple back overboard or into the ship, and then looks around. Thurid was disconcerted to find my mother sitting impassively on a large chest on the stern deck, regarding her with flat disinterest as she balanced unsteadily on the edge of the vessel. Thorgunna made no effort to come forward to greet her or to help. My mother's lack of response piqued Thurid, and as soon as she had composed herself she came straight to the point and made the mistake of treating my mother as an itinerant pedlar.

'I would like to see your wares,' she announced. 'If you have anything decent to sell, I would consider paying you a good price.'

My mother's calm expression scarcely changed. She rose to her full height, giving Thurid ample time to note the expensive cloth of her well-cut cloak of scarlet and the fine Irish enamelwork on the brooch.

'I'm not in the business of buying and selling,' she replied coolly, 'but you are welcome to see some of my wardrobe if that would be of interest here in Iceland.' Her disdain implied that the Icelandic women were out of touch with current fashion.

My mother then stepped aside and opened the chest on which she had been sitting. She riffled through a high-quality selection of bodices and embroidered skirts, a couple of very fine wool cloaks, some lengths of silk, and several pairs of elegant leather slippers – though it must be admitted that they were not dainty, my mother's feet being exceptionally large. The colours and quality of the garments – my mother particularly liked dark blues and a carmine red made from an expensive dye – put to shame the more drab clothing which Thurid was wearing. Thurid's eyes lit up. She was not so much jealous of my mother's wardrobe as covetous. She would have loved to obtain some of it for herself, and no one else on Iceland, particularly in the locality of Frodriver, was going to get the chance to buy it.

'Do you have anywhere to stay during your visit to our country?' she asked as sweetly as she could manage.

'No,' replied my mother, who was quick to discern Thurid's motives. 'It would be nice to spend a little time ashore, and have a chance to wear something a little more elegant than these sea clothes, though I may be a little over-dressed for provincial life. I assembled my wardrobe with banquets and grand occasions in mind rather than for wearing aboard ship or going on local shore visits.'

Thurid's mind was made up. If my mother would not sell her clothes, then at least she could wear them in Thurid's farmhouse for all visitors to see, and maybe in time this haughty stranger could be manoeuvred into selling some of her finery to her hostess.

'Why don't you come and stay on my farm at Frodriver?' she asked my mother. 'There's plenty of room, and you would be most welcome.'

My mother was, however, too clever to run the risk of being drawn into Thurid's debt as her invited guest, and she neatly side-stepped the trap. 'I would be delighted to accept your invitation,' she replied, 'but only on condition that I earn my keep. I would be quite happy to help you out with the farm work in return for decent board and lodging.'

At this point, I gather, I let out a squawl. Unperturbed, my mother glanced across at the bundle of blanket which hid me and continued, 'I'll be sending on my child to live with his father, so the infant will not disturb your household for very long.'

Thorgunna's clothes chest was snapped shut and fastened. A second, even bulkier coffer was hoisted out of stowage and man-handled into the rowboat, and the two women — and me — were carefully rowed to the beach, where Thurid's servants and horses were waiting to carry us back to the farm. I should add here that the horses of Iceland are a special breed, tough little animals, rather shaggy and often cantankerous but capable of carrying substantial loads at an impressive pace and finding their way over the moorlands and through the treacherous bogs which separate the farms. And some of the farms on Iceland can be very large. Their grazing lands extend a day's journey inland, and a successful farmer like Thurid's cuckolded husband Thorodd might employ as many as thirty or forty men and women, both thralls and freemen.

Thus my mother came to Frodriver under her own terms – as a working house guest, which was nothing unusual as everyone on an Icelandic farm is expected to help with the chores. Even Thurid would put off her fine clothes and pick up a hay rake with the rest of the labourers or go to the byres to milk the cattle, though this was more normally the work of thrallwomen and the wives of the poorer farmers, who hired out their labour. However, my mother was not expected to sleep in the main hall, where the majority of the farm workers settle down for the night among the bales of straw which serve as seats by day. My mother requested, and was given, a corner of the inner room, adjacent to the bedchamber where Thurid and her husband slept. When Thorgunna unpacked her large chest next day, Thurid, who had thought my mother wanted her own quiet corner so she could be alone with her baby, understood the real reason. My mother brought out from their wrappings a splendid pair of English-made sheets of linen, delicately embroidered with blue flowers, and matching pillow covers, also a magnificent quilt and a fine coverlet. She then asked Thurid if the farm carpenter could fashion a special bed with a high frame around it. When this was done Thorgunna produced a set of embroidered hangings to surround the bed, and even – wonders of wonders – a canopy to erect over the bed itself. A four-poster bed arrayed like this was something that Thurid had never seen before, and she was overwhelmed. She could not stop herself from asking my mother if perhaps, possibly, she would consider selling these magnificent furnishings. Once again my mother refused, this time even more bluntly, telling her hostess that she did not intend to sleep on straw. It was the last time Thurid ever asked Thorgunna to sell her anything, and Thurid had to be content, when Thorgunna was out working in the fields, with taking her visitors to give them surreptitious glances at these wonderful furnishings.

My mother, as I have indicated, had a predatory attitude towards the opposite sex. It was the story of Birsay all over again, or almost. At Frodriver she rapidly took a fancy to a much younger man, scarcely more than a boy. He was Kjartan, the son of one of the lesser farmers working for Thurid. Fourteen years old, he was physically well developed, particularly between the legs, and the lad was so embarrassed by Thorgunna's frequent advances that he would flee whenever she came close to him. In fact the neighbours spent a great deal of time speculating whether my mother had managed to seduce him, and they had a lot of fun chuckling over their comparisons of Thurid with her lover Bjorn, and Thorgunna in chase of young Kjartan. Perhaps because of their shared enthusiasm for sexual adventures, Thurid and Thorgunna eventually got along quite well. Certainly Thurid had no reason to complain of my mother's contribution to the farm's work. In the nearly two years that Thorgunna stayed at the Skattkaupandi farm, she regularly took her turn at the great loom at one end of the house where the women endlessly wove long strips of wadmal, the narrow woollen cloth which serves the Icelanders as everything from clothing to saddle blankets and the raw material for ships' sails when the strips are sewn side by side.

Thorgunna also pulled her weight — which was considerable — in the outside work, particularly when it came to haymaking. This is the crucial time in the Icelandic farming year, when the grass must be cut and turned and gathered and stacked for winter fodder for the animals, who will shortly be brought back from the outlying pastures where they have been spending the summer. My mother even had the carpenter make her own hay rake. It was longer, heavier and wider than most, and she would not let anyone else touch it.

Then came the day — it was late in heyannir, the haymaking season which occurs at the end of August in the second year of Thorgunna's stay — which the Frodriver people will never forget. The day was ideal for drying — hot with a light breeze. Thorodd mobilised the entire household, except for a few herders who were away looking after the sheep and cattle in the high pasture, to be out in the home meadow turning the hay. They were widely scattered, when just before noon the sky began to cloud over rapidly. It was a sinister sort of cloud – dark and ominous and heavy with rain. This cloud spread rapidly from the north-east and people began to glance up at it nervously, hoping that it would hold off and not spoil the haymaking. The cloud deepened and darkened until it was almost like night, and it was obvious that there would soon be a torrential downpour. Thorodd instructed the haymakers to stack their sections of hay to protect them from the rain, and was puzzled when Thorgunna ignored him. She seemed to be in a trance.

Then the rain started to pelt down and there was little point in staying outside, so Thorodd called in the workers for their midday break, to eat coarse bread and cheese in the main house. But Thorgunna again ignored Thorodd's instructions, nor did she pay any attention to the other workers as they trudged past her and back toward the farm. She kept on working, turning the hay with the wide slow powerful sweeps of her special rake. Thorodd called again, but it was as if Thorgunna was deaf. She kept working even as the rainstorm swept in, and everyone ran for shelter. It was a most unusual rainstorm. It fell on Frodriver, and only on Frodriver. All the other farms escaped the downpour and their hay was saved. But the Skattkaupandi farm was saturated. That in itself is not so strange. Any farmer has seen the same phenomenon when a summer cloudburst releases a torrent of rain which seems to drop vertically and strike just one small area. Then suddenly the rain ceases, the sun comes out and the ground begins to steam with the heat. But what was startling about the rainstorm at Frodriver was that it was not rain which fell from the cloud, but blood.

I know that sounds absurd. Yet it is no more fantastic than the contention that I have heard from apparently wise and learned men that fire and brimstone will pour from the sky in the great apocalypse. Certainly the people of Frodriver and the locality swear that the drops which hurtled from the sky were not rain, but dark red blood. It stained red the cut hay, it left pools of blood in the dips and hollows, and it drenched Thorgunna in blood. When she returned to the farmhouse, still as if in a daze and not saying a word, her clothes were saturated. When the garments were squeezed, blood ran out of them.

Thorodd asked her what was meant by the thunderstorm. Was it an omen? If so, of what? Thorgunna was slow in recovering from her confused state and did not reply. It seemed to Thorodd that she had been absent from her physical body and was not yet fully returned to it, and that something otherworldly was involved. His opinion was confirmed when the entire haymaking team went back into the field. The sun had re-emerged and the cut hay was steaming in the heat. All except one patch. It was the area where Thorgunna had been working. Here the hay still lay sodden, a dark blotch on the hillside, and though Thorgunna went back to work, turning the hay steadily, the workers noticed that the hay never dried out. It clung flat and damp on the ground, gave off a rank smell and the heavy handle of Thorgunna's hay rake stayed wet.

That evening Thorodd repeated his question. 'Was that strange thunderstorm an omen, Thorgunna?' he asked.

'Yes,' my mother replied. 'It was an omen for one of us.'

'Who is that?' asked Thorodd.

'For me,' came Thorgunna's calm reply. 'I expect I will shortly be leaving you.'

She went off to her splendid bed, walking stiffly as though her muscles were aching. In the morning she did not appear at breakfast to join the other workers before they returned to the haymaking, and Thorodd went to see her. He coughed discreetly outside the hanging drapes of the four-poster bed until Thorgunna called on him to enter. Immediately he noted that she was sweating heavily and her pillows were drenched. He began to make a few mumbled enquiries as to how she felt, but Thorgunna in her usual brusque fashion interrupted him.

'Please pay attention,' she said. 'I am not long for this world, and you are the only person around here who has the sense to carry out my last wishes. If you fail to do so, then you and your household will suffer.' Her voice was throaty and she was clearly finding it an effort to speak. 'When I die, as I soon will, you are to arrange for me to be buried at Skalhot, not here on this out-of-the-way farm. One day Skalhot will achieve renown. Just as important, I want you to burn all my bedding; I repeat, all of it.'

Thorodd must have looked puzzled, for Thorgunna went on, 'I know that your wife would love to get her hands on it. She has been hankering after the sheets and pillows, and all the rest of it from the very first day I got here. But I repeat: burn all of it. Thurid can have my scarlet cloak – that too she has been coveting since I first arrived and it ought to keep her happy. As for the rest of my possessions you can sell off my clothes to those who want them, deduct my burial costs from the money, and give the rest of the money to the church, including this gold ring,' and she removed the gold ring which she had been wearing since the day she arrived and handed it to Thorodd.

A few days later she died. One of the house women drew back the curtain and found her sitting up in bed, her jaw hanging slack. It took three strong men to lift her corpse and carry it out to the shed, where she was wrapped in a shroud of unstitched linen, and the same carpenter who had made her special bed nailed together a coffin large enough to contain her body.

Thorodd genuinely tried to carry out Thorgunna's last wishes. He had the bed frame knocked apart, and the pieces and the mattress and all the furnishings carried out to the yard. The carpenter took an axe to the bed frame and its four posts and made kindling, and the bonfire was ready. At that point Thurid intervened. She told her husband that it was a wanton waste to destroy such beautiful items, which could never be replaced. There would never be another chance to acquire such exotic goods. Thorodd reminded her of Thorgunna's express last wishes, but Thurid sulked, then threw her arms around him and wheedled. Eventually the poor man compromised. The eiderdown and pillows and the coverlet would be thrown on the flames; she could keep the rest.

Thurid did not lose a second in seizing the sheets and hangings and the embroidered canopy, and rushed them into the house. When she came back out, Thorodd had already left the yard and was walking away across the fields, so Thurid darted over to the fire and managed to salvage the coverlet before it was scorched, though it was some time before she dared to produce it before her husband.

Up to this point there seems to be an explanation for what happened in the events leading up to my mother's sudden death, including the red rain: she had caught a bad chill when she stayed out in the thunderstorm, then failed to change into dry clothes, and the chill developed into a mortal fever. Her insistence that her bedding was burned may have been because she feared that she had caught some sort of a plague and — if she had the medical knowledge that I was later to find among the priests and brithemain in Ireland — it was normal practice to burn the bedclothes of the deceased to prevent the illness spreading. As for the red rain, I observed when I was in the lands of the Byzantine emperor how on certain days the raindrops had a pinkish tinge and contained so many grains of fine sand that if you turned your face to the sky and opened your mouth the rain drops tasted gritty and did not slake your thirst. Or again, when I was employed at Knut's court in London, a south wind once brought a red rain which left red splotches on the ground like dried blood, as if the sky had spat from bleeding gums. Also I have heard how, in countries where the earth belches fire and smoke, there can be a red rain from the sky — and, Adam of Bremen should note, there are places in Iceland where holes and cracks in the ground vomit fire and smoke and steam, and even exude a bright crimson sludge. Yet the people of Frodriver will swear on any oath, whether Christian or pagan, that genuine blood, not tinted water, fell on them from the sky that day. They also affirm that in some mysterious way Thorgunna and the red rain were linked. My mother came from the Orcades, they point out, and as far as the Icelanders are concerned any woman who comes from there — in particular one as mysterious and taciturn as my mother – is likely to be a volva. And what is a volva? It is a witch.

Perhaps witch is not quite the right word. Neither Saxon English nor Latin nor the Norman's French, the three languages most used here in the scriptorium, convey the precise meaning of the word volva as the pagan Norse use it. Latin comes closest, with the notion of the Sibyl who can look into the future, or a seeress in English. Yet neither of these terms entirely encompasses what a volva is. A volva is a woman who practises seidr, the rite of magic. She knows incantation, divination, mysticism, trance – all of these things and more, and builds up a relationship with the supernatural. There are men who practise seidr, the seidrmanna, but there are not nearly so many men as there are women who have the knowledge and the art, and for the men the word magician would apply. When a volva or seidrman is about to die, there are signs and portents, and the red rain at Frodriver is a surer sign that my mother had seidr powers than any silly stories about love potions she used on my father.

And this is confirmed by what happened next.

Early the following morning my mother's coffin was lashed to the pack saddle on the back of the biggest horse in Thorodd's stables, and a little procession set out for Skalhot, where my mother had asked to be buried. Thorodd stayed behind on the farm as he had to oversee the rest of the haymaking, but he sent four of the farm labourers to manage the pack train. They took the usual route southward over the moorland. The going was quite easy as the moor was dried out at the end of summer and the usually boggy patches could carry the weight of the horses, so they made good progress. The only delays were caused when my mother's coffin kept slipping sideways and threatening to tumble to the ground. A coffin is an awkward load to attach to a pack saddle. If slung on one side like an enormous wooden pannier, you need a counter-weight on the opposite side of the horse to keep the load in balance. The men did not have a sufficiently heavy counterweight to balance my mother's coffin, and in the first half-hour the saddle itself kept slipping sideways, forcing the escort to tighten the girth straps until the poor pack horse could scarcely breathe. In desperation the men were on the point of hauling my mother's body out of its wooden box and draping it sideways across the pack saddle in its shroud, as it should have been in the first place. But they were far too fearful. They were already muttering amongst themselves that Thorgunna was a volva who would come to haunt them if they disturbed her. So they kept on as best they could, stopping every so often to tighten the lashings, and at noontime shifted the coffin to one of the spare pack horses as the first animal was on the point of collapse.

As the makeshift cortege climbed onto the higher ground, the weather got worse. It became squally with showers of rain and sleet, and by the time they reached the ford on the Nordur River the water was rising and the ford was deep. They waded across cautiously and late in the afternoon reached a small farm at a place called Nether Ness. At this point the man in charge, a steady farm worker called Hrolf, decided that it would be wise to call a halt for the day. Ahead lay the ford across the Hvit River, and Hrolf did not fancy trying to cross it in the dark, especially if the water was running high. He asked the farmer if they could stay the night. The farmer said they could bed down in the main hall, but it was late and as he had had no warning of their arrival, he would not be able to feed them. It was a churlish reply, but the Frodriver men were glad to get some sort of shelter even if they went to sleep hungry. So they unloaded my mother's coffin, stored it in an outhouse, fed and watered their horses and put them in a paddock near the farm, and brought their saddle bags into the hall.

The household settled down for the night, and the travellers were making themselves reasonably comfortable among the straw bales, which served as seats running the length of the main hall, when an odd sound was heard. It came from the larder. Going to investigate, one of the farm servants found my mother, stark naked, standing in the larder, preparing a meal. The unfortunate servant was too shocked even to scream. She rushed to the bed closet, where the farmer and his wife were just dropping off to sleep, and blurted out that she had seen a burly nude woman, her skin a deathly white, standing in the larder and reaching to take bread from the shelves, with a full pitcher of milk already beside her on the work table. The farmer's wife went to see, and there indeed was Thorgunna, calmly slicing thin strips off a leg of dried lamb, and arranging the slices on a wooden board. The farmer's wife did not know what to do. She had never met my mother, so did not recognise her, and she was utterly at a loss at this strange apparition. At this stage the corpse-bearers from Frodriver, awakened by the commotion, appeared. They, of course, recognised Thorgunna at once, or so they later claimed. Hrolf whispered to the farmer's wife that the apparition was Thorgunna's fetch or spirit, and it would be dangerous to interfere. He suggested that the farmer's wife should clear off the main dining table so that Thorgunna could set the table. Then the farmer himself invited the men to sit and take their missing evening meal. As soon as they had sat themselves at the farm table, Thorgunna in her usual taciturn way served them, placing down the food without a word and walking ponderously out of the room. She then vanished.

The Frodriver men remained at the table, taking care to make the sign of the cross over the food, and ate their delayed supper while the farmer hurriedly found some holy water and began sprinkling it in every corner of the building. Nothing was too much trouble for the farmer's wife now. She gave the travellers dry clothes and hung up their wet ones to dry, brought out blankets and pillows so they could sleep more comfortably and generally made as much fuss of them as possible.

Was the apparition of Thorgunna an elaborate hoax? Did the supper-less Frodriver men arrange for someone to play the part of Thorgunna? It was dark and gloomy in the farm building, and the candles were not lit until after Thorgunna had served the meal and withdrew, so a substitution and a bit of play-acting might just have succeeded. The nudity was a nice touch as most people are too shy to look closely at someone stark naked. On the other hand, who did the Frodriver men persuade to act the role of Thorgunna? A local farm woman would have been recognised at once, and the band of corpse-bearers were all male. Yet it is suspicious that her apparition was such a bonus for the corpse-bearers on the rest of their journey to Skalholt, where they delivered the coffin to the Christian priest at the brand-new church there, and handed over the money from Thorgunna's bequest. They lost no opportunity to recount the strange events of their evening at Nether Ness, and every farm they passed invited them in for a meal, for beer, for shelter if they needed it.

Do I believe that my mother's fetch appeared at Nether Ness? If I told that same story here in the scriptorium and changed the details, saying that she had reappeared emitting a strange glow and holding a copy of the Bible, my colleagues would accept my version of events without hesitation. So why would not the farmers of Snaefells be just as convinced that she had reappeared? Farmers can be as credulous as priests. There is hardly a soul in that remote farming community who doubts that Thorgunna came back to haunt the stingy farmer at Nether Ness, and while there might be an earthly explanation for the happenings at Nether Ness, until this explanation is supplied I am prepared to accept the supernatural. During my lifetime of travels I was to see many odd sights that defy conventional explanation. Within a few years of my mother's death I too encountered a fetch, and on the eve of a great battle I had strange and vivid forebodings which proved to be accurate. Often I've witnessed events which somehow I know that I have seen before, and sometimes my dreams at night recall events that are in the past, but sometimes they also bring me into the future. The facility for seidr is improved by apprenticeship to a practitioner, but there must be a natural talent in the first place, which is nearly always a question of descent. Volva and seidrmanna come from the same families down through the generations, and this is why I have spent so much time writing of the strange circumstances of Thorgunna's departure from this life and the hauntings: my mother gave me neither affection nor care, but she did bequeath to me a strange and disturbing gift – a power of second sight, which occasionally overwhelms me and over which I have no control.

THREE

ON HER DEATH bed Thorgunna made no mention of her son because she already had sent me off to join my real father. I was just two years old. I bear my mother no grudge on this score. Handing on a two-year-old child like a parcel may seem harsh, but there was nothing unusual about this. Among the Norsemen it is common practice for young children to be fostered out by their natural parents, who send them off to neighbouring families to be raised and educated. It binds the two families together, and this can be very useful when it comes to conducting local politics and intrigues among the Icelanders. Almost every family has its foster sons and daughters, foster brothers and sisters, and the attachments built up between them can be just as strong as between natural siblings. Besides, everyone at Frodriver had heard the rumour that my father was Leif Eriksson. So I was not being fostered, but merely sent to him where he lived with his father Erik the Red in Greenland. Indeed it turned out to be the kindest thing that my mother ever did for me because this second sea journey of my infancy placed me in the care of the woman who became more a mother to me than my own. Gudrid Thorbjornsdottir was everything that her reputation claims – she was kind, thoughtful, clever, hard-working, beautiful and generous of spirit.

Gudrid was travelling with her husband, the merchant Thorir, known as the Easterner, just at the time my mother at Frodriver was looking for someone to take her small child off to Greenland as she had long ago promised my father. And perhaps, too, my mother had a premonition of her own death. Thorir was pioneering a regular trading run between Iceland and Greenland, so when his ship called in at Snaefellsness Thorgunna put her request to Gudrid, and it was Gudrid who agreed to take me to my father.

Thorir's merchant ship was not one of the longships which have entered the sinister folklore of sheltered priests. The longships are warships, expensive to build, not particularly seaworthy and unsuitable for trading. At twenty paces' length, a longship offers barely four or five paces in the beam and, being like a shallow dish amidships, has little room for cargo. Worse, from a merchant's point of view, she needs a large crew to handle her under oars and even when she is sailing – which is how any sensible mariner makes progress – a longship must have a lively crew because these vessels have a treacherous habit of suddenly running themselves under or capsizing when under press of sail. Nor was Thorir's vessel one of those dumpy little coasters that farmers use when they creep round the Icelandic shore in fair weather, or to go out to the islands where they graze their sheep and cattle. His ship was a knorr, a well-found, full-bellied ship which is the most advanced of our deep-sea trading designs. She can carry a dozen cattle in pens in the central hold, has a single mast rigged with a broad rectangular sail of wadmal, and can cross from Iceland to Greenland in six dogur – a day's sailing – the standard length by which such voyages are calculated (Adam in Bremen might have difficulty in translating that distance onto a map, if that is what he proposes to do). Her chief cargo on that particular voyage was not cattle, but Norwegian timber. And that cargo of timber was about to save our lives.

Any sensible person who embarks on the voyage from Iceland to Greenland keeps the fate of the second settlement fleet in mind. Seventeen ships set out, nearly all of them knorrs. Less than half the ships managed to reach their destination. The others were either beaten back by adverse winds and limped into Iceland, or were simply lost at sea and no one ever heard of them again. As an experienced mariner, Thorir knew the risks better than most. The open water between Iceland and Greenland can be horrendous in bad weather, when a fierce gale from the south kicks up mountain-ous seas over the current that runs against it. Even the stoutest vessel can be overwhelmed in these conditions, and although the knorr is the most seaworthy ship that floats, she is just as much a plaything of the elements as any other vessel. Caught in heavy weather, a knorr has a fair chance of survival, but the crew must forget any idea of keeping a course. They spend their time franti-cally baling out the water that breaks aboard the ship, stopping leaks in the hull if they can, and preventing the cargo from being tossed about and bursting the planks, while the helmsmen struggle to keep the vessel at the safest angle to the advancing waves. If a storm continues for three or four days, the ship is often blown so far off course that no one has any idea of where they are, and it is a matter of guessing the most likely direction of land, then sailing there to try to identify the place.

Thorir had talked with men who had already sailed between Iceland and Greenland, so he knew the safest, shortest route. He had been advised to keep the tall white peak of Snaefellsjokul directly astern for as long as it was visible. If he was fortunate, he would see the high mountains of Greenland ahead before Snaefells-jokul had dipped below the horizon behind him. At worst he had only one or two days of open ocean between the landmarks until he had Greenland's huge white mass of ice in plain view and could steer larboard to skirt the southern tip of that huge and forbidding land. Then he planned to head north along the coast until he would arrive at Brattahlid, the centre of Greenland's most prosperous settle-ment and home of Erik the Red.

Thorir's knorr was well handled. She crossed the open straits and when she came in sight of Greenland's southern cape, it seemed that the ocean crossing had gone flawlessly. The vessel turned the southern cape and was heading for the fjord at Brattahlid, when as luck would have it she encountered a thick, clammy fog. Now a normal fog is associated with calm seas, perhaps a low swell. When the wind begins to blow, it clears away the fog. But a Greenland fog is different. Off Greenland there can be a dense fog and a full gale at the same time, and the fog stays impenetrable and dangerously confusing while the battering wind drives a vessel off course. This is what put paid to Thorir's ship. Running before the gale in bad visibility, trying to follow the coast, indeed almost within sight of Brattahlid if the weather had been kinder, the heavily laden knorr ran onto a reef with a crunching impact. She slid up on the rocks of a small skerry or chain of islands, the bottom tore out of her, and she was wrecked. Had the cargo been anything other than timber she would have filled and sunk. But the wedged mass of planks and logs turned her into a makeshift life raft. Her crew and passengers, sixteen including myself, were lucky to escape with their lives. As the waves eased, they scrambled up through the surf and spray and onto the skerry, with the shattered remnants of the knorr lurching and grinding on the rocks behind them until the tide dropped and the hulk lay stuck in an untidy heap. The castaways cautiously waded back aboard to retrieve planks and spars and enough wadmal to rig a scrap of tent. They collected some cooking utensils and food, and made a rough camp on a patch of windswept turf. With enough fresh water saved from the ship to last them several days, and a good chance of collecting rainfall later, they knew they would not die of thirst or hunger. But that was the limit of their hopes. They had been wrecked in one of the emptiest parts of the known world (indeed I wonder if Adam of Bremen knows about it at all) and their chances of rescue, as opposed to mere survival, were very bleak.

They were saved by a man's phenomenally keen eyesight.

Even now I can write this with a sense of pride because the man who possessed that remarkable eyesight was my father, Leif. I used to boast about it when I was a child, saying that I had inherited that gift of acute vision from him – as opposed to the second sight, which I possess through my mother and about which

I am far more reticent. But to explain how that remarkable rescue took place, I need to go back briefly to a voyage fourteen years earlier which had gone astray in another of those typical Greenland fog-cum-gales.

On that occasion a navigator named Bjarni Herjolfsson had overshot his destination at Brattahlid, and after several days in poor visibility and strong winds he was in that anxious condition the Norse sailors call hafvilla – he had lost his way at sea. When the fog lifted he saw a broad, rocky coastline ahead of him. It was well wooded but deserted and completely unfamiliar. Bjarni had kept track of his knorr's gyrations in the storm. He made a shrewd guess as to which way Greenland lay, put his ship about and after sailing along the unknown coast for several dogr eventually came back to Brattahlid, bringing news of those alluring woodlands. About the time my mother was thinking of sending me to my father, Leif had decided to sail to that unknown land and explore. Believing in the sea tradition that a vessel which had already brought her crew safely home would do so again, he purchased Bjarni's ship for the voyage.

By a remarkable coincidence he was on his way back from that trip even as Thorir's knorr shattered on the skerry. He was at the helm, battling a headwind and steering so hard on the wind that one of his crew, drenched by the resulting spray, complained, 'Can't we steer more broad?' Leif was peering ahead for his first glimpse of the Greenland coastline. 'There's a current from the north setting us more southerly than I like,' he replied. 'We'll keep this course for a little longer. We can ease the sheets once we are closer to land.'

Some time later another crew member called out a warning that he could see skerries ahead. 'I know,' Leif replied, relying on that phenomenal eyesight. 'I've been watching them for a while now and there seems to be something on one of the islands.' The rest of his crew, who had been curled up on deck to keep out of the wind, scrambled to their feet and peered forward. They could see the low black humps of the islands, but no one else could make

out the tiny dark patch that my father could already discern. It was
the roof of our makeshift shelter. My father, as I have said, was a
hard man to dissuade, and the crew knew better than to try to
make him alter course. So the ship headed onwards towards the
skerry, and half an hour later everyone aboard could make out the
little band of castaways, standing up and waving scraps of cloth
tied to sticks. To them it seemed a miracle, and if the story was
not told to me hundreds of times when I was growing up in
Brattahlid, I would scarcely believe the coincidence – a shipwreck
in the path of a vessel commanded by a man with remarkable
eyesight and sailing on a track not used for fourteen years. It was
this good fortune which earned Leif his nickname 'Heppni', the
'Lucky', though it was really the sixteen castaways who were the
lucky ones.

Expertly Leif brought his vessel into the lee of the skerry,
dropped anchor and launched the small rowboat from the deck.
The man who jumped into the little boat to help row was to have
a significant part in my later life – Tyrkir the German – and I
think it was because he was my rescuer that Tyrkir kept such a
close eye on me as I grew up. Tyrkir was to become my first, and
in some ways most important, tutor in the Old Ways, and it was
under Tyrkir's guidance that I made my first steps along the path
that would eventually lead me to my devotion to Odinn the All-
Father. But I will come to that later.

'Who are you and where are you from?' Leif shouted as he
and Tyrkir rowed closer to the bedraggled band of castaways
standing on the edge of the rocks. They backed water with the
oars, keeping a safe distance. The last thing my father wanted was
to take aboard a band of desperate ruffians who, having lost their
ship, might seize his own.

'We're from Norway, out of Iceland, and were headed for
Brattahlid when we ran on this reef,' Thorir called back. 'My name
is Thorir and I'm the captain as well as the owner. I am a peaceful
trader.' Tyrkir and Leif relaxed. Thorir's name was known and he
was considered to be an honest man.

'Then I invite you to my ship,' called Leif, 'and afterwards to my home, where you will be taken good care of.' He and Tyrkir spun the little rowing boat around and brought her stern first toward the rocks. The first person to scramble aboard was Gudrid and tucked under one arm was the two-year-old boy child she had promised Thorgunna she would deliver to his father. So it happened that Leif the Lucky unwittingly rescued his own illegitimate son.

FOUR

LEIF'S WIFE, GYDA, was not at all pleased to learn that the toddler Thorgils, saved from the sea, was the result of a brief affair between her husband and some middle-aged Orcadian woman. She refused to take me under her roof. She already had the example of her father-in-law's bastard child as a warning. My aunt Freydis, then in her late teens, was the illegitimate daughter of Erik and lived with the Erikssons. She was an evil-tempered troublemaker who, as it turned out, was to play a gruesome part in my story, though at the time she seemed to be no more than a quarrelsome and vindictive young woman always quarrelling with her relations. As Gyda did not want another cuckoo in her house, she arranged to have me fostered out, a real fostering this time. And this is how I came to spend my childhood not with my father but with Gudrid, who lived nearby. Gudrid, I suppose, felt responsible for me as she had brought me to Greenland in the first place. Also, I believe, she was a little lonely because soon after her arrival in Greenland she lost her husband, Thorir. He was in Eriksfjord for only a few weeks after his rescue before he went down with a severe fever. The illness must have arrived with his ship because Thorir and most of his crew were the first to begin coughing, spitting blood, and having bouts of dizziness. By the time the illness had run its course, eighteen people had died, among them Thorir and − finally − that old warhorse, my grandfather Erik the Red.

The gossips said that Gudrid took me in as a substitute for the child her body had failed to give her when she was Thorir's woman. I suspect these critics were jealous and only looking for a flaw to compensate for Gudrid's astonishing good looks − she possessed a loveliness of the type that endures throughout a woman's life. I remember her as having a pale translucent skin, long blonde hair, and grey eyes in a face of perfect, gentle symmetry with a well-defined nose over a delicious-looking mouth and a chin that had just the suggestion of a dimple exactly in the middle of it. At any rate I am sure that the young widow Gudrid would have taken me in even if she had children of her own. She was one of the kindest women imaginable. She was always ready to give help, whether bringing food to a sick neighbour, loaning out kitchen utensils to someone planning a feast and then doing half the cooking herself, or scolding children who were behaving as bullies and comforting their victims. Everyone in Brattahlid had a high opinion of her and I worshipped her. Never having known my real mother, I accepted Gudrid in that vital role as entirely normal, and I suspect that Gudrid made a far better job of it than gruff Thorgunna would have done. Gudrid seemed to have endless patience when it came to dealing with children. I and the other dozen or so youngsters of the same age made Gudrid's house the centre of our universe. When we played in the meadows or scrambled along the beach looking for fish and skipping stones on the cold water of the fjord, we usually finished by saying, 'Race you to Gudrid's!' and would go pelting across the rough ground like hares, bursting in through the side door which led to the kitchen, and arriving in a great clatter. Gudrid would wait till the last of us had arrived, then haul down a great pitcher of sour milk and pour out our drinks as we perched on the tall wooden benches.

Brattahlid was, for a child, an idyllic spot. The settlement lies at the head of a long fjord reaching deep inland. Erik had chosen the site on his first visit and chosen shrewdly. The length of the

fjord offers protection from the cold foggy weather outside, and it
is the most sheltered and fertile place to set up a farm in the area,
if not the whole of Greenland. The anchorage is safe and the beach
rises to low, undulating meadowland dotted with clumps of dwarf
willow and birch. Here Erik and his followers built their turf-
roofed houses on the drier hillocks, fenced in the home paddocks,
and generally established replicas of their former farms in Iceland.
There are no more than three or four hundred Greenlanders, and
so there is plenty of room for all those who are hardy enough to
settle there. Life is even simpler than in Iceland. At the onset of
winter we brought the cattle in from the meadowland and kept
them indoors, feeding them the hay we had prepared in the
summer. We ourselves existed on sour milk, dried fish, smoked or
salted meat and whatever else we had managed to preserve from
the summer months. As a result everything carried a rancid flavour,
particularly the lumps of whale and shark meat we buried in earth
pits for storage, then dug up, semi-putrid. The long, idle, dark
hours were spent with story-telling, sleeping, doing odd repair
jobs, playing backgammon and other games. In Greenland we still
played the older version of chess – a single king in the centre of
the board with his troops arranged against a crowd of opponents
who were spread around the edge. Not until I returned as a youth
to Iceland did I see the two-king style of chess, and I had to learn
the rules all over again.

Every youngster, almost from the time he or she could walk,
helped with day-to-day work and it made us feel valued. On land
we graduated from running errands and cleaning out the byres to
learning how to skin and butcher the beasts and salt down the
meat. On water we began by baling out the bilges of the small
rowing boats, then we were allowed to bait fishing lines and help
haul nets, until finally we were handling the sails and pulling on an
oar as the boats were rowed back to the landing place. We had
very little schooling, though Erik's widow, Thjodhild, did attempt
to teach us our alphabet and some rudimentary writing. We were
not enthusiastic pupils. Thjodhild's character was embittered by a

long-running disagreement with her husband. What irked her was that Erik had refused to become a Christian and this had set an example to many of his followers. Thjodhild was one of the earliest and most enthusiastic converts to the creed of the White Christ, and she was one of those querulous Christians who was always seeking to impose her beliefs on the rest of the community. But Erik was a dyed-in-the-wool pagan, and the more she nagged at him, the more stubborn he became. He had not left Iceland, he said, to bring with him in his baggage the newfangled religion. He had offered a sacrifice to Thor before he sailed to Greenland and, in return, Thor had looked after the colony very well. Erik told his wife in no uncertain terms that he was not about to abandon the Old Gods and the Old Ways. Eventually matters became so bad between the two of them that Thjodhild announced she would have as little as possible to do with him. They still had to live under the same roof, but she had a Christian chapel built for herself, very prominently, on a hillock near the farm just where Erik was sure to see it every time he left his front door. However, Erik refused to let his wife have much timber for the structure so the chapel remained a tiny building, no more than a couple of arm spans wide in any direction. It was the first Christian church in Greenland, and so small that no more than eight people could fit inside at once. We children called it the White Rabbit Hutch for the White Christ.

Halfway through the fifth summer of my life I learned that my foster mother was to marry again. After the hay gathering, the wedding was to be celebrated between the young widow Gudrid Thorbjornsdottir and another of Erik's sons, Thorstein. I was neither jealous nor resentful. Instead I was delighted. Thorstein was my father's youngest brother and it meant that my adored Gudrid was now to be a genuine relation. I felt that the marriage would bind her even more closely to me, and was only worried that after the wedding I would have to go to live in the main Eriksson household, which would put me in range of my detestable aunt Freydis. She had grown into a strapping young woman, broad shouldered and fleshy, with a freckled skin and a snub nose, so that she attracted men in a rather over-ripe way. She was also full of spite. She was always hatching plots with her girlfriends to get others into trouble and she was usually successful. On the few occasions I spent any time in my father's house I tried to stay clear of Freydis. Sixteen years older than me, she regarded me as a pest, and would think nothing of shoving me roughly into the darkness of the root cellar and locking me in there for hours, going off and not telling anyone. Luckily old Thorbjorn, Gudrid's father, who was still alive though weakly, was so pleased with the match that he agreed to let the newly-weds share his house, which was a short walk from the Eriksson home.

The wedding was a huge success. To satisfy grumpy old Thjodhild there was a brief Christian ceremony at the White Rabbit Hutch, but the main event was the exchange of ceremonial gifts, heavy beer drinking, raucous music and stamping dances which are the mark of the old-style weddings.

My next distinct memory of Greenland is a bright spring morning with the ice floes still drifting silently in our fjord. The glaring white fragments, so luminous on grey-blue water, made my eyes hurt as I stared at a little ship edging slowly towards us. She was a knorr, battered and seaworn, her planks grey with age. Some men were rowing, others handling the ropes as they tried to swing the rectangular sail to catch the cold breath of the faint wind that came from the north, skirting the great glacier behind us that is the heart of Greenland. I still recall how, from time to time, the oarsmen stood up to push with their blades against the floes, using the oars as poles to punt their way through the obstacles, and how slowly the boat seemed to approach. A crowd began to gather on the beach. Each person on the shore was counting the number of the crew and searching their faces to see who was aboard and if they had changed from the images we had been holding in our memories since the day they had gone to explore the mysterious land west across the sea, which Bjarni had first seen, and my father Leif had been the last person to visit. Then the keel grated on the shingle, and one by one her crew leapfrogged the upper strake and splashed ashore, ankle deep in the water. The crowd greeted them in near silence. We had already noticed that a man was missing, and the helmsman was not the skipper they had expected.

'Where's Thorvald?' someone in the crowd called out.

'Dead,' grunted one of the seamen. 'Killed by Skraelings.'

'What's a Skraeling?' I whispered to one of my friends, Eyvind. The two of us had wriggled our way through to the front of the crowd and were standing right at the water's edge, the wavelets soaking our shoes. Eyvind was two years older than me and I expected him to know everything.

'I don't know for sure,' he whispered back. 'I think it means someone who is weak and foreign and we don't like.'

Thorvald Eriksson, the second uncle of my tale, I remember only vaguely as a jovial, heavy-set man with large hands and a wheezing laugh, who often smelled of drink. Thorvald and his crew had departed westward eighteen months earlier to pick up where my father Leif had left off. My father had described an iron-bound low vista of slab-like grey rocks, long white-sand beaches extending back into boggy marshes and swamps, enormous still forests of dark pine trees whose scent the sailors could smell from a day's sail out to sea. Now Thorvald wanted to know whether anyone lived there, and if they did whether they had anything of value for trade or taking. If the place was truly deserted, then he would reoccupy the camp Leif had established on the Vinland coast and use it as a base to explore the adjoining territory. He would search for pasture, timber, fishing grounds, animals with fur.

Thorvald had taken with him a strong crew of twenty-five men and had the loan of my father's knorr, the same vessel which had plucked me off the rocks. He was a good navigator and several of his men had sailed with my father and were competent pilots, so his track brought him directly to the spot where Leif had overwintered four years before. There the Brattahlid men reoccupied the turf-and-timber huts that my father had built, and settled in for the winter. The following spring Thorvald sent the ship's small boat farther west along the coast on a voyage of enquiry. They found their journey very wearisome. The coast was a vast web of islands and inlets and shallows where they often lost their way. Yet the farther they went, the more the land improved. The wild grass grew taller, and there were strange trees which bled sweet juice when cut, or produced edible nuts whose buttery taste no one had encountered before. Despite the fertility of the land, they found no people and no trace of human habitation except at the farthest end of their exploration. There, at the back of a beach, they came across a ragged structure made of long, thin wooden poles which seemed to have been fashioned by man. The poles were fastened together with cords made from twisted tree roots and appeared to be a temporary shelter. Our men assumed that whoever had made the structure was living off the land, like our hunters in Greenland when they went north in summer to trap caribou. They found no tools, no relics, nothing else, but it made them nervous. They wondered if their presence had been noted by unseen watchers and feared an ambush.

Meanwhile Thorvald had spent the summer improving Leifsbodir, 'Leif's cabins' as everyone called them. His men felled timber to carry back to Greenland, and caught and dried fish as food for future expeditions. The quantity of fish was prodigious. The shore in front of the cabins had a very gentle slope, and low tide exposed an expanse of sand shallows runnelled with small gulleys. The men found that if they built fish traps of stakes across the gulleys, the fish – cod mostly – were trapped by the retreating tide and lay flapping helplessly. The fishermen had only to stroll across the sand and pick up the fish by hand.

After a second winter spent snug in the cabins, Thorvald decided to explore in the opposite direction – to the east and north, where the land was more like the Greenland coast, with rocky headlands, long inlets and the occasional landing beach. But the tides ran more powerfully there and this caught Thorvald out. One day the knorr swirled into a tide race and slammed against rocks beneath a headland. The impact was enough to break off the forward ten feet of

her false keel and loosen several of the lower strakes. Luckily there
was a beach nearby where the crew could land their craft safely,
and with so much timber around it was a simple matter to replace
the damaged keel with a fine clean length of pine. Thorvald found
a use for the broken-keel section. He had the piece carried to the
top of the headland and set vertically in a cairn of stones, where it
was visible from far out to sea. If strangers came to contest the
Greenlanders' discovery, it would be proof that the Erikssons had
been there before them.

This was the story of Thorvald's expedition as it emerged from
the reports of the returned crew that evening. Everyone in Brattahlid crammed into the hall of the Eriksson longhouse to hear the
details. We were listening with rapt attention. My father was sitting
in the place of seniority, midway down the hall on the right-hand
side. My uncle Thorstein sat beside him. 'And what about Thorvald? Tell us exactly what happened to him,' my father asked. He
put his question directly to Tyrkir, the same man who had been
rowing the small boat that rescued Gudrid and myself from the
skerries, and who had gone with Thorvald as his guide.

AT THIS POINT I should say something about Tyrkir. As a young
man he had been captured on the coast of Germany and put up for
sale at the slave market in Kaupang in Norway. There he had been
bought by my grandfather, Erik the Red, on one of his eastward
trips, and proved to be an exceptionally good purchase. Tyrkir was
hard working and tireless and grew to be intensely loyal to my
grandfather. He became fluent in our Norse language, the donsk
tunga, finding that it is not so far removed from his mother tongue
of German. But he never shed his thick accent, speaking from the
back of his throat, and whenever he got excited or angry he tended
to revert to the language of his own people. Eventually Erik trusted
Tyrkir so completely that, while my father Leif was growing up,
Tyrkir had the task of watching over him and teaching him all
sorts of useful skills, for Tyrkir was one of those people who has

gifted hands. He knew how to tie complicated knots for different
purposes, how to chop down a tree so that it fell in a certain
direction, how to make a fishing spear from a straight branch, and
how to scoop out a lump of soapstone so that it made a cooking
pot. Above all he possessed a skill so vital and wondrous that it is
closely associated with the Gods themselves – he could shape metal
in all its forms, whether smelting coarse iron from a raw lump of
ore or fusing the steel edge to an axe and then hammering a pattern
of silver wire into the flat of the blade.

We boys found the German rather frightening. To us he
seemed ancient, though he was probably in his late fifties. He was
short and puny, almost troll like, with a shock of black hair and a
ferocious scowl emphasised by a bulging, prominent forehead under
which his eyes looked distinctly shifty. Yet physically he was very
brave, and during Leif's earlier voyage to the unknown land it
was Tyrkir who volunteered for the scouting missions. His German
tribe had been a forest-dwelling people, and Tyrkir thought nothing
of tramping through the woodlands, wading across swamps, living
off berries and a handful of dried food. He drank from puddles if
he could find no clean running water, slept on the ground and
seemed impervious to cold or heat or damp. It was Tyrkir who had
first come across the wild grapes that some believe gave Vinland its
name. He came back into Leif's camp one day carrying a bunch of
the fruit, and so excited that he was rolling his eyes and muttering
in German until Leif thought he was drunk or hallucinating, but
Tyrkir was merely revelling in his discovery. He had not seen fresh
grapes since he had been a lad in Germany and indeed, if he had
not recognised the wild fruit, it is doubtful whether my father and
his companions would have known what they were. But the moment
Tyrkir explained what a fresh grape is, my father realised the significance of the moment. Here was evidence that the new-found
country had such a benign climate that grapes – an exotic plant for
Norsemen – actually grew wild. So he gave the land the name
Vinland, though of course there were cynics when he got home who
said that he was as big a liar as his father. To call a wilderness by

a name that evoked sunshine and strong drink was as misleading as to call a land of glaciers and rock Greenland. My father was canny enough to have an answer for that accusation too. He would reply that when calling the place Vinland he did not mean the land of grape vines but the land of pastures, for 'vin' in Norse means a meadow.

'TEN DAYS AFTER repairing the broken keel,' Tyrkir said in answer to my father's question about Thorvald, 'we came across the entry to a broad sound guarded by two headlands. It was an inviting-looking place, so we turned in to investigate. We found that the inlet divided around a tongue of land densely covered with mature trees. The place looked perfect for a settlement, and Thorvald made a casual joke to us that it was the ideal place, where he could imagine spending the rest of his life.' Tyrkir paused. 'He should never have said that. It was tempting the Gods.

'We put a scouting party ashore,' he went on, 'and when the scouts returned, they reported that on the far side of the little peninsula was a landing beach, and on it were three black hump-like objects. At first they thought that these black blobs were walruses, or perhaps the carcasses of small whales which had drifted ashore. Then someone recognised them as boats made of skin. Many years earlier he had been on a raiding voyage to plunder the Irish, and on the west coast he had seen similar craft, light enough to be carried on land and turned upside down.'

Here I should explain that the idea that these boats belonged to the wild Irish was not so incredible as it might seem. When the Norse first came to Iceland they found a handful of ascetic Irish monks living in caves and small huts laboriously built of stones. These monks had managed to cross from Scotland and Ireland aboard their flimsy skin boats, so perhaps they had also spread even farther. Thorvald, however, doubted that. Tyrkir described how Thorvald sent him with a dozen armed men to creep up on the strange boats from the landward side, while Thorvald himself

and most of the others rowed quietly round the coast to approach
from the sea. They achieved a complete surprise. There were nine
strangers dozing under their upturned boats. They must have been
a hunting or fishing party because they were equipped with bows
and arrows, hunting knives and light throwing lances. When they
heard the creak of oars they sprang to their feet and grabbed their
weapons. Some of them made threatening gestures, drawing back
their bows and aiming at the incoming Norse. Others tried to
launch their light boats into the water and escape. But it was too
late. Tyrkir's shore party burst out of the treeline, and in a short
scuffle all the strangers were overpowered, except for one. He
managed to flee in the smallest of the skin boats. 'I've never seen a
boat travel so fast,' said Tyrkir. 'It seemed to skim across the water
and there was no possibility that our ship's boat would have caught
up. So we let him go.'

The eight Skraelings our men had captured were certainly not
Irish. According to Tyrkir, they looked more like ski-running
people from the north of Norway. Short, they had broad faces with
a dark yellow skin and narrow eyes. Their hair was black and long
and straggly, and they spoke a language full of high sharp sounds,
which was like the chattering alarm call of a jay. They were
dressed entirely in skins: skin trousers, skin jackets with tails, skin
boots. Any part of their bodies not covered in these clothes was
smeared with grease or soot. They were human in form, but as
squat and dark as if they had emerged from underground. They
squirmed and fought in the clutch of the Norsemen and tried to
bite and scratch them.

Tyrkir's story now took a grim turn. One of the captive
Skraelings wriggled out of the grip of the man holding him, produced a bone harpoon head which he had hidden inside the front
of his loose jacket, and jabbed the point of the weapon deep into
his captor's thigh. The Greenlander roared with pain and rage.
He slammed the man's head against a rock, knocking him unconscious, and then in a fury plunged his short sword into the victim's
body. His action triggered a massacre. Thorvald's men fell on the

Skraelings, hacking and stabbing as if they were dispatching vermin, and did not stop until the last one of them was dead. Then Thorvald's men disabled the two remaining skin boats by gashing the hulls to shreds with their axes, and climbed through the woodland up to the top of the peninsula while the ship's boat rowed back to the knorr.

'On the highest point of the land we sat down to rest,' Tyrkir recalled. 'Thorvald intended to allow us only a few moments' breathing space, and we threw ourselves on the ground, and for some strange reason all of us fell asleep as if we were bewitched. About two hours later I was roused by a great voice howling, "Get back to the ship! If you are to save your lives, get back to your ship."'

At this point in Tyrkir's tale, several members of his audience exchanged sceptical glances. Everyone knew Tyrkir's other quirk: besides his quaint accent and bizarre appearance, he had a habit of mental wandering. From time to time he would slip off into some imaginary world where he heard voices and met strangers. On such occasions Tyrkir's face took on a glazed look and he would ramble off into long conversations with himself, invariably in German. It was a harmless habit, and everyone who knew him would look at one another and raise their eyebrows as if to say, 'There goes Tyrkir again, wool-gathering in his wits. What do you expect of a German winkled out of the woodlands?'

But that evening in Brattahlid Tyrkir insisted that he had been wakened from his drowsiness following the Skraeling deaths by a great bellowing voice. It had a strange reverberating rhythm. At times it seemed to come from far off, then from very close. It was impossible to tell from which direction. It appeared to fall from the sky or to come from all directions at once.

Even if Thorvald did not hear the mysterious voice, he must have realised that he and his men had been very foolish. He sent a man to a rocky vantage point where he could look across the fjord, and the sentry called down that a whole flotilla of skin boats was paddling towards them. Obviously the Skraelings were coming to seek their revenge. The shore party scrambled down the rocky slope, catching at the bushes to keep their balance and grabbing at trees as they bolted for their ship. The moment they were aboard, they unmoored and began to row, heading out of the bay and hoping for a wind to get them clear. Even the most lubberly among them knew that there was no way the knorr would out-row the pursuing skin boats.

There must have been at least thirty boats and each one contained three Skraelings. As soon as they were within range, two of the men stowed their paddles, took up light bows and began shooting arrows at the Norsemen. The third man paddled, keeping pace with the knorr and manoeuvring to give his companions the best angle for their shots. Thorvald and a couple of the sailors leapt up on their oar benches waving their swords and axes, challenging the Skraelings to come closer and fight hand to hand. But the natives kept their distance. To them the Norsemen must have seemed like giants. The Skraeling archers kept up a steady barrage. Slowly the knorr wallowed towards the mouth of the sound, where they could hoist sail. The natives kept abreast of them. Arrows hissed overhead, occasionally hitting with a thunk into the woodwork of the boat. The Skraeling archers stayed seated in their skin boats while they worked their bows, so they were lower to the water than their opponents on the higher-sided knorr, and at a disadvantage. Most of the arrows angled upwards and flew overhead harmlessly. A few rapped into the sail and stuck there like hedgehog quills.

After half an hour the natives broke off the attack. They were running out of arrows and they could see that the Norsemen were in full flight. The skin boats turned back one by one and the knorr was left to sail out to sea.

'It was only then,' Tyrkir told my father, 'that we realised that your brother Thorvald was wounded. A Skraeling arrow had found the gap between the topmost plank and his shield and hit him in the left armpit. It was scarcely more than a dart, but buried so deep that only an inch or two of the shaft was showing. Thorvald reached to pull out the arrow. But the arrow was designed for hunting seal and had triple barbs. He had to twist and tug violently to pull it and when it finally came free, there was a strong jet of dark red blood, and flesh stuck to the barbs. Thorvald gave one of his booming laughs – "That's my heart's fat there," he joked. "I said I would like to spend the rest of my days in this place, and I think that's what is going to happen. I doubt I will survive this wound. If I die I want to be buried here, up on that headland where every passing sailor will know my grave."

'I wish we could have done exactly what Thorvald wanted,' Tyrkir concluded in his thick accent. 'There was not much time. We buried Thorvald on the headland as best we could. We feared that the Skraelings would come back, so we could do little more than scrape out a shallow grave and pile a heap of stones over the corpse. Then we set course for Leif's huts to spend the winter – keeping a sharp lookout for Skraelings as soon as the weather improved.'

My uncle Thorstein spoke up. He was looking distressed. 'Leif,' he said, 'we can't leave Thorvald's body there. There's every chance that the Skraelings will find his body, dig it up and defile it. He deserves better. It's only a three-week sail to the spot, and I would like to take a crew of volunteers, sail to Thorvald's cairn, and recover the body so that we can have a proper burial here in Greenland. Your ship, which has just returned, isn't up to the job. She needs to be pulled ashore and recaulked, but my father-in-law Thorbjorn still has the knorr which brought him and his people from Iceland, and she could be ready to sail in two days' time. I'm sure that Thorbjorn will agree to loan her to me for the mission.'

Of course, both my father and old Thorbjorn, who was in the hall listening to the returnees, had to agree. This was a matter of family honour, and if there is one thing which the Norse are fanatical about it is the question of their honour. To a true Norseman his honour is something he places before all else. He will defend it or seek to enhance it by whatever means available, and that includes raiding for booty, exacting revenge for an insult, and lying or cheating to gain the advantage.

FIVE

DESPITE THEIR ORIGINAL plans, it was a full month before my uncle Thorstein set sail for Vinland. It seemed a pity to go all that distance and not bring back a cargo of timber and fish, so his expedition expanded into more than just a trip to recover Thorvald's body. There was equipment to gather, men to be summoned from the pastures, where they had gone with the cattle, stores to be loaded. Then someone suggested that it might be a good idea to leave a small group to overwinter at Leif's cabins, and this scheme delayed matters still further. When old Thorbjorn's knorr did finally set sail she looked more like an emigrant vessel than an expedition ship. There were six cows and several sheep standing in the hold, bales of hay to feed them, piles of farming gear, and on board were several women, including Gudrid, who had asked to accompany her husband. I, meanwhile, would stay behind with her father.

And by the time the preparations were all made it was too late. Thorstein Eriksson had a fine sense of family honour, but he lacked a sense of urgency and that essential gift of all good sea captains — weather luck. Intending for Vinland, he and his crew set out from Brattahlid but encountered such strong headwinds that they spent most of the summer beating uselessly about the ocean. At one stage they were in sight of Iceland and on another occasion glimpsed

birds which they judged came from the Irish coast. At the end of
the sailing season, without ever having set foot in Vinland, they
limped back to Greenland. Simple-minded folk claim that a ship or
boat has a mind and a spirit of its own. They believe that a vessel
can 'see' its way back home like a domestic cat or dog that has
been lost, or a horse to its stable, and that it can retrace the same
routes that it has previously sailed. This is nonsense, the dreaming
of landlubbers. Vessels which make several repeat journeys usually
do so because they are in the hands of the same experienced crew
members or there is some characteristic of the particular vessel –
shallow draught, ability to sail to windward, or whatever – which
makes it best suited to the task in hand. Seamanship and weather
luck make for a successful second or third voyage along a particular
track, not a boat's own acquired knowledge. Thorstein's failure to
fetch back his brother's bones goes to prove this very well.

They eventually made their Greenland landfall not at Brattahlid
but at Lyusfjord some three days' sail to the north-west. Here a
small group of Norse had already established a few coastal farms,
and Thorstein struck up a friendship with a namesake, who invited
him to stay and help him work the land, which was plentiful.
Perhaps my uncle was ashamed to return to Brattahlid with so little
accomplished and without Thorvald's body, so he accepted the
offer. That autumn a small coaster came down from Lyusfjord with
a message. My uncle was asking for his share of the family's cattle
herd and other stores to be sent to Lyusfjord, and – in a note
added by Gudrid – there was an invitation to send me along as
well. It seemed that I was still high in Gudrid's affections and her
substitute child.

My uncle's new-found partner was remarkably swarthy for a
Norseman, hence his nickname Thorstein the Black. This giving of
a nickname which identified him from all the other Thorsteins,
including my uncle, is a sensible Norse custom. Most Norse derive
their names, simply enough, from the parents. Thus, I am Thorgils
Leifsson, being the son of Leif Eriksson, who is the son of Erik.
But with so many Leifs, Eriks, Grimms, Odds and others to choose

from, it is helpful to have the extra defining adjective. The easiest way is to say where he or she comes from – not in my own case, though – or refer to some particular characteristic of the individual. Thus my grandfather Erik the Red's hair was a striking strawberry red when he was young and, as we have seen, Leif the Lucky was extraordinarily fortunate in his early career, always seeming to be in the right place at the right time. During my time in Iceland I was to meet Thorkel the Bald, Gizur the White and Halfdan the Black, and heard tales of Thorgrimma Witchface, who was married to Thorodd Twistfoot, and how Olaf was called the Peacock because he was always so vain about to his clothing, and Gunnlaug Serpent Tongue had a subtle and venomous way with words.

To return to Thorstein the Black: he had done remarkably well in the five or six years that he had been farming at Lyusfjord. He had cleared a large area of scrubland, built a sizeable longhouse and several barns, fenced in his home pasture, and employed half a dozen labourers. Part of his success was due to his wife, an energetic, practical woman by the name of Grimhild. She ran the household very competently, and this left Thorstein the Black free to get on with overseeing the farming and the local fishery. Their farmhouse was easily large enough to accommodate my uncle Thorstein and Gudrid, so rather than waste time and effort building their own home my uncle and aunt moved in with them. By the time I arrived, I found the two families sharing the same building amicably.

So I now come to an event which makes me believe that the mysterious hauntings which accompanied my own mother's death were not as implausible as they might seem. That winter the plague came back to the Greenland settlements for the second time in less than five years. It was the same recurring illness which was the curse of our existence. Where it came from, we could not tell. We knew only that it flared up suddenly, caused great suffering and then died away just as rapidly. Perhaps it is significant that both times these plagues visited us in autumn and early winter when we were all living cooped up, close together in the longhouses, with little light, no fresh air and a tremendous fug. The first person to contract the illness in Lyusfjord this time around was the overseer on the farm, a man named Gardi. Frankly, no one was too sorry. Gardi was a brute, untrustworthy and with a vicious streak. He could be civil enough when he was sober, but turned nasty when he was drunk, and was even worse the following morning when he had a hangover. In fact, when he first fell sick, everyone thought that he was suffering from yet another drinking binge until he began to show all the signs of the fever — a pasty skin, sunken eyes, difficulty in breathing, a dry tongue, and a rash of purple-red spots beginning to blotch his body. When, after a short illness, he died there was very little mourning. Instead the settlers around Lyusfjord began to wonder who would be afflicted next. The illness always picked its victims randomly. It might attack a man but leave his wife unscathed, or it would carry off two children from a brood of five, and the other three siblings never even had a sniffle. My uncle Thorstein contracted the sickness, but Gudrid escaped. Thorstein the Black was spared, yet his wife, Grimhild, succumbed. The progress of the sickness was as erratic as its selection was unpredictable. Sometimes the patient lingered for weeks. Others died within twenty-four hours of showing the first pustules.

Grimhild was one of the rapid victims. One day she was complaining of headaches and dizziness, the next she could hardly walk. She was so unsteady on her feet that by evening she could barely get to the outside privy a few steps away from the main farmhouse. Gudrid offered to accompany Grimhild in case she needed help and, as I was nearby, beckoned to me to assist. I took my place beside Grimhild so she could put her arm over my shoulder. Gudrid was on the other side with her arm around Grimhild's waist. The three of us then made our way slowly out of the door, and we were not halfway across the farmyard when Grimhild came to an abrupt halt. She was deathly pale and swaying on her feet so that Gudrid and I had to hold her from falling. It was bitterly cold and Gudrid wanted to get Grimhild across to the privy as fast as possible, then bring her back into the warmth. But

Grimhild stood rigid. Her arm was tense and trembling along my shoulders, and the hair rose on the back of my neck.

'Come on,' urged Gudrid, 'we can't stand out here in this cold. It will only make your fever worse.'

But Grimhild would not move. 'I can see Gardi,' she whispered in horror. 'He's over there by the door and he has a whip in his hand.' Gudrid tried to coax Grimhild to take a step forward. But Grimhild was petrified. 'Gardi is standing there, not five paces away,' she muttered with panic in her voice. 'He's using the whip to flog several of the farmhands, and near him I can see your husband. I can see myself in the group as well. How can I be there and yet here, and what about Thorstein? We all look so grey and strange,' She was about to faint.

'Here, let me take you back inside, out of the cold,' said Gudrid, half-lifting the delirious woman so that the three of us could turn in our tracks and stumble back into the main hall. We helped Grimhild into the bed closet, which had been turned into a makeshift sanatorium. My uncle Thorstein was already lying there. Fever-struck for the past week he had been shivering and slipping into occasional bouts of delirium.

Grimhild died the same night, and by dawn the farm carpenter was already planing the boards for her coffin. Our burial customs were very brusque. Under normal circumstances a wealthy farmer or his wife, particularly if they followed the Old Ways, might merit a funeral feast and be interred under a small burial mound on some prominent spot like a hillside or favourite beach. But in times of plague no one bothered with such niceties. People believed that the sooner the corpses were got out of the house and put underground, the quicker their wandering spirits would vacate the premises. Even the Christians received short shrift. They were buried in a hastily dug grave, a stake was driven into the ground above the corpse's heart, and when a priest next visited the settlement a few prayers were said, the stake was wrenched out and a bowl of holy water was emptied down the hole. Occasionally a small gravestone was erected, but not often.

That same morning Grimhild's husband went about the day-to-day chores of the farm as if nothing had happened. It was his way of coping with the shock of his wife's sudden death. He told four farmhands to go to the landing place where we kept our small boats and be ready to do a day's fishing. Trying to make myself useful and not wanting to stay in the same house as Grimhild's corpse, I accompanied the men as they headed to the beach to begin preparing the nets and fishing lines. We had loaded up the fishing gear into the two small skiffs, and were just about to push off for the fishing grounds when a runner came stumbling down from the farmhouse. In a lather of sweat and fear, he told Thorstein the Black to come quickly, something very odd was happening in the sick room. Thorstein dropped the sculls he was about to put into the boat and ran, clumping back up the narrow track to the farm. The rest of us stood there and stared at one another.

'What's happening in the farm?' someone asked the messenger, who was not at all in a hurry to get back to the longhouse.

'Grimhild's corpse started to move,' he replied. 'She sat up in bed, slid her feet to the floor and was trying to stand. I didn't see it myself, but one of the women came running out of the bed closet screaming.'

'Better stay away for a while,' said one of the farmhands. 'Let Grimhild's husband sort it out, if the story's true. I've heard about corpses coming alive, and no good ever comes of it. Come on, let's shove off the boats and go fishing. We'll find out what's happened soon enough.'

But it was difficult to concentrate on the fishing that day. Everyone in the two boats kept glancing back at the farmhouse, which could be seen in the distance. They were very subdued. I had gone along in one of the boats, helping bail out the bilges with a wooden scoop when I wasn't baiting hooks – my fingers were small and deft – but every time I caught sight of one of the men looking back at the farmhouse, I shivered with apprehension.

By mid-afternoon we were back on the beach, and had cleaned and split the few cod and saithe that we had caught, and hung

them up in the drying house. I walked very slowly back to the
house, staying at the rear of the group as we tramped up the path.
When we came to the front door, no one would go in. The
farmhands held back, fidgeted and looked at me meaningfully.
I was just a boy, but they thought of me as a member of their
employer's family, and therefore I was the one who should enter
the house first. I pushed open the heavy wooden door and found
the long hall strangely deserted. At the far end three or four of the
workers' wives were huddled together on benches, looking very
troubled. One of them was sobbing quietly. I tiptoed to the door
of the bed closet and peered in. Thorstein the Black was sitting on
the earth floor, his knees drawn up to his chest and his head
bowed. He was staring at the ground. On the bed in front of him
lay the corpse of his wife. A hatchet was buried in her chest, the
haft stuck up in the air. To my left, Gudrid was seated on the side
of the bed where her husband lay. Thorstein Eriksson was propped
up on a pillow, but looked very odd. I ran to Gudrid and threw
my arms around her waist. She was deathly calm.

'What's happened?' I croaked.

'Grimhild was on her feet. Her fetch must have come back and
entered her body,' Gudrid replied. 'She was stumbling slowly
round the room. Knocking into the walls like a blind person. She
was bumping and fumbling. That was when I sent for her husband.
I feared she would do harm. When her husband came into the
room, he thought that Gudrid was possessed. That she had been
turned into a ghoul. He picked up the hatchet and sank it into her.
To put an end to her. She has not moved since.'

Gudrid pulled me closer. 'Your uncle Thorstein is dead as
well,' she said quietly. 'He stopped breathing during the afternoon
and I thought he had passed away. But then he did come back to
us briefly. He called me over to him and told me that he knew
he was about to die, and that he did not want to be buried here,
but back in Brattahlid. I promised him that would be done. Then
he told me not to forget the volva's prophecy about my own
future. He said he was not the man who had been promised to

me. It was the last thing he said. Then he fell back and did not stir again.'

I was half-kneeling beside Gudrid with my head on her lap. 'Don't worry,' I told Gudrid, trying to console her. 'Everything will be all right now. You will not die from the plague. Nor will Thorstein the Black. Only old Amundi is going to die, and Sverting, who was with me in the boat this afternoon. That's all the people who were with Gardi last night in the yard.'

She put her hand under my chin, and gently turned my face so she could look into my eyes. 'How do you know?' she said softly.

'Because I saw them too, just as Grimhild did, all of them were there with Gardi and his whip. Last night, in the yard,' I answered.

'I see,' said Gudrid, and let her hand fall as she looked away.

I was too confused and frightened to make any sense of what was happening. I had never intended to tell anyone that I too had seen the group of fetches in the darkness of the farmyard. It was something which I did not understand. If I could see them, what did it mean about me and my responses to the spirit world? I had heard the rumours about my real mother Thorgunna and the ominous circumstances of her death. Would I see her fetch next? It was a terrifying prospect. But had I glanced up and seen Gudrid's expression when I made my confession, I would have been reassured. I would have realised that Gudrid too had seen the not-yet-dead, and that she had the gift of seidr, far more than me.

SIX

SEVEN-YEAR-OLDS are remarkably quick to adapt. Naturally enough, the farm workers at Lyusfjord refused to spend the winter cooped up in a building where such supernatural events had occurred, so our household moved back to Brattahlid, and within days I was back into the normal routines of childhood, playing with the other children. There were more of them than there had been at Lyusfjord so our games were more complicated and rowdy. I was smaller in stature than most of my contemporaries, but I made up for my lack of brawn with clever invention and quickness of thought. I also found I had a talent for mimicry and an imagination more vivid than most of my friends. So in our group I was the one who tended to invent new games or embellish the existing games with variants. When spring came and the days lengthened, we children moved out of doors to play the more boisterous games that the adults had forbidden indoors during the winter months. Most of our games involved a lot of play-acting with loud shouts, makeshift wooden shields and blunt wood swords. It was only natural that one we invented was based on my uncle Thorvald's voyage. Of course Thorvald's heroic death was a central feature of the make-believe. The oldest, strongest boy – his name was Hrafn as I remember – would play the leading role, staggering around the yard, clutching his armpit dramatically and pretending to pull out an arrow. 'The Skraelings have shot me,' he would yell. 'I'm dying. I will never see home again, but die a warrior's death in a far land.' Then he would spin round, throw out his arms and drop in fake death on the dirt and the rest of us would pretend to pile up a cairn of stones around his body. My own contribution came when we all boarded an imaginary boat and rowed and sailed along the unknown coast. I invented a great whirlpool which nearly sucked us down and a slimy sea monster whose tentacles tried to drag us overboard. My friends pretended to scan the beaches and called out what they saw – ravening wolves, huge bears, dragon-snakes and so forth. One day I created for them a monster-man who, I said, was grimacing at us from the beach. He was a troll with just one foot and that as big as a large dish. He was bounding along the strand, taking great leaps to keep pace with us and – to demonstrate – I left my companions to one side, and hopped along, both feet together until I was out of breath and gave up the pretence.

It was a harmless bit of play-acting, which was to draw attention to me in a way that I could never have anticipated.

The following day I got a really bad scare. I was walking past the open door to the main cattle shed when a thin arm reached out of the darkness, and seized me by the shoulder. I was yanked inside, and in the gloom found myself staring close up at the sinister face of Tyrkir. I was convinced he was about to batter me for some fault, and I went numb with fear as he briskly hefted me to the back of the cow byre and twisted me round to face him. He was still gripping my shoulder and it hurt. 'Who told you about the uniped?' he demanded in his heavy accent. 'Did you speak with any of the crew about it?'

'Turn the boy so I can look at his eyes,' said a voice with a deep rumble, and I saw another man, seated on the hay at the back of the byre. I had not noticed him before, but even without looking at his face I knew who he was, and my fright only increased. He was Thorvall, known as 'the Hunter'.

Of all the men in Brattahlid Thorvall was the one we boys

most feared and respected. He was the odd man out in our
community of farmers and fishermen. A huge, weatherbeaten man
now in his late fifties but still as fit and tough as a twenty-year-old,
he was disfigured by a scar which ran from the corner of his left
eye back towards his ear. The ear had been partly torn away and
healed with a ragged edge so that Thorvall looked like a tattered
tomcat that had been in numerous fights. The injury was the result
of a hunting accident in which Thorvall had been mauled by a
young polar bear. Standing in front of him in the cowshed, I tried
to keep my glance away from that terrible scar, while I thought to
myself that Thorvall had been lucky not to lose the eye itself. As
it was, the lid of his left eye drooped, and I wondered if it affected
his vision when he was drawing his hunting bow.

Thorvall was dressed in his usual hunting clothes, heavy
leggings bound with thongs, stout shoes and a jerkin with a hood.
I had never seen him wear anything else, and to be frank the
clothes did smell strongly even over the stench of the cow byre.
Thorvall had no one to look after his laundry. He was a bachelor
who lived by himself in a small house on the edge of the settlement
and he came and went as he pleased. His only personal ornament
was a necklace made of the teeth of polar bears he had killed. At
that moment, he was looking at me steadily and I felt I was being
scanned by some sort of predatory bird.

'Maybe the woman told him. She has the sight and knows a
good deal of the ways,' he said.

Tyrkir was still gripping my shoulder in case I made a dash for
the open door behind me. 'We know about her qualities, but she's
only his foster mother. Besides she wasn't there either. I think the
boy saw the uniped himself. They say that Leif's Orcades woman
had seidr powers. More likely the boy has his abilities from her.'
He gave me a slight shake as if to check whether these mysterious
'abilities' would somehow clank together inside me.

'You'll only scare him more if you rattle him around. Let him
speak for himself.'

Tyrkir relaxed his grip slightly, but did not release my arm. 'Have you talked with Gudrid about the uniped?' he asked.

I was puzzled. I had no idea what a uniped was.

'That creature who hopped along on just one foot.'

I now realised what this interrogation was about, but was completely baffled why Tyrkir and Thorvall would be interested in my childish antics. Surely I had done nothing wrong.

'What else do you see? Do you have any strange dreams?' Tyrkir was asking the question so intently that his German accent was all the more obvious. I did not know how to reply. Of course I had dreams, I thought to myself, but so did everyone else. I had nightmares of being drowned, or pursued by monsters, or that the room was squeezing in on me, all the usual terrors. In fact I was rather ashamed of my nightmares and never spoke about them to anyone. I had no idea where my vision of the so-called uniped had come from. It was not something I had dreamed in the night. The image had simply popped into my head at the time when I was playing with the other children and I had acted it out. I was still too scared to speak.

'Anything else unusual in your head, any odd sights from time to time?' Tyrkir rephrased his question, trying to adopt a more soothing tone.

My mind stayed a blank. I wanted desperately to answer, just to save myself, but I couldn't recall a single dream out of the ordinary. But I was beginning to understand that these two gruff men meant me no harm. With a child's acuteness of observation I was becoming aware that in some mysterious way they needed me. There was an undercurrent of respect, and of something else – of awe – in their attitude to me. Clamped in the rough grip of Tyrkir, and faced by the scarred face of Thorvall, I realised that the two men were expecting me to supply something they could not achieve, and it was something to do with the way I saw things.

'I can't remember any of my dreams,' I stammered. I had the good sense to look straight at Thorvall. A deliberately level gaze is a great help in persuading an interlocutor that one is telling the truth, even if one isn't.

Thorvall grunted. 'Have you talked about the uniped or any other dream like that with your foster mother?'

I again shook my head, still trying to understand why the two men were so interested in Gudrid's role.

'Do you know what this is?' Tyrkir suddenly brought his free hand in front of my face, and showed me what he had been holding in his palm. It was a small metal pendant, squat and T-shaped. The creases and lines on his hand, I noticed, were deeply ingrained with soot and grime.

'Mjollnir—' I ventured.

'Do you know what Thor uses it for?'

'Sort of,' I murmured.

'He uses his hammer to crack the heads of those who disobey him, and to obliterate his enemies. He'll use it on you, if you tell anyone about our little talk.'

'Let the boy go,' said Thorvall, and then, looking at me, he asked in a matter-of-fact tone, 'how would you like to know more about Thor and the other Gods? Would that interest you?'

I felt strangely drawn to his suggestion. I had now controlled my fear and nodded my agreement. 'All right, then,' said Tyrkir, 'Thorvall and I will teach you when we have time. But you don't tell anyone else about it, and we want you also to describe us any other dreams that you have. Now go on your way.'

Looking back on that little episode so long ago when two grown men trapped and questioned a frightened small boy in the cattle byre, I can see what Tyrkir and Thorvall were trying to achieve, and why they behaved in the odd way they did. They feared that knowledge of the Old Ways was fading from Greenland, and had been jolted into action when they detected in me someone who might possess the seidr power. They may even have heard about Christian missionaries rounding up the schoolchildren and the women and preaching at them. By imitation Thorvall and Tyrkir must have been thinking that they should do the same, but in a secret and select fashion, picking a child who seemed to have special powers and was therefore already gifted with seidr ability by the Gods. Then they would teach him what they knew of the old wisdom so that the knowledge and practice of the Old Ways would survive. If that is how they felt, at least a part of my subsequent life would have been their justification, though they would be scornful to see me now, skulking here in a Christian monastery pretending to be one of the faithful.

The uniped, Tyrkir told me in one of my first lessons, was the creature he had seen during the trip with Thorvald Eriksson to Vinland. The uniped had been skulking at the edge of the woods, close to the beach, as their ship sailed by. It looked exactly as I had described it to the other children – a bizarre, hunched body of a man standing on a single thick leg, which ended in a single broad foot. It had hopped along the strand, just as I had done in my childish game, keeping pace with the Norsemen and their boat. But when the visitors turned their vessel and began to make for shore, intending to land and capture the uniped – whether it was beast or man they could not tell – it abruptly swerved away, and had gone leaping off into the undergrowth until it had vanished underground, or so it seemed from a distance.

The sighting of the uniped was curious and inexplicable. Perhaps it was just one of Tyrkir's eccentricities, and he was citing another of his hallucinations. But several of the crew also claimed they had seen the strange creature, though not as clearly as Tyrkir. Nor could they describe it in such detail. None of them had mentioned the incident when they got back to Brattahlid for fear of being considered foolish. So my imitation of the creature – even the exact way it had kept pace with the knorr – had led both Tyrkir and Thorvall to think that somehow my other-spirit had been on that exploring ship off the coast of Vinland, and yet back at home in Brattahlid at the same time, and – as every Old Believer knows – the ability to be in two places at once is a true mark of seidr power. A seidr-gifted person is born with this trick of spirit flying through the air, invisible and at supernatural speed to places far distant and then returning to the mortal body. Judging by what happened to me in Vinland soon afterwards, Thorvall and Tyrkir were right in detecting a spirit link between me and that unknown land in the west. On the other hand, I have to admit that it could have been pure coincidence that I imitated a hopping One Foot in the children's game because no one ever saw a uniped ever again.

But that doesn't mean that unipeds do not exist. Recently I came across one here in the monastery's library. I was preparing a sheet of vellum, scraping off the old ink before washing the page. Vellum is so scarce that we reuse the pages when their writings are too faded or blurred, or the content of the text is out of date or unimportant. This particular page was from Ezekiel, on the demons Gog and Magog, and had become detached from its original book. As I removed the old writing, I noticed a small, simple drawing in the margin. It was rather crudely done, but it caught my attention at once. It was a uniped, just as Tyrkir had described it to me in that cattle shed sixty years ago, except that the creature in the margin was drawn with giant, flapping ears as well as a giant foot. And, instead of hopping, it was lying on the ground on its back with the single large foot held up in the air. I could just make out the faint word '... ped sheltering ...' and then the rest of the caption was a blur. What the uniped was sheltering from was not clear. If it was a Vinland uniped then it might have been the snow and rain. But there was nothing in the adjacent text to explain the mystery.

Over the next months Thorvall or Tyrkir frequently picked on me for some chore or other, ostensibly because they wanted me to help them, but in fact they were looking for opportunities to tell me something of their beliefs out of earshot of the others. Neither of my tutors were learned men and Tyrkir in particular was very artless. But they both possessed the enormous advantage that they were not in the least hypocritical in their beliefs. Their genuine conviction made a stronger impression on me than all the sophistry imaginable. And the pagan world of the Old Ways was so easy to imagine, so logical, so attractive, and so apt to our situation on the remote shore of Greenland, backed by its immense and mysterious hinterland of ice and mountains, that it would have been a very dull student who failed to respond.

Tyrkir told me of the Aesir, the race of heroes who migrated out of the east long ago and established their capital at Asgard, with Odinn as their chief. With the twin ravens Hugin and Munin – Thought and Memory – perched on his shoulders, Odinn was – and is, so Tyrkir insisted to me – cunning and ruthless, a true king. Dedicated to the pursuit of advantageous knowledge, even sacrificing the sight of one eye so he could drink a draught of water from the well of wisdom, he still treads the world in a variety of disguises, always seeking more and more information. But his role is doomed, for in his wisdom he knows he is leading the other Aesir in the ultimately hopeless task of defending the world against the powers of darkness, the frost giants and mountain giants and other grim monsters who will finally crush them, to the hideous baying of the monstrous hound, Gorm. In his palace at Valholl Odinn entertains the departed heroes of our human race, proven warriors who are provided with feasting and drinking and the company of splendid women, until they will be summoned forth for the last, fatal battle at Ragnarok. Then they and all the Gods will be overwhelmed.

There is no doubt in my mind that Tyrkir's eerie tales of Odinn and his deeds were the original inspiration for my later devotion to the All-Father, as Tyrkir always called him. To a seven-year-old there was a morbid fascination in how Odinn interviewed the dead or sat beside men hanging on the gallows to learn their final secrets or consorted with the maimed. His skill as a shape-shifter was no less beguiling, and I easily imagined the Father of the Gods as he changed himself into a bird of prey, a worm, a snake, a sacrificial victim, according to whatever stratagem he had in mind. Being still a youngster I had no inkling of his darker side – that he can trick and cheat and deceive, and that his name means 'Frenzy'.

Thorvall's hero, unsurprisingly given his own name, was red-haired Thor, Odinn's son, who rides across the sky in his goat-drawn chariot, his passage marked by rolls of thunder and flashes of lightning, hurling thunderbolts, controlling the sea, and laying about him with Mjollnir, his famous hammer. Thorvall was an ardent member of the Thor cult, and once he got started on one of his favourite Thor-stories, he became very animated. I recall the day he told me how Thor went fishing for the Midgard serpent, using an oxhead for bait, and when the serpent took the hook Thor pulled so hard on the line that his foot broke through the planking of the boat. At that point in his story Thorvall stood up and, as we were in the cattle shed at the time, put his foot against one of the stalls and heaved back to imitate his hero. But the stall was poorly made, and collapsed in a cloud of dust and splinters. I can still hear Thorvall's great bellowing laugh and his triumphant cry of 'Just like that!'

Despite Thorvall's enthusiasm for Thor – and my boyhood respect for the tough hunter – I still preferred Odinn. I savoured the idea of creeping about in disguise, picking up intelligence, observing and manipulating. Like all children, I liked to eavesdrop on the adults and try to learn their secrets, and when I did so and stood hidden behind a door or a pillar, I would close one eye in imitation of my one-eyed hero God. Also, if my foster mother had searched under my mattress she would have found a square of cloth I had hidden there. I was pretending it was *Skidbladnir*, Odinn's magic ship, which received a favourable wind whenever it was launched and could carry all the Aesir, fully armed, yet when Odinn no longer needed it, he could fold it up and tuck it in his pocket.

Several years later, when I was in my teens, it slowly dawned on me that I myself might be a part of Odinn's grand design. By then it seemed that the path of my life was increasingly directed by the All-Father's whim, and whenever possible I paid him homage, not only by prayer and secret sacrifice, but also by imitation. That is one reason why, as a callow youth, I sought to become a poet, because it was Odinn, disguised as an eagle, who stole the mead of poetry from its guardian Suttung. More important, my growing devotion to Odinn was in harmony with my natural wanderlust. Whenever I have set out on any journey I have done so in the knowledge that the All-Father is the greatest of all far-farers, and that he is watching over me. In that regard, he never played me false, for I have survived when many of my travelling companions fell.

TYRKIR ALSO TAUGHT me the details of the mysterious prophecy which Gudrid had mentioned on that dismal day in Lyusfjord when she sat beside Thorstein's deathbed, and I had let slip that I had seen the fetches of the not-yet-dead. Tyrkir had been delayed late in his workshop, where he made and repaired the metal tools essential to our farming. Gudrid had sent me to take the little German his supper. 'She's a good woman, your foster mother,' Tykir said as he set aside the empty bowl and licked his fingers. 'Far too good to fall under the influence of those crazy White Christ fanatics. No one else can sing the warlock's songs so well.'

'What do you mean, the warlock's songs?' I asked. 'What are they?'

Tyrkir looked at me from under his bulging forehead, a momentary gleam of suspicion in his eyes. 'You mean to say that your foster mother hasn't told you about her and the Little Sibyl?'

'No, I've never even heard of the Little Sibyl. Who was she?'

'The old woman Thorbjorg. She was the Little Sibyl, the volva. She died four years ago, so you really never knew her. But plenty still do, and they all remember the night when Gudrid Thorbjorns-dottir revealed herself.'

Tyrkir settled himself on the low stool near his anvil, and pointed for me to make myself comfortable on a pile of sacks that had held charcoal for his simple furnace. It was obvious that his story would be a long one, but he considered it important that I know the details about my foster mother. Anything which concerned my adored Gudrid was important to me, and I listened so attentively that I still remember every detail of Tyrkir's explanation.

THE LITTLE SIBYL, Tyrkir began, had come to Greenland in the earliest days of the colony to avoid the turbulent White Christ followers who were causing such ructions in Iceland by insisting that everyone should follow their one true God. She was the last of nine sisters, all of whom had possessed the seidr skills, and being the ninth she had more of the gift than all the others. She could foretell the weather, so farmers planned their activities according to her advice. Their wives asked her about the propitious names they should give their babies and the health and prospects of their growing children. Young women quietly enquired about their love lives; and mariners timed their voyages to begin on the auspicious days the Little Sibyl selected. Thorbjorg knew the correct offerings to the Gods, the right prayers, the proper rituals, all according to the Old Ways.

It was in the autumn of the year that my foster mother Gudrid first arrived in Greenland that a black famine had gripped the colony. After a meagre hay harvest the hunters, who had gone inland or along the coast looking for seals and deer, came back with little to show for their efforts. Two of them failed to come back at all. As the cheerless winter months wore on, our people began to die of starvation. The situation became so bad that a leading farmer, a man named Herjolf, decided he should consult the Little Sibyl to ask whether there was any action that the settlers could take to bring the famine to an end. Herjolf arranged a feast to honour the Little Sibyl and, through her, the spirit world she would have to enter if she was to answer their plea for advice. Also, consuming their last reserves of food in such a feast was a signal to the Gods that the people placed their trust in them.

Herjolf supplied the banquet from his final stocks of dried fish and seal blubber, slaughtered the last of his livestock and brought out his stores of cheese and bread. Naturally the entire community was invited to attend the feast, not just for food to fill their aching bellies but to hear what the Sibyl would say. Herjolf's wife arranged a long table running the full length of their hall. Crosswise at the head of the table and raised slightly above it where it could be seen by everyone, a seat of honour for the Little Sibyl was placed — a carved wooden chair with a cushion stuffed with hens' feathers.

While the guests were assembling, a man was sent to escort Thorbjorg from her home. When she arrived, it was immediately clear that the Little Sibyl had acknowledged the gravity of the emergency. Normally when called upon to practise seidr she arrived dressed in her everyday homespun clothes, and carrying only her seidr staff, a wooden stick about three feet long carved with runes and hung with withered strips of cloth. But when Thorbjorg was led into the great hall that evening she was dressed in clothes no one had ever seen her wear before: a long overmantle of midnight blue reaching almost to the ground and fastened across the chest with cloth straps worked with intricate designs in red and silver thread. The entire surface of the cloak was encrusted with patterns of small stones, not precious stones but pebbles, mottled and marbled and all smooth from lying underwater. They shimmered as if still wet. They were magic 'waterstones' said to contain the spirits of the river. Around her throat the volva wore a necklace of coloured glass beads, mostly red and blue. Her belt was plaited from the dried stalks of mushrooms and fungi, and from it hung a large cloth pouch, in which she kept her collection of dried herbs, charms and the other ingredients for her sorcery. Her feet were encased in heavy shoes made of calfskin, the hair still on them, and laced with heavy thongs with tin buttons on the ends. Her head was hidden within a dark hood of black lambskin lined with the fur from a white cat. On her hands were mittens also of catskin, but with the fur turned to the inside.

Had it not been for her familiar seidr staff the guests would have found it difficult to recognise Thorbjorg. The staff was of pale honey-coloured wood, much worn and slick with handling, and the knob at the end was bound in brass and studded with more of the 'waterstones'. There were, it seemed, more ribbons than usual.

As she arrived, Herjolf, who had been waiting to greet her at the door of the long hall, was surprised to find himself looking at the back of her black hood. Thorbjorg was walking backwards. The entire assembly fell silent as her host escorted Thorbjorg down the length of the hall, still facing the main entrance door. Herjolf named each person who was present as they drew level. The Sibyl responded by peering out from under her black hood and into their faces but saying little, only giving the occasional sniff as if smelling their presence.

When the volva was safely settled on her high seat, the meal was served and everyone ate with gusto, though many kept glancing up at Thorbjorg to see how she was behaving. She did not eat with the everyday utensils, but pulled from her pouch a brass spoon and an ancient knife with a handle of walrus ivory bound with two copper rings. The blade of the knife was very worn and pitted, as if it had been buried in the earth a long time, and the onlookers noted the point was broken. Nor did she eat the same food as everyone else. She asked for, and was given, a bowl of gruel prepared with goat's milk and a dish made of the hearts of all the animals slaughtered for the feast.

When the meal was over and the tables cleared, Herjolf stood up. 'Sibyl, I hope that everything that has been arranged this evening has been to your satisfaction,' he announced in a voice that carried the length of the hall. 'We have all assembled here in the hopes that in your wisdom you will be able to tell us how long the famine will last, and whether there is anything we can do to end our difficulties.'

'I need to spend longer in this house,' she answered. Her voice was thin and wheezing as if she had difficulty in breathing. 'I have yet to absorb its spirit, to learn the portents, to feel its soul. It is too early to give any judgement. I will stay here on this seat, all this night, and tomorrow afternoon I believe I will be able to reply to your question.'

There was a general sigh of despondency. Those who lived close enough to be able to walk to their homes through the dark left the building. The others bedded down for the night in Herjolf's hall and waited anxiously for the long, slow spread of dawn, which comes so late at that season that the light begins to fade almost as soon it reaches the earth.

The next afternoon, when the audience had reassembled, a hitch arose. The Sibyl unexpectedly declared that she needed the help of an assistant. She required someone to sing the proper seidr chants as her spirit began to leave her body. The chants would help free her spirit to start on its journey to the otherworld. There was consternation. The Sibyl had never requested an assistant before. Herjolf turned to face the crowd and appealed to everyone in the hall – if anyone could help, please would they step forward. His appeal was met with silence. The Sibyl sat on her high seat, blinking and peering down impatiently. Herjolf repeated his appeal, and to everyone's surprise Gudrid stepped forward quietly. 'Do you know any seidr?' Herjolf asked in astonishment. Gudrid's own father, Thorbjorn, must have been equally startled. He was gaping with surprise. 'Yes,' replied Gudrid quietly. 'When I was a foster child in Iceland to my father's friends Orm and Halldis, it was Halldis who taught me the warlock songs. If Halldis were here today, she would do it better, but I think I can remember all the words.' The Little Sibyl gave a sceptical grunt, and beckoned Gudrid close to her. She leaned over and must have asked the young woman to say a sacred verse to test her because Gudrid sang some refrain in a voice so low that no one could make out more than a few words, most of which seemed to be in some strange sort of language. The Sibyl nodded curtly, then settled back on her cushion.

At that point Gudrid's father, Thorbjorn, normally very easy-going, broke in. 'I'm not having my daughter involved in any witchcraft,' he announced loudly. 'That's a dangerous game. Once started, no one knows where it will end.'

'I'm neither a witch, nor a seeress, but if it will help our situation I am prepared to take part,' Gudrid told him firmly.

Thorbjorn took this rebuff badly, turned on his heel and pushed his way out of the crowd and left the building, muttering that at least he would not have to witness his daughter's disgrace.

'The spirits are still wary and obscure to me,' the Sibyl said after a short silence when the audience had settled down. 'They must be calmed and called to attend us.' She gestured to Gudrid, who exchanged glances with several of the farmers' wives. As their husbands looked either curious or uncomfortable, these women pushed through the crowd, and under Gudrid's instructions formed a small circle. There were perhaps half a dozen women facing inwards, Gudrid standing in the centre. As the crowd hushed, she began to sing the words of the warlock song. She had a high clear voice and sang without any trace of embarrassment. The women around her began to sway quietly to the rhythm of the voice, then their hands reached out and joined, and their circle began slowly to shuffle sideways, the direction of their rotation against the sun. Husbands and sons looked on, half-fearful and half-amazed. This was woman's work, something that few of the menfolk had ever guessed. Gudrid sang on, verse after verse, and the older women, softly at first, then more loudly, began to echo the refrain. To some of the audience the songs seemed at times like a lullaby that they had heard as children, though only Gudrid appeared to know all the verses and when to change the rhythms. She sang without a tremor until finally her voice died away, the women slipped back into the crowd and the volva looked down at Gudrid. 'I congratulate you,' she announced. 'Whoever taught you, taught you well, and the spirits have responded. I can feel them now, assembling around us and ready to carry my spirit to the Gods.'

She beckoned Gudrid to stand closer and began to croon softly. Gudrid must have recognised the chant, for she began to respond, catching the refrain, repeating the stanzas, changing a line, adding a line. Back and forth went the chant between the two women, their voices weaving together, and the volva began to rock back and forth in her chair. Then the words made a circle on themselves. There were repetitions and long pauses. People in the crowd began to shuffle their feet, glance at one another, then turn their gaze back to the blue-cloaked figure on its high seat. Not a person left the hall. Finally, after a little more than half an hour, the Sibyl's voice slowed. Gudrid, still standing beside her, seemed to sense that her role was at an end. The volva's head sank forward on her chest, and she appeared to be both awake and asleep. For a long moment nothing happened, and then very slowly the volva raised her head and looked straight down the crowded room. She nodded to Gudrid, and Gudrid quietly walked back to the edge of the crowd of onlookers, turned and faced the Little Sibyl.

Herjolf cleared his throat with a nervous cough. 'Can you tell us the answer to the question we all ask?' he said. The volva's reply was matter of fact. 'Yes, my dream was clear and cloudless. My spirit circled up through the air and I saw ice breaking in the fjord. I saw the first signs of new grass even though the migrating birds had not yet come to feed and prepare their nesting sites. The air was warm around me though the day was still short. Spring will come very early this year and your trials will finish within a few days. The hunger you are suffering will be at an end and no one else will die. You have put your trust in the Gods, and you will be rewarded.'

Unexpectedly the volva turned towards Gudrid and spoke directly to her. 'And for you,' she said, 'I also have a prophecy. My spirit messengers were so charmed by your seidr knowledge and the songs you sang that they have brought me news of your destiny. I can now reward you for the help you have given me. You are fated to make a distinguished marriage here in Greenland, but it will not last for long. Rather, I see how all your links lead you towards Iceland and its peoples. In that land you will give rise

to an illustrious family line and, through its people, you will attain
an enduring renown.'

TYRKIR CAME TO the end of his story.

'So you see, Thorgils,' he said, 'that's why Thorvall thought,
when you imitated the hopping One Foot in your game, that you
might have inherited seidr skill, the power of spirit flight, through
your foster mother. Gudrid herself could be a skilful volva, if only
she did not consort so much with White Christ fanatics.'

I knew what Tyrkir meant. Ever since Gudrid had come back
from Lyusfjord, she had been spending time with Leif's wife Gyda,
a zealous Christian. The two women were often seen visiting the
White Rabbit Hutch together. Tyrkir and Thorvall found it worrying that someone so gifted with the skills and knowledge of the
Old Ways was drifting towards the newfangled Christian beliefs.
Gudrid's interest in Christianity shook their own faith in the Old
Gods, and they felt uneasy. They did not realise, as I do now, that
the underlying truth is that good pagans make good Christians and
vice versa. The choice of religion is less important than the talents
of the person who is involved. The same is true of generals and
politicians, as I have noticed during my travels. I have seen that it
makes no difference whether an outstanding military commander is
clad only in skins and painted woad, or in a gilded helmet and a
beautifully tailored uniform of Persian silk as worn by the horse-
warriors of the kingdom between the two great rivers. The martial
genius is identical, and the brilliant, decisive reaction to the moment
is the same whatever the dress. Similarly with politicians. I have
listened to speeches delivered at a flea-infested tribal council meeting held around a guttering campfire in a bare forest glade which,
if prettified with a few well-polished phrases, could have been the
same as I heard from a conclave of the highly trained and perfumed
advisers to the Basileus. I am talking about Christ's supposed representative on earth when he sits on his gilded throne in a chamber

banded with porphyry and pretends that he is the incarnation of a thousand years of learning and refined civilisation.

The saddest aspect of Gudrid's drift towards the White Christ ways, now that I look back on it, is what a waste it proved to be. My foster mother would have made a truly remarkable priestess of the Old Ways if she had preferred to study under the Little Sibyl. For it is a striking feature of the old beliefs – and it would appal the monks around me if they knew – that the majority of its chief experts were women. There are fifteen different words in the Norse language to describe the various female specialisms in seidr, but fewer than half that number of words for male practitioners. Even Odinn the shape-changer has a strong element of the female about him, and you wonder about his enthusiasm for disguising himself as a woman. By contrast the White Christ expects his leading proponents to be male and women are excluded from their inner priesthood. Thus Gudrid diminished her horizons on the day she formally professed the faith of the White Christ. If she had followed the Old Ways she could have been respected and influential and helped those among whom she lived. But as a devout and saintly Christian she was finally obliged to become an anchoress and live on her own. However, that brings me far ahead of my story . . .

Thorvall and Tyrkir tried their best to make me understand that unless the Old Ways continued to be practised, they would soon be submerged by the advancing tide of White Christ beliefs. The speed with which the White Christ faith had taken hold in Iceland alarmed my tutors, and they feared that the same would happen in Greenland. 'I don't know how the White Christ people can claim to be peaceful and gentle,' said Thorvall sourly. 'The first missionary they sent to Iceland was a ruffian named Thang-brand. He swaggered about the countryside browbeating the farm-ers into taking his faith, and when he was teased about his crazy ideas, he lost his temper and killed two Icelanders in fights. To try to control him, a meeting was arranged between him and a learned

volva at which the two of them would debate the merits of their
beliefs. The volva made Thangbrand look an utter fool. He felt so
humiliated that he took ship for Norway, and the volva proved her
worth by asking Thor to send a storm, which nearly sank his ship
on his journey home.

'The Icelanders were far too easy-going,' Tyrkir added. 'When
the missionaries came back to Iceland some years later and began
their preaching all over again, the farmers had no more stomach
for the endless debates and quarrels between those who decided to
take the new faith and those who wanted to stay with the old ways.
They got so fed up that their delegates met at the Althing with
instructions to ask the Lawspeaker to come up with a solution. He
went off, sat down and pulled his cloak over his head, and thought
about it for nearly a day. Then he climbed up on the Law Rock
and announced that it would be less bother if everyone accepted
the new religion as a formality, but that anyone who wanted to
keep with the Old Ways could do so.

'We completely failed to see that the White Christ people
would never give up until they had grabbed everyone. We were
quite happy to live side by side with other beliefs; we never
presumed to think that our ideas were the only correct ones. We
made the mistake of thinking that the White Christ was just
another God who would be welcomed in among all the other Gods
and would coexist with them peaceably. How wrong we were.'

Inevitably, my education in paganism was patchy. Thorvall and
Tyrkir often confused folklore with religion, but in the end it did
not matter much. I soaked up the welter of information they gave
me. Tyrkir, for example, showed me my first runes, cutting the
rune staves on small flat laths of wood and making me learn his
futhark, the rune alphabet, by heart. He taught me also to read the
staves with my eyes shut, running my fingers over the scratches
and translating them in my mind. 'It's a skill that can come in
handy,' he said, 'when you want to exchange information secretly,
or simply when the message is so old and worn that you cannot
see it with the naked eye.' I tried hard to repay my tutors by

having significant dreams which they could interpret. But I found that such dreams do not come on demand. First you have to study the complex paths of the Old Ways, and then you must know how to enter them, sometimes with the help of drugs or self-mortification. I was still too young for that, and I was reluctant to approach my foster mother to ask about her seidr knowledge because she was growing more Christian by the day, and I was uncertain if she would approve of my growing interest in the Elder Faith.

Besides, that next winter Gudrid was distracted by much more down-to-earth events. Her father, old Thorbjorn, had died not long after our return from Lyusfjord, and Gudrid, as his only surviving child, had inherited everything. Next, Thorstein the Black announced that he would not return to the farm in Lyusfjord. He felt it was an unlucky spot for him and he did not feel like starting there all over again as it would mean finding a new partner to help run the farm. So by January he had found a buyer to purchase the farm as it stood, paying him in instalments, and this meant he could reimburse Gudrid for her deceased husband's share. The result was that Gudrid, who was still without a child of her own, still beautiful, still young, was now a wealthy woman. No one was much surprised when, within a year of being made a widow, my glamorous foster mother was approached by an eligible new suitor and that she agreed to his proposal of marriage. What did surprise everyone was that her husband announced soon afterwards that he was fitting out a ship to travel to Vinland and establish a new and permanent settlement at the same spot where the two Eriksson brothers, Leif and Thorvald, had previously set their hopes.

SEVEN

WHY DID GUDRID's new husband, Thorfinn Karlsefni, decide to
try his luck in far-off Vinland? Partly, I think, because he felt he
owed a debt of honour to my father, Leif. By Norse custom, when
a man wishes to marry, he first seeks formal permission from the
bride's senior male relation. In Gudrid's case this was Leif and he
readily agreed to the match. When Leif suggested the Vinland
project to Thorfinn soon afterwards, I believe that Thorfinn, who
had an old-fashioned sense of family loyalty, felt that he should
take up the project. Leif still believed that Vinland could be a new
and prosperous colony for the Greenlanders and, though he was
too busy as head of the family at Brattahlid to go there himself, he
did everything he could to support the new venture. He offered
Thorfinn the loan of the houses he had built there, which were
technically still his property, as well as the help of several key
members from his own household. Among them were my two
secret tutors – Thorvall the Hunter and Tyrkir the Smith – and
two slaves Leif had acquired on the same fateful voyage which
brought him to my mother's bed in Orkney.

I had always been curious about Haki and Hekja because I
saw them as a link to my own enigmatic past. They were husband
and wife, or that is what everyone took for granted. On the other
hand, they may have had no choice but to live together as a

couple since fate had thrown them together. They had been captured in a viking raid somewhere on the Scottish coast and
shipped to Norway, where, like Tyrkir, they were put up for sale
in the slave market at Kaupang. One of King Olaf Tryggvason's
liegemen bought them as a pair. He presumed the two captives
were Christians and thought that he could get into the good
graces of his king if he made a gift of them to his monarch. King
Tryggvason could then gain public credit and reputation by giving
the two slaves their freedom. To their owner's dismay, it turned
out that Haki and Hekja were not Christians at all, but adherents
of some pagan belief so obscure that no one had any idea what
their mutterings and incantations meant. Olaf kept them at his
court for only a few months, but the two Scots showed no
aptitude for household work. They were only happy when they
were out on some high moor or open fell that reminded them of
their homeland. So when my father Leif visited the court, the
Norwegian king got the two seemingly useless slaves off his hands
by presenting them to Leif with the remark that he hoped that
one day he would find some use for these two 'wild Scots', as he
put it, whose only skill seemed to be how swiftly they could run
across open country. Leif found the perfect work for Haki and
Hekja as soon as he got back to Greenland. The couple made
excellent sheep and cattle herders. They would spend each summer on the farthest heath lands, where they made themselves
temporary shelters by thatching over natural hollows with
branches and dried grass. Here they lived snugly like summer
hares in a form, a resemblance enhanced by their extraordinary
speed on foot. They could run down a stray sheep with ease, and
they were particularly valuable when it came to chasing wayward
animals during the autumn drive, when the livestock had to be
brought down from the hinterland and put into the winter barns.
For the rest of the year they busied themselves with odd jobs
round the farm, where I used to watch them surreptitiously,
wondering if my mother with her Irish blood had possessed the
same mixture of fair skin and dark hair, and I tried without much

success to understand the words that passed between the two Scots in their guttural, rippling language.

Karlsefni's expedition was the largest and best-equipped venture for Vinland up to that time. It numbered nearly forty people, including five women. Gudrid insisted on accompanying her new husband and she took along two female servants. There were also two farmers' wives, whose husbands had volunteered to help clear the land during the early days of the settlement in return for a land grant later. These two couples were too young to have had children of their own and Thorbjorn, Karlsefni's five-year-old son by an earlier marriage, was left behind in Brattahlid with foster parents. So the only child on board the knorr was myself, aged nearly eight. I had lobbied my father Leif to let me join the expedition and he readily agreed, to the open satisfaction of his harridan wife, Gyda, who still could not stand the sight of me.

The knorr which was to carry us westward belonged to Thorfinn. She was a well-found ship and had served him for several years in trade. Now he purchased a second smaller boat to serve as a scouting vessel. With characteristic competence Karlsefni also set about compiling a list of what was needed to establish the pioneer farm. After talking with Leif and the other men who had already been to Vinland, he loaded a good stock of farm implements – hoes, axes, saws and spades and the like – blacksmith's tools, a supply of rope and several bags of ship's nails in case we had to make repairs, as well as three dozen rolls of wadmal. This wadmal was an essential. It is cloth made from wool hand-plucked from our sheep and steeped in tubs of urine to remove the worst of the sticky wool grease. The women spin this fibre into yarn, then weave long bolts of the cloth on a simple loom suspended from the ceiling of the main room. The better-quality wadmal is set aside to make the sails of our ships while the coarser grade is turned into garments, blankets, sacks, anything that requires a fabric. Most wadmal is the same dingy brown as when the sheep had worn the wool, but sometimes the cloth is dyed with plant juice or coloured earth to produce more cheerful reds, greens and yellows. A special wadmal soaked in a mixture of sheep's grease and seal oil is nearly waterproof. This was the cloth we used to make our sea-going cloaks for the voyage – the same garment that my father gave my mother as his going-away present.

Downwind, anyone would have thought we were a mobile farm when we set sail. A small bull and three milch cows took up most of the central hold, and the smell of the cattle and wisps of dried hay from their stack of feed drifted out across the water in our lee. For the first few hours there were farmyard sounds as well because the cows kept up a low, distressed mooing before they settled to their strange new routine.

With youthful zeal I had expected instant adventure and excitement the moment we cleared the land, but like the cattle I soon found that life aboard followed the same routine as at home. I had chores to do – give the animals fresh water to drink, keep their hay topped up, clear the cattle dung. Our knorr proceeded at a stately pace, towing the scouting boat behind on a thick cable. The sea was calm, and there was nothing to see except for the escort of seabirds hovering over us and an occasional flock of black and white waterfowl with massive thick beaks, which swam along the surface of the sea beside us, occasionally ducking down and speeding ahead underwater. When I asked Thorvall why these birds did not take to the air and fly, he laughed. 'They do not know how to fly,' he said. 'The Gods gave them wings more like fish flippers. They swim when they want to travel, even from one country to another, from Iceland to Greenland, from Greenland to Vinland. That's how our sailors first guessed that there must be land to the west. When they saw the swimming birds heading out in that direction.'

This was the third of the many, many voyages of my lifetime, and I believe that Odinn had a hand in sending me upon the journey as he deliberately provoked in me the wanderlust which would bind me to him as the Far-Farer. I had been a babe in arms when my mother sailed with me from Birsay to Iceland, and still too young to remember much when I went with Gudrid from

Iceland to Greenland and suffered shipwreck. But now the crossing
from Brattahlid to Vinland made a deep and lasting impression on
me. There was a sense of travelling towards the new and unknown,
and it was a drug. Once tasted, I could never forget it, and I
wanted more. It would make me a wanderer all my life, and that is
what the All-Father intended.

My first sensation on the westward journey was the slow,
rhythmic motion of the fully laden knorr. She swayed up and down
over the long, low swells in a seemingly endless repetition of the
same movement, rising and falling, and giving a slight lurch as
each swell passed beneath her keel. Looking up at the mast top, I
saw the pattern repeated constantly in the steady elliptical circles
that the weathervane made against the sky. And just behind each
movement came the same sequence of sounds – the regular creak
of the mast stays taking up the strain each time the vessel rose, the
slight thump as the mast moved in its socket, the wash of the bow
wave as the prow of the knorr dug into the sea and, when the
vessel checked, the soft thud of a loose item rolling across the bilge
and striking the hull. I found something hypnotic and comforting
about the way that life on board took on its own rhythm, set by
the timing and order of our meals. The sequence began at dawn
with rismal when the night watch ate a cold breakfast of dried
bread and gruel; in mid-morning came dagmal when the entire
crew, except for the helmsman and lookout, gathered round the
little charcoal fire lit on a stone slab balanced on the keelson and
out of the wind and consumed the only hot meal of the day,
usually a broth, though sometimes there was fresh fish or boiled
seagull if we had been able to catch anything. Finally, as the sun
went down, we ate the nattmal, again a cold meal of skyr, sour
milk, and gruel.

On the very first night, as soon as it was dusk, Thorvall
brought me to a quiet corner of the deck and made me gaze
upwards past the dark outline of our sail. It was still early in the
season so the night was dark enough for the stars to be visible.
'The vault of the sky,' he said, 'is the inside of Ymir's skull, the

ancient frost giant. Four dwarves, Austri, Vestri, Nordri and Sudri, sit in the four corners and they took molten particles and sparks and placed them as stars, both wandering and fixed, to illuminate the earth. That way the Gods made it possible for us to guide our way at night.' He pointed out to me the leidarstjarna, the Pole Star, and how it was always at the same height in the sky on our right hand as we moved through the night. Thorvall was in his element when he was on the sea, and every day at noon he would produce a little wooden disc with small notches on the rim and lines scratched on its surface. He held it up in the sunlight so the shadow from a small pin in the centre of the disc fell across the engraved face, then he grunted directions to the helmsman.

'Trust the Gods,' he told me. 'As long as the wolves chase Sol, she will move across the sky and we can follow beneath her.'

'What if it is too cloudy and we cannot see the sun?' I ventured.

'Be patient,' he growled.

It was not cloud but a dense fog which shrouded the sun two days later. The fog was so thick that we seemed to be gliding through a bowl of thin milk. Drops of water condensed on the walrus-hide ropes of the rigging, the deck planks were dark with moisture, and we could not see farther than fifty paces. We could have been sailing in circles for all we knew, and the helmsman was edgy and nervous until Thorvall produced a flat stone from a pocket in his sea cloak. The stone was thin and opaque. Thorvall held it up to the light and peered through it, turning the stone this way and that, his arm held out straight. Finally he pointed ahead, slightly to the steering-board side of the ship. 'That course,' he ordered and without question the helmsman obeyed him.

Apart from two days spent groping our way through the fog and relying on what Thorvall called his sunstone, we had remarkably good weather and a smooth passage. Thorvall had absolute faith in Thor's power over the weather and the sea conditions, and whenever he caught a fish on the hook and line he always trailed behind the boat, he made a point of throwing a small part of the

catch back into the sea as a sacrifice. No one dared to scoff at him
openly for doing this, though I did notice some of the crew
members, the baptised ones, exchange amused glances and snigger.

Certainly Thorvall's gifts to Thor seemed to be remarkably
effective. No one was seasick except for Gudrid, whose servants
looked after her as she vomited, and it was on the morning of the
ninth day after leaving Brattahlid that Thorvall gave a deep sniff
and said firmly, 'Land.' By evening we could smell it too, the
unmistakable scent of trees wafting to us from the west. On the
morning of the tenth day we saw on the horizon the thin flat
smudge that was the edge of Vinland, and twenty-four hours later
we were close enough for Tyrkir and Thorvall and the other
veterans to establish our exact position. With the help of Thorvall's
wooden disc our knorr had made a near-perfect landfall. By general
opinion we were only a day's sail from the place where we would
find Leif's cabins.

The land was vast. The coastline extended across our ship's
bow, as though the country would go on for ever in each direction.
Behind the coast, in the interior, I could see the dark green swell
of an immense forest, where the land rose in a succession of low
hills as far as the eye could see. The shore itself was one low, grey
headland after the another, divided by deep bays and inlets.
Occasionally there were beaches of sand, but for the most part the
foreshore was a jumble of sea-worn rocks, where the waves
rumbled and surged. The colours of the stones were drab except
where a crust of seaweed and lichens added touches of green and
brown. To anyone from more southerly climates, the shore of
Vinland would have looked like a bleak and forbidding place. But
we had come from barren Greenland and, before that, from Iceland
with its equally harsh landscape. Vinland showed great potential to
the farmers among us. They noted the early growth of wild
meadow-grass speckling the land behind the beach and the first
flush of shoots on the low bushes of willow and alder. The bull
and three cows on board also sensed the pasture and became
restless to get ashore. We kept a sharp lookout for signs of

Skraelings and Tyrkir probably kept an eye open for his mysterious unipeds. But nothing moved. The land seemed empty.

Neverthless Karlsefni was cautious. He remembered Thorstein's death at the hands of the Skraelings and summoned our two 'wild Scots', Haki and Hekja. He told them that he was going to put them ashore so they could make a wide sweep inland. If they encountered Skraelings, they were to avoid contact, stay hidden, and try to assess the numbers of these strange people. After three days the two scouts were to report back to the beach, where our vessel would be anchored close by. Haki and Hekja each filled a satchel with dried food, but took nothing else. They were both wearing their usual dress, nothing more than a coarse blanket with a slit through which to put the head. There was a hood for when it rained, but otherwise the garment was so basic that it was open at the sides except for a single loop to fasten the cloth between the legs. Underneath they were naked. Both scouts clambered down into our small tender, and Thorvall and a small crew rowed them to the beach. There the Scots slipped into the water and waded to land before walking up the beach and disappearing into the scrub. Apart from a knife, they carried no weapon or tool, not even a steel and flint for making fire. 'If the Skraelings catch them, they'll think we've come from a tribe more wretched than themselves,' someone said as we backed our oars and manoeuvred the knorr to a safe distance, well out of arrow range.

Those three days seemed like an eternity for an eight-year-old boy. Karlsefni flatly refused to let anyone go ashore. We had to sit on the knorr, impatiently watching the run of the tide, trying to catch fish but without much success, and looking for signs of movement on land and seeing nothing until, suddenly, the slim figures of the two runners reappeared. Thorvall and a couple of the men went in the scouting boat to pick them up, and the two Scots returned with encouraging news. They had seen no Skraelings, they said, nor any sign of them.

We arrived at Leif's cabins at noon on the second day of coasting, but did not go ashore until Thorvall and four of the men had gone ahead, armed and alert, to check the abandoned huts, looking for strangers. But they found no sign that anyone had been there since the unlucky expedition two years earlier. Our scouts waved to us to bring the knorr into the anchorage, and by nightfall the entire expedition was safely ashore and setting up the wadmal tents which would be our homes until we had refurbished the semi-derelict cabins.

Three winters of rain and wind and snow had beaten on the turf and stone walls of Leif's cabins until they were slumped and crumbled. The rafters had fallen in. Weeds and wild grass grew on the floors. The original cabins had been constructed only for short-term occupation, so they had been roofed over with wadmal to keep out the weather. Now that we were here to stay, we needed something much more sturdy and permanent. So we began to mend and enlarge the cabins, build a big new longhouse, clear the land for our cattle, dig latrines. Our knorr, which had appeared to be so amply laden when we started out, now seemed to be a meagre source of supplies. The cattle had taken up most of the available cargo capacity, and Karlsefni had brought tools for the future, not food for the present. So we nearly starved during that first month. Of course there was no question that we would kill and eat the cattle. They were the beginning of our herd, or so we hoped. We had no time to investigate the fishing or check the forest to see if there was any wild game. Instead we laboured from dawn to dusk to cut and carry and stack hundreds of turf blocks for the main walls of our new longhouse. Soon people began to complain of hunger and how they needed proper food, not thin watery porridge, if they were to work so hard. The Christians among us began to pray to their God, seeking his help to alleviate their distress. They set up their cross-shaped symbol at one edge of the settlement, and when Thorvall – rather provocatively, I thought – built a little canopied shelter on the opposite edge of the settlement and made a pile of stones under it as his altar to Thor, there was very nearly a fight. The Christians accused him of being an arch-pagan. Thorvall warned them that he would knock down any man who interfered with his Thor altar.

Karlsefni had assigned Thorvall to help the house-builders rather than hunt. His great strength was very useful when it came to lifting up the turf sods as the walls grew higher and higher. But everyone could see that Thorvall was itching to explore. Finally, when hunger was really pinching, Karlsefni gave Thorvall permission to go hunting, though most of us wondered how just one man could find and kill enough wild game to feed forty hungry mouths. Thorvall said nothing, but gave one of his unsociable grunts, gathered up his spear and made ready to leave. As he left the camp, he went first to his little altar, took off one of the polar-bear teeth from his necklace and laid it as an offering on the top stone. Then he walked off into the thick brushwood. Within moments he had vanished.

Thorvall was away for three days, and when he did not reappear Karlsefni and the other senior men began to worry. Once again there was talk of the Skraelings and speculation that they had captured or killed our hunter. Finally Karlsefni called for volunteers to join a small search party to look for Thorvall. Karlsefni announced that he himself would lead the searchers. They were to take weapons and be on the lookout for Skraelings as well as Thorvall. There was a certain amount of reluctance to join the search party because Thorvall was not a popular figure, particularly among the Christians. Some said that if the Skraelings had got the surly curmudgeon, then it was good riddance. Naturally Tyrkir was willing to look for his friend, so too were the two Scots, and I managed to attach myself to the little group because I could be spared from the house-building.

After all this, finding Thorvall was very easy. Haki and Hekja ranged ahead, quartering back and forth through the undergrowth like a pair of hounds, and to all our surprise returned on the third day to say that they had found Thorvall on a nearby headland, but he had refused to come back with them. Thinking that Thorvall might be injured, we fought our way through the underbrush and arrived, exhausted and scratched, to find Thorvall lying stretched out on the ground on the flat crest of a small headland overlooking the sea. To the fury of the Christians, and the relief of his friends, Thorvall was in good health. Indeed, he looked remarkably relaxed as he lay on his back, gazing up at the sky and apparently talking to himself, occasionally itching himself rudely. For a moment I thought our hunter had leave of his senses or had got hold of some alcohol and was drunk. One of our group, a Christian named Bjarni, began shouting angrily at Thorvall, demanding what on earth he was playing at. Thorvall rose to his feet, and scowled at his interrogators.

'There's nothing to hunt here,' he told them, 'at least, not enough to feed forty people in a hurry. Just some small animals and birds. Maybe later, when I've more time to explore the land, I'll find the places where I can set traps for the larger animals. So I composed a poem to Thor's honour, and was reciting it for him, and asking him to provide for us.'

'Thor! You heathen!' yelled Bjarni. 'How do you imagine that your blundering oaf of a God can help us. You might as well pray to the sea to give us some food.'

'Maybe he will,' Thorvall replied gruffly.

We all walked back to the camp and Thorvall received black looks from many of the settlers. Several of them turned their backs on him. I heard a number of comments that he was a cantankerous fool, riddled with superstition, too lazy to go hunting properly, and had been idling away his time, while others had been doing all the hard work on the house-building.

Next morning one of the men went out along the strand to gather driftwood for our cooking fires and came stumbling excitedly back into camp.

'Everyone, bring your knives and axes. There's a dead whale lying on the beach,' he shouted. 'It must have been washed up in the night. There's enough meat there to feed us for a couple of weeks!'

Thorvall, who had been sitting near the campfire, raised his shaggy head and let out a great roar of triumph. 'There, you White Christ fanatics, Old Red Beard liked his praise poem and he's sent us food from the sea. Now go and fill your envious bellies.'

We all hurried along the beach and were soon hacking up the whale. It was perhaps twenty-five feet in length, and of a type that none of us had ever seen before, not even Karlsefni, who had seen many different types of whale during his travels as a merchant. But the carcass cut like any other whale's, with a good three-inch-thick layer of blubber which we peeled away in strips to get at the rich, dark red meat. It was a magnificent find. The blubber we would use as fat for cooking or eat salted, while the dark red meat we grilled and ate straight away – it tasted like well-hung beef. Thorvall took his chance to gloat over the Christians, teasing them about how Thor had turned out to be more generous than their Christ. Eventually they became so exasperated that they said that the meat was cursed and that it gave them stomach cramps and we should throw away the profane flesh. But I noticed that they ate a full meal before they made a gesture of throwing some of the offal into the tide.

The stranded whale ended our famine because over the next few weeks the land began to reward us with her bounty. Leif had sited his cabins on the lip of an estuary, where two small rivers merged before emptying into a shallow tidal estuary. Both rivers teemed with fish. One of my earliest tasks was to dig a series of trenches in the sand shallows at low tide. Shoals of halibut and other flat fish regularly came swimming into the lake on the high tide to feed and as the water receded were left stranded in my trenches. For variety I also picked up clams and mussels on the wide curve of the beach, or helped the adults set nets for the magnificent salmon and sea trout which swam up the rivers. By our Greenlandic standards nature was extraordinarily bountiful. The meadows by the river mouths were covered in tall wild grasses and gave good pasture for our cattle, which usurped the deer whose tracks we could clearly see on the river banks. The most travelled of our colonists had never laid eyes on such stands of trees, mostly softwoods, but with some trees completely unknown. One yellow tree, very like our birch, provides timber as tough as our native oak, and another tree with a three-pointed leaf gives a beautiful ingrained wood that Tyrkir gloated over, turning and polishing it so that it glowed with a deep honey colour. As a timber-starved people, we scarcely knew what to do first: whether to cut down small trees to make our houses or to fell the larger ones and set them aside to season so that we could take a precious cargo across to Greenland.

By late summer there was an almost continuous natural harvest along the fringes of the forest. The wild cherries were the first to bear fruit, followed by an abundance of hazelnuts and then an array of wild berries swelling and ripening on the bushes and shrubs, speckling them with red and purple, dark blue, crimson and gold. Many plants we recognised – blueberries, cloudberries, raspberries, loganberries and cranberries. But there were several which were new to us, and sometimes so highly coloured that at first we were suspicious they were poisonous. I was given the job of hiding in the undergrowth and watching to see whether the wild birds fed on them. If they did, then we gathered this fruit as well, drying what we could not eat immediately for our winter provisions.

Only the soil was a little disappointing: it was light and thin and not as rich as we had hoped, lying in a shallow skin over the estuary sand and gravel. But it was no worse than much of the soil in Greenland and Iceland, and our farmers did not complain because they were compensated by the excellence of the hunting. In the long days of summer we trapped deer on the edges of the meadows and snared wild duck, which gathered in vast numbers on the meres and bogs. Scarcely a month after we landed there was a whale drive. A small school of pilot whales ventured into the bay at high water, and we managed to get behind them in the rowing boats and drive them up into the shallows just at the critical moment when the tide turned, so that the animals were unable to retreat and lay awkwardly in the shallows. It was a slaughter. The

water was striped with wavering red bands of blood as every able-
bodied person waded into the water, knife or axe in hand. We
must have dispatched at least twenty of the animals in a gory
frenzy, with the beasts thrashing in their last agonies and the foam
pink with their blood. After we had tugged the corpses ashore,
skinned and cut them into pieces, we had enough meat to last three
months.

Tyrkir set up his workshop and a smithy down by the river.
Digging in the swamp behind the settlement, he turned up loaf-
shaped lumps of a hard encrusted stone which he said he could
smelt into soft iron for replacement tools when they were needed.
He announced that he required an assistant to help him with the
work and made sure that I became his apprentice. In his little
smithy he showed me how to build the small kiln of clay and stack
it with alternate layers of charcoal and the bog iron, then ignite the
mixture and wait until the fierce heat had done its work, before
breaking open the kiln and scraping out the lump of raw iron from
the embers. As I supplied more charcoal and operated the bellows,
and he refined and forged and shaped the metal, he talked earnestly
to me about the Old Gods and their ways. Watching Tyrkir heat
and hammer the metal, then quench it in water, I was fascinated by
the almost magical process whereby our metal tools were produced,
and I readily accepted Tyrkir's central theme that there is an
indissoluble bond between knowledge of metalwork and magic.
Tyrkir would mutter simple charms through the smoke and steam,
and grunt invocations to the Gods as he scrupulously observed his
craft's taboos. He never allowed two blades to lie one across the
other. He sprinkled a pinch of salt on the fire when we began work
in the morning, and at the end of the day he always placed his
working hammer on the small altar he had built for Thor. And
when he finished an item, whether a billhook or a spearhead, he
would mutter a small prayer and gather a few leaves, then pound
them into a green paste and smear them on the hot metal as an
offering. 'The juice gives strength to the metal,' he told me as I
held the cooler end of some spearhead or sickle with a cloth around

my hand and plunged it into the quenching tub with its hiss of steam.

In the smoke-grimed little smithy Tyrkir took breaks from pounding at the glowing metal to tell what he knew of the galdra, the charms and spells that make up the bulk of seidr lore. 'There are hundreds,' he told me. 'Each produces a different result suitable for a different occasion. How effective they are depends on the user's experience and skill. I know only a few, perhaps a couple of dozen, and they are mostly related to my work with metal. I never complete a sword for war, a sea knife for a sailor, or a spearhead for a hunter without reciting the correct galdra for the purpose it will serve. But these are craftsmen's galdra. There are more powerful ones, above all at times of combat. There is one to calm the rage in a warrior's heart, another to sing behind a shield as the charge is launched, which will guarantee that all your comrades-in-arms emerge from the fray unscathed, while a third gives the enchanter the quickness to catch an arrow flying through the air. A fourth, if spoken over a goblet of water which is then thrown over a warrior, ensures that he survives the forthcoming battle, perhaps wounded, but alive.'

Tyrkir failed to notice that I was not attracted by martial prowess and muscular feats and stories of bloodshed. To tell the truth I was always a little frightened of my dwarfish mentor and the hard-edged bitterness he sometimes showed when he told the more gory tales. He relished telling me how Volund, the master smith and 'prince of elves', had lured the young sons of King Nidud into his forge and, as they peered into his chest of treasure, lopped off their heads. 'You know why he did that, Thorgils?' Tyrkir asked as he fused a strip of harder steel into the soft iron blade of a sickle to give it a sharper edge. 'Volund did that to revenge himself on Nidud. Volund was so skilled at metalwork that the evil Nidud kidnapped him, then lamed him so he could not escape and forced him to work as a royal goldsmith. Volund bided his time until he could lure Nidud's greedy and stupid sons into his workshop. There he killed them and made splendid jewels from their eyeballs, brooches from their teeth and silver-plated bowls from their skulls. To their mother he presented the jewels, to their sister the brooches and to their father the bowls.' Tyrkir gave a grim smile of satisfaction. 'And in the end he seduced the Princess Bodvild and left her with child, before he cunningly fashioned wings of metal and flew away from his captivity.'

Gudrid was pregnant. People now understood why she had been seasick on the outward voyage and why she had insisted on bringing two serving women with her from Brattahlid. Most of the settlers took her pregnancy as a good omen. It meant that our little colony would flourish and grow. I wanted to be happy for Gudrid, like everyone else, but I was confused and unsure. For most of my young life I had seen myself as Gudrid's true son, and now it seemed that I was to have a rival for her affections.

In the late autumn of that first year in Vinland Gudrid gave birth to a healthy, squalling male child. He was given the name Snorri, which means 'unruly' or 'argumentative', and he was the first of our race to be born in that distant Norse outpost. Perhaps he is the only one ever to be born there. I do not know because for many years I have not had any direct news from Vinland. Nor, I suppose, has anyone else. Instead I have only the memory of the great rejoicing and excitement on the day when Snorri arrived in this world and how Thorfinn, the proud father, gave a birthday feast in our fine new longhouse. Perhaps it was the first stirring of jealousy within me, or perhaps it was my sixth sense that produced a sense of foreboding within me. But that evening, as we all gathered in the longhouse and sat along the side benches and listened to Thorfinn call toasts to celebrate the arrival of our first child, I felt a nagging certainty that those golden early days of our colony were numbered.

EIGHT

THE HERALDS OF our failure came just three days later. It was almost noon on a mild sunny day and the colonists were spread out doing their usual daily tasks, some fishing, a few absent in the forest hunting and tree-felling, the majority working in and around the houses or clearing gardens. The women, I remember, were preparing food, for I recall the smell of venison roasting on a spit over an open fire. One of the builders was up on the roof of a house, checking that the turves were binding together properly to make a watertight seal, when he straightened to ease his back and happened to glance out to sea. He stopped in surprise and shouted, pointing out along the coast. His cry alerted all of us in the settlement and we turned to look. Around the end of the farthest low spit of land a cluster of small boats was approaching. At that distance they looked no more than black needles, but it was quite obvious what they were: Skraelings. Everyone stopped whatever they were doing, and a shiver of apprehension passed through the crowd. It must be remembered that we were farmers and fishermen, not seasoned warriors, and the arrival of these strangers in this isolated land sent a chill of fear down our spines. 'Be as friendly as possible. Act normally,' warned Thorfinn. 'Don't make any sudden movements, but don't let them come too close either. We'll just wait to see what they want.'

The little Skraeling flotilla – there were nine of their skin boats – slowly paddled closer. The boatmen seemed to be as surprised and cautious as we were. They slackened their pace and drifted their boats gently through the shallows, keeping about fifty paces offshore as they watched us, staring curiously. Neither side said a word. There was a tense silence. Then one of the Skraelings stood up in his boat – it was a narrow, trough-shaped vessel, not very well made – and began to wave his arm in circles above his head. In his hand was some sort of blade, which made a low humming sound, halfway between a gentle roar and a mutter.

'What do you think that means?' Thorfinn asked his second-in-command, a man called Thorbrand Snorrisson.

'It could be a sign of peace,' he replied, 'They don't seem very hostile.'

'Then we had better respond in the same way,' answered Thorfinn. 'Take a white shield and go into the water up to your knees. Hold up the shield so they can see it clearly.'

A white shield is our standard signal of peace, recognised and used even among the wild Irish and distant German tribes. A red shield displayed means war. Anyhow, the Skraelings seemed to understand the gesture; they gently turned their boats towards us and paddled inshore. We all stood motionless as they touched land, and the men climbed out of their boats and advanced hesitantly up the beach.

We could see that they were exactly like the people that my uncle Thorvald's crew had attacked and killed. The men – there were no women in the party – were dark-skinned and a little smaller than us in stature. They had the same almond-shaped eyes and lank, very black hair worn long and loose, right down to their shoulders. Their cheekbones were high and prominent, and this gave their faces a menacing look. I noticed that their eyes were uniformly dark brown, almost black. They must have been a hunting party because there was very little in the boats except for some hunting spears and nondescript bundles wrapped in rawhide. Thorfinn suspected that they were as startled as we were by the encounter. At any rate, there was a very long silence, while both parties looked one another over, and then the leader of the Skraelings called out something in an unintelligible language and the entire group deliberately got back into their boats, shoved off and paddled away, from time to time looking back over their shoulders.

As the Skraeling boats disappeared on their original route up the coast, we returned to our chores. You can imagine the chatter and speculation about when the Skraelings would reappear and what they intended. No one doubted that this was only the pre-liminary encounter.

The Skraelings took us even more unawares on their next visit by appearing from the landward side of the settlement. It must have been about six months later, and how they got so close to the settlement without being detected was alarming. At one moment we were going about our usual routine, and the next instant a couple of dozen Skraelings were walking down from the edge of the woods towards us. They seemed to have sprung from the ground. It was lucky that they came peacefully for we were taken totally off guard. Indeed, we were all dithering, not knowing whether to run for our weapons, cluster together or go forward to meet the Skraelings with another peaceful gesture, when, as luck would have it, our bull began to bellow. He was with the cows in the nearby meadow, and possibly the scent of the Skraelings – for they did smell rather powerfully – disturbed him. He let out a series of thunderous bellows and this terrified our visitors. Glancing back over their shoulders, they scampered for the safety of our houses as though pursued by a monster. Several of our more timid men had already taken up position inside the houses, the better to defend themselves, and had already shut the doors. The next thing they knew, the terrified Skraelings were beating on the door planks, crying out in their strange language, pleading to be let in. The Norsemen, thinking that an attack was in progress, pushed desper-ately against the doors from the inside, trying to keep them shut. For us who were outside the situation, once so fraught, was now totally comic. It was clear that the Skraelings meant no harm, and the fainthearts inside the houses were in a panic at the unseen onslaught. Those of us who could see what was happening burst into roars of laughter. Our guffaws reassured the Skraelings, who calmed down and began to look sheepish, and after a few moments the frightened house defenders began to peek out to see what had happened, only to make us scoff even more loudly. This ludicrous situation proved to be the ideal introduction – there's nothing like two sides making public fools of themselves and accepting the fact for a sense of mutual understanding to develop. With sign language and smiles the Skraelings began to open the packs they had been carrying. They contained furs, splendid furs, the pelts of fox and marten and wolf and otter. There were even a couple of glossy black-bear pelts. The quality was like nothing we had seen before, and we knew they would fetch a premium price in any market in Norway or Denmark. There was not one of us who did not begin to wonder what we might trade with the Skraelings in exchange.

The obvious item was metal – for we had noted that the Skraelings possessed only stone-tipped weapons. But Thorfinn was quick off the mark. He ordered sharply that no one was to trade weapons or metal tools to the Skraelings. Better weaponry was the only advantage we possessed against their superior numbers. Everyone was standing around racking their brains about what to do next and the Skraelings were gazing around curiously, when one of the women in a gesture of hospitality fetched a pail of milk and a wooden dipper. She offered a dipper of the milk to the leader of the Skraelings. He stared at the liquid in puzzlement, sniffed it suspiciously and then cautiously tried a sip, while the woman indicated that he should drink it. The Skraeling was delighted with the taste of milk. He must have also believed that it was a rich and rare substance, for he delved in his pack and offered the woman a marten skin. She had the wit to accept it. Another Skraeling stepped forward and gestured he wanted to try drinking milk, and before long the entire group were clustering around, reaching for the ladle and handing over valuable furs and pelts in exchange.

Even as an eight-year-old lad, I had seen the drunks at Brattahlid so desperate as to give their last coins for a draught of wine or strong mead, but this was the only time in my long and varied life that I have ever seen anyone pay so handsomely for mere cow juice. What is more, the Skraelings were totally happy with the bargain. After they had parted with their entire stock of furs, even leaving behind their empty packs, they were content to walk back into the forest, carrying their barter profit in their bellies, while we gleefully stowed away a small fortune in Vinland furs.

But however peacefully the Skraeling visit had turned out, their arrival had a more sinister implication. The following day Thorfinn told us to stop all our other work and start building a palisade around the settlement. We did not need urging. All of us had an uncomfortable feeling that our peaceful and profitable relationship with the Skraelings might not last. Everyone remembered how the Skraelings had killed Thorvald Eriksson with their darts on his earlier expedition to this land, and that a massacre by our men of eight Skraelings from their hunting party had preceded his lone death. If the Skraelings behaved like us, then they might still be looking for more blood vengeance to balance the account. Like one of those sea anemones who retract their tentacles when they sense danger, we shrank back inside a safer perimeter. The outlying houses were abandoned and the entire community shifted to live within the shelter of the palisade, just in case the Skraelings returned with less peaceable intentions. The only structure to remain outside the stockade was Tyrkir's little smithy down by the river, where he needed access to the bog iron and running water.

THE SKRAELINGS DID not return until the beginning of the following winter, when baby Snorri was nearly a year old. By then we felt we were getting the measure of this new land. We had cleared back the surrounding brushwood for additional pasture, fenced two small paddocks for our cattle, which now included three healthy calves, improved and strengthened the walls and roofs of our original hastily built dwellings, and our people were beginning to talk about the prospect of sending our knorr back to Greenland with a cargo of timber and furs, and attracting more settlers to join us. We had lived through the full cycle of the seasons, and though the winter had been cold and dreary, it had been no worse than what we had known in Greenland. Our settlement had begun to put down roots, but – as we soon learned – those roots were shallow.

This time the Skraelings came in much greater strength, and by land as well as by water. One group of about a score of hunters emerged from the forest, while their comrades paddled directly into the bay in glistening, grease-treated skin boats. Their visit seemed to have been planned well ahead of time because both groups were seen to be carrying no weapons, only their packs of furs. This time one of our fishermen had spotted the Skraelings at a distance and come ashore to warn us. Thorfinn, worried by their greater numbers, had already ordered the entire community to enter the stockade and shut the gate. So when the Skraelings approached they found no one to greet them. The fields and the beach were deserted. They came up to the palisade and hesitated. Thorfinn called out, asking what they wanted, but of course they did not understand a word of our language and we had no way of understanding their reply. Then one of the Skraelings, a tall, good-looking man who must have been their chieftain, lobbed his pack over the top of the palisade. It landed on the earth with a soft thump and we found it contained five grey wolf pelts. Clearly this was the result of their summer trapping and the Skraelings had come again to trade. 'Let's see if we can sell them only milk again,' Thorfinn warned us. 'Remember: on no account let them get their hands on our weapons.' The stockade gate was cautiously open and we began to trade.

It was not quite as easy as before. The strange dark-skinned men were still eager to barter furs for milk, but when the milk was all drunk they still had more pelts for sale, and pointed to the red wadmal, which one of the colonists was wearing as garters. In the beginning we offered a hand's span of red cloth cut from the bolt for every pelt. This they accepted and immediately tied the pieces of cloth around their heads, preening in the gaudy decoration. But then the supply of red cloth ran low and it was only possible to offer them a single ribbon of red cloth, barely a finger wide, for each pelt. To our astonishment, the Skraelings were just as happy as before to make the bargain, and kept on dealing until their stock of fur was used up.

When the trading for milk and red cloth had ended, the Skraelings lingered. They strolled among our men, gingerly picking up various implements and testing their weight and wondering at their purpose. Clearly these were people who had never handled a spade or sickle, though I suspect that, hidden in the edge of the forest, they had often watched us farming. They did not mean any harm, I'm sure, and were merely inquisitive. But quick as a flash one of them leaned forward and tugged a scramsaxe from the belt of a man called Hafgrim. Startled, Hafgrim gave a shout of surprise and tried to seize the culprit Skraeling in order to retrieve his long knife. But the Skraeling was too quick for him and twisted away. The entire group of Skraelings scattered like a shoal of frightened minnows and began to run back towards the woods, several of them still with our farm tools in their hands. One Skraeling was so terrified that he ran in the wrong direction, past the smithy, and Tyrkir, who had gone back to work, emerged from the doorway just at the right moment to stick out his foot and trip him up. As casually as if he were in a salmon stream, Tyrkir then reached inside the smithy, produced a heavy fish spear he had been mending and killed him. I shall never forget the sight of my first battle corpse, the half-naked Skraeling, suddenly a pathetic, scrawny, broken figure, sprawled half in and half out of the peat stream, his bright red headband smeared with mud.

Thorfinn immediately called an assembly to discuss what we should do next. Everybody crowded into the open space in front of the longhouse and in the nervous aftermath of that tragic brawl it was not long before people were shouting irritably at one another, arguing about the best tactics to defeat the Skraelings. No one doubted that the Skraelings would return and seek revenge.

I do not know whether the next, and final, visit of the Skraelings was an accident or intentional and if they came to exact retribution for the man killed outside Tyrkir's smithy. For more than a year we mounted guard over the colony. Day and night there was a watcher stationed on the headland to keep a lookout for Skraeling boats, and another lookout scanned the edge of the forest, where it lapped down towards our stockade. Then came the fateful day when the coast watcher came panting up from the beach to announce that a large Skraeling fleet was rounding the headland. He had counted at least thirty of the needle-shaped boats and half a dozen larger canoes, each paddled by a dozen men. No one seemed to have noticed that the new Skraeling threat came from the south, and that the men we had driven off had run away in the opposite direction, to the north.

Thorfinn had planned it all out. As the Skraeling fleet aproached the beach, a handful of our men, led by the same Thorbrand Snorrisson who had stood alongside Thorfinn at the first encounter with the Skraelings, took up position on the foreshore, displayed their red shields and called out a fighting challenge. For a short while the Skraeling fleet hung back, the paddlers either suspicious or puzzled by the belligerent behaviour of the white men. Then, as our champions continued to shout defiance and wave their weapons, the Skraelings decided to accept the challenge. The Skraeling men rose to their feet in the skin boats and began to wave the same thin-bladed implements over their heads that they had employed on their very first visit, the flail-like implements that might have been mistaken for the flat wooden lath known as a weaver's sword. Only this time the sound they produced was entirely different. Instead of a low muttering hum, the noise was a loud and angry buzz, almost the sound of an enraged swarm of bees. Then, as more and more of the whirling flails joined in, the sound swelled in volume until it became a cataract of noise, filling the air until it seemed that the blood was roaring in our ears. Finally, the noise altered again as the sound-makers began to coordinate the movements of their flails, and the sound began to come rushing towards us in wave after wave, rising and falling in volume as it beat upon our senses.

Presumably, this extraordinary resonance was intended to frighten or dismay our small group of men down on the beach and it worked. Numbed by the vibrating din, they stood rooted to the ground. This was their error. While the Skraeling boats were still some distance away from the shoreline, a shower of darts suddenly came skimming through the air from the flotilla and began to patter down around our men in a deadly hail. The Skraelings were using some sort of dart launcher, a flat board a cubit long that made an extension to their throwing arm and gave an astonishing range to their missiles. Three of our men were struck by the darts, two were killed outright, and scarcely a member of our advance party was not injured in some way. As the Skraelings came into close range, they began to fling another strange weapon at us – spears which pulled behind them some sort of round float attached by a short length of line. The weird and startling appearance of these floats hurtling through the air frightened our men as much as the war sound of the flails. As they went skimming through the air over their heads and bounced on the ground, our men feared that the Skraelings were unleashing some sort of magic weapon.

Now the Skraelings were climbing out of their boats and running up the beach, waving lances and stone-edged knives, trying to come to grips with our advance guard. The Norsemen turned and fled, as was Thorfinn's plan, for they were really decoys. When the Skraelings came level with the dead bodies of our two slain, their leader was seen to reach down and pick up the axe from the corpse of Thorbrand Snorrisson. The Skraeling leader must never have seen a metal axe before, because he hefted it and then hacked experimentally at a nearby rock. The axe head broke, and thinking it was useless because it did not cut the rock, the Skraeling leader threw it into the sea with a gesture of disgust. A few moments later he learned what a metal blade can do on human flesh because by then the decoy party of colonists, with the Skraelings in pursuit, had fallen back as far as the edge of the forest, where Thorfinn had hidden the main body of the settlers in his ambush. The bulk of our men came charging out of the brushwood at full tilt, waving their weapons and roaring their war shouts. The Skraelings did not have a chance. They were lightly clad, held no shields, and even their lances could be sheered through with a swingle sweep of a metal sword. The rush of Norsemen bowled over the Skraelings, and before they could flee four Skraelings were killed, two of them victims to the heavy axes of the Norse farmers. The whole encounter was over in an instant. The Skraelings took to their heels in panic and either ran for the edge of the woods or back to their boats, which they pushed off and fled in as fast as they could paddle.

When I helped bury the corpse of Thorbrand Snorrisson I found that the small dart which had killed him looked more like a hunting weapon than a man-killing implement. As for the mysterious spears and their attached floats, they proved to be sealing harpoons with an inflated bladder attached to mark the spot where the seal has dived when it is wounded. I did not voice my opinion to the jubilant settlers – they would have thought me utterly impertinent – but I came to the conclusion that the Skraelings had not come prepared for war and we did not deserve our victory. The Skraelings were a large hunting party and would have passed by us peaceably if we had not challenged them with our red war shields and shouted defiance.

Yet, in the greater scheme of our Norse involvement in Vinland, I don't think it would have made any difference in the end. Even if we had realised that the Skraelings meant us no harm on that occasion, they would probably have come back on a later visit to drive us away from the lands where they lived. And, of course, we took the Skraelings to have the same responses as ourselves – when the Norse feel threatened, their natural reaction is to turn and fight, to protect their territory. They seldom consider the long-term consequences of such action, and they rarely back

down. That day on the beach at Vinland our men were too
frightened and too desperate to act in any other way than with
violence.

It was that feeling of being under threat that lost us Vinland.
We stayed for the winter – the season was too advanced to think
of moving anywhere – but all through the winter months we
worried and fretted that the Skraelings would return. 'This is a rich
and fertile land,' was how Thorfinn put it to us on the day we
assembled to make a final decision about leaving. 'Of course, we
can visit from time to time and cut shiploads of fine timber for
ourselves. But we would be foolish to think that we can establish
ourselves here in the face of superior numbers of hostile Skraeling.
In the end they would overwhelm us.' There was no dissenting
voice. We knew we were too isolated and exposed. In the spring
we reloaded our knorr with the products of our labour – seasoned
timber, dried fruit, a rich store of furs, carved souvenirs of that
splendid honey-coloured wood, the dried skins of some of the
more colourful birds complete with their feathers – and we set sail
for Greenland.

As our travel-worn knorr felt the wind and began to gather
speed, I looked back at the gently sloping beach in front of Leif's
cabins. On the very last morning of our stay I had stood barefoot
in the sand and dug a final channel in the hopes of trapping a
flounder, just as I had done when we first came there. Already the
incoming tide which had floated the knorr off the landing beach,
had washed away every trace of my labour. The only mark of my
efforts to harvest the sea were a few piles of empty mussel shells
just above the line of seawrack. A hundred paces farther up the
beach, over the first swell of the dunes, I could just see the roofs
of the turf houses we had abandoned. Already their humped shapes
were merging into the distance, and soon they would be lost to
view against the forest background. Everyone of us aboard the
knorr was looking back, even the helmsman was glancing over his
shoulder. We felt regretful but we did not feel defeated, and the
one unspoken thought in our minds was that perhaps there were

Norsemen still left alive in that vast land and we were abandoning them to their fate.

I was thinking of one person in particular – my hero and tutor, Thorvall the Hunter. He had disappeared midway through our time at Leif's cabins when the bickering between ardent Christians and Old Believers reached such a pitch that Thorvall announced that he did not intend to stay any longer with the group. He would explore along the coast and find a more congenial spot. Anyone who wanted to accompany him was free to do so. Four of our men chose to go with him and Thorfinn gave them our small scouting boat, possibly because Gudrid encouraged him to do so. More than once she said that she did not want Snorri growing up in the company of men like Thorvall with their heathen ways. I was downcast for several days after Thorvall and his few companions rowed off, heading north along the coast. When we heard nothing more from them, I presumed with everyone else that Thorvall and his companions had been captured and killed by the Skraelings. It was what we Norse would have done to a small group of interlopers.

NINE

BACK IN BRATTAHLID, we received a muted greeting from the Greenlanders. The general opinion was that our expedition had been a wasted effort and it would have been better if we had stayed at home. Faced with this dispiriting reception, Thorfinn announced that he would spend only a few weeks in Greenland, then head onwards with his ship to Iceland. There he proposed to return to his family in Skagafjord, and set up house with Gudrid and their two-year-old son. This time I was not invited to accompany them.

Abandoned – or so I felt – by Gudrid and with only wizened Tyrkir as my mentor, I became morose and difficult. After nearly three years' absence in Vinland, my moodiness deepened when I found I had drifted apart from my circle of boyhood friends in Brattahlid. Eyvind, Hrafn and the others had continued to grow up as a group while I was away. They showed an initial curiosity about my descriptions of life in Vinland, but soon lost interest in what I had seen or done there. The boys had always regarded me as being a little odd, and now they judged that my lonely life in Vinland as the only child of my age, had made me even more solitary. We no longer had much in common.

The result was that I began to nurse a secret nostalgia for Vinland. My experiences in that strange land helped define who I was. So I yearned to return there.

The opportunity to go back to Vinland was a complete surprise when it came, because it was arranged by the last person in the world whom I would have expected: my aunt Freydis. While I had been away in Vinland, she had matured from a scheming nineteen-year-old into a domineering woman, both physically and mentally. She had put on weight and bulk, so now she was big and buxom, full-bosomed and with heavy arms and a meaty face that would have been better suited to a man. She even had a light blonde moustache. Despite her off-putting appearance she had managed to find a husband, a weak-willed blusterer by the name of Thorvard, who ran a small farm at a place called Gardar. Like the majority of the people of the area, he lived in fear of Freydis's temper, with its violent mood swings and bouts of black anger.

Freydis, who never lost the chance to remind people that she was the daughter of the first settler of Greenland, took it into her head that Thorfinn and Gudrid had been incompetent as pioneers in Vinland and that she, Freydis, could do better. She was so vehement on the topic that people listened to her. Leif's cabins, Freydis pointed out, were still the property of her half-brother, and she announced that the Eriksson clan should return to their property and make it flourish, and she was the person to do it. She began by asking my father for permission to reoccupy the huts. Leif prevaricated. He had decided that he would not waste any men or resources in Vinland after his failed investment with Thorfinn. So he put off Freydis with the promise that he would lend her the buildings and even loan her the family knorr, but only if she managed to raise a crew. However, when Freydis put her energies into a project there was nothing and no one who could stand in her way.

To everyone's astonishment Freydis produced not one crew, but three, and a second vessel as well. The way it happened was this: the spring after my return from Vinland with Gudrid and Thorfinn, a foreign ship jointly owned by two brothers from Iceland, Helgi and Finnbogi, put in to Brattahlid. She was the largest knorr that anyone had ever seen, so big that she carried

sixty people on board. Helgi and Finnbogi had decided to emigrate
to Greenland and had brought along their families, goods, cattle,
and all the necessary paraphernalia. Naturally the two brothers
went to see Leif to seek his advice on where they should settle.
But on meeting the new arrivals, Leif was not at all keen to
welcome them, for it was abundantly clear that the Icelanders were
a very rough lot. Like Erik the Red before them, they had left
Iceland to escape a violent blood feud which had involved several
deaths. Three of the men had murder charges hanging over them.
Leif could easily imagine the quarrels and violence if the newcomers tried unsuccessfully to settle the marginal lands, and then started
to edge towards the better lands closer to the water. So while my
father greeted the two brothers with a show of hospitality, he was
very anxious that they should not stay too long. He advised them
to proceed farther along the coast and find new land to the north –
the farther away from Brattahlid the better was his unspoken
opinion.

At that crucial stage, just when Leif was hoping to be rid of
the newcomers and the Icelanders were getting restless, Freydis,
the born schemer, saw her chance. She travelled from her home in
Gardar to call on Helgi and Finnbogi.

'I'm putting together an expedition to sail to Vinland and
reoccupy Leif's cabins,' she said to them. 'Why don't you join
forces with me? There is plenty of good land there, which I can
allocate to you as soon as we are established.'

'What about the Skraeling menace?' Finnbogi asked. 'We heard
that Thorfinn Karlsefni reckoned that no Norseman could ever
hold Vinland in the face of Skraeling hostility.'

Freydis brushed the question aside. 'Karlsefni was a coward,'
she said. 'All his talk of the danger from the Skraelings and how
numerous they were was just an excuse to cover up the fact that he
and his settlers had been incompetent. If you join with me, our
group will be too numerous for the Skraelings to attack.'

She proposed that Helgi and Finnbogi supply thirty settlers.
She would match this number and their combined force would

discourage the Skraelings. She already had her own list of volunteers from Brattahlid and Gardar. They were mostly her cronies, one or two malcontents and several failed farmers who had nothing to lose by throwing in their lot with Freydis. Personally I disliked Freydis as much as ever and trusted her even less, but my name was also on her list. Against my better judgement and, in a fit of discontent and longing for Vinland, I had volunteered to join my aunt's crew. Like my father Leif, I had never thought Freydis would succeed in mustering a full expedition, and when she succeeded, I feared I would seem cowardly if I had backed out at the last moment. My immaturity also had something to do with the decision to go with Freydis. At the age of twelve I was being both fickle and obstinate. Joining her expedition seemed to me the only way of escaping from my troubles now that Gudrid and Thorfinn had left for Iceland and I felt depressed at the prospect of living out my life in the confines of Brattahlid. Once again the wanderlust that Odinn had implanted in me was stirring.

So for the third time Leif's venerable knorr sailed for Vinland, the very same vessel which ten years earlier had rescued me as an infant from the reef. My destiny seemed intimately connected with that vessel, though by now she was distinctly shabby and worn. Her mast had snapped in a heavy gale and been fished with heavy splints. Her hull was out of true, with a distinct droop where she had been overloaded so often that she sagged amidships. Many of her planks were rotten or had been damaged, and due to the shortage of good timber locally, they had been replaced with short lengths which made a clumsy patchwork. Even when recaulked and rerigged, she was barely fit for sea, and as we sailed west, I found myself not just cleaning cattle dung, but joining every able-bodied man in the crew to bail out the bilges every four hours to keep our vessel afloat. Our consort, the big new Icelandic ship, did nothing to help us. From the start there was no cohesion in our expedition whatsoever. The larger knorr would draw close as we lay there wallowing on the swell, tipping water over the side from buckets, and her ruffianly crew would jeer at us.

Tyrkir did not come with us. He had finally been given his formal freedom from slavery. A stickler for tradition, Tyrkir held a little ceremony to mark his manumission. He obtained a supply of grain and some malt and brewed a great cauldron of beer, then he invited every one of the Erikssons and their children to Thorvall the Hunter's old empty cabin, where Tyrkir had now installed himself. When everyone was gathered, he formally presented my father Leif with the first drinking horn of the new beer and a small loaf of bread and salt, which he had obtained by burning seaweed. Then he handed beer, bread and salt to all the other senior members of the family, one by one, and they pronounced him to be a free man and his own master and offered their congratulations. Considering that Tyrkir was still far from his German birthplace, from where he had been kidnapped as a youth, it was remarkable how emotional and happy he was. When the ceremony was over, he hung up the drinking horn by a leather thong on a peg just beside the entrance to his cabin, a proud reminder that he was now a free man.

No such camaraderie marked the arrival of our two knorrs at Leif's cabins. The Icelanders and the Greenlanders might as well have belonged to two different expeditions. Ashore the two groups bickered constantly. It all began with an argument about who was to occupy the longhouse which Karlsefni had built. Helgi and Finnbogi wanted to claim it, but Freydis retorted that all the buildings, including the cowsheds, belonged to her family and she would exercise her right to occupy all of them. She pointed out that she had never offered the Icelanders free accommodation, only a chance to settle the land. If they wanted shelter, they should build it for themselves. Helgi and Finnbogi's people were so enraged that they almost started a fight on the spot. But they paused after they counted up the men that Freydis had mustered. It seemed that Freydis had cheated. Instead of manning her ship with thirty men as agreed, she had smuggled aboard five extra settlers to Vinland, some of the most turbulent characters from Brattahlid, and her faction had the advantage of numbers. So the

Icelanders had to build two longhouses to accommodate themselves and their wives and children, and of course the Greenlanders did not help them. One group laboured at the building, while the other went fishing and hunting and tended their cattle. This time it was the Greenlanders who did the jeering at the sweating Icelanders.

What had begun with mere selfishness degenerated into unconcealed malice. Freydis's people not only refused to assist the Icelanders with their house-building but would not lend them tools for the work. They even demanded to be paid for any share of the fish and game they caught, insisting that the Icelanders pledge future profits from the colony. Very soon the two groups were not on speaking terms, and the Greenlanders were deliberately angering the Icelanders by ogling their women and passing lewd remarks. Freydis's husband Thorvard was too weak and hesitant to stop this reckless behaviour, and Freydis herself seemed positively to approve of it.

I stayed well out of this quarrel. I wanted no part of the growing animosity and I began to appreciate how Thorvall felt when there was bad blood between the Christians and the Old Believers. Obdurate bloody-mindedness is characteristic of the Norse. If someone receives a slight, or even imagines that he or she has done so, then they never forget. If they do not obtain immediate satisfaction, they nurse the grudge until it overshadows their daily lives. They plan revenge, seek allies for their cause and eventually take their retribution.

To avoid the poisonous atmosphere of the settlement, I began making long excursions deep into the forest. I claimed that I was going hunting, but I seldom brought back anything more than the wild fruit and roots that I had collected. Nevertheless, I would stay away from the settlement for two or three days at a time and my absence was barely noticed. Everyone was too engrossed in their own selfish concerns. On one of these trips, heading in a direction that I had never tested before, I heard a sound which puzzled me. It was a gentle, steady, rhythmic beat. I was following a deer path through dense underbrush and walked in the direction of the noise, feeling curious rather than fearful. Soon I smelled wood-smoke and, coming into a small clearing, saw that smoke was rising from what appeared to be a large pile of branches heaped up against a tall tree on the far side of the clearing. Looking closer, I realised that the pile of branches was in fact a simple lean-to shelter and the sound was coming from inside it. I had stumbled upon Skraelings.

Looking back on that moment, I imagine that most people would have stepped quietly back into the cover of the underbrush and quickly put as much distance as possible between themselves and the Skraeling hut. This would have been logical and sensible. Yet this thought never occurred to me. On the contrary, I knew with absolute certainty that I had to go forward. I knew, also, that no harm would come to me if I did. Later I was to come to understand that this sense of invulnerability mingled with curiosity and trust is a gift that I have naturally. I felt no fear or alarm. Instead a strange numbness ran right down through my legs, almost as if I could not feel my feet, and I felt I had no control over what my limbs were doing. I simply walked forward into the clearing, went across it to the entrance of the shelter, stooped down and pushed my way in.

As I straightened up inside the smoke-filled interior of the little lean-to, I found myself face to face with a small, thin man, who was flicking some sort of rattle steadily from side to side. It was this rattle which had made the rhythmic chinking sound I heard. The man must have been about sixty years old, though it was difficult to tell because he looked so different from any other human I had yet seen. He was no taller than me, and his narrow face was very brown and deeply lined, and framed with long, lank, black hair which hung down to his shoulders. He was dressed entirely in deerskin, from the jacket to the slippers on his feet. Above all he was very, very thin. His hands, his wrists where they emerged from the sleeves of his rough jacket, and his ankles were like sticks. He glanced up as I entered and the expression in his narrow brown eyes did not change as he looked straight into my face. It was almost as if he was expecting me, or he knew who I was. He gave me a single, long glance, then looked down again. He was staring down at the figure of another Skraeling, who was lying on a bed of branches and was obviously very ill. He too was dressed in animal skins and covered with a deerskin wrap. The man seemed barely conscious and was breathing erratically.

How long I stood there I have no recollection. All notion of time was absorbed into the hypnotic beat of the Skraeling rattle and I was completely relaxed. I too looked down at the invalid, and as I gazed at his recumbent body, something strange happened to my senses. It was as if I was looking through a series of thin veils arranged within the man's body and, if I concentrated hard enough, I could shift aside a veil and pass forward and see deeper and deeper inside, past his external form and into the man's interior. As each veil was passed, my vision became more strained until I could progress no further. By then I knew that I was seeing so far inside the sick Skraeling that I could distinguish the interior shape of his spirit. And that shape, his inner soul, was emitting a series of thin flickers, too light and frail to be sustained. At that moment I knew he was mortally ill. He was too sick to be saved and no one could help him. Nothing like this insight had ever happened to me before, and the impact of the premonition broke through my own inner calm. Like someone struggling to come awake from a deep sleep, I glanced around to try to grasp where I was, and I found myself looking into the eyes of the Skraeling with the rattle. Of course I did not know a single word of his language, but I knew why he was there. He was a doctor for his sick comrade, and he too had been peering into the invalid's soul. He had seen what I had seen. I shook my head. The Skraeling looked back at me quietly and I am sure he understood. Without any hurry I pushed my way out of the lean-to, then walked back across the clearing and away into the underbrush. I was confident that no one would follow me, that the Skraeling would not even mention my presence to his fellows, and that he and I shared something as close as any ties of tribe or race.

Nor did I tell Freydis, her husband, Thorvard, or anyone else
in the camp about my encounter with the two Skraelings. There
was no point in trying to explain it. They would have thought that
I was hallucinating or, in view of what happened a month later,
they would have seen me as a traitor who had failed to warn them
that the Skraelings were closing in.

They came when the leaves on the trees had turned to the
vivid reds and russets and yellows which herald the arrival of
winter in those lands. Later we guessed that the Skraelings had
needed to assemble their menfolk, who had dispersed to hunt and
gather food for the winter, before they made their united effort to
drive us away. Certainly the fleet of canoes which came paddling
towards us that late autumn morning was twice the number of
anything we had expected, though many of our more belligerent
settlers had been waiting eagerly for the encounter. For weeks they
had endlessly discussed their tactics and boasted how they would
crush the Skraelings. So when the Skraeling canoes eventually
approached the land, our main force rushed down to the beach and
showed their red shields in defiance. For their part, the Skraelings
stood up in their canoes and – as they had done the first time I
ever saw them – they began to whirl their strange humming sticks
through the air. Only now I noticed that they did not swing them
with the sun as before, but in the opposite direction, and as they
they whirled them faster and faster the air was again filled with a
dreadful droning sound that seemed to work right inside our heads.

Our men were still on the edge of the surf, shouting insults and
defiance, when the first Skraeling missiles struck. Once again the
range of their dart throwers took our men unawares. Two grunted
in surprise and slumped down so suddenly that their comrades
turned round in puzzlement.

Unnerved, our men began to fall back. They retreated up the
beach in disorder, leaving the corpses at the water's edge. We
watched the Skraeling flotilla paddle right up to the beach unopposed and their warriors step ashore.

The mass of the Skraelings advanced up the beach towards us.

There must have been nearly eighty of them and they kept no particular order or discipline, but neither did our men, who were scampering back towards the settlement. What followed was a chaotic and deadly brawl, which I watched from the shelter of a dense willow thicket, where I had been sent by Freydis's husband Thorvard when the Skraeling boats first appeared. Earlier I had told Thorvard how the Skraelings had been terrified by the bellowing of our bull on my first visit to Vinland. Now Thorvard told me to run and catch one of the bulls we had brought with us and produce the animal as our secret weapon. But by the time I had brought the animal to the willow thicket, ready to drive it into the open, our forces were about to gain an even more spectacular advantage.

Our men were fleeing back along the bank of one of the small rivers leading up from the strand. Later they claimed that a second band of Skraelings had emerged from the forest and was blocking their line of retreat towards the settlement, though this was a fabrication. The real problem was that our men had no leadership or cohesion. Once again the Icelanders and Greenlanders were behaving as though they were complete strangers to one another, and neither group showed any sign of helping the other. In their panic-stricken haste men were tripping over and picking themselves up, then running onward and bumping into one another as they glanced over their shoulders to see if any more of the Skraeling darts were on their way, or if the Skraelings were pressing home the attack. At this point, when it seemed that our forces were beaten, we were saved by a berserk.

The term berserk has now such common currency that it is known to nations far beyond the Norse world. All agree that the word describes someone so brimming with fighting rage that he performs extraordinary deeds on the battlefield with no regard for his own safety. Some say that in his fury the berserker howls like a wolf before he attacks, others that he foams at the mouth and bites the rim of his shield, glares at his foe, snarls and shakes before he strikes. A true berserk scorns any notion of armour or self-protection and wears only a bearskin shirt as a mark of his role. Sometimes he wears no shirt at all and goes half-naked into battle. This I have heard, and much more besides, but I have never heard tell of what appeared that day as our men fought the Skraelings – a female berserk.

Our situation was desperate. Our ill-disciplined men were degenerating into a worse rabble. A few of them had turned to skirmish with individual Skraelings, while others were scrambling along the river bank, fleeing ignominiously. One or two were shouting for help, or standing open-mouthed and apparently shocked by the reality of hand-to-hand fighting. It was shameful.

Just at that moment the gate of the settlement palisade banged open, and out rushed a frightful figure. It was Freydis. She had been watching the rout and was appalled by the cowardice of our men. She was in a fury. She came running full tilt down the slope towards the battle, roaring with anger and cursing our men as cowards and poltroons. She made an awesome sight, with her massive bulk, thick legs like tree trunks pounding the ground, red-faced, sweaty and her hair streaming behind her. She was wearing a woman's underdress, a long loose shift, but had discarded her overmantle so as to be able to run more swiftly, and now the undershift flapped around her. She thundered down the slope like an avenging heavyweight Valkyrie and, coming on one of the Norsemen who was standing futilely, she gave him a hefty blow with her meaty arm, which sent him flying, and at the same time snatched the short sword from his hand. She was in a blinding rage, more with her own men than with the Skraelings, many of whom had stopped and turned to look in shocked amazement at this huge, blonde woman raging with obscenities. Freydis was incandescent with anger, her eyes rolling. 'Fight like men, you bastards!' she bellowed at our shamefaced settlers. 'Get a grip on yourselves, and go for them!' To emphasise her rage, to shame our men and work herself into an even greater frenzy, Freydis slipped aside her shift, pulled out one of her massive breasts and gave it a great stinging slap with the flat of her sword. 'Come on!' she screamed to her followers. 'A woman could do better.' And she flung herself at the nearest Skraeling and slashed at him with the weapon. The wretched man, half her size and strength, put up his spear shaft to ward off the blow, but Freydis's sword chopped through the timber cleanly and dealt him such a terrific blow on his neck that he crumpled up instantly. Freydis then swung round and began lumbering at full speed at the next Skraeling. Within seconds the invaders broke and ran back towards their canoes. They had never seen anything like this, and neither had our men. Puffing and panting, Freydis churned along the beach, taking wild swipes at the backs of the departing Skraeling, who did not even attempt to turn and throw darts at her. Our attackers were utterly nonplussed, and they left a panting Freydis standing in the shallows, her loose shift soaked at the hem, great patches of sweat staining her armpits, and splashes of Skraeling blood across her chest.

It was the last time we saw the Skraelings. They left seven of their number dead on the beach, and when we examined them I found that they were not like the healer I had met in the branch shelter in the woods. These Skraelings who had attacked us were shorter in stature, broader, and their faces were generally flatter and more round than the man I had met. They also smelled of fish and wore clothes more suited to the sea than the forest – long sealskin jerkins and heavy leggings. We stripped their bodies of any useful items – including some finely worked spearheads of bone, then carried their bodies to the top of a nearby cliff and threw them into the tide. Our own dead – there were three of them – were buried with little ceremony in shallow graves scraped out of the thin soil.

Our victory, if such an inglorious encounter deserves the name, made the resentment within our camp even worse. Icelanders and Greenlanders heaped blame on one another for being cowards, for failing to come to help, for turning and running instead of making a stand and fighting. No one dared look Freydis in the face, and people slunk about the settlement looking thoroughly ashamed. To make matters worse, winter came on us within a few days and so swiftly that we were caught unprepared. One morning the weather was crisp and bright, but by afternoon it began to rain, and the rain soon turned to sleet, and the following morning we woke up to find a heavy covering of snow on the ground. We managed to get the cattle rounded up and put into the sheds, but we knew that if the winter proved to be long and hard we had not gathered sufficient hay to feed the cattle through to springtime. And the cattle would not be the only ones to suffer. The Icelanders had spent so much time on the construction of their new longhouses during the summer months that they had not been able to catch and dry enough fish for a winter reserve or save a surplus of sour milk and cheese. Their winter rations were very meagre, and when they suggested to Thorvard and the Greenlanders that they should share their food supplies, they were brusquely told that there was not enough to go round. They would have to fend for themselves.

That winter did prove to be exceptionally long and bitter, and in the depths of it we were hardly able to stir from our longhouses for the deep snow, ice and bitter cold outside. It was the most miserable episode of our entire Vinland experience. In the long-house of the Greenlanders, where I lived, life was hard. Our daily intake of food was quickly reduced to tiny portions of gruel with a handful of dried nuts which we had gathered in the autumn, and perhaps a few flakes of dried fish as we huddled around the central fire pit, nursing the embers of our small stock of firewood. All our cattle were dead by midwinter. We were feeding them such short rations that they never gave any milk anyhow, and we killed them when the fodder ran out entirely, though by then they were so scrawny that there was hardly any flesh on their bones. I missed my two mentors, Tyrkir and Thorvall. Before, in Vinland, they had been on hand to help pass the long dark hours with their tales of the Old Gods or instructing me in the Elder Lore. Now, with both men gone, I was reduced to empty daydreaming, turning over in my mind the tales they had told and trying to apply them to my own circumstances. It was at this time, in the depths of uncom-monly harsh Vinland winter, that I first began to pray to Odinn, making silent prayers partly for my own solace, and partly in the hopes that he would come to help, to make the winter pass away, to reduce the pangs of hunger. I made sacrifices too. From my tiny ration of food, I would set aside a few dried nuts, a shred of meat, and when no one was looking I would hide them in a crevice in the longhouse wall. They were my offerings to Odinn, and if the mice and rats came and ate them, then – as I told myself – they were either Odinn in disguise or at least his ravens, Hugin and Munin, who would report back that I had made my proper obedience.

If our lives were pinched in the longhouse of the Greenlanders, the conditions in the two houses occupied by the Icelanders were far, far worse. Two of their men had received crippling wounds in the Skraeling attack, and while in summertime they might have been able to recover from their injuries with adequate food and warm sunshine, they failed to survive the fetid gloom of their longhouses. They lay wrapped in their lice-ridden clothes and with almost nothing to eat until they died a lingering and famished death. Theirs were not the only Icelandic deaths that winter. One of the longhouses was infected with some sort of coughing sickness which killed three of the settlers, and then a child, driven to desperation by hunger, wandered out into the black winter night and was found a few paces from the entrance next morning, frozen to death. A malignant silence settled over the three longhouses, which became no more than three long humps in the snow. For days on end nothing stirred.

Our longhouse was the most westerly of the three, and only occasionally did someone venture outside and walk through the thick snow to visit our immediate neighbours. For two months no one at all from our longhouse went as far as the second of the Icelandic houses, and when someone did – it was Thorvard, Freydis's husband – he found the door was banked up with snow as if no one had emerged for days. When he levered open the door and went inside, he found the place was a mortuary. A third of the people were dead of cold and hunger, and the survivors looked no more than bundles of rags, scarcely able to raise themselves from where they lay on the side benches.

There was more bad news when one of our own men came back from the beach, where we had stored the two knorrs for the winter. At the time of the first, unexpected snow we had dragged the two vessels on rollers up above the high-tide line, propped them up on wooden baulks, and heaped banks of shingle around them as a protection from the blizzards. Then we covered them with tents of wadmal. But a winter gale had stripped away the covers from the elderly vessel that Leif had loaned us, and snow had filled her. A false spring day with its sudden thaw had melted the snow to water, which filled the bilge. That same evening a sudden drop in temperature turned the water into ice, which expanded and split the garboard plank, the key plank which ran the length of her keel. When our carpenter tried to mend the long and dangerous crack he found that the bottom of our ship was entirely rotten. Every time he tried to replace a section of plank, the adjacent area of hull crumbled away. The carpenter was a grouchy and bad-tempered man at the best of times, and now he reported to Thorvard that he refused to waste his time trying to make the decayed old vessel seaworthy.

By that stage, I think, Freydis had already made up her mind that the colony was a failure and that we would have to evacuate Leif's cabins yet again. But she kept the idea to herself and, with typical guile, prepared for the evacuation without alerting anyone else. Her immediate problem was the damage to our knorr. We needed a vessel to carry us away from Vinland and our ancient and rickety knorr was no longer seaworthy. One possible solution was for all the settlers, both Icelanders and Greenlanders, to evacuate the colony by cramming aboard the Icelanders' large, newer vessel. But given the history of bad blood between the two groups it was very unlikely that the Icelanders would agree to this arrangement. Alternatively the Icelanders might lend us their vessel for the evacuation if we promised to send the ship back to them once we had safely arrived in Greenland. Though why the Icelanders should trust us to do this was an open question. And even if the Icelanders were so generous, Freydis knew that there was a more acute problem to confront: if the Icelanders stayed behind in Vinland and somehow managed to make a success of the venture, then by customary law the possession and ownership of the entire settlement would pass away from the Erikssons and transfer to Helgi and Finnbogi and their heirs. They would no longer be Leif's cabins, but Helgi and Finnbogi's cabins, and this was a humiliation which Freydis, the daughter of Erik the Red, could not bear.

Her solution to the dilemma was as artful as it was demonic. It depended on that fatal Norse belief in personal honour.

Very soon after the spring thaw, a real one this time, she walked over to visit the nearest Icelandic longhouse. It was early in the morning, at first light, and I saw her go because I had slipped out of the longhouse to get some badly needed fresh air after a fetid night spent among the snoring Greenlanders. I was loitering near one of the empty store sheds. I always tried to stay well clear of Freydis, so when I saw her I stepped behind the shed until she walked past. I watched her push open the door of the Icelanders' longhouse and go inside. When she reappeared she was accompanied by Finnbogi, who was wearing a heavy coat to keep out the cold. The two were intending to walk in my direction, and once again I shrank back from view. They halted, less than ten paces away, and I heard Freydis say, 'I've had enough of Vinland. I've made up my mind that my people should leave the colony and return home. For that I need to buy your knorr because our vessel is no longer fit for the journey to Greenland. We'll sail away from here, and if you, Helgi and your people want to stay on, then the settlement is yours.'

Finnbogi must have been taken by surprise, for there was a long pause and then he answered that he had no objection to her proposal but would first have to check it with his brother. I heard the soft crunch of his footsteps receding on the slushy snow as he returned to the Icelanders' house. I waited to give Freydis time to get back to our own longhouse, and then scuttled there as fast as I could, knowing instinctively that something was very wrong. It was not my second sight which warned me. It was my long experience of Freydis. Speaking to Finnbogi, her voice had carried that hint of treachery and manipulation that had preceded the unpleasant tricks she had inflicted on me back in Brattahlid in my father's house. That tone of deceit convinced me that Freydis was planning something unpleasant. Quite how foul her plan was soon became apparent.

I got into the longhouse just in time to hear Freydis deliberately provoke her weak-willed husband Thorvard into losing his temper. That was another of Freydis's techniques I recognised. Thorvard must still have been in bed when Freydis returned to the longhouse and climbed in beside him, for he kept repeating his question. 'Where have you been? Where have you been? You have got cold, wet feet, and the hem of your shift is damp, so you must have been outside.' At first Freydis refused to answer. Then finally, when Thorvard was truly irritated with her grudging silence, she said that she had been to see Finnbogi and his brother to ask them for the sale or loan of their knorr.

'They refused my request outright,' she said. 'They laughed in my face, and then insulted me. They said I was becoming more like a man every day, and that you, not I, should have come to discuss the matter with them. Finnbogi even went so far as to hit me, knocking me to the ground.'

Thorvard began to bluster. He had a good mind to go out and give the brothers a good thrashing, he said. Freydis pounced on his bravado. 'If you were more than half a man,' she retorted scathingly, 'you would do more than just lie in bed threatening the two ruffians who have humiliated me. A real man would go off and avenge my honour. But you, you little worm, you are such a coward that you will do nothing. I know you and your faint-hearted ways, and so too do half the people in Brattahlid. When we get home, I'm going to divorce you on the grounds of cowardice, and there's no one who would not sympathise with me.'

As usual, my aunt knew how to twist the knife. Cowardice is

almost the worst and most shameful ground for summary divorce in Norse society, exceeded only by homosexual acts. Her goading was more than Thorvard could bear. He leapt out of bed, threw on his clothes and grabbed an axe and a sword. Moments later, with Freydis at his heels and calling on the other Greenlanders to follow their leader, Thorvard was slipping and slithering along the muddy path to the Icelanders' longhouse. He slammed his way into the building, ran across to where Helgi was sitting on his bed, sleepily thinking over Freydis's proposal to buy the knorr, and with a great swipe he sank his axe into Helgi's chest, killing him. Within moments a massacre was in progress. More and more of the Greenlanders appeared, brandishing their weapons and hacking and stabbing at the unfortunate Icelanders, who were taken by surprise. There were curses and shouts as the Icelanders rolled off their sleeping benches and scrabbled to find their weapons and defend themselves. But they were at too much of a disadvantage. Most of them were killed while they were sleepy or unarmed.

Too young to have been called upon to join the attack on the Icelanders, I heard the shrieks and clamour of the massacre and ran to the side entrance of the Icelanders' longhouse, arriving on the scene just in time to see Freydis pick up Helgi's sword from under his bed and make sure that his brother Finnbogi did not have a chance to reveal the truth by running him through so powerfully that the blade emerged a hand's breadth out of his back. She then wrenched the blade clear and joined in the general bloodbath.

Again Norse custom had its malign influence. Once the massacre had started, there was no going back. Every man knew the pitiless truth. The moment that the first mortal blow had been struck, it was better to kill every last Icelander. Any survivor was a potential witness, and his or her evidence about the murders would lead to a cycle of revenge if a report of the atrocity reached their families back in Iceland. Contributing to this stark policy was the killing frenzy which now gripped the Greenlanders. They killed and killed and killed until they were tired. Only when every adult Icelander, male or female, was dead did they stop the slaughter. By then only five Icelanders were left alive, three boys and two girls, and they were huddled in a corner, wide-eyed and speechless with shock as they watched their parents cut down. Murdering the children was beyond the capacity of even the most blood-crazed Greenlander, but not Freydis. She ordered the men to complete the job. They looked back at her, panting with exhaustion, their swords and axes streaked with gore, their clothes spattered with blood, and the red madness slowly fading from their eyes. They looked drained and tired, and did not move. Freydis raised her borrowed sword, and screamed at them. 'Kill the brats! Kill them! Do as I say!'

I was well inside the longhouse. Appalled by the sight of what seemed like so many limp and blood-soaked bundles of clothing lying on the floor, I crept along the side wall and sank down into a corner, wishing that I was somewhere else. I sat with my back to the wall, trying to make myself invisible, with my arms around my knees and my head down. Hearing Freydis's harridan shriek I raised my head and saw her become grim and calm. Her sway over the men became almost diabolic. She seemed to dominate them like some awful creature from the Hel of the Gods, as she ordered the men to bring the children one by one before her. Such was her authority that the men obeyed, and they led the children to stand in front of her. Then, teeth clenched, she beheaded each child.

I vomited pale, acid bile.

FREYDIS NOW ORDERED that everything that would burn was to be collected and heaped around the bases of the heavy timber posts supporting the turf roofs of the longhouses. Wooden benches, scraps of timber, old rags, anything combustible was piled up. Then Freydis herself went down the line of pillars, setting fire to the materials. She was the last person to leave each building and heave the big door shut. By midday we could see that smoke, which had been issuing from the smoke hole, was also seeping out from the sides of the building, where the turf wall joined the roof.

The whole structure of the longhouse began to look like a smouldering charcoal burners' mound as the turf and wattle interior walls eventually caught fire. The heat steadily built up until we could feel it from forty paces away. Around the fire the last of the snow melted and turned to slush, and in the end the long curved roofs simply fell in with a soft thump, a few sparks curled up into the sky, and the remains of the longhouses which the Icelanders had spent three months building became their funeral pyres. Looking at the ruins, it was obvious to us that in a few winters there would be scarcely any trace that they had ever existed.

Freydis summoned us to a meeting in our own longhouse late that evening. We gathered in a glum silence. Many of us were ridden with guilt, a few were trying to boost their spirits by bragging that it was exactly what the Icelanders had deserved. But Freydis was clear-headed and unmoved. 'The only trace of the Icelanders' existence now lies in our heads,' she told us fiercely. 'No one else will know what has happened, if we keep our mouths shut about the events of this day. We, who are responsible, are the only witnesses. Here on the edge of the world there is no one else to observe and report. We control the only knowledge of what has happened.' Freydis promised us that we had been justified in destroying the Icelanders. Again she produced the lie that she had asked Finnbogi for the loan of the knorr and been refused. 'The Icelanders denied us their knorr,' she said. 'If we had not seized the initiative, they would have sailed away, leaving us behind to our deaths. We acted in self-defence by striking first. What we have done was to save our own lives.'

I do not know how many of us believed her, perhaps a few. Those who did not were either too ashamed or too shocked or frightened of what might happen if they disagreed to speak out. So we kept quiet and followed Freydis's orders when she told us to load the knorr with our possessions and a cargo of valuable Vinland timber to take back to Greenland, for even at that late stage Freydis was determined to make a profit from her venture.

We were so keen to get away from that sinister place that we had the boat loaded and ready to sail within a week. Then Freydis ordered that our longhouse, too, should be set on fire. She told us that when we returned to Greenland we were to say that we had decided to abandon the colony, but the Icelanders had elected to stay, that Freydis and Thorvard had purchased the knorr, and when last seen the Icelanders had been thriving and prosperous and alive. Should anyone in later years visit the site, all they would find would be the burnt-out ruins of the longhouses, and of course they would presume that the Skraelings had overwhelmed the settlement and destroyed every last colonist.

TEN

SUCH A MONSTROUS event could never be kept a secret. When we reached Brattahlid, our people were delighted to see us safely back, though disappointed to hear that once again our plans for a permanent settlement in Vinland had been abandoned. Freydis went immediately to her farm at Gardar, taking her followers with her. Some she bribed to keep quiet about the massacre of the Icelanders, others she threatened with death if they should reveal the details. Given her reputation for violence, these threats were very effective. But rumours soon began to leak out, like the smoke which rose from the smouldering longhouse. Some former Vinlanders blurted out the grisly details when they were drunk. A few shouted aloud during their nightmares. Most were clumsy liars, and inconsistencies in their stories were noticed. Finally, the swirl of rumour and doubt became so powerful that Leif himself decided he must get at the truth of what was happening with his property in Vinland. He asked his half-sister to visit him at Brattahlid, and when she refused, he had three of her thralls arrested and tortured to reveal what had really gone on at Leif's cabins. They quickly revealed the horrors of Vinland, and Leif was appalled. He could not bring himself to punish his half-sister directly, for that would violate his ties of kinship. But he pronounced a curse on her and her progeny and shunned her for the rest of his life.

He also refused to have under his roof anyone who had been involved in these despicable events. The result was that I, who had been an innocent bystander to the massacre, was banished from his household.

For me, it was out of the question to live in Gardar with Freydis. We had a mutual dislike and my presence would have reminded her of the blood-stained episode which was to blight the rest of her life. For a few weeks I lived with Tyrkir, now an old man with failing eyesight, in his cabin on the outskirts of Brattahlid, until my father Leif could make plans for me, his bastard child, to be shipped away. He arranged a passage for me aboard the next trading vessel that arrived and made it clear to me that it did not much matter where I went. I said goodbye to Tyrkir, who was probably the only person genuinely sorry to see me leave, and at the age of thirteen began yet another sea journey, this time heading eastward.

Deep down, I suppose I was hoping that I might be able to find Gudrid again and be accepted back into her affections. I had heard nothing from her since she and Thorfinn and young Snorri had left Greenland to return to Thorfinn's people in Iceland. But for me Gudrid was still the person who had shown me the greatest kindness in my childhood, and I had no plan save for a vague notion of presenting myself at her new household to see if she would take me in. So when the ship called in at Iceland I told the captain that I would be going no farther with him. It may have seemed a rash decision to set foot in a country, several of whose people had been victims in Vinland, but news of the massacre had not yet spread and I discovered within days that the extermination of the Vinlanders was not the unique atrocity that I had imagined. Every farmer in Iceland was talking about the climax to a more local feud which, in its gruesome details, provided a freakish echo of the Vinland atrocity.

The feud had been going on for years, driven by the hatred of Hallgerd, the malevolent wife of a farmer named Gunnar Hamundarson, for her neighbour Bergthora, wife of Njal Thorgeirsson.

The feud had started with a quarrel over a dowry and had spread to include dozens of kinsmen and outsiders, leading to a series of killings and revenge murders. The autumn before I arrived a gang of Hallgerd's faction had surrounded the farmhouse in which Njal and his wife lived, blocked up the doors and set it on fire, burning to death nearly everyone inside, including Njal's three sons.

For me the story was a grisly reminder of Vinland, but for the sweating farmer from whom I heard the tale after I came ashore it was the juiciest gossip of the day. I was helping him stack hay in his barn to pay for my night's lodging. 'It'll be the high point of the next Althing, of that you can be sure,' he said as he wiped the back of his hand across his shiny forehead. 'It'll be a confrontation the like of which has not been seen for ages. Njal's people are bringing a lawsuit against the Burners, seeking compensation for his death, and the Burners are sure to bring along as many of their own supporters as they can muster to defend their action. And if that maniac Kari Solmundarson also shows up, the Gods only know what is likely to happen. I wouldn't miss it for all the looted silver in the world.'

Kari Solmundarson was the name which kept cropping up whenever people discussed the possible repercussions of the Burning, as people had taken to calling it. He was Njal's son-in-law and had escaped from the blazing building after the roof fell in by running up a fallen rafter, where it lay aslant against the gable wall, then leaping out through the smoke and flames as his makeshift ladder collapsed behind him. The Burners had surrounded the building and were waiting to kill any fugitives. But they failed to spot Kari in the gathering darkness, and he slipped through the cordon, though his clothes and hair were so charred by the heat that he had to plunge into a small lake to extinguish the embers. Now he had sworn to exact revenge and was criss-crossing Iceland, rallying Njal's friends to the cause and swearing bloody vengeance. Kari was a foe the Burners would have to take seriously according to everything I heard. He was a skilful warrior, a vikingr who had seen plenty of action overseas. Before he came to Iceland and married Njal's daughter, he had lived in Orkney as a member of the household of Earl Sigurd, lord of that country, and had distinguished himself in several sharp battles, including a famous encounter with a gang of pirates when he had rescued two of Njal's sons.

The moment I heard Kari's story, my half-formed idea of trying to track down Gudrid was replaced by a new and more attractive scheme. I added up the years and calculated that when Kari Solmundarson had served the Earl of Orkney, he might well have met my mother, Thorgunna. He was in Orkney at about the time she seduced Leif the Lucky, to the amazement of all at Earl Sigurd's court, and conceived a son. If I could locate Kari and ask him about those days in Birsay, maybe I would have the chance to learn more about my mother and who I was.

The place to find Kari, if the farmer was correct, was at the next Althing.

As this memorial is intended, if only in my fantasy, to redress some of the lapses which the good Adam of Bremen is likely to make in his history and geography of the known world, perhaps I should say something about the Althing, because I doubt if the cleric of Bremen has ever heard of it, and it is a remarkable institution. Certainly I never came across the like of it elsewhere in my travels. The Althing is how the Icelanders rule themselves. Every year the leading farmers in each quarter of the island hold local meetings, where they discuss matters of common interest and settle disputes among themselves. Important topics and any unresolved lawsuits are then brought to the Althing, a general conclave, which always assembles in July after ten weeks of summer have passed. Only the wealthier farmers and the godars or chieftains have any real role in the actual law-making and courts of justice. The common folk merely look on and support their patrons when called upon to do so. But the gathering is such a combination of fairground, congress and gossip shop that every Icelander who can make the journey to Thingvellir does so. Listening to the lawsuits is a spectator sport. Plaintiffs and defendants, or their representatives, appear before sworn juries of their equals and make their appeals to the customs of the country. This is where the Law-speaker has an important role. He acts as umpire and decides whether the customs are fairly quoted and applied. In consequence the arguments often take on the flavour of a verbal duel, and the Icelanders, who enjoy courtroom revelations as much as anyone else, cluster round to listen to the rhetoric, while analysing who is being most skilled in twisting the law to their own ends or outsmarting the opposition. If they are looking for such lawyers' tricks, they are rarely disappointed.

Some might say that the Althing is an ill-advised way to run a country's affairs, and feel that these are best conducted by a single wise ruler, whether king or queen, emperor, lord or regent. If a single ruler cannot be found, then a small council of five or six is more than enough. The notion that Iceland's affairs should be conducted by the mass of its citizens assembling once a year on a grassy pitch does seem very odd. But this is how the Icelanders have arranged matters ever since the country was first settled nearly two hundred years ago, and in truth its way of government does not differ so very much from the councils of kingdoms where the barons and nobles form their rival factions and compete with one another for the final verdict or advantage. The only difference is that Iceland lacks a single overlord, and this leaves the factions to settle the scores directly among themselves when legal arguments are exhausted. This is when the weapons take over from words.

Thingvellir, the site of the annual Althing, is an impressive location. In the south-west of the country and about five days' ride inland from Frodriver, where my mother spent her last days, it is a grassy area at the base of a long broken cliff, which provides sheltered spots for pitching tents and erecting temporary cabins among scattered outcrops of rock. One particular rock, known as the Lawgiver's Rock, makes a natural podium. Standing on top of this, the Lawspeaker opens the proceedings by reciting from memory the traditional laws and customs of the land to the assembled crowd. There is so much law for him to remember that the process can take two or three days, and when I was there the White Christ priests were already suggesting that it would save time just to write down the laws and consult them as necessary. Of course, the priests knew very well this meant that they, the book-learned priests, would eventually control as well as interpret the legal system. But as yet the change from memory to the written page had not been made, and to the irritation of the White Christ faction the Lawspeaker still went to the nearby Oxar River on the first day of the Althing and hurled a metal axe into the water as an offering to the Old Gods.

THE FACTION SUPPORTING the Burners arrived in style. They came as a group, about forty of them, riding those small and sturdy Icelandic horses. They were armed to the teeth because they feared an ambush organised by Kari. Their leader was a local chieftain, Flosi Thordarson. He had planned and organised the incendiary attack, though he did not boast about it as much as several of the other Burners, who arrived at Thingvellir gloating over the death of Njal and bragging that they would finish the job by putting paid to Kari as well, if he dared show his face. By contrast Flosi preferred to work with his head rather than by brawn. He knew that the Burners had a very weak case when it came to defending their actions before the courts set up at the Althing. So he used a classic strategy: he resolved to bribe the best lawyer in Iceland and rely on his legal hair-splitting to get the Burners acquitted.

The lawyer he picked was Eyjolf Bolverksson, generally considered to possess the most wily legal mind in the country. Eyjolf had already set up his booth at Thingvellir when Flosi went looking for him. Flosi, however, had to be careful about being seen negotiating in public with Eyjolf because Icelandic custom dictates that a lawsuit can only be conducted by the party directly concerned or by a deputy with a recognised relationship such as kinship or a debt of honour. Legal advice is not meant to be for profit or hire. Eyjolf had no prior connection with the Burners, and it is very unlikely that he believed in their innocence. But Eyjolf had a reputation for avarice and, like many lawyers, he was perfectly willing to sell his skills if the payment was high enough. So initially he rebuffed Flosi, telling him that he would not act on his behalf. At most he was allowed to act as a friend of the court and give impartial advice. But when Flosi quietly took him off to one side and offered him an arm bracelet of solid gold, Eyjolf accepted the bribe and agreed to act for him, assuring Flosi that no one else knew so intimately the twists and turns of the back alleys of Icelandic custom and that he would find a way which would allow the Burners to escape punishment.

I know all this because, by then, I had been set to spy on Flosi.

Four days before the Burners arrived at the Althing, Kari Solmundarson slipped quietly into Thingvellir. I would not have guessed from his appearance that Kari was the formidable warrior of his reputation. He was only of average height and rather slim, and he scarcely looked as if he could heft a battleaxe to good effect. He had a narrow face with a long nose above a small mouth, and his brown eyes were rather close set. Unusually for a fighting man, he kept his beard very neat and trim and tied back his hair with a browband of dark grey. Only when he was ready to do battle did he remove the browband and his magnificent head of hair become a warrior's mane. But if you looked past the sober style of Kari's dress, his movements gave him away. He was as supple as an athlete, always quick and fluid, and constantly alert like some sort of hunting animal. A bystander pointed Kari out for me just as Kari was about to enter the booth of one of his potential allies. I walked up behind him, out of his line of vision. Yet he sensed my presence, suddenly whirled about to face me, and dropped his hand to the hilt of the short sword in his belt. When he saw only an unarmed boy, he relaxed.

'Are you Kari Solmundarson?' I asked.

'I am,' he replied. 'Who are you, lad? I don't think I have seen you before.'

'I'm Thorgils Leifsson, though perhaps it might be more accurate if my name was Thorgils Thorgunnasson.'

He looked more than a little startled. 'Thorgunna the w—' He stopped himself. 'Thorgunna, who came from Ireland to Earl Sigurd's court?' he asked.

'Yes, I grew up in Greenland and the west, and only arrived here recently. I was hoping you could tell me something about my mother.'

'Well, well, you're Thorgunna's son. I did know your mother, at least by sight, though we exchanged only a few words,' Kari replied, 'but right at this moment I don't have time to spend chatting about those days. I've got much to do here at the Althing, but if you want to tag along with me, perhaps there will be a moment when I will be able to tell you a little of what you want to know.'

For the rest of that day, and the next, I followed Kari as he went from booth to booth, talking to the godars who had known his murdered father-in-law. Sometimes he was successful in enlisting their support for the case against the Burners, but just as often he was told that he would have to look after his own interests as the Burners were too powerful and anyone helping Kari would be victimised. In one booth we found a tall, rather gaunt man, lying on a bed with his right foot wrapped in bandages. The invalid was Thorhall Asgrimmsson, Njal's foster son.

'Thank the Gods that you managed to get here,' said Kari, obviously pleased.

'The travelling was painful, but I managed it by taking it in slow stages,' Thornhall replied. 'The infection is so sore that I can hardly walk.'

He pulled aside the bandages and showed his right ankle. It was swollen to three times its normal size. In the centre of the swelling a great pus-filled boil seemed to pulsate with heat. In the centre of the boil, I could see the focus of the infection: a black spot like an evil fungus ringed with a fringe of angry red.

'The court case against the Burners will probably be called the day after tomorrow. Do you think you will be able to attend?' asked Kari.

'I doubt it, unless the boil bursts by then,' Thorhall replied. 'But even if I can't attend in person, I can follow the case from my bed here and offer advice if you keep me informed of the details of each day's proceedings.'

'I'm really grateful, and can't thank you enough for coming to the Althing,' Kari said.

'It's the least I can do,' Thorhall said. 'It was your father-in-law Njal who taught me nearly everything I know about the law and I want to see justice done to his murderers.' He paused and thought for a moment. 'In fact, my disability could be useful. Very few people know that I am here, cooped up on this bed, and I think that it should stay that way. We might work a surprise on them.' He glanced at me. 'Who's this youngster?'

'He's just come from Greenland, grew up there and in a place called Vinland.'

Thorhall grunted. 'What do you know about the arrangements Flosi and the Burners are making for their defence at the trial?'

'It's said that they are going to try to get Eyjolf Bolverksson to lead their defence.'

'Officially he shouldn't be taking the case,' said Thorhall, 'but knowing how greedy he is for money, I expect he will be bought. If he is lining up against us, then it would be helpful to know.' His glance fell on me. 'Perhaps this lad could make himself useful. I doubt if anyone around here knows who he is, and he wouldn't stand out in a crowd.'

Then, speaking directly to me, he asked, 'Could you do something for us? If you had Flosi and the chief Burners pointed out to you, do you think you could stick close to them and report back to us how they are getting on in their campaign to recruit allies for their court hearing?'

It was the first time that anyone had ever showed such confidence in me and I was flattered. Equally important, Thorhall's suggestion appealed to my sense of identity. Odinn, as I mentioned earlier, is the God of disguises, the listener at the door, the stealer of secrets, and the God whose character and behaviour appeals to me most. Here was I, alone in a new country, being asked to spy in a matter of real importance. To accept the invitation would be a homage to Odinn and, at the same time, it would be a way of earning the confidence of the man who could tell me about my mother.

So it was that, three days later, I was crouching in a cleft of rock, barely daring to breathe. Not ten paces away was Flosi Thordarson, leader of the Burners, together with two of his leading supporters, who I would later learn were Bjarni Brodd-Helgason and Hallbjorn the Strong. With them was the eminent legal expert Eyjolf. He was easy to recognise because he was a dandy who liked to strut around the Althing wearing a flashy scarlet cloak and a gold headband, and carrying a silver-mounted axe. We were all a short distance behind the lip of the Almmana Gorge, out of sight of the meeting place below. Clearly the four men had come to this isolated spot for a private conference, thinking it an ideal place to talk freely, after they had left their retainers to keep a lookout. I had seen the group leave the cluster of booths at the Althing and begin to walk along the path leading to the clifftop, and I had guessed where they were going. Scrambling up ahead of them, I flung myself down on the grass so I was not visible against the skyline. After catching my breath and waiting for the pounding of blood in my ears to cease, I raised my head cautiously and looked to my right. A moment later I was wriggling backwards anxiously and trying to burrow into cover. The four men had chosen to sit down alarmingly close to me and begin their discussion. Fortunately the Thingvellir cliff is made of the rock the Icelanders call hraun. It oozes from the ground as a fiery torrent when the Gods are angry and, when it cools and hardens, develops cracks and slits. Into one of these clefts I slid. I was too far away to hear anything more than the occasional scrap of conversation when one or another raised his voice, but it was clear that some negotiations were going on. The outcome must have been satisfactory because the next thing I saw as I peeked cautiously from my hiding place, was Flosi pull off his own arm a heavy gold bracelet, take Eyjolf's arm and slip the bracelet onto it. I could tell that the bracelet was valuable from the way it gleamed briefly in the watery sun, and Eyjolf lovingly ran his finger over it. Then Eyjolf carefully slid the bracelet farther up his arm, under the sleeve of his coat where it would not be seen.

At this point I had no idea of the significance of the transaction. When the four men got to their feet and walked back along the path to rejoin their waiting retainers, I waited silently, still pressed to the ground, until I guessed that the others must be gone. Then I slipped quietly back to the booth, where Kari was conferring with Thorhall, and reported what I had witnessed. Kari scowled and muttered something about making sure that Eyjolf did not live to enjoy his bribe. Thorhall, lying on his cot, was more phlegmatic. 'Eyjolf's a tricky customer,' he said, 'but he may not be quite the invincible lawyer that he thinks he is.'

The eagerly awaited lawsuit began next morning before a large and expectant audience. One after another, various members of Kari's faction stood at the foot of the Law Rock and took it in turns to pronounce the accusations. The most eloquent speakers had been chosen, and the legal formulae rolled out sonorously. They accused Flosi Thordarson and his allies of causing the death of the Njalssons 'by internal wound, brain wound, or marrow wound' and demanded that the culprits be neither 'fed nor forwarded nor helped nor harboured' but condemned as outlaws. Further, they demanded that all the goods and properties of the accused be confiscated and paid as compensation to the relatives of the dead family and the people living in their area. It was then that I noticed how the crowd assembled round the law court were standing in separate groups. If I had not been a newcomer, I would have identified much sooner how those who supported the Burners were standing well apart from the band of men allied with Kari and the Njalsson faction. Between them, acting as a buffer, stood a large crowd of apparently neutral bystanders, and it was just as well they did so because both Kari's men and the Burners had come fully armed to the Law Rock and were wearing tokens – ribbons and emblems attached to their clothes – which signalled their loyalty and that they were ready for a fight.

For the moment, however, both sides were prepared to let the lawsuit take its course. The first day of the court case was occupied entirely with Kari's people laying accusations of murder or conspiracy to murder against the Burners. The second and third days saw legal arguments over which court had the power to try the cases, and who should be on the juries. Eyjolf proved to be every bit as slippery as his reputation suggested. He tried every wily trick in law to delay or deflect the accusations, and even came up with several variations which were entirely new. He fastened on tiny procedural irregularities which he claimed rendered the prosecution irrelevant. He discredited witnesses on minor technical points and had so many jurors disqualified for the most arcane reasons that Kari's side were driven to summoning up and enrolling nearly a dozen substitute jurors. Eyjolf bent and twisted the law this way and that, and the Lawspeaker, a man named Skapti, was constantly being called on to adjudicate. Invariably he found in favour of the clever Eyjolf.

At the end of each day the crowd, who greeted each new legal subtlety with a murmur of appreciation, judged that the Burners had the upper hand. But then next morning the spectators had to reverse that opinion because they had not reckoned with Kari's hidden adviser, Thorhall, lying in his booth nursing his grotesque boil. I was kept employed constantly running back and forth to Thorhall to report every latest twist in the legal wrangling. Thorhall, grimacing with discomfort, red-faced and tears of pain running down his cheeks, would listen to what I had to say, though the legal wording was so ornate that half the time I did not know what it was that I was reporting. Then he would wave me away to return to the law court and wait my next errand while he mulled over the fresh scrap of news. That evening he and Kari would have a consultation, and Kari or his representative would appear before the Lawspeaker the following morning and produce Thorhall's counter-argument, which would save the day and allow the prosecution to proceed. The Lawspeaker several times remarked that he did not know there was anyone who knew the laws so thoroughly. One little wrangle, I remember, turned upon whether the ownership of a milch cow entitled an individual to sit on the jury as a person of property. Apparently it did.

After four labyrinthine days, the case finally ended with a verdict. Despite all his twisting and turning Eyjolf had failed to get the case thrown out and the Burners were found guilty by the forty-two members of the jury. At that moment Eyjolf produced his master stroke: the verdict was invalid, he pointed out, because the jury was too large. It should have had thirty-six members, not forty-two. Kari and his faction had fallen into the trap that Eyjolf had set right at the beginning. His strategy had been to challenge repeatedly the composition of the jury, until he had lured Kari's faction into agreeing to an excess of jurors. On this technicality, the case against the Burners collapsed. Promptly Eyjolf turned the case on its head. He announced that Kari's prosecution had been malicious and that he was indicting Kari and his followers for false accusation and demanded that they, not the Burners, should be pronounced outlaws.

Kari came with me this time as we hurried back to Thorhall's booth to report the disaster. It was just past noon, and we left a crowd of onlookers clustering round Eyjolf and the Burners and excitedly offering their congratulations. Kari pushed past the door flap and summarised the situation in a few words. Thorhall, who had been lying back on his cot, swore loudly, sat up and swung his tender foot onto the ground. I had never seen a man look so angry. Thorhall groped under the cot and pulled out a short stabbing spear. It was, I remember, a particularly fine weapon, razor sharp, its blade inlaid with some fine silver work. Lifting up the spear with both hands, Thorhall brought it plunging down on the enormous boil on his ankle. There was a sickly squelching sound and I could almost hear the pus and blood as it burst out. A fat gob of pus slopped on the earth and there was a splatter of black blood across the earth floor as the putrefaction exploded. Thorhall let out a brief moan of pain as the boil was lanced, but a moment later he was on his feet, spear in hand and with bits of his own flesh still on the blade, striding out of the door, not even with a limp. Indeed, he was walking so fast that I found it difficult to keep up with him. I noticed that Kari, who was matching Thorhall stride for stride, had pulled off his browband, shaken out his hair, and had clapped a helmet on his head.

Thorhall came barging into the back of the crowd loyal to the Burners. The first person he encountered was one of Flosi's kinsmen, a man called Grim the Red. One look at Thorhall's furious expression and the spear in his hand, and Grim raised his shield to protect himself. Barely pausing, Thorhall rammed the spear into the shield with such force that the shield, an old and badly maintained wooden one, split in two. The spear blade carried right through Grim's body so that the point came out of his back between his shoulders. As Grim dropped to the ground, someone from the far side, from Kari's faction, shouted out, 'There's Thorhall! We can't let him be the only one to take revenge on the Burners!' and a furious melee broke out. Both sides drew their weapons and flung themselves at their opponents. So I saw what, in the end, is the deciding factor of Icelandic justice.

I also understood how Kari had got his reputation as a fighter. He came face to face with two of the Burners – Hallbjorn the Strong and Arni Kolsson. Hallbjorn was a big brute of a fellow, heavy-boned and broad-set. He was armed with a sword, which he swung at Kari, a low scything sweep at his legs, hoping to cripple or maim him. But the big man was too ponderous. Kari saw the blow coming. He leaped high in the air, drawing his knees up to his chest, and the sword swept harmlessly under him. Even as Kari landed, he struck with his double-bladed battleaxe at Arni Kolsson, a hit so shrewdly directed that it caught the victim in the vulnerable spot between shoulder and neck, chopping through the collarbone and splitting open his chest. Mortally wounded, Arni fell. Turning towards Hallbjorn, who was getting ready to take a second swing at him, Kari sidestepped and used his axe backhanded. The blade glanced off the lower edge of Hallbjorn's shield and carried downward, severing the big toe from Hallbjorn's left foot. Hallbjorn gave a howl of pain and hopped back a step. One of Kari's friends now rushed in and gave Hallbjorn such a shove with his spear that the big man toppled backwards in a heap. Scrambling back to his feet, Hallbjorn limped back in the crush of people as fast as he could set his injured foot on the ground. With each step he left a small splash of blood.

Next I witnessed something I have seen only four or five times in my life, even though I was to take part in quite a number of battles. Standing a little behind Kari, I saw a spear came hurtling at him, thrown by one of the Burners. Kari, who was not carrying a shield, sidestepped and caught the weapon left-handed in mid-air. At that instant I realised that Kari was ambidextrous. He caught the spear, as I say, left-handed, turned it and flung it back straight into the crowd of Burners and their supporters. He did not take aim, but threw as a reflex. The spear plunged into the crowd, killing a man.

By this stage men from both factions were trading blows with swords and axes and daggers, slamming shields in one another's faces, headbutting, wrestling hand to hand. This was not a military encounter between trained soldiers, disciplined and skilled in the use of arms. It was an ugly brawl between enraged farmers, and no less dangerous for being so.

The Burners and their friends began to fall back in disorder, and as the retreat began, Kari, the experienced fighter, picked his targets. He looked around for the men whom I had identified to him, those who bribed Eyjolf at the meeting at the gorge. One – Hallbjorn the Strong – was already in retreat with his injured foot, the other was Bjarni Brodd-Helgason. Seeing Bjarni in the scrimmage, Kari began to press towards him. There was no room for Kari to use his axe in the thick of the turmoil. Instead, again with his left hand, he snatched up a spear which someone had thrown and which was sticking up from the ground, and slithered the weapon through a gap between two men. His intended victim swung his shield round just in time to deflect the stab, which otherwise would have spitted him. With Kari extended fully forward, Bjarni saw his chance. As a space opened up, he darted his sword at Kari's leg. Once again Kari's remarkable agility saved him. He jerked back his leg, pivoted like a dancer, and in a moment was poised again and making a second spear thrust. As he lunged forward, Bjarni's life was saved by one of his retainers running forward with a shield. Kari's spear penetrated the shield and gashed the man in the thigh, a deep wound which was to make him a cripple for the rest of his life. Kari swayed back, preparing to strike a third time. He had dropped his axe and, holding the spear with both hands, thrust straight at Bjarni. The Burner threw himself sideways, rolling on the ground so the spear passed over him, then got back on his feet and ran for his life.

The fighting was now getting hazardous for the onlookers. The retreating Burners had to pass between the booths of several godars who had been friends with their victim, Njal. These godars and their retainers deliberately blocked the way, jostling and taunting the unfortunate Burners. Their taunts soon turned to blows and it seemed that the entire Althing was about to disintegrate into a general battle. A man named Solvi, who belonged to neither faction, was standing beside his booth as the Burners streamed by. Solvi was cooking a meal and had a great cauldron of water boiling over the cook fire. Unwisely he made a remark about the cowardice of the Burners, just as Hallbjorn the Strong was passing by. Hallbjorn heard the insult, picked up the man bodily and plunged him head first into the cauldron.

Kari and his allies chivvied the Burners through the booths and back towards the bank of the Oxar River. Both sides began to suffer losses. Flosi hurled a spear which killed one of Kari's men; someone else wrenched the same spear from the corpse and threw it back at Flosi, injuring him in the leg, though not badly. Once again it was Kari, the professional fighter, who did the most damage. Of the men who had almost humiliated him at the court, the key figure was Eyjolf the lawyer. Now Kari was out for revenge. As the Burners began to cross the river to safety, splashing their way through the milky-white shallows, Thorgeir Skora-Geir, who had been fighting alongside Kari all the time, saw the lawyer's scarlet cloak.

'There he is, reward him for that bracelet!' Thorgeir shouted, pointing to Eyjolf.

Kari seized a spear from a man standing beside him and threw it. The trajectory was flat and low, and the spear took Eyjolf in the waist and killed him.

With Eyjolf's death, the fighting began to subside. Both sides were exhausted, and Kari's faction were unwilling to cross the river and advance uphill against the Burners. One last spear was thrown – no one saw who flung it – and it struck down one more Burner. Then several of the leading godars arrived, among them Skapti the Lawspeaker, with a large band of their followers. They placed themselves between the two groups of combatants and called a halt to the fighting. Enough blood had been spilled, they said. It was time to make a temporary truce, and try to settle the dispute by negotiation.

To my astonishment, I now learned that conflict and killing in Iceland can be priced. Half a dozen godars assembled before the Law Rock and formed a rough-and-ready jury to calculate who had killed whom, how much the dead man was worth, and who should pay the compensation. It was like watching merchants haggle over the price of meat.

The weary fighters, who had been hacking at one another a moment before, were now content to lean on their shields or sit down on the turf to rest while they listened to the godars make their tally. The killing of this man was balanced by the killing of someone on the other side, the value of that wound was set at so many marks of silver, but that sum was then set against an injury on the opposite side, and so forth. In the end the godars decided that the losses that the Burners had sustained at the Althing brawl made up for the deaths they had inflicted on Kari's faction on previous occasions, and that both sides should make a truce and waive their claims for compensation. The original outstanding matter – the Burning of Njal and his family – was also settled. Compensation was to be paid for Njal's death, also for the death of his wife, and the Burners were to suffer outlawry. Flosi was banished for three years, while four of the more belligerent Burners – Gunnar Lambason, Grani Gunnarsson, Glum Hildisson and Kol Thorsteinsson – were banished for their lifetimes. However, in a spirit of compromise, the sentence of outlawry was not to take effect until the following spring, so that the chief malefactors could spend the winter arranging their affairs before beginning their period of banishment from Iceland.

The one man for whom no compensation was either sought or paid was Eyjolf. His underhand ways, it was commonly agreed, had brought the law into disrepute. One by one, the various farmers shook hands on the agreement, and thus ended what was, by all accounts, the most violent battle ever to take place before Logberg, the Law Rock.

ELEVEN

'OUTLAWRY FOR THREE years – that I can accept, but it's not for a youngster,' Kari explained later that evening. He had remembered me, even after all the violence of the day, and summoned me to the booth where he was staying. There he told me as much as he could remember about my mother Thorgunna in Orkney – including the details which I have given earlier – and now he was trying to make me understand why I had to fend for myself. When the godars announced their decisions at the Law Rock, Kari had been the only person to reject their judgement. He refused to acknowledge that the killings and maimings of the recent skirmish could be equated with the murders committed by the Burners on Njal and his family. 'In front of the most influential godars in the land, I declared that I refused to give up my pursuit of the Burners,' he went on, 'That means that sooner or later they will condemn me to outlawry and force me to leave Iceland. If it is lesser outlawry, then I must stay away for three years. If I come back before the time is complete, then my sentence is increased to full outlawry and I will be banished for life. Anyone declared an outlaw and still found in Iceland can be treated as a criminal. Every man's hand is against him unless he has friends willing to take the risk of protecting him. He can be killed on sight, and the executioner can take his property. It is no life for you.'

I still asked Kari if I could continue to serve him. But he refused. He would have no retinue or following. He would act alone in pursuing his vengeance, and a thirteen-year-old lad would be a hindrance. But he did have a suggestion: I should travel to Orkney, to the earl's household, and find out more details about my mother for myself. 'The person there who might have some more information for you is the earl's mother, if she is still alive. Eithne is her name, and she and Thorgunna got on particularly well. Both came from Ireland and they used to sit for hours at a time, quietly talking in Irish to one another.'

And he promised that if he himself was ever going to Orkney, then he would take me with him. It was my reward for spying on the Burners during the Althing.

Kari's revelation that on Orkney, in the person of the earl's mother, I might find a source of direct information about my mother completely eclipsed my earlier, ill-formed scheme of trying to rejoin Gudrid and Thorfinn. There were another six days before the Althing would be closed and the people dispersed to their homes, and I spent those six days going from booth to booth of the more important landowners, looking for work. I offered myself as a labourer, willing to spend the autumn and winter on a farm doing the same humdrum jobs I had performed in Greenland. In return I would receive my board and lodging and a modest payment when spring came. I realised that the payment would probably be in goods rather than cash, but it should be enough to buy my passage to Orkney. As I was rather weakly looking, I encountered little enthusiasm from the farmers. Winter was not the season when they needed extra hands, and an additional employee in the house had to be fed from the winter stocks of food. My other failing was that no one knew who I was. In Iceland's close-knit society that is a great disadvantage. Most people are aware of a person's origins, where he or she comes from, and what is their reputation. The people I spoke to knew only that I had been raised in Greenland and had spent some time in Vinland, a place few of them had even heard of. They were puzzled that I did not speak with the vocabulary of an ordinary labourer – I had Gudrid to thank for that – and I was certainly not slave-born, though once or twice people commented that my green-brown eyes made me look foreign. I supposed that I had inherited their colour from Thorgunna, but I could not tell them that I was Thorgunna's son. That would have been disastrous. I had made a few discreet enquiries about my mother, without saying why I wanted to know. The reactions had been very negative. My informant usually made some comment about 'foreign witches' and referred to something called 'the hauntings'. Not wanting to seem too curious, I did not pursue my enquiries. So, with the exception of Kari, I told no one about my parentage.

Thus my anonymity, which had been a help when Kari set me to spy on the Burners, was now a handicap, and I became anxious that I would not find a place to spend the autumn and winter. Yet, someone had made a very accurate guess as to who I was, and was keeping an eye on me.

He was Snorri Godi, the same powerful chieftain whose half-sister Thurid Barkadottir had stolen my mother's bed hangings at Frodriver.

Thus when I arrived from Greenland, bearing the name Thorgils, and of the right age to be Thorgunna's son, Snorri Godi guessed my true identity at once. Typically, he kept the knowledge to himself. He was a man who always considered carefully before any action, weighed up the pros and cons, then picked the right moment to act. He waited until I approached him at his booth on the penultimate day of the Althing, looking for work. He gave no indication that he knew who I was, but told me to report to his farm at a place called Tung five or six days' distance to the north-west at the head of a valley called Saelingsdale.

Snorri's bland appearance belied his reputation as a man of power and influence, and it would have been difficult to give him a nickname based on his physical looks. Now in late middle age, he was good-looking in a neutral way, with regular features and a pale complexion. His hair, once yellow, had turned grey by the time I met him, and so had his beard, which once had a reddish tinge. In fact, everything about Snorri was rather grey, including his eyes. But when you looked into them you realised that the greyness was not a matter of indifference, but of camouflage. When Snorri watched you with those quiet, grey eyes and with his expression motionless, it was impossible to know what he was thinking. People said that, whatever he was thinking, it was best to be on his side. His advice was sound and his enemies feared him.

Snorri turned that quiet look on me when I reported to him on the day I arrived at his farmhouse. I found him seated on a bench in the farthest shadowy corner of the main hall. 'You must be Thorgunna's son,' he said quietly, and I felt my guts coil and tighten. I nodded. 'Do you possess any of her powers?' he went on. 'Have you come because she sent you?'

I did not know what he was talking about, so I stood silently.

'Let me tell you,' continued Snorri, 'your mother left us very reluctantly. For months after her death, there were hauntings at Frodriver. Everyone knows about your mother's reappearance stark naked when they were taking her corpse for burial. But there was more. Many deaths followed at Frodriver. A shepherd died there under mysterious circumstances soon afterwards, and his draugar, his undead self, kept coming back to the farm and terrifying everyone living in the house. The draugar even beat up one of the farm workers. He met the worker in the darkness of the stable yard and knocked him about so badly that he took to his bed to convalesce and never recovered. He died a few days later, some said from pure fright. His draugar then joined the shepherd's draugar in tormenting the people. Soon half a dozen of the farm workers, mostly women, got sick and they too died in their beds. Next, Thorodd, the man who had given your mother a roof over her head when she came from Orkney, was drowned with his entire boat crew when they went to collect some supplies. Thorodd's ghost and the ghosts of his six men also kept reappearing at the house. They would walk in and sit down by the fire in their drenched clothes and stay until morning, then vanish. And for a long time afterwards there were mysterious rustlings and scratching at night.'

I remained silent, wondering where Snorri's talking was leading. He paused, eyeing me as if to judge me.

'Have you met my nephew, Kjartan?' he asked.

'I don't think so,' I replied.

'He was the only person who seemed to be able to quell the hauntings,' Snorri went on. 'That is why I'm sure your mother's spirit was responsible because in her life she really desired that young man. I think that even as a ghost she still lusted for him until finally she understood that he had no wish for her. She came back one last time, in the form of a seal, and poked her head up through the floor of the farmhouse at Frodriver. She was looking at him with imploring eyes, and Kjartan had to take a sledgehammer and flatten her head back down into the earth with several strong blows before she finally left him alone.'

I still did not know what to say. Had my mother really been so enamoured of a young teenager, scarcely three years older than I was now? It was unsettling for me to think about it, but I was too naive as yet to know how a woman can become just as hopelessly attracted by a man, as the other way around.

Snorri looked at me shrewdly. 'Are you a follower of the White Christ?' he asked.

'I don't know,' I stammered. 'My grandmother built a church for him in Brattahlid, but it wasn't used very much, at least not until Gudrid, who was looking after me, took an interest in going there. We didn't have a church in Vinland, but then we didn't have a temple to the Old Gods either, we only had the small altar that Thorvall made.'

'Tell me about Thorvall,' Snorri asked, and I found myself describing the cantankerous old hunter – how he had placed his trust in Thor, and vanished mysteriously, and was believed killed by the Skraelings. Snorri made no comment, except to ask an occasional question that encouraged me to talk further. When I told Snorri about Tyrkir and how I had worked alongside him in the smithy and learned something of the Old Ways, Snorri cross-examined me about Tyrkir's background, what the wizened German had told me of the various Gods and of their different legends, and how the world was formed. Occasionally he asked me to repeat myself. It was difficult to guess what Snorri was thinking, but eventually he stood up and told me to follow him. Without another word, he led me out of the house and across to one of the cattle byres. It was little more than a shed and from the outside looked like a typical cattle stable, except that it was round not oblong, and the roof was higher and rather more steeply pitched than usual. Snorri pushed open the wooden door and closed it behind us when we went in, shutting out the light.

When my eyes had adjusted to the dim interior, I saw that there were no cattle stalls. Instead the building was empty. There was only a bare earth floor and rising from it a circle of wooden poles supporting the steep cone of the roof, with a hole at the apex to let in the light. Then I realised that the poles were not necessary to the structure of the building.

'I built this four years ago when I moved here from my father's home,' Snorri was saying. 'It's a bit smaller than the original, but that does not matter. This does.' He had walked to the centre of the circular earth floor, and I now saw there was a low, round stone, very ancient and almost black, directly under the sky hole. The rock seemed to be natural, and was not carved or shaped in any way. There were irregular bumps and protuberances so that it was slightly misshapen. There was a shallow depression on its upper surface, like a basin.

Snorri walked over casually and picked up something which had been left lying in the basin. It was an arm ring, apparently made of iron and without any markings. Snorri handled its smooth surface, for it was much worn, then slipped it on his right arm, pushing it up just above his elbow. He turned to me. 'This is the priest's ring, the ring of Thor. It was my father's, and it is as precious to me as the cross of the White Christ. I continue to use it because

I know that there are times when Thor and the other Gods can help us here in Tung as they did my father and my grandfather before him.'

He was standing in the shaft of light that came in through the smoke hole so I could see his expression. His voice was utterly matter of fact, not in the least mystical or reverential. 'When Kjartan and the others came to ask my advice about the hauntings I went to the temple and put on the arm ring. Thinking about the hauntings and deaths, it came into my mind that the deaths might have something to do with the bed hangings that your mother left. She had said they were to be burned, but Thorodd, egged on by his wife Thurid, failed to do so. They kept some of the bedlinen, and somehow that brought the deaths and sickness. So I ordered that every last scrap of linen, sheets, hangings, drapery, everything, should be taken down and committed to the flames, and when that happened the sickness and death stopped. That is how Thor helped me to understand.'

'And did that stop the hauntings also? Was my mother ever seen again?' I enquired.

'Your mother's fetch was never seen again. The other hauntings ended when the White Christ priests went to the house and held a service to drive out the draugars and ghosts they like to call godless demons,' Snorri told me. 'They knew their job well enough to perform the matter correctly in the old way. The ghosts were summoned to appear and stand trial, just like in a law court, and told to leave the house. One by one the ghosts came, and each promised to return to the land of the dead. If the Christians believe that the White Christ himself appeared as a draugar after his death, then it is not so difficult to believe in ghosts that rise up through the floor as seals.'

Snorri slid the ring of Thor off his arm and replaced it on top of the altar.

'What made Thorvall and Tyrkir take so much trouble to teach you about the Old Ways?' he asked.

'They began after I became a uniped,' I said, and explained how my childish game had led them to believe that I could spirit-fly.

'So it seems that, like your mother, you do have seidr powers. That's how it usually is. The gift passes down through the family,' Snorri commented.

'Yes, but Tyrkir said that my spirit, my inner self, should also be able to leave my body and travel through space to see what is happening in other places. But that has never happened. It is just that at times I see people or places in a way that others do not.'

'When was the last time?' Snorri asked quietly.

I hesitated because it had been very recently. On the way to Tung I had stayed overnight at a large farm called Karstad. The farmer had been away when I called at the door and his wife had answered. I had explained that I was walking to Tung and asked if I could sleep the night in a corner of the main hall. The farmer's wife was old-fashioned; for her a stranger on the road was always to be given shelter, and she had put me with the household servants, who had provided me with a wooden bowl of sour whey and a lump of bread. Shortly before dusk the farmer had come in, and I was puzzled to see when he took off his cloak that the left side of his shirt was heavily soaked with fresh blood. But instead of enquiring what was the matter, his wife ignored the bright red stain and proceeded as if everything was normal. She produced the evening meal and her husband sat at the table, eating and drinking as if nothing was the matter. After the meal he walked over to be nearer the fire, pulled up a bench and began mending some horse harness. As he walked across the room, he came right past me where I was seated, and I could not keep my eyes off his blood-stained shirt. The gore still glistened. 'You see it too?' asked a thin, cracked voice. The questioner was so close that I jumped with fright. Turning, I found that an old woman had seated herself beside me and was looking at me with rheumy eyes. She had the mottled skin of the very elderly. 'I'm his mother,' the old woman said, nodding towards the farmer, 'but he won't listen to me.'

'I'm sorry, I'm a stranger,' I replied. 'What won't he listen to?'

I expected to hear the usual ramblings of an aged mother about her grown-up son, and I was preparing to invent some sort of an excuse — that I needed to visit the latrine — so that I could avoid this crazy old crone, when she went on, 'I've warned him that he will be hurt and hurt badly.'

Suddenly I felt giddy. Did she mean that she also saw how the man was bleeding heavily? And why had she spoken in the future tense? The blood seemed real enough to me.

I glanced across at the farmer. He was still unconcerned, pushing the awl through a broken horse harness. His shirt was sticking to his side it was so wet with blood. 'Why doesn't he take off the shirt so someone can attend the wound and staunch the bleeding?' I said in a low voice.

She laid a withered hand on my wrist and held tight. 'I knew you could see,' she said fiercely. 'I've been watching your face just as I've been watching that stain on his shirt for nearly three years past and still he won't listen to my warning. I told him to kill the creature, but he hasn't done so.'

This did not make sense, and I began to revert to my idea that the old woman was addled. 'Haven't you heard it?' she enquired, still holding me with her claw of a hand, thrusting her head forward until it was only a few inches from my face.

At this point her mutterings had lost me completely, and I was feeling uncomfortable, shifting in my seat. The farmer, sitting by the fire, must have noticed because he called out, 'Mother! Are you still going on about Glaesir. Leave the youngster alone, will you. I told you I don't believe there's any harm in the animal, and if there is I can deal with it.'

The old woman made a sniff of disgust, got slowly to her feet, and moved off down the hall. I was left to myself.

'Ignore her, young fellow,' called the farmer. 'And I wish you a safe journey wherever it is that you are going.'

'Was the farmer's name Thorodd?' asked Snorri, who had been standing silently, listening to my account.

'Yes, I think so,' I answered.

'He farms over at Karstad all right and there's a young bull in his herd called Glaesir. It's an animal you couldn't miss, spotted, very handsome. Frisky too. Some people think the animal is inhabited by the spirit of another Thorodd, a man called Thorodd Twistfoot. I had several quarrels with him. The worst was about the right to cut timber in a small woodland he owned. He got in such a rage that he went home and had a fit. Next morning they found him dead, sitting in his chair. They buried him twice. After the first time, when his ghost began plaguing his old farm, they dug up the corpse and shifted him to a hilltop, where they buried him under a big cairn. Then, when that didn't work and his ghost kept reappearing, they dug him up again. The grave diggers found that the body had not rotted away but just turned black and stank, so they burned the corpse to ashes on a pyre. Some say that the ash blew onto a nearby beach and was licked up by a cow feeding near the shoreline. The cow later gave birth to two calves, a heifer and a young bull calf. That's the one they call Glaesir. The Thorodd you met has a mother with second sight, or so it's said, and ever since that bull calf got on the farm, she's been wanting someone to kill it, saying that it will do terrible damage. Did you see the calf? He's a young prize bull now. Quite remarkable colouring.'

'No, I left the farm at first light next morning,' I replied. 'I wanted to get on my way early, and I didn't see Thorodd's mother again. I expect she was still asleep when I left. And there was nobody about, except for a few farm servants. I don't know anything about Glaesir. I just know that the farmer looked as if he had a serious injury to his side.'

Snorri was trying to assess what I had just told him. 'Maybe you do have second sight,' he said, 'but it's not quite in the usual way. I don't know. You seem to have it only when you are with others who also possess the gift. Like a mirror or something. You are young, so perhaps that will change. Either the sight will grow stronger or you will lose it altogether.'

He shrugged. 'I don't have the sight, though some people think

I do,' he said. 'My common sense tells me what is likely to happen, and the result is that many believe that I can see into the future or into men's minds.'

Whether Snorri believed I had the sight or not, from that moment onward he treated me as something more than a itinerant farm labourer. At the end of the day's work I was seated not among the farmhands down the far end of the hall, but alongside Snorri's large and rather boisterous family, and when he had free time – which was not often because he was such a busy man – he would continue with my education in the lore of the Old Gods. He was more knowledgeable in these matters than either Tyrkir or Thorvall the Hunter had been, and he had a more elegant way of explaining the intricacies of the Old Ways. Also, whenever Snorri went into the Thor temple, he expected me to go with him.

Such visits were surprisingly frequent. Local farmers came to pay their respects to Snorri as the local chieftain and ask his advice, and they spent hour after hour in the evenings, talking politics, negotiating land rights, discussing the weather and fishing prospects, and mulling over whatever news reached us via travellers or traders. But when the talking was over, and especially if the farmers had brought their families, Snorri would beckon to me and we would all walk across the farmyard to the temple shed, and there Snorri would hold a small ceremony to Thor. He would put on the iron arm ring, say prayers over the altar stone and present to Thor the small offerings brought by the farmers. Cheese, chickens, haunches of dried lamb were placed on the altar, or hung from nails driven into the ring of surrounding wooden pillars. These pillars were tied with ribbons brought by the farmers' wives, together with scraps of children's clothing, milk teeth wrapped in packets, embroidered belts and other personal articles. Frequently the women would ask Snorri to look into the future for them, to prophesy what would happen, what marriages their children would make, and so forth. At such moments Snorri would catch my eye and look slightly embarrassed. As he had warned me, his prophesies were largely based on common sense. For example, when a mother

asked whom her young son would marry I noticed that Snorri
often identified – though not exactly by name – the daughter of a
neighbour who, like as not, had visited the temple the previous
week and asked exactly the same question about her young
daughter. I never found out whether any, or all, of Snorri's
matrimonial prophecies came true, but the fact that the parents
thenceforward nurtured the probability of a particular match for
their offspring must have helped to bring it about.

However, on one particular occasion which I will always
remember, Snorri behaved differently. A small group of farmers –
there were about eight of them – had come to see him because
they were worried about the weather for the hay harvest. That
year there had been little sunshine and the hay growth was
exceptionally slow. But eventually the long grass in the meadows
was ready to be cut and dried, and everyone was waiting for a
spell of good dry weather to do the work. But the days continued
cloudy and damp, and the farmers were increasingly worried. If
they did not get in their hay crop, they would be obliged to
slaughter many of their cattle for lack of winter feed. A bad hay
crop, or worse, no hay crop at all, would be a major misfortune.
So they came to Snorri to ask him to intercede on their behalf
because, of course, Thor controls the weather. Snorri led the
farmers into the temple building and I went with them. Once
inside, Snorri made offerings, rather more lavish than usual, and
called on Thor, using the fine rolling phrases and archaic Norse
vocabulary which are a mark of respect to the Gods. But then
Snorri did something more. He called forward the farmers to stand
around the central altar stone. Next he made them form a circle
and join hands. Snorri himself was a member of the circle and so
was I. Then Snorri called out to the men and they began to dance.
It was the simplest of the stamping dances of the Norsemen, an
uncomplicated rhythm, with a double step to the left, then a pause,
a step back, a pause, and then two steps more to the left, their
clasped hands swinging out the rhythm. The men swayed down
and then arched back at the end of each double step.

As I joined in, I had a strange feeling of familiarity. Somewhere I had heard that rhythm before. For a moment I could not recall when and where. Then I remembered the sound that I had heard while wandering in the forest of Vinland, the strange rhythmic sound that had led me to the shelter of branches with the sick Skraeling inside, and the older man chanting over his body and shaking his rattle. It was the same cadence that I now heard from the Icelandic farmers. Only the words were different. Snorri began a refrain, repeating over and over the same phrases, and this time he was not speaking archaic Norse. He was using a language that I could not recognise. Again there seemed to be something distantly familiar about it. Several of the farmers must have known the same spell language because they began to chant in time with Snorri. Eventually, after nine circuits of the altar, left-handed against the sun, we stopped our dance, straightened up and Snorri turned to face north-west across the altar. He raised his arms, repeated another phrase in the same strange language, and then the spell session was over.

The next four days, as it happened, were bright and sunny. There was a perfect drying wind and we gathered and stacked the hay. Whether or not this was because we had performed our nature-spell I have no idea, but every farmer in the Westfjords managed to save his hay for the winter, and I am sure that each man's faith in Thor increased. Later, at a discreet moment, I dared to ask Snorri whether he thought the fine weather was the result of our incantations, and he was non-committal. 'I had a feeling in my bones that we were finally due for a dry spell,' he said. 'There was a change in the air, the moon was entering a new phase and the birds began to fly higher. Maybe the dry weather was already on its way and our appeal to Thor only meant that we were not disappointed.'

'What was the language you used when we were dancing in a circle?' I asked him.

He looked at me pensively. 'Under other circumstances you would know it already,' he said. 'It is the language of many spells and incantations, though I only know a few words of it. It is the native language of your mother, the language of the Irish.'

Four days later a messenger arrived from Karstad to ask Snorri to officiate at a burial. Farmer Thorodd was dead. During the haymaking on his farm, the young bull Glaesir had been kept confined to a stall as he was troublesome, and the labourers needed to mow the home meadows without being disturbed by the aggressive young bull. As soon as the hay was put up in haycocks, they had let Glaesir out on the stubble. First they took the precaution of tying a heavy block of wood over his horns to restrain and tire him. Glad to be free, the animal had charged up and down the largest of the home meadows. Within moments he had shaken off the block of wood and, something he had never done before, he began assaulting the carefully stacked haycocks. Ramming his horns into the stacks, he shook his head and scattered the hay in all directions. The farm workers were angry to see their work destroyed, but too fearful of the young bull to interfere. Instead they had sent word to Thorodd at the main house. He arrived, took one look at the situation and seized a stout wooden pole. Then he vaulted the low wall into the paddock and advanced on Glaesir.

Previously Glaesir had shown a unique respect for Thorodd. Alone of all the people on the farm, Thorodd was able to handle the young bull. But this time Glaesir had dropped his head and charged the farmer. Thorodd stood his ground and, as the bull closed with him, brought the heavy wooden pole down with a massive thump, striking Glaesir on the crown of the head right between the horns. The blow stopped Glaesir in his tracks and the animal stood there shaking his head in a daze. The force of the blow had broken the wooden pole in half, so Thorodd – confident of his mastery over the bull – strode forward and grasped Glaesir by the head, seeking to twist the horns and bring the animal to his knees. For a few moments the tussle went on. Then Thorodd's foot slipped on the short cut grass, and he lost his purchase. Glaesir jerked backwards and gave his head a shake which partially broke

Thorodd's grip. Thorodd managed to keep one hand on the left horn and, stepping behind the bull, boldly vaulted onto Glaesir's back, putting his body right forward on the animal's neck, intending that his weight — for Thorodd was a big, heavy man — would eventually subdue the young bull. Glaesir bolted down the field, swerving and twisting from side to side in an attempt to dislodge the burden on his back. The bull was quick and agile and stronger than Thorodd had anticipated. An unlucky leap, a change of direction in mid-air, unseated Thorodd and he began to slip to one side. Glaesir must have sensed the change, for he turned his head, placed a horn under Thorodd and got enough leverage to throw the farmer up into the air. As Thorodd fell back down towards the animal, Glaesir raised his head and the farmer fell straight onto one of the horns, which pierced his gut on the left side, low down. The horn drove deep. Thorodd fell off the bull and lay in a heap, as Glaesir, suddenly quiet, trotted off and began grazing. The farmhands ran into the field and picked up their master. They placed Thorodd on a hurdle and carried him up to the farmhouse. As they reached the door, Thorodd insisted on getting off the hurdle and walking into his own house upright. He lurched into the hall, the right side of his shirt drenched in blood. That night he died.

When the messenger finished his story, Snorri dismissed him, and waved away the small crowd who had gathered to hear the gruesome tale. Then he beckoned to me to follow him and led me to the small sleeping closet at the side of the hall. It was unoccupied and the only place where he could speak to me privately.

'Thorgils,' he asked, 'how many people did you tell about your vision of Thorodd in his blood-stained shirt?'

'No one apart from yourself.' I replied. 'I am sure that Thorodd's mother saw the blood too, but we were the only people to see it.'

'Let me give you some advice,' Snorri went on. 'Don't ever tell anyone else that you saw Thorodd's blood-stained shirt before his accident happened. In fact, I advise you not to talk to people whenever your second sight foretells anything that can be interpreted in a sinister way, particularly if there is any hint of death in it. People become fearful and nervous. Sometimes they think that a seer can cause an event to happen, and that once a seer has seen a vision, he or she shapes the future to make the vision come true, and they do this to enhance their reputations as visionaries. When ordinary people start to think like this, and some tragedy does occur, things can get very ugly. Fear leads to violence. People take revenge or try to remove the source of their fear by hurting the seer.'

'But aren't seers and volva and seidrmanna respected?' I asked, 'I thought that it was forbidden to spill their blood.'

'So it is. The last time that the people of this area mistrusted a magician, it was a man named Kolmek. He was another half-Irish like yourself, just a small farmer, who could see portents and make forecasts. A gang of his neighbours grabbed him one evening, pulled a sack over his head and bound it so tight that he choked to death. That didn't spill a drop of his blood. Nor did the way they dealt with Kolmek's wife. They accused her of black witchcraft. They carried her to a bog, tied a heavy stone round her feet and dropped her in.'

Already reticent about my dreams and second sight, I made a silent promise to myself that only in the most extreme circumstances would I disclose what my second sight revealed to me and not to others. Also I began to suspect that my flashes of second sight came from Odinn himself and, like all of Odinn's gifts, they could cause both help and harm.

TWELVE

HALLBERA WAS SNORRI'S fourth daughter. She had light freckles on healthy pale skin, rounded arms with a light fuzz of golden down, blue-grey eyes, blonde hair worn long and a face that was perfectly symmetrical. In short, she was the epitome of a normal, wholesome, good-looking Norse maiden. She adored her brothers, of whom she had eight, and she got on well with her sisters, of whom she also had eight. Indeed, if any proof is needed that Snorri Godi was more pagan than Christian, it is the fact that he had one official wife, and a second wife, whom he never married but made clear was his second consort. And he treated all their children equally. Hallbera's background in such a large and well-to-do family could scarcely have been more different from mine as an impoverished newcomer living on the fringes of her father's household. There were many times when I felt overawed by the energy and self-confidence of the Snorrissons and Snorradottirs. But I was smitten. I did everything I could to stay in her father's favour so that I could be close to this honey-gold girl. For the first time in my life I was in love.

Quite why Hallbera accepted my infatuation is something I have never been able to explain fully. There was really no reason for her to take up with such a modest prospect as myself. The only explanation that I can find is that she was bored and perhaps curious as to how to manage the opposite sex, and I was conveniently on hand to experiment with. There was nothing improper about our relationship. Hallbera and I began to meet quietly, exchange kisses and indulge in some gentle cuddling. These physical contacts made my head spin and I would feel weak for half an hour afterwards, though Hallbera never seemed to experience similar surges of emotions. She was always so robust and crisp and energetic. She was capable of emerging from an embrace, suddenly announcing that she had promised to help one of her brothers in some task, and go bouncing off in her athletic stride, her blonde hair swinging, leaving me dazed with emotion and completely baffled. I am sure that Snorri guessed at the relationship between his daughter and myself, and there is no doubt that it was known to Hallbera's mother. But neither of them chose to interfere because there were so many other children and more important matters to occupy their attention.

In the throes of calf love, I would go off for hours to some quiet corner and fall into a trance, meditating on how I could spend the rest of my life close to that glorious, milk-and-honey girl. Now I realise that I wanted more than just Hallbera. I was longing to be absorbed for ever into the embrace of a large family, where everything seemed to be in a perpetual state of sunny commotion and bustle, where there were few problems which, when they did arise, were solved in moments by mutual help and support. In short, I was feeling lonely and insecure, and my view of Snorri's family was a fantasy which overlooked the fact that my darling Hallbera was no more than a thoroughly normal, conventional young woman in the blush of her maidenhood.

The conversation that autumn was all about a local bandit by the name of Ospak, and what should be done about him. Listening to the discussions, I learned that Ospak had plagued the region for many years. He had always been a bully. A brute by nature and in stature, he had started his mischief when he was still in his teens, knocking about his neighbours and generally terrorising them. As he grew to middle age, he graduated to systematic oppression of

the people living within reach and a gang of similar-minded ruffians
soon clustered around him. On one notorious occasion he and a
gang of his toughs showed up when a dead fin whale had been
stranded on a beach. By Icelandic law the division of anything
washed up on a beach is strictly controlled. Each stretch of rocky
foreshore belongs to the farmers who own the driftage rights there.
Dead whales, lengths of driftwood, bits and pieces from boat
wrecks, are all considered valuable. They are so precious, in fact,
that the first pioneers developed an ingenious system of selecting
where to build their homes. Sailing along the new-found coast, the
captain of the vessel would throw overboard the carved wooden
panels that traditionally stand on each side of the high chair in a
Norse hall. Later, going ashore, the new arrivals would range the
coast looking to see where the panels had washed up. There they
built their home and claimed the beach rights because they knew
that the sea currents would supply an endless source of bounty at
that spot.

On the day the fin whale washed up, the farmers who owned
the driftage rights went down to the beach early in the morning to
check what the sea had cast up. The previous night there had been
a great gale from the direction which normally brought the best
flotsam, and sure enough the carcass of the whale, dead from
natural causes, was found lying in the shallows. The farmers went
home, fetched their cutting spades and axes and began to butcher
the dead whale. They had peeled back the blubber and got as far
as cutting up large chunks of the meat, stacking it in piles ready to
be shared out, when Ospak appeared. He had no driftage rights,
but knew the wind and waves as well as anyone and had rowed
across the bay with fifteen of his gang, all heavily armed. They
came ashore and demanded a share of the meat, only to be told by
one of the farmers, a man named Thorir, that if the other workers
agreed they would sell Ospak what he wanted. Ospak gruffly told
Thorir that he had no intention of paying and instructed his men
to begin loading their boat. When Thorir objected, Ospak struck
him on the ear with the flat of an axe blade and knocked him

unconscious. The rest of the farmers, outnumbered, were in no position to resist. They had to look on while Ospak and his men filled their boat with as much meat as they could carry, and rowed off, taunting their unfortunate victims.

The following year Ospak's behaviour became even more wild. He and his men took to raiding isolated farms and looting them, often tying up the farmer and his family. They carried off whatever valuables they could find, all spare stocks of food, and drove away the cattle and horses. They operated with impunity because the farmers were poorly organised, and Ospak had taken the trouble to fortify his own farmhouse so strongly that it was dangerous to counter-attack. His following increased to at least twenty men, all desperadoes attracted by the chance of easy pickings. But the more men Ospak recruited, the more he had to extend his raids to obtain them enough supplies. So the vicious cycle continued unabated. Some time before I joined Snorri's household, Ospak and his men had raided Thorir's farm, pillaged it and dragged Thorir outside and killed him. The raiders then headed on towards a farm owned by another of the men who had been at the whale kill, and against whom Ospak bore a grudge. Fortunately Alf, known as Alf the Short, was fully dressed and still awake when the raiders arrived, though it was late in the evening when most people would have been in bed and asleep. Alf managed to slip out of the rear of the house as the raiders battered down the front door, and he ran off across the moor, heading for refuge with Snorri, who was one of the few men in the district too powerful for Ospak to meddle with.

Snorri heard Alf's tale and his plea for help. But though he gave Alf shelter for as long as he wanted to stay, Snorri waited several months without taking any action against Ospak. For this Snorri was criticised by many, but it was typical of his style. Snorri never did anything in haste, and only after he had made meticulous preparations did he reveal his hand. He wanted more information about Ospak's defences, and asked if I would visit Ospak's fortified farm. Ostensibly I was calling to look for work. In reality I was, once again, a spy and – as Snorri made this request just when I was in the full fever of my passion for Hallbera and badly wanted to impress her – I accepted without hesitation.

It took me two days to walk across country to Ospak's stronghold, and as I approached his farmhouse I could see that he had built a tall palisade made of timber and closed the entrance to the stockade with massive double gates. Round the inside of the palisade ran an elevated walkway, which would allow the defenders to stand at the rampart and hurl missiles down at any attackers who came too close. Even more daunting was the garrison. I saw at least twenty heavily armed men, including one ugly specimen who affected the old-fashioned style of weaving his long beard in plaits, which he arranged in a mat down his chest. Snorri had already told me about this flamboyant villain, who went by the name of Hrafn the Vikingr. He was a simple-minded, lumbering sort of oaf who drank away his spoils and was already under sentence of full outlawry for committing a random murder.

I also laid eyes, for the first time, on a second, rather more intriguing outlaw at Ospak's farm. When I walked in through the massive wooden gates I saw a young man sitting in the farmyard on a bench, moodily carving a piece of wood with his knife. I remember he was wearing a brown tunic and blue leggings, and that he seemed to control a repressed fury. The pale shavings were curling up from his knife blade and jumping into the air like nervous insects. Only the breadth of his shoulders, his long arms and powerful hands gave a hint of how he had earned his name, Grettir the Strong. I was interested to meet him because he was only two years older than myself, yet already infamous throughout Iceland. He was not a member of Ospak's band but visiting the fortified farm with his sister, who was betrothed to Ospak's son. All sorts of stories were circulating about Grettir the Strong. Even as a young boy he had been uncontrollable. He wilfully disobeyed his parents, refused to help on the family farm and spent most of his time sprawling lazily in the house. When forced to get to his feet and carry out any chore, Grettir made sure he did it in such a way that he was never asked to do the same job again. Sent to lock up the poultry for the night, he left the chicken-shed door ajar so the birds escaped onto the moors. Told to groom the prize stallion, he deliberately scored its back with a sharp knife point so the wretched animal was invalided. He was an impossible youth, wayward and perverse. Nor was he affable with his contemporaries. He was always picking fights, quarrelling and brawling, and he made few friends. I had first heard his name mentioned that winter when I and several of Snorri's younger children were out on the frozen fjord, playing an ice game. We had divided into two teams and were using shaped sticks to hit a small ball through a mark. One of my team lost his temper and rushed at an opponent, threatening to smash him on the head with his stick. It was called 'doing a Grettir'. I found out that Grettir had famously attacked an opponent during the ice game and nearly killed him when he hit the boy so hard that his skull cracked. Three months later Grettir killed a man in a quarrel over, of all things, a leather flask of skyr, sour milk. After that brawl, Grettir was sentenced to lesser outlawry, and when I met him he was in the second grace year, preparing to leave Iceland and seek service with the King of Norway. At that time I had no inkling that one day Grettir would become perhaps my closest friend.

Ospak bluntly turned me away, saying that he had no work for me. However, in the few hours I spent inside his stockade I was able to glean enough information to report on Ospak's force and defences to Snorri when I got back to Saelingsdale.

I told Snorri what I had seen, and as usual he made little comment. He had been talking with the local chieftains about organising a unified attack on the brigands, and he was prepared to wait until all his allies were free to join him, and also for an excuse to assemble them without arousing Ospak's suspicions. The one person he did summon to Saelingsdale in advance of his attack was a former member of his household who had now set up as a farmer on his own account – Thrand Stigandi.

Thrand was the sort of person who causes people to lower their voices nervously when they catch sight of him. A head taller than any other man in the neighbourhood, he had a leathery, competent air and was known to be handy with sword and axe. He also looked formidable, with a craggy face, a great prow of a nose, and bushy eyebrows that he could pull down in a ferocious scowl. Anyone facing Thrand in a quarrel would have second thoughts about resorting to physical violence. But within moments of Thrand walking into Snorri's house I knew that there was another, hidden reason why Snorri had summoned him. When Thrand entered the main hall, I was standing slightly to the left of the entrance, and as he came into the room, he glanced to one side and caught my eye. The moment that happened he paused in his stride and waited for the space of a heartbeat. In that instant I recognised the same cool, calm look I had seen eighteen months before in Vinland, on the day I had stumbled across the two Skraelings in the forest. It was in the eyes of the Skraeling shaman when I blundered into the sick man's shelter. I guessed at once that Thrand was a seidrman, and my intuition was confirmed when Snorri and Thrand went that same evening to Thor's temple and spent many hours there. Thrand, I was sure, was communing with the God.

Thrand's arrival had the same effect on me as when I saw the blood-stained shirt in the company of Thorodd's mother, or when I saw the ghost of my dead uncle with Gudrid. The presence of someone who could also see into the spirit world aroused the spirit energy within me. On the second night after Thrand's arrival I had my first omen dream.

I dreamed of a farm that was under attack. Half awake, half asleep, I was in a dimness that was neither night nor day. The attackers had surrounded the building and were pressing home their assault with great ferocity, and I was conscious of the shouts of the combatants and the screams of women inside the building. Several times the thud of blows jolted me part awake, though they were sounds that could only have existed within my dream. The first time I woke, I told myself that my nightmare was a memory of all the horrors that I had heard about the Burning when Njal and his family had been massacred. But as I slipped back into the nightmare I realised that the farm I was watching was not being attacked with fire. There were no flames, no smoke, only the figures of men running here and there, occasionally hurling themselves at the rampart. Then I saw that it was Ospak's farm, and among the assailants was Thrand. His tall form was unmistakable, but he seemed to have an owl's head, and there was something about the conflict which reminded me of how the Skraelings had fought when they attacked us in Vinland. I woke up sweating.

In the morning I recalled Snorri's warning about keeping silent about my visions, particularly if they involved death or harm, and I told no one.

Snorri moved against Ospak's farm some three weeks later and with overwhelming force. Every able-bodied worker from the farm, including myself, joined the expedition. On our march across the moor we met a column of fifty farmers led by a neighbouring chieftain, Sturla, who had brought his people to assist in the campaign. Our joint company must have amounted to at least eighty combatants, though, as usual, there were very few trained fighters among them. Everyone carried a sword or an axe, plus his dagger, but there was a noticeable shortage of defensive armour. A few men wore leather jackets sewn with small metal plates, but most of the farmers were relying on their wooden shields and thick leather jerkins to protect them from any missiles that Ospak and his cronies would hurl at them from the rampart. In our entire war band I counted only a dozen metal helmets, and one of those was an antique. Instead of the conical modern style with its noseguard, it was round like a pudding bowl and the wearer's face was hidden behind two round eyepieces. I was not in the least surprised that the man who carried that helmet was Thrand.

Ospak's scouts must have been watching the trail because when we came in sight of the farmhouse the gates were already shut and barred, and we could see his men had taken up their positions on the elevated walkway. Snorri and Sturla held a short council and agreed that to make the best use of our own superior numbers all four sides of the farm should be attacked simultaneously. Snorri found that he was facing the forces commanded by Hrafn the Vikingr, while Sturla and his men attacked the section of the rampart where Ospak led the defence.

The siege of the farmhouse opened with a barrage of rocks and small boulders which the opposing forces hurled at one another. In this phase of the battle, the defenders on the elevated walkway held a considerable advantage, as they were able to drop boulders on any of the attackers who came too close. Their weakness was their limited supply of boulders and other missiles, so Snorri's and Sturla's forces spent the first hour or so of their attack making quick feints up to the palisade, shouting insults and throwing stones, then turning to run back as they dodged the counter-hail of missiles. When the defenders' supply of stones ran low, the attackers began to run right up to the palisade, concentrating on the fortified gateway and attempting to break through by hacking and levering at the planks. This tactic, however, had little success as the gates were too stoutly built, and the assaults were beaten back. The attackers threw few spears because they tended to bounce off the ramparts, or if one flew over the wall and landed in the compound, one of the defenders was likely to pick it up and hurl it back with more dangerous effect. Only a couple of men on either side used bows and arrows because, quite simply, they are seldom used among Icelanders in their quarrels – they much prefer hand-to-hand fighting.

The rather untidy assault had been in progress for a couple of hours when it seemed to me that the enthusiasm of the attackers was waning. It was at that moment that Thrand showed his worth. Wearing his antique helmet, he sprinted forward from our group, ran up to the palisade and, using the advantage of his great height, sprang into the air so that he leaped high enough to hook the blade of his battleaxe over the top of the palisade. He then grabbed the handle of the axe in both hands and pulled himself upwards, so that he got a leg over the rampart and was able to jump down on the walkway on the far side. There he came face to face with Hrafn the Vikingr, who rushed at him with a great roar of anger. Thrand dodged the Viking's clumsy spear thrust, knocked the plait-bearded warrior off balance, and hacked at the outstretched arm that held the spear. The axe blow was perfectly aimed. It struck Hrafn on the right shoulder and severed his arm from his body. Hrafn reeled sideways, slipped from the walkway and fell with a heavy thud into the compound below. As Ospak's men looked at the fallen body of their champion in shock, Thrand took advantage of the moment to vault back over the rampart, drop to the ground and run back to rejoin us. His intervention demoralised the defenders. Ospak's men began to fight with less bravado and, seeing this, Snorri sent me with a message for Sturla, who was attacking the opposite side of farm. I was to tell him to launch an all-out assault now that the defence was in disarray.

I ran round the side of the farm, scrambling over the low sod walls that marked out the home pasture, and reached Sturla just in time to see him step forward holding a weapon that I vaguely recognised. It was a thin, flat board, about as long as a man's arm, and I had first seen it when the Skraelings attacked us in Vinland and, most recently, it had appeared in my nightmare. It was a spear thrower. Where Sturla had obtained this device I do not know. But he knew how to use it, for he ran forward until close enough to the rampart to deliver an accurate strike. Ospak must not have known what Sturla was carrying because when he saw Sturla come so close, Ospak jumped up on the lip of the rampart, made an obscene gesture, and raised a large rock above his head with both hands, ready to toss it on Sturla's head. Ospak was wearing protective armour that few Icelanders could afford – a thigh-length shirt of chain mail, which protected almost his entire body. But the action of raising the rock lifted the skirt of the chain mail and exposed his upper thigh. Seeing his target, Sturla swung the spear thrower in its arc and delivered its projectile. The spear shot upward. The iron head of the spear was long and slender, with two small flanges to serve as wings. Behind it uncoiled a loop of line. The spear's point passed clean through Ospak's thigh and, as he staggered, Sturla gathered the line in both hands and gave a tremendous jerk. Like a fish that has been harpooned, Ospak was literally plucked off the wall and pulled down to the ground. Gesturing to his companions to stand back, Sturla ran forward, drew his dagger and stabbed Ospak through the heart.

The death of their leader ended all resistance from Ospak's gang. They lowered their weapons and began shouting out that they would leave the building if they were allowed to go unharmed. A moment later the double gates of the stockade were tugged open. Snorri, Sturla and the rest of us walked into the compound to find the bandits looking frightened and exhausted. Hrafn, Ospak and one other man were the only fatalities, but many of the defenders had minor wounds and bruises. Snorri kept his word and was remarkably lenient with their punishment. He held a brief court hearing on the spot, and in his capacity as the local godi condemned the worst culprits to exile. He did not have the power to exile them from Iceland, but he could forbid them to come ever again into Westfjords on pain of being prosecuted as full outlaws at the next Althing. The men were obliged to leave their weapons behind and quit the farm immediately, never to return. Snorri treated Ospak's widow and son magnanimously. The widow, he said, had not had any choice in her husband's behaviour, and though the son had fought in the defence of the farm, he was honour-bound to do so for his family's reputation. He had not been involved in his father's brigandage, and in consequence Snorri pronounced that the widow and son could continue in possession of the farm and its lands.

Thrand Stigandi stayed on at Snorri's farm for several weeks after Ospak's defeat at the battle of Bitra, as it came to be called, and there were many who came to congratulate him on his bravery and some, more discreetly, to thank him for interceding with Thor on behalf of the law-abiding people of the Westfjords. Snorri must have told Thrand about me and I was flattered when Thrand beckoned to me one evening as supper was being cleared from the table and led me to a quiet corner, where we could not be overheard. He sat down on a storage chest and said in his deep, husky voice, 'Snorri tells me that sometimes you see things which others cannot see.'

'Yes, occasionally,' I replied, 'but I don't understand what I am seeing, and I never know when it will happen.'

'Can you give me an example?' he asked.

I thought of Snorri's warning never to reveal dreams of death to anyone, but the events were in the past and Snorri had assured me that Thrand was seidr-skilled so I told him about my dream of the battle at Ospak's farm, the owl-headed man, and the rest.

Thrand did not interrupt, and when I had finished my account, he said, 'And how many days before the fight did you have this dream?'

'Soon after your arrival here, on the night after you and Snorri spent so much time in Thor's temple,' I answered.

'I wonder if you would have had the dream earlier, in the temple itself, if the conditions had been right,' Thrand commented, almost speaking to himself. 'Some seers are lucky. Dreams come to them so easily that they need only to withdraw to some quiet place, close their eyes and empty their minds, and the visions enter their consciousness. Others must get fuddled on strong drink, or chew strong weeds, or breathe the smoke of a sacred fire, or listen to sacred chants repeated over and over again until their spirit floats free from their body.'

He got up and went to where his sword and helmet were hanging from a peg on the wall. He brought them over and showed the flat of the sword's blade to me. 'What does that mean?' he asked.

The runes were easy to decipher and simple. 'Ulfbert made,' I replied.

'Now, what about this?' he continued, holding out his antique helmet with its quaint eye protectors. He had turned the helmet upside down so I could see inside the metal bowl. From the centre, radiating down to each side, was incised a plain, thin cross, its arms ending in arrow heads which pointed back towards the intersection.

'That's the aegishjalmr,' I said, 'the helm of awe.' 'Yes,' replied Thrand, 'but what about the marks around the edge?'

I looked more closely. Around the inner rim of the helmet I could see a number of small scratches. They were badly worn, but they had been put there deliberately. Several of them I recognised immediately as rune staves in the futhark, but others were more difficult to decipher. I ran my finger round them, to feel their shapes, as Tyrkir had taught me. Several I identified as letters which Tyrkir had said were little used nowadays. In the end, I did manage to puzzle them out.

'I don't know what it means, but if I try to read out the message it would sound something like . . . a g mod den juthu pt fur . . . but I cannot be sure.'

Thrand looked thoughtful. 'No more than half a dozen people in Iceland know how to read the archaic runes,' he said. 'That's galdrastafir – rune spell. It was put there soon after the helmet was forged, and the staves make the helmet a talisman against harm to the wearer, as well as a physical protection. I would never exchange this antique helmet for a modern one. Who taught you the archaic runes?'

'An old German, a metalsmith named Tyrkir, instructed me in how to read and cut rune staves while I was in Greenland.'

Thrand said solemnly, 'The message you carve in runes is more important than just knowing what each stave represents. Quite a few people know how to carve their name, but only the initiated know the spells and charms and curses that can be written. Odinn showed rune writing to mankind and now it is merely a matter of passing the knowledge from one person to the next.'

He seemed to make up his mind about something, turned towards me and, speaking to me as if I was an adult and not a fourteen-year-old lad, he went on:

'The greatest and most profound visions require pain and sacrifice. Odinn gave one of his eyes in order to drink from the fountain of Mimir and learn the secret wisdom which allows the Gods to survive. He also impaled himself on a spear and hung for nine days from Yggdrasil, the world tree, in order to learn the secret of the runes. Only through the sacrifice and pain could he open his mind and spirit to wisdom. That is one thing which distinguishes us from the Christians. They believe that the soul lives in the heart, but we hold that it resides in the mind, and that when the mind is set free the spirit also is liberated.'

Unwittingly I had allowed my rune literacy to impress Thrand in a way that was to have painful consequences. When he was ready to return to his own farm, he suggested to Snorri that I go with him and become his pupil in seidr skills. Snorri summoned me and, watching me with those quiet grey eyes, said, 'Thrand has offered to take you on as a pupil. I believe that this is your chance to develop a talent that you were born with and which may yet compensate for the disadvantages you have already faced in your young life. For that reason I am closing my house to you and sending you away.'

Thus I began to appreciate how the acquisition of knowledge can mean pain and sacrifice, for I was heart-broken to be parted from my adored Hallbera. Years later, long after my departure from Snorri's household, I learned that she married an eminently suitable husband, the son of a neighbouring landowner whose help Snorri needed at a session of the Althing. Her young man was ideal – respectable, well-connected, reliable. He was also decidedly dull. I am sure that Hallbera was very happy with him. The last I heard was that they had their own family of seven or eight children, lived on a well-run farm on the Westfjords, and were similarly looking for suitable matches for their numerous offspring. On the few occasions when I imagine myself as that young man Hallbera could have married, I wonder whether it was Hallbera's wish to have a more settled future that made her marry her worthy husband, or whether once again it was Odinn's intervention that led her family to judge me to be no more than a pleasant and temporary diversion for their fourth daughter.

THE SUMMER THAT I spent with Thrand at his farm in the uplands behind Laxadale was perhaps the most formative period of my life.

Thrand lived by himself on a small homestead, no more than a single cabin with a barn nearby. His dwelling was sparsely furnished with only a couple of stools, a pair of wooden cots, his iron cooking pot and griddle – he did all his own cooking – and a few large storage chests, always kept locked. The walls of his cabin were bare except for several foreign-looking wall hangings with strange patterns, which I could not decipher, and a row of pegs from which Thrand hung his weapons and various satchels and cloth bundles containing his seidr materials. The place was so orderly that it was stark, and this reflected the character of its owner. My teacher in seidr was reserved and self-controlled to the point of austerity and as a result he was very difficult to get to know. I am sure he never meant to seem unfriendly but if I plucked up enough courage to ask a question, the answer was sometimes so slow in coming that I feared he thought me stupid or that he had not heard the question. When the answer came – and it always did, though I might have to wait until the next day – it was terse, accurate and clear-cut. It was to take me a long time to grow fond of Thrand, but from the start I respected him.

He was a methodical teacher. Patiently he built on the foundation of the knowledge that Tyrkir and Thorvall had imparted. Sometimes he found it necessary to correct errors. My earlier mentors had occasionally muddled the roles of the Aesir, the family of Gods, and at other times I had misunderstood their lessons. So Thrand began by putting my chaotic knowledge in some sort of order and then went on to expand and deepen the details. I progressed from my basic knowledge of the main Gods and Goddesses of the Aesir and Vanir, and became aware of an entire pantheon, and this in addition to the Norns and light-elves and dark-elves and dwarves, and frost giants and the otherworld creatures and the roles they played in the ancient cosmology. 'Everything interlocks,' Thrand was fond of saying. 'Think of the braiding roots of the World Tree, where one root tangles with another, and then reaches out to a third, and then doubles back and binds on itself, or the spreading branches above which do the same. Yet all the roots and branches have a function. They sustain Yggdrasil and they are Yggdrasil. This is how it is with ancient lore. If you have the foundation knowledge, you can follow the path of a single root or just one strand, or you can stand back and see the whole pattern.'

Committing the lore to memory was surprisingly easy. It seemed that every deed, every deity, every detail, had been set into a language that flowed and rippled seductively, or laid out in lists that marched to a steady beat. Even now, half a century later, I can count off all forty-eight names of Odinn – from Baleygr, Harbardr and Herblindi, to Herian, Hialmberi, Thekkr, Thriggi, Thundr, Unnr, Viudurr, Yrungr, and so forth. The ones that still make my heart beat faster when I hear them in my head are: Aldafadr, All-Father; Draugadrottin, Lord of the Dead; Grimnir, the Masked One; Farmognudr, Maker of Journeys and Gangleri, the Wanderer.

Tyrkir and Thorvall had told me the simple tales that illustrate the deeds of the Gods – that the earth quakes when Loki writhes in his bonds, that the gales arise from the flapping wings of the great eagle giant Hraesvelg, and that lightning is the flash of Mjollnir when Thor hurls his hammer. Now Thrand placed these tales in their wider context. He explained the relationship between deeds past and the events that still lie in the future, and how at their intersection lies what happens today. And always he emphasised that everything interweaves, so that while those who were gifted with second sight might look into the future, there was little we could do to avert what had been ordained by the Norns. Those three supernatural women hold the ultimate power, for they have decided the fate of every living creature and even of the Gods themselves.

'The greater pattern cannot be altered,' Thraud emphasised to me. 'Even the Gods themselves know that they must inevitably face Ragnarok and the destruction of the world. With all their power they can only delay that fatal time, not avoid it. How much less can we, mere mortals, alter the web that the Norns have spun for us or the marks they have cut in the timber of our lives.'

Thrand was a firm believer in divination. If fate was set, then it could be revealed by skilled interpretation. He owned a casting set of rune blocks, carved from whalebone and yellow with age. He would spread out a white sheet and throw the blocks on the sheet like dice, then puzzle over the way the symbols fell, reading the message in their random patterns and then explaining their symbolism to me. Often the message was obscure, even more frequently it was contradictory. But that, as he explained to me, was in the nature of the runes themselves. Each owned two meanings, at the very least, and these meanings were opposites; whether they occurred in light or dark conjunctions determined which was the correct sense. I found it all very confusing, though I managed to grasp most of the basic principles.

Galdrastafir, the rune spells, were more straightforward and reminded me of the smith's galdr that Tyrkir had taught me. Thrand would take practice pieces of timber and show me how to carve correctly the sequence of runes, dividing my lessons into categories: mind runes for bringing knowledge, sea runes for safe journeys, limb runes for healing, speech runes to fend off revenge, the helping runes for childbirth. 'Don't be surprised if they are ineffective sometimes,' he warned me. 'Odinn himself only learned eighteen rune spells when he was hanging on Yggdrasil, and we are presumptuous to think that we can achieve more.' The accuracy of cutting was not all, he stressed. Every stave had its own spoken formula, which I had to recite as I made the mark, and Thrand made me repeat the formula until I was word-perfect. 'Speak the words right,' said Thrand, 'and you will not have to resort to such tricks as rubbing the marks with your own blood to make the spell more potent. Leave such devices to those who are more interested in doing harm with the rune spells, not achieving good.'

Thrand also had a warning. 'If galdrastafir is done badly, it is likely to have the reverse effect from what was intended. That arises from the double and opposing nature of the runes, the dual nature of Odinn's gift. Thus a healing rune meant to help cure an invalid will actually damage their health if incorrectly cut.'

Thrand, who was by nature an optimist, refused to teach me any curse runes. And, as a precaution, he insisted that at the end of every lesson we put all the practice rune staves into the fire and burn them to ashes, lest they fell into malevolent hands. On these occasions, as we watched the flames consume the wood, I noticed how Thrand stayed beside the dying fire, gazing into the embers. I had the impression that he was far away in his thoughts, in some foreign country, though he never talked about his past.

THIRTEEN

A HORSE FIGHT marked the end of my stay with Thrand. The match between the two stallions had been eagerly awaited in the district for several months, and Thrand and I went to see the spectacle. The fight, or hestavig, was held on neutral ground for the two stallions. To encourage them, a small herd of mares was penned in the paddock immediately next to the patch of bare ground where the two stallions would fight. Naturally a small crowd had gathered to place bets on the outcome. When we arrived, the owners of the stallions were standing facing each other, holding the halters. Both animals were already in a lather, squealing and lunging and rearing to get at one another. A visiting farmer — he had probably backed the animal to win — had boldly walked behind one of the stallions and was poking at his testicles with a short stick to enrage the animal still further, which led Thrand to comment to me, 'He wouldn't be doing that if he knew his lore. He could be making an enemy of Loki and that will bring bad fortune.' I didn't know whether Thrand was referring to the story in which the trickster God Loki changed himself into a mare to seduce a malignant giant in the shape of a huge stallion, or the comic scene in Valholl when Loki is given the task of amusing the visiting giantess Skadi. Loki strips off, then ties one end of a rope round the beard of a billy goat, and the other end round his testicles, and the pair tug one another back and forth across the hall, each squealing loudly until the normally morose giantess bursts into laughter.

There was a sudden shout from the crowd as the two stallions were given slack and immediately sprang forward to attack one another, teeth bared and snorting with aggression. Their squeals of anger rose to a frenzy as they clashed, rising up on their hind legs to lash out with their hooves, or twisting round with gaping jaws to try to inflict a crippling neck bite. When all eyes were on the contest, I felt a discreet tug on my sleeve and turned to see a soberly dressed man I did not recognise. He nodded for me to follow him, and we walked a short distance to one side of the crowd, which was cheering as the two stallions began to draw blood. "Kari sent me with a message,' said the unknown visitor. 'He plans to go to Orkney, and has arranged to board a ship leaving from Eyrar two weeks from today. He says that if you want, you can travel with him. If you do decide to make the journey, you are to find your way to Eyrar and ask for the ship of Kolbein the Black. He's an Orkney man himself and an old friend of Kari's.'

I had heard nothing from Kari since the day at the Althing when he had refused to accept the godi's proposed settlement with the Burners. But plenty of rumours had reached me. It seemed that, as soon as the Althing ended, Kari launched himself on a personal and deadly campaign of revenge. He intercepted a party of Burners and their friends as they rode home from the Althing and challenged them to fight. They took on the challenge because Kari had only a single companion, a man named Thorgeir, and the Burners were eight in number. But Kari and Thorgeir had fought so skilfully that three of the Burners were killed and the remainder fled in panic. The leader of the Burners, Flosi, again offered to settle the blood feud and pay a heavy compensation for Burned Njal's death. But Kari was not to be placated. He persuaded his colleague Thorgeir to accept the settlement, saying that Thorgeir was not directly concerned in the blood feud, but that he, Kari, was a long way from settling the debt of honour that he owed to his dead family.

Kari was now outside the law and every man's hand was against him, but he refused to give up his campaign of retribution. Driven by the Norse sense of honour I mentioned earlier, he skulked in hiding for months, either living on the moors or staying with friendly farmers. He found another comrade-in-arms in a smallholder named Bjorn the White, a most unlikely associate as Bjorn was known as a braggart who boasted much and did little. Indeed, Bjorn's reputation was so low that even his wife did not think he had the courage for a stand-up fight. But Kari was a natural leader and he inspired Bjorn to excel. The two men ranged the island, tracking down the Burners and confronting them. Each time the combination of Kari and Bjorn won the day. Bjorn guarded Kari's back while the expert dueller tackled the Burners. By now fifteen of the original gang of Burners had been killed, and the rest had decided that it was wiser to begin their own period of exile and leave Iceland rather than be hunted down by Kari. In late summer the last of the Burners had departed from Iceland, intending to sail to Norway, and nothing more had been heard from them. Now, I guessed, Kari was planning to begin his own period of exile.

I told Thrand of Kari's message as soon as we got back to Thrand's cabin. My mentor's response was unhesitating. 'Of course you have to go with Kari,' he said decisively. 'There is a bond between you. Kari has kept in mind his promise he made to you at the Althing. With this offer of a passage to Orkney, he is honouring his pledge. In turn, you should acknowledge his nobility of spirit, accept his offer and go with him.' Then he made a remark which showed how – all this time – he had been aware of what was troubling me. 'If there is to be a final lesson which I want you to take away with you, let it be this: show and maintain personal integrity towards any man or woman who displays a similar faith and trust in you and you will find that you are never truly on your own.'

KOLBEIN THE BLACK sailed south from Eyrar at the end of November. It was late in the year to be making the voyage, but we had weather luck and the trip was uneventful. En route to Orkney Kari asked if we could stop at the Fair Isle, which lies between Orkney and Shetland, as he wanted to visit another of his friends, David the White, whom he had known from the days when both men were in the service of Earl Sigurd of Orkney. It was while we were staying at Fair Isle that a fisherman brought news that the Burners were nearby on Mainland, as the chief island in Orkney is called. The Burners had sailed from Iceland two weeks before us, but where we had good weather the Burners had encountered a heavy gale. Driven off course, their vessel was wrecked on the rocks of Mainland in poor visibility and they only just managed to scramble ashore. The mishap put Flosi and his colleagues in a real predicament. One of their victims at the Burning, Helgi Njalsson, was formerly a member of Earl Sigurd's retinue. There was every chance that if they were caught by the earl's people, the earl would put them to death for murdering one of his sworn men. The worried Burners spent a very uncomfortable day on the seashore, hiding in rocky clefts, camouflaging themselves under blankets of moss and seaweed, before Flosi decided that they had no choice but to walk across the island to Earl Sigurd's great hall, present themselves before the ruler of Orkney and throw themselves on his mercy.

Earl Sigurd knew at once who they were when the Burners arrived. Most of the Norse world was talking of the Burning of Njal. The earl was renowned for his violent temper and, as the Burners had feared, his initial reaction was to fly into a rage and order the visitors to be arrested. But Flosi courageously spoke up, admitting his guilt for Helgi Njalsson's death. Then, invoking an old Norse tradition, he offered to serve in Helgi's place in the earl's retinue. After some grumbling, Earl Sigurd agreed. The Burners had then pledged obedience to the earl and now were under his protection.

'Sigurd the Stout', as he was popularly known, was a pagan Norseman of the old school and proud of it. He always attracted fighting men. It was said that his two favourite seasons of the year were spring and autumn because at the first sign of spring he would launch his warships and go raiding his neighbours. He then came home for the summer to gather the harvest, and as soon as that was done he promptly put to sea again for a second round of viking. His most celebrated possession was the battle banner that his mother, a celebrated volva, had stitched for him. Its insignia was Odinn's emblem, the black raven. It was claimed that whoever flew the banner in battle would be victorious. However, in keeping with Odinn's perverse character, the person who carried the banner in battle would die while winning the victory. Given this warning, it was hardly surprising, that only the most loyal of Earl Sigurd's retainers was prepared to be his standard-bearer.

This was the man, then, in whose long hall at Birsay my mother had conducted her affair with my father Leif the Lucky, and the woman who had stitched the raven banner was my mother's confidante, Eithne the earl mother. According to the fisherman who brought us the news about the Burners, the earl mother was well advanced in years but still very much alive.

Kari decided that the most prudent time for us to cross to Mainland and arrive at Sigurd's great hall was during the Jol festival, when there should be several days of feasting and oath-taking. Sigurd still followed the old-fashioned tradition of having a large boar – an animal sacred to the fertility God Frey – led down his great hall so that the assembled company could lay hands on the bristly animal and swear their solemn oaths for the coming year. Then that evening the oath boar would be served up roast at a great banquet, at which the earl displayed his bounty by distributing vast quantities of mead and beer for his retainers and guests. For Sigurd the festival was a proper celebration in honour of Jolnir, another of Odinn's names, but he had no objection if the Christians chose to combine the earthy celebration of Jol with one of their holy days, provided they did not interfere with the priorities of eating, drinking, story-telling and carousing. Indeed, it occurred to me that it might have been under similar circumstances, fifteen years earlier, that I was conceived.

Kolbein's boat had a favourable tide under her and carried us across the strait between Fair Isle and Mainland in less than ten hours. Kolbein knew of a quiet sandy beach for our landing place, and he, Kari and I went ashore in the boat's tender, leaving a few men aboard at anchor watch. It was less than a half-hour walk over the rolling sand dunes to reach the earl's long hall, and there was still enough daylight left for me to have my first glimpse of an earl's residence. After hearing so much about the wealth and power of an earl, for which there is no equivalent rank in Iceland, I was frankly rather disappointed. I had expected to see a grand building, something with towers and turrets and stone walls. What I saw was nothing more than an enlarged version of the longhouses that I already knew from Iceland to Vinland. The only difference was that Earl Sigurd's long hall was considerably bigger. In fact it was almost three times larger than the largest home I had yet seen, with side walls that were over four feet thick. But the rest of it, the stone and turf walls, the wooden supports and the grassy roof, were identical to the domestic structures I had known all my life. The interior of this huge building was just as gloomy, smoky and poorly illuminated as its more humble cousins, so Kari, Kolbein and I were able to slip quietly in through the main doors without being noticed in the crowd of guests. We took up our positions just a few paces inside. There we could see down the length of the great hall, yet we were far enough from the central hearth, where Sigurd, his entourage and chief guests were seated. In the half-light and surrounded by a jostle of visitors, there was little chance that Kari would be recognised.

I had forgotten about Kari's exalted sense of self-honour. We arrived in the interval between the parading of the oath boar and the time when it would be served up with an apple in its mouth. This long intermission lasts at least three hours, and the assembled company is normally entertained with a programme of juggling, tumbling and music. It is also a tradition for the host of the Jol banquet to call on each of his chief guests to contribute a tale from his own experience. Scarcely had the three of us found our places in the audience than Earl Sigurd called on one of the Burners, a tall, gangling man by the name of Gunnar Lambason, to recount the story of Njal's death and the events leading up to it. Clearly Earl Sigurd thought that a first-hand account of this famous and recent event, told by one of the chief participants, would impress his guests.

From the moment Gunnar Lambason started speaking, I knew he was a poor choice for a saga teller. The Icelanders can be somewhat long-winded when it comes to narration, but Gunnar made particularly heavy going. He had a nasal voice that grated on the ear, and he often lost the thread of his tale. He also skewed the story so that it showed the deeds of the Burners in the most favourable light. As Gunnar Lambason recounted it, the Njalssons had brought their fate on themselves and throughly deserved to die in the flames and smoke of their home. When Gunnar finished his recitation, Sigurd's most important guest, a sumptuously dressed chieftain with a splendidly lustrous beard, asked how the Njalsson family had endured their final hours. Gunnar answered dismissively. They had fought well at first but then begun to cry out, begging for quarter, he said. His reply was more than Kari could stomach. Standing next to him, I had heard his deep, angry breathing as Gunnar's dreary tale proceeded. Now Kari gave a roar of fury, broke out from the little knot of bystanders and raced half the length of the hall. Like everyone else, I stood and gaped as Kari jumped over the outstretched legs of the men seated at the side benches until he was level with Gunnar Lambason, who had just seated himself and turned to see what was the commotion was.

Everyone was so startled that there was no time to react. Kari had his famous sword Leg Biter in his hand. With a single sweep of the blade Kari cut Gunnar Lambason's head from his shoulders.

Sigurd, the veteran warrior, was the first to react. 'Seize that man!' he shouted, pointing at Kari, who stood there confronting the crowd, with a pool of Gunnar Lambason's blood seeping around his feet. There was a shocked murmuring, followed by an uncomfortable silence. No one got up from their seats. At banquets it is customary for weapons to be hung up on the walls as a precaution against drunken brawling leading to bloodshed. Kari had only managed to bring Leg Biter into the hall because we arrived so late that the gatekeepers were already drunk and had failed to search him. The only other people with any weapons were Sigurd's bodyguard, and they were men who had previously served with Kari and were wary of his prowess as a fighter. Kari looked straight at Sigurd and announced loudly, 'Some people would say that I have just rendered you a service by killing the murderer of your former servant, Helgi Njalsson.' There was a mutter of approval from the onlookers and Flosi, the leader of the Burners, rose to his feet. He too turned towards Sigurd and said, 'I can speak on behalf of the Burners. Kari has done no wrong. He never accepted any settlement or compensation we offered for the deaths of his family, and he has always made it public that he intends to seek blood revenge. He only did what is his duty.'

Sigurd quickly sensed the mood of the assembly. 'Kari!' he thundered. 'You have offended our hospitality gravely, but in a just cause. With my permission, you may leave this hall unharmed. But I declare that by your action you have brought upon yourself the same outlawry for which you were condemned in Iceland. For that reason you must leave Orkney without any delay, and not return until your sentence of exile has been fully served.'

Kari said nothing, but turned on his heel and, the blood-streaked sword still in his hand, walked back quietly down the hall to where Kolbein and I were still standing. As he passed us, we both made a movement to step forward and join him. Kari nodded to Kolbein and said quietly, 'Let's go,' but to me he said firmly, 'you are to stay. I have brought you to Orkney as I promised, but you have not had time to carry out your own mission. I hope everything goes well for you. Perhaps we will meet again some day.' With those words, he stepped out of the door and into the darkness of the night. I stood watching him walk away, with Kolbein at his shoulder, until I could no longer see them in the gloom.

The earl was quickly back to his role as a genial host. Even as Sigurd's guards hauled away Gunnar Lambason's body, the earl was calling for more drink to be brought and a moment later was shouting at the cooks, demanding to know how much longer it would be before they could serve up the oath boar. I suspect that he was secretly delighted that the spectacular events would make his Jol festival remembered for years to come. The housemaids and thralls washed down the tables, and to his great credit Flosi stood up and in a loud voice asked the earl if he might have permission to retell the story of Njal's Burning, but this time with proper regard for the heroism of Njal and his family. When Earl Sigurd waved his hand in agreement, Flosi turned to the audience and announced that he would start the tale all over again, right from the beginning. His listeners nodded approvingly and settled themselves down for a lengthy discourse. Not only do Norsemen have an insatiable appetite for such narratives, but the more often a tale is told the better they seem to like it.

Flosi had barely started when Sigurd's steward was pushing through the crowd to where I was standing. 'Are you the young man who arrived with Kari Solmundarson?' he asked. 'Come with me,' he said. 'The earl wants a word with you, and so does his guest of honour.' I followed the steward through the crush of people, and found myself standing beside the earl's high seat.

Sigurd looked me up and down and asked my name.

'Thorgils,' I replied.

'How long have you known Kari?' asked the earl.

'Not very long, sir,' I answered respectfully, 'I helped him last

year before the Althing, but just for a few days. Then he invited
me to join him on his voyage to Orkney.'

'Why was that?' asked Sigurd.

'Because he knew that I wanted to come here to enquire about
my family.'

Before Sigurd could ask me what I meant, the man seated on
his right interrupted, 'What a remarkable fellow that Kari is,' he
said, 'walking straight in, and carrying on his blood feud under our
noses, with no thought for his own safety. Great courage.'

'Kari has always been known for his bravery,' replied Sigurd,
and his slightly deferential tone made me look more closely at his
guest. He was the most expensively dressed man I had ever seen.
He wore at least three heavy gold rings on each arm, and his finger
rings glittered with magnificent coloured stones. Every item of his
clothing was of the finest material and in bright colours. His shoes
were of soft leather. He even smelled richly, being the first man
I had ever met who used body perfume. His sky blue cloak was
trimmed with a broad margin of gold thread worked in an ornate
pattern, and the precious brooch that held the cloak to his left
shoulder was astonishing. The pattern of brooch was common
enough. The pin pivoted on a slotted ring, and the wearer drove
the pin through the cloth, turned the ring and the cloth was held
in place. My father Leif had worn one very similar at feasts. But
he had never worn one anything like the brooch displayed so
ostentatiously by Sigurd's guest. The brooch was enormous. Its pin
was nearly the length of my forearm, and the flat ring was a hand's
span across. Both the pin – spike would be a better description –
and the flat ring were of heavy gold. Even more amazingly, the
surface of the gold ring was worked with intricate interlacing
patterns, and set into the patterns was a galaxy of precious stones
carefully picked for their colours – amethyst, blue, yellow and
several reds from carmine to ruby. The brooch was a masterpiece.
I guessed that there was probably no other piece of jewellery quite
like it in all the world. It was, I thought to myself, a work of art
fit for a king.

Earl Sigurd had already turned back to his dandified guest without waiting to hear my further explanation about why I wanted to visit Orkney. He was deep in conversation with him, and I caught a scowl from Sigurd's steward, who had been hovering in the background. Realising that my presence next to the high seat was no longer required, I made my way quietly back to the steward.

'No eavesdropping on matters of state,' he growled, and for a moment I thought he might know about my role as a spy for Kari at the Althing.

'Who's the man wearing the superb brooch?' I asked him.

'That's Sigtryggr, King of Dublin, and he's come here to negotiate with Earl Sigurd. Sigtryggr's looking for allies in his campaign against the Irish High King, Brian. Knowing Sigurd the Stout, I doubt that he'll be able to resist the chance of winning loot, even without the added attraction of that meddling hussy, Kormlod.'

The steward noticed that I had not the least idea what he was talking about, and beckoned to one of the hall servants. 'Here, you. Look after this lad. Find him something to eat and a place to sleep. Then something useful to do.' With that I was dismissed.

The Jol ended with the ceremonial quenching of the Julblok, a large burning log whose flames were doused with ale to ensure the fertility of the coming year, and when most of the guests had left I found myself assigned to domestic duties. Twelve days of uninterrupted revelry had left a remarkable mess in the great hall and the surrounding area. I was employed in sweeping up the debris, collecting and burning the rushes that had been fouled on the floor, raking out the long hearth, swabbing down benches, and digging out patches of sodden earth where the guests had relieved themselves without bothering to go to the outside latrines. At times I wondered whether the cattle in the byres at Brattahlid had not been more sanitary.

King Sigtryggr was still with us and some sort of negotiation was going on because I noticed that he and Sigurd the Stout spent

a good deal of time in Sigurd's council room, often accompanied
by their advisers. Among these advisers was Sigurd's mother Eithne.
As had been reported, the celebrated volva was surprisingly well
preserved for her advanced age. She must have been over seventy
years old, but instead of the bent old crone that I had expected,
Eithne was a small, rather rotund old woman full of energy. She
bustled about, turning up at unexpected moments and casting quick
glances everywhere and missing very little that went on around
here. Only her thin, scraggly grey hair gave away her age. Eithne
was almost bald, and she had a nervous habit of adjusting her
headscarf every few moments so that no one would see her pate.

Her ears, as well as her eyes, were collecting information. I had
barely begun to question the older servants about their memories
of a certain Thorgunna, who had stayed at Birsay one winter fifteen
years before, when I received another summons. This time it was
to Eithne's retiring room at the back of the great hall. I found the
earl mother standing so that the light from a small window fell
directly on my face as I entered. Most windows in Norse houses
are no more than open holes in the wall, which can be closed with
a shutter in bad weather or when it is cold outside, but it was a
mark of Sigurd's wealth and status that the window in his mother's
chamber was covered with a sheet of translucent cow horn, which
allowed a little of the dreary north light of winter to fall on me.

'I'm told you've been asking about Thorgunna, who stayed
here a long number of years ago,' Eithne said. 'I suppose you are
her son.'

My mouth must have dropped open with shock, for she went
on, 'Don't look so surprised. You have the same colour of eyes and
skin as she had, and perhaps the shape of your face is the same.'

'I never knew my mother,' I said. 'She sent me away to live
with my father when I was still a babe in arms, and she had died
by the time I came back to where she lived.'

'And where was that?' asked Eithne.

'At Frodriver in Iceland,' I answered. 'She died there when I
was only three years old.'

'Ah yes, I had heard something about that,' this strange, rotund little woman briskly interrupted.

'It was said that there were portents shortly before she died and hauntings afterwards.' I ventured. 'It was something to do with her goods, with the things she brought with her, her clothes and bed hangings. At least that was what I was told. When these things were finally burned, the troubles ceased.'

Eithne gave a little snort of impatience. 'What did they think! No wonder there was trouble if someone else got their hands on a volva's sacred possessions.'

She gave another sniff. 'Your mother may have been nothing to look at, but she was skilled in other ways and I don't mean just at needlework. Those wall hangings she owned, she brought them with her from Ireland and she had stitched them herself and chanted the spell-words over them.'

'You mean like rune writing,' I commented.

Eithne gave me a patient look.

'Yes, like rune writing, but different. Men and women can both cut runes, but women often prefer to stitch their symbols. In some ways it is more painstaking and more effective. Those cloths and hangings and garments your mother cherished were powerful seidr. In the wrong hands they caused the spirits to be uneasy.'

I was about to make some comment about the earl's mystical raven flag, but thought better of it. 'I was told that you and my mother spent time together, so I was hoping you would be kind enough to tell me something about her. I would truly appreciate any details.'

'Most of our discussions were on trivial matters – or on matters which do not concern men,' she replied crisply. 'Your mother kept herself to herself nearly all the time she was here. She was a big woman – as I expect you know – and rather fierce, so most people kept out of her way. I had more to do with her than anyone else because we spoke Irish to one another, and of course she recognised that I have the sight, just as I knew she was a volva.'

'Did she say where she came from? Who her family were?' I

persisted. 'If I knew that, perhaps I could find out if I have any living relatives.'

Eithne looked at me with a hint of pity. 'Don't expect too much. Everyone thinks that they are descended from some special line, princes or great lords. But most of our forebears were ordinary folk. All I know is that your mother spoke excellent Irish and she could be well mannered when she was not being peevish, which might mean she came from a family with good social standing. She did once mention that she belonged to a tribe who lived somewhere in the middle of the island of Ireland. I don't remember its name but it might have been Ua Ruairc or Ua Ruanaid, or something like that. But the Irish tribes love giving themselves new titles and names, even changing where they live. The Irish are a restless and wandering people. I've been living in Orkney so long that I'm out of touch with what goes on there. It's possible that King Sigtryggr might recognise your mother's clan name. But, on the other hand, he may not have any idea at all. Although he's King of Dublin and has his home there, he's a Norseman through and through. You would be better advised to find your way to Ireland yourself and make enquiries there. Though don't be in a hurry, there's already war in the west and it will soon get worse. But why am I telling you this? You know that already, or you should.'

Again I must have appeared puzzled because the old woman shot me a glance and said, 'No, perhaps not. You're still too young. Anyhow, I can arrange for you to accompany Sigtryggr when he returns home, which should be some time very soon – that doesn't require second sight to anticipate. He and his men are locusts. They'll eat up our last stocks of winter food if Sigurd doesn't make it obvious that they have outstayed their welcome. I've advised him to serve up smaller and smaller portions at mealtimes, and resurrect some of the stockfish that half rotted when the rain got into the storehouse last autumn. If the smell doesn't get rid of them, nothing will.'

The old lady was as good as her word and her dietary stratagem was effective. Sigtryggr and his followers left Birsay within forty-eight hours, and I was added to the royal entourage at the earl mother's particular request. I had failed to learn anything more about Thorgunna, but was glad to leave Orkney because I had noticed how one of the Burners had started giving me occasional puzzled glances, as if he was trying to remember where he had seen me before. I recognised him as one of the men on whom I had eavesdropped at the Althing, and was nervous that he would make the connection. If he did so, it was likely that I could finish up with my throat cut.

FOURTEEN

SIGTRYGGR'S SHIP WAS a match for his magnificent dress brooch. The Norsemen may not be able to weave gossamer silks into gorgeous robes or construct the great tiled domes and towers of the palaces that I was later to see in my travels, but when it comes to building ships they are without peer. Sigtryggr's vessel was a drakkar, sleek, sinister, speedy, a masterpiece of the shipwright's craft. She had been built on the banks of the Black River in Ireland, as her crew never tired of boasting. The Ostmen, the word the Norse in Ireland use to describe themselves, build ships every bit as well as the shipwrights in Norway and Denmark because the quality of native Irish timber equals anything found in the northern lands. Coming as I did from two countries where big trees were so rare that it was unthinkable to build a large ocean-going vessel, the moment I clambered aboard the drakkar I could not resist running my fingertips along the handpicked oak beams and the perfect fit of the flawless planking. I would have been a complete ignoramus not to appreciate the gracefully sweeping lines of the long black-painted hull and the perfect symmetry of the rows of metal fastenings, the ingenious carving of the wooden fittings for the mast and rigging, and the evident care which the crew lavished on their vessel. The drakkar – her name was *Spindrifter* – was deliberately flamboyant. At anchor her crew rigged a smart wadmal tent to cover her amidships, a tent sewn from strips of five different colours, and set it up so tautly that she looked like a floating fairground booth. And as soon as we were at sea with a fair wind, they set a mainsail of a matching pattern so that the vessel crested along like a brilliant exotic bird. As a king's ship, *Spindrifter* was prettified with fancy carvings and bright paint. There were intricately cut panels each side of the curling prow, a snarling figurehead, blue, gold and red chevrons painted on the oar blades, and the intricate decorative lashing on the helmsman's rudder grip was given a daily coat of white chalk. Even the metal weathervane was gilded. *Spindrifter* was meant to impress, and in my case she did.

Most mariners, I have noticed, share a particular moment of weakness. It comes in the first hour after a ship safely clears the land and is heading out to open sea. That is when the crew lets out a collective breath of relief, sensing that they are back in their closed world that is small, intimate and familiar. The feeling is particularly strong if the crew has previously sailed together, gone ashore for a few days and then returned to their vessel. They are eager to re-establish their sense of comradeship, and that is their moment of indiscretion. As the last rope is coiled down and the ship settles on her course, they begin to talk about their time ashore, compare their experiences, comment on sights they saw and the people they met, perhaps boast of the women they encountered and speculate about the immediate future, and they do so openly. They are a crew binding together and, as our ship sailed down the inner channel from Orkney, the crew of *Spindrifter* overlooked the fact that among them was a stranger. Too insignificant to be noticed, I heard their unguarded thoughts on the success of their visit to Birsay, the prospects for the coming war and the manoeuvrings of their lord and master, King Sigtryggr.

What I heard was puzzling. Sigtryggr's kingdom of Dublin is small, but it is the richest and most strategic of all the Norse domains scattered around the rim of Ireland, and Sigtryggr was savouring its prosperity to the full. Dublin's thriving commerce was the milch cow providing him with the money for the luxuries he enjoyed so much – his jewellery and fine clothes, his splendid ship, and the best food and wine imported from France. Indeed, his income from taxing the Dubliners was so great that Sigtryggr had taken the unique step of minting his own money. No other ruler in Ireland, even their own High King, was wealthy enough to do that, and I saw one of the drakkar sailors produce a leather pouch and double-check his wages by counting out a small stack of silver coins struck by Sigtryggr's moneyers.

The more I heard the sailors brag about the wealth of their lord, the more rash, it seemed to me, that he should be about to risk such a comfortable sinecure by joining a rebellion against a grizzled Irish veteran who styled himself 'Emperor of the Irish'. This was the same High King Brian whom Sigurd's steward had mentioned, a warlord who had been rampaging up and down the country with a sizeable army, imposing his authority and winning battle after battle.

Brian Boruma claimed to be driving out the foreign invaders from his land. Yet a large part of his army was made of foreigners, chiefly Ostmen, so what really distinguished his actions was that he was as virulent a Christian in his own way as 'St' Olaf of Norway had been. He travelled everywhere with a cluster of White Christ priests. Wild-looking creatures, they seemed as convinced of their own invincibility as any berserker. These Irish holy men, according to one of the drakkar sailors, were by no means as peaceable as their profession might suggest. The sailor had been in Dublin some fifteen years earlier when Brian Boruma had entered the city and ordered the destruction of a sacred grove of trees, a temple site for Thor. A group of Old Believers had stood in the way of the woodcutters, and the Irish holy men had rushed forward and beaten them back, wielding their heavy wooden croziers like clubs. The sailor's mention of Thor's sacred grove reminded me of Snorri and his twin role as priest and ruler, and it seemed to me that this Irish High King who mixed rule and religion was a grander version of my more familiar godi, and perhaps even more ruthless.

King Sigtryggr's informers had warned that the plan for

Boruma's next campaign was to overrun Dublin once again and bring to heel the provincial ruler, the King of Leinster. So Sigtryggr was scurrying around to build up a grand alliance to defeat the expected invasion. He was using his ample war chest to hire mercenaries and looking for assistance from overseas. In Birsay he had set a clever snare, according to the crew of *Spindrifter*. He had promised Sigurd the Stout that if the Earl of Orkney came to his help, then he would arrange for Sigurd to marry Kormlod, Brian Boruma's ex-wife. This Kormlod was an irresistible bait. She was not only the divorced wife of the High King, but also the sister of the Irish King of Leinster. Whoever married her, according to Sigtryggr, would be able to lay claim to the vacant throne of Ireland after the defeat of Brian Boruma, and his claim would be supported by the Leinster tribes. Yet I noted that when the crew of *Spindrifter* talked about this scheme, they chuckled and made sardonic comments. Listening to them, it seemed to me that the Lady Kormlod was not the meek and willing consort Sigurd would have been led to expect and neither did Sigtryggr himself set much store by the plan.

Thor sent our drakkar the wind she loved – a fine quartering breeze that brought us safely past the headlands and the tide races, and into the mouth of Dublin's river without the need to shift sail or even get out our oars until we were closing the final gap across the dirty river water ready to tie up at the wooden jetty which was the royal landing place.

I had never even seen a town before, let alone a city, and the sight of Dublin astounded me. There are no towns or large villages in Greenland or Iceland or Orkney, and suddenly here in front of me was a great, grey-brown untidy sprawl of houses, shops, laneways, roofs, all spilling down the side of the hill to the anchorage in the river. I had never imagined that so many people could exist, let alone live together cheek by jowl in this way. The houses were modest enough, little more than oversized huts with walls of wattle and daub and roofed with straw or wooden tiles. But there were so many of them and they huddled so close together

that it seemed there were more people living in one spot overlooking the south bank of Dublin's river than in the whole of Iceland.
It was not just the sight of the houses which amazed me. There
was also the smell. The river bank was thick mud littered with
rotting, stinking matter, and it was clear that many of the citizens
used the place as their latrine. On top of the stench of putrefaction
was laid an all-pervading odour of soot and smoke. It was an early
January evening when we moored and the householders of Dublin
were lighting fires to keep warm. The smoke from their hearths
rose through holes in the roofs, but just as often it simply oozed
through the straw covering so it seemed as if the whole city was
smouldering. A light drizzle had begun to fall, and it pressed down
the smoke and fumes of the fires so that the smell of wood smoke
filled our nostrils.

Sigtryggr's steward was waiting at the quayside to greet his
master and led us up the hill towards the royal dwelling. The
roadway was surfaced with wooden planks and woven wicker
hurdles laid on top of the mud, but even so we occasionally slipped
on the slick, damp surface. Through open doorways I caught
glimpses of the interiors of the houses, the flicker of flames from
an open hearth, dim shapes of people seated on the side benches or
a woman standing at a cooking pot, the grimy faces of children
peering round the doorpost to see us go by until unseen hands
reached out and dragged them back out of sight. Sigtryggr and his
cortege were not popular. The reception for the King of Dublin
was very muted.

We passed through the gateway of a city wall which I had not
noticed before because the cluster of houses had outgrown Dublin's
defensive rampart. Then we had reached the centre of Dublin,
where the houses were more spread out, and here stood Sigtryggr's
residence, similar in size and shape to Earl Sigurd's hall though it
was built of timber rather than turf. The only unusual feature was
a steep, grassy mound slightly to the rear and right of Sigtryggr's
hall. 'Thor's Mound,' muttered Einar, the sailor, who had spoken
about the warlike Irish priests earlier, and who now saw me

looking in that direction. 'Those mad fanatics chopped down the sacred trees, but it will take more than few axe blows to get rid of every last trace of his presence. Silkbeard still makes an occasional sacrifice there, just for good luck, though his real worship should be for Freyja. There's nothing he would like better than to be able to weep tears of gold.' Tyrkir had taught me long ago in Vinland that the Goddess of wealth shed golden tears at the loss of her husband, but I didn't know who Silkbeard was, though I made a shrewd guess. When I asked the sailor, he guffawed. 'You really are from the outer fringes, aren't you? Silkbeard is that dandy, our leader. He loves his clothes and perfume and his fine leather shoes and his rings, and haven't you noticed how much time he spends combing and stroking and fondling his chin whiskers.'

But I hardly heard his reply. I had come to a dead stop and was staring at a woman standing at the entrance to Sigtryggr's hall among the group of women and servants waiting to greet the king formally. I guessed her age at about fifty. She was very richly dressed in a long blue gown with expensive shoulder clasps, and her grey hair was held back in a matching silk scarf. She must have been important because she was standing in the front rank, next to a younger woman, who I guessed was Sigtryggr's wife. But it was not the older woman's dress which had caught my eye; it was the way that she stood, and the way that she was looking at Sigtryggr, who was now walking towards her. There was a sense of exasperation and determination on her face. I had seen precisely that look before and that same posture. I felt that I was seeing not the grey-haired matron in front of me, but another person. It was a memory that made me feel queasy. I had seen exactly that expression on the face of Freydis Eriksdottir.

'Get along and stop gawping,' Einar said from behind me.

'Who's the grey-haired woman standing in the front row?' I asked him.

'That's Sigtryggr's mother Kormlod, the Irish call her Gorm-laith.'

I was utterly confused. 'But I thought that she was the person

Earl Sigurd was supposed to marry as a reward if he came to help
Sigtryggr. The person who would help him become High King.'

'Precisely. Until last year she was the wife of the High King
Brian, but he divorced her after some sort of a row. Now she says
that Brian doesn't deserve to remain on his throne. She hates him
so much that she would support whoever marries her in a bid to
replace him. She's got a lot of influence because she also happens
to be the sister of King Mael Morda of Leinster, and at one time
she was even married to Malachi, another of the important Irish
chieftains who's spent years intriguing and fighting against Brian to
become the High King himself. Whatever happens in high politics
in this part of the world, you can be sure that Kormlod is involved.
Now you'd better report to Sigtryggr's steward and see if he can
find a place for you.'

Ketil the steward gave me an exasperated glance when I finally
managed to get his attention. He was bustling here and there in a
self-important manner, organising the storage of various boxes and
bundles that his master's embassy had brought back from Orkney,
calling for food to be brought from the kitchen and served, and
generally trying to give the impression that he was essential to the
smooth running of the royal establishment, though in fact he
seemed to be more of a hindrance. 'You can be a temporary dog
boy,' he snapped at me. 'One of those Irish chiefs the king is
negotiating with has sent a couple of hairy wolfhounds as a present.
Apparently it's a compliment, though I call it more of an aggrava-
tion. I'm told the brutes can only be exchanged between kings and
chieftains, so you'd better be sure they are kept healthy in case the
donor comes on a visit. Feed them before you feed yourself.' He
waved me away and a moment later was berating one of the
household servants for setting out the wrong goblets for the king's
meal.

My charges were hard to miss. They were skulking around the
back of the hall – tall, hairy creatures, occasionally loping in
embarrassed confusion from one corner to the next. I had no
experience whatsoever of looking after dogs. But even I could see

from the way their tails were curled tightly down between their legs and their large flappy ears were pressed close to their skulls that they were unhappy in their new surroundings. I had come across a few of the same breed of dog in Iceland, where they had been imported in much the same way as Irish slaves, so I was aware that they were not as lethal as they looked. I succeeded in coaxing them outside the king's hall and giving them some scraps which I wheedled from the kitchen staff. The dogs looked at me mournfully, their great dark, oval eyes blinking through their drooping fur, obviously recognising an incompetent, though well-meaning, dog keeper. I was grateful to the lanky beasts because they gave me an excuse to stay in the background and pretend to be busy. Whenever anyone looked in my direction, I made a show of brushing their rough, harsh coats, and the hounds were decent enough to let me do so, though I did wonder if there might not come a moment when, fed up with my incompetence, they would sink their teeth into me.

Fortunately my role as royal dog boy was never put seriously to the test. King Sigtryggr lacked any real affection for the animals, regarding them as decorative accessories akin to his fine footwear or personal jewellery. My only real duty was to see that the two hounds were prettily presented, sitting or lying near his seat whenever he held court or had meals.

Queen Mother Gormlaith scared me, and not simply because she reminded me so often of Freydis, the organiser of the Vinland massacre. There was a calculating coldness about Gormlaith which occasionally slipped out from under her elegance as the gracious queen mother. She was still a very handsome woman, slim and elegant, and she had retained her youthful grace so that with her green eyes and haughty stare she reminded me of a supercilious cat. She had exquisite manners – even condescending to make the occasional remark to the lowly dog boy – but there was a flinty hardness to her questions and if she did not get the answer she sought, she had a habit of ignoring the response and then putting on the pressure until she got the reply she wanted. I could see that she was manipulative, calculating, and that she could twist her son, the showy Sigtryggr, into doing precisely what she wanted.

And what she wanted was mastery. Eavesdropping on the high table conversations, and casually questioning the other servants, I learned that Gormlaith was not so much a woman scorned as a woman thwarted in her ambitions, which were vaunting. 'She married Boruma hoping to control the High King of Ireland,' one of the other servants told me, 'but that didn't work. Brian had his own ideas on how to run the country and soon got so fed up with her meddling that he had her locked up for three months. Brian's an old man now, but that doesn't mean he would allow himself to be manipulated by a scheming woman.'

'Is the Queen Mother really that ambitious?' I asked.

'You wait and see,' the servant replied with a smirk. 'She sent her son off to Orkney to recruit Fat Sigurd, offering herself as the meat on the hook, and she'll do anything to get even with the High King.'

Not until the middle of March, nearly seven weeks later, did I understand what the servant meant. I spent the interval as a member of Sigtryggr's household, carrying out domestic duties, learning to speak Irish with the slaves and lower servants, as well as feeding and exercising his two dogs as their guardian. If I have given the impression that the Norse people are uncouth and unwashed savages with their raucous drinking bouts and rough manners, then my descriptions have been misleading. The Norse are as meticulous in their personal cleanliness as circumstances will allow and, though it may seem unlikely, their menfolk are great dandies. And of course King Sigtryggr fancied himself as an arbiter of good taste and style. The result was that I spent a good deal of my time pressing his courtiers' garments, using a heavy, smooth stone to flatten the seams of the surcoats and cloaks from their extensive wardrobes which they changed frequently, and combing not just the rough hair of the two dogs, but also the heads of the royal advisers. They were very attentive to their hairstyles, and would even specify the length and fineness of the teeth on the combs I used. There was a special shop in Dublin, where I was sent to purchase replacement combs, specifying that they should be made of red-deer antler and not common cattle horn.

It was at a noon meal, one day in early spring, that I fully grasped the extent of the ambitions of Gormlaith, and how ruthlessly she worked her way towards achieving them. I had led into the great hall my two wolfhounds, settled them near the king's chair and stood back to keep an eye on them. King Sigtryggr was jealous of his regal dignity, and the last thing I wanted was for one of the big grey dogs to leap up suddenly and snatch food from the royal hand while the king was eating.

'Are you sure that Sigurd is going to keep his word?' Gormlaith was asking him.

'Positive,' her son replied, worrying at a chicken leg with his teeth and trying to stop the grease dripping onto his brocaded shirt. 'He's one of the old breed, never happier than when he's got a war to plan and execute. Cunning too. He's got a bunch of hard men at his court, Icelanders, renegade Norwegians and so forth. He knows that a campaign in Ireland will keep them occupied so they don't start plotting against him in Orkney.'

'And how many men do you think he will be able to bring?'

'He claimed he could raise eight hundred to a thousand.'

'But you're doubtful?'

'Well, Mother, I wasn't there long enough to count them,' Sigtryggr answered petulantly, wiping his hands on a linen cloth that a page held out for him. Sigtryggr was a great one for aping foreign etiquette.

'My information is that the Earl of Orkney can probably raise five hundred men, possibly six hundred, no more – and that's not enough,' she said. It was evident that his mother already knew the answer to her own question.

Sigtryggr grunted. He had detected the stern tone in his mother's voice, and knew that an order was coming.

'We need more troops if we want to be sure of dealing with that dotard Brian,' Gormlaith continued firmly.

'And where do you expect to find them?'

'A merchant recently arrived from Man mentioned to me this morning that there's a sizeable vikingr fleet anchored there. They are operating under joint command. Two experienced leaders. One is called Brodir and the other is Ospak Slant-eye.'

Sigtryggr sighed. 'Yes, Mother. I know both men. I met Brodir two years ago. Fierce looking. Wears his hair so long that he has to tuck it into his belt. Old Believer, of course. Said to be a seidr master.'

'I think you should recruit the two of them and their men into our forces,' his mother said firmly.

Sigtryggr looked stubborn, then decided to concede the point. I suspected that he had long since given up trying to dissuade his mother from her schemes, and it was obvious what was coming next.

'Good,' she said. 'It's less than a day's journey to Man.'

For a moment I thought that the king would raise some sort of objection, but he hesitated only briefly, then petulantly threw the chicken bone at one of the two wolfhounds and, forgetting the page with the napkin, wiped his hands on his tunic and ostentatiously turned to open a conversation with his wife.

Gormlaith's wish was Ketil's command. He was terrified of her, and that evening the steward was fluttering around warning the palace staff. *Spindrifter*'s crew were to be aboard by dawn, ready to take Sigtryggr to Man. 'And you,' he said to me spitefully, 'you're going too. You can take the big dogs with you. The king thinks that they will make a handsome present for those two pirates. I expect he'll tell them that they are war dogs, trained to attack. But from what I've seen of them they're happier to lie on the rushes all day and scratch for fleas. At least we'll be rid of them.'

The voyage to Man was cold, wet and took twice as long as we had expected. My two charges were miserable. They scrabbled on the sloping deck, threw up and shivered, and after falling into the bilges for the twentieth time, just lay there and were still looking wretched when *Spindrifter* rounded the southern headland of Man and under oars crept slowly into the sheltered bay where the vikingr fleet lay at anchor. We approached warily, all our shields still hung on the gunnels, the crew trying to look submissive, and Sigtryggr and his bodyguard standing on the foredeck weaponless and without body armour, making it clear that they came in peace. *Spindrifter* was easily the largest vessel in the bay, but she would not have withstood a concerted attack from the vikingr. Ospak and Brodir had assembled thirty vessels in their war fleet.

Neither side trusted the other enough to hold a parlay on one of the ships, so the council was held on the beach in a tent. Naturally Sigtryggr wanted his two hounds to be on display. Dragging along the two seasick dogs, I felt almost as cold and wretched as they did when I took up my station in the entourage. Ospak and Brodir paid no attention to the cutting wind and the occasional bursts of rain, which slatted and battered the tent as they stood listening to Sigtryggr's proposal. By now I knew his methods well enough to know what was coming. He spoke at length about the extent and prosperity of the Irish High King's realm, and how Brian Boruma had grown too old really to protect the kingdom's wealth effectively. An example of his fading powers, Sigtryggr pointed out, was how he had mistreated his wife Gormlaith. He had locked her up for three months, recklessly disregarding that this would be an insult to her family, the royal house of Leinster. Brian Boruma was old and feeble and losing his touch. It would take only a well-managed attack to remove him from power and lay Ireland open to pillage.

The two Viking leaders listened impassively. Brodir was the more imposing of the two. Ospak was slender and ordinary-looking, apart from the odd angle of his left eye socket which gave him his nickname, Slant-eye. But Brodir was huge, taller by nearly a head. Everything about him was on a massive scale. He had a great rough face, legs like pillars, and he had the largest hands and feet that I had ever seen. His most distinctive feature, however, was his hair. As Sigtryggr had told his mother, Brodir grew his hair so long that it came to his waist and he was obliged to tuck it into his belt. Unusually for a Norseman, this tremendous cascade of hair was jet black.

The meeting ended without reaching any firm conclusion. Both Ospak and Brodir said they needed to consult with their chief men and would let Sigtryggr have a decision the following morning. But as we made our way back down the shingle beach to our small boats, Sigtryggr took Brodir on one side and invited him to continue the discussions privately. An hour later the viking giant was clambering aboard *Spindrifter* and ducking in under the striped awning of the tent, which we had rigged to protect ourselves from the miserable weather. Brodir stayed for nearly an hour, deep in conversation with Sigtryggr. In the confined space there was little privacy, and every word of the discussion could be heard by the men on the nearest oar benches. Brodir wanted to know more about the political situation in Ireland, who would be supporting the High King and what would be the division of spoils. In his answers Sigtryggr sweetened the terms of the proposed alliance. He promised Brodir first choice in the division of any booty, that he would receive a special bonus, and that his share was likely to be greater than Ospak's because Brodir commanded more ships and more men. Finally, as Brodir still sat, cautiously refusing to commit himself to the venture, Sigtryggr made the same grand gesture that he had made in Orkney: he promised that Gormlaith would marry Brodir if Brian Boruma was defeated and that would open the way to the throne of the High King. As he made this empty promise, I noticed several of our sailors turn away to hide their expressions.

Brodir was not fooled. 'I believe you made the same offer to the Earl of Orkney recently,' he rumbled.

Sigtryggr never faltered. 'Oh yes, but Gormlaith changed her mind when I got back to Dublin. She said she would much prefer you as her husband to Sigurd the Stout – though he too is a fine figure of a man – and we agreed that there was no reason for Sigurd to know of the change of plan.'

At that precise moment Sigtryggr noticed that I was within earshot. I was crouched against the side of the vessel, with one of the hounds despondently licking my hand. Belatedly it must have occurred to Sigtryggr that perhaps I was a spy for the Earl of Orkney. 'As a token of my regard,' he went on smoothly, 'I would like to leave you with these two magnificent Irish wolf-hounds. They will remind you of the homeland of your future wife. Come now, let us make a bargain on it and seal it with this present.' He reached forward, clasped Brodir's brawny right arm, and they swore an oath of friendship. 'You must come to Dublin with your ships within the month, and try to persuade Ospak to come too.'

Brodir rose to his feet. He was such a colossus that he had to stoop to avoid brushing his black head on the wet tent cloth. As he turned to go, he said to me, 'Come on, you,' and I found myself once more dragging the unfortunate dogs out of the bilges and over the edge of the drakkar. When they refused to jump down into the little boat and paused, whimpering, on the edge of the gap between longship and tender, Brodir, who had already gone ahead, simply reached up and grabbed each dog by the scruff of the neck and hauled them down as if they had been puppies.

I awoke next morning, after an uncomfortable night curled up between the two hounds on the foredeck of Brodir's warship, and looked across to where *Spindrifter* had lain at anchor. The great drakkar had gone. Sigtryggr had decided that his mission was accomplished and had slipped away in the night, setting course for Dublin doubtless to report to his mother that she was now on offer to two ambitious war leaders.

In mid-afternoon Brodir beckoned to me to join him. He was sitting at the foot of the mast, a chunk of wind-dried sheepmeat in one hand and a knife in the other. He cut off slivers of meat and manoeuvred them into his mouth past his luxuriant beard as he cross-examined me. I think he suspected that I was a spy placed by Sigtryggr.

'What's your name and where are you from?' he enquired.

'Thorgils, sir. I was born in Orkney, but I grew up in Greenland and spent time in a place called Vinland.'

'Never heard of it,' he grunted.

'Most recently I've been living in Iceland, in the Westfjords.'

'And who was your master?'

'Well, I was in the service of Snorri Godi at first, but he sent
me to live with one of his people, a man called Thrand.'

Brodir stopped eating, his knife blade halfway to his mouth.

'Thrand? What does he look like?'

'A big man, sir. Not as big as yourself. But tall and he's got a
reputation as a warrior.'

'What sort of helmet does he wear?'

'An old-fashioned one, bowl-shaped with eye protectors, and
there are runes inside which he showed me.'

'Did you know what the runes read?' Bordir asked.

'Yes, sir.'

Brodir had put aside the lamb shoulder and looked at me
thoughtfully. 'I know Thrand,' he said quietly. 'We campaigned
together in Scotland a few years ago. What else did he tell you
about himself?'

'Not much about himself or his past, sir. But he did try to teach
me some of the Old Ways.'

'So you're an apprentice of seidr?' Brodir said slowly.

'Well, sort of,' I replied. 'Thrand taught me a little, but I was
with him for only a few months, and the rest of my knowledge I
have picked up by chance.'

Brodir turned and peered out from under the longship's awning
to look at the sky. He was checking the clouds to see if there
would be a change in the weather. There was still a thick overcast.
He turned back to face me.

'I was once a follower of the White Christ,' he said, 'for almost
six years. But it never felt right. I was baptised by one of those
wandering priests, yet from that moment on my luck seemed to
falter. My eldest son – he must have been a little younger than you
– was drowned in a boating accident, and my vikingr brought little

reward. The places we raided were either too poor or the inhabitants were expecting us and had fled, taking all their property with them. That was when I met up with Thrand. He was on his way to visit his sister, who was married to a Dublin Ostman, and he joined my war band for a quick raid on one of the Scots settlements. Before we attacked, he made his sacrifices to Thor and cast lots, and he predicted that we would be successful and win a special reward. It was a hotter fight than we had anticipated because we did not know that the King of Scotland's tax collector happened to be staying in the village that night, and he had an escort with him. But we chased them off, and when we dug in the spot of churned earth, we found where they had hastily buried their tax chest containing twenty marks of hack silver. My men and I were delighted, and I noticed how Thrand took care to make an offering of part of the hoard to Thor. Since then I have done the same before and after every battle. I asked Thrand if he would stay on with me as my seidr master, but he said he had to get back home to Iceland. He had given his word.'

'That would be to Snorri Godi, sir,' I said. 'Snorri still consults Thrand for advice before any sort of conflict.'

'And you say that you studied seidr under Thrand?'

'Yes, but just for a few months.'

'Then we'll see if you can be more than a dog boy. Next time I make a sacrifice to Thor, you can assist me.'

Brodir and Ospak held their combined flotilla at Man for another ten days. There was much coming and going between the two men as Brodir tried to persuade Ospak to join him in King Sigtryggr's alliance. The two men were sworn brothers, but Ospak took umbrage at Brodir's grand plan to become Gormlaith's consort and felt that the new scheme had now replaced their own original agreement for a vikingr campaign. Ospak's ambitions were more down to earth than Brodir's. He wanted booty rather than glory, and the more enthusiastically that Brodir spoke about the wealth of King Sigtryggr and his potential as an ally, the more Ospak saw the assets of Dublin as something waiting to be plundered. So he prevaricated, repeatedly pointing out that an alliance with King Sigtryggr was dangerous. The High King Brian, Ospak noted, had the more impressive record as a warrior, and even if King Brian was now getting old, he had four strapping sons, all of whom had shown themselves as capable commanders on the battlefield.

Eventually Brodir became so exasperated with this hesitation that he suggested to Ospak they should take the omens and see which way the forthcoming campaign would turn out. Ospak was also an Old Believer, and he agreed to the idea at once, so a sweat cabin was set up on the beach. I have mentioned that the Norse are as clean a people as circumstances allow. Among their habits is to take baths in hot water, quite a regular occurrence in Iceland, where water already hot emerges from the ground; they also bathe in steam, though this is more complicated. It involves constructing a small and nearly airtight cabin, bringing very hot stones and then dashing fresh water on the stones so that steam fills the chamber. If the process is excessive, more and more steam fills the room until the occupants become giddy from heat and lack of air and sometimes lose their senses. In Iceland Thrand had told me how this could be done to induce a trance-like state and, if one is fortunate, bring on dreams or even spirit flying.

While the steam hut was being prepared on the beach, Brodir set up a small altar of beach stones very like the one I had seen Thorvall construct in Vinland, and asked me to cut invocation runes on several pieces of driftwood. When the heated steam stones were placed inside the steam hut with a bucket of water, Brodir took my rune sticks and, after approving the staves I had cut, added them to the embers. As the last wisps of grey smoke curled up from the little pyre, he removed all his clothes, coiled his hair around his head and squeezed his great bulk into the hut. I covered the doorway with a heavy blanket of cloth, reminded of the similar structure where I had met the Skraeling shaman.

Brodir stayed in the steam cabin for at least an hour. When he emerged he was looking dour and did not say a word, but dressed quickly and ordered his men to row him out to his ship. Seeing his expression, no one on board dared ask him whether he had seen visions and, if so, what they were. The following day he repeated the process with much the same result. If anything, he emerged from the ordeal looking even more solemn than before. Later that evening he called me over and told me that next day it was my turn. 'Thrand would not have wasted his knowledge on someone who has not the sight. Take my place in the steam cabin tomorrow and tell me what you see.'

I could have told him that there was no need. I already knew. On both nights after Brodir had undergone his ordeal in the steamhouse, I had violent dreams. By now I knew enough about my own powers of sight to realise that my own dreams were echoes of his earlier visions. In the first dream I was aboard an anchored ship when there was a roaring noise in my ears and the sky began to rain boiling blood. The crew around me tried to seek shelter from the downpour and many of them were scalded. One man was so badly burned that he died. The dream on the second night was similar except that after the shower of blood the men's weapons leapt from their sheaths and began to fight, one with the other, and again a sailor lost his life. So when the flap dropped down behind me in the steam cabin, and I poured the water on the stones and felt the steam sear my lips and nostrils and burn deep into my lungs, I had only to close my eyes and I was immediately back in my dream. Now the sky, instead of spewing bloody rain, disgorged flight after flight of angry ravens like fluttering black rags. The birds came cawing and swooping, their beaks and claws were made of iron, and they pecked and struck so viciously at us that we were obliged to shelter beneath our shields. And for the third time we lost a sailor. His eyes pecked out and his face a bloody mess, he stumbled blindly to the side of the vessel, tripped on the coaming and, falling into the water, drowned in the spreading pink tendrils of his own blood.

Brodir woke me. Apparently I had been lying in the steam hut for six hours and there had been no sound. He had broken in and found me insensible. Brodir did not question me but waited until I had recovered sufficiently, then sent for Ospak to come to the beach. The three of us withdrew to a quiet spot, out of earshot of the other men, and there Brodir described his visions in the sweat hut. As I suspected, they were almost exactly what I had seen in my own dreams. But only I had the nightmare of the iron-beaked ravens. When Brodir rumbled, 'The lad has the sight. We should listen to him as well,' I described how Odinn's crows had attacked my shipmates and caused such ruin and disaster.

Only a fool would have been blind to the omens and Ospak was no fool. When Brodir asked whether he would be joining with him in King Sigtryggr's alliance, Ospak asked only for time to think things over. 'I need to consult with my shipmasters,' he told Brodir. 'Let us meet again on the beach this evening after dusk, and I will give you my answer.'

When Ospak returned to the beach that evening, there was barely enough light to see by. He was accompanied by all his ship's captains. It was not a good sign. They were all armed and they looked wary. I realised that they were frightened of Brodir, who, besides being very burly, was also known to be quick-tempered. I reassured myself with the thought that there is a prohibition among the Old Believers – not always obeyed – that it is unwise to kill someone after dark because their ghost will come to haunt you. Even before Ospak started speaking, it was obvious what had been decided. 'The dreams are the worst possible omen,' he began. 'Blood from the sky, men dying, weapons fighting among themselves, war ravens flying. There can be no other explanation than that there will be death and war, and that brother will fight brother.' Brodir scowled. Right up to that moment, he had been hoping that Ospak and his men would join him, and that he would be able to keep the combined flotilla together. But Ospak's blunt interpretation of the dreams left no doubt: Ospak and his ships would not only leave the flotilla, but he and his men intended to throw in their lot with the Ostmen fighting for King Brian. With the High King, they thought, lay their best chance of victory and reward.

Brodir did lose his temper, though only for a moment. It was when Ospak referred to the ravens again, almost as an afterthought. 'Perhaps those ravens are the fiends from hell the Christians are always talking about. They are supposed to have a particular appetite for those who have once followed the White Christ and then turned away.' Brodir had been some sort of priest during his Christian phase, I later learned. Stung by this jibe, he took a step forward and moved to draw his sword. But Ospak had stepped quickly back out of blade range, and his captains closed up behind him. 'Steady,' he called, 'remember that no good will come of killing after dark.'

Killing a man after sunset might be forbidden, but departing in the dark is not. That same night Ospak and his captains quietly unmoored. Their vessels had been anchored in a group, close inshore, and their crews poled them out into the ebb tide so that they silently drifted past us as we slept. Later some of our men said that Ospak had practised some sort of magic so that none of us awoke. In truth several of our sailors did glimpse Ospak's squadron gliding past in the blackness, but they did not have the heart to wake their colleagues. All of us knew that, soon enough, we would meet again in battle.

FIFTEEN

'NONE OF US can escape the Norns' decision,' said Brodir heavily. He was fastening the buckles and straps of his mail shirt. 'We can only delay the hour and even then we need the help of the Gods.' Brodir's fingers were shaking as he did up the straps, and I thought to myself that he was not as trusting as Thrand. Brodir's mail shirt was famous. Like Thrand's helmet, it was reputed to have supernatural qualities. It was said that no sword or javelin could penetrate its links, rendering its wearer invulnerable. Yet I judged that Brodir did not believe in the magic qualities of his armour but wore it only as a talisman to bring good luck. Or perhaps there were few mail shirts large enough to fit the leader from Man.

Brodir's contingent, nearly seven hundred men, was getting ready for battle. Our position was on the extreme right of Sigtryggr's grand alliance of Dublin Ostmen, Sigurd's Orkneymen, King Mael Morda's Leinstermen and sundry Irish rebels who had taken this chance to challenge the domination of the Irish High King. Behind us, an arrow-shot away, was the landing beach of sand and shingle onto which the keels of our ships had slithered at first light that morning.

The plan had been to catch Brian Boruma off guard. For the past ten days the allies had been gathering in Dublin in response to King Sigtryggr's request that they arrive before the great Christian festival at the end of March. I thought this was an odd calendar to set for such staunch Old Believers as Sigurd the Stout and Brodir, but at the long, long war council in the king's hall which preceded our deployment Sigtryggr had explained there was a reason for this unusual deadline, a reason based on intelligence which Gormlaith had supplied. While married to Brian Boruma, she had detected that her ex-husband was becoming more and more obsessed with his religion as he grew older. Apparently the Irish High King had vowed to her that he would no longer fight on the high and holy days of the Christ calendar. It was blasphemy, he had said, to do battle on such sacred occasions and such days were ill-fated. When Sigtryggr mentioned this, some of the Norse captains exchanged nervous glances. Sigtryggr had come closer to the mark than he knew. Rumours of Brodir's raven dream had spread among the Norse and there were many who thought we had no business pursuing our campaign after such an ill-starred start. Brodir had not revealed the content of our visions on the beach at Man, nor had I – the source had been Ospak. From Man he had promptly sailed to Ireland and marched to Brian Boruma's camp to offer his services to the Irish High King. Ospak must have expected a vast haul of loot from Dublin because, that very day, he cheerfully submitted to being baptised by the Irish priests. On the other hand he put such little store by his conversion that he lost no time in spreading word about the raven dreams and how they foretold that Brodir and his men were doomed.

Gormlaith herself spoke at Sigtryggr's council of war and she was very persuasive. Brian Boruma's personal prestige had been vital to his previous military success, she told the hard-bitten war captains. His army rallied to him personally. That was the Irish habit. Their warriors flock to a clan chief considered to be lucky, and when it comes to a battle they like to see their leader at the forefront of the charge. So Sigtryggr's grand alliance would hold a crucial advantage if it brought the High King's army to battle when Boruma himself was unable to participate for his misguided religious reasons. The one day of the Christian calendar that Boruma was

sure to refuse to carry weapons was the gloomy anniversary of the
White Christ's death. Brian Boruma regarded it as the holiest day
of the year, and there was no possibility that he could personally
lead his men into battle on that day. Gormlaith had also pointed out
that the morbid nature of such an anniversary would further dishearten the High King's forces. Some of his more devout troops
might even follow their master's example in refusing to bear arms.
Her logic impressed even the most sceptical of the council, and there
was not a single voice raised in objection when Sigtryggr set Good
Friday as the day most suitable for our attack. Sigtryggr also suggested that Earl Sigurd and Brodir might go back aboard their ships
the previous evening and pretend to sail off. The hope was that
Boruma's spies stationed on the hill overlooking the river would
report that many of Sigtryggr's allies were deserting him, and the
High King would be further lulled into inaction.

But such a commonplace deception had clearly failed. Already
depressed by whispers about Odinn's ravens, our troops were
further discouraged by the sight which greeted us as we came
ashore. Drawn up on the hill facing us were the massed ranks of
the High King's army and clearly they had been expecting us.
Even more clearly, they had no compunction about spilling blood
on the holy day. 'Would you look at that?' said one of Brodir's
men who was standing next to me as we began to form up. He
must have been a shiphandler rather than a fighting man as he was
poorly equipped, carrying only a javelin and a light wooden shield,
and had neither helmet nor mail shirt. 'I can see some of Ospak's
men in the line right opposite us. That fellow with the long pike
and the grey cloak is Wulf. He owes me half a mark of silver,
which he never paid after our last dice game, and I didn't dare
press him for the debt. He's got a foul temper, which is why
everyone calls him Wulf the Quarrelsome. One way or another,
that's a debt he and I are likely to settle today.' Like me, the
shiphandler had been assigned to the rearmost of the five ranks in
our swine array, the standard formation for a Norse brigade. It
places the best armed and most experienced fighters in the front

rank, shield to shield and no more than an arm's length apart. Youngsters like myself and the lightly armed auxiliaries fill up the rearmost ranks. The idea is that the shield wall bears the brunt of any charge and is too dense for the enemy to penetrate, while the lightly armed troops can make some minor contribution to the contest by hurling spears over the heads of their fighting colleagues. Quite what I was supposed to do, I had no idea. Brodir had told me to bring the two so-called 'fighting dogs' on shore, but there was no role for such fanciful creatures in the swine formation. Not that the the two hounds were in the least interested in biting enemy flesh. They were nervously darting from side to side and getting their leads in a tangle. As I hauled on the dogs' collars, I glanced across to my left, and with a sudden shock of surprise I recognised at least a dozen of the Burners among Earl Sigurd's Orkneymen. The Burners had sworn their oath to Sigurd the Stout and now they were obliged to do their duty. Just beyond their little group rose Earl Sigurd's famous battle standard with its symbol of the black raven. The sight caused me to have a sudden doubt. Had I misinterpreted my dream? I wondered. The iron-beaked birds who had swooped into the attack from far afield and torn men's flesh, were they Brodir's enemies? Or did they symbolise the arrival of Sigurd and his Orkneymen across the Irish Sea, following the raven banner to wreak havoc on Boruma's host?

My confusion was increased by this familiarity of friend and foe. Here I was fighting alongside men who would have counted me their enemy if they had known of my role in Kari's vengeance. And the sailor at my side was standing in the battle line facing a companion with whom, until a month ago, he had rolled dice. Nor was this mutual recognition restricted to the Norse warriors. 'Are you there, Maldred?' bellowed one of our front-rank men. He was a big, round-shouldered, grey-haired warrior, well armoured and carrying a heavy axe, and he was shouting his question across the gap that separated the two armies. 'Yes, of course I am, you arsehole!' came an answering cry from the High King's forces. From the opposing rank stepped a figure who, apart from his stature – he was slightly shorter – and the fact that he wore a patterned Irish cloak over his chain mail, was almost indistinguishable from our own man. 'No more farting about, now's the time to see who is the better man,' called our champion, and while the two armies looked on and waited as if they had all the time in the world, the adversaries ran forward until they came within axe swing, and each man let loose a mighty swipe at the other.

Each deflected the blow with his shield, and then the two men settled down to a bent-kneed crouch as they circled one another warily, occasionally leaping forward to deliver a huge blow with the axe, only for the other man to block the blow with his round shield and take a retaliatory swing which failed to connect because his enemy had jumped back out of range. When the two men lost patience with this alternate thud and leap, it seemed as if they reached some mutual pact of self-destruction, for in the instant that one man flung aside his shield so he could raise his axe with both hands his opponent did the same. Suddenly the contestants were charging at one another like a pair of mad bulls, each determined to deliver the mortal blow. It was the man with the cloak who struck first. He knew he had the shorter reach, so he let go of his axe as he swung. The weapon flew across the last two feet and struck the Norseman a terrific blow on the side of his face, laying bare the bone. The Norseman staggered, and blood sprayed from the wound, yet the surge of his charge and the momentum of his blow carried him forward so that the strike of his axe smashed down on the Irishman's left shoulder, cutting deep into the neck. It did not behead the victim, but it was a killer blow. The Irishman fell first to his knees, then slowly toppled forward face down on the mud. His conqueror, dazed and disorientated, with blood pouring down his face, lasted only a few moments longer. As the two armies looked on, the Norseman wandered in a circle, tripping and lurching, the side of his face smashed open by the axe, and he too fell and did not rise again.

'Can you see the High King anywhere?' I heard someone ask in front of me.

'I think I caught a glimpse of him earlier, on horseback, but he's not there now,' a voice replied. 'That's his son Murchad over there on the left. He seems to be in charge. And his grandson is that cocky youngster dressed in a red tunic and blue leggings.' I squinted in that direction and saw a lad, younger than myself, standing in front of one of the enemy divisions. He was turned to face his men, Irishmen to judge by their dress, and he was waving his arms as he declaimed some sort of encouraging speech.

'Dangerous puppy,' said a third voice, 'like all his family.'

'But no sign of the High King himself, are you sure? That's a bonus.' It was the same man who had asked the first question, and by the plaintive tone in his voice I guessed he was trying to find some courage to cheer himself up.

'Not much different from us then,' said a voice sourly. We all knew what he was talking about. King Sigtryggr had not expected to dupe the High King with the fake withdrawal of his Norse allies; he preferred to dupe his own allies. When the longships had withdrawn the previous evening, Sigtryggr had promised to be ready on the beach next morning to join forces with us. But we found waiting for us only Mael Morda's Leinstermen and several bands of bloodthirsty Irish volunteers from the northern province, Ui Neills they called themselves. From Dublin's garrison there was just a handful of troops, but the best of them, Sigtryggr's personal bodyguard, were entirely absent. They had stayed behind to protect Sigtryggr himself and Gormlaith, who had chosen to watch the outcome of the battle from their vantage point behind the safety of Dublin's walls. It was hardly a cheerful beginning for our own efforts, and I suspected that some of our men would have been happy if King Sigtryggr's face had been at the opposite end of the blows from their battleaxes.

I had little time to ponder King Sigtryggr's duplicity. At that moment the enemy line began to move. It came at us not in a single organised rush, but as a ragged, rolling charge, the Irish first letting loose a high keening scream, which overlaid the deeper roar of their Norse allies. They ran forward in a broken torrent, brandishing axes, swords, pikes, spears. A few tripped on the rough ground and went sprawling, vanishing under the feet of their companions, but the ones on top rushed on, determined to gather as much speed as possible before they hit the shield wall. When the collision came, there was a massive, shattering crash like oak trees falling in the forest, and into the air flew an eerie cloud of grey and white sprinkled with bright flecks. It was the dust and whitewash from several thousand shields that had been carefully cleaned and repainted before the battle.

The thunderous opening crash immediately gave way to a confused, indiscriminate chaos, the sound of axes thudding into timber and stretched cowhide, the ringing clash of steel on metal, shouts and curses, cries of pain, sobs of effort, the scuffling grunts of men fighting for their lives. Somewhere in the distance I heard the high, wild, urgent notes of a war horn. It must have come from the High King's army because we had no war trumpeters as far as I knew.

The two opposing battle lines lost all formation within moments. The conflict broke into swirling groups, and I noticed how the Norsemen tended to fight with Norsemen and the Irish with Irish. There was no cohesion, only larger clumps of fighters clustered around their own war leaders. Sigurd's raven banner was the centre of the largest and most unified group, and Brodir's contingent appeared to be the chosen target for the men who followed Ospak. My own role in the conflict was minimal. The two war hounds panicked at the sound of the initial collision between the armies and bolted. Foolishly I had tied their leads around my wrist and the dogs were so strong that I was plucked off my feet and dragged ignominiously over the ground, until the leather thongs snapped and the two dogs raced free. I never saw them again. I was scrambling back to my feet, rubbing my aching wrist to restore the circulation, when a light spear thudded into the ground beside me, and I looked up to see an Irish warrior not twenty paces away. He was one of their kerns – lightly armed skirmishers – and thankfully both his aim and courage were inadequate to the situation. Just as I was realising again that I was unarmed, apart from a small knife hanging inside my shirt, the Irishman must have thought he had ventured too far inside the enemy lines, and he turned and scampered away, his bare feet flying over the turf.

Already the opposing armies were growing exhausted. First the skirmishers disengaged and withdrew, and then the knots of hersirs, the Norse warriors, began to disentangle as both sides fell back to their previous positions, and paused to count the cost of this first engagement. The losses had been severe. Badly injured men sat on the ground, trying to staunch their wounds; those who were still on their feet were leaning over, propped on their spears and shields, as they gasped for breath like exhausted runners. Scattered here and there were dozens of corpses. Mud and blood were everywhere.

'Seems that we're not the only ones to have slippery allies,' said a tall, thin soldier who was trying to stop the blood running down into his eyes from a sword slash that had nicked his forehead just below the brow line of the helmet. He was looking across at a large Irish contingent of the High King's army, which now stood some distance away from the rest of his battle line. It was apparent from their fresh appearance that these cliathaires as the Irish call their fighters, had not joined in the charge, but had stood by, watching. 'That's Malachi's lot,' explained one of our Ostmen. 'He laid claim to be the High King before Brian Boruma pushed him off the throne, and he would dearly like to have it back. The moment Malachi joins in the battle, then we'll know who's winning. He'll throw in his troops to join whoever is about to be victorious.'

'Form shield wall!' bellowed Brodir, and his men moved into line and began to lock shields again. A concerted ripple of movement among the High King's troops farther up the gentle slope of the hill showed that our opponents were getting ready for a second charge.

This time they picked their targets. The elite of the Irish forces was Murchad's bodyguard. As the High King's eldest son, he was entitled to an escort of professional men-at-arms, many of them battle-hardened from years of fighting in his father's numerous campaigns. The most menacing among them were the Gall-Gael, the Irishmen known as the 'Sons of Death', who had been adopted into Ostmen familes as youths and trained in Norse fighting methods. They combined their weapons skill with the fanaticism of re-converts, and of course their Norse opponents regarded them as turncoats and traitors, and never gave them any quarter. The result was the Gall-Gael were as feared as any berserk. In their earlier charge Murchad's bodyguard had singled out Mael Morda's Leins-termen. Now they shifted their position along the Irish battle line to join forces with Ospak's raiders and strike at Brodir and the contingent from Man.

They came screaming and bellowing at us, running downhill with the advantage of the slope, and the shock of their charge broke our shield wall. I found myself being bundled here and there in a shouting, swearing mass of men as Murchad and his bodyguard erupted through the first and second ranks of the swine array, closely followed by chain-mail-clad troops from Ospak's division, who surged into the gap torn in our line. I thought I recognised the face of Wulf, the cantankerous card player, over the upper rim of a red and white shield when the tall, gangling warrior behind whom I was standing, took a direct hit in the chest from a spear. He gave a surprised grunt and fell backwards, knocking me to the ground. As I squirmed out from under his body, one of the Gall-Gael careering into the attack took a moment aside from the more serious fighting to glance down and casually club at me with the back of his battleaxe. Even in the hubbub of the battle he must have heard the loud snapping crack as the axehead struck my spine. I caught a glimpse of his teeth as he bared them in a grimace of satisfaction before turning away, satisfied that he had broken my back. The shocking thump of the blow sent a terrible pain searing through me and I let out a gasp of agony as I fell face forward into the earth. I was dizzy with pain and when I tried to move, I found I could only turn my face far enough to one side to breathe.

As I lay there semi-paralysed, I watched from ground level the fight raging above and around me. I recognised instantly the Irish leader, Murchad. He was armed with a long, heavy sword and using it two-handed to thrust and sweep as he carved his path through the disorganised swine formation. He had no need for a shield because fully armoured bodyguards kept pace with him on each side, blocking the counter-blows and leaving Murchad the glory of killing his opponents. I saw two of Brodir's best men go down before him, no more than five paces from where I lay, and then Murchad was called away by someone shouting urgently in a tongue which, even in the waves of pain coming from my spine and ribs, I could understand as Irish. Then someone trode heavily on my outflung arm, and the edge of a grey cloak passed across my field of vision. I closed my eyes, pretending to be dead, and after a moment's pause I opened them a slit and saw that it was Wulf the Quarrelsome who had tramped over me. He still held his long pike in his hand and was headed for the huge figure of Brodir, who was sweeping with his battleaxe to fend off a frontal attack from two more of Ospak's men. I was too tired and in a state of shock to shout a warning, even if I had thought to do so. It probably would have been the death of me, for Gall-Gael and Ostmen thought nothing of spearing a wounded man lying on the battlefield. Instead I watched Wulf come within pike thrust of Brodir and pause, waiting for his chance. As Brodir's axe swept down on one of his adversaries, Wulf lunged. He was aiming for the weakest spot in Brodir's famous mail shirt, the place in the armpit where even the most skilful armourer finds it impossible to make a flawless join between the metal rings which protect the shoulder and the torso. The point of the pike pierced the mail and carried into Brodir's side. The huge Manx leader staggered for a moment, then turning, pulled the weapon free. His face had gone deadly pale, though I could not tell whether it was from the pain of the stab or the shocking realisation that his talisman, the famous mail jacket, had failed him. Wulf had stepped back half a pace, still holding the pike, its point wet with Brodir's blood, and then stabbed again, hitting the same spot, probably more by good luck than judgement. I had expected Brodir to counter-attack, but to my dismay he began to retreat. He switched his battleaxe to his uninjured arm, and took several steps backwards, his body hunched over to protect his wounded side while still swinging his battleaxe to keep off his attackers. From his ungainly posture it was clear that he was hurt, and even more obvious that he was strongly right-handed and not at all accustomed to using a battleaxe with his left hand.

As Brodir backed away slowly from his attackers, it dawned on me that he should not have been fighting alone. Members of his war band should have been on hand to protect their leader's retreat, but no one was coming to his assistance. Cautiously I twisted my head around to see what was going on elsewhere. The sound of battle was ebbing, and I guessed that there would soon be another lull in the fighting to allow the two armies to pull back and regroup. Lying prone on the ground, I could not see what had happened on the rest of the battlefield, who had sustained the heaviest losses or who had gained the upper hand. But the fighting between Brodir's men and Ospak's followers must have been murderous. Beyond the body of the tall soldier whose collapse had knocked me down lay three dead men. Judging by their armour, they were from the front line of our swine array, and they had not given up their lives cheaply. In front of them were two enemy corpses and one casualty, whether he was friend or foe I could not tell, who was still alive. He was lying on his back and moaning with pain. He had lost an arm, chopped off at the elbow, and was trying to sit up, but was so unbalanced by his maiming, that he never managed to rise more than a few inches before falling with a small whimper. Soon he must bleed to death. Cautiously I began to check my own injuries. I stretched out one arm, then the other, and half-rolled onto my side. The pain from my back pierced deep into me, but I was encouraged to find that I could feel sensation in my right leg. My left leg was completely numb and then I saw that it was still trapped under the dead soldier. Cautiously I worked the leg free and, like a crab, pulled myself away from the corpse. After

a pause to gather more strength, I struggled up onto my hands and
knees, and reached back to feel the spot where the axe had struck
me. Under my shirt my hand touched a hard, jagged edge and for
one awful moment I thought I was touching the end of a broken
rib emerging from my flesh. But I was imagining. What I was
feeling was the broken haft of the small knife, which I usually
wore out of sight, protected in a wooden sheath and hanging
loosely from a thong around my neck. During the turmoil of the
battle, the knife must have swung round behind my back, and it
had taken the full force of the axe blow. The crack that the Gall-
Gael thought was my spine breaking was the knife and wooden
sheath snapping in two.

Slowly I rose to my feet as waves of dizziness swept over me,
and set off at a hobbling run, weaving my way between the scatter
of dead and wounded men and heading for the one symbol that I
could recognise: the black raven banner of Earl Sigurd, which
marked where the Orkneymen still rallied to their leader. There
were not nearly as many of them as I had remembered, and at least
half of those who were still on their feet appeared to be wounded.
Sigurd himself was in the centre of the group and unharmed, so I
guessed that his bodyguard had done their duty. Then I noticed
that most of his surviving bodyguard were Burners. They must
have stood together in the battle as fellow Icelanders and that is
what had saved them. To my surprise, Sigurd the Stout noticed me
at once. 'Here's Kari Solmundarson's young friend,' he called out
cheerfully. 'You wanted to come to Ireland and find out what it is
like. Now you know.' At the mention of Kari's name, several of
the Burners glanced round and I was sure that the Burner who had
been puzzling over my identity finally realised who I was and that
he had seen me at the Althing. But there was nothing he could do,
at least for the moment.

Sigurd was demanding everyone's attention. An overweight
butterball of a man, he did not look as if his place was among the
cut and thrust of the battlefield, but his courage matched his
corpulence. Purple in the face and hoarse from shouting, he began

to stamp up and down, exhorting his men to get ready for the next clash, to fight boldly and to maintain their honour. His mother's seidr spell on the black raven banner was holding true, he told them. The Orkneymen had been the most successful of Sigtryggr's allies on the battefield. They had withstood the enemy onslaught better than anyone else, and he praised the sacrifice of the three men who had been cut down while carrying the standard.

'Even now the Valkyries are escorting them to Valholl, where each man has rightly earned his place. Soon he will tell the tale of how he defended Odinn's raven though it meant his own certain death.' Few of the Orkneymen seemed impressed. They looked utterly exhausted and when Sigurd called for a volunteer to carry the banner at the next assault, there was no response. There was an awkward silence into which I stepped. Why I did this, I still cannot say for sure. Perhaps I was dizzy and disorientated from the battering I had received; perhaps I had decided that I had nothing to lose now that I had been recognised by the Burners. I only know that as I walked unsteadily to where the flagstaff was stuck in the ground I was feeling the same sensation of calm and inevitability that I had felt years earlier when, as a boy, I had crossed the clearing in the wood in Vinland and entered the hut of the Skraelings. My legs were acting on their own and my body was separate from my mind. I felt as if I was floating at a little distance outside and above my physical self and calmly looking down on a familiar stranger. I tugged the flagpole from the earth. For a moment Sigurd looked astonished. Then he gave a roar of approval. 'There you are,' he called to his men 'we've got our lucky bannerman! The lad's unarmed, yet he'll carry the black raven for us.'

My role as the earl's standard bearer was brief and inglorious. For a third time the High King's forces came swarming down the slope at us, and once again it was Murchad's shock troops who led the way. We had now been on the battlefield all morning and both sides were torn and weary, but somehow Murchad's people seemed to find the strength to smash down at us as fiercely as ever. Sigurd's raven banner was their supreme prize. First it was a half-crazed, kilted Irish clansman leaping down the hill determined to show his courage to his colleagues by seizing the standard. Then came a pair of grim-faced Norse mercenaries heavily chopping their way through the shield wall, concentrating at the spot nearest to the raven banner. For a short interval Fat Sigurd's Orkneymen held firm. They stood solid, shields locked together, resisting the onslaught and exchanging axe sweeps with the enemy. Two paces behind them, for I was in the second rank of the swine array now, I could do no more than use the banner staff as my crutch, leaning on it for support with my head bowed and one end of the pole resting on the ground. I was in agony from my damaged back and I tried desperately to think of a galdr spell chant that might help me, but my mind was in turmoil. I heard and felt the conflict rather than saw it. Once again there was the shouting of voices, much hoarser now, the clang of metal, the thump and thud of bodies meeting and falling, the press and jostle as our formation bent and buckled. I do not even know who struck – Gall-Gael, kern or Ostmen. But suddenly there was a terrible pain in the hand that held the staff and the banner was wrenched from my grasp as I doubled over, clasping my injured hand into my belly. Someone swore in Norse, and I was aware of a tussle as two men fought over the flag, each trying to wrench the shaft from the other. Neither won the contest. I looked up to see one of Sigurd's bodyguards, it was one of the Burners – Halldor Gudmundsson, receive a killing sword thrust in his left side, just as another of the Burners stepped behind the other man and crippled him with a downward blow behind the knee. The man fell sideways and was lost beneath the stamping feet.

'Rally to the Raven!' It was Sigurd's voice, shouting over the tumult, and the tubby earl himself pushed through the brawl and grabbed the banner staff. 'Here! Thorstein, you may carry our emblem,' and he held it out to a tall man standing nearby. It was another of the Burners.

'Don't touch it if you want to live,' warned a voice sharply. An

Icelander, Asmund the White, chose this moment to desert his lord.

Thorstein hesitated, then turned away. At that moment I understood that my first interpretation of my omen dream had been correct. We had spurned our own emblem of Odinn, and the war ravens were our enemies.

Overweight and out of breath, Sigurd might have been a poor foot soldier but he was not a coward. 'Right then,' he growled, 'if no one else will carry the banner, then I will do so even if it means my death. It is fit that the beggar bears the bag, and I would prefer to die with honour than to flee, but I will need both hands if this is to be my final fight.' He pulled the red and black banner from the staff, folded it lengthways, and wrapped it around his waist as a sash. Then, with a sword in one hand and a round shield on the other arm, he stumped forward, puffing and wheezing. Only a handful of men followed him, and at least half of them were Burners. Perhaps they too realised that their lives were over and that, forbidden to ever return to Iceland, they might as well die on the battlefield. The final encounter was very brief. Sigurd lumbered straight towards the nearest Irish chieftain. Once again it was Murchad, who seemed to be everywhere during the battle. There was little contest. Murchad took a spear from a solder nearby, levelled it and when Sigurd came within range thrust forward so the weapon took Sigurd in the throat. The Earl of Orkney fell, and the moment he went down those who remained of his contingent turned and began to retreat towards the ships. A moment later I heard a deep baying cry and the wilder rattle of light drums. It was Malachi committing his fresh troops on the side of Brian Boruma.

I ran. Hugging my injured hand to my chest, I fled for my life. Twice I tripped and fell sprawling, crying out with pain as my spine was wrenched. But each time I got back on my feet and blundered forward, hoping to reach the safety of the boats. My eyes were filled with tears of pain so I could barely see where I was going. I knew only to run in the same direction as my fellows, and try to keep up with them. I heard a choking cry as someone close to me received an arrow or javelin in the back. And suddenly I was splashing through water, the salty drops flying up in my face, and my headlong rush slowing so I almost pitched forward. I looked up and saw that I had reached the beach, but was far from safety. During the battle the tide had come in, and the sand flats to which we had brought the longships that dawn were now submerged. To get to the ships our defeated men would have to wade, then swim.

I laboured forward through the pluck of the water, my feet slipping on the unseen sand and mud. Not all the men around me were fugitives. Many were hunters. I saw Norsemen who had taken Brian Boruma's pay catch up with their countrymen who had fought for Sigtryggr and cut their throats as they floundered in the sea. Blood oozed across the tide. The retreat was becoming a massacre. I watched a young Irish chieftain – he was the same man who had been pointed out as the High King's grandson – come bounding out through the shallows, his hair flying and his face alight with battle craziness. He closed with two Orkneymen, each far bigger than himself, and without a weapon his hand, he grabbed and pulled them down underwater to drown. There was a terrible thrashing in the water, and the three contestants surfaced several times before all three grew weaker until the youth and one of the Norse failed to come back and gulp for air. Their two waterlogged corpses were floating face down even as the third man, now too tired to swim the final gap, threw up his arms and sank from view.

As I watched him drown, I knew that my injured arm and hand would prevent me from swimming to the waiting boats. Turning, I waded back to land and by some intervention of the Gods I was left alone. Soaking wet, shivering with cold and shock, I emerged on the beach and, like a wounded animal, looked around me to seek shelter from my enemies. Halfway up the slope of the hill I saw a thicket of bushes at the edge of the wood overlooking the battle-field. Aching with tiredness, I laboured up the hill towards this refuge. For the last hundred paces I was panting with exhaustion and dreading the shout of discovery. But nothing came and as I reached the bushes I did not stop, but blundered forward until the tearing of the thorns slowed me. I dropped to my knees and crawled forward, holding my injured hand to my chest as a fox with a wounded leg seeks shelter after the trap. Reaching deep into the thicket, I collapsed on the ground and lay panting for breath.

I must have lost consciousness for some time, before the sound of singing penetrated through my nausea, and I thought that my ears were deceiving me. I heard the words of a hymn that my grand-mother, Erik the Red's wife, had sung in the White Rabbit Hutch back in Greenland. Then the sound came again, but not in a woman's voice. It was a male choir. I crawled a few feet forward to find that my refuge was not as deep and effective as I thought. The bushes made only a thin fringe on the edge of the woods. On the far side of the bushes began a forest of young oak trees. There were wide open spaces between the tree trunks, and at that moment the nearest trunks gave the impression of being the columns of a church because, set on the forest floor, was a large portable altar. The sound of singing came from half a dozen White Christ priests who were celebrating some sort of ceremony, holding up sacred symbols, a cross, a bowl and even several candles as they sang. One of the celebrants was about my age and he was carrying a large dish covered with a cloth. The leading figure standing beside the altar was an old man, perhaps in his early sixties, grey-haired and gaunt. He was the high priest, I thought, because all the other priests were treating him with great respect and, though he was bareheaded, he was richly dressed. Then I heard the whicker of a horse and to my left I saw a large tent, half hidden among the trees, placed where it had a commanding view of the battlefield I had just left. Loitering beside the tent were half a dozen Norsemen. My brain was fuzzily trying to work out the connection between the tent and the religious ceremony when there was a great crashing sound. Out from the bushes, like an enormous enraged bear, burst Brodir. He too must have been hiding from enemy pursuit. Now he came lumbering out of the bushes and I caught a glimpse of the crusted streak down his right side where blood had leaked from his wound. Brodir still had his battleaxe in his ungainly left hand, but why he had burst from cover in this suicidal manner did not occur to me at once. I watched as Brodir ambushed the priests, and the young man with the dish tried to block his charge. The boy stepped into Brodir's path and held up the metal dish like a shield, but Brodir swept him aside with a single awkward blow from the battleaxe, and I cringed in sympathy as the boy's right hand was cut off, leaving a stump which spurted blood. Brodir gave a curious low growl as with another ungainly left-handed sweep he swung his axe at the old man's neck, half-severing his head from his body. The old man seemed to shrivel to a bunch of rags as he collapsed to the ground even as the men-at-arms came running forward, too late. Some knelt to pick up the fallen priest, the others, awed by Brodir's immense size, cautiously formed a half-circle around him and began to close in. Brodir offered no resistance, but just stood there, swaying slightly on his feet, the battleaxe hanging straight down from his weak left hand. He threw back his head and shouted, 'Now let man tell man that it was Brodir who killed King Brian.' At that moment I knew that the seidr magic of the black raven banner had been a hoax worthy of Odinn the Deceiver. I, the last person to carry the banner on high, had survived, yet we had lost the battle. By contrast our enemy, who had won the victory, had sacrificed their leader. I had witnessed the victory of the High King but the death of Brian Boruma.

Brodir was pressed back slowly by his enemies. It seemed that the men-at-arms wanted to take the killer of the High King alive. They held their shields in front of them as they advanced deliberately and cautiously, forcing Brodir back towards the thicket in which I lay. More than ever Brodir seemed like a great wounded bear, but now it was a beast that has been cornered at the end of a forest hunt. Finally he could back away no farther. His retreat was blocked by the thicket and as he took one more step backwards, still facing his enemies, he caught his heel and fell. The hunters leapt forward, literally throwing themselves on their quarry, smothering Brodir in a crackling smash of branches and twigs. Overcome in the confusion, I lost consciousness once again and the final image in front of my eyes was of the iron-beaked ravens swarming in until the entire sky went black.

SIXTEEN

I AWOKE TO a jolt of excruciating pain in my arm. I thought at first that the source was my injured hand. But the pain was now coming from the other side. I opened my eyes to find a cliathaire leaning over me, clumsily hammering a rivet to close a fetter on my right wrist. He had missed his stroke and struck my arm with the hilt of his sword, which he was using as a makeshift mallet. I twisted my head to look around. I was lying on the muddy ground not far from the bush, out of which I had been dragged unconscious. About a dozen Irish and Norse soldiers were standing with their backs to me, staring at something which lay at the foot of one of the oak trees. It was Brodir's corpse. I recognised it from the lustrous long black hair. He had been disembowelled. Later I was told that this had been done at the request of the mercenaries in the High King's bodyguard. They claimed that Brodir's murderous ambush of the unarmed High King had been the mark of a coward and should be punished in the traditional way – his stomach slit and his guts pulled out while he was still alive. So his entrails had been nailed up to the oak tree. The truth, I suspected, was that the mercenaries were trying to divert attention from their own deficiency. They should never have left the High King unguarded.

The Irishman hoisted me to my feet, then tugged the fetter's chain to lead me away from the scene of Brian Boruma's death.

'Name?' he asked in dansk tong. He was a short, wiry man of about forty, dressed in the usual Irish costume of leggings bound with gaiters and a loose shirt, over which he wore a short brown and black cloak. He slung his small round shield onto his back by its strap so that he had one hand free to hold my leading chain. In his other hand he still held his sword.

'Thorgils Leifsson,' I replied. 'Where are you taking me?'

He looked up in surprise. I had spoken in Irish. 'Are you one of Sigtryggr's people, from Dublin?' he demanded.

'No, I came here with the ships from Man, but I didn't belong to Brodir's contingent.'

For some reason, the Irishman looked rather pleased with this news. 'Why were you fighting alongside them, then?' he asked.

It was too complicated to explain how I had come to be with Brodir's men, so I replied only, 'I was looking after a pair of wolf hounds for him, as their keeper.' And, unwittingly, with those words I sealed my fate.

After a short walk we reached the area where the remnants of the High King's army were gathering together the plunder of battle. The simple rule was that the first person to lay hands on a corpse got to keep his spoil provided he stripped the victim quickly and made it clear that he had established his claim to the booty. Many victors were already dressed in several layers of garments, a motley collection of captured finery worn one on top of another, with many of the outer layers blood-stained. Others were carrying four or five swords in their arms as if collecting sticks of firewood in the forest, while their colleagues were busy stuffing looted shoes into their sacks, together with belts and shirts, which they had stripped from the slaincluding the dead from their own side. One Irish fighter had assembled a gruesome collection of three severed heads, which he had thrown on the ground, their hair knotted together. Clusters of men were disputing the more valuable items – chain-mail shirts or body jewellery. These arguments were frequently between Malachi's fresh troops and Boruma's battle-stained soldiers, who had done most of the fighting. The latter usually won the argument because they had an ugly, tired gleam in their eyes which indicated that after so much slaughter they were fully prepared to keep their rewards even if it meant taking arms against their own side.

My captor led me to a small group of his colleagues who were clustered around a campfire, preparing a meal. A jumble of their booty lay on the ground beside them. It was rather meagre, mostly weaponry, a few helmets and some Ostman clothes. They looked up as he approached. 'Here,' he said, jerking on my chain, 'I've got the Man leader's aurchogad.' They looked impressed. An aurchogad, I was to learn, was a keeper of hounds. This is an official post among the Irish and found only in the retinue of a senior chief. By the Irish custom of war it meant that, as far as my captors were concerned, I had been a member of Brodir's personal retinue. Therefore I was a legitimate captive, an item of war booty, and thus I was now my captor's slave.

Our little group did not linger on the battlefield. Word quickly spread that Malachi, who was now effectively the leader of the victorious army, was already in negotiations with King Sigtryggr, still safe behind his city walls with Gormlaith, and that there would be no attack on the city, so no booty there. With Brian Boruma dead, Malachi had lost no time in laying claim to the title of High King, and Sigtryggr was promising to support his claim on condition that Malachi spared Dublin from being plundered. So the real victors of our momentous battle were the two leaders who had taken the least part in the fighting and, of course, Gormlaith. As matters turned out, she was to spend the next fifteen years in Dublin as the undisputed power behind the throne, telling King Sigtryggr what to do.

The losses among the real combatants had been horrific. Nearly every member of Boruma's family who took part in the battle had been killed, including two of his grandsons, and Murchad's reckless courage had finally brought about his own death. He had knocked one of Brodir's men to the ground and was leaning over him, about to finish him off when the Norseman thrust upward with his own dagger and gutted the Irish leader. One-third of the High King's fighters lay dead on the battlefield. and they had inflicted a similar level of damage on their opponents. Mael Morda's Leinstermen had been annihilated, and only a handful of the Norse troops from overseas survived the desperate scramble through the tidal shallows to get back to their ships. Earl Sigurd's Orkneymen suffered worst of all. Fewer than one man in ten managed to escape with his life, and Earl Sigurd's entire personal retinue had fallen, including fifteen of the Burners, though, for me, that was little consolation.

My owner, I learned as we marched into the interior of Ireland, went by the name of Donnachad Ua Dalaigh, and he was what the Irish call a ri or king. This does not mean a king as others might know it. Donnachad was no more than the leader of a small tuath or petty kingdom located somewhere in the centre of the country. By foreign standards he would have been considered little more than a sub-chieftain. But the Irish are a proud and fractious people and they cling to any level or mark of distinction, however modest. So they have several grades of kingship and Donnachad was of the lowest rank, being merely a ri tuathe, the headman of a small group who claim descent from a single ancestor of whose semi-legendary exploits they are, of course, extremely proud. Certainly Donnachad was much too unimportant to have rated an aurchogad of his own. Indeed, he was fortunate even to have the services of the single elderly attendant, who helped to carry his weapons and a dented cooking pot, as we travelled west with his war band of no more than twenty warriors. Donnachad himself proudly held the chain attached to his one and only slave.

I had never seen such a verdant country in all my life. Everywhere the vegetation was bursting from bud to leaf. There were great swathes of woodland, mostly oak and ash, and between the forests stretched open country that brimmed with green. Much of the ground was soggy, but our track followed a ridge of high ground that was better drained and on either hand I looked out across a gently rolling landscape with thorn trees so heavy with white blossoms that the sudden gusts of winds created little snowstorms of white petals that drifted down onto the path. The verges on each side of the track were speckled with small spring flowers in dark blue, pale yellow and purple, and every bush seemed to hold at least one pair of songbirds so intent on their calls that they ignored our approach until we were nearly close enough to touch them. Even then they only hopped a few feet into the upper branches to continue to announce their courting. The weather itself was utterly unpredictable. In the space of a single day we experienced all seasons of the year. A blustery grey morning brought an autumn gale that buffeted us so fiercely that we had to walk leaning into the blast, and the squall was succeeded by a spring-like interval of at least an hour when the wind suddenly dropped and we heard again the shouting of the small birds, only for a swollen black cloud to throw down on us a rattling attack of winter sleet and hail that had us pulling up the hoods of our cloaks and pausing for shelter under the largest and leafiest tree. Yet by mid-afternoon the clouds had cleared away entirely and the sunshine was so hot on our faces that we were rolling up our cloaks to tie them on top of our packs as we tramped, sweating, through the puddles left by the recent downpour.

After all, Donnachad proved to be a rather good-natured man and not the least vindictive. On the third day of the journey he abandoned the practice of holding my lead chain, and let me walk along with the rest of his band, though I still wore the fetters on each wrist. This was particularly painful for my left arm because the hand in which I had held the staff of the black raven banner when I was struck was puffed up and swollen and had turned an ugly purple-yellow. At first I had thought I would lose the use of the fingers entirely, for I could not bend them and I had no sense of touch. But gradually the swelling receded and my hand began to mend, though it would always ache before the onset of rain. The small bones, I suppose, had been fractured and never knitted together properly.

We passed a succession of small hamlets, usually set off at

some distance to one side of the road. They were prosperous-looking places, groups of thatched farms and outbuildings often protected by a palisade, but their vegetable patches and grazing pastures were outside the defensive perimeter so evidently the land was not entirely lawless. From time to time Donnachad and his men turned aside to tell the farmers about the outcome of the great battle and to purchase food, paying with minor items of their spoil, and I looked for the barns where the farmers stored the winter hay for feeding their cattle, but then realised that the Irish winters were so mild that the herders could allow the cattle to graze outside all year long. We were travelling along a well-used road, and frequently met other travellers coming towards us – farmers with cattle on their way to a local market, pedlars and itinerant craftsmen. Occasionally we met a ri tuathre, a chieftain one step up the hierarchy from Donnachad. These mid-ranking nobles ruled over several smaller tuaths, and whenever we met one on the road I noted how Donnachad and his people stood respectfully aside to allow the ri tuathre to trot past on his small horse, accompanied by at least twenty outriders.

After the fourth or fifth of these self-important little cavalcades had splashed past us, the hooves of their horses sprinkling us with muddy water from the puddles, I ventured to ask Donnachad why the ri tuathre travelled with such large escorts when the land seemed so peaceful.

'It would be very wrong for a ri tuathre to travel alone. It would diminish the price of his face,' Donnachad answered.

'The price of his face?' I enquired. Donnachad had said 'log n-enech', and I knew no other way to translate it.

'The price of his honour, his worth. Every man has a value whenever he is judged, either in front of the arbitrators or by his own people, and a ri' – and here he sucked in his breath and tried to look a little more regal, though that was difficult in his shabby and mud-spattered clothes – 'should always act in measure with the price of his face. Otherwise there would be anarchy and ruin in his tuath.'

'So what would be the price of Cormac's face?' I meant this as
a joke. I had noted that the Irish have a quick sense of humour
and Cormac, one of Donnachad's cliathaires, was particularly ugly.
He had bulging eyes, broad flat nostrils, and an unfortunate
birthmark running down the left side of his face from his ear to
disappear under his shirt collar. But Donnachad took my question
entirely seriously. 'Cormac is a cow-freeman of good standing –
he has a half-share in a plough team – so his face price is two and
a half milch cows, rather less than one cumal. He renders me the
value of one milch cow in rent every year.'

I decided to take my luck a little further. A cumal is a female
slave, and Donnachad's reply would have some bearing on my
own future as his property. 'Forgive me if I am being impolite,' I
said, 'but do you also have a face price? And how would other
people know what it was?'

'Everyone knows the face price of every man, his wife and his
family,' he answered without even a moment's pause for thought,
'from the ri tuathre whom we saw just now, whose honour is eight
cumals, to a lad still living on his parent's land whose face would
be valued at a yearling heifer.'

'Do I have a face price too?'

'No. You are doer, unfree, and therefore you have neither price
nor honour. Unless, that is, you manage to obtain your freedom
and then by hard work and thrift you accumulate enough wealth.
But it is easier to lose face price than to gain it. A ri endangers his
honour if he even lays his hand to any implement that has a handle,
be it hammer, axe or spade.'

'Does that include using a sword hilt as a mallet?' I could not
refrain from answering, and Donnachad gave me a cuff around the
head.

It was on the fourth day of our walk that I had my most notable
encounter with this strange Irish notion of face price. We came to
a small village where normally we might have stopped and bought
some food. Instead we marched straight forward even though, as
I knew, our supplies were running low. The brisk pace made my

back hurt. It was still sore from the blow received in the battle, but my companions merely told me to hurry up and not delay them and that I would soon have medicine to reduce the pain. They quickened their pace and looked distinctly cheerful as if anticipating some happy event. Shortly afterwards we came in sight of a building, larger than the usual farmhouse and set much closer to the road. I saw that it had a few small outhouses, but there were no cattle stalls nor any sign of farming activity around it. Nor did it have a defensive palisade. On the contrary, the building looked open to all and very welcoming. Without a moment's hesitation my companions veered from the track, approached the big main door and, barely pausing to knock, pushed their way inside. We were in a large, comfortable room arrayed with benches and seats. In the centre of the room a steaming cauldron hung over a fire pit. A man who was evidently the owner of this establishment came forward to greet Donnachad most warmly. Using several phrases of formal welcome, he invited him to sit down and take his ease after the weariness of the highway. He then turned to each of the cliathaires – ignoring me and Donnachad's servant, of course – and invited them likewise. Scarcely had our group found their seats than our host was providing them with flagons of mead and beer. These drinks were soon followed by loaves of bread, a small churn of butter and some dried meat. There was even some food for myself and Donnachad's elderly servant.

I ate quickly, expecting that we would soon be on our way. But to my puzzlement Donnachad and his cliathaires appeared to be settling in to enjoy themselves. Their host promised them a hot meal as soon as his cook had fired the oven. Then he served more drinks, followed by the meal itself, and afterwards made another liberal distribution of mead and beer. By then the cliathaires had settled down to story-telling, a favourite pastime among the Irish, where – as at Earl Sigurd's Jol feast in Orkney – each person at a gathering is expected to tell a tale to keep the others entertained. All this time more travellers had been entering the room, and they too were seated and fed. By nightfall the room was full to capacity, and it was obvious to me that our little party would be spending the night at this strange house.

'Who is the owner of the house? Is he a member of Donnachad's tuath?' I asked Donnachad's servant.

He was already drowsy with tiredness and strong drink. 'Doesn't even come from these parts originally. Set up here maybe four years ago, and is doing very well,' the old man replied with a gentle hiccup.

'You mean he sells food and drink to travellers, and is making his fortune?'

'No, not making his fortune, spending his fortune,' the old-timer answered. 'He's made his fortune already, cattle farming somewhere to the north, I think. Now he's earning a much higher face price and he well deserves it.' I thought the old fellow's wits were fuddled and gave up the questions. There would be a better time to solve the mystery in the morning.

In fact next morning was not the right time to ask questions either. Everyone had fierce headaches, and the sun was already high before we were ready to set out on the road again. I loitered, waiting for Donnachad to pay our host for all the food and drink we had consumed, but he made no move to do so, and our host seemed just as good-natured as when we first arrived. Donnachad muttered only a few gracious phrases of thanks and then we rejoined his men, who were trudging blearily forward. I sidled across to the elderly servant and asked him why we had left without paying. 'You never pay a briugu for hospitality,' he answered, mildly shocked. 'That would be an insult. Might even take you to court for looking to pay him.'

'In Iceland, where I come from,' I said, 'a farmer is expected to be hospitable and give shelter and food to travellers who come to his door, particularly if he is wealthy and can afford it. But I didn't see any farming near the house. I'm surprised that he doesn't move away to somewhere a bit more remote.'

'That's precisely why he's built his house beside the road,' explained the old man, 'so that as many people as possible can visit him. And the more hospitality he dispenses, the higher will rise his face price. That's how he can increase his honour, which is much more important to him than the amount of wealth he has accumulated.'

What the briugu would do when all his hoarded savings ran out, he did not explain. 'A briugu should possess only three things,' concluded the old man with one of those pithy sayings of which the Irish are fond, 'a never-dry cauldron, a dwelling on a public road and a welcome for every face.'

We arrived at Donnachad's tuath in the second week of Beltane, the month which in Iceland I had known as Lamb-fold-time. After trudging halfway across Ireland in the mud with Donnachad and his slightly shabby band, I was not expecting Donnachad's home to be very grand. Even so, its air of threadbare poverty was flagrant. His dwelling was merely a small circular building with walls of wattle and daub and a conical thatch roof, and the interior was more sparsely furnished than the briugu's roadside hostel. There were a few stools and benches, and the sleeping arrangements were thin mattresses stuffed with dried bracken, while the beaten-earth floor was covered with rushes. Outside were some cattle byres, a granary and a small smithy. There was also a short line of stables of which Donnachad was proud, though there were no horses in them at the present moment.

From the conversation of his cliathaires I gathered that Donnachad and his warriors had gone to fight alongside the Irish High King not from loyalty, but in the hope of bringing back enough booty to improve the hardship of their daily lives. The land on which their clan or fine lived was unproductive at the best of times, being waterlogged and boggy, and there had been so much rain during the last three summers that their ploughings had been flooded and the crops ruined. At the same time a recurring murrain had afflicted their cattle herds, and because petty kings like Donnachad and his chief farmers counted their wealth in cattle, this loss had brought them very low. The victory at the weir of

Clontarf, as the battle was now being called, had been the only cheerful event in the past five years.

Donnachad put me to work as a field labourer, and he treated me fairly, even though I was a slave. He allowed me rest time at noon and in the evening, and the food he provided – coarse bread, butter and cheese, and an occasional dish of meat – was not much different from his own diet. He had a wife and five children, and the homespun clothes they wore were a sign of their very reduced means. Yet I never saw Donnachad turn away any stranger who came to the farm – the Irish expectation of hospitality extended farther than the briugus – and twice during that summer I was called in as a house servant when Donnachad entertained his clansmen at the banquets which they expected from a man with his log n-enech. The food and mead, I knew, were almost everything that Donnachad held in his storerooms.

That summer in the open air, herding cattle, minding sheep and pigs, making and mending fences, changed me physically and mentally. I filled out and grew in strength, my back healed, and my command of the Irish improved rapidly. I found I had a gift for learning a language quickly. The only disappointment was that my injured hand still troubled me. Though I flexed and massaged it, the fingers remained stiff and awkward, and it was a particular handicap when I had to grip a spade handle to cut and stack turf for Donnachad's winter fire or grapple with boulders that we pulled from the rough fields and heaped into boundary walls.

The harvest was poor but not disastrous, and soon afterwards I began to notice that Donnachad was showing signs of gathering anxiety. His normally cheerful conversation dried up, and he would sit for an hour at a time, looking worried and distracted. In the night I woke occasionally to hear the low murmur of voices as he talked with his wife, Sinead, in the curtained-off section of the house they called their bed chamber. In the scraps of their conversation I often heard a word I did not know – manchuine – and when I asked its meaning from Marcan, the elderly servant, he grimaced. 'It's the tax Donnachad must pay to the monastery in the autumn. It's levied every year, and for the past five years Donnachad has not been able to pay. The monastery allowed him more time, but now the debt has grown so large that it will take years to clear, if ever.'

'Why does Donnachad owe money to a monastery?' I asked.

'A small tuath like ours must have an over-ruler,' Marcan replied. 'We are too small to survive on our own, and so we pledge allegiance to a king who can give us protection when we need it, in a local war or a dispute over boundary lands or something of the sort. We give the over-king our support, and he gains in honour if he is acknowledged as over-king to several tuaths. Also he supplies us with cattle which we look after for him. At the end of the farming year we give back an agreed amount of interest, in goods such as milk and cheese or calves, and we do some service for him.'

'But how does a monastery get involved in all this?'

'The arrangement seemed sensible when Donnachad's grand-father made it. He thought the abb would be a more considerate overlord than our previous ri tuathre, who was always asking us to provide him with soldiers for his endless squabbles with other ri tuathre, or he would suddenly show up with a band of his retainers and stay for two or three weeks, treating our houses as his own and generally reducing us to beggary. Donnachad's grandfather came up with the notion of transferring our loyalty to a monastery. The monks weren't going to ask for soldiers to join in their wars, and they wouldn't come visiting so often either.'

'So what went wrong?'

'The new arrangement worked well for nearly twenty years,' Marcan replied. 'But then the new abb got grand ideas. He and his advisers began claiming a special sanctity for their own saint. He must have precedence over other monasteries with their patron saints. The abb started bringing in stonemasons and labourers to build new chapels and erect imposing monuments, and he began to purchase expensive altar cloths and employ the best jewellers to design and make fancy church fittings. It all cost a great deal.'

More log n-enech, I thought.

'That was when the monastery treasurer began asking for increased returns on the cattle that had been loaned to us and, as you know, our cattle herding has not been lucky. Next, his successor came up with a new way of raising revenue. The monks now go on a circuit of their tuaths every autumn, bringing with them their holy relics to show the people. They expect the faithful to provide them with the manchuine, the monastery tax, so that the abb can continue the building programme. If you ask me, it will take another couple of generations for the job to be done. They're even asking for money to pay for missionaries whom the monks will send abroad to foreign countries.'

Marcan's remark about the missionaries reminded me of Thang-brand, King Olaf's belligerent missionary to Iceland, who had made such a nuisance of himself. But I wasn't sure of the old man's religious views so I kept silent.

'When are the priests due to make their next visit?'

'Ciaran is their special saint and the ninth day of September is his feast. So we'll probably see them in the next couple of weeks. But one thing's sure: Donnachad won't be able to settle the debt that the tuath owes.'

For some reason I expected St Ciaran's relics to be part of the saint – a thigh bone and a skull, perhaps. I had heard rumours that White Christ people revered these macabre remnants. But it turned out that the relics which the monks brought with them ten days later were much less personal. They were the crooked head of a bishop's staff and a leather satchel, which, they claimed, still held the Bible that their saint had studied. Certainly the crozier was proof of Marcan's assertion that the monastery had spent huge sums on glorifying their saint. The bent scrap of ancient wood was enshrined in a magnificent filigreed case of silver gilt, studded with precious stones and cleverly fashioned into the shape of a horse's head. This, the monks claimed, was the staff that Ciaran himself had used, and they held up the glittering ornament for all of us who gathered outside Donnachad's house to see and revere.

Strangely, they were even more reverential of the book. They affirmed that it was the very same miraculous volume that Ciaran had always carried with him, studying it at every available moment, rising at first light to begin reading, and poring over its pages far into the night, rarely setting it aside. And, unwittingly, they reminded me of the day my mother's hay had failed to dry after the downpour of rain at Frodriver, as they recounted the tale of how Ciaran had been sitting outside his cell one day when he was unexpectedly called away. Thoughtlessly he placed the book on the ground, lying open with its pages exposed to the sky. In his absence, a heavy shower had fallen; when he came back to collect the book all the ground was sodden wet, but the fragile pages were bone dry and not a line of the ink had run.

To prove it to us, the monks unfastened the satchel's leather thongs, solemnly withdrew the book and reverentially showed us the pristine pages.

Such tales made a great impression on Donnachad's people, even if they were not capable of reading and had no idea how to judge the age of the book. It made for an awkward interview as the little party of monks in their drab gowns stood in the centre the earth floor of Donnachad's home and asked for payment of their dues. The abb, or abbot, was represented by the treasurer, a tall, lugubrious man who exuded a sense of sad finality as he made his request. From where I was standing against the side wall with Marcan, I saw that Donnachad looked embarrassed and ashamed. I guessed that his log n-enech was at stake. Humbly Donnachad asked the monks to allow him and his people to pay off their obligation in small stages. He explained how the harvest had been a disappointment once again, but he would gather together as much produce as could be spared and deliver the food to the monastery throughout the coming winter. Then he delivered his pledge: as an earnest of his intention he would loan to the monastery his only slave, so the value of my work would be a surety to set against the annual debt.

The sad-looking treasurer looked at me where I stood against the far wall. I no longer wore a chain or manacles, but the scars on my wrists made my status obvious. 'Very well,' he said, 'we will accept the young man to come to work for us on loan, though it is not our custom to employ slaves in a monastery. However, the blessed Patrick himself was a slave once, so there is a precedent.' And with that I passed from the ownership of Donnachad, ri tuathe of the Ua Dalaigh, into the possession of the monks of St Ciaran's foundation.

SEVENTEEN

To this day I look back on my time at St Ciaran's monastery with immense gratitude as well as heartfelt dislike. I do not know whether to thank or curse those who were my teachers there. I spent more than two years among them and had no inkling that the knowledge made available to me was such a privilege. My existence seemed pointless and confined and there were many days when, in my misery, I feared that Odinn had abandoned me. With hindsight I am now aware that my suffering was only a shadow of what the All-Father endured in his constant search for wisdom. Where he sacrificed an eye to drink at Mimir's well of wisdom, or hung in agony upon the world tree to learn the secret of the runes, I had only to bear loneliness, frustration, bouts of cold and hunger, and the repetition of dogma. And I was to emerge from St Ciaran's monastery equipped with knowledge that was to serve me well every day of my life.

Of course, it was not meant to be like that. I came to St Ciaran's monastery as a slave, a non-person, a nothing, a doer. My prospects were as bleak as the grey autumn day on which I arrived, with the air already holding the chill promise of winter. I was a down payment against a debt, and my only value was the manual work I was able to perform to reduce the arrears. So I was assigned to the stonemasons as a common labourer and I would have

remained with them, hauling and cutting stone, sharpening chisels
and heaving on pulley and tackle until I was too old and feeble to
perform these simple manual tasks, if the Norns had not woven a
different fate for me.

The monastery stands on the upper slope of a ridge facing west
and overlooks a broad, slow-flowing river which is the chief river
of Ireland. Just as Donnachad's royal home was not a palace in the
accepted sense, so too St Ciaran's monastery is not the imposing
edifice which might be imagined from its name. It is a cluster of
small stone-built chapels on the hillside, interspersed with the
humble buildings which house the monks and contain their books
and workshops, and surrounded by an earth bank which the monks
call their vallum. In physical size everything is on a modest scale,
small rooms, low doors, simple dwellings. But in ambition and
outlook the place is immense. At St Ciaran's I met monks who had
travelled to the great courts of Europe and preached before kings
and princes. Others were deeply familiar with the wisdom of the
ancients; several were artists and craft workers and poets of real
excellence, and many were genuine Ceili De, servants of God, as
they called themselves. But inevitably there were also dullards in
community, as well as hypocrites and sadists who wore the same
habits and sported the same tonsures.

The abb in my time was Aidan. A tall, balding and colourless
man with pale blue eyes and a fringe of curly blond hair, he looked
as though all the blood had drained out of him. He had spent his
entire adult life in the monastery, entering when little more than a
child. In fact, it was rumoured that he was the son of an earlier
abb, though it was more than a century since monks were allowed
to have wives. Strict celibacy was now the outward show, but there
were still monks who maintained regular liaisons with women in
the extensive settlement which had grown up around the holy site.
Here lived the lay people who provided casual labour for the monks
– as their carters, ploughmen, thatchers and so forth. Whatever his
origins, Abb Aidan was a cold fish, conservative yet ambitious. He
ran the monastery along the same unwavering guidelines that he

had inherited from his predecessors and he shunned innovation. His great strength, as he would have seen it, was his devotion to the long-term interests and continuity of the brotherhood. He intended to leave the monastery stronger and more secure than when he was first made abb, and if such a stiff figure recognised the frailty and impermanence of human existence, it was in order to concentrate his energy on longer-lasting material foundations. So Abb Aidan strove to increase the reputation of the monastery by adding to its material marvels rather than its sanctity.

He was fixated on finances. Brother Mariannus, the treasurer, saw the abb more than any other member of the community, and he was expected to render an almost daily account of the money that was owed, the taxes due, the current value of the possessions, the costs of administration. Abb Aidan was not avaricious for himself. He was interested only in enhancing the prestige of St Ciaran's, and he knew that this required a constant flow of income. Anyone who threatened that revenue was dealt with harshly. Most of the monastery's income came from renting out livestock, and in the year before I arrived a thief was caught stealing the monastery's sheep. He was hanged publicly on a gibbet just outside the holy ground. An even greater stir came in the second year of the abb's rule. A young novitiate absconded, taking with him a few articles of minor value – a pair of metal altar cups and some pages from an unfinished manuscript in the scriptorium. The young man disappeared in the night and managed to travel as far as the lands of his tuath. Abb Aidan guessed his destination and sent a search party after him, with orders that the stolen items be recovered and the miscreant brought back under guard. When I arrived at St Ciaran's, one of the first stories I was told in scandalised whispers was how the young monk had arrived on the end of a leading rope, his wrists bound, his back bloody from a beating. The other monks had expected that he would suffer a strict regime of mortification to atone for his sins, and they were puzzled when the young man was only held overnight at the monastery, then led away to an unknown destination across the river. A month later news filtered through that the young man had been placed in a deep pit and left to starve to death. Apparently it would have been profane to shed the blood of someone who had been about to promise himself to the Church, so the abb had revived a method of execution rarely used.

The yield from Abb Aidan's meticulous husbandry of the monastic finances was spectacular. The monastery had long been known for its scriptorium – the exquisite illumination of its manuscripts was famed throughout the land – but there was now a whole range of other skills devoted to the glorification of the monastery and the service of its God. Abb Aidan encouraged work in precious metals as well as in enamel and glass. Many of the craftsmen were the monks themselves. They created objects of extraordinary beauty, using techniques they sifted from the ancient texts or had learnt in foreign lands during their travels. And often they exchanged ideas with the craftsmen who came to the monastery, attracted by its reputation as a generous patron of the arts. I was put to work for one of these craftsmen, Saer Credine the master stonemason, because our abb believed that nothing could express immutable devotion better than monuments of massive stone.

Saer Credine was surprisingly frail-looking for someone whose life was spent carving huge blocks of stone with mallet and chisel. He came from a distant region to the south-west where the rocks break naturally into cubes and plates, and his tuath was a place where stoneworkers have been reared and respected for time out of mind. Any fool, he would say, could attack a lump of stone with brutish strength, but it took skill and imagination to see the finished shape and form within the rock and know how to coax that shape from the stone. That was the God-given gift. When he first made this remark, I thought he meant that the White Christ had endowed him with his skills.

Abb Aidan had commissioned him to produce an imposing new stone cross for the monastery, a cross to be the equal of any of the splendid crosses which already stood in the monastic grounds. The base was to show scenes from the New Testament and the shaft would be incised with the most renowned of St Ciaran's many miracles. The senior monks had provided the stonemason with rough sketches of the scenes – the resurrection of the White Christ from his tomb, of course, and the wild boar bringing branches in its jaws to make St Ciaran's first hut – and they checked that the tableaux had transferred correctly to the face of the stone before Saer Credine gouged the first groove. But from that moment onward there was little that the monks could do, and everything depended on Saer Credine's competence. Only the master stone-mason knew how the stone would work, and by subtle distinction how to lead and instruct the eye of the beholder. And, of course, once the carver's blow had been struck there was no going back, no rubbing out, starting again and altering the moment.

By the time I joined his labour force, Saer Credine had the massive rectangular base nearly complete. It had taken him five months of work. On the front panel a shrouded Christ was emerging from his coffin watched by two helmeted soldiers; on the rear panel Peter and Christ shared a net while fishing for the souls of men. The two smaller end panels were simple interlace carved by Saer Credine's senior assistant because the master craftsman was already working on the great vertical shaft. It was of a hard granite, brought by raft down the great river and laboriously hauled up the hill to the shed where we worked. When I arrived, the stone lay on its side, sheltered by a roof. It was supported on huge blocks of wood so as to be at a convenient height for Saer Credine to strike the surface. My first task was no more than to pick up the stone chips that dropped into the muddy ground, and at dusk my duty was to cover the half-completed work with a layer of straw against the frost. I was also, by default, the nightwatchman because no one had assigned me a sleeping place and I slept curled up on the straw bales. At breakfast time I went to stand in line with the other servants and indigents who came to the monastery kitchens to seek charity of milk and porridge, then I carried the food back to eat as I squatted beside the great block of stone that rapidly became the

fixed point of my slave's existence. After a few days of gathering
stone chips it was a short step to being given the task of brushing
clean the worked face of the stone whenever the master craftsman
stepped back to view his work or take a break from his labour.
Saer Credine never made any comment on how he thought his
work was progressing, and his face was expressionless.

Within a month I had graduated to the task of sharpening Saer
Credine's chisels as well as wielding the sweeper's brush, and he
even let me strike a few blows on the really rough work, where
there was not the slightest chance that I could do any harm.
Despite my stiffened left hand, I found that I was fairly deft and
could cut a true facet. I also discovered that Saer Credine, like
many craftsmen, was a kindly man beneath his taciturn exterior,
and extremely observant. He noted that I took a more than usual
interest in my surroundings, wandering round the monastery
enclosure whenever possible to see what was going on, examining
the other stone crosses that already stood with their instructional
scenes. But, typically, he said nothing. After all, he was a master
craftsman, and I was a doer, nothing.

Late one evening, when the butt of the shaft was finished,
neatly flattened across the base and precisely squared on each of its
corners ready to be dropped into its socket on the base, Saer
Credine cut some marks which puzzled me – they looked like
scratches, twenty or thirty of them. He made them after the other
workmen had left, and he must have thought himself unobserved
when he took his chisel and lightly chipped the lines across one of
the corners. He made the marks so delicately that they could hardly
be seen. Indeed, once the shaft was set into its socket hole the lines
would be buried. Had I not observed him doing the work, I would
not have known where to look, but I glimpsed him stooping over
the stone, fine chisel in hand. When he had gone home I went to
where he had been working and tried to puzzle out what he had
been doing. The lines were certainly nothing that the abb and his
monks had ordered. At first I thought they might be rune writing,
but they were not. The lines were much simpler than the runes

with which I was familiar. They were straight scratches, some long, some short, some in small clusters and several at a slant. They had been cut so that some were on one face of the squared-off stone, others on the adjacent face, and a few actually straddled both faces. I was completely baffled. After gazing at them for some time, I wondered if I was missing any hidden details. I tried running my fingertips over the scratches and could feel the marks, but they still made no sense. From the ashes of the midday cooking fire, I took a lump of charcoal and, laying a strip of cloth over the corner of the shaft, I rubbed the charcoal on the cloth to reproduce the pattern on the material. I had peeled the cloth away from the stone and laid it out flat on the ground so that I could kneel down and study it, when I became aware of someone watching me. Standing in the shelter of one of the monks' huts was Saer Credine. He had not gone back to his house, which was his usual custom, but must have returned to check on the final details for the stone shaft which was to be erected next day.

'What are you doing?' he demanded as he walked towards me. I had never heard him so gruff before. It was too late to hide the marked strip of cloth as I scrambled to my feet.

'I was trying to understand the marks on the cross shaft,' I stammered. I could feel my face going bright red.

'What do you mean "understand"?' the stonemason growled.

'I thought it was some sort of rune writing,' I confessed.

Saer Credine seemed surprised as well as doubtful. 'You know rune writing?' he asked. I nodded. 'Come with me,' he stated bluntly and set off at a brisk walk, crossing the slope of the hill to the site where many of the monks had been buried, as well as visitors who had died on pilgrimage to the holy place. The hillside was dotted with their memorial stones. But it was not a monk's last resting place that interested Saer Credine. He stopped in front of a low, flat, marker stone, set deep in the ground. Its upper surface had been carved with symbols.

'What does that say?' he demanded. I did not hesitate with my reply. The inscription was uncomplicated and whoever had cut it used a simple, plain form of the futhark. 'In the memory of Ingjald,' I replied and then ventured an opinion, 'he was probably a Norseman or a Gael who died while he was visiting the monastery.'

'Most of the Norse who came to visit this place didn't get a memorial stone,' the stonemason grunted. 'They came upriver in their longships to plunder the place and usually burned it to the ground, except for the stone buildings, that is.'

I said nothing, but stood waiting to see what my master would do next. It was in Saer Credine's power to have me severely punished for touching the cross shaft. A mere slave, and a heathen at that, who touched the abb's precious monument could merit a whipping.

'So where did you learn the runes?' Saer Credine asked.

'In Iceland and before that in Greenland and in a place called Vinland,' I replied. 'I had good teachers, so I learned several forms, old and new, and some of the variant letters.'

'So I have an assistant who can read and write, at least in his own way,' said the stonemason wonderingly. He seemed satisfied with my explanation, and walked back with me to where his great cross shaft lay on its trestles. Picking up the nub of charcoal I had left behind, he searched for a flat piece of wood, then shaved a straight edge with his chisel.

'I know a few of the rune signs, and I've often wondered whether the runes and my own writing are related. But I've never had a chance to compare them.' He made a series of charcoal marks along its edge. 'Now you,' he said, handing me the wooden stick and the charcoal. 'Those are the letters I and my forebears have used through the generations. You write your letters, your futhark or whatever you call it.'

Directly above my master's marks I scratched out the futhark that Tyrkir had taught me so long ago. As the letters formed I could see that they bore no resemblance to the stonemason's writing. The shapes of my runes were much more complicated, cut at angles and sometimes turning back on themselves. Also there were several more of them than the number of Saer Credine's

letters. When I had finished copying, I handed the stick back to
Saer Credine and he shook his head.

'Ogmius himself could not read that,' he said.

'Ogmius?' It was a name I had not heard before.

'He's also called Honey Mouth or Sun Face. Depends who you
are talking to. He's got several names, but he's always the God of
writing,' he said, 'He taught mankind how to write. Which is why
we call our script the ogham.'

'It was Odinn who acquired the secret of writing, according to
my instructors, so perhaps that is why the two systems are different,' I ventured. 'Two different Gods, two different scripts.' Our
conversation made me feel bolder. 'What is it that you wrote on
the cross shaft?' I asked.

'My name and the name of my father and my grandfather,' he
replied. 'It has always been the custom of my family. We carve the
scenes that men like Abb Aidan decide for us, and we take pride in
such work and we do it as well as our gifts allow. But in the end
our loyalty goes back much farther, to those who gave the skill to
our hands and who would take away that skill if we did not pay
proper respect. So that is why we leave our mark as Ogmius
taught. The day that this cross is set in the foundation stone I will
leave him a small offering beneath the shaft in thanks.'

Saer Credine gave me no hint of what he must have decided
that evening when he learned that I could read and write the runes.

Three days later I received word that Brother Senesach wanted
to speak with me. I knew Brother Senesach by sight and reputation.
He was a genial and vigorous man, perhaps in his fifties. I had seen
him frequently, striding around the monastery grounds, ruddy-
faced and always with an air of unhurried purpose. I knew that he
was in charge of the education of the younger monks, and that he
was popular with them on account of his good nature and his
obvious concern for their well-being.

'Come in,' Senesach called out as I paused nervously at the
doorway of his little cell. He lived in a small hut made of wattle
and daub and furnished with a desk, a writing stool and a palliasse.

'Our master stonemason tells me that you can read and write, and that you take an interest in your surroundings.' He looked at me keenly, noting my ragged shift and the marks left on my wrists by the manacles from Clontarf. 'He also says that you are hard-working and good with your hands, and suggested that you might one day become a valuable member of our community. What do you think?'

I was so surprised that I could scarcely think what to reply.

'It's not only the sons of the well-to-do who join us,' Senesach went on. 'In fact we have a tradition of encouraging young men of talent. With their skills they often contribute more to our community than the material gifts which the richer recruits bring.'

'I'm very grateful for your thoughtfulness and to Saer Credine for his kind words,' I replied, seeking to gain a moment's thinking space. 'I have never even imagined such a life. I suppose my first worry is that I am not worthy to devote my life to the service of Christ.'

'Few newcomers to our community are completely certain of their calling when they first arrive, and if they are, that is something of which I personally would be rather wary,' he answered gently. 'Anyhow, humility is a good place to start from. Besides, no one would expect you to become a fully observant monk for years. You would begin as a trainee and under my instruction learn the ways of our brotherhood, as scores have done before you.'

It was a suggestion which no slave could possibly have turned down. I had no one to pay a ransom for me, I was far from the places where I had grown up, and until a moment ago I had no prospects. Suddenly I was being offered an identity, a home and a defined future.

'I've already talked to the abb about your case,' Senesach continued, 'and although he was not very enthusiastic to begin with, he agreed that you should have a chance to prove your worth. He did say, however, that you might find that being a servant of God was more demanding than being slave to a stone-cutter.'

It occurred to me that perhaps Odinn had at last observed my plight and arranged this sudden opportunity. 'Of course I shall be happy to join the monastery in whatever capacity you think fit,' I said.

'Excellent. According to Saer Credine your name was Thorgils or Thorgeis, something like that. Much too heathen sounding. You had better have a new name, a Christian one. Any suggestions?'

I thought for a moment before replying, and then – silently acknowledging Odinn the Deceiver – I said, 'I would like to be called Thangbrand, if that is possible. It is the name of the first missionary to bring the White Christ's teachings to Iceland, which is where my people came from.'

'Well, no one else here has got a name like that. So Thangbrand it will be from now on, and we'll try to make it appropriate. Maybe you will be able to go back one day to Iceland to preach there.'

'Yes, sir,' I mumbled.

'Yes, Brother. Not sir. And we don't talk of the White Christ here, it is simply Christ or Jesus Christ, or Our Lord and Saviour,' he answered, with such sincerity that I felt a little ashamed. I hoped he would never discover that Thangbrand had failed completely in his battle against the Old Ways.

As the abb had warned, the physical life of a young novitiate at St Ciaran's monastery was little different from my days working for Saer Credine. I found that my previous chores as a slave were mirrored in my duties as a trainee monk. Instead of sweeping up the stonemason's chippings, I swept out the senior monks' cells and emptied their slops. In place of hammer and chisel, I grasped a hoe and spent hours stooped and hacking away at the rocky soil in the fields which my brethren and I prepared for planting. Even my clothing was much the same: previously I had worn a loose tunic of poor stuff held in at the waist with a bit of string. Now I had a slightly better tunic of unbleached linen with a waist cord, and a grey woollen cloak with a hood to go over it. Only my feet felt different. Previously barefoot, now I wore sandals. The major change was in discipline and for the worse. As a slave I was expected to rise at dawn and work all day, with a break for a midday meal if I was lucky, then curl up for a good night's rest so that I would be fit and strong for the next day's labour. A monk, I found, got far less rest. He had to rise before dawn to say his prayers, work in the fields or at his desk, repeat his prayers at regular intervals, and often went to bed far more exhausted than a slave. Even his diet was little consolation. A slave might be inadequately fed, but the monk ate coarse food that was little better. Worse than that, he often had to fast and go hungry. Wednesdays and Fridays were both fast days at St Ciaran's, and the younger ones among us ate double portions of food on Thursday, if we could.

But none of this mattered. Senesach's benevolence threw open the door of learning, and I walked in and revelled in the experience. As a slave I had been credited with the mind of a slave and offered only the knowledge that was relevant to my work – how best to scour a cooking pot with sand, stack a pile of turf, straighten a warped plough handle by soaking it in hot water. Now as a monk in preparation I was offered schooling in an extraordinary range of skills. It began, of course, with the requirement to learn to read and write the Roman script. Senesach produced a practice book, two wax tablets held in a small wooden folder, and he drew for me the letters, scratching them with a metal stylus. I think that even Senesach was astonished that it took me less than three days to learn the entire alphabet, and that I was writing coherent and reasonably well-spelt sentences within the same week. Perhaps my mind was like a muscle already exercised and well developed when I learned the rune writing and the rune lore – of which I said nothing – and had gone slack from disuse. Now all it needed was sharp stimulus and practice. My fellow students, as well as my teachers, soon came to consider me something of a prodigy when it came to the written or the spoken word. Maybe my combination of Norse and Irish ancestry, both peoples who relish the rhythms of language, also accounted for my fluency. In less than six months I was reading and writing Church Latin and was halfway to a working knowledge of French, which I was learning from a brother who had lived in Gaul for several years. Both the German tongue and the language of the English posed little difficulty, for they were close enough in pronunciation and vocabulary to my own donsk tong for me to understand what was said. By my second year I was also reading Greek.

My talent with words kept me on the right side of Abb Aidan. I had the feeling that he was waiting for me to falter and disgrace myself, but he could only acknowledge that I was among the star pupils of the community when it came to that prime requirement of memory – the learning of the psalter. There were some one hundred and fifty psalms and they were our chief form of prayer, chanted at holy service. Normally it took years for a monk to have the entire psalter word-perfect, and most of my contemporaries knew only the most popular psalms, those that we repeated again and again. But for some reason I found that I could remember almost every word and line more or less at the first hearing, so I found myself singing out the verses, line by line, while most of my colleagues were mumbling or merely joining in the refrain. My memory for the psalms was uncanny, though, as someone remarked, it was closer to the devil's work because, although I could remember the words, my singing of them was discordant and grating and offended the ears.

My new-found mastery of the Roman script meant that I was able to soak up all manner of information from the written page, though at first it was difficult to gain access to the monastic library because Brother Ailbe, the librarian, believed that books were more valuable than the people who read them, and he discouraged readers. In a way he was justified, as I came to appreciate when I was assigned to labour in the scriptorium. The manuscripts in his care were the glory of St Ciaran's and exceedingly valuable, even in the physical sense. The skins of more than a hundred calves were required to make sufficient vellum for a single large volume, and in a land where wealth is counted in cattle this is a prodigious investment. Eventually Brother Ailbe did come to trust me enough to let me browse the shelves where the books were stored and I found most of the volumes were Holy Scripture, mainly copies of the Gospels with their canon tables, breves causae and argumenta and paschal texts. But there were also writings from classical authors such as Virgil, Horace and Ovid, and works of Christian poetry by writers such as Prudentius and Ausonius. My favourite was a book of geography written by a Spanish monk named Isidore, and I spent hours dreaming of the exotic lands he described, little knowing that one day I would have the chance to see many of them for myself. I had a magpie's facility to select and carry away bright scraps of unrelated information in my head, and my erratic robbery from these solemn texts quickly irritated my teachers, the older and more learned monks who were assigned to give the novices their classes in such subjects as history, law and mathematics.

As novices, we were expected not just to acquire knowledge, but also to preserve and transmit its most precious elements, namely the Holy Scripture. That meant copying. We were issued once again with the wax tablets from which we had learned the alphabet, and shown how to form our letter with the help of a metal stylus and ruler. Over and over again, we practised, until we were deemed fit to mark the surface of reused vellum, over-writing the faint and faded lines left by earlier scribes until we had the gist of it. At that stage we were mixing our own ink from lamp black or chimney soot. Only when we could write a perfect diminuendo, starting with a large initial letter and then progressively writing smaller and smaller along the line, until the eye could scarcely distinguish the individual letters, were the most deft of us permitted to work on fresh vellum. It was then I appreciated why the monastery needed a never-ending supply of younger monks for the famed scriptorium just as much as it needed flocks of calves and lambs to produce the vellum skins. Young animals provided unblemished skin, and young monks provided sharper eyes. Our finest copyists were men of early to middle age, deft, clear-eyed and with remarkable artistic imaginations.

Strangely, the materials designed to please the eye remain in my memory according to their smells. The raw calfskins had been steeped in a fetid concoction of animal dung and water to loosen the hairs so they could be scraped off easily, and they gave off a pulpy, fleshy odour while stabilising in a wash of lime. Oak galls had a bitter stink when crushed to provide our best red ink, and as for greens and blues I still smell the sea whenever I see those colours. They were made by squeezing out the juice from certain shellfish found on the rocks. We then left the liquid to fester in the sun, which made the extract alter from green, to blue, to purple, all the while giving off the pungent smell of rotting bladderwrack. It complemented the fishy odour of the fish oil we employed to bind the ink.

The transformation of these reeking originals to such beauty on the page was a miracle in itself. I was never an outstanding copyist or illustrator, but I acquired enough of the techniques to appreciate the skill involved. Observing one of our finest illuminators decorate the initial letter of a Gospel would make me hold my breath in sympathy in case he made a slip. He required a steady hand as well as the finest brush – the hair from the inside of a squirrel's ear was favoured for the most delicate work – and a rare combination of imagination and geometric skill to interweave the lacing patterns that twined and curved like tendrils of some unearthly plant. Curiously, I was reminded of the patterns that I had seen – it seemed so long ago – carved on the curling stem post of King Sigtryggr's royal ship when he sailed from Orkney. How or why the patterns, Christian initial and Viking prow, were so similar I did not know. What was even stranger was that so many of the bookish trellis patterns ended in a snarling figurehead. That I could understand on the high bow of a ship of war, designed to frighten the enemy, but how the motif was found in a book of Holy Scripture was beyond my understanding. Still, it was not a topic on which I dwelt. The extent of my contribution in penmanship was to write the occasional line in black, using the tiny script which Abb Aidan favoured because it meant more words could be squeezed on each expensive square inch of vellum, and I was delegated to fill in the red dots and lozenges which were liberally scattered across the page as decoration. This kept me occupied for hours as they could number in the hundreds on a single page.

It would be wrong if I gave the impression that my life as a novice monk was spent in the fields, the schoolroom or the scriptorium. Religious instruction was severe and unfortunately was the responsibility of Brother Eoghan, who was at the opposite remove from the kindly Brother Senesach. Brother Eoghan's appearance was deceptive. He looked benign. Rotund and jovial-seeming, he had dark hair and very dark eyes that seemed to gleam with a humorous twinkle. He even had a booming, cheerful-sounding voice. But any of his pupils who presumed upon his good nature were quickly disillusioned. Brother Eoghan had a vicious temper and a grinding sense of self-righteousness. He taught not through reason, but strictly by rote. We were required to memorise page after page of the Gospels and the writings of the Church Fathers, and he tested us on our acquisition of the texts. His favoured technique was to pick out an individual in his class, demand a recitation, and when the victim stammered or erred, to suddenly turn to another student and shout at him to continue. Terrified, the second performer was sure to make a mistake, and then Brother Eoghan would swoop. Seizing the two novices, each by his hair, our tutor would complete the quotation himself, grinding out the words through gritted teeth, his face set grimly, and punctuating each phrase by banging together the two heads with a steady thump.

Every novice, and there were about thirty of us, reacted in his own way to the unyielding world in which we found ourselves. Most were meekly acquiescent and followed the rules and routines laid down. Only a handful were genuinely enthusiastic for the monkish life. One young man – his name was Enda and he was a little simple – sought to model himself on the Desert Fathers. Without informing anyone, he climbed to the top of the round tower. This was St Ciaran's most spectacular edifice, a slim spike of stone which had been a lookout in the days of the Viking raids, but now mostly used as a bell tower. Enda clambered to the very top, where, naturally, he was out of sight from the ground, and sat there for four days and four nights while the rest of us searched for him uselessly. It was only when we heard his weak calls for a supply of bread and water and saw the end of a rope he had lowered down – he had misjudged the height and his rope was dangling far too short – that we knew where he was. Brother Senesach organised a rescue party, and we clambered up and retrieved Enda, who by then was too feeble to move. He was taken to the infirmary and left there to recover, but the experience seemed to have left him even weaker in the head. I never knew what finally became of him, but in all likelihood he became a monk.

EIGHTEEN

I MADE ONLY one real friend among my fellow novices in the two years I spent at St Ciaran's. Colman had been sent there by his father, a prosperous farmer. Apparently the farmer had prayed to St Ciaran for relief when a severe cattle murrain had affected his herd. As a remedy he had smeared his sick animals with a paste made from earth scraped from the floor of the saint's oratory. When the cattle all recovered, the farmer was so grateful that he enrolled the lad – the least promising of his six sons – with the monks as a thank offering for the saint's beneficial intervention. Solid and reliable, Colman stood by me when the other novices, jealous that I outshone them in the classroom, ganged up to bully me about my own alien origins. I repaid Coleman's loyalty by helping him with his studies – he was something of a plodder when it came to book learning – and the two of us made an effective team when it came to breaking the bounds of monastic discipline.

Our dormitory huts were situated on the northern side of the monastery grounds, and at night the bolder ones among us would sometimes scramble over the monastery bank to see what the outside world was like. Slinking among the houses that had grown up around St Ciaran's, we watched from the shadows how ordinary people lived, eavesdropped on quarrels and conversations heard through the thin walls of their dwellings, listened to the cries of

babies, the drinking songs and the snores. We were discreet because
there were townsfolk who would report our presence to the abb
if they saw us. When that happened the punishment was harsh.
Spending three or four hours flat on your face on the earth floor
reciting penances was the least of it. Worse was to be made to
stand with your arms outstretched as a living cross until the joints
creaked with pain, supervised by one of the more callous senior
brothers, while reciting, over and over again, 'I beseech pardon of
God,' 'I believe in the Trinity,' 'May I receive mercy.' Little mercy
was available. One of the novices, reported for the second time for
a nocturnal excursion, received two hundred lashes with a scourge.

A short walk from the monastery was a small stone-built
chapel, sheltering in a wood. No one knew who had built it there
or why. The monks at St Ciaran's denied any knowledge of its
origins. The place was nothing to do with them, and they never
went there. The little chapel was abandoned and falling into
disrepair and housed, as we discovered, a hidden attraction. Which
novice first found the lewd sculpture, I do not know. It must have
been someone with remarkably sharp eyesight, for the carved stone
was tucked away among the stones forming the entry to the chapel,
and under normal circumstances it would have been invisible.
Whoever found the carving mentioned it to his friends and they in
turn passed on the knowledge to other students, so that it became
a sort of talisman. We called the stone the Sex Hag, and most of
us, at some stage, crept down to the chapel to gaze at it. The
carving was as grotesque as any of the strange and leering beasts
which appeared in our illuminations. It showed a older and naked
woman, with three pendulous breasts sagging from a rugged rib-
cage. She was seated with her legs apart and knees open, facing the
observer. With her hands she was pulling apart the lips of her
private entry and on her face was a seraphic smile. The effect was
both erotic and demonic.

Of course, there was a good deal of salacious talk inspired by
the Sex Hag's revelations, but for the most part it was ignorant
speculation as we had few occasions to meet any women. Indeed

the frightening posture of the Sex Hag acted as a deterrent. Several of the novices were so disturbed and repelled by the graphic quality of the carving that I doubt they ever touched a woman thereafter.

The same cannot be said for me. I was intensely curious about the opposite sex and spent a good deal of time trying to devise a way of striking up an acquaintance with a female of my own age. This was well-nigh impossible. Our community was all male, and our only regular women visitors were those who came from the nearby settlement to visit the infirmary or to offer prayers at the various oratories. Unfortunately they seldom included anyone who was youthful and nubile. Sometimes a young and unmarried woman was glimpsed among the pilgrims who came to St Ciaran's shrine, and we younger monks would gaze in fascination, telling ourselves there was nothing wrong in our curiosity because the temptation was only momentary as the pilgrims would linger just a few hours, then vanish out of our lives for ever.

It was Brother Ailbe the librarian who, unwittingly, provided me with the long-desired chance to meet a female of my own age. Our keeper of books was so solicitous about the well-being of the precious volumes that he wrapped all the important books in lengths of linen, then stored them in individual leather satchels to protect them from harm. One day he decided that the satchel which contained St Ciaran's own copy of the Bible – the same book which had been paraded before Donnachad on the day I was handed over to the monastery as a slave – needed attention. For any other book in his library Brother Ailbe would have ordered a replacement satchel from the best leather-worker in the town, sending a note with the necessary dimensions of the volume and waiting for the finished satchel to be delivered. But in this case the existing satchel was something very special. It was claimed that St Ciaran himself had sewn the satchel. So there was no question of throwing it away and ordering a new one. Yet the existing satchel was so shabby that it did no honour to the saint's memory, and there was an ugly rip in the leather that cut right across the faint marks which, it was said, were the fingerprints of the saint himself.

Brother Ailbe decided to entrust the repair to a craftsman living in the town, a man by the name of Bladnach, who was a master of the long blind stitch. In this technique the needle, instead of passing straight through the leather, is turned and runs along within the thickness of the skin to emerge some distance away from where it entered so that the thread itself is invisible. But using a long blind stitch on old and brittle leather is a risk. There is only one opportunity to run the needle in. There can be no second chance, no withdrawing the point and trying again, as this destroys the original substance. Yet this is how Brother Ailbe wanted St Ciaran's satchel to be mended so that it would appear to the uneducated eye that the satchel had never been damaged. Bladnach was the only craftsman capable of the work.

Bladnach was a cripple. Born without the full use of his legs, he moved about his workroom on his knuckles, though with remarkable agility. This way of motion had, of course, developed the strength and thickness of his arms and shoulders to an extraordinary degree, and this was no disadvantage for a man who needs all his power to drive a needle through heavy, stiff leather. But Bladnach's disability also meant that it was more logical for Brother Ailbe to bring the damaged book satchel to Bladnach's workshop than for Bladnach to be carried to the monastery each day to make the repairs. Yet St Ciaran's bible satchel was so precious that Ailbe could not possibly leave it unguarded. The librarian's solution was to ask Abb Aidan for permission for someone from the monastery to accompany the satchel to Bladnach's workshop and stay with it until the repair was done. By that time I was a familiar figure in the library, reading my texts, and Brother Ailbe suggested that I would make a suitable envoy. Abb Aidan agreed and stipulated that I was not to live in the leatherworker's house but to live, eat and sleep within the workshop itself, not allowing the satchel out of my sight.

Neither our abb nor our librarian were aware that when it comes to the sewing of the very finest leather, the most elegant stitching of delicate lambskin or the threading of a single twist of flax so fine that you cannot use a needle to insert it but make the merest pinprick of a hole, the work is almost invariably done by a woman. In the case of Bladnach the work was done by his daughter, Orlaith.

How can I describe Orlaith? Even after all these years I feel a slight tightening sensation in my throat as I remember her. She was sixteen and as fine-boned and delicately formed as any woman I have ever seen. Her face was of the most exquisite shape, where delicate cheekbones emphasised the slight hollows of the cheeks themselves and the gentle sweep of her jaw led to a small and perfect chin. She had a short, straight nose, a flawless mouth and the most enormous dark brown eyes. Her hair was chestnut, yet you could mistake it for being black, and it made an almost unreal contrast with her pale skin. By any standards she was a truly beautiful woman, and she took meticulous care with her appearance. I never saw her with a hair out of place or wearing a garment that was not perfectly cleaned and pressed and selected for its colours. But the strangest thing of all is that, when I first laid eyes on her, I did not think her beautiful. I was shown into her father's workshop, where she sat at her bench stitching a woman's belt, and I barely gave her a second glance. I utterly failed to appreciate her stunning beauty. She seemed almost ordinary. Yet within a day I was captivated by her. There was something about the fragile grace in the curve of her forearm as she leaned forward to take up a thread of flax, or the flowing subtlety of her body as she rose to her feet and walked across the room, which had me in thrall. She stepped as delicately as a fawn.

She was in the early bloom of her womanhood and responsive to my admiration. She was also, as I later understood, in despair for a private reason and that made her all the more alert to the chance of happiness. There was little that either of us could do during those first few days to progress our feelings. It took her father a week to mend the precious satchel, most of the time being spent applying coat after coat of warmed wool grease to soften and restore the desiccated leather. There was nothing for me to do but sit in the workroom, watching father and daughter at their work, trying to make myself useful in small ways. When Orlaith left the room for any reason, the room seemed to lose its colour and turn lifeless, and I would ache for her return just to be close to her, sensing her presence so powerfully that it was almost as if we were in physical contact. Two or three times we managed to speak to one another, awkward, shy words, each of us stumbling and mumbling, sentences fading away and left unfinished, both of us fearful of making a mistake. But these stilted conversations were only possible when Bladnach was out of the room, which happened rarely as it was a great effort for him to swing on his knuckles, hauling his useless lower limbs as he left the workshop to go to relieve himself. All three of us took our meals together, Orlaith fetching the food from her mother's cooking fire. We would sit in the workroom, eating in quiet, shared company, and I am sure that Bladnach was alert to what was happening between his daughter and myself, but he chose to ignore it. I suspect that he too wanted his daughter to have some happiness in her life. With his own disability he knew how to value any small chance that occurred.

When the satchel was repaired, Bladnach sent word to the monastery, and our librarian came down to collect the precious relic. As Brother Ailbe and I walked back to the monastery, my heart was close to bursting. On that last morning Orlaith had whispered a suggestion that we try to meet a week later. She had grown up around St Ciaran's, where all the sharp-eyed children knew about the novice monks and how they came out at nights to spy on the community. So she proposed that we meet at a certain spot outside the monastery vallum a week later, soon after nightfall. She thought that she could slip quietly out of the house and she would be free for an hour or two, if I could meet her there. This first tryst was to become a defining moment in my lifetime's memories. It was a night in early spring and there were a few stars and enough light from a sliver of new moon for me to see her standing in the darker pool of shadow cast by an ash tree. I approached, trembling slightly, aware even of the scent given off by her clothing. She reached out and touched my hand in the darkness and gently drew me towards her. It was the most natural, most marvellous and most tender moment that I could ever have imagined. To hold her, to feel her warmth, the yielding softness of her flesh and the wondrous life and structure of her fine bones within my arms was a sensation that made me dizzy with elation.

For the next weeks I felt as if I was sleep-walking through my daily routines of prayer and lessons, the sessions in the scriptorium and the hours spent labouring in the fields. My thoughts dwelt constantly on Orlaith. She was everywhere. I placed her in a thousand imaginary situations, speculating on her gestures, her words, her presence. And when I came back to reality, it was only to calculate where she was at that particular moment, what she was doing, and how long it might be before I held her in my arms again. My trust in Odinn, which had begun to falter among so much Christian fervour, came surging back. I asked myself who else but Odinn could have arranged such a wondrous development in my life. Odinn, among all the Gods, understood the yearnings of the human heart. He it was who rewarded those who fell in battle with the company of beautiful women in Valholl.

I should have been more wary. Odinn's gifts, as I knew full well, often conceal a bitter core.

Our love affair lasted nearly four months before catastrophe arrived. Every one of our clandestine meetings produced intoxicating happiness. They were preceded by a giddy sense of anticipation, then followed by a numbing glow of fulfilment. Our meetings became all we lived for. Nothing else mattered. Sometimes, returning through the darkness from the tryst, I found it difficult to keep walking in a straight line. It was not the darkness which confused me, but the physical sense of being so happy. Of course, the three companion novices who shared our sleeping hut noticed my night-time excursions. At first they said nothing, but after a couple of weeks there were some approving and slightly wistful comments, and I knew there was little risk of betrayal from that direction. My friend Colman stood by me one night, when an older monk noticed

I was missing. It was Colman who made some plausible excuse for my absence. As spring passed into summer – it was now the second year of my time as a novice – I grew bolder. My nocturnal meetings with Orlaith were not enough. I thirsted to see her by day, and I managed to persuade Brother Ailbe that two more satchels might need the leather-worker's attention. They were humdrum items of little value, and I offered to take them to Bladnach's workshop for his inspection, to which the librarian agreed.

My reception when I arrived at Bladnach's workshop was deeply unsettling. There was an awkward atmosphere in the workshop, a sense of strain. It showed on the face of Orlaith's mother as she greeted me at the door, and it was repeated in Orlaith's response to my arrival. She turned away when I entered the workshop and I saw that she had been crying. Her father, normally so quiet, treated me with unaccustomed coldness. I handed over the two satchels, explained what needed to be done and left the house, puzzled and distressed.

At the next meeting by the ash tree I asked Orlaith about the reason for the strange atmosphere in the house. For several harrowing moments she would not tell me why she had been crying, nor why her parents had been in such evident discomfort, and I came close to despair, faced with some unimaginable dread. I continued to press her for an answer, and eventually she blurted out the truth. It seemed that for many years both her parents had needed regular medical treatment. Her father's deformity racked his joints, and her mother's hands had been damaged by years of helping her husband at the leather-worker's bench. The smallest finger on each of her hands was permanently curved inward from the strain of tugging on thread to pull it tight, and her hands had become little more than painful claws. Initially they had used home-made remedies, gathering herbs and preparing simples. But as they aged these medicines had less and less effect. Eventually they had presented themselves at the monastery's infirmary, where Domnall, the elderly brother who worked as a physician, had been very helpful. He had made up draughts and ointments which had worked what seemed a genuine miracle, and the leather-worker and his wife were deeply grateful. In the years that followed, they began to made regular visits, every two or three months in summer and more frequently in winter when the pains were worse. Blad-nach would be carried to the monastery on a plank, and it was on one of his early visits that he first came to Brother Ailbe's attention and received his initial commission to work on the library satchels.

But Brother Domnall had paid for his selfless work at the infirmary with his life. A yellow plague had swept through the district, and the physician had been infected by the invalids who came to him for help. Willingly he made the final sacrifice, and the running of the infirmary had passed to his assistant, Brother Cainnech.

When Orlaith mentioned the yellow plague and Cainnech's name, my heart plummeted. I knew all about the yellow plague. It had struck in the late winter, and to my sorrow it had carried off the stoneworker Saer Credine. His commission from the abb, the grand cross, still stood half finished as there was no one skilled enough to complete the carving. The yellow plague had left Brother Cainnech as our new physician in its wake, and there were many in the monastery who considered that he was a reminder of the pestilence. Brother Cainnech was a clumsy, coarse boor who seemed to enjoy hurting people under the pretext of helping them. Among the novices it was generally considered preferable to endure a minor broken bone or a deep gash than let Cainnech near it. He seemed to enjoy causing pain as he reset the bone or cleaned out the wound. Often we thought that he was under the influence of alcohol, for he had the blotched skin and stinking breath of a man who drank heavily. Yet no one doubted his medical knowledge. He had read the medical texts in Brother Ailbe's library, spent his apprenticeship as Domnall's assistant, and stepped naturally into the chief physician's role. After the outbreak of the yellow fever it was Cainnech who insisted that every scrap of our bedding, blankets and clothes were thrown on a bonfire, leading me to wonder if this is what my mother had intended at Frodriver when she had insisted that her bedding be burned.

One day, Orlaith told me, she had accompanied her father and mother on their regular visit to the infirmary for their treatment and she had come to Cainnech's attention. The following month Cainnech informed her parents that it was no longer necessary for them to come to the infirmary. Instead he would call at their house, to bring a fresh supply of medicines and administer any treatment. It would save Bladnach the difficult trip to the monastery. Cainnech's decision seemed a selfless act, worthy of his predecessor. But the motive for it soon became clear. On the very first visit to Bladnach's home, Cainnech began to make approaches to Orlaith. He was shamelessly confident. He presumed on the complicity of her parents, making it clear to them that if they thwarted his visits or hindered his behaviour while in their home, they would not be welcome back at the infirmary for treatment. He also emphasised to Bladnach that if he complained to the abb, there would be no further work from the library. Cainnech's visits quickly became a frightening combination of good and harm. He always remained the conscientious physician. He would arrive at the house punctually, examine his two patients, provide their medicaments, make careful notes of their condition, give them sound medical advice. Under his care both Bladnach and his wife found their health improving. But as soon as the medical consultation was over, Cainnech would dismiss the parents from the workshop and insist that he be left alone with their daughter. It was hardly surprising that Orlaith felt she could not divulge to me what went on during the sessions when she was shut up with the monk; she had never told her parents. What made the nightmare even worse, for both Orlaith and her parents, was Cainnech's absolute certainty that he could repeat his predatory behaviour for as long as he liked. As he left the house, leaving an abused Orlaith weeping in the workshop, he would pause solicitously beside Bladnach and assure him that he would return within the month to see how his patient was progressing.

Orlaith's wretched story made me all the more passionate about her. For the rest of that dreadful rendezvous, I held her close to me, feeling both protective and helpless. On the one hand I was outraged, on the other I was numbed by an acute sense of shared hurt.

Worse followed. Even more anxious to see Orlaith, I risked visiting the leather-worker's house in broad daylight, pretending that I was on an errand for the library. No one stopped me. The following week I repeated my foolhardy mission and found Orlaith by herself at her workbench. For an hour we sat side by side, mutely holding hands, until I knew I had to leave and get back to the monastery before my absence was noticed. I was aware that my luck would eventually run out, but I felt powerless to do anything else. I was so desperate to find a solution, I even suggested to Orlaith that we should run away together, but she dismissed the idea out of hand. She would not leave her parents, particularly her invalid father, who depended on her skill with the fine needle now that her mother was unable to work.

So it was an irony that her mother, unintentionally, caused the calamity. She came with a group of her friends to the monastery to pray at the oratory of St Ciaran. As she was leaving the oratory, she chanced to meet Brother Ailbe and mentioned to him how much she appreciated his continuing to send me to her house to assist her husband. Of course, Brother Ailbe was puzzled by this remark, and that evening sent for me to come to the library. He was standing beside his reading desk as I entered, and I thought he was looking slightly pompous and full of his own authority.

'Were you at the house of Bladnach the leather-worker last week?' he asked in a flat tone.

'Yes, Brother Ailbe,' I answered. I knew that I had been seen by the townsfolk on my way there and that the librarian could easily check.

'What were you doing? Did you have permission from anyone to go there, away from the monastery?'

'No, Brother Ailbe,' I replied. 'I went on my own initiative. I wanted to ask the leather-worker if he could teach me some of his

craft. In that way I thought I could learn how to repair our leather
Bible satchels here in the monastery, and then there would be no
need to pay someone for outside skills.' My answer was a good
one. I saw from Ailbe's expression that he anticipated a favourable
response if he put the same proposal to the abb. Anything which
saved the monastery money was a welcome suggestion to our abb.

'Very well,' he said, 'The idea has merit. But you broke our
rule by leaving the monastery without authorisation. In future you
are not to visit the town without first asking permission from me
or from one of the other senior monks. You are to make amends
by going to the chapel and reciting psalm one hundred and nineteen
in its entirety, kneeling and cross figel.'

He made a gesture dismissing me. But I stood my ground. It
was not because the punishment was severe, though the hundred
and nineteenth psalm is notoriously long and would make the cross
figel – kneeling with arms outstretched – very painful. I faced
down the librarian because a strange and wild spirit of rebellion
and superiority was welling up within me. I was overcome with
scorn for Brother Ailbe for being so gullible. It had been so easy
to dupe him. 'I just told you a lie,' I said and I did not bother to
hide the contempt in my voice. 'I did not go to the leather-
worker's house to ask to be his apprentice. I went there to be with
his daughter.' Brother Ailbe, who had been looking rather smug,
gaped with surprise, his mouth open and closed without making a
sound, and I turned on my heel and left the room. As I did so, I
knew that I had irreversibly destroyed my own life. There was no
going back on what I had said.

Months later I realised that the spirit of defiance which had
overwhelmed me had came from Odinn. It was his odr, the frenzy
which throws aside caution and pays no heed to sense or prudence.

As I walked away from the library, I knew that I would be
severely punished for breaking monastery discipline, above all for
consorting with a female. That was the worst offence of all as far
as the senior monks were concerned. But I found some consolation
in the thought that at least I had brought Bladnach and his family

to the attention of Abb Aidan, and it would be unlikely that Cainnech would risk continuing his abuse of their daughter until the scandal of my behaviour had died down. Maybe he would be warned off for ever.

I underestimated Cainnech's viciousness. He must have realised that, through Orlaith, I knew about his degenerate behaviour, and he decided that I should be put out of the way for good. That evening Abb Aidan called a conclave of the senior monks to discuss my fate. The meeting was held in the abb's cell and lasted for several hours. Rather to my surprise, there was no immediate decision on my punishment, nor was I called to give an explanation for my actions. Very late in the evening my friend Colman whispered to me that Senesach wanted to see me, and I was to go, not to his cell, but to the small, newly built oratory on the south side of the monastery. When I arrived, Senesach was waiting for me. He looked so despondent that I felt wretched. I owed so much to him. Yet I had failed to live up to his hopes for me. It was Senesach – it seemed so long ago – who had persuaded the abb that I should be released from slavery as the stonemason's assistant and given a chance to train as a monk, and Senesach had always been a fair and reasonable teacher. I was sure that if anyone had argued my case for me during the discussion of my transgressions, it would have been Senesach.

'Thangbrand,' he began, 'I don't have time to discuss with you why you chose to do what you did. But it is evident that you are not suited for life within the community of St Ciaran's. For that I am heartily sorry. I hope one day you will regain your original humility enough to pray for forgiveness for what you have done. I have asked you here for another reason. During the discussion of your misbehaviour, Brother Ailbe spoke up to say that he believed you may be a thief as well as a fornicator. He claimed that several pages are missing from the library copy of Galen's *De Usum Partium*, which you were studying as an exercise to improve your Greek. Did you steal those pages?'

'No, I did not,' I replied. 'I looked at the manuscript, but the

pages were already missing when I consulted the text.' I had a
shrewd suspicion who would have stolen them: Galen's writings
were the standard authority for our medical work, and I wondered
if Cainnech had taken the missing pages – as monastery physician
he had regular and unquestioned access to the volume – and then
drawn the librarian's attention to their absence.

Senesach went on, 'There was another complaint, a more
serious one. Brother Cainnech' – and here my heart sank as usual
– 'has raised the possibility that you have a Satanic possession. He
pointed out that your association with the leather-worker's daughter has a precedent. When you first came to us you said your name
was Thorgils, and we have learned that you were captured at the
great battle at Clontarf against the Norsemen. Another Thorgils
defiled this monastery in the time of our forefathers. He too came
from the north lands. He arrived with his great fleet of warships
and terrorised our people. He was an outright heathen and he
brought with him his woman, a harlot by the name of Ota. After
Thorgils's troops captured the monastery, this Ota seated herself
on the altar and before an audience she uttered prophesies and
disported herself lewdly.'

Despite the seriousness of my situation, an image of the Sex
Hag sprang into my mind and I could not help smiling,

'Why do you have that stupid grin on your face?' Senesach
said angrily. His disappointment in me came boiling to the surface.
'Don't you understand the gravity of your situation? If either of
these accusations is found to be true, you will suffer the same fate
as that stupid fool who ran off with the relics a couple of years
ago. You can be sure of that. I've never told anyone this before,
but when our abb condemned that youngster to death, I broke my
vow of unquestioning obedience to my abb's wishes, and asked
him to reduce the penalty. You know what he replied? He said
that St Colm Cille himself was banished from this country by his
abb because he was found guilty of copying a book without the
owner's permission. Stealing the pages themselves, our abb told
me, was a far worse crime because the misdeed permanently

deprived the owner. So he insisted that the culprit had to suffer the greater penalty.'

'I am truly sorry that I have distressed you,' I answered. 'Neither accusation has any truth in it, and I will await the judgement of Abb Aidan. You have always been kind to me and, whatever happens, I will always remember that fact.'

The finality in my tone must have caught Senesach's attention, for he looked at me closely and said nothing for several seconds. 'I will pray for you,' he said and, after genuflecting to the altar, he turned and strode out of the chapel. I heard the brisk footfalls of his sandals as he marched away, the last memory of the man who had given me the chance of bettering myself. That chance I had taken, but it had led me onto a different path.

NINETEEN

I WAS CERTAIN that the conclave would find me guilty. And, as I
had no wish to be left to starve in a pit like my predecessor, that
night I gathered together my few belongings – my monk's
travelling cloak, a workmanlike knife that Saer Credine had given
me, and a sturdy leather travelling pouch that I had made for
myself while sitting in Bladnach's workshop. I clasped Colman's
hand in farewell, then crept out of our dormitory hut and found
my way to the library. I forced the door, and took down the
largest of the bible satchels from where it hung on its peg. I knew
that it contained a ponderous copy of the Gospel of St Matthew.
Sliding the great book out of the case, I took out my knife and
with the point I prised out several of the stones which had been
inset as decoration into the heavy cover. They were four large
rock crystals as large as walnuts, and a red-coloured stone about
the size of a pigeon's egg. The stones were of little value in
themselves. I just wanted to hurt the monastery in the only way I
knew, by stealing something which would cause Abb Aidan a
moment of financial pain. I wrapped my booty in a strip of linen
rag torn from the Gospel's slip cover, and dropped it into my
satchel. Then I made my way to the earth vallum that marked the
monastery boundary, and clambered over it, as I had so many
times before on my way to meet Orlaith.

In my flight I had one single advantage over the wretched runaway novice who had been starved to death in a pit. He had been caught because he had fled back to his tuath, and Abb Aidan had easily guessed his destination. This was the natural course for any fugitive. Among the native Irish the only place that an ordinary man or woman has any security is on the territory of their own tuath, among their own kinsfolk, or on the land of an allied tuath which has agreed mutual recognition of rights. But such rights are worthless when confronted with the power of an important abb capable of making his own laws and regulations. So the fugitive had been handed over meekly by his own people and led away to his death. But I had no tuath. I was a foreigner. I had neither clan nor family nor home. So while everyone's hand was against me, my lack of roots also meant that the abb and his council would have no idea where to send their people to look for me.

For one stupid moment, as I dropped down on the ground on the outer side of the vallum, I thought that I might make a brief visit to Bladnach's house to say goodbye to Orlaith. But I quickly put the idea out of my mind. It would only make matters worse for her. The monks would surely interrogate her and her family about where I might have gone. It was better that they remained ignorant of any details of my departure, even the hour when I had disappeared. Besides, any time spent visiting Orlaith reduced my chances of getting away cleanly. I had already decided that my best route lay to the west and that meant I had to get across the great river before dawn.

St Ciaran's stands on the east bank, on the flank of the hill where the great road follows the line of the ridge then dips down to the river crossing. Here the monks had built a bridge, famous for its length and design. It stood on massive tree trunks driven deep into the soft mud as pilings, and approached by a long causeway laid across the marshy ground. Stout cross-pieces of timber held the main structure together, and the surface was made of layers of planks interleaved with brushwood and laid with rammed earth. Everyone used the bridge. The river was so broad, its banks so soft and treacherous and the currents so unpredictable, especially in the winter and spring floods, that the bridge was the natural choice for any traveller. For this reason the monks maintained a toll keeper on the bridge to collect money for the upkeep of the structure, which needed constant maintenance. Few people travelled at night, but the monastery profited from any surplus income, so Abb Aidan insisted that the toll keeper stayed on duty during the hours of darkness. He lived in a small hut on the eastern side of the bridge.

The events on the beach after the battle at Clontarf had taught me that very few of the Irish know how to swim. Those of our men who had escaped the defeat that day did so by swimming out to the longships, and I had seen how few of the Irish fighters had been able to follow them. Even Brian Boruma's grandson had drowned in the shallows because he was a poor swimmer. By contrast there is hardly a single Norseman who is not taught to swim when he is a boy. It is not just as a matter of survival for a seafaring people. At home in Iceland we considered swimming a sport. Besides the usual swimming races, a favourite game was water wrestling, when the two contestants struggled to hold one another underwater until a victory was declared. Though I was a rather indifferent swimmer by Norse standards, I was positively a human otter when compared to the Irish. Yet my ability to swim was something the monks could not possibly have known. So the bridge, which ought to have proved an obstacle, in fact served me as a friend.

I crept cautiously down to the river bank. A half moon gave enough light for me to select a path. Unfortunately the moonlight was also strong enough for the nightwatchman on the bridge to see me if I attracted his attention. With each step the ground grew softer until I was ankle-deep in the boggy ground. The stagnant water gave off a rich, peaty smell as I gently pulled my feet from the ooze. There was insufficient wind to cover any noise if I blundered so I moved very, very gently, dreading that I would startle a night-nesting bird in the reeds. Very soon I was half walking, half wading. The water was quite warm, and when I was almost out of my depth, I rolled up my travelling cloak and tied it in a bundle with my leather satchel and strapped them both on my back. Then I launched out into the river. I was too cautious to risk swimming the entire width of the river in a single attempt. I knew that my cloak and satchel would soon become a soggy burden, and hamper me. So I swam from piling to piling of the bridge, keeping in the shadow. Each time I reached a piling I hung on quietly, listening for any sounds, feeling the pluck of the current sucking at my body. When I had almost reached the far bank, where the causeway began again, I paused.

This was the riskiest part of the crossing. The west bank of the river was open ground and there was no question of leaving the river here. In the moonlight I would have been in full view. I took a deep breath, submerged, then released my grip. Immediately the current swept me downstream. I lost all sense of direction as I was spun in the eddies. A dozen times I came to the surface for a gulp of air, then let myself sink again. I did not even try to swim. I only surfaced, sucked in air, then used my arms to push myself back underwater. Gradually my strength faded. I knew that I would have to begin to swim again if I was not to drown. The next time I came back to the surface, I glanced up at the moon to find my direction and struck out for the shore. The diving had tired me more than I had anticipated. My arms began to ache, and I wondered if I had left it too late. Cloak and satchel were weighing me down badly. I kept lowering my feet to try to find the ground, only to be disappointed and I was so tired that each time I took a swallow of muddy water. Finally my feet did touch bottom, though it was so soft that I could not support myself, but floundered, lurching and flailing with my arms, for I was too tired to care any longer about keeping silent. I only wanted to reach safety. With a final effort I staggered through the shallows until I could grasp at a clump of sedge grass. I lay there for at least five minutes until I felt strong enough to slither forward on my stomach and pull myself onto firmer ground.

Next morning I must have looked like some ghoul of the marsh. My clothing was slimed with mud, my face and hands scratched and bloody where I had hauled myself face down through the swamp. Occasionally I gave a retching cough to try to dislodge the foul residues in my throat from all the muddy water I had swallowed. Yet I was confident that my crossing of the river had gone undetected. When the abb of St Ciaran's sent out word that I was to be stopped and brought back to the monastery, his messengers would first go to check with the keeper of the bridge if I had been seen, and then alert the people living on the east side of the river. By the time the news spread to the west bank, I should have put some distance between myself and any pursuit. Equally, I had to admit that my long-term chances of evasion were slim. A single, desperate-looking youth, wandering through the countryside, skulking past villages and hamlets, would be the object of immediate suspicion. If caught, I would be treated as a fugitive thief or an escaped slave and I still had the faint scars of the manacles that had been hammered on my wrists by Donnachad after Clontarf.

An image came to my mind from my childhood in Greenland. It was the memory of my father's two runners, the Scots slaves Haki and Hekja, and how the two of them would set off each spring and travel up into the moors, barefoot and with no more than a satchel of food between them, and live off the land all summer. And there was the tale, too, of how Karlsefni had set them ashore when he first arrived in Vinland with instructions to scout out the land. They had gone loping off into the wilderness, as if nothing could have been more normal, and returned safely. If Haki and Hekja could survive in unknown Vinland, then I could do the same in Ireland. I had no idea what lay beyond the great river, but I was determined to do as well as my father's own slaves. I got up and, bending double, began picking my way through the tussocks of grass towards a line of willow bushes that would provide cover for the first few steps of my flight to the west.

The next five days blur together so I have no way of knowing the order of the events, or what took place on which day. There

was the morning when I tripped over a tree root and twisted my
ankle so painfully that I thought I was crippled. There was the lake
that I came across unexpectedly, forcing a wide detour. I remember
standing for at least an hour on the edge of the woods, gazing at
the water and wondering whether I should circle around to my left
or my right and, having made my decision and started walking,
how I spent the next few hours wondering whether I was going in
the right direction or doubling back on my path. Then there was
the night when I was asleep on the ground as usual, wrapped in
my cloak and with my back to a tree trunk, and I was startled
awake by what I thought was the howling of wolves. I sat up for
the rest of the night, ready to climb the tree, but nothing came
closer. At dawn I was so drowsy that I set out carelessly. I had
walked for an hour before I noticed that my knife was not in its
sheath. Alarmed by the howling, I had pulled the knife out and
laid it on the ground beside me. I turned back and retraced my
steps. Luckily I found the knife within moments, lying where I had
left it.

I never lit a fire. Even if I had carried a flint and steel to make
a spark, I would not have risked the telltale smell of wood smoke.
The autumn weather was mild so I did not need a fire for warmth,
and I had no food which required cooking. I lived off wild fruit.
This was the season for all manner of nuts and berries to ripen –
hazelnuts, cranberries, blackberries, whortleberries, rowan berries,
plums, sloes, wild apples. Of course, I still went hungry and sometimes my gut ached from eating only acid fruit. But I made no
attempt to catch the occasional deer or hare that crossed my path.
I was as shy as the animals themselves. I crouched back into the
undergrowth when I observed them, fearful that the alarmed flight
of game would attract hunters who might then find me by accident.

I was never far from human settlement, at least during the first
part of my journey. The countryside was a mixture of woodland,
cleared fields, pasture and bogland. There were frequent villages
and hamlets, and twice I came across crannogs, places where a ri
tuath had built himself a well-protected home on an artificial island

in the middle of a lake. The village guard dogs were my chief worry. From time to time they detected my presence and raised a furious barking of alarm, forcing me to retreat hurriedly and then make a wider circuit round them. Once or twice gangs of children playing at the edge of the forest nearly discovered me, but in general their presence was useful. Their shouts and cries during their games often alerted me to the existence of a village before I blundered into it.

I had no idea how far to the west I was progressing. I noted, however, that the landscape was slowly changing. The forest was not nearly so dense and there were many stretches of open, scrubby ground. Increasingly the hills showed bald caps of rock, and there were broad expanses of barren moorland. It was a more harsh and unforgiving land so there were fewer settlements, yet the lack of forest cover made me more vulnerable to detection. After five days I had become so accustomed to slinking across the countryside that I began to think of myself as almost invisible. Perhaps made light-headed by lack of food, I found myself again recalling the fantasies of my Greenlandic childhood and how I had fancied myself in the role of Odinn the Invisible, travelling the world without being seen.

So my discovery on the sixth day of my flight was all the more shocking. I had spent the previous night in a little shelter that I made by laying branches to form a roof over a cleft between two large rocks on a stretch of open moorland. Soon after daybreak I emerged from my lair and began to descend the valley that sloped down from the edge of the moor. Ahead I could see a grove of trees on the bank of the little stream which ran through the dale. The trees would give me some cover, I thought, and if I was lucky I might also find some which were fruiting. I entered the wood and penetrated far enough to come to the bank of the stream itself. The water was clear and shallow, rippling prettily over brown and black pebbles, and overhung with vegetation. Shafts of sunlight speckled the greenery of the undergrowth, and I could hear birdsong from several directions. The place seemed as innocent as if no human had ever stepped there. I pushed aside the bushes, placed my satchel on the ground beside me on the bank and lay down flat on the earth so that I could submerge my face in the water and feel it run cool against my skin. Then I drank, sucking in the water. Finally I got back on my knees, reached down to scoop up a palmful of water and splashed it on the back of my neck. As I wiped away the drops, I looked up. On the far side of the stream, no more than ten feet away from me, stood a man. He was absolutely motionless. With a shock I realised that he must have been standing there even when I first arrived and that I had failed utterly to notice him. He had made no attempt to conceal himself. It was only his stillness which had deceived me, and the fact that the wood was full of the natural sounds of birds singing, insects chirping and rustling, the ripple of the stream. As I looked directly into the man's face, his expression did not change. He stood there, considering me calmly. I felt no alarm because he seemed so relaxed and self-contained.

The stranger was wearing a long cloak rather like my own, of grey wool, and he carried no weapon that I could see, though he did have a plain wooden staff. I guessed his age at about fifty, and his face was clean-shaven with weatherbeaten skin and regular features that included a pair of grey eyes now regarding me steadily. What made me gaze at him in complete astonishment was his hair. From ear to ear the man had shaved his head. From the back of his head the hair hung right down to his shoulders, but the front half of his scalp was bald except for some stubble. It was a hairstyle that I had read about while browsing in the monastery library, but had never expected to see in real life. The monks at St Ciaran's — those who still had any hair — used the Roman tonsure, shaving the central patch. The man in front of me still wore his hair as a monk would have done if the style had not been outmoded and forbidden by the Church for nearly two hundred years past.

TWENTY

'IF YOU ARE hungry as well as thirsty, I can offer you some food,' said this apparition.

Feeling foolish, I got to my feet. The stranger barely glanced back at me as he walked away through the undergrowth. There was no path that I could see, but I meekly splashed across the stream and followed him. Before long we came to a clearing in the wood which was obviously where he had set up his home. A small hut, neatly made of wattle and thatched with heather, had been built between the trunks of two large oak trees. Firewood was stacked beside the hut, and streaks of soot up the face of a large boulder and a nearby blackened pot showed where he did his cooking. A water bladder hung from the branch of a thorn tree. The stranger ducked into his hut and reappeared with a small sack in one hand and a shallow wooden bowl containing a large knob of something soft and yellow in the other. He tipped some of the contents of the sack into the bowl, stirred it with a wooden spoon, and handed the bowl and spoon to me. I took a mouthful. It proved to be a mix of butter, dried fruit and grains of toasted barley. The butter was rancid. I was not aware until then just how hungry I was. I ate everything.

The stranger still said nothing. Looking at him over the edge of the wooden bowl, I guessed he must be a hermit of some kind.

The monks at St Ciaran's had occasionally spoken of these deeply devout individuals who set themselves up in some isolated spot, far away from other humans. They wanted to live alone and commune in solitude with their God. St Anthony was the inspiration for many of them, and they tried to follow the customs of the Desert Fathers, even to the point of calling their refuges 'diserts'. They were not far removed in their behaviour from the pillar dwellers whom poor Enda had tried to emulate at St Ciaran's. What was odd was that this half-shaven hermit was so hospitable. True hermits did not welcome intruders. I could see no sign of an altar or a cross, nor had he blessed the food before passing it to me.

'Thank you for the meal,' I said, handing back the bowl. 'Please accept my apologies if I am trespassing on your disert. I am a stranger to these regions.'

'I can see that,' he said calmly. 'This is not a hermitage, though I have been a monk in my time as, I suspect, you have been.' He must have recognised my stolen travelling cloak, and maybe I had a monkish way about me, perhaps in my speech or in the way I had held the bowl of food.

'My name is—'. I paused for a moment, not knowing whether to give him my real name or my monastery name, for fear that he had heard about the fugitive novice called Thangbrand. Yet there was something in the man's shrewd gaze which prompted me to test him. 'My name is Adamnan.'

The corners of his eyes crinkled as he took in the implication of my reply. Adamnan means 'the timid one'.

'I would have thought that Cu Glas might be more appropriate,' he replied. It was if we were speaking in code. In the Irish tongue cu glas means literally a 'grey hound' but it also signifies someone fleeing from the law or an exile from overseas, possibly both. Who-ever he was, this quiet stranger was extremely observant and very erudite.

I decided to tell him the truth. Beginning with my capture at Clontarf, I sketched in the story of my slavery, how I had come to be a novice monk at St Ciaran's and the events that had culminated in my flight from the monastery. I did not mention my theft of the stones from the Gospel. 'I may be a fugitive from the monks and a stranger in this land,' I concluded, 'but I originally came to Ireland hoping to track down my mother's people.' He listened quietly and when I had finished said, 'You would be wise to give up any hope of tracing your mother's family. It would mean travelling from tuath to tuath all across the country, asking questions. People don't like being cross-examined, particularly by strangers. Also, if you do manage to trace your mother's people, you may be disappointed in what you hear, and your curiosity will certainly have aroused suspicion. Sooner or later you would come to the attention of the abb of St Ciaran's, and he will not have forgotten the unfinished business between you and the monastery. You will be brought back to the monastery to stand punishment. Frankly, I don't think you would find much pity from him. The Christian idea of justice is not so charitable.'

I must have looked doubtful. 'Believe me,' he added. 'I know something about the way the law works.' This was, as I learned later, an extreme understatement.

The man I had mistaken for a hermit was, in fact, was one of the most respected brithemain in the land. His given name was Eochaid, but the country people who encountered him in the course of his work often referred to him as Morand, and this was a great compliment. The original Morand, being legendary as one of their earliest brithemain, was renowned as a man who never gave a flawed verdict.

My teachers at St Ciaran's had warned us about the brithemain, and with good reason. The brithemain are learned men – judges is not quite the right word – who trace their authority to a time long before any of the Irish had even heard of the White Christ. Many Irish – perhaps the majority – in the remoter parts still retain a profound respect for a brithem, and their deference galls the monks because the brithem lineage goes back to those early physicians, lawgivers and sages commonly known among the Irish as drui, a name the monkish scholars have been at pains to blacken. Yet the nearest word in their clerkly Latin that the monks could find to describe the drui was to call them magi.

I can write about these matters with some familiarity because, as it turned out, I was to spend almost as long in the company of Eochaid as I did with the brothers of St Ciaran's and, truth be told, I learned as much from him as I did from all the more erudite brothers put together. The difference was that in the monastery I had access to books, and the books provided me with most of my monastic education. Eochaid, by contrast, looked on book learning almost as a weakness. The brithemain did not write down the laws and customs — they remembered them. This required prodigious feats of memory, and I recall Eochaid saying to me one day that it needed at least twenty years of study to learn brithem law, and that was just the basics.

I would be proud to claim that Eochaid took me on as his apprentice, but that would not be true. I stayed with Eochaid because he invited me to remain for as long as I wished, and I found sanctuary in his company. For the next two years I served him in the capacity of an assistant or orderly, and at times as a companion. He had no ambitions for me as his student. He probably thought my memory was already too weak for that. The brithemain begin their studies when they are very, very young. Formerly there were official schools for the brithemain but they are nearly all gone and now the knowledge passes from father to son, and to daughters as well, for there are female brithemain of distinction.

I was lucky to stumble on him. Each year he spent only a few months in his forest retreat. The rest of the time he was a wanderer, travelling the country. But retreat to the forest was essential to him, and as a result he could identify the tune of every songbird, recognise the tracks left by deer or wolf or otter or hare or squirrel, name each shrub and herb and flower, and knew the medicinal properties of each of them. He was a herb doctor as well as a brithem, and as well as dispensing justice to the people we visited he also gave out medical advice. In his forest hut he was so calm and peaceable that the wild animals seemed to sense little danger near him. The deer would wander into the clearing by our hut to nose about the cooking fire, looking for grains that had dropped from our plates, and a tame badger lumbered unafraid around our feet and became a pet. But Eochaid was not sentimental about these animals. My second winter with him was bitterly harsh. Snow lay on the ground for a week – a most unusual event – and the ponds turned to ice. It was freezing cold in the hut and we came close to starving. The badger saved us – as a stew.

'The wilderness is where the inspiration for the first brithem laws arose,' he once told me, and 'natural justice' was a phrase he often used. 'It is a heavy responsibility to interpret the Fenechas, the laws of freemen. False judgements ruin men's lives and the evil consequences live on for generations. So I need to return regularly to the ultimate source, to the rhythms and mysteries of Nature.' He smiled his self-deprecating smile and mocked himself. 'How much easier if I could wear one of those heavy iron collars which the first brithemain had around their necks. If they made a poor judgement the collar tightened until they could scarcely breathe. When they amended the judgement to make it fair, the collar loosened.'

'But how could the early brithemain make false judgements?' I asked him. 'The monks at St. Ciaran's told me that the brithemain were really drui in secret, and communed with evil spirits and, besides being able to fly through the air, made profane prophecies. So they must have been able to foresee the future and would have known if they were in error.'

'It is true that in the earlier days some drui were trained as seers and soothsayers,' he answered. 'But those days are gone, and much of what appeared to be their prophesy was really only a prolonged observation. For example, by watching the animals in the forest I can foretell the coming weather. Those who study the movement of the stars learn how they behave. From that knowledge they can predict events like the eclipses of the sun or moon.

Such predictions impress people who fail to notice the signs or who
do not understand the value of accumulated wisdom. Six hundred
and thirty years is the length of time our star watchers use when
measuring a single cycle of star movements in the sky. You can
imagine the power of so much stored wisdom.'

Eochaid's journeys were determined by his own celestial calendar. The first occasion he left the forest after my arrival was shortly
before the start of the thirteenth month of his year. A thirteenth
month, of course, has no equivalent in the White Christ calendar,
but for those who measure time by the waxing and waning of the
moon it obviously does exist and occurs three or four times every
decade. Eochaid called it the elder month, and he invited me to
accompany him on his journey. It would be a tiring walk, he
warned, but he had a duty to perform for a confederation of four
tuaths some distance to the north-west. The people of this region
were so respectful of the Old Ways that they had named their
territory Cairpre, to commemorate one of the greatest drui, reput-
edly the son of the God Ogmius.

It was indeed a long walk, six days' striding across an increasingly bleak countryside of moorland and rock to our destination,
a substantial crannog. At Eochaid's suggestion I took along my
battered leather satchel with a spare change of clothes for myself, a
white gown belonging to Eochaid, and a small supply of dried nuts
and grain for food. Eochaid himself carried nothing of value, no
symbols of his profession. He had only a small cloth bag slung
over his shoulder and a sharp sickle, which he used to clear a space
in the undergrowth when we slept out in the open or to cut
medicinal herbs that he noticed growing by the wayside. Plants
which heal, he explained, are available at all times of the year if
you know where to look. Some are best gathered in the spring
when their sap is full, others when they show their summer flowers,
and several when their roots are dormant or they are bearing
autumn fruit. On that journey he was collecting the roots of
burdock thistles for making an infusion to treat skin diseases and

boils, and with the point of his sickle he dug up the roots of something he said was a cure for ringworm. He called it cuckoo plant.

'That broken hand of yours,' he commented to me one day, 'would have healed much quicker if you had known how to treat it.'

'What should I have done?'

'Found the root which people call boneset or knitbone – it's very common – then made a paste and applied it to the wound as a poultice. It would have reduced the swelling and the pain. The same paste, dissolved in water, can be used as a treatment for diseases of the stomach or even given as medicine to children who have whooping cough.'

With his medical skill Eochaid was welcome at every settlement we passed. He seemed to be able to produce a remedy for any malady, even if it was severe. He gave an invalid, who was coughing as if to burst his lungs, an oily drink made from the fruit of water fennel, and an unfortunate who suffered from fits was calmed with an extract of all-heal root. 'Valerian is another name for it,' Eochaid said to me as he prepared the fetid-smelling drug, 'which comes from the Latin "to be in health". But you want to be careful with it. Too big a dose and you'll put a person to sleep for good.' I was about to ask Eochaid how he came to know Latin, when we were interrupted. A distraught mother arrived to say her child was suffering from a very sore throat, and Eochaid despatched me to fetch haws from a whitethorn bush we had seen not far back down the road so she could make hawthorn broth for the youngster.

The inhabitants of the hamlets and villages treated Eochaid with a deference bordering on awe. If we needed shelter, we were always given a place of honour in the home of the leader of the community, and no one ever asked where we were going or what our business was. I commented on this to Eochaid, and the fact that he carried no weapon and did not ask permission of any of the tuath people to cross their lands, though this would have been a dangerous act of folly for any stranger. He answered me that the brithemain were privileged. They could walk the trackways and be certain that they would not be impeded or molested, even by brigands. This immunity, he explained, arose from a belief among the country people that to harm a brithem would result in terrible misfortune. 'It's one of the beliefs which date back to the early days of the drui, and which the Christian priests, though they complain that the drui were sent by the devil, have been shrewd enough to turn to their advantage. They now say that harming a priest will also bring a curse on the evildoer, and they sometimes carry and display holy relics to strengthen the aura of their protection. Mind you,' he added, 'if the relic is too valuable, that doesn't always prevent thieves from robbing them.' Thinking of the ornamental stones that I had prised from the big Gospel book and still carried, I said nothing.

The chieftains of the four allied tuaths were waiting for Eochaid to decide their backlog of legal cases. Having seen how the Icelanders dispensed justice at their Althing, I was interested to observe how the Irish applied their laws. The lawsuits were heard in the crannog's council hall, where Eochaid sat on a low stool flanked by the chieftains. They listened to what the plaintiffs had to say, then called on the defendants for their versions of events. Sometimes a chieftain would ask a question or add a piece of corroborating detail, but Eochaid himself said very little. Yet, when the moment for a judgement arrived, the entire assembly would wait for the brithem to pronounce. Invariably Eochaid began his remarks with a reference to earlier custom in a similar case. He would quote 'the natural law', often using archaic words and phrases that few of his listeners could comprehend. Yet, such was their esteem for brithem law that they stood respectfully and they never disputed his decision. Eochaid rarely imposed a sentence of imprisonment or physical punishment. He dealt mainly in compensation. When he found a genuine offence had been committed, he explained its gravity and then suggested the correct compensation that should be paid.

The first cases he heard were fairly trivial. People complained of horses and oxen that had broken into neighbouring pastures, pigs trespassing on a vegetable patch, and even the case of a pack of hounds, not properly restrained, which had entered a yard and defiled it with their droppings. Patiently Eochaid listened to the details, and decided who was at fault – the landowner for not fencing his property more securely, or the animals' owner for allowing the creatures to stray. Then he would deliver his judgement. The pigs' owner was obliged to pay a double fine because his animals had not only eaten the vegetables but had rooted up the earth with their snouts and this would make the garden more difficult to restore. The man complaining about a neighbour's cattle in his field lost his case because he had failed to build his fence to the approved height and strength to stop the oxen pushing through it. In the case of the errant dogs, Eochaid found for the plaintiff. He recommended that the dogs' owner pick up the droppings, and then produce restitution in the form of the same amount of butter and dough as the quantity of dog turds retrieved. This particular arbitration raised broad smiles of approval from his audience.

As the day wore on, the cases before the brithem became more serious. There were two divorce cases. In the first a woman sought a formal separation from her husband on the grounds that he had become so fat that he was impotent because he was no longer capable of intercourse. One look at the obesity of the husband made that an easy case to settle. Eochaid also awarded the woman most of the joint property on the grounds that the fat man was also lazy and had clearly contributed little to the income of the household. The second case was more finely balanced. The husband claimed that his wife had brought shame on his honour by flirting with a neighbour, and she counter-claimed that he had done likewise by gossiping to his friends about the intimate details of their own sexual relationship. The pair became increasingly strident until Eochaid cut short their quarrelling by announcing that neither side was at fault, but it was obvious that the marriage was over. He recommended that they separate, each taking back whatever property they had originally brought into it. The woman, however, was to retain the family home as she had children to rear.

'How do you know that your judgements will be obeyed?' I asked Eochaid that evening. 'There is no one to enforce your decisions. Once you leave this place, who will oblige the guilty party to carry out the terms you have laid down?'

'Everything depends on the respect that the people have for the brithem law,' he answered. 'I cannot oblige people to do what I say. But you will have noticed that I try to produce a settlement that both parties can accept. My intention is to restore equilibrium within the community. Even in the extreme case of a murder I would not suggest a death sentence. Executing the murderer will not bring the dead victim back to life. It is surely more sensible that the killer and his kinsfolk pay restitution to the family of the deceased. In that way people will think before committing murder, knowing that their own kinsfolk will have to suffer consequences.'

'And what if the compensation is so severe that the kinsfolk cannot find the money to pay?' I asked.

'That is part of the brithem's proper training,' he replied. 'It is our responsibility to know the face price of every person and the value of every misdeed, and how to vary the compensation according to a myriad of circumstances. A ri, for example, has a greater face price than an aithech, a commoner. So if the ri receives an injury, then the compensation awarded to him is higher. But at the same time if it is the ri who is at fault then he must pay a greater amount of compensation than I would award against an aithech.'

While Eochaid was hearing the cases, more and more people kept arriving at the crannog, until the latecomers were so numerous that they were obliged to camp on the surrounding lands. To add to the congestion the cowherds and shepherds brought in their animals from the outlying pastures in preparation for the forthcoming winter season. Surplus animals were slaughtered, and any meat which was not preserved was being cooked over open fires. A holiday atmosphere developed as the people gorged themselves and drank copious amounts of mead and beer. A number of market stalls appeared. Though the gathering was far smaller than the Althing I had witnessed in Iceland when I first met the Burners, I was struck by the similarity. There was a difference, though: among the Irish I became aware of a certain underlying nervousness. It was the eve of their Samhain, the Festival of the Dead.

On the last day of Eochaid's law court a great crowd gathered at the causeway leading to the crannog. Many of the people were carrying bundles of firewood and there was a strange mixture of jubilation and apprehension. Eochaid emerged from the gate of the crannog wearing a plain white surcoat over his normal tunic. He held a long staff in one hand and his small sickle in the other. Behind him came the chieftains of the allied tuaths. The little group crossed the causeway and headed off across the fields with the crowd following them. In the distance stood a clump of trees. I had noticed the trees earlier because all the surrounding land had been cleared for farming, but this small copse had been left untouched. It was primeval woodland.

I fell into step behind Eochaid as he entered the wood, which was composed almost entirely of hazel trees. In the middle was a small lake, scarcely more than a pond. Behind us the crowd spread out among the trees and laid down their burdens. A dozen of the chieftain's servants began cutting back the undergrowth at the edge of the pond, clearing a space for Eochaid. He stood there calmly, sickle in hand, watching the preparations. Then, as dusk fell, he moved to the edge of the little lake. Soon it was so dark that it was only just possible to make out the dim shapes of the watching crowd amid the darker shadows of the trees. The whole copse was silent except for the occasional crying of a baby. Eochaid turned towards the lake and began to declaim. He spoke sentence after sentence in a language that I did not understand. His voice rose and fell as if reciting poetry, his words producing a flat, dull echo from the surrounding trees. The entire crowd seemed to be holding their breath as they listened. The water in the pond was inky black and an occasional whisper of breeze ruffled the surface, dissolving the reflected circle of the moon. As the clouds slid by, the moon's image appeared and disappeared randomly.

After about half an hour Eochaid stopped speaking and leaned forward. The white overgown he was wearing made it possible to see his movements clearly, and I glimpsed the glint of the sickle in his right hand. He reached forward and cut a wisp of dried reeds from the edge of the pond. A moment later, by a process I could not detect, a flicker of flame danced in his grasp as the wisp began to burn. As the flames grew brighter, they reflected off the white cloth of his gown and illuminated Eochaid's face so that his eyes seemed in deep shadow. He walked over to a pile of hazel twigs and thrust the burning tinder among them. At once the twigs burst into flame. Within moments the fire was burning so vigorously that orange tongues of flame were twisting and wavering to head height. As the fire took increasing hold, the chieftains of the tuaths stepped forward with their bundles of wood and threw them on the fire. I heard the rapid crackle of blazing timber and sparks began to fly upwards in the hot air currents. Soon there was so much heat radiating from the fire that my face was scorching, and I put up an arm to shield my eyes. There was a low appreciative murmuring from the crowd, and looking across the flames I could see that someone had come forward out of each family group. Each face was lit by the blazing fire and had an expression so intent that it seemed as if the person was enraptured by the swirling of the flames. Several stepped so close to the fire that I thought they would be burned. They all cast small items onto the fire – I could make out a tiny rag doll, a child's shoe, a handful of seeds, a ripe apple. They were offerings from those who sought to have children and bountiful crops in the coming year, or making thanks for their past blessings. The fire burned down quickly. One moment it was a high blaze, then next moment it collapsed on itself in a cascade of sparks. That was when the heads of families each thrust a brand into the flames. As soon as the brand had caught alight, they turned and, gathering up their families, began to walk away, heading back to their homes and tents, each carrying a burning flare. They would guard the brand through the night, and use it to relight their hearth fires, which they had extinguished to mark the passing of summer. The flares being carried out across the countryside made a remarkable spectacle, a sprinkle of bobbing light in the darkness. A hand touched my elbow. I looked round and recognised the steward of one of the tuath chieftains. He nodded for me to follow him, and we began to walk back to the crannog. Halfway there I paused and turned to look at the hazel copse. I could see the glow of the embers, and standing beside them the white-clad figure of Eochaid. He had his back towards us and was looking out at the lake. He had both arms outstretched to the sky, and I fancied that I saw the arcing glint of his sickle as he threw it into the pond.

These were mysteries to which I could not be privy, and the steward kept hold of my arm to make sure that I did not double back to rejoin Eochaid. Instead my guide led me to where his own people were waiting. They were from the farthest of the federate tuaths and had set up their camp at a little distance from the crannog. My escort brought me into the circle where the families had gathered to celebrate the successful conclusion of the ceremony. They had lit a central bonfire with their sacred flame and were seated on the ground, eating and drinking and enjoying themselves. I was greeted with nods and smiles. Someone put a wooden cup of mead in my hand, someone else handed me a rib of roasted sheep, and space was made for me in the circle to sit down and join the feast. I started to gnaw at the tendrils of mutton and looked around at the ring of faces. This was the first time that I had been exposed to the society of the true Irish, the ordinary people from the remotest fringes of their island, at a time when they were most relaxed. Now I was a guest, not a war captive, or a slave, or a novice. I savoured the mood of the gathering. Abruptly I felt a shocking lurch of recognition. Seated about a third of the way around the circle was Thorvall the Hunter. I knew it was impossible. The last time I had seen Thorvall had been when he had left our Vinland settlement, angry with Karlsefni and Gudrid, and sailed off in our small boat with five companions to explore farther along the coast. We had never heard anything more of him, and presumed he had been killed by the Skraelings or drowned, though someone did say that Thor would never let someone drown at sea who was so robust in his belief in the Old Ways.

I stared at the wraith. Not since I had seen the fetch of Gardi the overseer in Greenland eleven years before had I seen a dead man come back among the living. Thorvall looked older than when I had last seen him. His beard and hair were shot with grey, his face was deeply lined and his massive shoulders had acquired a slight stoop of age. But the lid of his left eye drooped as it had always done, and I could still see the mark, much fainter now in the creases and folds of his ageing face, where the bear claws had left the hunting scar that had made such an impression on me as a child. A leather skullcap was pulled down on his head and pressed his hair over his ears so I could not see whether, like the Thorvall I knew from Vinland, he had also lost the top of his left ear. He was dressed in the clothing of an Irish cliathaire, laced leggings and a heavy jerkin of sheepskin over a rough linen shirt. Laid on the ground in front of him was an expensive-looking heavy sword. I tried to remain calm. I had taken to heart what Snorri Godi had warned me about: that when you experience second sight it is wiser to pretend that all is entirely normal, even though you are seeing something invisible to others. I continued to chew on my meat, occasionally glancing across at Thorvall and wondering if his ghost would recognise me. Then I noticed the man seated on Thorvall's right turn towards him and say something. My flesh tingled. I was not alone in seeing the wraith. Others were aware of his presence. Then it occurred to me that perhaps I had let my imagination run away with me. The man seated on the other side of the fire was not Thorvall, but someone who looked very like him.

Getting to my feet, I backed away from the circle, then walked round to where I could approach the seated stranger from one side. As I came closer, the more certain I was that it really was Thorvall. He had the same big-knuckled, gnarled hands that I remembered, and I glimpsed around his neck a necklace of bear claws. It had to be him. Yet how did he come to be seated among Irish clansmen, dressed like a veteran Irish warrior?

'Thorvall?' I enquired nervously, standing a little behind his right shoulder.

He did not respond.

'Thorvall?' I repeated more loudly, and this time he did turn round and looked up at me with a questioning expression on his face. He had the same pale blue eyes that I remembered staring at me in the stable all those years ago when I was first interrogated about my second sight. But the eyes looking at me had no sense of recognition.

'Thorvall,' I said for the third time and then, speaking in Norse, 'I am Thorgils, don't you recognise me? It's me, Leif's son from Brattahlid in Greenland.'

Thorvall continued to stare at me with no reaction except for a slightly puzzled frown. He had not understood a word I said. People were starting to take notice of my behaviour and glancing curiously at me. I began to lose my nerve.

'Thorvall?'

My voice trailed away in confusion. The man gave a grunt and turned back to face the fire, ignoring me.

I crept back to my place by the fire, thoroughly embarrassed. Luckily the tide of mead was rising and my strange actions were forgotten in the general merriment. I kept glancing across at Thorvall, or whoever he was, trying to resolve my confusion.

'Who's that man over there, the one with the big sword on the ground in front of him?' I asked my neighbour.

He looked across to the man with the scar on his face. 'That's Ardal, the ri's champion, though he's had very little to do ever since we allied with the other tuaths,' he replied, 'Just as well. He's getting a bit long in the tooth to do much duelling.'

I remembered Eochaid's warning about not asking too many questions and decided that it would be better to wait till next day to consult the brithem about the mysterious clansman.

'King's champion?' Eochaid replied next morning. 'That's an

old title, not used much today. He's usually the best warrior in the tuath, who acts as the ri's chief bodyguard. He also represents the ri if there is a quarrel between two tuaths which is to be decided by single combat between two picked fighters. Why do you want to know?'

'I saw a man yesterday evening who I thought was someone I knew long ago when I was living in the Norse lands. I was told his name was Ardal and that he is, or was, the king's champion. But I was sure he was someone else. Yet that seems impossible.'

'I can't say I know him. Who did you say he was with?' Eochaid asked.

'He was seated among the people who came from the farthest tuath, the one near the coast.'

'That'll be the Ua Cannannain.' Eochaid and I were standing in the mead hall of the crannog, waiting to say a formal farewell to the ri. Eochaid turned to the ri's steward. 'Do you know this man called Ardal?'

'Only by reputation,' he replied. 'A man of very few words. Not surprising. He was half dead when he was washed ashore and it was thought that he would never live. But he was nursed back to health in the ri's own house and became a servant there. Then it turned out that he was so good with weapons that he eventually became the king's champion. Quite an advancement for someone who was fuidir cinad o muir.'

It was a phrase I had never heard before. A fuidir is someone half-free or ransomed, and cinad o muir is 'a crime of the sea'. I was about to ask the steward what he meant, when the man added, 'If you want to meet Ardal, it will have to wait till next year. Early this morning most of the Ua Cannannain set out to return to their own tuath.'

Eochaid looked at me. 'What makes you think that you knew this man Ardal previously?'

'He and his friend, a smith named Tyrkir, were my first tutors in the Old Ways,' I replied, 'but I thought he was dead.'

'He may well be dead,' Eochaid observed. 'We are now in

Samhain, the season when the veil between the living and the dead is at its thinnest, and those who are no longer with us can pass most easily through the veil. What you saw may have been your friend who has returned briefly to this world.'

'But the steward said that he had been in this land for several years, not just at this season.'

'Then perhaps you were imagining your friend in the form of this man Ardal. It seems an appropriate name for the king's champion. It means someone who has the courage of a bear.'

A berserker, I thought or was it because of the bear-claw necklace? And this thought distracted me from asking what the steward meant by a fuidir cinad o muir.

I never solved the mystery of Ardal because on the next celebration of Samhain I fell sick during the six-day walk to Cairpre. I developed a shivering fever, probably caught from too many damp days spent in Eochaid's forest retreat during what was a very wet summer, even by Irish standards. Eochaid left me in the care of a roadside hospitaller, whose wife fed me – as he had instructed – on a monotonous diet of celery, raw and in watery broth. The cure worked, but it gave me a lasting dislike for the taste of that stringy vegetable.

TWENTY-ONE

I WAS NOW in my nineteenth year, and my situation in the company of a forest-dwelling brithem, offered little opportunity for contact with the opposite sex. My heartbreak over Orlaith had left its mark, and I often wondered what had become of her. A sense of guilt for what had happened made me question whether I would ever achieve a satisfactory relationship with a woman, and Eochaid's attitude towards women only served to increase my confusion.

Eochaid regarded women as subject to their own particular standards. There was the day when two women appeared before him for judgement after one had stabbed the other with a kitchen knife, causing a deep gash. They were both wives of a minor ri, who had exercised his right to have more than one wife. When the two women were brought before Eochaid, he was told that the wounded woman was the first wife and that she had initiated the affray. She had attacked the new wife a few days after her husband had married for the second time.

'How many days afterwards?' Eochaid asked gently.

'Two days later, when the new and younger wife first came into the home,' came the reply.

'Then culpability is shared equally,' the brithem stated. 'Custom states that a first wife has the right to inflict an injury on a new wife provided it is non-fatal and it is done in the first three days. Equally, the second wife has the right to retaliate, but she must limit herself to scratching with her nails, pulling the hair, or abusive language.'

An assault with words was, in brithem law, as serious as an attack with a weapon of metal or wood. 'Language,' Eochaid once said to me, 'can be lethal. A tongue can have a sharper edge than the best-honed dagger. You can do more damage by inventing a clever and hurtful nickname for your enemy than by burning his house or destroying his crops.' He then cited a whole catalogue of verbal offences, ranging from the spoken spells of witchcraft uttered in secret, through hurtful satire, to the jibes and insults which flew in a quarrel. Each and every one had its own value when it came to arbitration. 'If the monks ever told you that the drui used spells and curses,' he said to me on another occasion, 'they were confusing it with the power of language. A drui who aspired to be a fili ollam, a master of words, was striving for the highest and most difficult discipline, to deploy words for praise or poetry, irony or ridicule.'

That was the day he told me about his own time as a monk. We were seated on a log outside his forest hut after returning from an expedition to net small fish in the stream, when a blackbird burst into full-throated song from somewhere in the bushes. Eochaid leaned back, closed his eyes for a moment to listen to the birdsong and then began to quote poetry,

> 'I have a hut in the wood, none knows it but my Lord;
> an ash tree this side, a hazel on the other,
> a great tree on a mound encloses it.
> The size of my hut, small yet not small, a place of familiar
>   paths;
> the she-bird in its dress of blackbird colour sings a
>   melodious strain from its gable.'

He stopped, opened his eyes, and looked at me. 'Do you know who composed those lines?' he asked.

'No,' I answered. 'Are they yours?'

'I wish they were,' he said. 'They were spoken to me by a Christian hermit in his disert. He was living here, on this very same spot, when I first came across these woods. It is his hut which we now occupy. He was already an old man when I found him, old, but at peace with himself and the world. He had lived here for as long as he could remember, and he knew that his time would soon be over. I met him twice, for I came back a couple of years later to see how he was getting on and to bring him some store of food. He thanked me and rewarded me with the poem. The next time I came back he was dead. I found his corpse and buried him as he would have wished. But the poetry stayed echoing in my head, and I decided that I should go to the monastery where he had been trained, to visit the place where the power of such words is nurtured.'

Eochaid had enrolled at the monastery as a novice and within months was its star pupil. No one knew his brithem background. He had shaved his head completely to remove his distinctive tonsure, telling the monks he had suffered from a case of ringworm. With his phenomenal trained memory, book learning came easily to him and he quickly absorbed the writings of the early Christian authors. 'Jerome, Cyprian, Origen and Gregory the Great . . . they were men of acute perception,' he said. 'Their scholarship and conviction impressed me profoundly. Yet, I came to the conclusion that much of what they wrote was a retelling of the far earlier truths, the ones in which I had already been schooled. So in the end I decided that I would prefer to stay with the Old Ways and left the monastery. But at least I had learned why the Christianity has taken hold so easily among our people.'

'Why is that?' I asked.

'The priests and monks build cleverly on well-laid foundations,' he answered, 'Samhain, our Festival of the Dead, becomes the eve of their All Saints' Day; Beltane, which for us is the reawakening of life and celebrated with new fire, is turned into Easter even with the lighting of their Paschal Fire; our Brigid the exalted one, of whom I am a particular adherent, for she brings healing, poetry and learning, has been transmuted into a Christian saint. The list goes on and on. Sometimes I wonder if this means that the Old Ways are really still flourishing beneath the surface, and I could have stayed a monk and still worshipped the Gods in a different guise.'

'Didn't anyone at the monastery ask after the hermit who lived here? After all, he had been one of them.'

'As I warned you, the monks can be harsh towards people who abandon their way of life. They had a nickname for him. They called him Suibhne Geilt, after the "Mad Sweeney" who was driven insane by a curse from a Christian priest. He spent the rest of his life living among the trees and composing poetry until he was killed by a swineherd. Yet, such is the power of words that I have a suspicion that Mad Sweeney's verses will be remembered longer than the men who mocked him.'

On the eve of my third Samhain in Eochaid's company he announced that, instead of going to Cairpre that year, he would travel east to the burial place of Tlachtga, daughter of the famed drui Mog Ruth. A distinguished drui in her own right, Tlachtga had been renowned for the subtlety of her judgements, and it was custom that those brithemain who were adepts in arbitration should assemble at her tomb every fifth year to discuss the more intricate cases they had heard since their last conclave and agree on common judgements for the future. The hill of Tlachtga lies only a half-day's travel from the seat of the High King at Tara, so it is here that the High King of Ireland also comes to celebrate the Samhain feast. 'It is one of the great gatherings in the land,' Eochaid told me, 'so perhaps Adamnan the Timid might be better advised to stay away. Equally, it might be a chance for you to learn whether you should begin using Diarmid as your alias.' It was an old joke of his. With his usual keen observation he had noted how I kept glancing at the younger women whenever we went to the settlements. In legend Diarmid carried on his forehead a 'love spot', a

mark placed there by a mysterious maiden which caused women to
fall madly and instantly in love with the handsome young man.

The great gathering at the foot of the hill of Tlachtga was a
spectacle that surpassed anything I had anticipated. The bustle and
flamboyance of the Irish who came to the High King's festivities
made a lively impression. There were several thousand participants,
and they arrived in their kin groups, with each chieftain trying to
impress his equals. Their retinues swaggered through the crowds,
flaunting the expensive finger rings, torcs and brooches which their
leaders had awarded them. By regulation long-bladed and long-
handled weapons had to be set aside during the festivities, but
daggers were permitted and were worn to show off their workmanship or decoration. There were displays of horses and hounds, and
even a few chariots came bouncing and swaying in behind their
teams of shaggy war ponies; the wheels of these old-fashioned
contraptions were brightly painted in contrasting colours so as they
spun they looked like children's toys. In the presence of the Irish,
wherever there are horses and dogs in any number, there will be
racing and contests and gaming. By the time Eochaid and I arrived,
a wide circle of wooden posts had been driven in the ground to
create a race track, where crowds of spectators jostled each morning
and afternoon to watch the contests.

Sometimes just two riders settled a personal challenge by racing
their mounts. More often it was a general match with an honour
prize to the winner, a wild stampede of a score of lathered,
sweating horses thundering round the course, urged on by the
shouts of the crowd and the flailing whips of their riders, usually
skinny young lads. On my second day at Tlachtga I also came
across an event which, to an outsider, might have seemed like a
mock battle. Two squads of wild-looking men were milling
together and striking at one another with flat clubs. Occasionally a
man fell to the ground, bleeding from a head blow, and it seemed
that the fighters were hitting out with unrestrained viciousness.
Yet, the object of their attention was only a small hard ball which

each side was trying to propel into the opponents' territory and then through an open mark. The blows to the head were accidental, or allegedly so. The reason for my fascination was that I had seen a similar sport being played – though with less riot and fervour – by my youthful companions in Iceland and I had once played it myself.

I was standing on the sidelines, watching the contest closely and trying to detect the differences from the Icelandic version of the game, when I received a shattering blow on the back of my own head. It must have been a harder stroke than anything being dealt on the games field because everything went dark.

I awoke to the familiar sensation of lying on the ground with my wrists tied together. This time the pain was not as bad as it had been after the battle of Clontarf because my bonds were leather straps, not iron manacles. But the other difference was more serious. When I opened my eyes, I knew my captor: I found myself looking up into the face of the treasurer of St Ciaran's.

Brother Mariannus was gazing down at me with an expression in which distaste matched satisfaction. 'What made you think you would get away with it?' he asked. I shook my head groggily. I had a violent headache and could feel the large bruise swelling up where someone had struck me with a weapon. I wondered if I had been hit with a games stick. A clout on the head with a heavy crozier would have done the job just as well. Then I remembered Eochaid. While I was watching the Irish at their sports, he had gone in search of other brithemain and he probably did not know what had happened to me. He had important business to attend to and when I failed to show up would probably surmise that I had departed in search of strong drink or female diversion. I had left my cloak and travelling satchel in the hut where we were staying, but he might even think that I had taken the chance to part company with him altogether.

'You'll discover that it's both a sin and a crime to steal Church property,' the treasurer was saying grimly, 'I doubt you have any respect for the moral consequences of the sin, but the criminal repercussions will have more impact on someone of your base character.'

We were in a tent, and two of the monastery servants were standing over me. I wondered which of them had hit me on the head. The younger man had the stolid gaze of an underling who would do unquestioningly as he was told, but the older servant looked as if he was positively enjoying seeing me in trouble.

'My men will take you back to the monastery, where you will be tried and receive punishment. You'll start out tomorrow,' Brother Mariannus went on. 'I presume that you have disposed of the property you stole, so you can expect the maximum penalty. Would you not agree, Abb?'

I turned my head to see who else was in the tent, and there, standing with his hands clasped behind his back and looking out of the tent flap as if he wished to have nothing to do with this sordid matter of theft and absconding from his rule, was Abb Aidan. The sight of him brought to mind something that Eochaid had once explained to me about the laws of the Christians. The monastery abbs, he said, had created most of their statutes and regulations as ways of raising money locally. Shrewdly they had adopted the brithem principle that whenever a rule was broken, then the transgressors had to pay a fine. So their cana, as they called their laws, were only valid within the territories the abbs controlled. Farther afield, Eochaid had stated, it was not monastery law which applied, but the king's law.

'I claim my right to trial before the king's marshal,' I said. 'Here at Tlachtga I am not subject to the cana of St Ciaran's. I am outside the monastery's jurisdiction. More than that, I have the right to protection from the king's law because I am a foreigner, a fact acknowledged when I was first interviewed for admission into the community at St Ciaran's.'

Brother Mariannus glowered at me. 'Who taught you anything about the law, you impudent puppy . . .' he began.

'No, he's right,' Abb Aidan interrupted. 'Under the law he is entitled to a hearing before the king's marshal, though that will not make any difference to the verdict.' I felt a faint stir of satisfaction. I had judged the abb correctly. He was such a stickler for custom and correctness that I had avoided being transported back to St Ciaran's and within range of Brother Cainnech, whom I knew was my real foe.

'Take him outside and tie him up securely, feet as well as hands, to make sure he doesn't disappear a second time,' Abb Aidan ordered and then, addressing the treasurer, 'Brother Mariannus, I would be obliged if you would contact the officials of the royal household and ask if the case of Thorgils or Thurgeis, known sometimes as Thangbrand, can be heard at the first opportunity, on a charge of theft of Church property.'

So, late the next day, I found myself at a legal hearing once again. But this time I was not an observer. I was the accused. The trial was held in the mead hall of the local ri, a modest building that could scarcely hold more than a hundred spectators, and which that afternoon was far from full. Of course, the High King himself was not there. He was represented by his marshal, a bored-looking man in late middle age, with a sleek, round face, straggling moustache and large brown eyes. He reminded me of a tired seal. He had not expected an extra case to be brought before him so late in the day and wanted it to be dealt with quickly. I was pushed into the centre of the hall and made to stand facing the marshal. He sat at a plain wooden table and on his right was a scribe, a priest, making notes on a wax tablet. Farther around the circle from the penman were about a dozen men, some seated, others standing. They were clearly clerics, though I could not tell whether they were there as advisers, jury, prosecutors, or merely onlookers. Opposite to them, and fewer in number, were a group of brithemain. Among them, to my relief, I could see Eochaid. He was standing in the rear of the group and made no sign that he knew me.

The proceedings went briskly. The treasurer recounted the charges against me, how I had joined the monastery, how I had betrayed their trust and generosity, how I had disappeared one

night, and the next day the library was found broken into and
several holy and precious ornaments to a Gospel book had been
torn from their mountings. Earlier some pages had gone missing
from an important manuscript, and I was suspected of being responsible for that theft as well.

'Has any of the stolen material been recovered?' the marshal
asked without much interest.

'No, none of it. The culprit disappeared without trace, though
we looked for him widely and carefully. It was only yesterday,
after an interval of two years, that he was seen here at the festival
by one of our people and recognised.'

'What penalty are you seeking?' the marshall enquired.

'The just penalty – the penalty for aggravated theft. A death
penalty.'

'Would you consider some sort of arbitration and a payment of
compensation if that could be arranged?' The question came from
the marshal's left, from one of the brithemain. The question had
been addressed to the treasurer and I saw several of the Christians
stir and come alert. Their hostility was obvious.

'No,' replied the treasurer crisply. 'How could the wretch
possibly pay compensation? He has no family to stand surety for
him, he is a foreigner, and he is obviously destitute. In his entire
life he could never repay the sum that the loss represents to the
monastery.'

'If he is so destitute, would it not be appropriate to forgive a
pauper for his crime? Isn't that what you preach – forgiveness of
sins?'

The treasurer glared at the brithem. 'Our Holy Bible teaches us
that he who absolves a crime is himself a wrongdoer,' he retorted.
To the marshal's left I saw the churchmen nod their agreement.
They looked thoroughly pleased with the treasurer's response. No
one asked me a single question. Indeed they barely glanced at me.
I knew why. The word of a runaway novice counted for nothing
against the word of a senior monk, particularly someone with the
status of the treasurer. Under both Church law and brithem custom,

the value of testimony depends on the individual's rank, so whatever I said was of no import. If the treasurer stated I was the culprit, then it was useless for me to deny it. For my defence to be effective, I needed someone of equal or superior status to the treasurer to speak for me, and there was no one there who appeared willing to act on my behalf. As I had known from the beginning, it was not a question of whether I was innocent or guilty, but of what my sentence would be.

'I find the culprit guilty of theft of Church property,' the marshal announced without any hesitation, 'and order that he should suffer the penalty as sought by the plaintiff.' He began to rise from his chair, clearly eager to close the day's hearings and leave for his supper.

'On a matter of law . . .' a voice interjected quietly. I could recognise Eochaid's voice anywhere. He was addressing the marshal directly and, like everyone else, ignored me completely. The marshal gave an exasperated grimace, and sat back down again, waiting to hear what Eochaid had to say. 'It has been stated by the plaintiff that the accused is a foreigner and that he has no family or kin in this land, and therefore there is no possibility of compensation or restitution for the theft. The same criteria must surely apply to the court's sentence: namely, any individual without family nor kin to guide or instruct him in what is right and what is wrong, must – by those circumstances – be regarded as having committed his or her crime out of a natural deficiency. In that case, the crime is cinad o muir and must be punished accordingly.'

I had no idea what Eochaid was talking about.

But Brother Mariannus clearly did know what the brithem had in mind because the Treasurer was looking wary. 'The young man has been found guilty of a major felony. His offence was against the monastery of St Ciaran, and the monastery has the right to carry out the appropriate sentence,' he said.

'If it is the monastery which is the injured party,' Eochaid replied calmly, 'then punishment should be carried out in accordance with monastic custom, should it not? And what could be more appropriate than allowing your own God to decide this young man's fate. Is this not how your own saints were willing to demonstrate their faith?'

The treasurer was clearly irritated. There was a short silence as he searched for a retort, when the marshal intervened. He was getting bored with the continuing discussion. 'The felon is judged to have committed a cinad o muir,' he announced, 'He is to be taken from here to the nearest beach and the sentence to be carried out.'

I thought I was to be drowned like an unwanted cur, with a stone about my neck. However, the following day, when I was brought to the beach, the boat drawn up on the shingle was so small that I could not imagine how I would fit into it as well as the person who was to throw me overboard. The tiny craft was barely more than a large basket. It was made of light withies lashed together with thongs to form an open framework and then covered over with a skin sewn of cowhides. The boat, if such a flimsy vessel could be called that, was in very poor condition. The stitching was broken in several places, there were cracks and splits in the leather cover, and the thongs of the basketwork were so slack that the structure sagged at the edge. It looked as if its owner had abandoned the craft on the beach as being totally unfit for the sea and that, I gathered, was precisely why it had been selected.

'We'll have to wait for the wind,' said the senior of the two monastery servants who had escorted me. 'The locals say that it usually gets up strongly in the afternoon and blows hard for several hours. Enough to see you on your way for a final voyage.' He was relishing his role. On the half-day's walk to the beach he had lost no chance to make my journey unpleasant, tripping me up from time to time, then jerking viciously on the leading halter as I struggled to get back on my feet. Neither Abb Aidan nor the treasurer had thought it worth their while to come to the beach to witness my sentence being carried out. They had sent the servants to do the work, and there was a minor official from the marshal's court to report back when the punishment had been completed.

Apart from the three of them, there was just a handful of curious bystanders, mostly children and old men from the local fishing families. One of the old men kept handing a few small coins from one gnarled paw to the other, his lips moving as he counted them again and again. I guessed he was the previous owner of the semi-derelict little boat, which, like me, had been condemned.

'Are you from the settlement outside St Ciaran's?' I asked the older servant.

'What's that to you?' he grunted disagreeably.

'I thought you might know Bladnach the leather-worker.'

'And so what? If you think he'll show up here by some holy miracle and sew up the boat before you set sail in her, you must be even more optimistic than Maelduine sailing for the Blessed Islands. Without his legs, Bladnach would really need a marvel to get here so briskly.' He laughed bitterly. 'You would have thought he had suffered enough without losing his daughter as well.'

'What do you mean, losing his daughter?'

He shot me a glance of pure loathing. 'Don't think your antics with Orlaith didn't get noticed by her neighbours. Orlaith got pregnant, thanks to you, and there were complications. She ended up by having to go to the monastery for treatment, but the hospital couldn't help her. Both she and the baby died. Brother Cainnech said there was nothing he could do.'

His words sickened me. Now I knew why the servant had been so vicious to me. It was no good protesting that I could not have been the father of her child.

'I'm sorry,' I said feebly.

'You'll be more than sorry when the wind changes. I hope you die at sea so slowly that you wish you had drowned; and, if your wreck of a boat does float long enough for you to come ashore, that you fall into the hands of savages who make your life as a fuidir unbearable,' he retorted, and kicked my feet from under me so that I fell heavily on the shingle.

Now I knew what Ardal had been when he was described as fuidir cinad o muir. He had been a castaway, found in a rudderless boat which had drifted onto the coast. The tribesmen of Cairpre had presumed that he was a criminal deliberately set adrift as punishment. If such a person came back to land, then whoever found him could treat him as his personal property, whether to kill or enslave him. That was what it meant to be fuidir cinad o muir – human flotsam washed up by the waves, destined for a life of servitude.

As predicted, the wind changed in the early hours of the afternoon and began to blow strongly from the west, away from the land. The two monastery servants roused themselves and, picking up the battered little boat with ease, carried it down the beach and set it afloat. One man held the boat steady, and the other came back to where I sat, kicked me hard in the ribs and told me to get down to the water's edge and climb into the boat. The tiny coracle tipped and swivelled alarmingly as I got aboard, and water began to seep in through the leather hull. Within moments there were several inches of water in the bilge. The older servant, whose name I gather was Jarlath, leaned forward to cut the leather thong binding my wrists, and handed me a single paddle.

'I hope God does not grant you any more mercy than he gave Orlaith,' he said. 'I'm personally going to give your boat such a shove that I hope it carries you to Hell. Certainly you cannot paddle back to land against this wind, and in a few hours it may even raise waves big enough to swamp your vessel if you have not already capsized. Think about it and suffer!'

He was about to send the boat into deeper water when someone cried, 'Wait!' It was the court official, the man deputed to report on the conduct of my punishment. He waded out to where I sat rocking on the waves.

'The law allows only a single oar, a sail and no rudder, so that you cannot row to shore but are dependent on the weather that God sends. However, you are also permitted one bag of food . . . here . . .'

He handed me a well-worn leather satchel filled with a thin

gruel of grain and nuts blended with water. I recognised Eochaid's favourite diet, the produce of what he called the briugu caille, the hospitaller trees of the forest. I also identified the leather satchel. It was the same one that I had carried away with me from the monastery when I fled from St Ciaran's. Old and stained and battered, it had been repaired many times because the original leather was thick and stout enough to take the needle. I clutched it to me as Jarlath and his colleague began to push the little cockleshell of a boat out into deeper water, and my fingers slid down the fat seams of the satchel so I could feel the hard lumps. They were the stones I had stolen from St Ciaran's. My time spent sitting in Bladnach's workshop waiting for him to blind stitch the book satchels had not been wasted. I had practised how to slit and close leather so neatly that the stitches could not be seen, and that is where I had hidden my loot. Now, belatedly, I understood that Eochaid must have known all along about my hidden hoard.

Jarlath was so determined that I never come back to land that he kept on wading after his colleague had turned back, until he was chest deep in the sea and the larger waves were threatening to break over his head. He gave the boat a final shove, then I was adrift and the wind was rapidly carrying me clear. Still clasping the satchel, I slid myself down to sit in the bilge of the coracle and make her more stable. There was no point in looking back because the man who had helped me was not there. Without Eochaid's intervention at my trial before the king's marshal, I knew I would have finished up like the unfortunate sheepstealer at St Ciaran's, hanging from a gibbet in front of the monastery gate. I found myself wishing that somehow there had been a moment when I had thanked Eochaid for all he had done for me, ever since that morning on the day we first met when he had stood silently regarding me drink water from the woodland stream. Yet, probably I would not have found the right words. Eochaid remained an enigma. I had never penetrated his inner thoughts, or learned why he had chosen to be a brithem, or what sustained him along that demanding path. He had kept himself to himself. His Gods were

different from mine and he had never discussed them with me,
though I knew they were complex and ancient. His studies of their
mysteries made him wise and practical and gave him a remarkable
insight into human nature. Had he been an Old Believer, I would
have taken him for another Odinn, but without the darker, cruel
side. My silent homage to him as I drifted out to sea was to admit
that if there was one man on whom I wished to pattern my life it
would be Eochaid.

At first I clung fiercely to the sides of the little coracle as it
lurched and swivelled crazily in the waves, then tilted and hung at
a steep angle, so that it seemed on the point of capsizing at any
moment and throwing me into the sea. With each gyration I braced
myself in the bottom of the little vessel, and tried to counter-
balance the sudden movement. But soon I discovered it was better
to relax, to lie limp and let the coracle flex and float naturally to
the waves. My real worry was the constant intake of water. It was
seeping through the cracks and splits in the leather and splashing
over the rim of the little vessel with each wave crest. Unless I did
something, the coracle would swamp and founder. I gulped down
the gruel in the satchel and began to use the empty leather bag as
a scoop, steadily tipping the bilge water back into the sea. It was
this action, repeated again and again and again, which distracted
me from my fear of capsize and death. As I bailed, I found myself
thinking back to my fellow fuidir cinad o muir – Ardal, the
mysterious clansman who had been found adrift on the western
coast. The more I thought of Ardal, and how closely he had
resembled Thorvall the Hunter, the more I convinced myself that
they were one and the same man. If so, I told myself as I carefully
poured another satchelful of water back into the sea, then Thorvall
had drifted across the ocean from Vinland in an open boat, a
voyage of many weeks riding the wind and current. The terrible
ordeal must have destroyed his memory so he no longer knew his
own identity or recognised who I was, but he had survived. And if
Thorvall could live through such a nightmare, then so could I.

It was impossible to tell when the sun went down. The sky was

so overcast that the light merely faded until I could no longer
make out the distant line of the coast far astern. My horizon was
reduced to a close circle of dark, restless sea, out of which appeared
the white flashes of wave crests. I kept bailing steadily, my arms
aching, my skimpy gown soaked against my skin, and the beginnings of a thirst brought on by licking away the spray which struck
my face. It must have been nearly midnight when the cloud cover
began to break up and the first stars appeared. By then I was so
tired that I scarcely noticed that the waves were diminishing. They
broke less frequently into the coracle. I found myself setting aside
the satchel and relaxing until the rise of bilge water from the leaks
obliged me to go to work again.

In these intervals, resting from the labour of bailing, I thought
back to the eerie coincidences that had occurred in my life. From
the time that my mother had sent me away as an infant, it seemed
that there had been a pattern. I had been brought into contact,
repeatedly, with people who possessed abnormal qualities – my
foster mother Gudrid with her volva's powers could see draugar
and fetches; Thrand knew the galdrastafir spells; Brodir had shared
with me the vision of Odinn's ravens on the battlefield; Eochaid
had spoken of his mystic inheritance from the ancient Irish drui;
and there had been the brief encounter with the Skraeling shaman
in the Vinland forest. The more I thought upon these coincidences,
the more calm I became. My life had been so strange, so discon-
nected from the humdrum progress of other men, that it must have
a deeper purpose. The All-Father, I concluded, had not watched
over me through so many vicissitudes only to let me drown in the
cold, grey waters of the sea of Ireland. He had other plans for me.
Otherwise, why had he shown me so many wonders in such far-
flung places, or let me learn so much? I sat in the water swilling in
the bottom of the coracle and tried to determine what that design
might be. As I brooded on my past, I scarcely noticed the wind
was dying away. A stillness settled on the water until even the
swell was barely felt. In that tiny coracle, motionless save for a
very gentle rocking motion, I was suspended on the surface of

black sea, the darkness of the night around me, the inky depths below. I began to feel that I was leaving my own body, that I was spirit flying. From exhaustion, from exposure, or because it was Odinn's will, I went into a trancelike stupor.

A hand grasping my shoulder broke the spell.

'Sea luck!' said a voice. I looked up into a heavily bearded Norse face.

It was broad daylight, my coracle was nuzzling against the side of a small longship, and a sailor was leaning down to grab me out of the coracle.

'Look what we've got here,' said the sailor, 'a gift from Njord himself.'

'Pretty miserable gift, I would say,' commented his companion, helping drag me aboard still clutching my satchel, then sending the coracle on its way with a contemptuous kick so that the little vessel tilted and sank.

'May Odinn Farmatyr, God of Cargoes, reward you,' I managed to blurt out.

'Well, at least he speaks good Norse,' said a third voice.

My rescuers were savages. Or that is what the monks of St Ciaran's would have called them, though my word for them was different – they were vikingr, homeward bound after a season on the coast of what I later knew as Breton land. Their luck had been fair, a couple of small monasteries surprised and looted, some profitable trading for wine and pottery in the small ports farther south and now they were headed north again in their ship. They were proper seamen, so the lookout with the dawn light behind him had spotted the tiny black speck of the coracle appearing and disappearing on the gentle swells. They had rowed across to check what they had found and as they approached they had seen me sitting there, so motionless that they thought I was a corpse.

The Norse consider it propitious to rescue someone from the sea, as much for the rescuer as the rescued. So I received a kindly welcome. I was shivering with cold and they wrapped me in a spare sea cloak and gave me chunks of dried whale blubber to chew, their diet for someone who has been exposed to the cold and wet. After I was recovered, they asked me for my story and discovered that I had abundant tales to tell. This made me popular. My stories helped to pass the long hours of the homeward trip and Norsemen love a good yarn. I found myself telling my tales again and again. With each repetition I became more fluent, more able to pace the run of my narrative, to know which details caught the attention of my hearers. In short, I began to understand how satisfying it is to be a saga teller, particularly when the content of your tales has an appreciative audience. I learned that I was one of only a handful of Norse survivors from the great battle at Clontarf, so I was asked repeatedly to describe the progress of the great battle, where each man fought in the line, how each warrior had dressed for the combat, what weapons had proved best, who had said what and to whom, whether such-and-such had died with honour. And always when I came to describe how Brodir of Man had ambushed the High King and slain him in the open, though he knew it would mean his own certain death, my audience would fall silent and, as often as not, greet the conclusion of my story with a sigh of approval.

As I told the story for perhaps the twentieth time, the thought occurred to me that this might be what Odinn was intending – that I should be an honest chronicler of the Old Ways and the truth about the far-flung world of the Norsemen. Was it really Eochaid who had told me that words hold greater power than weapons? Did Senesach at St Ciaran's encourage me to learn to read the Roman and Greek scripts and write with the pen and stylus? Was it Tyrkir who showed me the cutting of runes in Greenland and taught me so much of the Elder Lore. Or were all of them really Odinn in his many disguises equipping me for my life's path?

If it was Odinn, then I am keeping his faith by writing this account, and I will describe how I travelled even farther afield in the next phase of my life and took part in events that were even more remarkable.

AUTHOR'S NOTE

THORGILS, SON OF Leif the Lucky and Thorgunna, did exist. According to the Saga of Erik the Red, 'The boy ... arrived in Greenland, and Leif acknowledged him as his son. According to some people this Thorgils came to Iceland the summer before the Frodriver Marvels. Thorgils then went to Greenland, and there seemed to be something uncanny about him all his life.'

The events of Thorgils's life imagined here derive mostly from the Icelandic sagas, one of the great collections of world literature and widely translated, notably in the Penguin Classics. Eochaid's poem of the hermit's hut is taken from Kenneth Hurlston, *A Celtic Miscellany*, first published by Routledge & Kegan Paul, 1951; revised edition published by Penguin Books, 1971, reprinted 1973, 1975.

VIKING
Sworn Brother

MAPS

Westfjords
Skagafiord
Drang Island
Hvit river
Reykholt
ICELAND

FAEROES

Birsay
Caithness

IRELAND

Northumbria

York

Derby
King's Ly
Northampton
ANGLIA
Norwich

R. Thames
Winchester
London

NORWAY

Nidaros

Tonsberg

Sigtuna

Bjorko

Gothland

Limfiord

JUTLAND

Roskilde

SKANE

Ringsted

Holy river

Hedeby

Steye
Bight

SJAELLAND

Rugen

Jomsburg

NGLISH
SEA

BALTIC SEA

Thorgil's Journeys

-------------- London – Tonsberg – Nidaros – Tonsberg
——————— Tonsberg – Iceland – Jomsburg – Iceland
·················· Iceland – Baltic Sea – Skridfinni – Miklagard

PERMIA

KARELIA

IDFINNI

Aldeijuborg

RUS

GARDARIKI

LAND

BOLGARS

Kiev

PECHENEGS

KHAZARIA

Miklagard

MIYAN

Baghdad

SERKLAND

To my holy and blessed master, Abbot Geraldus,

As requested of your unworthy servant, I send this, the second of the writings of the false monk Thangbrand. Alas, I must warn you that many times the work is even more disturbing than its antecedent. So deeply did the author's life descend into iniquity that many times I have been obliged, when reading his blasphemies, to set aside the pages that I might pray to Our Lord to cleanse my mind of such abominations and beseech Him to forgive the sinner who penned them. For here is a tale of continuing deceit and idolatry, of wantonness and wicked sin as well as violent death. Truly, the coils of deception, fraud and murder drag almost all men down to perdition.

The edges of many pages are scorched and burned by fire. From this I deduce that this Pharisee began to write his tale of depravity before the great conflagration so sadly destroyed our holy cathedral church of St Peter at York on 19 September in the year of our Lord 1069. By diligent enquiry I have learned that the holocaust revealed a secret cavity in the wall of the cathedral library, in which these writings had been concealed. A God-fearing member of our flock, making this discovery, brought the documents to my predecessor as librarian with joy, believing them to contain pious scripture. Lest further pages be discovered to dismay the unwary, I took it upon myself to visit the scene of that devastation and search the ruins. By God's mercy I found no further examples of the reprobate's writings, but with a heavy heart I observed that nothing now remains of our once-great cathedral church, neither the portico of St Gregory, nor the glass windows nor the panelled ceilings. Gone are the thirty altars. Gone too is the great altar to St Paul. So fierce was the heat of the fire that I found spatterings of once-molten tin from the bellcote roof. Even the great bell, fallen from the tower, lay misshapen and dumb. Mysterious indeed are the ways of the Lord that these profane words of the ungodly should survive such destruction.

So great is my abhorrence of what has emerged from that hidden pustule of impiety that I have been unable to complete my reading of all that was found. There remains one more bundle of documents which I have not dared to examine.

On behalf of our community, I pray for your inspired guidance and that the Almighty Lord may keep you securely in bliss. Amen.

Aethelred
Sacristan and Librarian
Written in the month of October in the Year of our Lord One thousand and seventy-one.

ONE

I LOST MY virginity — to a king's wife.

Few people can make such a claim, least of all when hunched over a desk in a monastery scriptorium while pretending to make a fair copy of St Luke's gospel, though in fact writing a life's chronicle. But that is how it was and I remember the scene clearly.

The two of us lay in the elegant royal bed, Aelfgifu snuggled luxuriously against me, her head resting on my shoulder, one arm flung contentedly across my ribs as if to own me. I could smell a faint perfume from the glossy sweep of dark chestnut hair which spread across my chest and cascaded down onto the pillow we shared. If Aelfgifu felt any qualms, as the woman who had just introduced a nineteen-year-old to the delights of lovemaking but who was already the wife of Knut, the most powerful ruler of the northern lands, she did not show them. She lay completely at ease, motionless. All I could feel was the faint pulse of her heart and the regular waft of her breath across my skin. I lay just as still. I neither dared to move nor wanted to. The enormity and the wonder of what had happened had yet to ebb. For the first time in my life I had experienced utter joy in the embrace of a beautiful woman. Here was a marvel which once tasted could never be forgotten.

The distant clang of a church bell broke into my reverie. The sound slid through the window embrasure high in the queen's chambers and disturbed our quiet tranquillity. It was repeated, then joined by another bell and then another. Their metallic clamour reminded me where I was: London. No other city that I had visited boasted so many churches of the White Christ. They were springing up everywhere and the king was doing nothing to obstruct their construction, the king whose wife was now lying beside me, skin to skin.

The sound of the church bells made Aelfgifu stir. 'So, my little courtier,' she murmured, her voice muffled against my chest, 'you had better tell me something about yourself. My servants inform me that your name is Thorgils, but no one seems to know much about you. It's said you have come recently from Iceland. Is that correct?'

'Yes, in a way,' I replied tentatively. I paused, for I did not know how to address her. Should I call her 'my lady'? Or would that seem servile after the recent delight of our mingling, which she had encouraged with her caresses, and which had wrung from me the most intimate words? I hugged her closer and tried to combine both affection and deference in my reply, though I suspect my voice was trembling slightly.

'I arrived in London only two weeks ago. I came in the company of an Icelandic skald. He's taken me on as his pupil to learn how compose court poetry. He's hoping to find employment with . . .' Here my voice trailed away in embarrassment, for I was about to say 'the king'. Of course Aelfgifu guessed my words. She gave my ribs a little squeeze of encouragement and said, 'So that's why you were standing among my husband's skalds at the palace assembly. Go on.' She did not raise her head from my shoulder. Indeed, she pressed her body even more closely against me.

'I met the skald – his name's Herfid – last autumn on the island of Orkney off the Scottish coast, where I had been dropped off by a ship that rescued me from the sea of Ireland. It's a complicated story, but the sailors found me in a small boat that

was sinking. They were very kind to me, and so was Herfid.'
Tactfully I omitted to mention that I had been found drifting in
what was hardly more than a leaky wickerwork bowl covered
with cowskin, after I had been deliberately set afloat. I doubted
whether Aelfgifu knew that this is a traditional punishment levied
on convicted criminals by the Irish. My accusers had been monks
too squeamish to spill blood. And while it was true that I had
stolen their property – five decorative stones prised from a bible
cover – I had only taken the baubles in an act of desperation and
I felt not a shred of remorse. Certainly I did not see myself as a
jewel thief. But I thought this would be a foolish revelation to
make to the warm, soft woman curled up against me, particularly
when the only item she was wearing was a valuable-looking
necklace of silver coins.

'What about your family?' asked Aelfgifu, as if to satisfy
herself on an important point.

'I don't have one,' I replied. 'I never really knew my mother.
She died while I was a small child. She was part Irish, I'm told,
and a few years ago I travelled to Ireland to find out more about
her, but I never succeeded in learning anything. Anyhow, she
didn't live with my father and she had already sent me off to stay
with him by the time she died. My father, Leif, owns one of the
largest farms in a country called Greenland. I spent most of my
childhood there and in an even more remote land called Vinland.
When I was old enough to try to make my own living I had the
idea of becoming a professional skald as I've always enjoyed
story-telling. All the best skalds come from Iceland, so I thought
I would try my luck there.'

Again, I was being sparing with the truth. I did not tell
Aelfgifu that my father Leif, known to his colleagues as 'the
Lucky', had never been married to my mother, either in the
Christian or pagan rite. Nor that Leif's official wife had repudiated
her husband's illegitimate son and refused to have me in her
household. That was why I had spent most of my life being
shuttled from one country to the next, searching for some stability

and purpose. But it occurred to me at that moment, as I lay next
to Aelfgifu, that perhaps my father's luck spirit, his hamingja as
the Norse say, had transferred to me. How else could I explain
the fact that I had lost my virginity to the consort of Knut, ruler
of England, and royal claimant to the thrones of Denmark and
Norway?

It all happened so suddenly. I had arrived in London with my
master Herfid only ten days earlier. He and the other skalds had
been invited to a royal assembly held by King Knut to announce
the start of his new campaign in Denmark, and I had gone along
as Herfid's attendant. During the king's speech from the throne, I
had been aware that someone in Knut's entourage was staring at
me as I stood among the royal skalds. I had no idea who Aelfgifu
was, only that, when our eyes met, there was no mistaking the
appetite in her gaze. The day after Knut sailed for Denmark,
taking his army with him, I had received a summons to attend
Aelfgifu's private apartments at the palace.

'Greenland, Iceland, Ireland, Scotland . . . you are a wanderer,
aren't you, my little courtier,' Aelfgifu said, 'and I've never even
heard of Vinland.' She rolled onto one side and propped her head
on a hand, so that she could trace the profile of my face, from
forehead to chin, with her finger. It was to become a habit of
hers. 'You're like my husband,' she said without embarrassment.
'It's all that Norse blood, never at home, always rushing about,
constantly on the move, with a wanderlust that wants to look
beyond the horizon or incite some action. I don't even try to
understand it. I grew up in the heart of the English countryside,
about as far from the sea as you can get. It's a calmer life, and
though it can be a little dull at times, it's what I like. Anyhow,
dullness can always be brightened up if you know what you are
doing.'

I should have guessed her meaning, but I was too naive;
besides, I was smitten by her sophistication and beauty. I was so
intoxicated with what had happened that I was incapable of asking
myself why a queen should take up with a young man so rapidly.

I was yet to learn how a woman can be attracted instantly and overwhelmingly by a man, and that women who live close to the seat of power can indulge their craving with speed and certainty if they wish. That is their prerogative. Years later I saw an empress go so far as to share her realm with a young man – half her age – who took her fancy, though of course I never stood in that relationship to my wondrous Aelfgifu. She cared for me, of that I am sure, but she was worldly enough to measure out her affection to me warily, according to opportunity. For my part, I should have taken heed of the risk that came from an affair with the king's wife, but I was so swept away by my feelings that nothing on earth would have deterred me from adoring her.

'Come,' she said abruptly, 'it's time to get up. My husband may be away on another of those ambitious military expeditions of his, but if I'm not seen about the palace for several hours people might get curious as to where I am and what I'm doing. The palace is full of spies and gossips, and my prim and prudish rival would be only too delighted to have a stick to beat me with.'

Here I should note that Aelfgifu was not Knut's only wife. He had married her to gain political advantage when he and his father, Svein Forkbeard, were plotting to extend their control beyond the half of England which the Danes already held after more than a century of Viking raids across what they called the 'English Sea'. Aelfgifu's people were Saxon aristocracy. Her father had been an ealdorman, their highest rank of nobility, who owned extensive lands in the border country where the Danish possessions rubbed up against the kingdom of the English ruler, Ethelred. Forkbeard calculated that if his son and heir had a high-born Saxon as wife, the neighbouring ealdormen would be more willing to defect to the Danish cause than to serve their own native monarch, whom they had caustically nicknamed 'the Ill-Advised' for his uncanny ability to wait until the last moment before taking any action and then do the wrong thing at exactly the wrong time. Knut was twenty-four years old when he took Aelfgifu to be his wife, she was two years younger. By the time Aelfgifu invited me to her bedchamber four years later, she was a mature and ripe woman despite her youthful appearance and beauty, and her ambitious husband had risen to become the undisputed king of all England, for Ethelred was in his grave, and – as a step to reassure the English nobility – Knut had married Ethelred's widow, Emma.

Emma was fourteen years older than Knut, and Knut had not bothered to divorce Aelfgifu. The only people who might have objected to his bigamy, namely the Christian priests who infested Emma's household, had found a typically weasel excuse. Knut, they said, had never properly married Aelfgifu because there had been no Christian wedding. In their phrase it was a marriage 'in the Danish custom', *ad mores danaos* – how they loved their church Latin – and did not need to be set aside. Now, behind their hands, they were calling Aelfgifu 'the concubine'. By contrast Knut's earls, his personal retinue of noblemen from Denmark and the Norse lands, approved the dual marriage. In their opinion this was how great kings should behave in matters of state and they liked Aelfgifu. With her slender figure and grace, she was a far more attractive sight at royal assemblies than the dried-up widow Emma with her entourage of whispering prelates. They found that Aelfgifu behaved more in the way that a well-regarded woman in the Norse world should: she was down to earth, independent minded and at times – as I was shortly to discover – she was an accomplished schemer.

Aelfgifu rose from our love bed with typical decisiveness. She slid abruptly to the side, stepped onto the floor – giving me a heart-melting glimpse of her curved back and hips – and, picking up the pale grey and silver shift that she had discarded an hour earlier, slid the garment over her nakedness. Then she turned to me, as I lay there, almost paralysed with fresh longing. 'I'll arrange for my maid to show you discreetly out of the palace. She can be trusted. Wait until I contact you again. You've got another journey to make, though not nearly as far as your previous ones.' Then she turned and vanished behind a screen.

Still in a daze, I reached the lodging house where the royal skalds were accommodated. I found that my master, Herfid, had scarcely noticed my absence. A small and diffident man, he wore clothes cut in a style that had gone out of fashion at least a generation ago, and it was easy to guess he was a skald because the moment he opened his mouth you heard the Icelandic accent and the old-fashioned phrases and obscure words of his profession. As usual, when I entered, he was in another world, seated at the bare table in the main room talking to himself. His lips moved as he tried out various possibilities. 'Battle wolf, battle gleam, beam of war,' he muttered. After a moment's incomprehension I realised he was in the middle of composing a poem and having difficulty in finding the right words. As part of my skald's apprenticeship, he had explained to me that when composing poetry it was vital to avoid plain words for common objects. Instead you referred to them obliquely, using a substitute term or phrase – a kenning – taken if possible from our Norse traditions of our Elder Way. Poor Herfid was making heavy weather of it. 'Whetstone's hollow, hard ring, shield's grief, battle icicle,' he tried to himself. 'No, no, that won't do. Too banal. Ottar the Black used it in a poem only last year.'

By then I had worked out that he was trying to find a different way of saying 'a sword'.

'Herfid!' I said firmly, interrupting his thoughts. He looked up, irritated for a moment by the intrusion. Then he saw who it was and his habitual good humour returned.

'Ah, Thorgils! It's good to see you, though this is a rather lacklustre and empty house since the other skalds sallied forth to accompany the king on his campaign in Denmark. I fear that I've brought you to a dead end. There will be no chance of royal patronage until Knut gets back, and in the meantime I doubt if we'll find anyone else who is willing to pay for good-quality praise poems. I thought that perhaps one of his great earls whom he has left behind here in England, might be sufficiently cultured to want something elegantly phrased in the old style. But I'm told they are a boorish lot. Picked for their fighting ability rather than their appreciation of the finer points of versifying.'

'How about the queen?' I asked, deliberately disingenuous. 'Wouldn't she want some poetry?'

Herfid misunderstood. 'The queen!' he snorted. 'She only wants new prayers or perhaps one of those dreary hymns, all repetitions and chanting, remarkably tedious stuff. And she's got plenty of priests to supply that. The very mention of any of the Aesir would probably make her swoon. She positively hates the Old Gods.'

'I didn't mean Queen Emma,' I said. 'I meant the other one, Aelfgifu.'

'Oh her. I don't know much about her. She's keeping pretty much in the background. Anyhow queens don't employ skalds. They're more interested in romantic harp songs and that sort of frippery.'

'What about Thorkel, the vice-regent, then? I'm told that Knut has placed Thorkel in charge of the country while he is away. Wouldn't he appreciate a praise poem or two? Everyone says he's one of the old school, a true Viking. Fought as a mercenary, absolute believer in the Elder Faith, wears Thor's hammer as an amulet.'

'Yes, indeed, and you should hear him swear when he's angry,' said Herfid cheering up slightly. 'He spits out more names for the Old Gods than even I've heard. He also blasphemes mightily against those White Christ priests. I've been told that when he's drunk he refers to Queen Emma as Bakrauf. I just hope that not too many of the Saxons hear or understand.'

I knew what he meant. In Norse lore a bakrauf was a wizened old hag, a troll wife, and her name translates as 'arse hole'.

'So why don't you attach yourself to Thorkel's household as a skald?' I insisted.

'That's a thought,' Herfid said. 'But I'll have to be cautious. If word gets back to Knut that the vice-regent is surrounding himself with royal trappings, like a personal skald, the king may think that he is putting on airs and wants to be England's ruler. Knut delegated Thorkel to look after the military side of things, put down any local troubles with a firm hand and so forth, but Archbishop Wulfstan is in charge of the civil administration and the legal side. It's a neat balance: the heathen kept in check by the Christian.' Herfid, who was a kindly man, sighed. 'Whatever happens, even if I get an appointment with Thorkel, I'm afraid that there won't be much of an opportunity for you to shine as my pupil. A vice-regent is not as wealthy as a king, and his largesse is less. You're welcome to stay on with me as an apprentice, but I can't possibly pay you anything. We'll be lucky if we have enough to eat.'

A page boy solved my predicament three days later when the lad knocked at the door of our lodgings with a message for me. I was to report to the queen's chamberlain ready to join her entourage, which was leaving for her home country of Northampton. It took me only a moment to pack. All the clothing I owned, apart from the drab tunic, shoes and hose that I wore every day, was a plum-coloured costume Herfid had given me so that I could appear reasonably well dressed at court. This garment I stuffed into the worn satchel of heavy leather I had stitched for myself in Ireland when I had lived among the monks there. Then I said goodbye to Herfid, promising him that I would try to keep in touch. He was still struggling to find a suitable substitute phrase to fit the metre of his rhyme. 'How about "death's flame"? That's a good kenning for a sword,' I suggested as I turned to leave with the satchel over my shoulder.

He looked at me with a smile of pure delight. 'Perfect!' he said, 'It fits exactly. You've not entirely ignored my teaching. I hope that one day you'll find some use for your gift with words.'

In the palace courtyard Aelfgifu's entourage was already waiting, four horse-drawn carts with massive wooden wheels to haul the baggage and transport the womenfolk, a dozen or so riding animals, and an escort of a couple of Knut's mounted huscarls. The last were no more than token protection, as the countryside had been remarkably peaceful since Knut came to the throne. The English, after years of fighting off Viking raiders or being squeezed for the taxes to buy them off with Danegeld, were so exhausted that they would have welcomed any overlord just as long he brought peace. Knut had done better. He had promised to rule the Saxons with the same laws they had under a Saxon king, and he showed his trust in his subjects – and reduced their tax burden – by sending away his army of mercenaries, a rough lot drawn from half the countries across the Channel and the English Sea. But Knut was too canny to leave himself entirely vulnerable to armed rebellion. He surrounded himself with his huscarls, three hundred of them all armed to the teeth. Any man who joined his elite guard was required to own, as a personal possession, a long two-edged sword with gold inlay in the grip. Knut knew well that only a genuine fighter would own such an expensive weapon and only a man of substance could afford one. His palace regiment was composed of professional full-time fighting men whose trade was warfare. Never before had the English seen such a compact and lethal fighting force, or one with weaponry so stylish.

So I was surprised to observe that the two huscarls detailed to escort Queen Aelfgifu were both severely maimed. One had a stump where his right hand should be, and the other had lost a leg below the knee and walked on a wooden limb. Then I remembered that Knut had taken the huscarl regiment on his campaign in Denmark; only the invalids had been left behind. Even as I watched the huscarls prepare to mount their stallions, I was already revising my opinion of their disabilities. The one-legged man limped to his horse, and though he was encumbered with a round wooden shield slung across his back, he bent down and removed his wooden leg and, with it still in his hand, balanced for a moment on a single foot before he gave a brisk, one-legged hop and swung himself into the saddle. There he tucked the false limb into a leather loop for safe keeping, and began to tie a leather strap around his waist to fix himself more firmly in place.

'Come on, stop fiddling about. It's time to ride!' he bellowed cheerfully at his companion, who was using one hand and his teeth to untangle his horse's knotted reins, and getting ready to wrap them around the stump of his arm, 'Even Tyr didn't take so long to get Gleipnir ready for Fenrir.'

'Shut up, Treeleg, or I'll come across and knock that stupid grin off your face,' came the reply, but I could see that the one-handed man was flattered. And rightly so. Every Old Believer knows that Tyr is the bravest of the Old Gods, the Aesirs. It was Tyr who volunteered to put his hand into the mouth of the Fenrir, the hell wolf, to lull the beast's suspicions while the other Gods placed Gleipnir, the magic fetter, on the hell wolf to restrain him. The dwarves had made the fetter from six magical ingredients – 'the sound of a cat's footfall, a woman's beard, a mountain's roots, a bear's sinews, a fish's breath and a bird's spit' – and Gleipnir did not burst even when the hell hound felt his bonds tightening and struggled with a fiend's strength. Meanwhile brave Tyr lost his hand to the hell wolf's bite.

Aelfgifu's chamberlain was glaring at me. 'Are you Thorgils?' he asked curtly. 'You're late. Ever ridden a horse before?'

I nodded cautiously. In Iceland I had occasionally ridden the sturdy little Icelandic horses. But they stood close enough to the ground for the rider not to get hurt when he fell off, and there were no roads, only tracks across the moors, so the landing was usually soft enough if you were not so unlucky as to fall on a rock. But I did not fancy trying to get on the back of anything resembling the bad-tempered stallions the two huscarls were now astride. To my relief the chamberlain nodded towards a shaggy and dispirited-looking mare tied up to the tail of one of the carts. Her aged head was drooping. 'Take that animal. Or walk.' Soon our motley cavalcade was creaking and clopping its way out of the city, and I was wondering whether there had not been a change of plan. Nowhere could I see my adored Aelfgifu.

She joined us in a thunder of cantering hooves when we had already crawled along for some five miles. 'Here she comes, riding like a Valkyrie as usual,' I heard the one-handed huscarl remark approvingly to his colleague, as they turned in their saddles to watch the young queen approach. On my plodding creature I twisted round as well, trying not to make my interest obvious, but my heart was pounding. There she was, riding like a man, her loose hair streaming out behind her. With a pang of jealousy I noted that she was accompanied by two or three young noblemen, Saxons by the look of them. A moment later the little group were swirling past us, chattering and whooping with delight as they took up their places as the head of the little group, then reined in their horses to match our trudging progress. Clumping along on my ugly nag, I felt hot and ashamed. I had not really expected that Aelfgifu would even glance at me, but I was so lovelorn that I still hoped she would catch my eye. She had ignored me entirely.

For four unhappy days I stayed at the back of the little column, and the most I ever saw of Aelfgifu was an occasional glimpse of her shapely back among the leading horsemen with her companions. It was torture for me whenever one of the young men leaned across towards her to exchange some confidence, or I saw her throw back her head and laugh at a witty remark. Sour with jealousy, I tried to learn who her companions were, but my fellow travellers were a taciturn lot. They could only tell me that they were high-born Saxons, ealdormen's spawn.

The journey was torture for another reason. My lacklustre mount proved to be the most leaden-footed, iron-mouthed creature that ever escaped the butcher's knife. The brute plodded along, slamming down her feet so that the impact of each hoof fall rattled up my spine. My saddle, the cheapest variety and made of wood, was an agony. Each time I dismounted I hobbled like a crone, so stiff that I could not walk properly. Life on the road was no better. I had to work for every yard of progress, kicking and slapping at the flanks of the sluggish creature to make her go forward. And when the mare decided to leave the main track and

head for a mouthful of spring grass, there was nothing I could do
to prevent her. I hit her between the ears with a hazel rod I cut
for the purpose, and heaved on the reins. But the creature merely
turned her ugly head to one side and kept walking in a straight
line towards her target. On one embarrassing occasion she tripped
and the two of us went sprawling in the dirt. As soon as the mare
had her head down and started eating, I was helpless. I pulled on
the reins till my arms ached and kicked her in the ribs, but there
was no response. Only when the obstinate brute had eaten her fill
would she raise her head and lumber back to the main track while
I swore in rage.

'Try to keep up with the group,' One Hand warned me gruffly
as he rode back down the column to see that all was in order. 'I
don't want any stragglers.'

'I'm sorry,' I replied. 'I'm having difficulty controlling my
horse.'

'If it *is* a horse' commented the huscarl, regarding the ill-
shapen monster. 'I don't think I've ever seen such an ugly nag.
Has it got a name?'

'I don't know,' I said, and then added without thinking, 'I'm
calling her Jarnvidja.'

The huscarl gave me a funny look, before wheeling about and
riding off. Jarnvidja means 'iron hag' and I realised, like Bakrauf,
it is the name of a troll wife.

My dawdling horse allowed me plenty of opportunity to
observe the countryside of England. The land was astonishingly
prosperous despite the recent wars. Village followed village in
quick succession. Most were neat and well tended – a dozen or so
thatched houses constructed with walls of wattle and daub or
wooden planks and set on either side of the muddy street or at a
crossroads. Many had gardens front and back and, beyond their
barns, pigsties and sheep sheds, were well-tended fields stretching
away to the edge of forests or moorland. If the place was
important enough there might be a larger house for the local
magnate with its little chapel, or even a small church built of

wood. Sometimes I noticed a stonemason at work, laying the foundations for a more substantial church tower. It seemed that the worship of the White Christ was spreading at remarkable speed, even in the countryside. I never saw a shrine to Old Ways, only tattered little strips of votive rags hanging from every great oak tree we passed, indicating that the Elder Faith had not entirely vanished.

Our party was travelling across country in an almost straight line and I thought this strange. The roads and tracks I had known in Iceland and Ireland meandered here and there, keeping to the high ground to avoid boglands and turning aside to shun the thickest forests. But the English road cut straight across country, or nearly so. When I looked more closely, I realised that our heavy carts were rolling and creaking along a prepared track, rutted and battered but still discernible, with occasional paving slabs and a raised embankment.

When I enquired, I was told that this was a legacy of the Roman days, a road called Watling Street and that, although the original bridges and causeways had long since collapsed or been washed away, it was the duty of the local villages to maintain and repair the track. They often failed in their task, and we found ourselves splashing across fords or paying ferrymen to take us across rivers in small barges and row boats.

It was at a water splash that the appalling Jarnvidja finally disgraced me. As usual, she was plodding along at the rear of the column when she smelled water up ahead. Being thirsty, she simply barged her way forward past the wagons and other horses. Aelfgifu and her companions had already reached the ford, and their horses were standing in the shallows, cooling their feet while their riders chatted. By then I had lost all control over Jarnvidja, and my hideous mount came sliding and slithering down the bank, rudely shouldering aside a couple of horses. As I tugged futilely on the reins, Jarnvidja splashed monstrously through the shallows, her great hooves sending up a muddy spray which drenched the finery of the Saxon nobles, and spattered across the queen herself.

Then the brute stopped, plunged her ugly snout into the water and began to suck up her drink noisily, while I was forced to sit on her broad back, crimson with embarrassment, and Aelfgifu's companions glared at me as they brushed off the muck.

On the fifth day we turned aside from Watling Street and rode down a broad track through a dense forest of beech and oak until we came to our destination. Aelfgifu's home was more heavily protected that earlier settlements I had seen. It was what the Saxons call a burh and was surrounded by a massive earth bank and a heavy wooden palisade. All around for a space of about a hundred paces the forest had been cleared back to allow a field of fire for archers in case of attack. Inside the rampart the ground was laid out to accommodate a lord and his retinue. There were dormitories for servants, a small barracks for the soldiery, storehouses and a large banqueting hall next to the lord's own dwelling, a substantial manor house. As our travel-stained group entered the main gate, the inhabitants lined up to greet us. Amid the reunions, gossip and exchanges of news, I saw the two huscarls head straight for the manor house, and – to my disappointment – Aelgifu and her attendant women disappear into a separate building, the women's quarters. I dismounted and stretched my back, glad at last to be rid of my torment on the Iron Hag. A servant came forward to take the mare from me, and I was heartily glad to see her gone. Her final act of treachery was to step heavily on my foot as she was led away, and I hope never to see her again.

I was wondering what I should do and where I should go, when a man whom I guessed was the local steward appeared. He had a list in his hand. 'Who are you?' he asked.

'Thorgils,' I replied.

He looked down his list, then said, 'Can't see your name here. Must have been a last-minute addition. Until I get this sorted out, you can go and help out Edgar.'

'Edgar?' I queried.

But the steward was already waving me away, too busy to

explain details. He had pointed vaguely towards a side gate. Whoever Edgar was, it seemed that I would find him outside the palisade.

My satchel slung over my shoulder, I walked out through the gate. In the distance I could see a low wooden building, and a small cottage. I walked towards them and as I drew closer my heart sank. I heard the barking and hubbub of dogs and realised that I was approaching a kennel. Earlier, in Ireland, I had been dog boy to the Norse king, Sigtryggr of Dublin, and it had not been a success. I had been put in charge of two Irish wolfhounds and they had run away from me. Now I could hear at least a dozen dogs, maybe more, and smell their unmistakably pungent odour. It was beginning to rain, one of those sudden heavy showers so frequent in an English spring time, and I looked for somewhere to shelter. I did not want to risk being bitten, so I swerved aside and ran towards a small shed set close to the edge of the forest.

The door was not locked and I pulled it open. It was gloomy inside, the only light coming through cracks in walls made from loosely woven wattle. When my eyes had adjusted to the darkness, I saw that the shed was completely empty except for several stout posts driven into the earth floor, over which had been strewn a thin layer of sand. From each post extended a number of short wooden poles, covered with sacking or bound with leather, and sitting on the poles were birds. They ranged in size from scarcely bigger than my hand to a creature as large as a barnyard cockerel. The shed was eerily quiet. I heard only the distant howling of the dogs and the patter of rain on the thatched roof. The birds were silent, except for the occasional rustle of a wing and a scratching sound as they shifted their claws on the perches. I stepped forward to examine them more closely, gingerly treading past them as they turned their heads to follow my progress. I realised that they were following me by sound not by sight, for they were blind. Or rather, they could not see me because they were wearing leather hoods on their heads. Then I stopped dead in my tracks and a great wave of homesickness suddenly swept over me.

In front of me, sitting on a perch well away from the others, was a bird I recognised at once. Its feathers were pale grey, almost white, and speckled with blackish brown spots, like a sheet of parchment on which a scribe had sprinkled spots of ink. Even in the half-light I could see that, though hunched up and miserable, it was a spear falcon.

The spear falcons are princes among the birds of prey. As a child in Greenland I had seen these magnificent birds hunting ptarmigan on the moors, and our trappers occasionally tangled them in nets or climbed the cliffs to take them as fledglings, for they are the most precious of our Greenlandic exports. We sent away five or six falcons in a year to the traders in Iceland, and I heard that they were then sold on for a great price to wealthy magnates in Norway or the southern lands. To see one of these birds, in the centre of damp, green England, cooped up and far from its natural home, made me feel it was a kindred soul, an exile, and the scene squeezed at my heart.

The spear falcon was in moult. That was why it was looking so dejected, its feathers dishevelled and awry. The bird sensed my presence and turned its head towards me. I crept forward and then I saw: its eyes were sewn shut. A thin thread had been stitched through each of the lower eyelids, and then led up over the bird's head, pulling the eyelid up. The two threads were tied together in a knot over the head, holding up the lids. Tentatively I stretched out my hand, fearing to frighten the bird, yet wanting to unpick the knot and release the eyes. I felt the creature's unhappy fate was a symbol of my predicament. My hand was hovering over the bird's head, no more than six inches away, when suddenly my left wrist was seized from behind and my arm twisted up violently between my shoulder blades. Wiry fingers clamped on the back of my neck, and a voice hissed ferociously in my ear, 'Touch that bird and I'll break first your arm and then your neck!' Then I was pushed forward so that I was forced to bend double at the waist. Next my attacker turned and marched me, still bent over, out through the shed door and into the open. There he deftly kicked my feet from under me so that I fell headlong in the mud. Winded, I lay gasping for a moment, shocked by the lightning attack. My assailant had dropped on top of me and was holding me face down, one knee in my back. I could not turn my head to see who he was, so I blurted out, 'I was looking for Edgar.' Above me, a voice seething with anger said, 'You've found him.'

TWO

MY ATTACKER RELEASED his grip and allowed me to roll over and look up. A small, thick-set man was standing over me, dressed in a patched and worn tunic, heavy hose and scuffed leather leggings. His grey hair was cropped close to his skull, and I guessed he must be in his mid-fifties. What struck me most was how battered and weatherbeaten he looked. Deep lines were etched across his face and his cheeks were mottled with dark red blotches as if someone had scoured them with sand. An angry scowl pulled his eyebrows so far down that his eyes almost disappeared into his skull. He looked thoroughly dangerous, and I noted a well-used dagger with a stag-horn handle tucked into his leather belt and wondered why he had not drawn it. Then I remembered how easily he had bundled me out of the shed, as if I was no more than a child.

'What were you doing in the hawk shed?' he demanded furiously. He spoke the language of the Saxons, close enough to my native Norse for me to understand, but with a country accent, deep and deliberate, so that I had to listen closely. 'Who gave you permission to go in there?'

'I told you,' I replied placatingly, 'I was looking for Edgar. I had no idea that I was doing any harm.'

'And the gyrfalcon? What were you doing near it? What were you trying? To steal it?'

23

'No,' I said. 'I wanted to remove the thread so that it could open its eyes.'

'And who said you could do that?' He was growing even more angry, and I was worried that he would lose control and give me a beating. There was no answer to his question, so I kept silent.

'Imbecile! Do you know what would have happened? The bird would have panicked, left its perch, thrashed around. Escaped or damaged itself. It's in no condition to fly. And that bird, for your information, is worth ten times as much as you are, probably more, you miserable lout.'

'I'm sorry,' I said. 'I recognised the bird and I've never seen them with their eyes sewn shut before.'

My reply set him off again. 'What do you mean "recognised?"' he snarled. 'There are no more than five or six birds like that in the whole of England. That's a royal bird.'

'Where I come from, there are quite a few.'

'So you're a liar as well as a thief.'

'No, believe me. I come from a place where those birds build their nests and raise their young. I only entered the shed to look for you, if you are Edgar, because I was told to find him and report to him for work.'

'I asked for a kennelhand, not a thieving Dane with sticky fingers like all the rest of them. I can recognise your ugly accent,' he growled. 'Get on your feet,' and he let loose a kick to help me up. 'We'll soon learn whether you're telling the truth.'

He marched me back to the burh and checked my story with Aelfgifu's harassed steward. When the steward confirmed who I was, Edgar spat deliberately – the gob of spittle just missed me – and announced, 'We'll see about that then.'

This time we returned to the kennels and Edgar lifted the latch on the low gate which led into the dog-run. Instantly a hysterical brown, white and tan cascade of tail-wagging confusion swirled forward and engulfed us. The dogs barked and howled, though whether with enthusiasm or hunger I could not tell. Some leaped up at Edgar in affection, others pushed and shoved to get closer, a few cringed back, or ran off into the corner and defecated in their excitement. The kennel smelled abominable, and I felt a sharp pain in my calf where one mistrustful dog had run round behind me to give me an experimental bite. Edgar was completely at ease. He plunged his hands into the heaving mass of dog flesh, petting them, rubbing ears fondly, calling their names, casually knocking aside the more exuberant animals which tried to leap up and lick his face. He was in his element, but for me it was a vision of the abyss.

'This is where you will work,' he said bluntly.

I must have looked aghast, for he allowed himself the glimmer of a smile. 'I'll show you your duties.' He crossed to the far side of the dog-run, where a long, low shed was built against the fence. He dragged open the ill-fitting door and we went inside. The interior was almost as bare as the hawk shed, only this time there was no sand on the earth floor and instead of bird perches, a wide wooden platform had been constructed down one side of the building. The platform was made of rough wooden planks, raised about a foot above the ground on short posts. Its surface was covered with a thick layer of straw, which Edgar pointed at. 'I want that turned over daily, so that it's well aired. Pick up any droppings and put them outside. When you've a sackful of turds, you'll be carrying it to the tannery for the leather-makers. Nothing like a strong solution of dog shit to soften the surface of hides. Then every three days, when the straw is too soiled, you change all the bedding. I'll show you later where to find fresh straw.'

Next he pointed out three low troughs. 'Keep these topped up with drinking water for the dogs. If they get fouled, you're to take them outside and empty them − I don't want the floor in here any more damp than it already is − then refill them.' As he made his remark about the damp floor, he glanced towards a wooden post hammered into the ground about halfway along the shed. The post was wrapped with straw and there was an obvious damp patch around it. I realised it was a urinating post. 'Every three days you change that straw as well. Let the dogs out into the run first thing every morning. That's when you will change their straw bedding. They're to be fed once a day – mostly stale bread, but also meat scraps from the main kitchen, whatever is left over. You are to check through the scraps to make sure that there's nothing harmful in the swill. If any dog is sick or off-colour, and there's usually one or two, you're to let me know at once.'

'Where will I find you?' I asked.

'I live in the cottage opposite the hawk shed. Behind my house you'll find the lean-to where the straw is kept. If I'm not at home, probably because I'm out in the forest, check with my wife before you touch any of the stores. She'll keep an eye on you to make sure that you're doing your job thoroughly. Any questions?'

By now we had re-emerged from the dog shed and were back at the entrance to the dog-run. 'No,' I said, 'you've made everything very clear. Where do I sleep?'

He gave me a look of pure malice. 'Where do you expect? With the dogs, of course. That's the right place for a kennelman.'

My next question was on the tip of my tongue, when the expression on his face decided me not to give him the satisfaction of asking it. I was going to enquire, 'What about my food? Where do I take my meals?' But I already knew the answer – 'With the dogs. You eat what they do.'

I was right. The next days were among the most vile that I ever spent and I have lived under some unspeakable conditions. I ate and I slept with the dogs. I picked out the better scraps from their food for my own meals, I caught their fleas and I spent a good deal of my time avoiding their teeth. I loathed them, and took to carrying a cudgel – which I hid under the dog platform whenever Edgar appeared – and used it to clout any dog that came too close to me, though some of the nastier ones still tried to circle round behind me and attack. The experience gave me ample time to wonder how on earth people could become fond of their dogs, least of all such unlovely hounds as these. In Ireland the clan chiefs had been proud of their wolfhounds, and I had understood why. Their dogs were resplendent, elegant animals, aristocratic with their long legs and haughty pace. But Edgar's pack was, to all appearances, a bunch of curs. Half the height of a wolfhound, they had short faces, sharp snouts and untidy fur. The predominant colour was a drab brown, though a few had patches of black or of tan, and one dog would have been all white if it had not kept rolling in the filthiness. It was incredible to me that anyone would take the trouble to keep a pack of them. Several months later I learned that they were known as 'Briton hounds' and their forebears had been greatly valued as hunting dogs by those same Romans who had built the Watling Street. My informant was a monk whose abbot was a sporting priest and ran a pack of them, and he told me that these Briton hounds were valued for their courage, their tenacity and their ability to follow the scent whether in the air or on the ground. How the dogs managed to follow a scent amazed me, for they themselves stank exceedingly. In an attempt to keep my purple tunic from being tainted, I took the precaution of hanging my faithful leather satchel from a peg in one of the upright posts, as high up as I could manage, for I knew for certain that, within hours, I reeked as much as my canine companions.

Edgar came to visit the kennel both morning and afternoon to check on me as well as his noxious hounds. He would enter the dog-run and wade nonchalantly through the riot of animals. He had an uncanny ability to spot any of them that were cut, scratched or damaged in any way. Then he would reach out and grab the dog and haul it close. With complete assurance he folded back ears, prised apart toes looking for thorns, and casually pulled aside private parts, which he called their yard and stones, to check that they were not sore or bleeding. If he found a gash, he produced a needle and thread, and with one knee pinned down the dog while he stitched up the wound. Occasionally, if the dog was troublesome, he would call on me to assist by holding it, and of course I got badly bitten. Seeing the blood dripping from my hand, Edgar gave a satisfied laugh. 'Teach you to stick your hand in his mouth,' he jeered, making me think instantly of the one-handed huscarl. 'Better than a cat bite. That'd go bad on you. A dog bite is clean and healthy. Or at least it is if the dog isn't mad.' The dog which had bitten me certainly didn't look mad, so I sucked at the puncture wounds left by its teeth and said nothing. But Edgar wasn't going to miss his opportunity. 'Do you know what you do if you get bitten by a mad dog?' he asked with relish. 'You can't suck hard enough to get out the rottenness. So you get a good strong barnyard cock, and strip off his feathers, all of them, until he is arse naked. Then you clap his fundament on the wound and give him a bad fright. That way he clenches up his gut and sucks out the wound.' He guffawed.

My ordeal would have lasted much longer but for the fact that I mislaid a dog on the fourth day. Edgar had told me to take the pack to a grassy area a few hundred paces from the kennel. There the animals were encouraged to chew the blades of grass for their health. During that short excursion I managed to lose track of the number of hounds I took with me, and when I brought them back into the dog-run I failed to notice that one was missing. Only when I was shutting the dogs up for the night and took a head count, did I realise my error. I closed the kennel door behind me, and walked back to the grassy area to see if I could find the missing hound. I did not call the dog because I did not know its name and, just as importantly, I did not want to alert Edgar to my blunder. He had been so hostile about the possible loss of a hawk that I was sure he would be furious over a missing dog. I walked quietly, hoping to spot the runaway lurking somewhere. There was no dog by the grass patch, and, thinking that the animal might have found its way to the back door of Edgar's cottage to scavenge, I went to check. Just as I rounded the corner of the little house, I heard a slight clatter, and there was Edgar.

He was kneeling on the ground with his back to me. In front of him was a square of white cloth spread on the earth. Lying on the cloth where he had just dropped them lay a scatter of half a dozen flat lathes. Edgar, who had been looking down at them intently, swung round in surprise.

'What do they say?' I asked, hoping to forestall the outburst of anger.

He regarded me with suspicion. 'None of your business,' he retorted. I began to walk away when, unexpectedly from behind me, I heard him say, 'Can you read the wands?'

I turned back and replied cautiously, 'In my country we prefer to throw dice or a tafl. And we bind our wands together like a book.'

'What's a tafl?'

'A board which has markers. With practice one can read the signs.'

'But you do use wands?'

'Some of the older people still do, or knuckle bones of animals.'

'Then tell me what you think these wands say.'

I walked over to where the white cloth lay on the ground, and counted six of the wooden lathes scattered on it. Edgar was holding a seventh in his hand. One of the lathes on the ground was painted with a red band. I knew it must be the master. Three of the wands on the ground were slightly shorter than the others.

'What do you read?' Edgar asked. There was a pleading note in his voice.

I looked down. 'The answer is confused,' I said. I bent down and picked up one of the lathes. It was slightly askew, lying across another wand. I turned it over, and read the sign marked on it. 'Tyr,' I said, 'the God of death and war.'

Edgar looked puzzled for an instant and then the blood drained from his face, leaving the ruddy spots on his cheekbones even brighter. 'Tiw? You know how to read the marks? Are you sure?'

'Yes, of course,' I replied, showing him the marked face of the wand. The symbol on it was the shape of an arrow. 'I'm a devotee of Odinn and it was Odinn who learned the secret of the runes and taught them to mankind. Also he invented fortune dice. It's very plain. That rune is Tyr's own sign. Nothing else.'

Edgar's voice was unsteady as he said, 'That must mean that she is dead.'

'Who?'

'My daughter. Four years ago a gang of your Danish bandits took her away during the troubles. They couldn't attack the burh – the palisade was too strong for them – so they made a quick sweep around the perimeter, beat my youngest son so badly that he lost an eye and dragged off the girl. She was just twelve. We've not heard a word from her since.'

'Is that what you wanted to know when you cast the wands? What had become of her.'

'Yes,' he replied.

'Then don't give up hope,' I said. 'The wand of Tyr was lying across another wand, and that signifies the meaning is unclear or reversed. So your daughter may be alive. Would you like me to cast the sticks again for you?'

The huntsman shook his head. 'No,' he said. 'Three casts at a time is enough. Any more would be an affront to the Gods and, besides, the sun has set and now the hour is no longer propitious.'

Then his suspicions came back with a rush. 'How do I know you're not lying to me about the runes, like you lied about the gyrfalcon.'

'There's no reason for me to lie,' I answered, and began picking up the wands, the master rod first and then the three shorter, calling out their names, 'rainbow, warrior queen, firm belief.' Then, collecting the longer ones, I announced, 'The key-holder, joy,' and taking the last one from Edgar's fingers I said, 'festivity.'

To establish my credentials even more clearly, I asked inno-cenctly, 'You don't use the wand of darkness, the snake wand?'

Edgar looked dumbfounded. He was, as I later found out, a countryman at heart, and he believed implicitly in the Saxon wands, as they are called in England where they are much used in divination and prophecy. But only the most skilled employ the eighth wand, the snake wand. It has a baleful influence which affects all the other wands and most people, being only human, prefer a happy outcome to the shoot, as the Saxons call the casting of the rods. Frankly I thought the Saxon wands were elementary. In Iceland my rune master Thrand had taught me to read much more sophisticated versions. There the wands are fastened to a leather cord, fanned out and used like an almanac, the meanings read from runes cut on both sides. These runes – like most seidr or magic – reverse the normal forms. The runes are written backwards, as if seen in a mirror.

'Tell my wife what you just said about our daughter,' Edgar announced. 'It may comfort her. She has been grieving for the girl these four years past.' He ushered me into the cottage – it was no more than a large single room, divided across the middle into a living area and a bedroom. There was an open fire at the gable wall, a plain table and two benches. At Edgar's prompting I repeated my reading of the wands to Edgar's wife, Judith. The poor woman looked pitifully trustful of my interpretation and timidly asked if I would like some proper food. I suspected that she thought that her husband had been treating me very unfairly. But Edgar's loathing was understandable if he thought I was a Dane, like the raiders who had kidnapped his daughter and maimed his son.

Edgar was obviously weighing me up. 'Where did you say you come from?' he asked suddenly.

'From Iceland and before that from Greenland.'

'But you speak like a Dane.'

'Same words, yes,' I said, 'but I say them differently, and I use some words that are only used in Iceland. A bit like your Saxon. I'm sure you've noticed how foreigners from other parts of England speak it differently and have words that you don't understand.'

'Prove to me that you come from this other place, this Greenland or whatever you call it.'

'I'm afraid I don't know how to.'

Edgar thought for a moment, and then said suddenly, 'Gyrfalcon. You said you come from a place where the bird builds its nests and raises its young. And I know that it does not do so in the Danes' country, but somewhere further away. So if you are really from that place, then you know all about the bird and its habits.'

'What can I tell you?' I asked.

He looked cunning, then said, 'Answer me this: is the gyrfalcon a hawk of the tower, or a hawk of the hand?'

I had no idea what he was talking about and when I looked baffled he was triumphant. 'Just as I thought. You don't know anything about them.'

'No,' I said 'It's just that I don't understand your question. But I could recognise a gyrfalcon if I saw it hunting.'

'So tell me how.'

'When I watched the wild spear falcons in Greenland, they would fly down from the cliffs and perch on some vantage point on the moors, like a high rock or hill crest. There the bird sat, watching out for its prey. It was looking for its food, another bird we call rjupa, like your partridge. When the spear falcon sees a rjupa, it launches from its perch and flies low at tremendous speed, faster and faster, and then strikes the rjupa, knocking it to the ground, dead.'

'And what does it do at the last moment before it strikes?' Edgar asked.

'The spear falcon suddenly rises, to gain height, and then come smashing down on its prey.'

'Right,' announced Edgar, finally persuaded. 'That's what the gyr does and that's why it can be a hawk of the tower and also a hawk of the fist, and very few hunting birds can be both.'

'I still don't know what you mean,' I said. 'What's a bird of the tower?'

'A bird that towers or waits on, as we say. Hovers in the sky above the master, waiting for the right moment, then drops down on its prey. Peregrine falcons do that naturally and, with patience, gyrfalcons can be taught to hunt that way. A hawk of the fist is one that is carried on the hand or wrist while hunting, and thrown off the hand to chase down the quarry.'

Thus my knowledge of the habits of the wild gyrfalcon and the art of divination rescued me from the ordeal of those noxious dog kennels, though Edgar confessed some weeks later that he would not have kept me living in the kennels indefinitely because he had recognised that I did not have the makings of a kennelman. 'Mind you, I can't understand anyone who doesn't get along with dogs,' he added. 'Seems unnatural.'

'They stink exceedingly,' I pointed out. 'It took me days to wash off their stench. Quite why the English love their dogs so much baffles me. They never stop talking about them. Sometimes they seem to prefer them to their own children.'

'Not just the English,' Edgar said, 'That pack belongs to Knut, and when he shows up here half his Danish friends bring along their own dogs, which they add to the pack. It's a cursed nuisance as the dogs start fighting amongst themselves.'

'Precisely,' I commented. 'When it comes to dogs, neither Saxon nor Dane seems to have any common sense. In Greenland, in times of famine, we ate them.'

By the time of that conversation I was being treated as a member of Edgar's family. I had been allocated a corner of their cottage where I could hang my satchel and find a sleeping place, and Judith, who was as trusting as her husband had been initially wary, was spoiling me as if I was her favourite nephew. She would fish out for me the best bits of meat from the stewpot that simmered constantly over her cooking fire. I have rarely been fed so well. Officially Edgar was the royal huntsman, an important post which made him responsible for arranging the hunts when Knut came to visit. But Edgar also had a neat sideline in poaching. He quietly set nets for small game – hares were a favourite prey

– and would come back to the cottage in the first light of dawn, his leggings wet with dew, and a couple of plump hares dangling from his hand.

As spring turned to summer, I realised that I was very privileged. July is the hungry month before the crops have been harvested, and normal folk must live on the sweepings of their storehouses and grain bins. They eat hard, gritty bread made from bran, old husks and ground-up peas. But in Edgar's house our stockpot was always well supplied, and with the hunting season approaching Edgar began to take me into the forest to scout for the biggest game of all – red-deer stags. This was Edgar at his best – quiet, confident and willing to teach me. He was like Herfid explaining the skald's techniques, or the monks in Ireland when they taught me French, Latin and a little Greek, and how to read and write the foreign scripts, or my seidr master Thrand in Iceland as he tutored me in the mysteries of the Elder Faith.

Edgar took me with him as he quietly followed the deer paths through the forest of oak and beech, and smaller thickets of alder and ash. He showed me how to judge the size of a deer from the size of the hoof prints, and how to tell whether the stag was walking, running or moving at a trot. After he had located a stag large enough to be hunted by the king's pack, we would return again and again to note the stag's regular haunts and observe its daily routine. 'Look closely,' he would say to me, pulling aside a bush. 'This is where he slept last night. See how the grass and weeds are flattened down. And here are the marks where his knees pressed the earth as he got to his feet at dawn. He's a big stag all right, probably twelve points on his antlers, a royal beast . . . and in good condition too,' he added, poking open one of the stag's turds. 'He's tall, that one, and holds his head well. Here's where his antlers scraped the tree when passing.'

Nor was Edgar confused when, as happened, the tracks of two stags crossed in the forest. 'The one we want is the stag who veered off to the right. He's the better one,' he told me quietly. 'The other one is too thin.'

'How do you know?' I whispered, for the size of the tracks looked the same to me.

Edgar made me kneel on the ground and sight along the second line of tracks. 'See anything different?' he asked.

I shook my head.

'Observe the pattern of the slots' – this was his name for the hoof marks – 'you can see the difference between the fore and back feet, and how this stag was running. His hind feet strike the ground in front of the marks made by his fore feet, and that means he is thin. A well-fed, fat stag is too big in the body for his legs to over-reach in this way.'

It was on one of these scouting trips into the forest that Edgar came close to treating me with deference, a far cry from his earlier harassment. He was, as I had noted, someone who believed deeply in signs and portents and the hidden world which underlies our own. I did not find this strange, for I had been trained in these beliefs through my education in the Elder Faith. In some sacred matters Edgar and I had much in common. He respected many of my Gods, though under slightly different names. Odinn, my special God, he knew as Wotan; Tiw was his name for Tyr the War God, as I had noted; and red-bearded Thor he referred to as Thunor. But Edgar had other gods too, and many of them were entirely new to me. There were elves and sprites, Sickness Gods and Name Gods, House Gods and Weather Gods, Water Gods and Tree Gods, and he was forever making little signs or gestures to placate them, sprinkling a few drops of soup on the flames of the fire, or breaking off a supple twig to twist into a wreath and lay on a mossy stone.

On the day in question we were moving quietly through beech forest on the trail of a promising stag, when his slots led us to a quiet glade among the trees. In the centre of the glade stood a single, great oak tree, very ancient, its trunk half rotten and moss-speckled. At the base of the oak someone had built a low wall of loose stones. Coming closer I saw that the wall protected the mouth of a small well. Edgar had already picked up a small stone and now he took it across to the trunk of the tree and pushed it into a crevice in the bark. I saw other stones tucked away here and there, and guessed that this was a wishing tree.

'Newly married couples come to ask for babies,' Edgar said. 'Each stone represents their desire. I thought a stone put there might help to bring my daughter back.' He gestured to the well itself. 'Before girls marry they come here too, and drop a straw down into the well, to count the bubbles that rise. Each bubble represents one year before they find their husband.'

His remark touched a raw spot in my feelings. I broke off a twig and leaned over to drop it into the well. Not far below, I could see the dark reflection of the black water. My wish, of course, was not to know my marriage date, but when I would next see Aelfgifu, for I had been pining for her and did not know why I had not heard from her. On every possible occasion I had taken the chance to go from Edgar's cottage up to the burh in the hopes of glimpsing her. But always I had been disappointed.

Now, as I leaned forward over the well, and before I dropped the twig, something happened which was totally unforeseen.

Since I was six or seven, I have known I am one of those few people who are gifted with what others call the second sight. My Irish mother had been famous for it and I must have inherited it from her. From time to time I had experienced strange presentiments, intuitions and out-of-body sensations. I had even seen the spirits of those who were dead or the shadows of those about to die. These experiences were random, unexpected. Sometimes months and even years would pass between one occurrence and the next. A wise woman in Orkney – herself the possessor of the sight – had diagnosed that I only responded to the spirit world when in the company of someone else who already had the power. She said that I was some sort of spirit mirror.

What happened next proved her wrong.

As I leaned over to drop the twig, I looked down at the glint of black water and suddenly felt ill. At first I thought it was that sensation which comes when a person looks down from a great height, and feels as if he or she is falling and is overtaken by sudden faintness. But the surface of the inky pool was hardly more than an arm's length away. My giddiness then changed to a numb paralysis. I felt an icy cold; a terrible pain shot through me, spreading to every part of my body, and I feared I was going to faint. My vision went cloudy and I wanted to retch. But almost as quickly my vision cleared. I saw again the silhouette of my head in the water below, framed by the rim of the well and the sky above it. But this time, as I watched, I saw – quite distinctly – the reflection of someone moving up behind me, holding something up in the air about to strike me, them a metallic flash, and I felt a terrible presentiment of fear.

At that moment I must have fainted away, because I came back to my senses with Edgar shaking me. I was lying on the ground beside the well. He was looking frightened.

'What happened to you?' he asked.

'I don't know,' I replied. 'I had a seizure. I went somewhere else.'

'Woden spoke to you?' he asked, awe in his voice.

'No. I heard nothing, only saw an attack. It was some sort of warning.'

Edgar helped me to my feet and guided me to a fallen log where I could sit down.

'Here, rest for a while. Is that the first attack you have had?'

'Like that one, yes.' I replied. 'I've had visions before, but never in a calm, quiet place like this. Only at times of stress or when I was in the company of a volva or seidrman.'

'What are those?' he asked.

'It's the Norse way of describing the women and men who communicate with the spirit world.'

Edgar understood immediately. 'There's a person like that over to the west, a good two days' walk. An old woman. She too lives by a well. Takes a sip or two of the water, and when the mood is on her, goes into a trance. Some people call her a witch and the priests have cursed her. But often her prophecies come true, though no one else would drink the water from this well. It gives you a bad gut if you do, and there's something mysterious about the well itself. The waters suddenly gush up and overflow as a warning that a dreadful catastrophe will occur. The last time that happened was before Ashington Battle, when the Danes defeated our men.'

'Were you there?' I asked, still feeling faint.

'Yes,' Edgar replied, 'with the Saxon levies and armed with my hunting bow. It was useless. We were betrayed by one of our own leaders and I was lucky to get away with my life. If the waters of the well had been able to warn us about traitors, I would have slit his throat for him, for all that he was an ealdorman.'

I hardly heard what Edgar was saying because, as my head cleared, I was trying to puzzle out what could have caused my vision.

Then, in a sudden flash of comprehension, I understood: I was sensitive to the spirit world not only when in the company of someone who also possessed the second sight, but *by place*. If I found myself where the veil between the real world and the spirit world is thin, then I would respond to the presence of mysterious forces. Like a wisp of grass which bends to the unseen wind, long before a human feels it on his skin, I would pick up the emanations of the otherworld. The realisation made me uneasy because I feared that I had no way of knowing whether I was in such a sacred place before another vision overcame me.

IT WAS A WEEK after my vision in the forest and Edgar was in high good humour. 'South wind and a cloudy sky proclaim a hunting morning,' he announced, prodding me with the toe of his shoe as I lay half-asleep among my blanket in the corner of his cottage. He was very fond of his proverbs.

'Time for your first hunt, Thorgils. I've got a feeling that you'll bring us luck.'

It was barely light enough to see by, yet he was already dressed in clothes I had never seen before. He was wearing green from head to toe. I struggled out from under my blanket.

'Here, put these on,' he said, throwing at me in succession a tunic, leggings and a cloak with a soft hood. They were all of green. Mystified, I dressed and followed him out into the cold morning air. Edgar was testing a hunting bow, drawing it back and then releasing it. The bow was painted green too.

'Should I get the dogs?' I asked.

'No, not today. We take only one.'

I said nothing, though I wondered what use it was to have a pack, feed them, clean them, exercise them, and then not use them when you went hunting.

Edgar guessed my thoughts. 'Hunting with a pack is playtime for kings, an entertainment. Today we hunt for meat, not fun. Besides, what we are doing is much more delicate and skilled. So mark my words and follow my instructions carefully. Ah! Here they are,' and he looked towards the burh.

Three green-clad horsemen were riding towards us. One man I did not recognise, though he seemed to be a servant. To my surprise, the other two riders were the huscarls who had accompanied us from London. I still thought of them as One-Hand Tyr and Treeleg. Edgar told me that their true names were Gisli and Kjartan. Both looked in a thoroughly good humour.

'Perfect day for the hunt!' called out Kjartan cheerfully. He was the one missing a hand. 'Got everything ready, Edgar?' They both seemed to be on familiar terms with the royal huntsman.

'Just off to fetch Cabal,' answered Edgar and hurried to the kennel. He returned, leading a dog I had noticed during my unhappy days as a kennelman because it was different from the rest of the pack. This particular dog did not bite or yap, or run around like a maniac. Larger than the others, it was dark brown with a drooping muzzle and a mournful look. It kept to itself and was a steady, quiet, sensible creature. I had almost liked it.

'Mount up!' Edgar said to me. I looked puzzled. I could see no spare horse. There were only three, and each already had a rider. 'Here, lad,' called out Kjartan, leaning down from his saddle and holding out his one remaining hand for me to grasp. It seemed that we were to ride two-up on the animals. Edgar had already sprung up on the saddle behind the servant. One thing about hunting, I thought to myself as I scrambled up behind the huscarl and grabbed him round the waist to steady myself, it's a great leveller – it makes huntsman, huscarl, servant and former kennelman all equal.

'Never been hunting like this before?' Kjartan asked me over his shoulder. He spoke kindly and was obviously looking forward to the day's events. I wondered how he could go hunting when he lacked a hand. He could not pull a bow, and he was not even carrying a spear. His only weapon was a scramsaxe, the long-bladed knife of all trades.

'No, sir,' I replied. 'I've done a bit of hunting on foot, small animals mostly, in the forest. But not from horseback.'

'Well, wait and see,' Kjartan said. 'This will be part on horse and part on foot. Edgar knows what he is doing, so it should be successful. We only have to do what he says, though luck plays a certain part, as well as skill. The red deer are just getting into their fat time. Good eating.' He began humming gently to himself.

We rode into the forest to an area where Edgar and I had recently noted the slots of a red-deer stag and his group of four or five hinds. As we approached the place, the dog, which had been running beside the horses, began to cast back and forth, sniffing the ground and searching. 'Great dog, Cabal, good fellow,' said Kjartan. 'Getting old and a bit stiff in the limbs, but if any dog can find deer, he can. And he never gives up. Great heart.' Another besotted dog lover, I thought to myself, but I had to admire the serious attention that old Cabal was giving to every bush and thicket, running here and there, sniffing. From time to time he halted and put his great muzzle up into the air, trying to catch the faintest whiff of scent.

'There!' said Kjartan quietly. He had been watching Cabal and the dog had dropped his muzzle very close to the ground and was moving forward through the forest, clearly tracking a quarry. 'Silent as he should be,' grunted Kjartan approvingly. When I failed to appreciate the compliment for the dog, he went on, 'Most dogs start to bark or whine when they catch the scent of deer, but not old Cabal. Specially trained to stay silent so as not alarm the quarry.'

We had slowed our horses to the gentlest of walks and I noticed that the riders were taking care to make as little noise as possible. Kjartan glanced across at Edgar, and when Edgar signalled with a nod, our little group stopped immediately. The servant dismounted, took Cabal's leash and led the dog quietly to where he could fasten the leash to a sapling. Cabal, still silent, lay contentedly down on the grass and lowered his head on his paws. It seemed his job was done.

The servant returned and we all closed up in a small circle to listen to Edgar. He spoke in a soft whisper.

'I think we'll find the deer just ahead and we've come to them upwind, so that's good. You, Aelfric,' here he indicated the servant, 'mount up with Gisli, Thorgils stays with Kjartan and I'll walk. We'll leave the extra horse here.'

At his signal, the five of us and the two horses moved forward cautiously. We emerged into an area of the forest where the trees thinned out. To our right, between the trees, I glimpsed a movement, and then another. It was a red-deer hind and her companion. Then I saw the little group – the stag and his four hinds.

'Now we go across the face of the deer,' Kjartan whispered to me. He clearly wanted me to appreciate the subtlety of the chase. I heard the brief creak of leather and to my astonishment one-legged Gisli unfastened his special leather belt, slid out of the saddle, and dropped to the ground. I noticed that he landed on the side of the horse away from the deer, shielded from their sight. He stood grasping the stirrup leather in one hand to keep himself upright as he strapped on his wooden leg. He did not carry a crutch, instead he had a heavy bow in his hand. Edgar moved up to stand beside him. He too was behind the horse and hidden from the deer. When Edgar gave his next signal, the two horses moved out in the open, three men riding and two men walking alongside and hidden from the deer. The stag and his hinds immediately raised their heads and watched our distant procession. Now I understood. The deer were not alarmed by men on horseback, provided they rode gently and quietly and kept their distance. They were accepted as another form of forest animal. I noticed how Edgar and Gisli timed their paces on foot so that they moved with the horses' legs.

'Not quite another Sleipnir,' I whispered to Kjartan. He nodded. Sleipnir, Odinn's horse, has eight legs so that it can travel at tremendous speed. To the deer, our horses must have looked as if they each had six legs.

Fifty paces further on I realised that one-legged Gisli was no longer with us. Glancing back, I saw he was standing in front of a young oak tree, motionless. Dressed in green, he was almost impossible to see. He had let go of the stirrup leather just as the horse passed the tree, used his bow as a crutch, and was now in position. A few paces further on, Edgar did the same. He too was almost invisible. We were setting an ambush.

Kjartan, Aelfric and I rode on, then began to circle to the right. We reached the far side of the clearing and at the edge of the trees Kjartan said quietly, 'Thorgils, this is where you drop off. Stand in front of that tree there. Stay absolutely still. Only move if you see the deer heading your way and not towards Edgar and Gisli.' I slipped off the horse and did as I had been ordered, waiting quietly as Kjartan and the servant rode on.

For what seemed a long time I stood, not moving a muscle, and wondering what would happen next. Then I heard it, a single faint sound – chkkk! Very, very slowly I turned my head towards the noise. I heard it repeated, softly, almost languidly from far away. A moment later I heard the gentle crack of a twig, and into my line of vision walked one of the red-deer hinds. She was perhaps twenty paces away, moving gently through the forest, stopping now and again to snatch a mouthful of food, then moving on. Then I saw another hind and caught a glimpse of the stag itself. All the animals were on the move, unhurried yet heading in the same direction. Chkk! Again I heard the strange sound, and behind the deer I saw Kjartan on his horse. He was riding on a loose rein, barely moving, drifting through the forest behind the deer, not hurrying, but turning his horse this way and that as if the animal was feeding. The sound was Kjartan softly clicking his tongue. A moment later I glimpsed the second rider, Aelfric, and heard a gentle, deliberate tap as he struck his saddle lightly with a willow switch. The soft sounds made the deer move forward, unalarmed. Directly ahead Edgar and Gisli waited.

With excruciating slowness the quarry moved forward. As they drew level with my position, I hardly dared to breath. Slowly I turned my head to look for Edgar. He was so motionless that it took me a moment to detect his position. He was standing with his bow pulled back and an arrow on the string as the leading deer approached him. An elderly hind, she was almost upon Edgar when she realised that she was staring straight into the eyes of her hunter. Her head came up suddenly, she flared her nostrils and tensed her muscles to leap away. At that instant Edgar loosed. From that short range I clearly heard the thunk of the arrow hitting her chest.

Now all chaos broke loose. The stag and other hinds awoke to their danger and began to run. I heard another thump and guessed that Gisli had shot an arrow. A young hind and the stag turned back and broke away towards me. They came bounding through the trees, the stag taking great leaps, his antlers crashing against the branches. I stepped forward so the deer could see me and raised my arms. The hind swerved in panic, slipped on the greasy ground, scrambled to her feet and darted away to safety.

But the great stag, fearing that his flight was blocked, doubled
back and headed to where Edgar stood. By then Edgar had a
second arrow nocked to his bow string and was waiting. The stag
saw Edgar, accelerated and veered past him. Smoothly Edgar
swivelled at the hips, his bow pulled so far back that the arrow's
feathers were at his right ear, and he loosed just as the prey sped
past. It was a perfect passing shot, which brought a shout of
approval from Kjartan. The arrow struck the great stag between
the ribs. I saw the beast falter in its stride, recover, and then go
bounding away through the bushes with a great thrashing of
branches which dwindled in the distance until the only sound was
the patter of twigs and leaves falling to the ground.

Gisli's shot had also hit its mark. Two hinds, his and Edgar's,
lay dead on the forest floor.

'Good shooting,' called out Kjartan as he rode up to the
ambush.

'Lucky the stag broke to my left,' said Edgar. He was trying
to sound matter of fact, though I knew he was delighted. 'Had he
gone the other side of me, it would have been a more awkward
shot, swinging away from my leading foot.'

Aelfric had already run off to retrieve Cabal and the dog
swiftly picked up the scent of the wounded stag. The trail of
blood was hard to miss, and after a couple of hundred paces we
came across Edgar's arrow, lying where it had fallen from the
wounded animal. 'Gut shot,' said Edgar, showing me the metal
barbs. 'You can see traces of his stomach contents. This won't be
a long pursuit. Bright clear blood would mean a superficial wound
and a long chase.'

He was right. We tracked the stag for less than a mile, and
found it dead in a thicket. Losing no time, the servant began to
skin the carcass and butcher the meat, and Edgar rewarded Cabal
with a choice titbit.

'Located the big stag without trouble, Gisli,' Kjartan called
out as we arrived back to where Gisli was standing at the ambush
site. The one-legged huscarl had been unable to join the pursuit.

'Five deer found and three killed. That was a nice shot of yours. Fifty paces at least.'

'One advantage to losing a leg, my friend,' Gisli replied. 'When you use a crutch to help you hobble around, it strengthens the arms and shoulders.'

THREE

WE DELIVERED THE venison to the burh, where the earldorman's cooks were preparing the great feast which, by Saxon custom, celebrates the binding of the harvest sheaves.

'The royal huntsman is always invited and gets an honoured place,' Edgar said to me. 'And so he should – he provides the best of the festival food. As my assistant, Thorgils, you're expected to be there as well. Make sure you're suitably dressed.'

So it was that I found myself at the door of the burh's great hall five days later, wearing my purple tunic, which had been freshly cleaned by Edgar's wife, Judith. I was having difficulty in controlling my excitement. Aelfgifu must surely be at the banquet, I thought to myself.

'Who's going to be at the high table?' I asked a fellow guest as we waited for the horn blast to signal that we could enter the hall.

'Ealdorman Aelfhelm is the official host,' he replied.

'Is he Aelfgifu's father?' 'No. Her father was executed by that fool Ethelred on suspicion of disloyalty long before Knut came to power. Aelfhelm is her uncle. He has an old-fashioned view of how to conduct a banquet so I expect Aelfgifu will be a cup-bearer.'

When the blaedhorn sounded, we filed into the great hall to

46

find our places. I had been allocated to sit at a long table facing towards the centre of the hall, which had been left clear for the servitors who brought our food and for the entertainment to follow. A similar long table had been placed on the far side, and to my right, raised up on a platform, was the table at which ealdorman Aelfhelm and his important guests would dine. Our humbler board was set with wooden plates, mugs and cowhorn spoons, but the ealdorman's guests had an embroidered linen tablecloth and their drinking vessels were expensive imports, goblets of green glass. We lesser folk had just taken our places when another horn blast announced the entry of the ealdorman. He came in with his wife and a cluster of nobles. Most were Saxons, but among them I noticed Gisli and Kjartan, wearing their gold-hilted huscarl swords and looking much more dignified than the green-clad hunters I had accompanied five days earlier. Still there was no sign of Aelfgifu.

The ealdorman and his party took their seats along one side of the high table, looking down at us. Then came a third horn blast, and from the left-hand side of the hall appeared a small procession of women. Leading them was Aelfgifu. I recognised her at once and felt a surge of pride. She had chosen to wear the same close-fitting sky-blue dress in which I had first seen her at Knut's Easter assembly in London. Then her long hair had hung loose, held with a single gold fillet. Now her hair was coiled up on her head, to reveal the slender white neck I remembered so well. I could not keep my eyes from her. She walked forward at the head of the procession, looking demurely down at the ground and holding a silver jug. Stepping up to her uncle's table, she filled the glass goblet of the chief guest, then her uncle's glass and then the noble next in rank. Judging by the colour of the liquid she poured, their drink was also a luxurious import – red wine. Her formal duty done, Aelfgifu handed the jug to a servant and walked to take her own seat. To my chagrin she was placed at the far end of the high table, and from where I sat my neighbour blocked my line of sight.

The cooks had excelled themselves. Even I, who was used to eating Edgar's game stews, was impressed by the variety and quality of the dishes. There were joints of pork and mutton, rounds of blood sausage and pies and pastes of freshwater fish – pike, perch, eel – with sweet pastries too. We were offered white bread, unlike the everyday rough bread, and of course there was the venison which Edgar had contributed, now brought in cere- monially on iron spits. I tried leaning forward and then back on my bench, attempting to get another glimpse of Aelfgifu. But my immediate neighbour on my right was a big, hulking man – the burh's ironworker as it turned out – and he was soon irritated by my fidgeting.

'Here,' he said, 'settle down and get on with the meal. Not often that you have a chance to eat such fine food –' he belched happily – 'or as much to drink.'

Of course, we were not offered wine, but on the table were heavy bowls made from local clay, which gave a deep grey sheen to the pottery. They contained a drink which I had not tasted before.

'Cider,' commented my burly neighbour as he enthusiastically used a wooden scoop to refill his wooden cup and mine. He had an enormous thirst and throughout the meal gulped cup after cup. I tried to avoid his friendly insistence to keep pace, but it proved difficult, even when I switched to drinking mead flavoured with myrtlewort in the hope that he would leave me alone. The leather mead bottle was in the hands of an overly efficient servant, and every time I put down my cup he topped it up again. Gradually, and for almost the first time in my life, I was getting drunk.

As the banquet progressed, the entertainers came on. A pair of jugglers skipped into the open space between the tables and began throwing batons and balls in the air and doing somersaults. It was uninspiring stuff, so there were catcalls and rude comments, and the jugglers left, looking cross. The audience perked up when the next act came on – a troop of performing dogs. They were

dressed in coloured jackets and fancy collars and had been trained
to scamper about in patterns, to duck and roll over, to walk on
two feet and jump through hoops or over a bar. The audience
shouted with approval as the bar rose higher and higher, and
threw scraps of meat and chicken into the arena as rewards. Next
it was the turn of the ealdorman's scop to come forward. He was
the Saxon version of our Norse skald, and his duty was to declaim
verses in praise of his lord and compose poems in honour of
the chief guest. Remembering my time as an apprentice skald, I
listened carefully. But I was not overly impressed. The ealdorman's scop had a mumbling delivery and I thought that his verses
were mundane. I suspected they were stock lines which he
changed to suit the particular individual at his lord's table, filling
in the names of whoever was present that day. When the scop
had finished and the final lines of poetry died away, there was an
awkward silence.

'Where's the gleeman?' called down the ealdorman, and I saw
the steward hurry up to the high table and say something to his
master. The steward was looking unhappy.

'The gleeman's probably failed to show,' slurred my neighbour. The cider was making him alternately cantankerous and
genial. 'He's become very unreliable. Meant to travel from one
festival to another, but often has too much of a hangover to
remember his next engagement.'

The steward was heading towards a small crowd of onlookers
standing at the back of the hall. They were mostly women, kitchen
workers. I saw him approach one young woman at the front of
the crowd, take her by the wrist and try to bring her forward.
For a moment she resisted and then I saw a harp being passed
to her from somewhere at the back of the room. She beckoned to
a youth sitting at the far table and he got to his feet. By now
an attendant had placed two stools in the middle of the cleared
space and the young man and woman – I could see that they
were brother and sister – came forward and, after paying their

respects to the ealdorman, sat down. The young man produced a bone whistle from his tunic and fingered a few experimental notes.

The crowd fell silent as his sister began to tune her harp. It was different from the harps I had known in Ireland. The Irish instrument is strung with twenty or more wires of bronze, while the harp the girl was holding was lighter, smaller, and had only a dozen strings. When she plucked it I realised it was corded with gut. But the simpler instrument suited her voice, which was pure, untrained and clear. She sang a number of songs, while her brother accompanied her on his whistle. The songs were about love and war and travel, and were plain enough, and no worse for that. The ealdorman and his guests listened for most of the time, only occasionally talking among themselves, and I judged that the stand-in musicians had done well.

When they finished, the dancing began. The young man on the whistle was joined by other local musicians, playing pan pipes, shaking rattles and beating tambourines. People left their benches and started to dance in the centre of the hall. Determined to enjoy themselves, men coaxed women out of the crowd of onlookers, and the music became more cheerful and spirited and everyone began to clap and sing. None of the august guests danced, of course, they merely looked on. I could see that the dancing was uncomplicated, a few steps forward, a few steps back, a sideways shuffle. To escape from my drunken neighbour, whose head was beginning to loll heavily against my shoulder, I decided to try. A little fuddled, I rose from my bench and joined the dancers. Among the line of women and girls coming towards me, I realised, was the girl harpist. She was wearing a bodice of russet red and a skirt of contrasting brown, which showed off her figure, and with her brown hair cut short and lightly freckled skin, she was the picture of fresh womanhood. Each time we passed she gave my hand a little squeeze. Gradually the music grew faster and faster, and the circles whirled with increasing speed, until we were short of breath. The music rose to a crescendo and then stopped abruptly. Laughing and smiling, the dancers staggered to a halt and there in front of me was the harpist girl. She stood before me, triumphant with her evening's success. Still intoxicated, I reached forward, took her in my arms and gave her a kiss. A heartbeat later, I heard a short, loud crash. It was a sound that few people in that gathering could have ever heard in their lives – the sound of expensive glass shattering. I looked up and there was Aelfgifu, standing up. She had flung her goblet on the table. As her uncle and his guests looked up in amazement, Aelfgifu stalked out of the hall, her back rigid with anger.

Swaying tipsily, I suddenly felt wretched. I knew that I had offended the woman I adored.

'WAR, HUNTING AND love are as full of trouble as they are of pleasure.' Edgar launched another of his proverbs at me next morning, as we were getting ready to visit the hawk shed, which he called the hack house, and feed the hawks.

'What do you mean?' I asked, though I had a shrewd idea why he had mentioned love.

'Our lady's got a quick temper.'

'What makes you say that?'

'Come on, lad. I've known Aelfgifu since she was a skinny girl growing up. As a youngster she was always trying to get away from the stuffiness of the burh. Used to spend half her days with my wife and me down at the cottage. Playing around like any ordinary child, though she tended to get into more mischief than most. A real little vixen she could be when she was caught out. But she's got a good heart and we love her still. And we were very proud when she was wed to Knut, though by then she had become a grand lady.'

'What's that got to do with her bad temper?'

Edgar paused with his hand on the door into the hack house, and there was a glint of amusement in his eyes as he looked straight at me. 'Don't think you're the first young man she's taken

a fancy to,' he said. 'Soon after you arrived, it was clear that you
were not cut out to be kennelman. I began wondering why you
were brought all the way from London and I asked the steward,
who told me that you had been included in my lady's travelling
party on her particular instructions. So I had my guess, but I
wasn't sure until I saw her tantrum last night. No harm in that,'
he went on, 'Aelfgifu's not been so well treated these past months,
what with that other queen, Emma, and Knut being away all the
time. I'd say she has a right to her own life. And she's been more
than good to me and my wife. When our daughter was taken by
the Danes, it was Aelfgifu who offered to pay her ransom if she
was ever located. And she would still do so.'

THE HAWKING SEASON was now upon us, and for the previous
two months we had been preparing Edgar's hunting birds as they
emerged from their moult. The hack house contained three
peregrine falcons, a merlin, and a pair of small sparrowhawks, as
well as the costly gyrfalcon which had first got me into trouble.
The gyrfalcon, Edgar pointed out, was worth its weight in pure
silver or 'the price of three male slaves or perhaps four useless
kennelmen'. He and I would go into the hack house every day, to
'man' the birds as he put it. This meant picking them up and
getting them used to being handled by humans while feeding them
special titbits to increase their strength and condition as their new
feathers grew. Edgar proved to be just as expert with birds as he
was with hounds. He favoured a diet of goslings, eels and adders
for the long-winged falcons and mice for the short-winged hawks.
Now I learned why there was sandy floor beneath their perches:
it allowed us to find and collect the droppings from each bird,
which Edgar examined with close attention. He explained that
hunting birds could suffer from almost-human ailments, including itch, rheum, worms, mouth ulcers and cough. When Edgar
detected a suspicion of gout in one of the peregrines, an older

bird, he sent me to find a hedgehog for it to eat, which he pronounced to be the only cure.

Most of the birds, with the exception of the gyrfalcon and one
of the sparrowhawks, were already trained. When they had their
new feathers, it was only necessary to reintroduce them to their
hunting duties. But the gyrfalcon had recently arrived in the hack
house when I first saw it. That was why its eyelids had been sewn
shut. 'It keeps the bird calm and quiet when it's being transported,'
Edgar explained. 'Once it arrives in its new home, I ease the
thread little by little so that the bird looks out on its surroundings
gradually and settles in without stress. It may seem cruel, but the
only other method is to enclose its head in a leather hood, and I
don't like to do that to a bird captured after it has learned to hunt
in the wild. Putting on the hood too soon can cause chafing and
distress.'

Edgar also had a warning. 'A dog comes to depend upon its
master, but a hunting bird keeps its independence,' he said. 'You
may tame and train a bird to work with you, and there is no
greater pleasure in any sport than to fly your bird and see it take
its prey and then return to your hand. But always remember that
the moment the bird takes to the air it has the choice of liberty. It
may fly away and never return. Then you will suffer falconer's
heartbreak.'

Their free spirit attracted me to the hunting birds and I
quickly found that I had a natural talent for handling them. Edgar
started me off with one of the little sparrowhawks, the least
valuable of his charges. He chose the one which had never yet
been trained and showed me how to tie six-inch strips of leather
to the bird's ankles with a special knot, then slip a longer leash
through the metal rings at their ends. He equipped me with a
falconer's protective glove, and each day I fed the hawk its diet
of fresh mouse, encouraging it to leap from the perch to the warm
carcass in my hand. The sparrowhawk was shrill and bad tempered
when it first arrived – a sure sign, according to Edgar, that it had

been taken from the nest as a fledgling and not caught after it had left the nest – yet within two weeks I had it hopping back and forth like a garden pet. Edgar confessed he had never seen a sparrowhawk tamed so fast. 'You seem to have a way with women,' he commented, slily because only the female sparrow-hawk is any use for hunting.

Not long afterwards he decided that I was the right person to train the gyrfalcon. It was a bold decision and may have been superstitious on Edgar's part, thinking that I would have some special understanding of the spear falcon because I came from its homeland. But Edgar knew that I had been brought to Northamp-ton at the express wish of Aelfgifu, and he may have been playing a deeper game. He made me the gyrfalcon's keeper. I handled her – she was also a female – two or three times each day, fed her, bathed her once a week in a bath of yellow powder to get rid of lice, gave her chicken wings to tug and twist as she stood on her perch so her neck and body muscles grew strong, and held out my glove, a much stouter one this time, so she could hop from perch to hand. Within a month the gyrfalcon was quiet enough to wear a leather hood without alarm, and she and I were allowed outside the hack house, where the splendid white and speckled bird flew on a long leash to reach lumps of meat I placed on a stump of wood. A week after that and Edgar was tossing into the air a leather sock dressed with pigeon's wings, and the gyrfalcon, still tethered, was flying off from my glove to strike the lure and pin it to the ground and earn a reward of gosling. 'You have the makings of a first-class falconer,' Edgar commented and I glowed with satisfaction.

Two days after Aelgifu's outburst at the banquet, we allowed the gyrfalcon to fly free for the first time. It was a critical and delicate moment in her training. Soon after dawn Edgar and I carried the falcon to a quiet spot, well away from the burh. Edgar whirled the lure on its cord. Standing fifty paces away with the gyrfalcon on my glove, I lifted off the leather hood, loosed the leather straps, and raised my arm on high. The falcon caught sight at once of the whirling lure, thrust off from the glove with a powerful leap that I felt right to my shoulder, and flashed straight at the target in a single, deadly swoop. She hit the leather lure with a solid thump that tore the tethering cord from Edgar's grasp, then carried the lure and its trailing cord up into a tree. For a moment Edgar and I stood aghast, wondering if the falcon would now take her chance to fly free. There was nothing we could do. But when I slowly held up my arm again, the gyrfalcon dropped quietly from her branch, glided back to my glove and settled there. I rewarded her with a morsel of raw pigeon's breast.

'So she finally comes to claim her royal prerogative,' Edgar said quietly to me as he saw who was waiting beside the hack house as we walked back. Aelfgifu was standing there, accompanied by two attendants. For a moment I resented the mischievous implication in Edgar's comment, but then a familiar feeling washed over me. I felt light-headed at being in the presence of the most beautiful and desirable woman in existence.

'Good morning, my lady,' said Edgar. 'Come to see your falcon?'

'Yes, Edgar,' she replied. 'Is the bird ready yet?'

'Not quite, my lady. Another week or ten days of training and we should have her fit for the hunt.'

'And have you thought of a name for her?' asked Aelfgifu.

'Well, Thorgils here has,' said Edgar.

Aelfgifu turned towards me as if seeing me for the first time in her life. 'So what name have you chosen to call my falcon?' she asked. 'I trust it is one I will approve.'

'I call the falcon Habrok,' I answered. 'It means high breeches, after the fluffy feathers on its legs.'

She gave a slight smile which made my heart lurch. 'I know it does; Habrok was also the "finest of all hawks" according to the tales of the ancient Gods, was it not? A good name.'

I felt as if I was walking on air.

'Edgar,' she went on, 'I'll keep you to your promise. In ten days from now I begin hawking. I need to get out into the countryside and relax. Two hunts a week if the hawks stay fit.'

So began the most idyllic autumn I ever spent in England. On hawking days Aelfgifu would arrive at the hack house on horseback, usually with a single woman attendant. Occasionally she came alone. Edgar and I, also mounted, would be waiting for her. The hawks we carried depended on our prey. Edgar usually brought one of the peregrines, myself the gyrfalcon, and Aelfgifu accepted from us the merlin or one of the sparrowhawks, which were lighter birds and more suitable for a woman to carry. We always rode to the same spot, a broad area of open land, a mix of heath and marsh, where the hunting birds had room to fly.

There we tethered the horses, leaving them in the care of Aelfgifu's servant, and the three of us would walk across the open ground with its tussock grass and small bushes, its ponds and ditches, ideal country for the game we sought. Here Edgar would loose his favourite peregrine, and the experienced bird would mount higher and higher in the sky over his head and wait, circling, until it could see its target. With the peregrine in position, we advanced on foot, perhaps startling a duck from a ditch or a woodcock from the brushwood. As the panicked creature rose into the air, the peregrine far above would note the direction of its flight and begin its dive. Plummeting through the air, making minute adjustments for the speed of its prey, it hurtled down towards its target like a feathered thunderbolt from Thor. Sometimes it killed with the first strike. At other times it might miss its stoop as the quarry jinked or dived, and then the peregrine would mount again to launch another attack or pursue the quarry at ground level. Occasionally, but not often, the peregrine would fail, and then Edgar and I would whirl our lures and coax the disappointed and angry bird to return to human hand.

'Would you like to fly Habrok next?' Edgar asked Aelfgifu halfway through our first afternoon of hunting and he set my heart racing. The gyrfalcon was a royal bird, fit for a king to fly, and a queen, of course. But Habrok was too heavy for Aelfgifu to carry, so it was I who stood beside her ready to cast the falcon off. As luck would have it, the next game we saw was a hare. It sprang out of a clump of grass, a fine animal, sleek and strong, and went bounding away arrogantly, ears up, a sure sign that it was confident of escape. I glanced at Aelfgifu and she nodded. With one hand I slipped Habrok's leash – the hood was already off – and tossed the splendid bird clear. For a moment she faltered, then caught a distant glimpse of her prey leaping through the rough grass and reeds. A few wing beats to gain height and have a clear sight of the hare, then Habrok sped towards the fleeing animal. The hare realised its danger and increased its pace, swerved and sought protection in a thicket of grass at the very instant the falcon shot by. Habrok curved up into the air, turned and swooped again, this time attacking from the other side. The hare, alarmed, broke cover and began to run towards the woods, ears back, full pace now, straining every sinew. Again it was lucky. As she was about to strike, the gyrfalcon was foiled by an intervening bush and forced to check her dive. Now the hare was nearing refuge and almost safe. Suddenly, Habrok shot ahead of her prey, turned and came straight at the hare from ahead. There was a tremendous flurry, a swirl of fur and feather, and predator and prey vanished into the thick grass. I ran forward, guided by the faint jingle of the bells on Habrok's legs. As I parted the grass, I came upon the hawk, standing on the dead carcass. She had bitten through the hare's neck, using the sharp point on her beak which Edgar called the 'falcon's tooth' and was beginning to feed, tearing open the fur to get at the warm flesh. I let Habrok feed for a moment, then gently picked her up and hooded her.

'Don't allow a hunting bird to eat too much from its prey, or it will not want to hunt again that day,' Edgar had instructed. Now he too came running up, delighted with the performance in front of Aelfgifu. 'Could not have done better,' he exulted. 'No

peregrine could have matched that. Only a gyrfalcon will pursue
and pursue its prey, and never give up,' and then he could not
resist adding, 'rather like its owner.'

But the hunt was not the main reason why I remember those
glorious afternoons. Our hunting took us deep into the marshy
heath, and after an hour or so, when we were a safe distance from
the attendant watching our horses, Edgar would hang back or
take a different path, tactfully leaving Aelfgifu and me alone
together. Then we would find a quiet spot, screened by tall reeds
and grasses, and I would set Habrok down on a temporary perch,
a branch curved over and the two ends pushed into the earth to
make a hoop. And there, while the falcon sat quietly under her
hood, Aelfgifu and I would make love. Under the vault of
England's summer sky we were in a blissful world of our own.
And when Edgar judged that it was time to return to the burh,
we would hear him approaching in the distance, softly jingling a
hawk bell to give us warning so that we were dressed and ready
when he arrived.

On one such hawking excursion – it must have been the third
or fourth time that Aelfgifu and I were walking the marshland
together – we came across a small abandoned shelter at the tip of
a tongue of land which projected into a mere. Who had made the
secluded hut of interlaced reeds and heather it was impossible to
know, probably a wild fowler come to take birds from the mere
by stealth. At any rate Aelfgifu and I claimed it for our own as
our love bower, and it became our habit to direct our steps towards
it, and spent the afternoon there curled up in one another's arms
while Edgar stood guard at the neck of land.

These were times of glorious pleasure and intimacy: and at
last I could tell Aelfgifu how much I longed for her and how
inadequate I felt, she being so much more experienced and high
born.

'Love needs no teaching,' she replied softly and with that
characteristic habit of hers she ran the tip of her finger along the
profile of my face. We were lying naked, side by side, so her

finger continued across my chest and belly. 'And haven't you ever heard the saying that love makes all men equal? That means women too.'

I bent over to brush my lips across her cheek and she smiled with contentment.

'And speaking of teaching, Edgar tells me that you trained Habrok in less than five weeks. That you have a natural way with hunting birds. Why do you think that is?'

'I don't know,' I replied, 'but maybe it has something to do with my veneration for Odinn. Since I was a child in Greenland I have been attracted to Odinn's ways. He is the God whose accomplishments I most admire. He gave mankind so much of what we possess – whether poetry or self-knowledge or the master spells – and he is always seeking to learn more. So much so that he sacrificed the sight of one eye to gain extra wisdom. He comes in many forms, but to any person who wanders as far from home as I have done, Odinn can be an inspiration. He is ever the traveller himself and a seeker after truths. That is why I venerate him as Odinn the wanderer, the empowerer of journeys.'

'So what, my little courtier, has your devotion to Odinn to do with birds and teaching them?' she enquired. 'I thought that Odinn is the God of War, bringing victory on the battlefield. That, at least, is how my husband and his war captains regard him. They invoke Odinn before their campaigns. While their priests do the same to the White Christ.'

'Odinn is the God of victories, yes, and the God of the dead too,' I answered. 'But do you know how he learned the secret of poetry and gave it to men?'

'Tell me,' Aelfgifu said, nestling closer.

'Poetry is the mead of the Gods, created from their spittle, which ran in the veins of the creature Kvasir. But Kvasir was killed by evil dwarves, who preserved his blood in three great cauldrons. When these cauldrons passed into the possession of the giant Suttung and his daughter Gunnlod, Odinn took it upon himself to steal the mead. He changed himself into a snake –

Odinn is a shape-changer, as is often said – and crept through a hole in the mountain which guarded Suttung's lair, and seduced Gunnlod into allowing him three sips, one at each cauldron. Such was Odinn's power that he drained each cauldron dry. Then he changed himself into an eagle to fly back to Asgard, the home of the Gods, with the precious liquid in his throat. But the giant Suttung also changed himself into a great eagle and pursued Odinn, chasing him as fast as Edgar's peregrine chases a fleeing hawk. Suttung would have overtaken Odinn, if Odinn had not spewed out a few drops of the mead and thus lightened of his precious load managed to reach the safety of Asgard just ahead of his pursuer. He escaped by the narrowest of margins. Suttung had come so close that when he swung his sword at the fleeing Odinn-eagle, Odinn was forced to dodge and dive and the sword cut away the tips of his tail feathers.'

'A charming story,' said Aelfgifu as I finished. 'But is it true?'

'Look over there,' I answered, rolling onto my side, and pointing to where Habrok sat quietly on her perch. 'Ever since Odinn lost his tail feathers to Suttung's sword, all hawks and falcons have been born with short tail feathers.'

Just then the gentle tinkle of Edgar's hawk bells warned us it was time to return to the burh.

Our idyll could not last for ever and there was to be just one more tryst at our hidden refuge before its sanctuary was destroyed. The day was sultry with the threat of a thunderstorm and, for some reason, when Aelfgifu arrived to meet Edgar and myself she had no attendant with her but had chosen to bring her lapdog. To most people it was an appealing little creature, brown and white, constantly alert, with bright intelligent eyes. But I knew Edgar's view of lapdogs – he thought they were spoiled pests – and I had a sense of foreboding which, mistakenly, I put down to my usual dislike of dogs.

Aelfgifu detected our disapproval and was adamant. 'I insist Maccus comes with us today. He too needs his fun in the country. He will not disturb Habrok or the other hawks.'

So we rode out, Maccus riding on the pommel of Aelfgifu's saddle, until we tethered our mounts at the usual place and walked into the marshland. Maccus bounced happily ahead through the undergrowth and long grass, his ears flapping. He even put up a partridge, which Habrok struck down in a dazzling attacking flight. 'Look!' said Aelfgifu to me, 'I don't know why you and Edgar made such long faces about the little dog. He's proving himself useful.'

It was when she and I were once again in our bower and had made love that Maccus barked excitedly. A moment later I heard Edgar's warning bell ring urgently. Aelfgifu and I dressed quickly. Hurriedly I picked up Habrok and tried to pretend that we had been waiting in ambush by the mere. It was too late. A servant, Aelfgifu's old nursemaid, had been sent to find her mistress as she was wanted at the burh, and Maccus's enthusiastic barking had led her to where Edgar was standing guard. Edgar tried to distract the servant from advancing along the little causeway leading to the bower, but the dog went dashing out from our little hut and eagerly led her servant to our trysting place. Not till much later did I know what harm had been done.

We were returning to our horses when Edgar glanced behind us and saw, high in the sky, a lone heron flying towards his roost. The bird was moving through the air with broad, measured wing beats, his winding course following the line of the stream that would lead him to his home. The arrival of the servant had ruined our sport so Edgar thought perhaps he could retrieve our day's enjoyment. A heron is the peregrine's greatest prey. So Edgar loosed his peregrine and the faithful bird began to mount. The peregrine spiralled upwards, not underneath the heron but adjacent to the great bird's flight so as not to alarm her quarry. When she had reached her height, she turned and came slicing down, hurtling through the air at such a pace that it was difficult to follow the stoop. But the heron was courageous. At the last moment the great bird swerved, and tilted up, showing its fearsome beak and claws. Edgar's peregrine swerved aside, overshot, and a moment later was climbing back into the sky to gain height for a second onslaught. This was the rare opportunity that Edgar and I had discussed a dozen times: the chance to launch Habrok against a heron.

'Quick, Thorgils. Let Habrok fly!' Edgar called urgently.

Both of us knew that a gyrfalcon will only attack a heron if there is an experienced bird to imitate. I fumbled for the leash and reached out to remove the leather hood, but a strange presentiment came over me. I felt as if my hands were shackled.

'Hurry, Thorgils, hurry! There's not much time. The peregrine's got one more chance, and then the heron will be among the trees.'

But I could not go on. I looked across at Edgar. 'I'm sorry,' I said. 'There's something wrong. I must not fly Habrok. I don't know why.'

Edgar was getting angry. I could see the scowl developing, the eyes sinking back into his head, his jaw set. Then he looked into my face and it was like the day at the well in the forest. The words died in his throat, and he said, 'Thorgils, are you feeling all right? You look odd.'

'It's fine,' I replied. 'The feeling is over. I don't know what it was.'

Edgar took Habruk from me, removed hood and leash, and with a single gesture let loose the falcon. Habrok rose and rose in the air, and for a moment we were sure that the gyrfalcon would join the waiting peregrine and learn its trade. But then, the white and speckled bird seemed to sense some ancient call, and instead of flying up to join the waiting peregrine, Habrok changed direction and with steady sure wingbeats began to fly towards the north. From the ground we watched the falcon disappearing, flying strongly until we could see it no more.

Edgar could not forgive himself for allowing Habrok to fly. For the next two weeks he kept on saying to me, 'I should have realised when I saw your face. There was something there that neither of us could know.' The shocking loss brought all our hawking to a halt. The spirit had gone out of us, we grieved and, of course, I had lost my link with Aelfgifu.

THE RHYTHM OF the hunting year had to go on. We fed and doctored the remaining birds, even if we did not fly them, and walked the dogs. There was a new kennelman, who was excellent at his job, taking the pack each day to an area of stony ground where the exercise toughened their paws. In the evenings he bathed any cuts and bruises in a mixture of vinegar and soot until they were fit to run on any surface. Edgar wanted the pack ready for the first boar hunt of the year, which takes place at the festival the White Christ devotees call Michael's Mass. He and I returned to our scouting trips in the forest, looking this time for the tracks of a suitable boar, old and massive enough to be a worthy opponent.

'The boar hunt is very different from the hunting of the stag and much more dangerous,' Edgar told me. 'Boar hunting is like training for a battle. You must plan your campaign, deploy your forces, launch your attack and then there is the ultimate test – close combat with a foe who can kill you.'

'Do many lose their lives?'

'The boar, of course,' he answered. 'And dogs too. It can be a messy business. A dog gets too close and the boar will slash him. Occasionally a horse slips, or a man loses his footing when the boar charges, and if he falls the wrong way then the files can disembowel him.'

'The files?'

'The tusks. Look closely when the boar is cornered, though not too closely for your own safety, and you will see him gnash his teeth. He is using the upper ones to sharpen his lower tusks, as a reaper employs his whetstone to put a keen edge on his scythe. The boar's weapons can be deadly.'

'It sounds as if you are less enthusiastic about the boar hunt than pursuing the stag.'

Edgar shrugged. 'It's my duty as huntsman to see that my

master and his guests enjoy their sport to the full, that the boar is killed so its fearsome head is brought on a platter into the banquet and paraded before the applauding guests. If the boar escapes, then everyone goes home feeling that their battle honour has been diminished, and the banquet is a dismal affair. But for the hunt itself, I personally don't find there is much skill to it. The hunted boar travels most often in a straight line. His scent is easy for the dogs to follow, unlike the canny stag who leaps beside his own track to confuse the trail, or doubles back, or runs through water to perplex the scenting pursuit.'

It still took us three days of searching the forest, and the help of Cabal's questing nose to find the quarry we were seeking. Edgar calculated from the mighty size of its droppings that the boar was enormous. His opinion was confirmed when we came across the boar's marking tree. The rub marks extended an arm's length above the ground and there were white gashes in the bark. 'See there, Thorgils, that is where he has marked his territory by scratching his back and sides. He's getting ready for the rutting season when he will fight the other boars. Those white slashes are file marks.' Then we found the wallow where the creature had rested and Edgar laid his hand on the mud to check how long the creature had been away. He drew his hand back thoughtfully. 'Still warm,' he said, 'the animal is not far off. We'd best leave quietly because I have a feeling that he is close by.'

'Will we scare him off?' I asked.

'No. This boar is a strange one. Not just big, but arrogant. He must have heard us approaching. A boar sees very poorly, but he hears better than any other creature in the forest. Yet only at the last moment did this one leave his bed. He fears nothing. He may still be lurking nearby, in some thicket, even preparing to rush on us – it has happened in the past, a sudden unprovoked attack – and we have not thought to bring our boar spears.'

Cautiously we withdrew and the moment we got back to Edgar's cottage he took down his boar spears from where they hung suspended on cords from the rafters. Their stout shafts were of ash and the metal heads were the shape of slender chestnut leaves, with a wickedly narrow tip. I noticed the heavy crosspiece a little way below the metal head.

'That's to stop the spear head piercing so deep into the boar that he can reach you with his tusks,' Edgar said. 'A charging boar knows no pain. In his fury he will spit himself even to his death, just to get at his enemy, especially if he is already wounded. Here, Thorgils, take this spear and make sure that you put a keen edge on it just in case you have to meet his charge, though that is not our job. Tomorrow, on the day of the hunt, our task is only to find the boar and run him until he is exhausted and turns to fight. Then we stand aside and let our masters make the kill and gain the honour.'

I hefted the heavy spear in my hand and wondered if I would be brave enough or capable of withstanding the assault.

'Oh, one more thing,' Edgar said, tossing me a roll of leather. 'Tomorrow wear these. Even if you are faced with a young boar, he can do some damage with his tusks as he slips by you.'

I unrolled the leather, and found they were a pair of heavy leggings. At knee level they were cut clean through in several places as though by the sharpest knife.

By coincidence, Michael's Mass of the Christians falls near the equinox when, for Old Believers, the barrier which separates the spirit world from our own grows thin. So I was not surprised when Judith, Edgar's wife, shyly approached me and asked if I would cast the Saxon wands at sunset. As before, she wanted to know if she would ever see her missing daughter again and what the future held for her sundered family. I took the white cloth that Edgar had used and with a nub of charcoal drew the pattern of nine squares as my mentors in Iceland had taught me before I laid the sheet upon the ground. Also, to please Judith, I carved and marked the eighth wand, the sinuous snake wand, and included it when I made my throw. Three times I threw the wands into the cloth's central square, and three times the answer came back the same. But I could not fathom it, and feared to explain it to Judith, not only because I was perplexed but because the snake wand was so dominant on each cast. That signalled some sort of death, and certain death because the snake wand lay across the master wand. Yet there was a contradiction too because all three times the wands gave me back, clearly and unambiguously, the signs and symbols for Frey, he who governs rain and the crops and rules prosperity and wealth. Frey is a God of birth, not death. I was baffled, and told Judith something bland, mumbling about Frey and the future. She went away happy, thinking, I suspect, that Frey's dominance – he is the God shown with the huge phallus – meant that perhaps her daughter would one day present her with grandchildren.

The morning of the hunt dawned with the dogs barking and baying in excitement, the kennelman yelling to keep them in order, and the boisterous shouts of our masters, who arrived to begin the chase. The hunt marshal was Aelfgifu's uncle, the earldorman, and it was his glory that was to be burnished that day. Aelfhelm had brought along a dozen friends, almost all of whom had attended the sheave-day feast, and once again I noticed the two huscarls. Even with their disabilities, they were prepared to pursue the boar. There were no women in the group. This was men's work.

We sorted out the chaos at the kennels and moved off, the lords mounted on their best horses, Edgar and myself on ponies, and a dozen or so churls and slaves running along beside us. They were to act as horse holders once we found our boar. From that moment forward the hunt would be on foot.

Edgar had already calculated the line the boar would run once he was moved so, as we rode, we dropped off small groups of dogs with their handlers at strategic spots, where they could be released to intercept and turn the fleeing boar.

Within an hour the first deep voices of the older dogs announced they had found their quarry. Then a crash of sound from the pack told us that they were onto the boar. Almost at once there was a piercing yelp of agony and I saw Edgar and the ealdorman exchange glances.

'Beware, my lord,' Edgar said. 'That's not a beast that runs. It stands and fights.'

We slipped from our horses and walked through the forest. But that day's hunting was a calamity. There was no chase, no hallooing or blasts on the horn, no occasion to use the dogs we had so carefully positioned. Instead we came upon the boar, standing at the foot of a great tree, champing its teeth, flecks of foam in its jaws. But this was not a boar at bay. It was a boar defiant. It was challenging its attackers, and the circling pack of dogs howled and barked in frustration. Not one dog dared to close with it and I could see why. Two dogs lay on the ground, disembowelled and dead. Another was trying to drag itself away, using only its forepaws, because its back was broken. The kennelman ran forward to restrain his other dogs. The boar stood, black and menacing, the ridge of bristle on his back erect, his head held low, looking with murderous short-sighted eyes.

'Watch the ears, my lord, watch the ears,' Edgar cautioned.

The ealdorman had courage, there was no doubt about that. He gripped the handle of his spear and walked forward towards the boar, defying it. I saw the beast's ears go flat against his skull, a sure sign that he was about to charge. The boar's black body quivered and suddenly exploded into action. The legs and hooves moved so fast that they seemed a single blur.

The ealdorman knew what he was doing. He stood his ground, the boar spear held at an angle sloping slightly downwards so as to take the charge on its tip. His aim was true. The boar impaled itself on the leaf-shaped tip and gave a mighty squeal of anger. It seemed to be a death strike, but the ealdorman was perhaps too slow. The sheer weight of the boar's charge knocked him off his feet and he was tossed aside. He fell and those near him heard his arm crack.

The boar rushed on, the spear projecting from its side. It darted through the circle of dogs and men unopposed. It ran in a frenzy of pain, a dark red stripe of blood oozing from its flank. We followed at the double, led by Edgar, boar spear in his hand, the dogs howling with fear and excitement. The beast did not go far, it was too badly hurt. We could easily follow the crashing sound of its reckless run. Then suddenly the noise stopped. Edgar halted immediately, and gasping for breath, held up his hand. 'All hold! All hold!' He walked forward very slowly and cautiously. I followed, but he waved at me to keep a safe distance. We moved between the trees and saw and heard nothing. The boar's blood trail led to a tangled thicket of briars and brushwood, a woven mass of thorn and branches, impossible to penetrate even for the dogs. We could see the battered and torn leaves and broken twigs which marked the tunnel of its blind, impetuous entry.

I heard the sudden intake of breath of a man in pain. Looking round, I saw the ealdorman clutching his broken arm, He had stumbled through the wood to find us. With him were three of his high-born guests. They looked drawn and shaken.

'Give me a moment to prepare myself, my lord,' said Edgar. 'Then I'll go in after him.'

The ealdorman said nothing. He was dizzy with pain and shock. Seeing what Edgar proposed, I made a move to join him, but a single firm hand fell on my shoulder. 'Stand still, lad,' said a voice and I glanced round. I was being held back by Kjartan the one-handed huscarl. 'You'd only get in his way.'

I looked at Edgar. He was removing his leather leggings so he would be less hampered. He turned towards his lord and saluted him, a short movement of the boar spear held up to the sky, then he faced the thicket, shifted his boar spear to his left hand holding it close to the metal head, dropped to his knees and began to crawl into the tunnel. Straight towards the waiting beast.

We held our breath, expecting any moment the boar's suicidal charge, but nothing came.

'Maybe the boar's already dead in there,' I whispered to Kjartan.

'I hope so. If not, Edgar's only chance will be to kneel and take the charge head on, the spear point in the boar's chest, butt planted in the ground.'

Still there was no sound except our breathing and the whimper of a nervous dog. We strained to hear any noise from the thicket. None came.

Then, incredibly, we heard Edgar's voice in a low, guttural chant, almost a growl. 'Out! Out! Out!'

'By the belt of Thor!' muttered Kjartan. 'I heard that sound when we fought King Ethelred at Ashington, The place I lost my hand. It's the war call of the Saxons. That is how they taunt their foe. He's challenging the boar.'

Suddenly there came a tearing, crashing, rushing sound, an upheaval in the thicket, and the boar came blundering out, unsteady on its feet, weaving and slipping on the ground, its legs losing purchase. It stumbled past us and ran another hundred paces, then slipped one more time and fell on its side. The yelping pack closed upon it now it was helpless. The kennelman ran up with a knife to cut the boar's throat. I did not see the end, for already I was on my hands and knees crawling through the tunnel to find Edgar. I came across him doubled up in agony, his boar spear tangled in the underbrush, his hands clasped across his belly. 'Easy now,' I told him, 'I have to get you clear.' Slowly I dragged him, crawling backwards until I felt helping hands reach over me to grab Edgar by his shoulders and pull him free.

They laid him on the ground and Kjartan reached down to draw Edgar's hands aside so he could inspect the wound. As Edgar hands came away, I saw that the tusks had gutted him. His entrails lay exposed. He knew he was dying, his eyes shut tight with pain.

He died without saying another word, at the feet of his master, the ealdorman whose honour he had protected.

Only then did I know the real message in the wands was not about Edgar's missing daughter. The wands had pointed to the truth, yet I had been too dull to see it. The snake wand had meant death; that much I had understood. But the appearance of Frey stood not for prosperity and fertility, but because the God's familiar is Gullinborsti, the immortal boar who pulls his chariot.

FOUR

LONDON WAS SOGGY and miserable under a rain-shrouded sky when I arrived back there a week after Michael's Mass. I was still trying to come to terms with Edgar's death. The festivities in the burh had been dismal, with the ealdorman injured, Edgar dead, and the premature onset of gales and heavy rain showers to remind us that the English countryside is no place to spend a winter. Edgar's death had hit me hard. The wiry huntsman had been so competent, so sure of himself, that he had seemed indestructible. I told myself that he would have accepted his death as a risk of his profession and that he had died honourably and would have found a place in Valholl, or wherever it was that his own Gods rewarded those who died a worthy death. His wife Judith, however, was left numbed by her loss. First her daughter and now her husband had been taken away from her, and she was distraught. Aelfhelm, the ealdorman, behaved nobly. When we brought Edgar's body back to the huntsman's cottage, he had promised Judith that he would remember her husband's sacrifice. She could continue to live in her home, and Edgar's son would be employed as assistant to whoever was appointed the new royal huntsman. If the young man proved as capable as his father had been, then there was every reason why he would eventually succeed his father. Yet when I went to say goodbye to Judith on the day Aelfgifu and her entourage set out for London, she could only press my hand in hers and murmur, 'Thorgils, take care of yourself. Remember your days with us. Remember how Edgar . . .' but she did not finish what she had to say because she choked and began to weep.

It had rained for most of our journey south-east as our glum little procession travelled the same road that had taken us to Northampton in the spring. And I had another worry. 'Far from court, far from care,' had been one of Edgar's many proverbs and, as the capital drew nearer, I began for the first time to appreciate the danger of my affair with Aelfgifu. I was still very much in love with her and I longed to see her and hold her. Yet I knew that the risks of discovery in London would be far greater than in our secluded rural world. There was a rumour that Knut was shortly to return from Denmark to England now that the summer campaigning season was over. Naturally Aelfgifu as his queen, or rather as one of his queens, should be on hand to greet him. She had chosen to come to London because Emma, the other wife, was installed in Winchester, which Knut regarded as his English capital. Naturally there was gossipy speculation as to which city, and which wife, he would return to if he did come. As events turned out, he did not return to England that winter, but continued to leave the affairs of the kingdom under the joint control of Earl Thorkel the Tall and Archbishop Wulfstan.

While the staff were unloading the carts at the palace, I approached Aelfgifu's chamberlain and asked if he had any orders for me, only to be told that he had no instructions. I was not on the official list of the queen's retinue. He suggested I should return to my original lodgings at the skalds' house, where he would send for me if I was wanted.

Feeling rejected, I walked through the sodden streets, skirting around the murky puddles in the unpaved roadway and ducking to avoid the dripping run-off from the thatched roofs. When I reached the lodging house, the place was shuttered and locked. I hammered on the door until a neighbour called out to say that the housekeeper was away visiting her family, and expected back that evening. I was soaked by the time she finally returned and let me in. She told me that all the skalds who had regular employment with Knut were still in Denmark. Those, like my absent-minded mentor Herfid who had no official appointment at court, had packed up and drifted away. I asked if I could stay in the lodgings for a few days until my future was clear.

It was a week before Aelfgifu sent a messenger to fetch me and I went with high hopes, remembering my last visit to her rooms in the palace. This time I was shown to an audience room, not to her private chamber. Aelfgifu was seated at a table, sorting through a box of jewellery.

'Thorgils,' she began, and the tone of her voice warned me at once that she was going to be businesslike. This was not a lover's tryst. I noticed, however, that she waited until the messenger who fetched me had left the room before she spoke. 'I have to talk to you about life in London.' She paused, and I could see that she was trying to find a way between her private feelings and her caution. 'London is not like Northampton. This palace has many ears and eyes, and there are those who, from jealousy or ambition, would do anything to damage me.'

'My lady, I would never do anything to put you at risk,' I blurted out.

'I know,' she said, 'but you cannot hide your feelings. Your love is written in your face. That is one thing that I found so appealing when we were in the country. Don't you remember how Edgar would joke about it – he used to say, "Love and a cough cannot be hid". He had so many of those proverbs.' Here she paused wistfully for a moment. 'So, however much you may try to conceal your love, I don't think you would be successful. And if that love was constantly on display before me, I cannot guarantee that I might not respond and reveal all.'

Anguished, I wondered for a moment if she would forbid me to see her ever again, but I had misjudged her.

She went on. 'I have been thinking about how it might be

possible for us to meet from time to time – not often, but at least when it is safe to do so.'

My spirits soared. I would do anything to see her. I would trust to her guidance, however much it might hurt me.

Aelfgifu was playing with the contents of the jewellery box, lifting up a necklace or a pendant, letting it slide back through her fingers, then picking up a ring or a brooch and turning it so that the workmanship or the stones caught the light. For a moment she seemed distracted.

'There is a way, but you will have to be most discreet,' she said.

'Please tell me. I'll do whatever you wish,' I replied.

'I've arranged for you to stay with Brithmaer. You don't know him yet, but he is the man who supplies me with most of my jewels. He came to visit me this morning to show me his latest stock, and I told him that in future I preferred to have my own agent staying at his premises, someone who knows my tastes' – she said this without a trace of irony – 'so that when anything interesting comes in from abroad, I will see it without delay.'

'I don't know anything about jewellery, but, of course, I'll do whatever is necessary,' I promised her.

'I've asked Brithmaer to give you some training. You'll have plenty of time to learn. Of course he won't instruct you himself, but one of his craftsmen will. Now go. I will send for you when I judge it to be safe.'

One of Aelfgifu's servants showed me the way to Brithmaer's premises, which was just as well because it was a long walk from the palace to the heart of the city, near the new stone church of St Paul, where the land slopes towards the Thames waterfront. Riverside London reminded me of Dublin, only it was very much bigger. Here was the same stench of fetid foreshore, the same jostle and tangle of muddy lanes leading inland from the wharves, the same dank spread of drab houses. However, London's houses were more substantial, stout timbers replacing Dublin's daub and wattle. The servant took me down a lane leading to the river, and

if he had not stopped at the door of the building, I would have
mistaken Brithmaer's home for a warehouse, and a very solid one
at that.

A small spy hatch opened in answer to our knock. When the
servant identified himself, the massive door was opened and, as
soon as I was inside, closed firmly behind me. The palace servant
was not allowed to enter.

I found myself blinking to adjust to the dimness. I was in an
antechamber. The place was dark because the barred windows
were small and high up in the walls. The man who had let me in
looked more like a rough blacksmith than a fine jeweller and I
quickly concluded that he was more of a guard than a doorkeeper.
He grunted when I gave him my name and gestured for me to
follow him. As I crossed the darkened room, I became aware of
a muffled sound. It was an uninterrupted chinking and clinking, a
metallic sound, irregular but insistent which seemed to come
through rear wall of the room. I could not imagine what was
causing it.

There was a small door to one side, which led on to a narrow
stairway, and that in turn brought us up to the upper floor of the
building. From the outside the house had seemed workmanlike,
even grim, but on the upper floor I found accommodation more
comfortable than in the palace I had just left. I was shown into
what was the first of a series of large, airy rooms. It was clearly a
reception room and expensively furnished. The wall hangings
were artfully woven in muted golds and greens and I imagined
they must have been imported from the Frankish lands. The
chairs were plain but valuable and the table was spread with a
patterned carpet, a fashion I had never seen before. Sculpted
bronze candle holders, even some glass panes in the windows
instead of the usual window panes of horn, spoke of wealth and
discreet good taste. The sole occupant of the room was seated at
the table, an old man quietly eating an apple.

'So you are to be the queen's viewer,' he said. By his dress
and manner he was clearly the owner of the establishment. He

was wearing a dark grey tunic of old-fashioned cut with comfort-able loose pantaloons. On his feet were well-worn but beautiful stitched slippers. Had he been standing, I doubted that he would have come only halfway up my chest, and I observed that he had developed the forward stoop of the very old. He held his head hunched down carefully into his shoulders and the hand that held the apple, was mottled with age. Yet his small, narrow face with its slightly hooked nose and close-set eyes, was a youthful pink, as if he had never been exposed to the wind and rain. His hair, which he had kept despite his age, was pure white. He looked very carefully preserved. It was impossible to read any expression in the watery, bright blue eyes which regarded me shrewdly.

'Do you know anything about jewellery and fine metals?' he asked.

I was about to tell this delicate gnome of a man that I had lived for two years in an Irish monastery where master craftsmen produced exquisite objects for the glory of God – reliquaries, platens, bishops' crosses and so forth – made in gold and silver and inlaid with enamel and precious stones. But when I saw those neutral, watchful eyes, I decided only to answer, 'I would be pleased to learn.'

'Very well. Naturally I am happy to accede to the queen's request. She is one of my best customers. We'll provide you with board and lodging – rent free of course, though nothing was said about paying any wages.' Then, speaking to the doorkeeper who had stood behind me, he said, 'Call Thurulf. Tell him that I want a word.'

The servant left by a different door from the one we had entered through and, as he opened it, that same puzzling sound came bursting in, at much greater volume. It seemed to be coming from below. Now I remembered a similar sound. As a boy, I had been befriended by Tyrkir the metalworker and had helped him at his forge. When Tyrkir was beating out a heavy lump of iron, he would relax between the blows by letting his hammer bounce lightly on the anvil. This is what I was hearing. It sounded as if a dozen Tyrkirs were letting their hammers tap idly in a continuous, irregular ringing chorus.

Another burst of the sound accompanied the young man who now stepped into the reception room. Thurulf was about my age, about eighteen or nineteen, though taller. A well-set-up young man, his cheerful countenance was fringed by a straggly reddish-orange beard which made up for the fact that he was going prematurely bald. His face was ruddy and he was sweating.

'Thurulf, be so kind as to show our young friend Thorgils to a guest room – the end room, I think. He will be staying with us for some time. Then you might bring him down to the exchange later in the afternoon.' With studied courtesy the old man waited until I was walking out of the door before he turned back to take the next bite of his apple.

I followed Thurulf's broad back as he stepped out onto an internal balcony, which ran the entire length of the building, and found myself looking down on a curious sight.

Laid out below me was a long workshop. It must have been at least forty paces in length and perhaps ten paces broad. It had the same small high windows protected with heavy bars which I had seen in the ground-floor antechamber. Now I noticed that the outer wall was at least three feet thick. A heavy, narrow work-bench, set high and securely fixed, ran for the full length of the wall. At the bench a dozen men sat on stools. They were facing the wall, away from me, so I could only see the backs of their heads and they were bowed over their work, so I could not make out what they were doing. All I could see was that each man held a small hammer in one hand and what looked like a heavy, blunt peg in the other. Each worker was making the same action, again and again and again. From a box beside him he lifted an item so small that he was obliged to pick it up carefully between forefinger and thumb, then he placed it in front of him. Next he set the peg in position and struck the butt end with his hammer. It was the metallic sound of this blow repeated regularly by a dozen men, which I had been hearing from the moment I had entered Brithmaer's premises.

Looking down on the line of stooped, hammer-wielding workmen as they beat out their rhythm, I wished Herfid the skald had been standing beside me. I knew exactly what he would have said: he would have taken one glance and burst out, 'Ivaldi's Sons!' for they would have reminded him of the dwarves who created the equipment of the Gods: Odinn's spear, Thor's hammer and the golden wig for Sif, Thor's wife, after she had been shorn by the wicked Loki.

Thurulf led me along the balcony to the last door on the right and showed me into a small sleeping room. It had a pair of wooden beds, set into the walls like mangers, and I put my leather satchel on one of them to claim it. The battered satchel was my only baggage.

'What are all those men with the hammers doing?' I asked Thurulf.

He looked puzzled by my ignorance. 'You meant with striking irons?'

'The men in the workshop down there.'

'They're making money.' I must have looked mystified, for Thurulf went on, 'Didn't you know that my uncle Brithmaer is the king's chief moneyer?'

'I thought he was the royal jeweller.'

Thurulf laughed. 'He's that also in a small way. He makes far more money by making money, so to speak, than by supplying the palace with gems. Here, I'll show you.' And he led me back to the balcony and down a wooden ladder, which led directly to the floor of the workshop.

We walked over to the heavy bench and stood beside one of the workmen. He did not lift his head to acknowledge our presence or break the steady rhythm of his hammer. In his left hand was the metal peg which Thurulf called the 'striking iron'. I could see that it was a blunt metal chisel about five inches long and square in section, with a flat tip. With the hand that held the striking iron, the man stretched out to a wooden box on the bench beside him, and used finger and thumb to pick up a small, thin, metal disc. He then placed the disc carefully on the flat top of a similar metal peg fixed into the heavy wooden bench in front of him. Then, as the little disc balanced there, the workman brought the striking iron into position on top of it, and gave the butt of the iron a smart blow with his hammer. Lifting the iron, he used his right hand to pick up the metal disc and drop it into a wooden tray on his right-hand side.

Thurulf reached out, took one of the metal discs from the first box and handed it to me. It was about the size of my fingernail and I saw that it was plain unmarked silver. Thurulf took back the disc, returned it to the box, then picked up a disc from the tray on the workman's right. This too he handed to me, and I saw that on one side the disc bore a stylised picture of the king's head. Around the margin were stamped the letters KNUT, a small cross, and a leaf pattern. Turning the disc over, I saw the leaf pattern repeated and over it was stamped a larger cross. This time the lettering read BRTHMR. I was holding one of Knut's pennies.

Thurulf took back the penny, carefully replaced it in the box of finished coins and, holding me by the arm, led me away from the workmen so we could speak more easily over the constant ringing of the hammers.

'My uncle holds the king's licence to make his money,' he said. He still had to raise his voice to make himself heard clearly. 'In fact, he's just been named a mint master, so he's the most important moneyer in London.'

'You mean, there are other workshops like this?'

'Oh yes, at least another dozen in London. I'm not sure of the exact number. And there are several score more moneyers in towns scattered all around England, all doing the same work, though each moneyer has his own mark on the coins he stamps. That's in case of error or forgery so the king's officials can trace a coin back to its maker. My own family are moneyers up in

Anglia, from Norwich, and I've been sent here to gain experience under my uncle.'

'It must cost the king a great deal to keep so many moneyers employed,' I said wonderingly.

Thurulf laughed at my naivety. 'Not at all. Quite the reverse. He does not pay them. They pay him.'

When he saw that I was baffled again, Thurulf went on, 'The moneyers pay the king's officials for the right to stamp money, and they take a commission on all the coins they produce.'

'Then who's paying the commission, and who supplies the silver which is turned into coins?'

'That's the beauty of it,' said Thurulf. 'Every so often, the king announces a change to the design of his coins and withdraws the old style from circulation. His subjects have to bring the moneyers all their old coins. These are then melted down for the new issue, and the new coins are given out, but not to the same value as those that were given in. There is a deduction of five to fifteen per cent. It's a simple and effective royal tax, and of course the moneyers get their share.'

'So why don't the people just keep their old pennies and use them amongst themselves as currency?'

'Some do and they value their old coins by their weight of silver when they come to trading. But the king's advisers are a clever lot and they've found a way round that too. When you pay royal taxes, whether as fines or trade licences or whatever, the tax collectors only accept the current issue of coins. So you have to use new coins and, of course, if you fail to pay the tax collectors, they impose more fines and that means you have to obtain more coins of the new issue. It's a system of pure genius.'

'Don't people complain, or at least try to melt down their own old coins and stamp out a copy of the new design?'

Thurulf looked mildly shocked. 'That's forgery! Anyone caught making false coins has their right hand cut off. The same penalty, incidentally, applies to any moneyer caught producing coins which are fake or under weight. And the merchants don't complain about the system because the royal stamp on coins is a guarantee of quality. All over Europe the coins of England are regarded as the most trustworthy.'

I looked at the number of men working at the benches, and the porters and assistants who were moving around, carrying bags of silver blanks and finished coins. There must have been at least thirty of them.

'Isn't there a risk that some of the workers will steal? After all, a single penny must represent at least a day's wage for them, and a coin or two would be very easy to carry away.'

'That's why my uncle has designed the premises with that balcony so he can appear from his rooms at any time and look down into the workshop to see what's going on, but the counting is far more effective. A moneyer's job might seem to be nothing but organising a lot of men to hammer out coins while he himself endures the din. But the real chore is the endless counting. Everything is counted in and out. The number of blanks issued to each worker, the number of finished coins he returns, the number of damaged coins, the number of coins received in for melting down, their precise weight, and so on. It's endless, this counting and recounting, checking and rechecking, and everything of value is stored in the strongrooms behind you.' He pointed to a row of small rooms located directly under his uncle's rooms. Brithmaer, I thought to myself, ate and slept on top of his money like a Norse troll guarding his most valuable possessions.

I saw what I thought might be a flaw in the moneyer's defences. 'What about the striking irons?' I asked. 'Couldn't someone copy one of them, or steal one, and start making coins that are indistinguishable from the genuine article?'

Thurulf shook his head. 'It takes great skill to craft a striking iron. The metal is particularly hard. The shank is of iron, but the flat head is steel. To engrave the right image takes a master craftsman. New striking irons are issued by the king's officers when the design of the coin changes. Each moneyer has to buy them from the iron-maker, and return all the striking irons of the older design. More counting out and counting in.' He sighed. 'But recently my uncle was authorised to have a master craftsman engrave irons here on the premises and that's a great relief. After all he's been a moneyer for nearly forty years.'

'You mean your uncle is a moneyer for the Saxon kings, as well as for Knut?'

'Oh yes,' said Thurulf cheerfully. 'He was a moneyer for Ethelred the Ill-Advised long before Knut came along. That's why my uncle has amassed such a fortune. Kings may change, but the moneyers stay the same and go on making their commissions.'

LATER THAT AFTERNOON Thurulf took me to see his uncle at what he called 'the exchange'. It was another sturdy building, closer to the waterfront, where the little stream called the Wal-brook empties into the Thames near the wharves. There I found Brithmaer sitting at a table in a back room, writing figures in a ledger. He glanced up as I came in, again with that bland and careful look. 'Did Thurulf show you the jewellery stock?'

'Not yet,' I answered. 'He showed me the coin makers, and then we went to eat at a tavern near the docks.'

Brithmaer did not react. 'No matter. Now that you're here, I'll explain how the jewellery side of my business operates, so you can do whatever it is that the queen wants.'

He nodded towards three or four locked chests on the floor beside him. 'This is where the preliminary assessment is made. When foreign merchants arrive in London port, they usually visit this office first of all. They need to pay the port dues to the harbour reeve and, as this is a royal tax, they have to pay in English coin. If they don't have any English coin they come to my office. I give them good English silver stamped with the king's head in exchange for their own foreign coins or whatever they have to offer. Most of the exchange work is straightforward, and done in the front office. My clerks know the comparative value of Frisian coins, Frankish coins, coins from Dublin and so forth. If they don't recognise a coin, they weigh it and place a value on the metal content. But occasionally we get items brought to us like this.'

He pulled out a heavy iron key and unlocked the largest of the chests. Opening the lid, he reached in and produced an ornate buckle, which glinted gold in the weak afternoon light.

'As you can see, this is valuable, but how valuable? What is it worth in English coin, do you think? Maybe you would care to give me an opinion.'

He passed the buckle over to me. I knew he was testing me so I looked at it cautiously. Compared to the metalwork I had seen in my Irish monastery, it was crude stuff. Also it had been damaged. I weighed it in my hand. For something that looked like gold, it was remarkably light. 'I have no idea of the value,' I said, 'but I don't think it would be worth very much.'

'It's not,' the old man said. 'It's not genuine gold, but gilt over a bronze base. I would say it was once part of a horse harness belonging to some showy chief, perhaps among the Wendish people. It's amazing what shows up in the hands of the merchants, particularly if they come from the northern lands. Everyone knows the reputation of the Norse as raiders. A merchant may come in from Sweden looking to exchange a pile of broken silver bits and some foreign coins, then find he has not enough value for what he needs, reach into his purse and produce this—'

The old man rummaged in the chest, and pulled out something I recognised at once. It was a small reliquary, no bigger than the palm of my hand and made in the shape of a tiny casket. It was crafted in silver and bronze, and decorated with gold inlay. Doubtless it had been looted from an Irish monastery. It was an accomplished piece of metalwork.

'So what do you think that one is worth?'

Again I exercised caution. Something about Brithmaer's attitude sent me a warning signal.

'I'm sorry,' I said, 'I have no idea. I don't know what it is used for or how much precious metal is in it.'

'Neither did the illiterate barbarian who brought it in to me,' said the old man. 'For him it was just a pretty bauble, and because his wife or mistress could not wear it as a brooch or hang it round her neck as a pendant, he couldn't find a use for it.'

'So why did you buy it?'

'Because I could get a bargain.'

Brithmaer dropped back the lid of the chest. 'Enough. I presume that your job is to be here at the exchange so that, when a merchant or a sailor comes in with something similar, you are on hand to assess whether the queen would like to add it to her jewellery collection. If you go to the front office, my clerks will find a space for you.'

So began a long, tedious spell for me. I was not born to be a shopkeeper. I lack the patience to sit for hours gazing vacantly out of the door or, when the weather allows, to stand in the street, hovering to greet a potential customer with an attentive smile. And because it was the start of winter and the sailing season was at an end, very few ships were working upriver with cargoes from the Continent. So there were very few clients. Indeed there were almost no visitors to Brithmaer's exchange, except for two or three merchants who seemed to be regular customers. When they arrived, they did not deal with the clerks in the front room but were shown directly to see Brithmaer in his office in the back. Then the door was firmly closed.

Whenever the boredom got too great to endure, I would slip out of the building, stroll down to the wharves and find a spot out of the wind. There I would stand and gaze at the waters of the Thames sliding past me with their endless patterns and ripples, and I would mark the slow passage of time by the inexorable rise and fall of the tideline on the river's muddy foreshore, and ache for Aelfgifu. She never sent me word.

FIVE

By MID-DECEMBER I was so racked by longing to see Aelgifu that I asked Brithmaer for permission to look through his existing stock of jewellery for items which might catch the queen's eye. He sent me to Thurulf with a note telling him to show me the inventory in the strongroom. Thurulf was glad to see me. We had adjacent rooms at Brithmaer's home, but each morning went our separate ways – I to the exchange, Thurulf to the workshop floor. Once or twice a week we met up after working hours and, if we could avoid Brithmaer's attention, slipped out of the house to visit the taverns by the docks. We always timed our return to be outside the heavily guarded door to the mint when Brithmaer's two night workers reported for duty, and we entered – unnoticed, we hoped – with them. The night workers were both veterans of the moneyer's bench, too old and worn-out for full-time labour. One had an eye disease and was nearly blind, so he sat at the bench and worked by touch. The other was stone deaf after years among the din of hammers. The men spent a few hours each night at their well-remembered places at the workbench, in lamplight, and I would often fall asleep to the patient clink, clink of their hammers. The general opinion was that it was an act of charity for Brithmaer to give them part-time employment.

'What are you doing here at this time of day?' said Thurulf, obviously pleased when I showed up mid-morning with Brithmaer's note. He was glumly counting up the contents of the bags of the old-issue coins stored in the strongroom before they were melted down for new coinage. It was a job he particularly loathed. 'The bags never seem to grow any less,' he said. 'Goes to prove that people are hoarders. Just when you think you've cleared the backlog, another batch of old coins comes in.'

Thurulf put aside the wooden tally stick on which he was cutting the number of bags of coin, a notch for each bag. Locking the door behind him, he took me to where the jewellery was kept. At the far end of the minting floor was the workroom for the craftsman who cut the faces of the striking irons. He was a suspicious, surly figure and unpopular with the other workers, who resented that he was paid far more than them. I never learned his name because he only came to the mint one day a week, went straight to his workroom and locked himself inside to get on with his job.

'There's not enough work in preparing striking irons to keep a craftsman employed, even one day a week,' explained Thurulf, relishing his chance to display his moneyer's expertise. 'When all the striking irons for a new coin issue have been made, another full set of irons won't be needed until the king decides a new design for his coin, and that might not be for several years. In the meantime the work is mainly repairing and refacing damaged and worn-out striking irons. So my uncle decided that his craftsman might as well make and repair jewellery during his extra hours.'

Thurulf pushed open the door to the workroom. It was a cubbyhole equipped with the same sort of heavy workbench that was used in the main workshop, a small crucible for melting metal and an array of punches and engraving tools for cutting the faces of the striking irons. The only difference was the large iron-bound chest tucked under the bench. I helped Thurulf tug this out and heave it up on the bench. He unlocked it, rummaged inside and produced some jewellery, which he spread out. 'It's mostly

repairs,' he said, 'replacing a missing stone in a necklace, tightening up the mounts, mending a clasp, straightening, cleaning and
polishing an item so that it will catch the customer's eye. A lot of
what is here is rubbish – imitation gold, low-grade silver, broken
odds and ends.'

He picked through the better pieces on the bench, and selected
a handsome pendant, silver with a blue stone set in its centre and
an attractive pattern of curved lines radiating from the mount.
'Here,' he said, 'you can see how this pendant is hung on a chain
through that loop. When my uncle acquired the piece, the loop
was cracked and flattened and our man had to reshape and solder
it. Then he went over the decoration lines again with his
engraving tool – they were a bit faded – and made them more
distinct.'

I took the pendant from Thurulf. It was easy to detect where
the mend had been done and the scratches of the new engraving.
'Your man's not very skilled, is he?' I commented.

'Frankly, no. But then most of our clients aren't too discern-
ing,' said Thrulf blithely. 'He's a working engraver,, not an artist.
Now look at this. Here's something he could repair if only he had
the right stones to fill the holes.' He handed me a necklace made
of red amber beads strung on a silver chain. After every third
bead a crystal, the size of half a walnut, was held in a fine silver
claw. Like nuggets of smooth, fresh ice, the crystals threw back
the light from flat surfaces cut and polished on them. Originally
there had been seven crystals, but now three of them were
missing, though the silver mounts remained. Had the necklace
been entire, it would have been spectacular. As it was, it looked
like a gap-toothed grin.

'I thought you said your uncle's workshop made jewellery,' I
commented.

'Nothing complicated,' Thurulf replied, lifting a leather pouch
from the chest and unfastening the drawstring. 'This is what we
specialise in,' and he pulled out a necklace.

My heart gave a little lurch. It was a necklace, made very

simply by joining a chain of silver coins together with links of gold. I had seen one around Aelfgifu's neck. It was the only item she had worn on the day we first made love.

'Your uncle said that I could look through the chest to pick out anything which I thought the queen might like.'

'Go ahead,' said Thurulf amiably, 'though I doubt that you'll find much that has been overlooked. My uncle knows his clients and his stock down to the tiniest item.'

He was right. I picked through the box of broken jewellery and managed to find no more than a couple of bead necklaces, some heavy brooches, and a finger ring which I thought might please Aelfgifu. They added up to a feeble excuse to visit her.

'Would it be possible to make up a coin necklace for her?' I enquired. 'I know that she would like that.'

'You'd have to ask my uncle,' Thurulf said. 'He's the coin expert. Even hoards them. But that's what you'd expect from a moneyer, I suppose. Here, I'll show you.'

He tipped the contents of a second pouch over the workbench and a cascade of coins tumbled out in a little pile. I picked through them, turning them over in my fingers. They were of all different sizes, some broad and thin, others as thick and chunky as nuggets. Most were silver, but some were gold or copper or bronze, and a few were even struck from lead. Some had holes in the centre, others were hexagons or little squares, though the majority were round, or nearly so. Many were smooth with handling, but occasionally you could still see the writing clearly and the images. On one coin I read the Greek script that the Irish monks had taught me; on another I saw runes that I had learned in Iceland. On several was a script with curves and loops like the surface of the sea riffled by a breeze. Nearly all were stamped with symbols – pyramids, squares, a sword, a tree, a leaf, several crosses, the head of a king, a God shown with two faces, and one with two triangles which overlapped to make a six-pointed star.

I slid the coins about on the bench like counters in a board game, trying to align a sequence that would make a handsome

necklace for my love. Instead I found my thoughts flying out like
Hugin and Munin, Odinn's birds, his scouts who fly out across
the world to observe and report to their master all that happens.
By what routes, I wondered, had these strange coins reached a
little box in a strongroom belonging to a moneyer for King Knut?
How far had they come? Who had made them and why were
these symbols chosen? My fingertips sensed a vast, unknown
world that I had never imagined, a world across which these little
rounds and squares of precious metal had travelled by paths I
would like to explore.

I assembled a row of coins, alternately gold and silver, that
looked well. But when I turned them over to check their reverse
sides, I was disappointed. Three of the coins were blemished.
Someone had dug fierce little nicks in the surface with something
sharp. 'A pity about those nicks and pits,' I said. 'They ruin the
surface and destroy the images.'

'You find those marks all the time,' Thurulf said casually.
'Nearly half the old-issue silver coins that we get from the
northern lands carry those cuts and scratches. It's something
foreigners do to them, especially in Sweden and the land of the
Rus. They don't trust coins. They think they might be fakes: a
lead base coated with silver, or a bronze core which has a gold
wash applied to make it look like solid gold. It's possible to
achieve that effect, even in this small workshop. So when they are
offered a coin in payment, they jab the point of a knife into it or
scratch the surface to check that the metal is genuine all the way
through.'

I abandoned the idea of making up a coin necklace for
Aelfgifu, and instead prepared a package of the necklaces and
brooches which I thought might please her. Thurulf wrote down
a careful list of what I was taking. Then we left and locked the
strongroom, and one of Brithmaer's burly watchmen escorted me
and the jewellery to the palace.

I asked to see the queen's chamberlain and told him that I had
samples of jewellery for the queen to view. He kept me waiting

for an hour before he returned to say that the queen was too busy. I was to return the same day the following week to seek another appointment.

As I was emerging from the palace gate, a leather stump tapped me on the shoulder and a voice said, 'If it isn't my young friend, the huntsman.' I turned to see Kjartan the one-handed huscarl. 'Someone said you had found a job with Brithmaer the moneyer,' he said, 'but by the glum look on your face, it would seem that you had found Fafnir's golden hoard and then lost it again.'

I mumbled something about having to return to Brithmaer's workshop. My escort, the watchman, was already looking impatient. 'Not so fast,' the huscarl said. 'At year's end we hold our gemot, the dedication feast. Most of the brigade is still in Denmark with Knut, but there are enough of us semi-pensioners and a few back on home leave for us to make a gathering. Each huscarl is expected to bring one orderly. To honour the memory of our good friend Edgar I would like you to be my attendant. Do you accept?'

'With pleasure, sir,' I replied.

'I've just one condition to make,' said Kjartan. 'For Aesir's sake, get yourself a new set of clothes. That plum-coloured tunic you wore last time at Northampton was beginning to look very shabby. I want my attendant to be turned out smartly.'

The huscarl had a point, I thought, as I pulled my much-worn tunic out of the satchel when I got back to my room. The garment was spotted and stained and a seam had split. The tunic was getting a little too small for me. I had filled out since coming to England, partly due to exercise and good meals when living with Edgar but more from all the ale I was drinking. For a moment I thought of borrowing something to wear from Thurulf, but I decided I would be adrift in his larger garments. Besides, I was already in his debt for our visits to the taverns. I received board and lodging from Brithmaer but no wage, so my friend was always buying the drinks.

If I was to have a new tunic, I had to pay a tailor, and I believed I knew how to raise the money. Better still, I would be able to show my love for Aelfgifu.

When Thurulf had shown me the amber necklace with its missing crystals, I had immediately thought of my satchel. Closed deep in a slit in the thick leather where I had stitched them three years earlier were the five stones I had prised from an ornate bible cover in a fit of rage against the Irish monks who I felt had betrayed me, before I fled their monastery. I had no idea what the stolen stones were worth, but that was not the point. Four of the stones were crystals and they matched the stones missing from the necklace.

I suppose only someone so much in love as I was would have dreamed what I now proposed: I would sell the stones to Brithmaer. With the money from the sale I could repay my debt to Thurulf and still have more than sufficient to purchase new clothes for the banquet. Best of all, I was sure that once Brithmaer had the stones he would tell his craftsman to set them in the necklace. Then, at last, I would have some jewellery worthy to offer the queen.

With a silent prayer of thanks to Odinn I took down the satchel from its peg, slit open the hiding place and, like squeezing roe from a fish, pressed out the stones into the palm of my hand.

'How many of these do you have,' asked Brithmaer. We were sitting in his private room at the rear of the exchange when I handed him one of the gleaming flat stones to inspect.

'Four in all,' I said. 'They match.'

The mint master turned the stone over in his hand, and looked at me thoughtfully. Again I noted the guarded expression in his eyes. 'May I see the others?'

I handed over three more stones, and he held them up to the light one by one. He was still expressionless.

'Rock crystal,' he announced dismissively. 'Eye-catching, but of little value on their own.'

'There's a damaged necklace in the jewellery coffer which lacks similar stones. I thought that—'

'I'm perfectly aware of what jewellery is in my inventory,' he interrupted. 'These may not fit the settings. So before I make you an offer I'll have to check if they suit.'

'I think you'll find they are the right size,' I volunteered.

I thought I detected a slight chill, a deliberate closeness in the glance that met this remark. It was difficult to judge because Brithmaer masked his feelings so well.

His next question was certainly one he asked every customer who brought in precious stones to try to sell.

'Have you got anything else you would like me to take a look at?'

I produced the fifth of my stolen stones. It was smaller than the others and dull by comparison. It was a very deep red, nearly as dark as the colour of drying blood. In size and shape it resembled nothing so much as a large bean.

Brithmaer took the stone from me, and once again held it up to the daylight. By chance – or maybe by Odinn's intervention – the winter sun broke through the cloud cover at that moment and briefly flooded the world outside with a luminous light, which reflected off the surface of the Thames and came pouring in through the window. As I looked at the little red stone held up between Brithmaer's forefinger and thumb, I saw something unexpected. Inside it appeared a sudden vivid flicker of colour. It reminded me of an ember deep inside the ashes of a fire which feels a draught and briefly gives off a radiant glow that animates the entire hearth. But the glow the stone gave off was more alive. It travelled back and forth as if a shard from Mjollnir's lightning flash when Thor throws his hammer lay imprisoned within the stone.

For the first and only time in my meetings with Brithmaer, I

saw him drop his guard. He froze, hand in the air, for a moment.
I heard a quick, slight intake of breath, and then he rotated the
stone and again the interior lit up, a living red gleam flickering
back and forth. Somewhere inside the jewel was a quality which
rested until summoned into life by motion and light.

Very slowly Brithmaer turned to face me – I heard him exhale
as he regained his composure.

'And where did you get this?' he asked softly.

'I would rather not say.'

'Probably with good reason.'

I knew that something untoward had entered our conversation.
'Can you tell me anything about the stone?' I asked.

Again there was a long pause as Brithmaer looked at me with
those washed-out blue, rheumy eyes, carefully considering before
he spoke.

'If I thought you were stupid or gullible, I would tell you that
this stone is nothing more than red glass, cleverly made but of
little value. However, I have already observed that you are neither
simple nor credulous. You saw the fire flickering within the stone,
as well as I did.'

'Yes,' I replied. 'I've had the stone in my possession for a
while, but this is the first time I've looked at it carefully. Until
now I kept it hidden.'

'A wise precaution,' said Brithmaer drily. 'Have you any idea
what you have here?'

I stayed silent. With Brithmaer silence was the wiser course.

He rolled the stone gently between his fingers. 'All my life I
have been a moneyer who also dealt in jewels. As did my father
before me. In that time I've seen many stones, brought to me
from many different sources. Some were precious, others not,
some badly cut, others raw and unworked. Often they were
nothing more than pretty lumps of coloured rock. Until now I
have never seen a stone like this, but only heard of its existence.
It is a type of ruby known vulgarly and for obvious reasons as a
fire ruby. No one knows for sure where such gems originate,

though I would make a guess. In my father's time we used to receive many coins, mostly silver but a few of gold, which bore the curling script of the Arabs. So many were reaching us that the moneyers found it convenient to base their system of weights and measures on these foreign coins. Our coins were little more than substitutes, reminted from their metal.'

Brithmaer was looking pensively at the little stone as it lay in his palm. Now that the sunlight no longer struck it directly, the stone lay lifeless, nothing more than a pleasant dark-red bead.

'At the time of the Arab coins I heard reports about the fire rubies, how they glow when the light strikes them in a certain way. The men who described these stones were usually the same men who dealt in the Arab coins, and I conjectured that fire rubies came along the same routes as the Arab coins. But it was impossible to learn more. I was told only that these gems originated even further away, where the desert lands rose again to mountains. Here the fire gems were mined.'

The mint master leaned forward to hand me back the little stone. 'I'll let you know whether I want to buy the rock crystals, but I suggest you keep this gem somewhere very safe.'

I took his hint. For the next few days I kept the fire ruby concealed in a crack behind the headboard of my manger bed, and when Brithmaer decided he would buy the rock crystals and have his workman repair the faulty necklace, I went to the pedlars' market. There, using a fraction of his purchase price, I bought a cheap and ugly amulet. It was meant to be one of Odinn's birds, but was so badly cast in lead that you could not tell whether it was eagle, raven, or an owl. Yet its body was fat enough for my purposes. I scraped out a cavity, inserted the ruby and sealed the hole. Thereafter I wore it on a leather thong around my neck and learned to smile sheepishly when people asked me why I wore a barnyard fowl as a pendant.

My other purchases took a little longer: a tunic of fine English wool, yellow with an embroidered border; a new set of hose in brown; gaiters of the same hue; and garters to match the tunic. I also ordered new footwear – a pair of soft shoes in the latest style, also in yellow with a brown pattern embossed across the toe. 'Don't you want to take away the leather scraps with you, young master, so you can make an offering for your Gods?' asked the cobbler with a grin. The cross displayed in his workshop denoted he was a follower of the White Christ. He had recognised me as a northerner by my accent, and was teasing me about our belief that on the terrible day of Ragnarok, when the hell wolf Fenrir swallows Odinn, it will be his son Vidar who will avenge him. Vidar will step onto the wolf's fanged lower jaw with one foot and tear away the upper jaw with his bare hands. So his shoe must be thick, made from all the clippings and scraps that shoe-makers have thrown away since the beginning of time. The cobbler had made his jibe good-humouredly, so I answered in the same spirit, 'No thanks. But I'll remember to come back to you when I need a pair of sandals that will walk on water.'

Kjartan raised an appreciative eyebrow when he saw my finery as I presented myself at the huscarl barracks on the morning of the gemot. 'Well, well, a handsome show. No one will think me poorly attended.' He was looking resplendent in the formal armour of a king's bodyguard. Over his court tunic he wore a corselet of burnished metal plates, and the helmet on his head had curlicues of gold inlay. In addition to his huscarl's sword at his hip, with its gold inlay handle, a Danish fighting axe hung from his left shoulder on a silver chain. In his left hand he gripped a battle spear with a polished head, which for a moment reminded me of Edgar's death facing the charging boar. But the item which caught my eye was the torc of twisted gold wire wrapped around his arm, the same one that lacked a hand. He noticed my glance and said, 'That was royal recompense for my injury at Ashington.'

Kjartan cautioned me as we walked towards the barrack's mess hall, and his words reminded me of Aelfgifu's mistrust of palace intrigue. 'I rely on you to keep silent about what you witness today,' he said, 'There are many who would like to see all the veteran huscarls purged. The tide of affairs is moving against us, at least in England. We have fewer and fewer opportunities to celebrate our traditions, and our enemies would use our ceremonies to denounce us as evil pagans. The Elder Ways offend the bishops and archbishops as well as the king's church advisers. So your task today will be to serve as my cup-bearer at the feast and to be discreet.'

Kjartan and I were among the last to enter the hall. There were no trumpet blasts or grand arrivals and no women. About forty huscarls were already standing in the room, dressed in their finery. There was no sense of rank or social standing. Instead an air of fellowship prevailed. One man I recognised instantly, for he stood a head taller than anyone else in the room, which was remarkable in itself because the huscarls were mostly big men. The giant was Thorkel the Tall, the king's vice-regent. When the group around him parted, I saw that his legs were freakishly long, almost as if he were wearing the stilts some jugglers use in their performances. It made him look ungainly, as his body was of normal proportions, though the arms were long and dangled oddly by his sides. When he listened to his companions Thorkel was obliged to bend over to bring his head closer. He reminded me of a bird I had occasionally seen when hawking in the marshes with Edgar – the wandering stork.

'Where do you want me to stand?' I said quietly to Kjartan. I did not want to disgrace him in etiquette. There was no division of the tables as at Ealdorman Aelfhelm's feast, where the seating arrangement distinguished between commoner and nobly born. Now a single large table stood in the middle of the room, one place of honour at its head, benches down each side. Service trestles had been set up in one corner for the tubs of mead and ale, and somewhere I could smell roasting flesh, so a kitchen was nearby.

'Stand behind me when the company moves to table. Huscarls are seated by eminence of military prowess and length of service, not because they are high born or well connected,' he replied. 'After that, just watch what the other cup-bearers do and follow their example.'

At that moment I saw Thorkel move towards the place of honour at the head of the table. When all the huscarls had taken their places on the benches, we cup-bearers placed before them their drinking horns already filled with mead. I could not see a single glass goblet or a drop of wine. Still seated, Thorkel called a toast to Odinn, then a toast to Thor, then a toast to Tyr, and a toast to Frey. Hurrying back and forth from the service trestles to refill the drinking horns for each toast, I could see that the cup-bearers were going to be kept busy.

Finally Thorkel called the minni, the remembrance toast to the dead comrades of the fellowship. 'They who died honorably, may we meet them in Valholl,' he announced.

'In Valholl,' his listeners chorused.

Thorkel unfolded his great length from his chair and rose to speak. 'I stand here as the representative of the king. On his behalf I will accept renewal of the fellowship. I begin with Earl Eirikr. Do you renew your pledge of allegiance to the king and the brotherhood?' A richly dressed veteran seated closest on the bench to Thorkel stood up and announced in a loud voice that he would serve and protect the king, and obey the rules of the brotherhood. I knew him as one of Knut's most successful war captains, who had also served his father Forkbeard before him. For this service Eirikr had received great estates far in the north of England, making him one of the wealthiest of Knut's nobles. Both his arms sported heavy gold torcs, which were marks of royal favour. Now I knew why Herfid the skald loved to refer to Knut as the 'generous ring giver'.

So it went on. One after another the names of the huscarls were called out, and each man stood up to renew his oath for the coming year. Then, after the pledges were all received, Thorkel called out the name of three of the huscarls who were in England but had failed to attend the gemot.

'What is your verdict?' he asked the assembled company.

'A fine of three mancus of gold, payable to the fellowship,' a voice said promptly. I guessed that this was customary forfeit.

'Agreed?' asked Thorkel.

'Agreed,' came back the response.

I was beginning to understand that the huscarls ruled themselves by general vote.

Thorkel moved on to a more serious violation of their code. 'I have received a complaint from Hrani, now serving with the king in Denmark. He states that Hakon was asked to look after his horse, specifically his best battle charger, for him. The horse was too sickly to be shipped with the army for Denmark. Hrani goes on to state that the horse was neglected and has since died. I have established these facts as true. What is your verdict?'

'Ten mancus fine!' shouted someone.

'No, fifteen!' called another voice, a little drunkenly I thought.

'And demotion by four places,' called another voice.

Thorkel then put the matter to a vote. When it was passed, a shame-faced huscarl stood up and moved four places further away from the head of the table before sitting down among his comrades.

'All that talk of horses reminds me that I'm getting hungry,' a wag shouted out. It was definitely a tipsy voice. It was beginning to be difficult to hear Thorkel above the general background hubbub.

'Who's the glum-looking fellow at the end of the table?' I asked Gisli's cup-bearer, a quiet young man with an unfortunate strawberry birthmark on his neck. He glanced across to the huscarl sitting silently by himself. 'I don't know his name. But he's in disgrace. He committed three transgressions of the rules and has been banished to the lowest end of the table. No one is allowed to talk to him. He'll be lucky if his messmates don't start throwing meat bones and scraps of food at him after the meal. That's their privilege.'

Suddenly a great cheer went up. From the side room where

the cooks had been at work four men appeared. They were
carrying between them the body of a small ox, spit roasted, which
they lifted over the heads of the revellers and placed on the centre
of the table. The head of the ox was brought in separately and
displayed on a long iron spike driven into the floor. An even
louder cheer greeted the four men when they appeared a second
time with another burden. This time the carcass they carried was
the body of a horse. This too had been roasted and its ribs stood
up like the fingers of a splayed hand. The roast horse was also
placed on the table and its head on a second spike beside the ox's.
Then the cooks withdrew, and the huscarls fell upon the food,
hacking it up with their daggers, and passing chunks up the table.
'Thank the Gods we can still eat real meat on feast days whatever
those lily-white priests say,' a whiskery veteran announced to no
one in particular, chewing heartily, his beard already daubed with
morsels of horse flesh. 'Makes no sense that the White Christ
priests forbid their followers to eat horse flesh. Can't think why
they don't ban mutton when they spend so much time talking
about the Lamb of God.'

As the pace of eating slowed, I noticed the cooks and other
servitors leave the mess hall. Only the huscarls and their cup-
bearers remained. Then I saw Thorkel nod to the disgraced
huscarl seated at the end of the table. It must have been some sort
of pre-arranged signal for the man got up from his place and
walked across to the double entrance doors. Closing them, he
picked up a wooden bar and dropped the timber into two frame
slots. The door was now effectively barred from the inside.
Whatever was now going to take place inside the mess hall was
definitely a private matter.

Someone hammered on the table with his sword hilt, calling
for silence. A hush fell over the assembled company, and into that
silence came a sound I had last heard in Ireland three years
before, at the feast of a minor Irish king. It was an eerie wailing.
At first it seemed to be unearthly, without rhythm or tune until
you listened closely. It was a sound that could make the hairs

stand up on the back of your neck – a single bagpipe, hauntingly played. I listened carefully, trying to locate the sound. It seemed to be coming from the side room where the cooks had worked. As I looked in that direction, through the doorway stepped a figure that made the blood rush to my head. It was a man and his head was completely invisible inside a terrifying mask made from gilded basketwork. It covered the wearer down to his shoulders, leaving only eye holes for him to see his way from as he advanced into the room. He man was wearing the head of a giant bird.

And there was no doubt that he was a man because, except for the mask, he was stark naked.

I knew at once who was represented. The man held in each hand a long spear, the symbol of Odinn, his ash spear Gungnir, the 'swaying one'.

As the bagpipe continued to play, the naked man began to dance. Deliberately at first, lifting each spear in turn and bringing its butt end down with a thump on the ground in time with the music. As the music quickened, so too did the dancing figure, turning and cavorting, leaping in sidelong jumps down one side of the table, then up the other. As the cadence of his dance became familiar, the huscarls took up the rhythm, beating gently at the start and then with increasing fervour on the table with their hands, their dagger handles, and chanting, Odinn! Odinn! Odinn!' The figure whirled, holding out the two spears so they whistled through the air, and he leaped and leaped again. I saw several of the older huscarls reach out and dip their hands in the bloody juices of the horse carcass and mark their own foreheads with a bloody stripe, dedicating themselves to the All-Father.

Then, as unexpectedly as he had arrived, the masked figure darted out of sight back into the room he had come from.

Again the bagpipe began to play, and this time the musician emerged from his hiding place. He was a young man and he was playing a smaller pipe than those I knew from Ireland. He took up his station behind Earl Eirikr and I guessed that the Northumbrian earl had brought the piper with him for our entertainment.

He had also hired a professional mimer, for the next person to appear from the side room with a dramatic leap was dressed in the costume of a hero, with helmet, armour and a light sword. It took only moments for the audience to recognise he was playing the role of Sigurd in the lay of Fafnir. They roared their approval as he mimed the ambush from the trench in which the hidden Sigurd stabs upwards into Fafnir's slithering belly and the gold-guarding dragon dies. Then, in a sinuous movement the actor changed character and became Regin, Sigurd's evil foster-father, who arrives upon the scene and asks Sigurd to cook the dragon's heart so he may eat it. Another leap sideways and the mimer became Sigurd, licking his burned thumb as he cooks the meat, and from that taste learns the language of birds, who tell him that the treacherous Regin intends to murder him. A sham sword fight, and Sigurd killed the evil foster-father, ending his display by dragging away two imaginary chests of dragon's gold. And not entirely imaginary gold either, for several of the huscarls threw gold and silver coins on the floor as a mark of their appreciation.

At this point Thorkel and several of the more senior huscarls left the hall. They must have known that the gemot could last far into the night, and into the next day as well, and that the celebrations would soon grow even more ribald and disorderly. But Kjartan made no move to go, so I kept to my cup-bearer's duties as the evening grew more and more raucous. Prodigious quantities of mead and ale were consumed, and the liquor loosened tongues. I had not anticipated the strength of dislike that the traditional huscarls showed towards the White Christ faction at court. They talked of the Christians as devious, smug and crafty. The special targets for their odium were the queen, Emma of Normandy, and the king's chief lawmaker, Archbishop Wulftstan. A very drunk huscarl pulled out a long white shirt – he must have brought it with him for that purpose – and waved it in the air to attract the attention of his drinking companions. Unsteadily he got to his feet, pulled it on over his own head and mimicked the act of Christian prayer, shouting, 'I've been prepared for baptism three times, and each time the priests paid me a month's wages and gave me a fine white shirt.'

'Easy money,' yelled a companion drunkenly. 'I collected four payments; it's a new version of the Danegeld'.

This drew a roar of drunken laughter. Then the assembly began to chant a name. 'Thyrmr! Thyrmr! Remember Thyrmr!' and the huscarl took off his white shirt and threw it into the corner of the room. 'Thyrmr! Thyrmr!' chanted the men, now completely intoxicated, and they began picking up the remnants of the meal, and throwing the chewed bones and discarded gristle in the direction of the crumpled cloth.

'I thought they were going to throw the bones at the disgraced huscarl,' I muttered to Gisli's cup-bearer.

'He's in luck tonight,' he answered. 'Instead they're celebrating the day that one of the Saxon high priests, an archbishop, I think his name was Alfheah, got himself killed. A man named Thyrmr did it, smacked the archbishop on the back of his head with the flat of his battleaxe at the end of a particularly boisterous feast after everyone had pelted the priest with ox bones.'

This drunken boasting was infantile and pointless, I thought to myself as I watched the stumbling drunkards. It was the response of men who felt outmanouevred by their rivals. This hollow mummery was not the way to protect the future veneration of the Old Gods.

I grew more and more depressed as the evening degenerated into brutishness. The only moment I raised a smile was when the company began to chant a lewd little ditty about Queen Emma and her priestly entourage. The words were clever and I found myself joining in the refrain, 'Bakrauf! Bakrauf!' I realised I was thick tongued and slurring my words, even though I had been trying to stay sober. So when Kjartan slumped from his seat, completely drunk, I beckoned to Gisli's cup-bearer to help me, and together we carried the one-armed huscarl back to his barracks bed. Then I started out on the long walk back through London to reach my own room, hoping that the chilly winter air and the exercise would clear my head.

I scratched quietly at the heavy door of the mint. It was long past the time that Thurulf and I normally returned from tavern, but I had bribed the door keeper, who was by now quite accustomed to my drinking excursions. He must have been waiting by the door, for he opened it almost at once, and I went in, walking as quietly and as straight as my drunkenness would allow. I was just sober enough to realise that it would be foolish to use the stairs to the upper floor that went past Brithmaer's chambers. A creaking floorboard or falling up the stairs would attract attention. I decided to go to my room by the far stair, which led directly from the workshop floor to the balcony. I removed my smart yellow shoes, and holding them in my hand, walked quietly along the length of the workshop, trying to keep in a straight line. In a pool of lantern light at the far end of the workshop, the two elderly men were still at the coining bench. I could see them bent over, tapping out the little coins. Neither of them was aware of my approach – one because eye disease had damaged his sight, the other because he was concentrating hard on his work and, being deaf, would not have heard me even if I had not been barefoot. I was more drunk than I thought and I swayed and swerved in my walk enough to brush against the deaf man. It gave him such a shock that he started upright and fumbled his work. The striking iron dropped to the floor, as he turned to see what was behind him. In tipsy embarrassment I put my finger to my lips, entreating silence. Then, concentrating ferociously as only a drunkard can, I managed to bend over without tumbling headlong, picked up his striking iron from the ground, and returned it to him. A glint of silver caught my eye. It was the coin he had just struck. It too had fallen to the floor. Risking another attack of sot's vertigo, I picked up the coin and put it in his hands. Then with an exaggerated salute, I turned and wove my way to the staircase, then climbed it hand over hand like a novice sailor, and eventually toppled into my manger bed.

I awoke next morning with a vile headache and the taste of stale mead in my mouth. As I was bent over a bucket of well water, trying to wash my bleary eyes, my position bent over the bucket reminded me of something that had puzzled me. I recalled something strange when I leaned down and picked up the old man's striking iron and the dropped coin. I could not remember exactly what it was. Then I remembered: as I placed the coin into the workman's palm, a gleam of lantern light had fallen across it. The freshly minted coin was a silver penny. But the face I saw stamped on the coin was not Knut's familiar image, but someone else's.

Or was I too drunk to know the difference? The mystery nagged at me all morning until I realised that I could check. The striking irons used at night were kept for safe keeping in the jewellery workshop, and so mid-morning I reminded Brithmaer that the crystal necklace should be repaired by now and asked if I might visit the workshop to examine it.

Thurulf opened the door to the strongroom and wandered off, leaving me on my own. A few moments was all the time I needed to locate the striking irons that the two night workers used. They were tucked away out of sight under the workbench, wrapped in a leather cloth. There was also a lump of old wax, tossed aside when the engraver had made moulds for repairing jewellery. I nipped off two little pellets of wax and pressed them between the faces of the striking irons and their counterparts, then replaced the nightworkers' tools. When Thurulf returned, I was admiring the rock crystals in their new settings.

I was so eager to examine the wax impressions that I had scarcely gone a hundred paces on my way back to the exchange when I shook them out from my sleeve. Even the simplest pedlar would have recognised the patterns pressed on them. There was no mystery: they could be found in half the markets in the land,

and they lay in the mint's storerooms by the thousand – the king's head on the striking irons was that of King Ethelred the Ill-Advised, dead these four years past. On their reverse, one wax impression bore the mark of a moneyer in Derby and the other a moneyer in Winchester. I was intrigued. Why would Brithmaer secretly be making coins that were out of date? Why would he want coins that were already valueless and should be melted down, and that at a discount?

There seemed no logic to it, and in the tavern that evening I casually asked Thurulf if he had heard of a moneyer in Derby by the name of Guner. He told that the name was vaguely familiar, but he thought that the man was long since dead.

I drank little, telling Thurulf that I was still queasy from the huscarls' gemot. In fact I wanted to look my best the following morning for that was when I had arranged with Aelfgifu's chamberlain that I would return with a selection of jewellery for her inspection.

Aelfgifu was in a mischievous mood. Her eyes sparkled when – at last – she managed to dismiss her attendants, telling them that she would try on the jewels in private. It seemed a feeble excuse to me, but she carried it off, and moments later we were in the private bedchamber where she had first taught me how to love.

'Let me look at you!' she gloated, making me stand back so she could admire the effect of my new tunic. 'Yellow and brown and black. The colours really suit you – you look good enough to eat. Come, let me taste you.' And she walked across and threw her arms around me.

Feeling the softness of her breasts, I was flooded by my own craving. Our mouths met, and I realised that if my longing had been acute, hers was also. Previously in that room our love had been tender and forbearing, with Aelfgifu leading my novice hesitancy. Now we both plunged into the certainty of our passion, greedy for one another, tumbling together on the bed. Within moments we were naked and making love with desperate urgency

until the first wave of passion had spent itself. Only then did
Aelfgifu disengage herself and, as always, run her finger down
my profile. 'What was it you wanted to show me?' she asked
teasingly.

I rolled over to the side of the bed and reached down to pick
up the bag of jewellery, and tipped it out on the sheet. As I had
hoped, she pounced immediately on the crystal and amber necklace.

'It's beautiful' she exclaimed. 'Here help me put it on,' and
she turned so that I could fasten the clasp at the nape of her neck.
When she turned back again to face me, her eyes shining to match
the crystals, I could have imagined no better place for the gems
that I had stolen. Now they lay supported on the sweet curves
of her breasts. What would the Irish monks have thought? I
wondered.

Somehow Aelfgifu had arranged that we could be alone
together for several hours, and in that time we were unrestrained.
We made love light-heartedly and often. We delighted in one
another's bodies. Aelfgifu was provocative in her response when
I covered her with jewellery – the necklace, of course, but also
bracelets on her ankles and wrists, a pendant as a belt, and two
magnificently gaudy brooches to cup her breasts, all at once.

When we had laughed and loved one another to exhaustion
and were lying side by side, I told her about the fire ruby hidden
in the amulet of lead – she had lifted it from my neck after the
first encounter, saying the lump would give her bruises. She
listened to my story and before I had finished, had guessed my
intention. 'Thorgils,' she said gently, 'I don't want to have that
stone. You are not to give it to me. I have a feeling that stone
should remain with you. It has your spirit. Somewhere inside you
flickers that same light, which needs someone to make it glow,'
and gently she leaned over and began to lick my chest.

SIX

GREAT HAPPINESS; GREAT danger – another of Edgar's proverbs. Only two days after my impassioned visit to Aelfgifu, I was shaken awake by Brithmaer's door keeper. A palace messenger was waiting for me in the street, he grunted, on an urgent matter. Groggy with sleep since it was not yet dawn, I dressed in my tunic, elated that this summons to the queen's apartments had come so soon after our last tryst.

But when I opened the door to the street, I did not recognise the messenger standing there in the half-dark. He was sombrely dressed and looked more like a minor clerk than a royal servant.

'Your name is Thorgils?' he enquired.

'Yes,' I replied, puzzled. 'What can I do for you?'

'Come with me, please,' the man said. 'You have a meeting with Archbishop Wulfstan.'

A chill came over me. Archbishop Wulfstan, co-regent of England, was no friend to followers of the Old Ways, and by reputation was the cleverest man in the kingdom. For an instant I wondered what business he had with someone as insignificant as myself. Then a hard knot formed in my stomch. The only person who connected me with matters of state was Aelfgifu.

The messenger led me to the royal chancery, a melancholy building at the rear of the palace where I was shown to an empty

waiting room. It was still only an hour after daybreak when I was
ushered into the archbishop's council chamber, yet the king's chief
minister was already deep in his work. Flanked by two priests as
his secretaries, Wulfstan was seated at a table listening to some
notes being read to him in Latin. He looked up as I entered, and
I saw that he must have been well past his sixtieth year. He had
a seamless face, scrubbed and pink, a few wisps of white hair
remained on his scalp and his hands, which were folded on the
table, were soft and white. His serene demeanour and the benign
smile he directed towards me as I entered gave him the appearance
of a kindly grandfather. But that agreeable impression withered
the moment he spoke. His voice was so quiet that I had to strain
to hear him, yet it carried a menace far more frightening than if
he had shouted aloud. Worse was his choice of words: 'The fly
that plays too long in the candle singes his wings at last.'

I felt as if I was about to faint.

One of the notaries passed a sheet of parchment to the archbishop. 'Your name, Thorgils, is a pagan one, is it not? You are
an un-believer?' Wulfstan asked.

I nodded.

'Would that be why you attended the banquet at the huscarls'
mess hall the other evening? I understand that certain gross ceremonies were conducted during the course of the meal.'

'I attended only as a cup-bearer, my lord,' I said, wondering
who was the informer who had told the archbishop about the
evening's events. 'I was a bystander.'

'Not entirely, I think,' said the archbishop consulting his notes.
'It is reported that at times you participated in the debauchery.
Apparently you also enthusiastically joined in the chorus of a blasphemous and scurrilous song, which might be said to be treasonable
and is certainly seditious.'

'I don't know what you mean, my lord,' I answered.

'Let me give you an example. The song noted here apparently
referred to our noble Queen Emma, and repeatedly, as a Bakrauf.'

I stayed silent.

'You know what Bakrauf means?'

Still I said nothing,

'You ought to be aware,' the archbishop went on unrelentingly, 'that for a number of years I served as Archbishop of York. In that city the majority of the citizens are Norse and speak their donsk tunga, as they call it. I made it my business to learn the langage fluently, so I do not need my staff to tell me that the word Bakrauf means the human fundament, or in a more civilised speech, an anus. Hardly a fitting description of the wife of the king of England, do you think? Sufficient cause for the culprit to suffer some sort of punishment — like having his tongue cut out, perhaps?' The archbishop spoke in little more than a gentle whisper. Yet there was no mistaking that he meant his threat. I recalled that he was famous for the virulent sermons he delivered under the name of 'the Wolf'. I wondered where this line of questioning was leading.

'Do you deny the charge? There are at least three witnesses to the fact that you participated in the chorus and with apparent relish.'

'My lord,' I answered, 'I was fuddled at the time, having taken too much drink.'

'Hardly an excuse.'

'I mean I misunderstood the meaning of the word Bakrauf,' I pleaded. 'I know that Bakrauf means anus in the donsk tunga, but I was thinking in Latin, and those who taught me Latin told me that anus means "an old woman". They never said that it might also mean part of the human body. Of course I humbly apologise for referring to the queen as an old woman.'

Wulfstan, who had begun to look bored, suddenly became more attentive. 'So Thorgils knows his Latin, does he?' he mumured. 'And how is that?'

'Monks in Ireland taught me, my lord,' I said. I did not add that, judging from his conversation in Latin with the notaries when I came in, my command of the language was probably better than his own.

Wulfstan grimaced. 'Those benighted Irish monks,' he observed sourly. 'A cluster of thorns in the flesh of the true Church.' He noticed the lead amulet hanging round my neck. 'If you studied with the Irish monks, how is it that you were not baptised? You should be wearing a Christian cross around your neck. Not a pagan sign.'

'I never completed the necessary instruction, my lord.'

Wulfstan must have accepted that I was not easily intimidated, for he tried another approach, still in the same soft, menacing voice. 'Whether Christian or not, you are subject to the king's laws while you are in his realm. Did those Irish monks teach you also about the law?'

His enquiry was so barbed that I could not resist replying, 'They taught me – "the more laws, the more offenders".'

It was a stupid and provocative reply. I had no idea that Wulfstan and his staff had laboured for the past two years at drawing up a legal code for Knut and prided themselves on their diligence. Even if the archbishop had known that it was a quotation from Tacitus expounded to me in the classroom by the monks, he would have been annoyed.

'Let me tell you the fifty-third clause in King Knut's legal code,' Wulfstan went on grimly. 'It concerns the penalty for adultery. It states that any married woman who commits adultery will forfeit all the property she owns. Moreover she will lose her ears and nose.'

I knew that he had come to the point of our interview.

'I understand, my lord. A married woman, you said. Do you mean a woman married according to the laws of the Church? Openly recognised as such?'

The 'Wolf' regarded me malevolently. He knew that I was referring to Aelfgifu's status as 'the concubine' in the eyes of the Church, which refused to consider her as a legal wife.

'Enough of this sophistry. You know exactly what I am talking about. I summoned you here to give you a choice. We are well informed of your behaviour with regard to a certain person close to the king. Either you agree to act as an agent for this office, informing this chancery of what goes on within the palace, or it will be arranged that you are brought before a court on a charge of adultery.'

'I see that I have no choice in the matter, my lord,' I answered.

'He that steals honey should beware of the sting,' said the archbishop with an air of smug finality. He rivalled Edgar in his love of proverbs. 'Now you must live with the consequences. Return to your lodgings and think over how you may best serve this office. And you may rest assured that you are being watched, as you have been for the past month and more. It would be futile to try to flee the king's justice.'

I returned to Brithmaer's mint just long enough to change out of my court clothes, pack them into my satchel and put on my travelling garments. I had come to a decision even as the archbishop set out his ultimatum. I knew that I could not betray Aelfgifu by becoming a spy for Wulfstan, nor could I stay in London. My position would be intolerable if I did. When Knut returned to England, Wulfstan would not need to bring an accusation of adultery against me, only to hint to the king that Aelfgifu had been unfaithful. Then I would be the cause of the disgrace of the woman I adored. Better I fled the kingdom than ruin her life.

My first step was to take the two little wax moulds pressed from the striking irons of Brithmaer's elderly workmen, and bring them to the huscarls' barracks. There I asked to see Kjartan. 'I've come to say goodbye,' I told him, 'and to ask a favour. If you hear that some accident has befallen me, or if I fail to contact you with a message before the spring, I want you to take these two pieces of wax and give them to Thorkel the Tall. Tell him that they came from the workshop of Brithmaer the moneyer while Knut was the king of England. Thorkel will know what to do.'

Kjartan took the two small discs of wax in his single hand, and looked at me steadily. There was neither surprise nor question in his eyes. 'You have my word on it,' he said. 'I have the feeling that it would be tactless of me to ask why your departure from London is so sudden. Doubtless you have your reasons, and anyhow I have a strong feeling that one day I will be hearing more about you. In the meantime, may Odinn Farmognudr, the jourey empowerer', protect you.'

Within the hour I was back at Brithmaer's exchange office on the waterfront and I asked if I could speak to him in private. He was standing at the window of the room where he met his private clients, looking out on the wintry grey river, when I made my request.

'I need to leave England without the knowledge of the authorities and you can help me,' I said.

'Really. What makes you think that?' he answered blandly.

'Because new-minted coins bear a dead king's mark.'

Slowly and deliberately Brithmaer turned his head and looked straight at me. For the second time that day an old man regarded me with strong dislike.

'I always thought you were a spy,' he said coldly.

'No,' I replied, 'I did not come to you as a spy. I was sent in good faith by the queen. What I learned has nothing to do with Aelfgifu.'

'So what is it that you have learned?'

'I know that you are forging the king's coinage. And that you are not alone in this felony, though I would not be wrong in believing you are the prime agent.'

Brithmaer was calm. 'And how do you think that this felony, as you call it, is enacted? Everyone knows that the coinage of England is the most strictly controlled in all Europe and the penalties for forgery are severe. Counterfeit coins would be noticed immediately by the king's officers and traced back to the forger. He would be lucky only to lose a hand, more likely it would be his life. Only a fool or a knave would seek to forge the coins of the king of England.'

'Of the present king of England, yes,' I replied, 'but not the coins of a previous king.'

'Go on,' said Brithmaer. There was an edge to his voice now.

'I discovered quite by accident that the two elderly workers who strike coins at night in your workshop are not producing coins with the head of Knut. They make coins which carry the head and markings of King Ethelred. At first it made no sense, but then I saw coins which had arrived from the northern lands, from Sweden and Norway. Many of them had the test marks, the nicks and scratches. Most of them were old, from Ethelred's times, when the English paid vast amounts of Danegeld to buy off the raiders. It seems that huge numbers of Ethelred's coins are in circulation in the north lands, and now they are coming back in trade. Thurulf spends a great deal of time counting them in the storerooms.'

'There's nothing wrong with that,' Brithmaer murmured.

'No, but Thurulf remarked to me how the numbers of the old coins never seemed to diminish, but kept piling up. That made me think about something else which was not quite right. I had noticed that here in the exchange you accept large amounts of inferior jewellery made with base metals and cheap alloys. You say it is for the jewellery business, yet your so-called jeweller is nothing more than a workaday craftsman. He is an engraver, familiar with the cutting and maintenance of striking irons and he knows nothing about jewellery. Yet I found very little of the broken jewellery. It had disappeared. Then I realised that the engraver had the skill and equipment in his workshop to melt down the low-grade metals, and turn out blanks for stamping into coins.'

'You seem to have done a great deal of imagining,' said Brithmaer. 'Your story is a fantasy. Who would want low-grade coins from a dead king?'

'That is the clever part,' I replied. 'It would be reckless to issue forged coins in England. They would be quickly identified. But forge coins which you then issue in the north lands, where the coins of England are regarded as honest, and few people would detect that the coins were counterfeit. Cutting or nicking the coins would not reveal the purity of the metal. And if it did, and the coins are revealed as fakes, then the coins carry the markings of long-dead moneyers, and could never be traced back to their maker. However, there has to be one more link in the chain.'

'And that is?'

'The link that interests me now. You can obtain the base metals from the cheap jewellery, make low-grade coins, forge the marks of other moneyers, but you still need to distribute the coins in the north lands. And for that you need the cooperation of dishonest merchants and ship owners who make regular trading voyages there and put the coins into general circulation. These, I suspect, are the people who visit your private office, even in winter. So my request to you now is that you will arrange with one of these men for me to be smuggled aboard ship, no questions asked. It is in your interests. Once I am out of England, I would no longer be in a position to report you to the authorities.'

'Would it not be more sensible for me to arrange for you to vanish permanently?' Brithmaer said. He was no more emotional than if he was suggesting a money-changing commission.

'Two wax impressions taken from the striking irons used in the forgery will be delivered to the king's regent if I vanish mysteriously or fail to report by springtime.'

Brithmaer regarded me thoughtfully. There was a long pause while he considered his alternatives. 'Very well. I'll make the arrangements you request. There's a merchant ship due to visit King's Lynn in two week's time. The captain trades from Norway and is one of the very few who makes the winter crossing of the English Sea. I will send you to King's Lynn with Thurulf. It's about time he returned to Norwich, which is nearby. If he meets up with any of the king's officials he will say that you are travelling as his assistant. I will also write a note to inform the ship captain that you are to be taken on as supercargo. It would be hypocritical to wish you a safe journey. Indeed, I hope I never see you again. Should you ever return to England, I think you will find no trace of the conspiracy which you say you have uncovered.'

And with that I left the service of Brithmaer the king's moneyer, and master forger. I never saw him again, but I did not forget him. For years to come, every time I was offered an English coin in payment or as change in a market place, I turned it over to see the name of the maker and rejected it if it had been minted in Derby or in Winchester.

SEVEN

'YOU ICELANDERS REALLY get around, don't you?' commented Brithmaer's accomplice as he watched the low coastline of England disappear in our wake. The Norwegian shipmaster had not informed the port reeve of our impending departure before he ordered his crew to weigh anchor on the early tide. I suspected the harbour official was accustomed to seeing our ship slip out of port at strange hours and had been bribed to look the other way.

I barely heard the captain's comment, for I was still brooding on the thought that every mile was taking me further away from Aelfgifu. Unhappiness had haunted me throughout the three-day journey to King's Lynn with Thurulf. We had travelled on ponies, with two servants leading a brace of packhorses and I did not know how much Brithmaer had told his nephew about why I had to travel posing as his assistant or the need for discretion. Our servants blew loudly on trumpets and rang bells whenever we approached settlements or passed through woodland, and I had suggested to Thurulf that it might be wiser to proceed with less ostentation, as I did not wish to attract the attention of the authorities.

Thurulf grinned back at me and said, 'Quite the reverse. If we used the king's highway in a manner that might be considered surreptitious, people would take us to be skulking criminals or robbers. Then they would be entitled to attack, even kill us. Honest travellers are required to announce their presence with as much fanfare as possible.'

Thurulf had brought me to the quay where the Norwegian vessel was berthed. There he handed me over to her captain with a note from Brithmaer to say that I was to be taken abroad, on a one-way trip, and that it would be wise to keep me out of sight until we left England. Then he had turned back to rejoin his family in Norwich. The gloom of parting from a friend was added to my heartache for Aelfgifu.

'Know someone by the name of Grettir Asmundarson, by any chance? He's one of your countrymen.' The captain's voice again broke into my thoughts. The name was vaguely familiar, but for a moment I couldn't place it. 'Got quite a reputation. They call him Grettir the Strong. Killed his first man when he was only sixteen and was condemned to three year's exile. Decided to spend part of it in Norway. He asked me to make some purchases for him while I was in England, but they cost rather more than I had anticipated. I'm hoping you could tell me the best way of dealing with him so he'll pay up without any trouble. He's a dangerous character, quick to anger.' The captain was trying to strike up a conversation so he could find out just who I was.

'I don't think I know him,' I answered, but the word outlaw had jogged my memory. The last time I had seen Grettir Asmundarson had been six years earlier in Iceland. I remembered a young man sitting on a bench in a farmyard, whittling on a piece of wood. He had been much the same age as myself, with middling brown hair, freckles and fair skin. But where I am quite slender and lightly built, he had been broad and thickset, though only of average height, and while I am normally self-possessed and calm by nature, Grettir had given the impression of being hot-headed and highly strung. I remembered how the little shavings had jumped up into the air with each slice of the sharp blade as if he was suppressing some sort of explosive anger. Even at that age Grettir exuded an air of violent, unpredictable menace.

'Troublemaker from the day he was born, and got worse as he grew up,' said the captain. 'Deliberately provoked his father at every turn, though his parent was a decent enough man by all accounts, a steady farmer. The son refused to help out with the farmyard chores. Broke the wings and legs of the geese when he was sent to put them in their house in the evening, killed the goslings, mutilated his father's favourite horse when he was asked to look after it. Cut the skin all along the animal's spine so the poor creature reared up when you laid a hand on its back. A thoroughly bad lot. His father would have thrown him out of the house, but for the fact that his mother was always asking that he should be given a second chance. Typical of a mother's spoiled pet, if you ask me.'

'What made him kill a man?' I asked.

'Quarrelled over a bag of dried food, would you believe. Hardly a reason to attack someone so viciously.'

I remembered the jumping wood shavings, and wondered if Grettir Asmundarson was touched in the head.

'Anyway, you'll soon have your chance to make your own judgement. If this wind holds steady on the quarter, our first landfall will be the place where he's staying with his half-brother Thorstein. Quite a different type, Thorstein, as even-tempered and steady as Grettir is touchy and wild. Got the nickname "the Galleon" because he has a rolling stride to his walk, just like a ship in a beam sea.'

I saw what the captain meant when we dropped anchor in the bay in front of Thorstein's farm in the Tonsberg district of Norway three days later. The two brothers met us on the beach. Thorstein, tall and calm, was waiting for us, feet planted stolidly on the shingle; Grettir, a head shorter, tramped back and forth nervously. He was a squat volcano, ready to erupt. But when our eyes met, I felt that shock of recognition I had experienced half a dozen times in my life: I had seen the same look in the eyes of a native shaman in Vinland, in the expression of the mother of the Earl of Orkney who was a noted sibyl, in the glance of the wife

of King Sigtryggr of Dublin, whom many considered a witch, and
in the faraway stare of the veteran warrior Thrand, my tutor in
Iceland, who had taught me the rune spells. It was the look of
someone who possessed the second sight, and I knew that Grettir
Asmundarson saw things hidden from more normal people, as I
do. Yet I had no premonition that Grettir was to become my
closest friend.

We began by treating one another warily, almost with distrust.
No one would ever call Grettir easygoing or amiable. He had a
natural reticence which people mistook for surliness, and he met
every friendly remark with a curt response which often caused
offence and gave the impression that he discouraged human
contact. I doubt if the two of us exchanged more than half a
dozen sentences in as many days as we sailed on along the coast
towards the Norwegian capital at Nidaros. Grettir had asked if
he might join our ship as he intended to present himself at the
Norwegian court and petition for a post in the royal household,
his family being distant relatives of the Norwegian king, Olaf.

Our passage was by the usual route, along the sheltered
channel between the outer islands and the rocky coast, with its
succession of tall headlands and fiord entrances. The sailing was
easy and we were in no hurry. By mid-afternoon our skipper
would pick a convenient anchorage and we would moor for the
night, dropping anchor and laying out a stern line to a convenient
rock. Often we would go ashore to cook our meal and set up
tents on the beach rather than sleep aboard. It was at one of these
anchorages as the sun was setting that I noticed a strange light
suddenly blaze out from the summit of the nearest headland. It
flared up for a moment as if someone had lit a raging fire in the
mouth of a cave, then quickly extinguished it. When I drew the
skipper's attention to the phenomenon, I was met with a blank
look. He had seen nothing. 'There's no one living up on that
headland. Only an old barrow grave,' he said. 'Burial place for
the local family who own all the land in the area. The only time
they go there is when they have another corpse. It has proved to

be a lucky place for them. The current head of the family is called
Thorfinn, and when he buried his father Kar the Old, the ghost
of the dead man came back and haunted the area so persistently
that the other local farmers decided to leave. After that, Thorfinn
was able to buy up all the best land.' Then he added tactfully,
'You must have seen a trick of the light. Maybe a shiny piece of
rock reflecting the last rays of the setting run.'

The rest of the crew looked at me sideways, as if I had been
hallucinating, so I let the matter drop. But after we had finished
our evening meal and the men had wrapped themselves in their
heavy sea cloaks and settled down for the night, Grettir sidled
across to me and said quietly, 'That blaze was nothing to do with
the sun's rays. I saw it too. You and I know what a fire shining
out from the earth means: gold underground.'

He paused for a moment then murmured, 'I'm going up there
to take a closer look. Care to come with me?'

I glanced round at the others. Most of the crew were half
asleep. For a moment I hesitated. I was not at all sure that I
wanted to go clambering around the dark countryside with a man
who had been convicted of murder. But then my curiosity got the
better of me. 'All right' I whispered. 'Let me get my boots on.'

Moments later Grettir and I had left the camp and were
picking our way between the black shapes of the boulders on the
beach. It was a dry, clear night, warm for that time of year, with
a few clouds moving across the face of the moon but leaving us
enough moonlight to see our way to the base of the headland and
begin our climb. As we moved higher, I could make out the
distinct humpbacked profile of the grave barrow up ahead of us,
curving against the starry sky. I also noticed something else: each
time clouds covered the moon and darkness suddenly cloaked us,
Grettir would hesitate, and I heard his breath come more quickly.
I felt his sudden onset of panic, and I realised that Grettir the
Strong, notorious murderer and outlaw, was desperately afraid of
the dark.

We followed a narrow path used by the funeral parties until

it brought us out onto a small, grassy area around the grave barrow itself. Grettir looked away to our left out over the black sheen of the sea, its surface pricked with the reflection of the stars. 'Fine place for a burial,' he said. 'When I die, I hope I'll finish up in a spot like this, where the helmsmen of passing ships can point out my last resting place.' Given Grettir's reputation as a youthful homicide, I wondered what his epitaph might be.

'Come on, Thorgils,' he said and began to clamber up the grassy side of the barrow mound. I followed him until we were both standing on the top of the whale-backed hillock. Grettir produced a heavy metal bar from under his cloak.

'What are you doing?' I asked, though the answer was obvious.

'I'm going to break in and take the grave goods,' he answered jauntily. 'Here, give me a hand.' And he began digging a hole down through the turf which covered the tomb. Grave-robbing was a new experience for me, yet when I saw the furious energy with which Grettir hacked and stabbed at the soil with his iron bar, I decided it would be wiser to humour him. I was frightened of what he might do if I tried to restrain him. Taking it in turns to excavate, we burrowed down to the outer roof of the tomb. When the point of the iron bar struck the roof timbers of the vault, Gettir gave a grunt of satisfaction, and with a few powerful blows punched a hole large enough for him to climb down into the tomb.

'Stand guard here for me, will you?' he asked. 'In case I get stuck down there and need help to climb out.' He was unwinding a rope from around his waist, and I realised that plundering the tomb had been his intention from the moment he had suggested that he and I climb to the headland.

A moment later Grettir was lowering himself down into the black hole and I could hear his voice as he vanished into the gloom. For a moment I thought he was speaking to me, and tried to make out what he was saying. But then I realised that he was talking to himself. He was making a noise to keep up his courage, to compensate for his terror of the dark. His words, echoing up from the entrance hole into the tomb, made no sense. Then came a sudden loud crash, followed immediately by a loud yell of bravado. There was another crash, and another, and I guessed he was flailing about in the dark, floundering and tripping over one obstacle after another, falling over the grave goods in the dark, driven by his determination to carry out the robbery, yet gripped by a sense of panic.

The racket finally ended and then I heard Grettir's voice call up to me, 'Hang onto the rope! I'm ready to climb up.'

I braced on the rope and soon Grettir's head and shoulders appeared through the hole in the roof of the tomb, and he hauled himself out onto the grass. Then he turned round and began to pull on the rope, until its end appeared attached to a bundle. He had used his tunic as a sack to hold the various items he had collected. He laid them out on the grass to inspect. There were several bronze dishes, some buckles and strap ends from horse harness, a silver cup, and two silver arm rings. The finest item was a short sword which the dead man would have carried if the Valkyries selected him for a warrior's afterlife in Valholl. Grettir slid the weapon out of its sheath and in a glimmer of moonlight I could see the intricate patterns a master swordsmith had worked into the metal of the blade.

'That's a noble weapon,' I commented.

'Yes, I had to fight the haugbui for it,' Grettir replied. 'He was reluctant to give it up.'

'The mound dweller?' I asked.

'He was waiting for me, seated in the dead man's chair,' Grettir said. 'I was groping around in the darkness, gathering the grave goods, when I put my hand on his leg and he jumped to his feet and attacked me. I had to fight him in the dark, as he tried to embrace me in his death grip. But finally I managed to cut off his head and kill him. I laid him out face down, with his head between his buttocks. That way he will never live again.'

I wondered if Grettir was telling the truth. Had there really been a haugbui? Everyone knows stories about the spirits of the dead who live in the darkness of tombs, ready to protect the treasures there. Sometimes they take substantial form as draugr, the walking dead who emerge and walk the earth, and frighten men, just as the ghost of Kar the Old had scared away the local farmers. Cutting off a haugbui's head and placing it on the buttocks is the only way to lay the creature finally to rest. Or was Grettir spinning me a tale to account for the noise and clatter of his robbery, his senseless loud talk and the shouts of bravado? Was he ashamed to admit that Grettir the Strong was terrified of the dark, and that all that had happened was that he had blundered into the skeleton of Kar the Old seated on his funeral chair? For the sake of Grettir's self-esteem I did not question his tale of the barrow wight, but I knew for sure that he was more fearful of the dark than a six-year-old child.

Grettir's self-confidence and bravado were still evident the next morning when the camp awoke and he made no attempt to hide his new acquisitions. I was surprised that he even took his loot with us when we went to visit Thorfinn's farm to buy ship's stores. When Grettir brazenly laid out the grave goods on the farmhouse table, Thorfinn recognised them at once.

'Where did you find these?' he asked.

'In the tomb on the hill,' Grettir replied. 'The ghost of Kar the Old is not that fearsome after all. You'd better keep hold of them.'

Thorfinn must have known Grettir's reputation because he avoided any confrontation. 'Well, it's true that buried treasure is no use to anyone,' he said amiably. 'You have my thanks for restoring these heirlooms to us. Can I offer you some reward for your courage?'

Grettir shrugged dismissively. 'No. I have no need for such things, only for an increase to my honour, though I will keep the sword as a reminder of this day,' he said. He then rudely turned on his heel and walked out of the farmhouse, taking the fine short sword and leaving the rest of the grave goods on the table.

I mulled over that answer as I walked back to the ship, trying to understand what drove Grettir. If he had plundered the barrow in order to gain the admiration of the others for his courage, why did he behave so churlishly afterwards? Why was he always so rude and quarrelsome?

I fell into step with him. Typically, he was walking by himself, well away from the rest of our group.

'That man whose death got you outlawed from Iceland, why did you kill him?' I asked. 'Killing someone over something as trifling as a bag of food doesn't seem to be a way of gaining honour or renown.'

'It was a mistake,' Grettir replied. 'At the age of sixteen I didn't realise my own strength. I was travelling across the moors with some of my father's neighbours when I discovered that the satchel of dried food I had tied to my saddle was missing. I turned back to the place where we had stopped to rest our horses, and found someone else already searching in the grass. He said that he too had left his food bag behind. A moment later he gave a cry and held up a bag, saying that he had found what he was looking for. I went over to check and it seemed to me that the bag was mine. When I tried to take it from him, he snatched out his axe without warning and aimed a blow at me. I grabbed the axe handle, turned the blade around and struck back at him. But he lost his grip and the axe suddenly came free, so I struck him square on the skull. He died instantly.'

'Didn't you try to explain this to the others when they found out what had happened?' I asked.

'It would have done no good – there were no witnesses. Anyhow the man was dead and I was the killer,' said Grettir. 'It goes against my nature to heed the opinions of others. I don't seek either their approval or their disdain. What matters will be the reputation I leave behind me for later generations.'

He spoke so openly and with such conviction that I felt he was acknowledging a bond between us, a comradeship which had started when we pillaged the barrow together. My intuition was to prove correct, but I failed to discern that Grettir was also casting the shadow of his own downfall.

The sailors thought Grettir had been a rash fool to interfere with the spirits of the dead. All day they kept muttering among themselves that his stupidity would bring down misfortune on us. One or two Christians among them made the sign of the cross to keep off the evil eye. Their disquiet was confirmed when we got back to where we had moored the ship. In our absence a gust of wind had shifted the vessel on her anchorage and brought her broadside to the rocky beach. The anchor had lost its grip and she had been driven ashore. By the time we got back, the boat was lying canted over, stoved in, sea water swilling in her bilge. The damage to her planking was so severe that her captain decided we had no choice but to abandon the vessel and march overland to Nidaros, carrying the most valuable of our trade goods. There was nothing to do but wade out in the shallows and salvage what we could. I noticed that the sailors took care to keep as far away from Grettir as possible. They blamed him for the calamity and expected that further disaster would follow. I was the only person to walk beside him.

Our progress was dishearteningly slow. By sea it would have taken two days to reach the Norwegian capital, but the land path twisted and turned as it followed the coast, skirting the bays and fiords. The extra distance added two weeks to our journey. Whenever we came to the mouth of a fiord, we tried to reduce the detour by bargaining with a local farmer to ferry us across, paying him with trade goods or, I supposed, some of Brithmaer's false coin. Even so, we had to wait for the farmer to fetch his small boat, then wait again as he rowed us across the water two or three passengers at a time.

Finally came an evening when we found ourselves on the beach at the entrance to a fiord, facing across open water to a farmhouse we could see on the opposite bank. We were chilled to the bone, tired and miserable. We tried to attract the farmer's attention so he would come across to fetch us, but it was late in the day and there was no reaction from the far shore, though we could see smoke rising from the smoke hole in the farmhouse roof. The spot where we were standing was utterly bleak, a bare beach of pebbles backed by a steep cliff. There were a few sticks of damp driftwood, enough to make a small fire if we could get one started, but our tinder was soaked. We slid our packs off our backs and slumped down on the shingle, resigned to spending a cold and hungry night.

It was at that moment that Grettir suddenly announced he would swim across the fiord to reach the farm on the other side. Everyone looked at him as if he was insane. The distance was too great for any but the strongest swimmer, and it was nearly dark already. But, typically, Grettir paid no attention. The farm would have a stock of dry firewood, he said. He would bring back some of it and a lighted brand so we could warm ourselves and cook a meal. As we watched in disbelief, he began to strip off his clothes until he was wearing nothing but his undershirt and a pair of loose woollen trousers, and a moment later he was wading into the water. I watched his head dwindle in the distance as he struck out for the far shore, and I recalled his words that he lived for honour and fame. I wondered if he might not drown in this new act of bravado.

It was well past midnight and a thick fog had settled over the fiord, when we heard the sound of splashes and Grettir reappeared out of the darkness. He was reeling with exhaustion but, to our astonishment, held in his arms a small wooden tub. 'Enough sticks to make a fire and there are some burning embers in the bottom,' he said, then sat down abruptly, unable to stand any longer. I noticed a fresh bruise on his forehead and that one hand was bleeding from a deep cut. Also he was shaking and I got the impression that it was not just from cold.

As the sailors busied themselves with making a campfire, I led Grettir to one side. 'What's the matter?' I asked, wrapping my warm sea cloak around him. 'What happened?'

He gave me an anguished look. 'It was like that business with the food bag all over again.'

'What do you mean?'

'When I reached the other side of the fiord there was just enough light for me to see my way to what we thought was a farmhouse. It turned out that it wasn't a farm, but one of those shelters built along the coast as refuges for sailors trapped by bad weather. I could hear sounds of singing and laughter inside, so I went up and pushed at the door. The lock was flimsy and broke easily. I stumbled in on about a dozen men, sailors by the look of them. Everyone was roaring drunk, lolling about and scarcely able to stand. There was a blazing fire in the middle of the room. I thought it was useless to ask the drunkards for help. They were too far gone to have understood what I wanted. Instead I went straight up to the fire and took the wooden tub of dry kindling that was next to it. Then I pulled a burning brand out of the hearth. That was when one of the drunks attacked me. He yelled out that I was some sort of troll or water demon appearing out of the night. He lumbered across the room and took a swipe at me. I knocked him down easily enough and the next moment all his companions were bellowing and lurching to their feet and trying to get at me. They picked up logs from the fire and tried to rush me. They must have been heaping straw on the fire, for there were a lot of sparks and embers flying about. I pulled a burning log out of the fire and kept swinging it at them as I backed away to the door. Then I made a dash for it, ran for the water, threw myself in and began swimming to get back here.' He shivered again and pulled the sea cloak tighter around him.

I sat with him through the rest of that black night. Grettir stayed hunched on a rock, brooding and nursing his injured hand. My presence seemed to calm him, and he took comfort from my stories as I passed the hours in telling him about my time as a youngster growing up in Greenland and the days that I had spent in the little Norse settlement in Vinland until the natives had driven us away. At first light the sailors began to stir, grumbling and shivering. One of the sailors was blowing on the embers to rekindle the fire when someone said in appalled tones, 'Look over there!' Everyone turned to stare across the water. The sun had risen above the cliff behind us, and the blanket of fog was breaking up. An early shaft of bright sunlight struck the far side of the fiord at the spot where the wooden building had stood. Only now it was gone. Instead there was a pile of blackened timber, from which rose a thin plume of grey smoke. The place had been incinerated.

There was a dismayed silence. The sailors turned to look at Grettir. He too was gazing at the smouldering wreckage. His face betrayed utter consternation. No one said a word: the sailors were scared of Grettir's strength and temper and Grettir was too shocked to speak. I held my tongue because no one would believe any other explanation: in everyone's mind Grettir the hooligan and brawler had struck again.

Within the hour a small boat was seen. A farmer from further along the fiord had noticed the smoke and was rowing down to investigate. When he ferried us across, we went to inspect the burned-out refuge. The devastation was total. The place had burned to the ground and there was no sign of the drunken sailors who had been inside. We presumed that they had perished in the blaze.

A sombre group huddled around the charred beams. 'It is not for us to judge this matter,' announced our skipper. 'Only the king's court can do that. And that must wait until a proper complaint has been made. But I speak for all the crew when I say that we will no longer accept Grettir among us. He is luck-cursed. Whatever the rights and wrongs of last night's events, he brings catastrophe with him wherever he goes and whatever he does. We renounce his company and will no longer travel with him. He must go his own way.'

Grettir made no attempt to protest his innocence or even to say farewell. He picked up his pack, slung it over his shoulder, turned and began to walk away. It was exactly what I had expected he would do.

A moment later I realised that it was what I would have done too. Grettir and I were very alike. We were two outsiders. To protect ourselves we had developed our own sense of stubborn independence. But whereas I understood that my sense of exclusion came from my rootless childhood and from scarcely knowing my parents, I feared that Grettir would grow only more bewildered and angry at misadventures which were unforeseen and apparently random. He did not realise how often he brought calamity upon himself by his waywardness or by acting without first considering the consequences. Grettir had qualities which I admired – audacity, single-mindedness, bravery. If someone was on hand to rein him in, stand by his side in times of crisis, Grettir would be a remarkable and true companion.

Another of Edgar's proverbs echoed in my memory. 'Have patience with a friend,' Edgar used to say, 'rather than lose him for ever.' Before Grettir had gone more than a few steps I shouldered my satchel and hurried to join him.

GRETTIR'S EVIL REPUTATION travelled before us. By the time the two of us reached Nidaros, the whole town was talking about the holocaust. The men who had perished in the blaze were a boat crew from Iceland, all members of a single family. Their father, Thorir, who was in Nidaros at the time, had already brought a complaint against Grettir for homicide. Nor had our former shipmates helped Grettir's case. They had arrived in Nidaros before us, and had spread a damning account of how he had returned battered and bruised from his swim across the fiord. Of course they barely mentioned that Grettir had risked his life to bring them fire and relieve their distress and, wittingly or not, they smeared his name further by adding lurid details of his grave robbery.

The Norwegian king, Olaf, summoned Grettir to the palace to stand judgement, and I went with him, intending to act as a favourable witness. The hearing was held in the great hall of the royal residence and King Olaf himself conducted the enquiry with proper formality. He listened to the dead men's father state his case, then asked our former companions to recount their version of that fateful evening. Finally he turned to Grettir to ask him what he had to say. Stubbornly Grettir remained silent, glowering at the king, and I felt it was left to me to speak up. So I repeated what Grettir had told me about the drunkards using burning firebrands as weapons. When I had finished, the king asked Grettir, 'Do you have anything to add?'

'The sots in the house were all alive when I left them,' was his only comment.

King Olaf was fair-minded as well as patient. 'All the evidence I have heard today is conjectural, as none of the participants survived except Grettir,' he said, 'and Grettir's statement must be treated with caution as he is the defendant in this case. So it will be difficult to arrive at the truth. My own opinion is that Grettir is probably innocent of the charge of deliberate murder because he had no motive to set fire to the building.'

I was about to congratulate Grettir on the royal verdict, when King Olaf continued. 'I have therefore decided that the best way to settle the matter is that Grettir Asmundarson submits himself to ordeal in my new church and in the presence of the faithful. The ordeal to be that of hot iron.'

I had completely forgotten that King Olaf never missed a chance to demonstrate the advantages of Christianity. A fervent believer in the White Christ, he wanted all his subjects to adopt the faith and follow Christian customs. Trial by ordeal was one of them. Of course, trials to test for guilt or innocence were also a part of the Old Ways, usually by armed combat, man to man, arranged between plaintiff and accused. But the Christians had come up with much more ingenious tests. They dropped the accused into narrow wells to see if the guilty sank or the innocent swam. They obliged others to pluck stones out of boiling water to observe whether the scald wounds then festered; or – as was proposed for Grettir – they made them hold a red-hot lump of iron and watched to see how far they could walk before their hands blistered mortally. And, for some curious reason, they thought it more authentic and righteous if the ordeals by steam and fire were conducted in a church.

A packed congregation assembled to witness Grettir's test. Their expectant faces revealed how notorious my friend had already become. Apparently the stories of his exploits were common knowledge: how he had tackled a rogue bear and killed the animal single-handed, and – in an uncomfortable echo of his present situation – how he had locked a marauding gang of dangerous berserks into a wooden shed and burned the place down, killing them all. Now the audience turned up to see whether Grettir could endure the pain of holding a lump of scorching iron in the palms of his hands while he walked ten paces. I slipped quietly into the church ahead of Grettir, though I had no idea how I could help him. The best I could do, while the congregation chanted a prayer to their God, was to repeat over and over again a galdr verse I had learned long ago, the seventh of Odinn's spells, which will quench a blazing fire.

Odinn heard my appeal, for when Grettir entered the church and began to walk up the aisle to where the priest and his assistant stood waiting by the brazier, a young man darted out from the congregation, and began to caper and dance beside Grettir. He was a fanatical Christian devotee. He was grimacing and shouting, waving his arms and cursing. Grettir was a vile heathen, the youth shouted, he should never be allowed inside a church or permitted to tread on sacred ground. Rolling his eyes and dribbling, he began to taunt Grettir, hurling a torrent of abuse until finally Grettir swung his arm and fetched his tormentor such a crack on the side of the head that the youth went spinning away, pitching face down in the aisle. The congregation gasped. They waited for the youth to get back to his feet, but he lay there motionless. Grettir said not a word, but stood patiently. Someone knelt down beside the lad and turned him over.

'He's dead' he said, looking up. 'His neck's broken.'

There was an awful silence, then the priest raised his voice.

'Violent death in God's House! Murder in the face of our Lord!' he screamed.

Grettir began to retreat slowly down the aisle towards the door. The people's fear of him was so great that no one dared to move. Before Grettir reached the door King Olaf, who had been in the front of the church to witness the ordeal, intervened. He must have realised that his show of Christian justice was turning sour. 'Grettir!' he called, 'no man is unlucky or as ill-fated as you. Your quick temper has destroyed your chance to prove your innocence or guilt. I hereby pronounce that you must leave this kingdom and return to your own country. In view of the provocation you have suffered, you will be permitted a grace period of six months. But you are never to return to Norway.'

For days Grettir and I searched for a ship that would take us back to Tonsberg, where his brother Thorstein lived. But it was hard to find a captain who would accept us aboard. Seamen are more superstitious than most and Grettir was said to be the most luckless man alive. If he did not cause mischief himself, his misfortune would drag down those around him. Nor were his enemies satisfied with King Olaf's verdict. Grettir and I were in a shoreside tavern, seated in a back room and whiling away one of those dark and dreary Norwegian winter afternoons when Thorir's family decided to take their revenge. Five of them burst into the room, armed with spears and axes. Four of the attackers made straight for Grettir, while the fifth turned his attention on me. I was taken completely unawares – before I could get to my feet my attacker had struck me hard on the side of the head with the butt of his spear. I crashed backward from my seat, my head so filled with pain that I could hardly see. When my vision cleared, I saw that Grettir had picked up a bench and was using it as his weapon. His strength was prodigious. He handled the heavy bench as if it was a fighting staff, first sweeping the legs from under two of his assailants, and then bringing the heavy furniture down on the shoulder of a third with a massive thump. The man howled and clutched at his now useless arm. The fourth man, seeing his opening, rushed at Grettir from one side with an axe. Grettir dodged and, as the man overreached, my friend effortlessly plucked the weapon from his grasp. The balance of the contest changed in an instant. Seeing that Grettir was now armed and dangerous, the attackers jostled one another as they headed for the door. The man who had knocked me down raised his spear to skewer me. Compared with Grettir, I was a helpless target. In a flash Grettir turned and used his free hand to wrench the spear from my attacker, and he too ran out of the door and slammed it hard behind him.

'Are you all right?' Grettir asked as I struggled groggily to my feet. My head felt as if it was split.

'Yes, I'll be fine. Just give me a moment.'

I could hear our opponents just outside the door, shouting insults and calling out that they had not finished with us. Grettir cocked his head on one side to listen. I saw him heft the captured spear in one hand to find its balance point and draw back his arm in the throwing position. Then he hurled the spear straight at the door. His strength was so great that the weapon splintered right through the wood panel. I heard a yelp of pain. Moments later the attackers had gone.

'I'm sorry. I didn't mean for our friendship to bring you into danger,' Grettir said to me quietly. 'That was not your quarrel.'

'What is friendship for if not to hold things in common, including another's battles?' I said. Despite my aching head, I felt a new self-confidence welling up within me. I knew that since Edgar's death and my parting from Aelfgifu, I had been adrift, and that my day-to-day existence had been aimless. But now my life had taken a new shape: Grettir had acknowledged me as his friend.

EIGHT

'IT'S THE STRENGTH in his arms that does it,' said Thorstein
Galleon to me two weeks later. Grettir and I had finally found a
ship, an Icelandic vessel and at a bandit's price, to take us to
Tonsberg, where the three of us – Thorstein, Grettir and I – were
now seated in the kitchen at Thorstein's farm. 'Look here, see my
arm.' And Thorstein rolled back his sleeve. 'People would say
that I'm well muscled. But take a look at Grettir's arms. They're
more like oxen's hocks. And he's got the strength in his chest and
shoulders to back them up. We used to have contests when we
were children, seeing who could pick up the heaviest stones or
throw them the furthest. Grettir always won and by the time he
was in his early teens people started taking bets on whether he
could lift a particularly heavy boulder they selected. Yet to look
at him you would never know how strong he is. Not until he
takes off his tunic, that is. That is why people misjudge him so
often. They get into a fight with him or an argument, and finish
up the worse off. If Grettir was a big man, massive and fearsome
to look at, he would not have half the trouble he seems to attract.
People would steer clear.'

Grettir, as usual, was adding little to the conversation. He sat
there, listening to his half-brother ramble on. I could see that
there was considerable affection between them, though for the

most part it was unspoken. We were lazing away the day, waiting
for the captain who had brought us to decide whether he would
risk sailing onward to Iceland. My friend had announced that he
had decided to go home, even if it meant breaking the terms of
his three-year exile. He had confided to me that although his
sentence of lesser outlawry still had six months to run, as far as
he was concerned the matter was over and done with. He felt he
had spent enough time abroad to cancel the blood debt to the
Icelandic family of the man he had killed. Now that I knew him
better, I realised that his unfinished sentence had become an
attraction rather than a deterrent. He was thinking he would gain
fame – or notoriety – as the man brave enough to adjust his time
of exile out of a sense of self-justice.

When Grettir told Thorstein of his decision to return home,
his half-brother pondered the matter for several moments, then
said in his deep rumbling voice, 'I doubt that your father will be
too pleased to see you, or even speak to you. But remember me
to our mother and tell her that I am well and prospering here in
Norway. Whatever happens, I want you to know that you can
always count on my support. And if worst comes to worst, and
you get yourself unjustly killed, I swear that I will hunt down the
killer and avenge you. This I pledge.'

Though Grettir had promised our avaricious captain that he
would double his usual fee for the passage to Iceland, the skipper
had already delayed his departure three times, not because he was
fearful of Grettir's bad luck, but because he was uneasy about
running into a late winter gale. He was mercenary but he was also
a good seaman. Even now he was aboard his ship in the little
creek close below Thorstein's farm, gazing up anxiously at the
sky, watching which way the clouds were going, and offering up
prayers to Njord, God of the winds and waves. He knew that an
open-sea crossing to Iceland was not something to undertake
lightly at that time of year.

Sailors give nicknames to their ships. I have sailed on 'Plunger',
which pitched badly in the waves; 'Griper' was almost impossible

to sail close to the wind, and 'The Sieve' obviously needed constant bailing. The ship we now expected to carry us to Iceland was known to her crew as 'The Clog'. The man who had built her many years earlier had intended a vessel nearly twice the size and he had constructed the fore part of the ship before realising that he was running out of funds. Iceland has no ship-building timber, and the wood for her vessels has to be imported from Norway. The price of timber soared that year, and 'The Clog's' builder was already deep in debt. So he had truncated his ship, making her stern with whatever material he had left over. The result was that the bow of 'The Clog' was a fine, sea-kindly prow. But the stern was a sorry affair, stunted, clumsy and awkward. And it turned out to be nearly the death of us.

Her captain knew that he needed six days of settled weather to make his passage in 'The Clog', as she was such a slow and heavy sailer. 'We could be lucky and have a week of favourable east winds at this season,' he said, 'but then again it can turn nasty in a few hours and we'd be in real trouble.'

Eventually his weather sense, or perhaps his enthusiasm for our passage money, persuaded him that the right moment had come and we set sail. At first everything went well. The east wind held and we plodded west, passing through an area where we saw many whales and knew we had cleared the rocks and cliffs of Farroes. Though I was a paying passenger, I took my turn to prepare meals on the flat hearth stone at the base of the mast, and I helped to handle sails, bail out the bilges, and generally showed willing. Grettir, by contrast, sank into one of his surly moods. He lay about the deck, wrapped in his cloak and picking the most sheltered spots, where he was in the way of the working crew. Even when it was obvious that he was a hindrance, he refused to shift, and the vessel's regular eight-man crew were too frightened of his brawler's reputation to kick him out of the way. Instead they glared at him, made loud remarks about lazy louts and generally worked themselves into a state of rightful indignation about his idleness. Grettir only sneered back at them and called

them lubberly clowns, no better than seagoing serfs. Being
Grettir's friend and companion I was thoroughly embarrassed by
his churlish behaviour, though I knew better than to interfere.
Anything I said when he was in that sullen mood was likely to
make him even more obstinate. So I put up with the scornful
remarks of my shipmates when they enquired how I managed to
maintain a friendship with such a boor. I held my tongue and
remembered how, without Grettir's intervention, I would probably
have ended my life in a Nidaros tavern brawl.

'The Clog' trudged along. Despite her age, she was doing all
that was asked of her thanks to the hard-working crew and the
good weather. Unfortunately, though, the weather proved a cruel
fraud. The same east wind which was pushing us along our route
so satisfactorily, gradually grew in strength. At first no one
complained. The increase in the wind was by small degrees and
easily handled. The crew reduced sail and looked pleased. 'The
Clog' was now moving through the water as fast as any of them
could remember and in the right direction. In the evening the
wind strength rose a little more. The sailors doubled the ropes
which supported the single mast, lowered the mainyard a fraction,
and checked that there was nothing loose on deck that might roll
free and do damage. The younger mariners began to look slightly
apprehensive. During the third night at sea we began to hear the
telltale sound of the wind moaning in the rigging, a sign that 'The
Clog' was coming under increasing stress. When dawn broke, the
sea all around us was heaving in rank upon rank of great waves,
their tops streaked with foam. Now the older members of the
crew began to be concerned. They checked the bilges to see how
much water was seeping through the hull's seams. The ship was
labouring, and if you listened closely you could hear the deep
groans of the heavier timbers in contrast to the shrieking clamour
of the wind. By noon the captain had ordered the crew to take
down the mainsail entirely and rig a makeshift storm sail on a
short spar just above deck level. This storm sail was no bigger
than a man's cloak, but by then the wind had risen to such

strength that the tiny sail was enough to allow the helmsman to steer the ship. Only the captain himself and his most experienced crewman were at the rudder because each breaking wave was threatening to yaw the ship and send her out of control. In those vile conditions there was no question of trying to steer our intended course, nor of heaving to and waiting for the gale to blow itself out. 'The Clog' was too clumsy to ride the waves ahull. They would roll her. Our best tactic was to steer directly downwind, allowing the great waves to roll harmlessly under her.

This was when the original failure of her construction began to tell. A deep-sea merchant ship, properly built to our favoured Norse design, would have had a neat stern, so she rose effortlessly to the following waves, as a sea-kindly gull sits on the water. But 'The Clog's broad, ugly stern was too ungainly. She did not lift with the waves, but instead squatted down awkwardly and presented a bluff barrier to the force of the sea. And the sea responded in anger. Wave after wave broke violently against that clumsy stern. We felt each impact shake the length of the little vessel. And the crest of every wave came rearing up and toppled onto the deck, washing forward and then cascading into the open hold. Even the least experienced seafarer would have seen the danger: if our vessel took on too much water, she would either founder from the added weight or the swirl of the water in the hold would make her dangerously unstable. Then she would simply roll over and die, taking all of us with her.

Without being told, our crew – myself included – bailed frantically, trying to return the sea water to where it belonged. It was back-breaking, endless labour. We were using wooden buckets, and they had to be hoisted up from the bilge by one man to a helper on deck, who then crossed to the lee rail, emptied the bucket over the side, lurched his way back across the heaving and slippery deck, and lowered back the bucket down to the man working in the bilge. It became a never-ending, desperate cycle as more and more water came gushing in over 'The Clog's' ill-begotten stern. Our skipper did what he could to help. He steered the ship to each wave, trying to avoid the direct impact on the stern, and he ordered the now-useless mainsail to be rigged as a breakwater to divert the crests that leaped aboard. But the respite was only temporary. After a day of unremitting bailing, we could feel 'The Clog' beginning to lose the battle. Hour by hour she became more sluggish, and the man who stood in the bilge to bail was now up to his thighs in water. The previous day he had been able to see his knees. Our ship was slowly settling into her grave.

All the time, as we struggled to save the ship, Grettir lay on deck like a dead man, his face turned to the bulwark, soaked to the skin and ignoring us. It was difficult to credit his behaviour. At first I thought he was one of those unfortunates who are so seasick that all feeling leaves them and they become like the living dead, unable to stir whatever the emergency. But not Grettir. From time to time I saw him turn over to ease his bones on the hard deck. I found his attitude inexplicable and wondered if he was so fatalistic that he had decided to meet calmly whatever death the Norns had decreed him.

But I had mistaken my friend. On the fourth morning of our voyage, after we had passed an awful night, bailing constantly until we were so exhausted that we could scarcely stand, Grettir suddenly sat up and stretched his arms. He glanced over to where we were standing, our eyes red-rimmed with tiredness, muscles aching. There was no mistaking our expressions of dislike as we saw him finally take an interest in our plight. He did not say a word, but got up and walked over to the edge of the open hatch leading to the hold and jumped down. Silently Grettir held out his hand to the man who was standing there, crotch deep in the water. He took the bailing bucket from him, waved him away, then scooped up a bucket full of water and passed it up to the sailor who had been emptying the bucket over the rail. Grettir made the lift look effortless even though he had to reach above his head. When the bucket was empty, it was handed back and Grettir repeated his action so smoothly and quickly that the full bucket was back on deck level before the startled sailor was ready to receive it. He staggered across the pitching deck and emptied its contents over the side, while my friend stood in the bilge and waited his return. Now Grettir caught my eye and gestured towards a second bucket lashed with its lanyard to the mast step. I saw immediately what he meant, so fetched the bucket and passed it down to him. He filled that bucket, too, and handed it back up to me so I could dump the water over the rail. Back and forth we went, the sailor and I, emptying our buckets as fast as the two of us could cross the deck while Grettir stayed below and went on scooping and filling our loads. When I was too tired to continue, I handed my bucket to a second sailor, as did my workmate. Grettir did not break his rhythm. Nor did he falter when the second pair of helpers had to rest, but kept on filling bucket after bucket with water from the bilge.

He kept up his amazing feat for eight hours, with only a short break after every five hundredth bucket. None of us would have believed such stamina was possible. He was tireless and kept pace with the crew as they worked in relays. The men who had glared and complained about his indolence, now looked at him in awe. Inspired, they found an endurance of their own and worked, turn and turn about, to win the race against the water level in the bilge. Without Grettir, they and their ship would be lost and they knew it. For my part, I knew that Grettir was saving my life for a second time and that I owed him my unswerving friendship.

'The Clog' nearly overshot Iceland altogether as she ran before that tyrannical east wind. When the gale finally eased, our shaken skipper managed to edge his ship into the lee of the land off the Hvit River and we found that, by 'The Clog's' lumbering standards, we had made a record passage. Our sailors went ashore boasting about their prowess, though their greatest applause was reserved for Grettir. He was the hero of the hour. The skipper went so far as to hand him back half our passage money and announced that Grettir was welcome to stay on board as long as he wished. After such a shockingly desperate voyage the skipper vowed that he would keep 'The Clog' safely at anchor until the proper sailing season.

'Why don't you take up his offer, at least for a day or two?' I suggested to Grettir. 'You stay on board. It will give me a chance to go ashore and find out what sort of a reception you may get when people learn that you have returned before completing your three-year exile.'

'Thorgils, you know very well that I don't care what people will do and say. I'm planning to go to see my mother, Gerdis, to bring her news about Thorstein, and find out how the rest of my family is getting on. I left two brothers here in Iceland when I went away, and I fear that I abandoned them just when they needed me most. We were in the middle of a feud with neighbours and there was talk of bloodshed and reprisals. I want to know how that quarrel turned out. If it is unresolved, then perhaps there's something I can do. So I'll find a good, swift horse to carry me across country to our family home.'

'Look, Grettir,' I told him. 'I spent some time in this district when I was a lad and I know the leading chieftain – Snorri Godi. Let me get his opinion about whether there is any way you can get the final part of your sentence waived.'

'It will be a wonder if Snorri Godi is still alive. He must be an old man now,' said Grettir. 'I know his reputation as a shrewd lawgiver. So he's not likely to approve of someone flouting the rules of outlawry.'

'Snorri always treated me fairly,' I answered. 'Maybe he'll agree to act as an intermediary if you offer to pay compensation to the family of the man killed in the quarrel over the bag of food. It wouldn't cost very much because you've already served most of the sentence.'

But when I put that suggestion to Snorri Godi two days later, his response came as a body blow. He said quietly, 'So you haven't heard the Althing's decision?'

'What do you mean?' I asked.

I had travelled a day's journey to Snorri's substantial farm-house, and the farm looked even more prosperous than I remembered it. Snorri himself now had a head of snow-white hair, but his eyes were as I remembered them — grey and watchful.

'At the last meeting of the Althing, Thorir of Gard, the father of those lads who died in the fire in Norway, brought forward a new complaint against Grettir. He accused him of murdering his sons in a deliberate act. He was very persuasive and provided complete details of the outrage. He contended that the deed was so foul that Grettir should be declared skogarmadur.'

The word skogarmadur dismayed me. In Iceland it is never used in jest. It means 'a forest man', and describes someone found guilty of a crime so repugnant that the offender is condemned to live outside civilised society for ever. It means full outlawry and banishment for life. If the annual lawgiving assembly of the Icelanders, the Althing, passes such a sentence, there can be neither an appeal nor a pardon.

'No one at the Althing wanted to convict Grettir of such a heinous crime without hearing his side of the affair,' Snorri went on, 'but there was no one to speak up for him, and Thorir was so vehement that in the end Grettir was made a full outlaw. Now there is nothing that can be done to reverse the verdict. You'd better go back and warn your friend Grettir that every man's hand is against him. He will be hunted down like vermin. Anyone who meets him is entitled to kill him, casually or deliberately. In addition, Thorir is offering a handsome reward to anyone who executes him.'

'But what about Grettir's family?' I asked 'Weren't they represented at the Althing? Why didn't they speak up for him?'

'Grettir's father died while his son was abroad. And the most competent of his brothers, Atli, whom everyone liked and would have listened to, was killed in that deadly feud which the Asmundarsons are pursuing with the faction led by Thorbjorn Oxenmight. And, Thorgils, you'd better be careful too. Don't let yourself get drawn into that feud because of your relationship with Grettir.

Remember that the law states that anyone who helps or harbours a forest man is an accessory to his crime and therefore forfeits his own goods. My advice to you is to have as little as possible to do with Grettir in the future. Once you have delivered your message to him, put as much space as possible between yourself and your murderous friend. Go and build yourself a normal life. Why don't you settle down, get married, raise a family, find your place in a community?'

I was aghast. Grettir had come home believing that he was entitled to live a normal life. Instead he stood condemned in his absence of a crime which I was convinced he did not commit. The effect of such injustice on his already brooding character would be calamitous. He would find himself even further isolated from normal society.

I knew that his chances of survival were negligible. No forest man had ever lived to old age unless he fled abroad and never returned to Iceland. In effect I had lost my friend. It was as if he was already dead.

To my surprise Grettir was not in the least perturbed to hear that he been declared a skogarmadur. 'Cheer up, Thorgils,' he said. 'Don't look so glum. If they are going to hunt down and kill their outlaw, they'll have to catch me first. I have no intention of running away and I've friends and allies in Iceland who'll ignore the Althing's decision and give me food and a roof over my head when I need it. I'll just have to be careful when I call on my mother. I'll have to do that in secret. Then I'll see how matters turn out once people hear that Grettir the Strong is back.'

'I'll go with you,' I said.

'No you won't, my friend,' he replied. 'Snorri was wise in that regard. You really ought to try settling down. You are at the right age for marriage, and you should look around for a wife and perhaps start a family. If I need your help, then I'll call on you for it. In the meantime I can look after myself very adequately.'

The two of us were standing on the brow of a low hill

overlooking the anchorage where 'The Clog' was riding at anchor. In contrast to the foul weather of our voyage from Norway, it was a warm and sunny day, almost spring-like. I had suggested to Grettir that we walk up there as I had important news to tell him in private. Grettir reached down to pluck a wisp of grass, and tossed it nonchalantly into the air as if he didn't have a care in the world. The breeze caught the blades of grass and carried them away. 'I like this country,' he said. 'It's my home, and no man will chase me away from it. I believe I can live off this land and it will take care of me.'

'You'll need more than just the ability to live off the land,' I said.

'There's a saying that goes "Bare is the back of the brother-less,"' Grettir answered. He was carrying the sword we had plundered from the barrow grave, and now he pulled it from its scabbard and used the point to carve out a long strip of turf. He did not cut the ends but left them attached to the ground. Then he picked up his spear – since the attack at the tavern he never went anywhere unless fully armed – and used it to prop up the strip of turf so that it formed an arch. 'Here, hold out your right hand,' he said to me. When I did so, he delicately drew the blade of his sword across the palm of my hand. It felt like the touch of a feather, yet the blood began to flow. He shifted the sword to his left hand, to make a similar cut on his right palm. He held out his hand, and our palms met and the blood mingled. Then we ducked under the arch of turf, straightening up as we emerged on the other side. 'Now we are fostbraedralag,' said Grettir. 'We are sworn brothers. It is a loyalty that cannot be sundered as long as either of us is alive.'

Looking back on that ceremony under the arch of turf, I realise that it was another of the defining moments of my adult life. I, who had never really known my mother and whose father had been aloof and distant, had found true kindred at last. Had my life been otherwise, perhaps I would have natural brothers and sisters or, in the manner of many Norse families, I would have been fostered out and gained an alternative family of foster-brothers and -sisters with whom I could have been close and intimate. But that never happened. Instead I had gained a sworn brother by a decision made between two adults and that made our bond even stronger.

'Well, sworn brother,' said Grettir with a mischievous glint in his eye, 'I've got my first request of you.'

'What's that?' I asked.

'I want you to help me steal a horse.'

So before the next daybreak Grettir and I dressed in dark clothes and crept to a meadow where he had seen a handsome black mare. Under cover of darkness, we managed to coax the mare away from the herd, far enough for Grettir to put a bridle on her, jump on her back and begin his journey home. Thus a friendship which began with grave robbery celebrated its formal recognition with a horse theft.

NINE

WRITING THIS MEMOIR of my life I now come to one of its less happy episodes, namely my first marriage. Brief and cheerless, that marriage now seems so distant that I have to strain to recall the details. Yet it was to have important consequences and that is why I must include it in my tale.

Her name was Gunnhildr. She was four years older than myself, taller by half a head and tending to overweight, with milky pale skin, blonde hair of remarkable fineness and pale blue eyes which bulged when she was angry. Her father was a moderately well-to-do farmer up in the north-west district, and while he was far from pleased with the match, he knew it was the best that could be managed. His daughter, the third of five, had recently been divorced for reasons which I never fully discovered. Perhaps I should have taken this as a warning and been more cautious, for – as I was to find out – it is far easier for a woman to divorce a man in Norse society than the other way around and divorce can be a costly affair – for the man.

Before a marriage is agreed in Iceland, two financial settlements are made. One comes from the bride's family and is a contribution to the couple to help them get started. That investment remains the bride's property. If the marriage fails, she keeps it. By contrast the price put into the marriage by her husband's

side, the mundur, is held as common property, and in the event
of divorce may be claimed by the bride if she can show that her
husband was in any way at fault. Understandably, the haggling
between the families of groom and bride over the size of the
mundur can take up a considerable time before a marriage, but
should the marriage collapse, the rancour over which partner was
at fault takes even longer.

Why did I get married? I suppose it was because Grettir had
recommended it and Snorri Godi, who was regarded as a very
astute man, had done the same. That, at least, would have been
my superficial reason, but deeper down I suppose that Grettir's
departure to seek his own family had left me feeling insecure.
Also Snorri, after making the initial suggestion, then proceeded
actively to find me a wife, which left little option. Like many
men who are approaching the loss of their prestige and power, he
could not resist meddling in the affairs of others, however insignificant they might be.

And I was certainly insignificant. Born illegitimate and sent
away by my mother at the age of two to a father who had
remarried and largely ignored me, I could offer neither support
nor prospects to a wife. Nor would it have been wise to tell her
that I was sworn brother to the most notorious outlaw in the land.
So, instead, I kept quiet and let Snorri do the negotiating for me.
I suppose his reputation as the foremost chieftain of the district
was in my favour, or perhaps he had some hidden understanding
with Gunnhildr's father, Audun. Whatever the background, Snorri
invited me to stay at his home while he arranged the details, and
all went smoothly until the matter of mundur came up. Old
Audun, a grasping and pompous man if there ever was one, asked
what bride price I was prepared to pay for what he called his
'exquisite daughter'. If Odinn had been kinder to me at that
moment, I would have said that I was penniless and the negotiations would have collapsed. As it was, I foolishly offered to
contribute a single jewel, but one so rare that nothing like it had
been seen in Iceland. Audun was sceptical at first, then curious,

and when I melted down the clumsy lead bird of my amulet and produced the fire ruby he looked amazed.

The greater impact was made on his daughter. The moment Gunnhildr saw that gem she had to have it. She was determined to flaunt it before her sisters. It was her way of paying them back for years of spiteful remarks about her frumpiness. And once Gunnhildr decided that she wanted something nothing would stop her, as her father well knew. So the last of old Audun's objections to our marriage disappeared and he agreed to the match. My future in-laws agreed to provide Gunnhildr and myself with a small outlying farmstead as her dowry, while the gem was my mundur. At the last moment, either because the thought of parting with my talisman and its association with my life in England was so painful, or because of a premonition, I made Gunnhildr and Audun agree that if the marriage failed I would be allowed to redeem the jewel on payment of a sum which was the equivalent value of the farmstead. The price of the gem was set at thirty marks of silver, a sum that was to cloud my next few years.

Our wedding was such a subdued affair that it was barely noticed in the neighbourhood. Even Snorri was absent, having taken to his bed with an attack of fever and Gunnhildr dressed up only in order to display the fire ruby. I was taken aback to discover that the ceremony was to be conducted by an itinerant priest. He was one of those Christian holy men who had begun to appear in increasing numbers in the countryside, travelling from farm to farm to persuade the women to accept their faith and baptise their children, and railing all the while against what they described as the barbaric and heathen Old Ways. During the wedding ceremony I realised that my bride was a rabid Christian. She stood beside me, sweating slightly in her wedding finery, and calling out the responses in her unmelodious voice so devoutly and harshly that I knew she believed the priest's every incantation. Now and again, I noticed, she fondled the fire ruby possessively as it dangled between her ample breasts.

The wedding feast was as skimpy as my father-in-law could

get away with, and then my wife and I were conducted to our farmstead by a small group of her relatives, then left alone. Later that evening Gunnhildr made it clear that physical relations between us were out of the question. She had given herself to the White Christ, she informed me loftily, and close contact with a non-believer like myself was repugnant to her. It was a reaction which I did not care to challenge. On the walk to our new home I had been pondering on the fact that my marriage was probably the worst mistake I had yet made in my life.

Matters did not improve. I quickly learned that my in-laws' wedding gift of the farmstead was self-serving in the extreme. The farm lay just too distant from their own home for them to work it themselves. My father-in-law had been too parsimonious to hire a steward to live there and run it, and too jealous of his neighbours to rent them the lands and pasture. By installing a compliant son-in-law he thought he had found his ideal solution. I was expected to bring the farm into good order, then hand on to him a significant portion of the hay, meat or cheese it produced. In short, I was his lackey.

Nor did Gunnhildr intend to spend much time there with me. Once she had acquired a husband or, rather, once she had got her hands on the fire ruby, she reverted to her previous way of life. To her credit she was a competent housekeeper, and she was quick to clean up the farmhouse, which had been left unoccupied for several years and make the place habitable in a basic way. But then she began to spend more and more time back at her parent's house, staying the nights there on the excuse that it was too far to return to her marital home. Or she went off on visits to her gang of women friends. They were an intimidating group. All were recent and ardent converts to Christianity, so they spent a good deal of their time congratulating one another on the superior merits of their new faith and complaining of the coarseness of the one they now spurned.

I must admit that Gunnhildr would have found me a thoroughly unsatisfactory helpmeet had she stayed at home. I was completely unsuited to farm work. I found it depressing to get up every morning and pick up the same tools, walk the same paths, round up the same cattle, cut hay from the same patch, repair the same rickety outhouse and return to the same lumpy mattress, which, thankfully, I had to myself. To put it bluntly, I preferred Gunnhildr in her absence because I found her company to be shallow, tedious and ignorant. When I compared her to Aelfgifu I almost wept with frustration. Gunnhildr had an uncanny ability to interrupt my thoughts with observations of breathtaking banality, and her sole interest in her fellow humans appeared to be based on their financial worth, an attitude she doubtless learned from her money-grubbing father. To spite him, I did as little work on the farm as possible.

Naturally the other farmers in the area, who were hard-working men, thought me a good-for-nothing and shunned my company. So rather than stay and mind the cattle and cut hay for the winter, I went on excursions to visit my mentor Thrand, who had instructed me in the Old Ways when I was in my teens. Thrand lived only half a day's travel away and, compared with white-haired Snorri, I found him remarkably little changed. He was still the gaunt, soldierly figure whom I remembered, plainly dressed and living simply in his small cabin with its array of foreign trophies hung on the wall. He greeted me with genuine affection, telling me that he had heard that I was back in the district. He had not attended my wedding, he added, because he found it difficult to support the prating of so many Christians.

We slipped back easily into the old routine of tutor and pupil. When I told Thrand that I had become a devotee of Odinn in his role as traveller and enquirer, he suggested I memorise the Havamal, the song of Odinn, 'Let the Havamal be your guide for the future,' he suggested. 'In cleaving to Odinn's words you will find wisdom and solace. Your friend Grettir, for example: he wants to be remembered for what he was, for his good repute, and Odinn has something to say on that very subject,' and here Thrand quoted:

'Cattle die, kinsmen die,
you yourself die,
But words of glory never die
for the man who achieves good name.

'Cattle die, kinsmen die,
you yourself die.
I know one thing that never dies,
the fame of each man dead.'

On another day, when I made some wry comment about Gunnhildr and her disappointing behaviour, Thrand promptly recited another of Odinn's verses:

'The love of women whose hearts are false
is like driving an unshod steed over slippery ice,
a two-year-old, frolicsome, badly broken,
or like being in a rudderless boat in a storm.'

This led me to ask, 'Have you ever been married yourself?'

Thrand shook his head. 'No. The idea of marriage never appealed to me, and at an age when I might have married, it was not allowed.'

'What do you mean "not allowed"?'

'The felag, the fellowship, forbade it and I took my vows seriously.'

'What fellowship was that?' I asked, hoping to learn something of Thrand's enigmatic past, which the old soldier had never talked about.

But Thrand said only, 'It was the greatest of all the felags, at that time at least. It was at the height of its glory. Now, though, it is much reduced. Few would believe how much it was once admired throughout the northern lands.'

On occasions like this I had the feeling that Thrand sensed that the beliefs he held, and had taught me, were in final retreat, that an era was drawing to a close.

'Do you think that Ragnarok, the great day of reckoning, is soon?' I asked him.

'We haven't yet heard Heimdall the watchman of the Gods blow the Gjallahorn to announce the approach of the massed forces of havoc,' he answered, 'but I fear that even with his wariness Heimdall may overlook the closer danger. His hearing may be so acute that he can hear the grass growing, and his sight so keen that he can see a hundred leagues in every direction by day or night, but he does not realise that true destruction often creeps in disguise. The agents of the White Christ could prove to be the harbingers of a blight just as damaging as all the giants and trolls and forces of destruction that have been foretold for so long.'

'Can nothing be done about it?' I asked.

'It is not possible to bend fate, nor can one stand against nature,' he replied. 'At first I thought that the Christians and the Old Believers had enough in common to be able to coexist. We all believe that mankind is descended from just one man and one woman. For the Christians it is Adam and Eve, for us it is Ask and Embla, whom Odinn brought to life. So we agree on our origins, but when it comes to the afterlife we are too far apart. The Christians call us pagans and dirty heathens because we eat horse-flesh and make animal sacrifice. But, for me, a greater filthiness is to dig a pit for the corpse of a warrior and put him in the ground to be eaten by worms and turned to slime. How can they do that? A warrior deserves his funeral pyre, which will send his spirit to Valholl to feast there until he joins the defenders on the day of Ragnarok. I fear that if more and more warriors take the White Christ faith, there will be a sadly depleted army to follow Odin, Frey and Thor at the great conflict.'

THROUGHOUT THAT SUMMER and autumn I heard reports of my sworn brother Grettir. His exploits were the main topic of conversation among the farmers of the region. Whenever I called on my father-in-law, Audun, to discuss my progress with the out-farm, I was regaled with the latest episode in Grettir's deeds. Audun's gossip made my visits bearable because I was missing my sworn brother, though I was very careful not to reveal that I knew that 'cursed outlaw', as Audun called him. I learned that Grettir had succeeded in visiting his mother without alerting anyone else in the household. He had called at her house after dark, approaching the farmhouse along a narrow ravine that led to the side door, from where he found his way along the unlit passage to the room where his mother slept. With a mother's intuition she had identified the intruder in the darkness, and after greeting him had told him the dismal details of how Atli his older brother had been murdered by Thorbjorn Oxenmight and his faction. Grettir had then hidden in his mother's house until he was able to confirm that Thorbjorn Oxenmight was on his own farm and accompanied by only his farm workers.

'And do you know what that scoundrel Grettir did then?' said Audun, snorting with indignation. 'He rode right over to the Oxenmight's place, in broad daylight, a helmet on his head, a long spear in one hand and that fancy sword of his at his belt. He came on Oxenmight and his son working in the hayfields, gathering up the early hay and stacking it. They recognised Grettir at once and knew why he had come. Fortunately they had brought their weapons with them to the meadow, and so Thorbjorn and his lad devised what they thought was an effective defence. Oxenmight would confront Grettir to distract him, while his son armed with an axe worked his way round behind the outlaw and struck him in the back.'

'And did the plan work?'

My father-in-law let out the self-satisfied grunt of a storyteller who knows he has his audience on tenterhooks. 'It nearly did,' he said. 'A servant woman saw the whole affair. She saw Grettir stop, then sit down on the ground and start fiddling with the head of the spear. Apparently he was removing the pin which holds the spear head to the shaft. If he missed his throw, he didn't want

Oxenmight pulling the spear out of the ground and using it against him. But when Grettir threw the spear at Oxenmight the head came off too early and the spear went harmlessly astray. That left Grettir armed with his sword and a small shield against the grown man and the youth. Oxenmight did not get his name for nothing, so it seemed that the odds were now against Grettir.'

'I've heard that Grettir is not the sort of man to back off from a fight,' I said.

'He didn't. Grettir went up to Oxenmight and the two men started to circle one another, holding their swords. Oxenmight's lad saw his chance to slip around behind Grettir and bury the axe in his spine. He was just about to make his stroke when Grettir lifted up his sword to hack at Oxenmight and saw the lad out of the corner of his eye. Instead of bringing the sword forwards, he kept swinging it up and over and brought it down back-handed on the boy's head. The blow split the lad's skull like a turnip. Meanwhile his father had seen his opening and rushed forward, but Grettir deflected his sword blow with his shield, and then took a cut at his opponent. That Grettir is so strong that his sword smashed right through Oxenmight's shield as if it was made of straw, and struck his opponent in the neck. Killed him on the spot. Grettir returned immediately to his mother's house and announced to her that he had avenged the death of her oldest son Atli. She was delighted and told Grettir that he was a worthy member of her family, but that he had better be careful as Oxenmight's people would be sure to seek retribution.'

'Where's Grettir now?' I asked, trying not to seem too interested.

'Can't be sure,' Audun answered. 'He went over to see Snorri Godi and asked if he could stay there, but Snorri turned him down. There's a rumour that Grettir is hiding out with one of the farmers over in Westfiords.'

Later my obnoxious father-in-law informed me that Grettir had surfaced on the moors, living rough and keeping himself fed by making raids on the local farmsteads or sheepstealing. He was moving from place to place, usually alone but sometimes in the company of one or two other outlaws.

It was not until the spring that I met Grettir again and then completely unexpectedly. I was on my way to visit Thrand when I encountered a large group of farmers, about twenty of them. From their manner I saw at once that they were very excited, and to my surprise I saw Grettir among them. He was in the middle of the group, being led along on a rope with his hands tied behind his back.

'Can you tell me what's going on?' I asked the farmer at the head of the group.

'It's Grettir the Strong. We finally caught him,' said one of the farmers, a big, red-faced man dressed in homespun clothes. He was looking very pleased with himself. 'One of our shepherds reported seeing him on the moors, and we got together and stalked him. We had been suffering from his raids and he had got over-confident. He was asleep when we found him, and we managed to get close enough to overpower him, though a couple of us got badly bruised in the scuffle.'

'So where are you taking him?' I asked.

'We can't decide,' said the farmer. 'No one wants to take charge of him until we can bring him before our local chieftain for judgement. He's too strong and violent, and he would be a menace if kept captive.'

I glanced over at Grettir. He was standing, with his hands still bound behind his back and looking stone-faced. He did not acknowledge that he knew me. The rest of the farmers had halted and were continuing with what was obviously a long-running argument, whether to hand Grettir over to Thorir of Gard for the reward or to the local chieftain for a trial.

'Let's hang him here and now,' said one of the captors. Judging by the bruise on his face, he was one of the men whom Grettir had hit during the capture. 'That way, we can take the corpse to Thorir of Gard and claim the reward.' There was a murmur of agreement from some of his companions, though the rest were looking doubtful. In a few moments they would reach a decision and there would be no chance to influence them.

'I want to speak up for Grettir,' I called out. 'I sailed with him last year, and if he hadn't been on board our ship would have foundered. He saved my life and the lives of the rest of the crew. He's not a common criminal and he was convicted at the Althing without a chance to defend himself. If any of you have suffered from his robberies, I promise I will make good the loss.' Then I had an inspiration. 'It will be to your credit if you are generous enough to spare his life. People will talk about how magnanimous you were and remember the deed. I suggest that you make Grettir swear that he will move away from this district, and not prey on you any more. And that he'll not take his revenge on any one of you. He's a man of honour and will keep his word.'

It was the mention of honour and fame that swayed them. In every farmer, however humble, there lurked a shred of that same sense of honour and thirst for fame that Grettir had expressed to me. There was a general muttering as they discussed my proposal. It became clear that they were relieved that they would not have the dirty work of taking the outlaw's life. Finally – after a long and awkward pause – their spokesman accepted my suggestion.

'All right, then,' he said. 'If Grettir clears off and agrees never to trouble us again, we'll let him go.' Looking at Grettir, he asked, 'Do you give us your word?'

Grettir nodded.

Someone untied Grettir's bonds, loosening the knots cautiously and then stood back.

Grettir rubbed his wrists and then walked across to embrace me. 'Thank you, sworn brother,' he said. Then he stepped aside from the path and struck out across the moor.

Grettir kept his word to the farmers. He never came back into the district, but stayed away and made his home in a cave on the far side of the moor. For my part, the revelation that I was Grettir's sworn brother put an end to my quiet life. Some of my neighbours now looked at me with curiosity, others gave me a wide berth, and Gunnhildr flew into a rage. When she heard what had happened, she confronted me. Not only was I an unbeliever, she shrilled, I was consorting with the worst sort of criminals. Grettir was the spawn of the devil, a creature of Satan. He was twisted and evil. She had heard that he was a warlock, in touch with demons and ghouls.

Accustomed to my wife's ready grievances, I said nothing, and was vaguely relieved when she announced that she would in future live with her parents, and that if I continued my friendship with Grettir she would seriously consider a divorce.

My promise to pay compensation to the farmers Grettir had robbed contributed significantly to Gunnhildr's anger. The truth was that I could not afford the reparations. I was penniless and little more than a tenant for my father-in-law. Gunnhildr was very much her father's daughter, so prising money out of her grasp in order to pay the farmers was nigh impossible. It was useless to ask if she would let me use any of our joint property to settle the farmers' claims, and the only item of value which I had ever owned – the fire ruby – was now Gunnhildr's mundur, and no longer mine, even as surety for a loan. For a few days after my encounter with Grettir I was hopeful that his victims would not hold me to my promise, and I would see nothing more of them. But though the farmers had an appetite for honour and renown, they were still peasants at heart and they valued hard cash. A succession of men showed up at my door, claiming that they had been robbed by my sworn brother and asking for recompense. One said he had been held up on the roadway and his horse stolen from him; another that valuable clothing had been stripped from him at knife point; several claimed that Grettir had rustled their sheep and cattle. Of course there was no way of knowing whether their claims were genuine. The sheep and cattle might have wandered off on their own, and I was fairly sure that the values the owners put on their losses were often exaggerated. But I had appealed to their sense of honour when obtaining Grettir's freedom and, after taking such a high-minded stance, I was hardly in a position to quibble over the precise cost of their claims. I found myself faced with a sum that I had no hope of paying off.

Thrand, of course, had heard what had happened. On my next visit to his house, he noticed that I looked distracted and asked the reason. When I told him that I was worried about my debts, he merely asked, 'How much is it that you owe?'

'A little less than seven marks in all,' I said.

He walked across to his bed where it stood against the wall, reached underneath and pulled out a small, locked chest. Placing it on the table between us, he produced a key. When he threw back the lid, I found myself looking at a sight I had last seen when I had worked for Brithmaer the moneyer. The strong box was two-thirds full of silver. Very little was in coin. I saw bits and fragments of jewellery, segments of silver torcs, broken pieces of silver plate, half a silver brooch, several flattened finger rings. They were jumbled together where Thrand had tossed them casually into his hoard chest. From my days as a novice monk I recognised part of a silver altar cross, and – with a little lurch of my heart – I saw a piece of jewellery inscribed with the same sinuous writing that had been on the silver coins of Aelfgifu's favourite necklace.

'You know how to use this, I imagine,' Thrand asked, picking something out from the clutter. At first sight I thought it was one of the metal styluses that I had used in my writing lessons in the monastery. But Thrand was searching for two more items. When he put them together I recognised a weighing scale, similar to the ones that Brithmaer had used, but smaller and constructed so that it could be dismantled, suitable for a traveller.

'Here,' Thrand said. 'Hold these.'

He sifted through his hoard, picking out the pieces for me to weigh as I told him how much I owed to each farmer. Once or twice, when he could not find a piece of silver that matched the sum, he took out his sword, laid a larger piece of silver on the table, and chopped off the correct weight. 'That's how we did it in the old days,' he commented, 'when we divided up the spoils. No bothering with coins; a mark of silver is just as good by weight as when it is stamped with a king's head.' Sometimes more so, I thought, remembering Brithmaer's forgeries.

I was tactful enough not to ask Thrand where he had acquired his treasure and said only, 'I give you my word that I will repay your generosity when I have the chance.'

In reply he said, 'This is a gift, Thorgils. It does me no good locked away here in a box,' and he quoted the Havamal again:

> 'If wealth a man has won for himself
> Let him never suffer in need
> Oft he saves for a foe what he plans for a friend
> For much goes worse than we wish.'

When I had paid off the last of Grettir's victims, I decided it was time to pay a visit to my sworn brother. I had no idea where to find him, so I set off across the moors in the direction that he had taken when I had saved him from the angry farmers. As it turned out, Grettir saw me coming from a distance away. He had made his lair in a cave on high ground, from where he could keep a watch for the approach of strangers, and he came down the hillside to greet me. He led me back to his cave, the two of us scrambling up a near-vertical rock face to reach his home. He had hung a grey blanket across the entrance, the colour matching the rock so that you did not realise that the cave was there until you were a few paces away. Inside were a fireplace, a place to sleep, where he had laid out his leather sleeping sack, and a store of dried food. He took his drinking water from a small rill that drained at the foot of the cliff. When I commented on a pile of fist-sized rocks that he had stacked near the entrance of the cave, he explained that he had collected them to use as missiles. 'If anyone tries to storm the cave,' he said, 'there's only one approach, and that is straight up the cliff. I can keep them at bay for hours.'

I noticed a second leather sleeping sack, thrown in a heap on the far side of the cave. 'Who does that belong to?' I asked.

'A man called Stuv Redbeard. He's an outlaw like myself. He's gone off to raid for food. He should be back soon.'

Redbeard returned that evening, carrying a shoulder of dried lamb and a bag of whey he had stolen from an unguarded shepherd's hut. From the moment that I laid eyes on Stuv Redbeard I was worried. There was a shiftiness about him which put me on my guard. When he left the cave for a moment, I took the chance to ask Grettir about him.

'How long have you known Stuv? Do you trust him?' I asked

'Not entirely,' Grettir replied. 'I know there are men who would kill me for the price on my head. Last autumn a man came to the moor and joined me, claiming to be an outlaw like myself and needing shelter. One night he crept up on me, thinking I was asleep. He had a dagger in his hand, and intended to stab me, but I awoke in time, and managed to grab the weapon from him. I made him confess that he was a professional killer, hoping to win my blood money from Thorir of Gard.'

'Thorir is offering twenty-four marks of silver for your head and Oxenmight's family have promised to match that sum for anyone who kills you,' I said. 'It's twice as much as the highest reward ever offered for the death of a skogarmadur.'

'Well, that night creeper didn't get to collect it,' Grettir said. 'I killed him with his own dagger, carried his body over to the nearest lake, weighed the corpse down with stones and dumped him in.'

'So why are you now taking the risk of sharing your lair with that Redbeard? He could also be after the reward money.'

'It's a risk I'm prepared to take,' Grettir replied. 'I make sure that I keep an eye on him, but I would rather have company, however suspect it might be, than live here out on the moors by myself. At least after sunset.'

I remembered that, for all his ferocity and reputation, Grettir was still mortally afraid of the dark. I knew it was useless to try to persuade him that his childish dread was putting his life in danger.

My fears were well-founded. Over the next few weeks I was rarely at my father-in-law's farm as I was spending most of my time on the moor. I brought Grettir regular deliveries of food and clothing, and the two of us would sit for hours at the entrance to the cave, looking out across the moor as I relayed to him news of what was happening in the outside world. Grettir's family and friends had been negotiating with Oxenmight's people in an attempt to settle their feud, and the two sides had agreed that the deaths of Oxenmight and Grettir's brother Atli should cancel each other out. Grettir's supporters even collected enough money to offer a heavy compensation to Thorir of Gard for the death of his sons. But Thorir refused to be placated. Nothing less than Grettir's death would satisfy him.

It was on one of these visits to carry supplies to Grettir that I found the cave unoccupied. It was a warm day and I guessed that he had gone to the nearby lake to bathe and wash his clothes. Leaving my parcel of food, I started off across the moor to find him. The lake lay on the far side of a low rise in the ground. As I came to the top of the slope, I found myself looking down on a shallow expanse of water fringed with reeds and with one or two small islands in the centre. From my vantage point I could see Grettir in the water, far out from the shoreline. Much closer to the bank was his fellow outlaw, Stuv Redbeard. Clearly they had both decided to go for a swim, stripped off their clothes and left them on the bank. I watched Redbeard wade out of the water, return to his pile of clothes and get dressed quickly. There was something about his hasty movements which was suspicious. I saw him pick up his sword, unsheathe it and then slink back to where he could crouch down among the reeds in ambush. The distance was too great for me to shout a warning to Grettir, who was now approaching the landing place. I saw him reach the shallows, stand up and begin to wade towards the bank, pulling at the reeds for support as his feet moved through the slippery lake bottom. He was naked and I realised that this was the moment that Redbeard had been waiting for, perhaps for months. He had Grettir at his mercy.

Even as I watched, I saw Redbeard suddenly rise up from his ambush and the flash of his blade as he slashed at Grettir. Grettir's reaction was astonishingly swift. He must have sensed the blow coming, for he flung himself backwards into the water with a tremendous splash, and the sword stroke missed. Redbeard immediately raised his sword for a second strike. But Grettir had disappeared. The ripples still spread out from where he had flung himself back into the water, and Redbeard stood poised, head thrust forward, watching for his prey to surface, his sword at the ready. He watched and watched, and both of us became increasingly puzzled as Grettir did not reappear. For a moment I wondered whether Grettir had been caught by the tip of the sword and drowned. It was too far for me to see whether there was any blood floating to the surface. The water of the lake was a dark peaty brown, and the only sign of the struggle was the broad patch of dirty yellow where Grettir's feet had disturbed the mud as he fell backwards. This opaque patch was my sworn brother's salvation. As time passed, Redbeard concentrated his gaze in that area.

Then I noticed the reeds quiver a short distance to Redbeard's left. From my vantage point I saw them bend and stir gently: their movement was tracing a line from the water's edge to where Redbeard was standing. I realised that Grettir must have swum underwater to the bank, hauled himself out and was stalking his prey. In his eagerness Redbeard stepped forward, wading up to his knees in the water, still holding his sword with the point downward, ready to stab. But now it was Redbeard who was edging into danger. He was facing the lake, ready to pounce, when Grettir burst from the reeds behind him. I was reminded of the way that the boar had charged from the thicket when I was hunting with Edgar in England. Once again the charging animal was lethal. Grettir, stark naked, flung himself out of the reeds and onto Redbeard's back. The force of the impact knocked Redbeard into the lake. I saw Grettir reach forward right-handed, and pluck the sword from his attacker's hand. Then with his left arm, Grettir spun Redbeard over in the water, and plunged the sword in the man's belly. By then I was running down the slope, heart pounding, until I slithered to a stop beside Grettir and clasped him to me. Redbeard's body lay face down where he had intended my sworn brother to die.

Again, I was more badly shaken by the attack than Grettir. He was so accustomed to violence and assault that he recovered quickly from the ambush. Nevertheless, seeing him so narrowly escape death made me distraught. I was shaking with relief as we walked back together to the cave, leaving his would-be killer's body drifting on the surface of the lake for all to see. 'It will be a warning to others,' Grettir said. 'My whereabouts is not a secret any longer.'

'You'll have to find another refuge,' I told him. 'Staying on the moor is getting too dangerous. Sooner or later, you'll be trapped here and find yourself outnumbered.'

'I know, Thorgils,' he answered. 'I need to find somewhere so remote that no one will plague me, a place where the landowner is discreet and willing to ignore my presence.'

'Why don't we consult your mother? She may know someone who will offer you the hideaway you need. Until we get her answer, come and stay with me. Gunnhildr, my wife, is hardly ever at home. I can smuggle you into the house and you can hide there until we can pick the moment to travel to your mother's place.'

As matters turned out, Grettir stayed with me for more than two weeks. Redbeard's body was found and Oxenmight's friends assembled to make a sweep of the moor nearby, looking for Grettir. They eventually discovered his cave, and I had a feeling that they suspected that I was harbouring the fugitive, for more than once I thought I saw a watcher on the hillside above my house. Only when the hunt had been abandoned did I think it safe for Grettir to make the journey to his mother's home, and even then I insisted that I accompany him in case we encountered trouble on the road.

My caution was justified. We had gone only half a day's travel when we came face to face on the path with a man I recognised. He was one of Snorri Godi's sons, a tall, well-set-up man in his thirties by the name of Thorodd. I remembered him as a rather quiet, decent fellow. Yet as he drew level with us, he suddenly stepped right into Grettir's path, drew his sword and announced, 'Guard yourself, skogarmadur.' I must have gaped with surprise, for I did not remember Thorodd as being the least belligerent.

'What are you doing, Thorodd?' I blurted. 'Don't you recognise me? I'm Thorgils. We used to know one another when I lived at your father's farm.'

'Stay out of this,' he snapped back at me. 'Everyone knows of your association with Grettir. I'll attend to you later. Right now I intend to deal with the outlaw.'

'Don't be mad,' I insisted. 'You've got no quarrel with Grettir. Let us pass on peacefully. Just forget you've seen us.'

For his response, Thorodd struck me hard in the stomach with the pommel of his sword, knocking the wind out of me. I sat down abruptly on the roadside, clutching my guts.

Grettir had not moved until he saw me hit. Then he drew his own sword and waited for Thorodd to strike the first blow. I could see from the way Thorodd advanced on Grettir that he was a competent fighter. The speed and accuracy of the hilt blow that had knocked me down was impressive and I guessed that Thorodd had received enough weapon-training to deal with the average farmer. But Thorodd was not fighting an ordinary opponent. He was attacking the man reputed to be the strongest in Iceland.

Thorodd launched his first blow, a high cut that, if it had landed, would have separated Grettir's head from his shoulders. Almost nonchalantly Grettir raised his small wooden shield and deflected the blow as if he was swatting aside an insect. Thorodd recovered his balance and launched a second stroke, this time aimed at Grettir's legs in the hopes of laming him. Again Grettir warded off the blow, using his sword to block the attack. The two sword blades met with a ringing clash. For his third stroke Thorodd tried using all his strength to swing back-handed at Grettir's right side. Without even moving his feet, Grettir moved his wooden shield across to stop the blow. Thorodd, now panting with exertion, tried a direct stab. He lunged, with the point of his sword aimed at Grettir's belly. Again, the shield blocked the attack.

Thorodd stepped back, calculating how he could get past Grettir's guard. At that moment Grettir decided he had had enough of the onslaught and that his opponent was serious about killing him. In absolute silence, which was more terrifying than if he had given a berserker's battle roar, my sworn brother advanced on Thorodd and rained down on him a series of heavy sword blows that resembled a blacksmith beating on a forge. There was nothing subtle about Grettir's assault. He did not bother to feint or conceal the direction of the next blow, but relied entirely on brute strength. He moved forward, striking downward repeatedly on his hapless victim's defence. Thorodd raised his shield to block the blows, but each time Grettir's sword struck the shield I saw the arm shake beneath it and Thorodd stagger slightly. Grettir could have swung below the shield to cut at Thorodd's body, or struck at Thorodd's head. But he did not bother. He simply hammered on the shield, his blows so fast and so hard that Thorodd was forced to give ground. Step by step Thorodd was driven back, and I saw that Grettir was not even trying to kill his enemy, only to pound him into submission. After twenty or thirty heavy blows, Thorodd could withstand the onslaught no longer. First his shield arm began to droop, then his backward steps became more and more shaky, until he sank to his knees, still desperately trying to keep up his defence. Finally his shield, which had begun to splinter and crack, broke in half, and Thorodd was left kneeling defenceless on the soggy ground.

'Stop!' I shouted at Grettir, for I had got my breath back. But my warning was unnecessary. Now that Grettir had belaboured his opponent into submission, he stood back. He was not even out of breath.

I went across to where Thorodd was still kneeling, his body bowed forward in exhaustion. Putting an arm around his waist, I helped him to his feet.

'What on earth possessed you?' I asked. 'Did you really think that you could defeat Grettir the Strong?'

Thorodd was gasping for air. His shield arm was so numb that it hung uselessly. 'I hoped to win back my father's favour,' he groaned. 'I quarrelled with him so badly that he ordered me out of his house, saying that I had to prove my worth before he would accept me back again. He shouted at me that I had to do something spectacular — like dealing with an outlaw. I had no idea that I would run into Grettir. That was something the Gods put in my way.'

'Go back to your father,' I advised him, 'and tell him what happened. The wreckage of your shield should prove that you are telling the truth, and surely he'll accept that anyone courageous enough to tackle Grettir single-handed has proved his worth. Tell him also that Grettir's quarrel is only with those who have harmed his family. If he has robbed others or caused them injury, the sole motive has been his own survival.'

When Thorodd had limped away, Grettir insisted that I turn back to my house. 'It's less than half a day's walk from here to my mother's place,' he said, 'and that is just where my enemies will be on the lookout for me. It will be easier for one man to approach unobserved than for two of us. And after I have spoken to her and decided where I will go next, I will send you word where to find me.'

'I think we should have some way of checking that any message that passes between us is genuine,' I said. 'Now I have been seen in your company, people may use our friendship to lure you out of hiding and trap you.'

'You're always the clever and cautious one, Thorgils,' said

Grettir with a slight smile. 'Any time a message passes between us, the bearer can begin by quoting one of Odinn's sayings. That should keep you happy.'

I walked back home, worrying that Grettir would fall into an ambush as he approached his mother's house. But it was I who found calamity waiting at my door.

I almost walked right past them without noticing. Only when I was level, within touching distance, did I realise they were there. They were waiting for me and, though they were motionless, they were as dangerous as any killer waiting to pounce with a dagger.

Scorn poles – two of them were planted upright in the ground just beside my front door. I could guess who had erected them there because one was a likeness of myself carved with physical details that only someone intimate could have known. The second wooden pole was less elaborate, but there was no mistaking the broad shoulders of the man it portrayed. To make sure, the carver had scratched in runes the name 'Grettir'. The two poles were adult height, very obviously male, and both faced in the same direction, towards the door. One scorn pole was placed close behind the other, almost touching. The message was explicit, obvious to every passer-by: Grettir and Thorgils were lovers.

My initial shock of comprehension was quickly replaced by cold fury. I was outraged. I felt cheated and damaged, my closest friendship defiled. I knew, of course, that Gunnhildr must have arranged for the scorn poles to be carved and then planted for all to see. It was a public accusation, and – worse – in the same way that the sentence of full outlawry can never be appealed against, so the public accusation of man-love can never be effectively denied if it is made from within a marriage. In that regard I now shared Grettir's fate: he had been found guilty of a crime he did not commit and which he had no opportunity to deny; I had been accused unjustly of acts against which there was no way to defend myself.

Disgusted, I pushed open the door of the house and gathered up a few clothes, thrusting them angrily into a travelling satchel.

I vowed that I would never again enter that odious house, or work one more hour on the farm for old Audun's benefit, or speak to my treacherous wife. Slinging the satchel over my shoulder, I stormed out of the building feeling utterly betrayed.

OF COURSE I went to Thrand. Of all the people who had ever guided and advised me, Thrand had always been the most staunch. When I told him about the scorn poles and asked how I could fight back against the slur, he brought me to my senses.

'The more you stamp on a turd,' he said bluntly, 'the further it spreads. Let the matter alone, there's nothing you can do about it.'

It was good advice, but I was too angry and resentful to accept it outright.

'What about Grettir?' I said. 'Should I tell him? And how will he react?'

'Grettir's got far more serious threats to think about,' said Thrand. 'Of course, he will get to know about the scorn poles like everyone else. All you can do is make sure that he hears the news before it is common gossip. Then it is for him to decide if he wants to do anything about it. But, as I said, a public denial is useless. Let the matter drop, ignore it, wait for the uproar to die down and for the next new scandal to erupt and smother it. If you tell me where to find him, I'll go to see Grettir and talk with him.'

'He'll still be hiding out at his mother's house,' I replied. 'Should I do anything about Gunnhildr?'

'Well, for a start you can expect that she will bring divorce proceedings against you. She's probably lined up some hostile witnesses already, rehearsing them to appear at the next district gathering to support her claim.'

'I'll go there myself and deny the accusation,' I said defiantly, still stung by the injustice of my predicament.

'I doubt that will do much good,' said Thrand calmly. 'For

any chance of success you'll need to be represented by skilful
advocates at the court, and there's no one you know who can act
in that capacity.'

'Maybe I could ask Snorri Godi,' I suggested.

'Snorri Godi is unlikely to act on your behalf. He helped to
arrange the match in the first place and he will look foolish trying
to act for an aggrieved spouse. The best you can expect from him
is that he might help to recover your mundur, the fire ruby. And
when it comes to keeping the jewel from falling permanently into
Gunnhildr's hands, I think I can be of use.'

'How can you help?' I asked, but Thrand did not answer. He
only advised me to get a good night's sleep so as to have a clear
head in the morning. That was impossible. It was long after
nightfall before I fell into a restless slumber, plagued by black
dreams in which I was pursued by a death hag. When I woke, it
was to find Thrand gone.

He came back four days later, and in his absence I alternately
seethed with anger at Gunnhildr and concocted wild plots to
avenge myself for her perfidy, or I felt sorry for myself and
wondered how to escape from this crisis.

Thrand was as calm as always when he returned. 'Gunnhildr
has announced publicly that she is seeking a divorce,' he confirmed. 'She and her father are claiming back the farm. It was her
dowry, so that is just a formality. But they also want to keep your
mundur, the fire ruby, as you are the one at fault.' My face must
have showed my vexation and despair.

'The divorce is all but guaranteed,' Thrand went on, 'but for
the moment you need not worry about the fire ruby. It is in safe
hands.'

'What do you mean?' I asked.

'Snorri Godi has it. I went to see Snorri Godi and reminded
him about the initial agreement at the time of your marriage: that
the mundur was to be valued at thirty marks and could be
redeemed in the event of a divorce. He said that his inclination

was not to get involved in such a messy business, but because Grettir had spared his son Thorodd's life he would use his influence to get Audun and Gunnhildr to hand the jewel over to him, and he would hold it in safe keeping until you could provide thirty marks to redeem it.'

'I'm surprised that Gunnhildr or that miserly father of hers agreed to such a proposal,' I said. 'They are so grasping that they wouldn't accept a verbal assurance. They know that I could never raise thirty marks.'

'Snorri Godi told them that the sum is guaranteed. He is holding a surety for that amount.'

'What do you mean? Snorri won't lie about something like that.'

'He didn't,' said Thrand. 'I've left thirty marks of hack silver with him.'

I was stunned.

But Thrand had not finished. 'I also went to see Grettir and had a talk with him, told him about the scorn poles and asked him what he wanted to do about it. As I expected, he took the matter in his stride. Commented that far worse things were being said about him and one more false accusation would make no difference. When I suggested that he could solve all his problems by leaving the country and that you would probably go with him, he answered that he had no intention of running away from his enemies, which you knew already. Also to tell you that his younger brother, Illugi, has now grown to manhood, and that he felt he should stay to protect him. Grettir still feels guilty that he deserted his older brother Atli, who was killed during his first outlawry. He asked me to wish you well on your travels.'

'My travels?' I asked.

'Yes,' Thrand replied 'I told Grettir that you and I were leaving Iceland for a while, long enough for the scandal to die down and for you to have a chance to win the thirty marks to redeem your mundur.'

'Thrand,' I said, 'I'm deeply grateful to you for the money you have left with Snorri Godi, but there's no reason for you to desert your farm.'

Thrand shrugged. 'I have been sitting too long in this quiet corner. I feel the wanderlust coming back, and I want to return to the places I knew as a young man, the places where I won my silver. Who knows – you may do the same.'

'You never told me where or how you got your hoard,' I said.

'Until now there was no need. Besides, I had my reasons for remaining silent,' he answered. 'But you should know that I fought with the felag, with the Jomsvikings.'

Every boy in Iceland who dreamed of plunder and martial glory had heard about the Jomsvikings, but I had not known whether they were mythical or whether they really existed. If Thrand said they were real, then I was prepared to take his word on it.

'What did Grettir say when you told him that you and I would be going abroad?'

'He quoted some lines from the Havamal:

> "A better burden may no man bear
> For wanderings wide than wisdom
> It is better than wealth on unknown ways
> And in grief a refuge it gives." '

Thrand looked at me and with a note of compassion in his voice said, 'Appropriate, don't you think?'

TEN

JOMSBURG WAS AN indistinct smudge on the horizon for half a day. Since first light our ship, a weather-beaten merchantman owned by a syndicate of Wendish traders, had been edging slowly towards the home of the Jomsvikings, yet by noon we did not seem to have come any closer. After the dramatic cliffs and rocky shores of Iceland and Norway, I was disappointed by the apparently featureless Baltic coast ahead. Its monotony was accentuated by the grey overcast sky reflected in murky water under our keel. Thrand and I had already spent two weeks on the voyage and I was impatient to reach our destination. I stood gripping the weather shrouds as if I could drag the vessel bodily forward.

'We'll arrive at the time the Gods have decided, and that will be soon enough,' said Thrand, noting my mood.

'Is that where you won your hoard?' I asked, staring towards the dark line on the horizon where the sky met the sea.

'Not here, but in the company of comrades who lived here,' he replied.

'When was the last time you saw them?'

'Not since the great battle in Jorunga Bay against Earl Haakon of Norway more than thirty years ago.'

'Do you have any idea what might have happened to them since then? Have you heard anything?'

'No, not after our defeat,' he answered and walked away to the far side of the deck and stood staring down into the water, his face expressionless.

I would have left the matter there if one of the Wendish sailors had not sidled up to me. Ever since Thrand and I had joined the ship as passengers, the man had been glancing at my taciturn companion, trying not to let his curiosity show. Now as our ship crept closer to Jomsburg, the sailor took his chance to ask the question that had been on his mind for days.

'Old Jomsviking, eh?' he enquired in his heavily accented Norse, jerking his head at Thrand.

'I don't know,' I replied.

'Looks Jomsviking, sure,' said the sailor. 'Going to Jomi. Maybe for his friends. But not many to find now. They liked to die.'

I waited for a few moments and then crossed to where Thrand stood watching the water rippling gently past our scuffed hull and asked him what the sailor had meant. There was a long silence before the tall Icelander finally replied and he spoke so quietly that I had to strain to hear him. For the first time in all the years I had known him, Thrand's voice had a tremor of emotion. Whether it was sorrow, pride or shame, I could not tell.

'Only eighty came out of the sea battle alive; eighty of all those who did not turn their backs on the enemy. They took refuge on an island and ten of them died of exposure before the enemy hunted them down and brought the survivors before their executioner. Thorkel Leira was his name. Earl Haakon had ordered that no Jomsviking was to be left alive. Their hands and legs were bound so tightly that a stick had to be thrust through their hair – they took great pride in braiding their hair before battle – and each man was half-carried to his fate, as if he was a dead animal brought home on a pole after the hunt. The headsman asked the same question of each man, "Are you afraid of dying?"'

'What did they reply?'

'Some answered, "I am content to die," or words to that

effect. Others insisted that they be allowed to face the headsman's sword so they could see the blow coming. One man's last request was that his hands should be untied so he could hold a dagger in the air while his head was lopped from his shoulders.'

'Why such a strange request?' I commented. 'What could he have been thinking of?'

'He said that in the Jomsviking barracks he and his companions had often discussed if the mind resides in the head or in the body, and now he had the chance to settle the matter. He had decided to hold up the dagger after death, so if he let it drop when his head left his body, then his head was the seat of his decision. However, if the dagger stayed clutched in his hand, then his body had made the decision and was sticking to it.'

'And what was the outcome of the experiment?'

'The dagger hit the ground before his body.'

'If I understood the Wend properly, he said that a few of the Jomsvikings survived. So why did Earl Haakon spare their lives when he had sworn to kill them all?'

Thrand smiled grimly. 'It was Sven the son of Bui's doing. He had exceptional yellow hair, long and glossy, and he was very proud of it. He grew it almost to his waist and spent a great deal of time combing and arranging it. When his turn came to go before the executioner he asked for someone to be assigned to hold up his hair so it did not get bloodstained when his head came off. Thorkel Leira agreed, and told his chief assistant to hold the hair to one side. Then just as Thorkel made his sword stroke, Sven jerked his head forward, pulling the assistant off balance so the sword struck the man's wrists, cutting off a hand. Of course Thorkel Leira was furious and was about to take a second cut at Sven and behead him properly when Earl Haakon, who had seen what happened, intervened. He said that the Jomsvikings were proving so awkward even in the manner of their death, that it would be easier to set the remainder free if they promised never to take up arms against him again. He knew that a Jomsviking honours his word.'

'How many were left alive to make that promise?'

'Just twenty-five of the eighty who were captured,' Thrand answered, and before I could put the obvious question he added, 'and, yes, I was one of them.'

It was dusk by the time our ship entered the channel leading to Jomsburg itself, and by then I realised I had been mistaken about the apparent monotony of the coastline. The final stages of our approach revealed a long line of cliffs, not ragged and raw as in Iceland, but a regular wall of brown and grey rock. At its foot a beach of rocks and boulders gradually changed to a long strip of white sand backed by dunes. Here we turned into a river mouth to find a town built on an island where a steep hill rose close to the bank. Its summit provided the site for the stronghold of the Jomsvikings. Watchtowers dominated a palisaded citadel and two long breastworks extended down the slope of the hill to enclose a military harbour within the protective perimeter. Heading for the commercial wharves, our ship continued upstream, and I noticed Thrand look into the mouth of the Jomsviking harbour as we passed. He must not have liked what he saw. The pilings which fronted the river were in poor condition, their timbers soggy and rotten. Two massive wooden gates faced with iron plates had formerly protected the entrance – in times of siege they could be swung closed, sealing off the harbour inside. Now they were sagging and askew, and the ramparts which had allowed the defenders to hurl missiles at their attackers were crumbling. The stronghold of the Jomsvikings looked rundown.

As soon as we docked, Thrand and I left the ship and set off for the citadel. The town looked prosperous enough and was far larger than I had expected, with a regular grid pattern of streets and numerous stalls, warehouses and shops, now shuttered up for the night. It was when we began to climb the hill towards the Jomsviking citadel that signs of neglect reappeared. The roadway was potholed and weeds grew along each side. Nor was the main gateway leading into the citadel properly guarded. A trio of bored soldiers made no attempt to stop us as we walked through the gate into the main enclosure. The space inside was a large oval and in its centre was a parade ground. On each side stood four large barn-like structures, which were clearly barracks. Each building was at least eighty paces in length, and solidly built from heavy tree trunks in blockhouse construction, with a roof of wooden shingles. I noted that three of the barracks were derelict. Their roofs had holes and in several places the roof ridges sagged. Only the fourth barrack block, the one nearest the entrance gate, was still in use. Its roof was neatly patched, smoke arose from several chimney holes, and at least a score of men were seated on benches at the main doorway, talking or playing a board game set on a trestle table between them.

As Thrand and I walked towards them, they looked up. Thrand was still twenty paces away when I saw one of the men rise to his feet. He was a leathery-looking character, dressed in sombre civilian clothes but with the unmistakable bearing of a professional warrior. Judging by his grey hair, he was about the same age as my companion. Suddenly he slammed his hand down on the table, making the game pieces jump into the air. 'Thrand!' he called. 'By the head of Hymir's ox! it must be Thrand. I would know those long shanks anywhere!' He hurried across to my companion and seized him in a bear hug. 'I never thought to see you again!' he cried. 'Where have you been all these years?' I heard rumours that you were with a raiding party in the Irish Sea, but that was at least ten years back and since then there was no further news.'

'I've been living quietly in Iceland,' answered Thrand, 'until I felt it was time to see what had happened to the old felag.'

'Things aren't at all what they used to be, as you can see,' said the old soldier, waving at the empty barrack buildings. 'But never mind, that will change. We're gaining recruits, though not as many as I would wish and we are not as strict as before about their qualifications. Here, let me introduce you.'

Proudly he steered Thrand towards the group of loungers and began to make introductions. Thrand, he boasted to them, had

been a member of the brotherhood in the glory days, had fought
Earl Haakon's men at Jorunga Bay and survived. He was a
warrior of experience and knew what it was like to be a true
Jomsviking. His description of my companion was so extravagant
that I began to wonder if there was a purpose behind it, and
looked more closely at his audience. They were a mixed lot. Some
were scarred warriors, while others were considerably younger
without a martial bearing. Nor, judging by their appearance, were
they all Norsemen. Several had square Wendish faces; others were
narrow jawed with foxy eyes and probably came from the Permian
regions further north. Their only common feature was that they
all wore good daggers, and many were dressed in the padded
jerkins which are worn beneath the chain-mail shirt the northerners call a byrnie.

'Who's your companion?' asked Thrand's acquaintance, whose
name I later found out was Arne.

'He is called Thorgils. He came with me from Iceland.'

'Is he a fighting man?'

'More of a traveller and observer,' said Thrand, 'He is a
devotee of Odinn the Far-farer.'

'Well, Odinn is the God of battles, too, so he may find himself
at home among us—'

Thrand interrupted him. 'To whom should I report?'

Arne checked his enthusiasm and looked a little awkward. He
drew Thrand away from the group, out of earshot, and I followed.

'It's not like the old days, at least not yet,' Arne told us. 'The
felag all but disintegrated after the disaster against Earl Haakon.
There were so few left to continue the fellowship – only a couple
of dozen who were on sick leave or had stayed behind to garrison
Jomsburg, plus the handful of battle survivors. And many of
them, like yourself, we never thought to see again. Of course, the
others were too ashamed to return.'

'You had better explain to Thorgils,' said Thrand. He had
noticed that I was listening. 'If you want to recruit him to the
fellowship, he should know the truth.'

Arne spat in the dust. 'Sigvaldi, Thorkel and the others – they and their crews withdrew from the battle line when they saw that our ships were heavily outnumbered by the Norwegians. They broke their solemn vow as Jomsvikings and retreated, leaving the likes of Thrand to face the enemy unsupported. Their bad faith did more damage to the felag than losing the battle. Defeat and death we were prepared for, but against cowardice and dishonour we had no defence.'

Thrand later told me his comrades were so ashamed when several Jomsviking ships deserted the battle line that they debated whether to challenge their colleagues and fight them in order to obliterate the dishonour. As it was, they hurled spears and stones at their retreating boats and shouted curses in their wake, before turning to face the Norwegian onslaught.

Arne continued. 'Sigvaldi was among the first to run away, and the worst thing about it was that he was our leader. In those days we all swore to follow just one man as our absolute commander. He decided everything for the felag, whether it was the division of our booty or the settlement of quarrels between us. And when a leader fails so abjectly, it is difficult afterwards to regain respect for leadership. That is why now we rule ourselves by council – a gathering of the senior men decides what we should do. I've little doubt, Thrand, that you will be elected to that council.'

Thrand was looking across at the barracks where a couple of women were loitering. 'I see there are other changes too,' he remarked.

Arne followed his gaze. 'Yes,' he said, 'but you know as well as I do that the regulation forbidding women into the fortress was frequently ignored. Women were smuggled into the barracks and Sigvaldi turned a blind eye to the practice. He said that it was better to have the women here than for the men to slip away into the town and stay there without permission.'

Thrand said nothing, but every line of his face showed his disapproval.

'There's one rule which you will be glad we have set aside,' Arne added slyly. 'We no longer insist that every member of the felag must be between the ages of eighteen and fifty. You and I are getting long in the tooth, and the council has agreed to admit every man who has battle experience, whatever his age, provided he is still fit enough to hold spear and shield in the first or second line. To back them up, we've put in place a training programme for all our new recruits.'

Over the next four weeks I learned what he meant. I was assigned to the training platoon, while Thrand was received back into the ranks of the Jomsvikings and, as Arne had predicted, voted onto their council within days. My fellow recruits were a ragbag assortment of volunteers – Saxons, Wagrians, Polabians, Pomeranians and others. Their reasons for joining the fellowship were as varied as their origins. I found myself learning the rudiments of warfare alongside malcontents and misfits, fugitives escaping justice and opportunists who had come to Jomsburg in the hope of winning plunder. There was also a handful of adventurers and romantics who genuinely hoped to restore the past glory of what had once been the most famous and respected military brotherhood of the northern lands.

We came under the authority of a crop-headed, irascible instructor who reminded me of one of Edgar's hunting dogs, the short-legged variety we put down a badger hole to flush out the occupant, which has a habit of suddenly twisting round and giving its handler a nasty bite. Like the little yapping dogs, our instructor had a loud and incessant bark. He was an Abodrite, a member of the tribe on whose territory Jomsburg had been built, and he never lost an opportunity to show up our ignorance. On the very first day of training he took us into the Jomsviking armoury. We looked around in awe. The Jomsviking weapons store had once equipped a battle group of a thousand men and it still held an impressive array of arms. Many were now rusty and blunt, but the best of them were still greased and arranged on their wooden racks by a crippled armourer, who remembered the days when a dozen smiths and their assistants had wrought and repaired hundreds of swords, axes and spearheads to equip the felag.

'Pick out the weapon you would take into battle if you could carry only one weapon and nothing else,' snapped our instructor, pointing to the largest man in our group, a big shambling Dane, who stood bemused by the choice. After a moment's hesitation, the Dane reached out and selected a heavy sword. Its blade was as long as my arm, and it had a workmanlike brass handle. It seemed a sensible selection.

Without a word our instructor took up a shield with a metal rim and told the Dane. 'Now take a swing at me.'

The Dane, irritated by the instructor's cocksure manner, did as he was told. He lashed out at the instructor, who deftly interposed his shield, edge on. The heavy sword blade met the metal rim and promptly snapped, the blade spinning away from the handle. The instructor stepped up close to the Dane, rammed his shield boss into the Dane's stomach, and the big man fell on the ground in a heap.

'Swords may look good,' announced the instructor, 'but unless you know their true quality don't trust them. They're treacherous in your hand, and you won't find the very best blades in an armoury.'

He caught my eye. 'Here you, the Icelander, what should he have chosen as his weapon?'

The answer was obvious. 'He should have chosen a good spear,' I said.

'And what would you do with it? Throw it at your enemy?'

I remembered how Grettir had lost the head of his spear when he threw it at Oxenmight. 'No, I would use it like a lance, thrusting at my opponent, keeping him at a distance, until I found an opening.'

'Right. So that's what I'm going to teach you lot. Swords are first-class weapons when they are in skilled hands and under the right circumstances. But for well-trained troops the real killing tool is the humble spear, straight and true, and with a shaft of hardened ash.'

So for the first ten days he drilled us only with the spear. He taught us to hold the weapon high in our right hands, the shaft projecting behind the shoulder, so that we could thrust downwards and use our body weight behind the thrust. It was tiring work, but nothing as exhausting as when we were issued with round limewood shields. 'Close up! Close up! Close up tighter!' he ranted as we shuffled sideways on the parade ground, shoulder to shoulder, holding our shields before us and trying to fill every gap in the line to make a wall. 'Closer together, you louts!' he would scream, and then come charging at us and deliver a massive flat-footed kick at the weakest man in the line. When his victim staggered back, leaving a gap, the instructor charged in, wielding a heavy baton and lashing out at the two men on each side who were now exposed. As they rubbed their bruises, he would bellow at the unfortunate man who had wilted, 'You fall and the comrades on each side of you die! Shoulder to shoulder, shield to shield, that's your only hope.'

Gradually we became better at withstanding his frenzied assaults. The line buckled, but did not break, and we learned when it was safe to stand with our shields rim to rim or – in the face of a massed charge – to form up in even closer order, our shields overlapping so that the rim touched the shield boss of the man to our left. Then our shield wall, the burg as our instructor called it, seemed to be nearly impregnable.

We became so confident in our defensive skills that the big Dane felt bold enough to question our instructor when he told us that we had to repeat all our training, but this time dressed in byrnies, the hot and heavy chain-mail shirts.

Our instructor smiled grimly. He ordered us to set up a shield on a wooden frame and place behind it a pig's carcass. He then went to the armoury and fetched a throwing spear. Marking off twenty paces, he took aim and threw the first javelin. The missile struck the shield, the metal head passed clean through and pierced the dead pig a hand's breadth deep. 'Now,' barked our instructor, 'you can see why in future you will drill wearing Odinn's web, your byrnies.'

So it was back to the armoury to try to find byrnies that would fit us, and then we spent an entire day scouring and oiling their metal rings so they slid more smoothly and restricted our movements to a minimum. I still felt like a crab in its shell after I had tugged the mail shirt over my head and put on the cone-shaped metal helmet that the armourer issued to me. The helmet's central noseguard made me squint and I tried easing the chin strap and shifting the helmet so that I could see straight. A moment later a blow from behind me sent the helmet spinning to the ground and my instructor was snarling in my face.

'See this scar here?' he yelled, pointing at a groove that ran across his scalp. 'Got that from Courlander's sword when I left my helmet strap too loose.'

Recalling those sweaty, dusty days of training on the parade ground, I now understand that our instructor knew we were too raw to be any use on the battlefield unless we could be trained to work in unison. So he made us rehearse again and again the basic battlefield manoeuvres – staying in a tightly packed group as we wheeled to left or right, retreating in good order one step at a time, or forming a disciplined front when the first rank dropped on one knee so the spears of the second rank projected over their shoulders in a bristling hedge. Then, on his command, we all sprang to our feet and went charging forward, spears at the ready. Even in close combat, our instructor did not trust us to fight singly, one on one. He made us fight as pairs, one man knocking aside his opponent's shield, while his comrade stabbed a spear through the gap.

Only after we were reasonably proficient with the spear did he allow us to handle axes and swords. Then he showed us how to aim our blows rather than chop, hack and thrust indiscriminately. For our graduation class we learned the 'swine array', an arrowhead formation, a single man at the point, two men behind him in the second rank, three men in the third rank, four men behind them and so forth. On his command we all lumbered forward and to our amazement, for we were rehearsing against a shield burg of the older men, the weight of our charge broke their line, and our point man, the beefy Dane again, was thrust right through the opposition.

Each day, after drill and training, the recruits joined the senior members of the felag for the evening meal. I never imagined that so many words could be expended on discussing, for instance, the relative merits of the spear with a broad flange against the narrow-bladed spear, or whether it is better to sling a sword scabbard from the right or the left shoulder, and whether it should hang vertically or horizontally. Usually these discussions were accompanied by practical demonstrations. Some burly warrior would get up from his bench and strike a pose, grasping his spear shaft or sword hilt to show what he considered the proper grip, then making a series of mock passes with the weapon. After much drink had been consumed and arguments arose, it was remarkable that these differences of opinion did not lead to open fights between armed men who were both boastful and belligerent. But the rules of the Jomsviking fellowship held: each man considered the others to be his brothers.

Thrand, like myself, found many of these discussions tedious, and the two of us would leave the barracks and spend the evening strolling about the town of Jomi. Our initial impression of its prosperity had been correct. The place was thriving. Traders came from as far afield as the Greek lands to purchase the amber carvings for which the place was famous, though the majority of the merchants were from the other major Baltic ports – Hedeby, Bjorko, Sigtuna and Truso. Besides their pottery, furs, leather goods and other wares, they brought news of what was going on in the outside world. Knut, it seemed, had grown so powerful and rich that there was talk he might proclaim himself emperor of the north. Already he held both England and Denmark, and he was

claiming sovereignty over Norway as well. The merchants, whose
trade depended on continued peace, were divided as to the merits
of Knut's ambition. Some thought it would be beneficial if all the
northern lands were united under a single ruler; others feared that
Knut's pretensions would lead to war. The traders who arrived
from Sweden were the most sceptical. They were followers of the
Old Ways and pointed out that Knut was increasingly under the
influence of the followers of the White Christ, and that where
Knut ruled the Christians followed. Among the townsfolk of Jomi,
the Swedes had a sympathetic hearing, for although Christians
were allowed to practise their religion in Jomi, the city council
had ruled that their observances must be done discreetly. No
church bells were allowed.

The traders had a finely tuned instinct for politics. One
evening Thrand and I had gone to visit the temple of Svantevit,
the local four-faced Wendish God. His sacred animal is a white
stallion used for divination, and we had seen the priests lead out
the horse and coax him between three rows of wooden stakes as
they watched anxiously, believing that if the horse steps first with
its right foot then their presaging is true. As Thrand and I re-
entered the Jomsviking citadel, we found a delegation from Knut
himself. To my delight the embassy was led by a man I recognised
– one-legged Kjartan who had stood beside me when Edgar died
in the boar hunt and had assisted my escape from London.

'Thorgils!' he exclaimed, thumping me on the shoulder with
his fist. 'Who would have thought to find you here! It's good to
see you.'

'How's Gisli the One Hand?' I asked.

'Fine, fine,' Kjartan replied, looking around at the parade
ground. 'You can't imagine how good it is to be here, away from
those canting Christians. I've still got those wax coins you gave
me. I suppose you know that Archbishop Wulfstan, that wily
schemer, died.'

'No, I hadn't heard.'

'Last year he finally went to meet his maker, as he would have put it, and good riddance. But sadly his departure to join his precious angels has had little effect on the king's court. There seem to be just as many Christians in positions of power, and they are making life difficult for the Old Believers. Queen Emma encourages them, of course. She goes nowhere unless she is accompanied by a pack of priests.'

'What about Aelfgifu?' It was a question I could not hold back.

Kjartan gave me a shrewd glance and I wondered just how much he knew.

'She's well, though we don't see much of her now. Either she's at her father's place in Northampton or she travels overseas as Knut's representative.'

At that point a trumpet sounded. The felag was called to attend to a meeting in the great hall and Kjartan turned to go. 'I hope we'll have the chance to remember our days in Northampton and London,' he said.

The meeting was packed. Every Jomsviking, whether veteran or recent recruit, had assembled to hear what Kjartan had to say. He was escorted into the hall by two leading members of the felag's ruling council, who introduced him to his audience. He spoke clearly and firmly, and his soldierly bearing and battle injury made his audience listen respectfully. His message was clear enough: King Knut, ruler of England and Denmark and rightful heir to the throne of Norway, invited the Jomsvikings to join his cause. War was looming. The enemies of the king – Kjartan described them as a league of resentful earls forgetful of their oaths of loyalty, warlords from Norway and Sweden, and a false claimant to the Norwegian throne – were assembling an army to challenge Knut's authority. King Knut, of course, would crush them, and in victory he would remember and reward those who had helped him. There would be much booty to distribute – here an appreciative murmur rose from the listening warriors – and there was fame to be won.

Kjartan reminded his listeners of the renown of the Jomsvikings, their illustrious history and their prowess as fighting men. Finally, he proffered the bait that, all along, he knew would most tempt his audience. 'King Knut holds you in such high regard,' he announced, 'that he has authorised me to offer each one of you fifteen marks of silver if you agree to fight on his behalf, half to be paid now, and half to be paid on the conclusion of the campaign.'

It was a munificent offer and characteristic of Knut's statecraft: silver coins rather than iron weapons were his tools of preference.

When Kjartan had finished speaking, a senior member of the Jomsviking council rose to reply. It was a generous proposal, worthy of a generous ruler, he began. He himself would recommend acceptance, but it was the custom of the Jomsviking assembly that any member of the felag could state his views, whether for or against, and he called upon anyone who wished to express an opinion to speak up. One after another, Jomsvikings came forward to address the assembly. All were in favour of accepting Knut's offer, which was not surprising. The advance payment of fifteen marks for every man was an enticing prospect and it seemed that further discussion was a mere formality. Until Thrand spoke.

He had been sitting with the other members of the council, and when he rose to give his opinion a hush fell on the gathering. Everyone in the hall also knew that he was a survivor of the original felag.

'Brothers of the felag,' he began, 'before you make your decision whether or not to accept the King of England's offer, I want his emissary to answer one question.' Turning to Kjartan, he asked, 'Is it true that in agreeing to join King Knut's army, we could find ourselves fighting alongside, or even under the command of, Knut's deputy in military affairs: the leader of the royal huscarls, his earl known as Thorkel the Tall?'

The man standing beside me abruptly sucked in his breath, as though a raw nerve had been exposed. Behind Thrand several older members of the council looked uncomfortable.

'And am I right in thinking,' Thrand continued, 'that this same Thorkel, more than thirty years ago, broke his Jomsviking vow when he, with his crew, turned tail and abandoned his brothers who were left, unaided, to fight the Norwegian Haakon and his fleet?'

A terrible hush had fallen over the assembly. A few paces from me someone was whispering to his neighbour the story of the disgrace, when the honour of the Jomsvikings was shattered.

Kjartan rose to give his answer. All could see that he had been shaken. He had not anticipated this. Thrand's question implied that no Jomsviking should go to the assistance of a man who had betrayed the fellowship. We waited expectantly. The pause lengthened slowly and became an embarrassment. I felt sorry for Kjartan. He was a soldier, not a diplomat, and he could not come up with the fine words to wriggle out of the dilemma.

When he finally spoke he was hesitant. 'Yes, Knut's most trusted earl is the same Thorkel who was a member of your fellowship. Thorkel has become a great war leader, won riches, earned the confidence of the king. I believe that you should be proud of what he has become, rather than remember what happened thirty years ago.'

His words made little impression. I could feel the scepticism of the crowd grow around me, their mood suddenly changed. Kjartan felt it too. He knew that his mission was on the verge of collapse. He scanned the faces of the crowd. I was standing close to the front, looking up at him and, like all the others, waiting for him to continue. Our eyes met, and suddenly Kjartan announced.

'You don't have to take my word for it. One of your own brotherhood has met Thorkel the Tall at King Knut's court, and he can tell you about him now.' He beckoned to me and, after a moment's surprised hesitation, I stepped forward to stand beside him. He gripped my elbow and whispered in my ear, 'Thorgils, for the memory of Edgar the huntsman, try to say something to make them accept my proposal.'

Turning to face my audience, my breath seemed to leave my

lungs. A couple of hundred warriors were looking at me curiously and I could scarcely breathe. For the first time in my life I had been called upon to address a large gathering and my mind was in turmoil. I realised that I held the balance between two men to whom I owed great debts: Thrand, who had been my mentor over the years, and Kjartan, who had stood by me when I was in desperate need in England. I had to find a middle way without dishonouring either man.

Odinn came to my rescue.

I cleared my throat and, stammering over the first few syllables, said, 'I am Thorgils, a follower of Odinn, and I have always let the High One be my guide – Kjartan is my friend and I know him to be an honest man, so I believe he is carrying an honest message. Thrand is also my friend and has told me of the cowardice of Thorkel and the others in the fight against Earl Haakon. Yet I have seen how high Thorkel the Tall then rose in the court of King Knut, and I know that he would never have achieved such fame and wealth if he had stayed to fight and die. So I say – let Odinn's wisdom guide you, and accept this as his sign. Seventy survivors of our felag came before Earl Haakon for judgement, and this is the seventieth of the High One's sayings.'

Here I paused to draw breath before reciting:

> 'It is better to live than to lie a corpse,
> I saw flames rise before a rich man's pyre
> and before his door he lay dead.'

Kjartan saw his chance. He quoted the next verse for me.

> 'The lame rides a horse, the handless is herdsman
> The deaf in battle is bold
> No good can come of a corpse.'

A low mutter of approval came from the crowd, and a voice from the back shouted, 'Forget about Thorkel. Odinn had other plans for him. I'm all for the accepting Knut's silver.'

One by one, the members of the council spoke up and all

were in favour of Kjartan's proposition. Only Thrand failed to speak. He sat there silent, and on his face was the same distant expression that I had seen while he gazed into the ship's wake and thought of the defeat at Hjorunga Bay.

As the assembly began to dissolve, Kjartan took me aside to thank me. 'Your speech made all the difference,' he said. 'Without it, the men would not have committed themselves to fight for Knut.' Then he smiled. 'With my wooden leg, I liked the bit about the lame being able to ride a horse. But I'm not sure that when I get back to London I should tell Gisli One Hand that, according to you and Odinn, he should become a cowherd.'

'It was All-Father Odinn who spoke through me and swayed the minds of the audience,' I replied. What I did not tell Kjartan was that, after a month in Jomsburg, I knew that the new order of Jomsviking could never resemble the felag Thrand had known. The new Jomsvikings were driven by their thirst for silver, not glory, and in the end they would have accepted Knut's bribe whatever Thrand had said. By citing the High One, I had given Thrand a reason to accept their decision with no loss to his own sense of honour or duty to his fallen comrades.

ELEVEN

WE WERE SUMMONED to earn our fifteen marks of silver early in September. Knut moved against the forces massing to oppose him, and sent a messenger to tell the Jomsvikings to join his fleet, now on its way from England. His messenger slipped into our citadel disguised as a Saxon trader because Knut's enemies already lay between us and the man whose pay we had taken. To the west of Jomsburg a great Norwegian force was raiding Knut's Danish territories, while their allies, the Swedes, were harrying the king's lands in Skane across the Baltic Sea. This left the felag dangerously isolated and our council met to discuss how best we should respond. After much debate it was decided to send two shiploads of volunteers, the most experienced warriors, to run the gauntlet and join the king. The rest of the Jomsvikings, fewer than a hundred men, would remain to garrison the citadel against any enemy attack.

'Stay and complete your training,' Thrand advised me. He was packing his war gear into the greased leather bag which also served as his sleeping sack while on campaign. As one of the most experienced fighters in the felag, he had been appointed second in command of one of the two ships in our little expeditionary force. My speech in defence of Thorkel the Tall at the assembly seemed to have done no damage to our friendship, though Thrand was so taciturn that it was difficult to tell what he was thinking.

'I've already volunteered to join the expedition,' I told him. 'If I'm to take Knut's silver, then I feel I ought to earn it. Besides, our battle drills are becoming very repetitive.'

'As you wish,' said Thrand. He slid his sword halfway out of its scabbard to check the blade for rust, and then carefully eased it back into the sheath. The scabbard was lined with unwashed sheep wool, the natural oils in the fleece protecting the metal from decay. As an added precaution he began to wind a linen strip around the hilt to seal the gap where the blade entered the scabbard. He paused from the work and looked up.

'Be warned: Knut wants the Jomsviking as warriors in his line of battle. That is what you have trained for. But if it comes to a sea action, all that training is next to useless. There's no chance for the swine array or shield walls. Ship fights are close up and brutal. Most of the engagement is pitiless and chaotic, with a good deal of luck as to who emerges the victor.'

That afternoon I went to the armoury to withdraw my weaponry for the expedition. When I had been a new recruit, the crippled armourer had been casual, issuing me with a mail shirt in need of repair and the weapons that were closest to hand. This time, knowing that I was going into action, he took greater care, and I emerged from the armoury with a helmet that fitted me properly and a byrnie of a new design. Attached to the helmet was a small curtain of mail that hung across my lower face, protecting my throat. He also produced for me a good sword with an inlaid metal handle, two daggers, half a dozen javelins, an ash spear and a round limewood shield, as well as a short-handled battleaxe. When I stacked this assortment of weaponry on the ground beside Thrand, he commented, 'if I were you, I would change the grip on that sword. Wrap that showy metalwork with tarred cord so that your hand does not slip when your palm gets sweaty. And you'll need a second shield.'

'A second shield?'

'Every man brings a second shield. Nothing fancy, just a light wooden disc. They'll be arranged along the side of the vessel –

there's a special slot along the upper strake to hold them — and they'll make a fine display. In my experience much of warfare is decided by appearances. Strike fear into your enemy by how you look or act before the first blow and you've won half the battle.'

A spoked wheel with alternating fields of red, black and white was the pattern that the council chose for our insignia, and I had to admit it looked imposing when the shields were set in place. They gave our two ships a professional air, though a trained eye would have noted that the vessels, like the Jomsviking harbour, were antiquated and in a poor repair. The two drakkar, longships of medium size, were all that now remained of a Jomsviking fleet of thirty vessels, the great majority of which had been sunk or captured in Earl Haakon's time. These two survivors were leaky and their timbers were suspect. The felag's shipwrights had struggled to make them seaworthy, caulking seams and applying a thick layer of black pitch to the outside of the hulls. But the deck planks were warped and cracked, and there were splits and shakes in the masts. Fortunately the Jomsburg lowlands grew flax so we were able to obtain new sails and rigging at short notice. But nothing could hide the fact, as we set out on a bright and crisp September day, that our two vessels were unhandy and slow, and their sixty-man crews were badly out of practice as sailors.

A fully manned drakkar offers little comfort to her crew. By the time we had loaded aboard all our weapons and equipment, the spaces between the sea chests which served as our oar benches were so crammed with gear that there was very little room to move about. Our only gangway was a walkway of planks, laid along the middle of the vessel to connect the small platform in the bows of the drakkar with the stern deck, where our captain stood. He was a squat thug of a man, a Jute who had lost one eye in a minor skirmish and the wound made him look like a bandit. Indeed, as I glanced round at my companions with their diversity of homelands and racial features, I thought they looked more like a pirate crew than a trained fighting unit. The truth was that we were hired mercenaries, setting out for money and the chance of

loot – I wondered how long our discipline and our loyalty to the
felag would last.

Our inexperience showed in the chaos of our embarkation.
We found our places about the drakkars, unlashed the oars from
their stowage and fitted them to the thole straps. Men took
practice pulls with their oars to test their length and find their
own best position. Unless they were careful, they knocked into
their neighbours or struck the man sitting directly in front, hitting
him in the back with the loom of the oar. There were oaths and
angry grumbling in several languages and it was some time before
our captain was able to order the lines to be cast off. Our drakkars
pulled slowly out of the harbour, their oars moving to an uneven
beat as though we were two crippled insects.

The current was in our favour once we emerged through the
disused harbour gates, and as we rowed towards the river mouth
it became obvious which of our oarsmen had learned to row on
rivers and lakes and which were proper seamen. Those from
calmer waters pulled their oars in a long flat sweep, while the
experienced mariners used a shorter, chopping action, and of
course the two styles did not match. So there were more oaths
and arguments among the rowers, until our drakkars began to
pitch and roll on the first waves from the sea, and one of the river
rowers sprained his wrist. Luckily there was a brisk east wind to
speed us on our way, so we hoisted our brand-new sail, hauled
the oars inboard and relaxed, leaving the Jutish captain and his
helmsman to steer.

'Thank Svantevit for this wind,' said the Wend beside me,
reaching inside his shirt and producing a little wooden image of
his God. He found a niche for the talisman beside his seat and put
it there, then nodded towards the flat shoreline on our left. 'Anyone know this coast?'

A man three places from us must have been a Sjaellander, for
he answered, 'Used to sail past it with my uncle when we were
bringing his farm produce to Rugen. Not much to see, but easy
enough once you know the channels. Have to watch out for sand

and mudbanks, but there are plenty of creeks and bays handy for shelter if the wind blows up.'

'Rich country?' asked another voice hopefully.

'No, just farmlands; nothing of note until you get to Ringsted and that's Knut's domain, so I guess we'll be on our best behaviour if we stop there.'

'We won't be making any stops,' said a heavily bearded Skanian, one of our Danish volunteers. 'Rumour has it that Knut's fleet has left Limfiord and is heading for the sound and we're to rendezvous with him there.'

He spat over the side, and watched the spittle float away in our wake, judging the speed of our vessel. 'She's no racer,' he commented. 'In a wind like this she ought to be half as fast again.'

'Ballast's all wrong,' said a voice from somewhere amidships. 'She's too heavy in the bow.'

'Reckon the mast isn't stepped quite right either,' came a third opinion. 'Should be shifted aft a hand's breadth and the main halyard set up tighter.' As the discussion gathered pace I realised that sailors could spend as much time discussing the rig of their vessels as warriors in barracks spent comparing the merits of weapons.

That evening we landed on a stretch of deserted shore to make a meal and rest. There is no cooking hearth aboard a drakkar, so the crew eat cold food if they do not land. We brought the vessels close inshore, turned stern on, and after setting anchors to haul them off next morning, we backed water with the oars until the sterns touched the sand. That way, if there was an emergency or we needed to depart in a hurry, we could scramble aboard and leave in double-quick time. Not that we expected trouble. Few villages could muster enough men or courage to dispute the landing of two shiploads of armed men. The only glimpse we had of the local inhabitants was the distant figure of a shepherd running away down sand dunes to take a warning to his people. He left his flock behind, so we butchered ten of his sheep and feasted.

Next morning the wind was fluky, changing in strength and direction as we resumed our coastal passage. But the sun shone in a sky flecked with high, fast-moving white clouds. It felt like a holiday as we headed onward under sail, keeping well offshore.

'Wish all campaigning was like this,' commented the Sjaelander, who was proving to be the ship's chatterer.

By now most of the crew had learned how to make best use of the cramped space, stretching out on the lids of the storage chests that held their war gear. Folded sails and padded jerkins were their cushions. Thrand, I noticed, never joined us. As we sailed onward, he took up his position on the little foredeck, standing there watching the forward horizon or, more often, scanning the shoreline as we moved steadily northward.

Shortly before noon I became aware that Thrand's gaze had not shifted for some time. He was looking towards the land, his attention fixed. Something about his posture alerted me to turn around and look back at our captain. He was glancing in the same direction too, and then looking astern at the waves and sky, as if to check the wind speed and direction, and watching the bronze weathervane on our stern post. Everything seemed to be in good order. Our two ships were moving steadily forward, nothing had changed.

The Sjaelander, who had been stretched out on his back enjoying the warmth of the sun on his face, lazily rolled over on his side and raised his head to peer over the side of the drakkar. 'Soon be passing the entrance to the Stege Bight,' he said, and then, 'ah yes, there it is, I can see sails on the far side of that little island. They must be coming out from West Sjaelland.' He rolled back on his side and settled himself comfortably. 'Probably merchantmen on their way out to the sound.'

'If so, they've come to trade with swords not purses. Those are warships,' said the big Dane. He was standing on the oar bench, an arm shielding his eyes from the sun's reflection on the water, as he looked towards the distant sails. There was a sudden stir among our crew. Men sat up and looked around, several got to their feet and squinted in the same direction.

'How do you know they're warships?' asked one of the Wends. He had been one of the river rowers and this was clearly the first time he had been to sea.

'Some of those sails have stripes. Sign of a fighting ship,' answered the Dane.

I looked at our own new sail. It was unmarked. 'Maybe they'll mistake us for merchant ships as well.'

'I doubt it,' said the Dane. 'Merchant ships don't carry low, broad sails like ours. Their sails are taller and not so wide. As soon as they clear the island and get a good view of us, they'll recognise the outline of a drakkar hull and know we're not a pair of harmless trading ships. However, this may be a piece of luck. West Sjaelland is ruled by Earl Ulf, one of Knut's liegemen, and those ships could be on the way to reinforce Knut's war fleet. We'll be able to sail in company with them and if we run into the king's enemies they'll think twice about attacking such a large force.'

When the strange ships emerged from behind the dunes and into plain view, we saw that the big Dane had been correct, at least in part. Five ships came out from the sound. Three were drakkars like our own and two were trading knorrs, apparently under escort. Their position put them slightly upwind of us, and we watched them set their course to match our track, gradually closing the gap between us, as if to join us.

It is a commonplace to say that everything happens slowly at sea until the last moment, then all is haste and flurry, but it is true. For a while very little happened as all seven vessels carried steadily on their way – the five Danish ships sailing in company while our own helmsmen kept the two Jomsviking vessels close together, no more than fifty paces apart. As the gap between us and the approaching squadron dwindled, we gazed across at the strangers trying to learn more about them, until eventually our own Dane was able to confirm that they were indeed Earl Ulf's men. He knew the earl's livery and even thought he recognised some of the warriors aboard. Their two knorrs were clearly troopships carrying Danish levies, and their slower speed meant that the junction between our squadrons was leisurely.

Finally, in early afternoon, the leading Danish drakkar had pulled slightly ahead of her consorts, and was close enough for our Jutish captain to call out a greeting. 'Well met,' he bellowed, cupping his hands around his mouth so the sound carried over the waves washing along his vessel's side. 'Any news of Knut's fleet? We go to join the king.'

There was a long delay and I saw the Danish captain turn to consult his colleagues on the aft deck. Then he looked back at us and shook his head to indicate that he had not understood. He gestured for us to slow down so the ships drew closer, and held his hand to his ear.

'We go to join the king!' our skipper called out yet again. The Danish captain stepped up on the bulwarks of his ship, and one of his men reached and gripped him by the belt to hold him steady as if a slightly smaller gap would make the sound carry more clearly. 'Have you news of the royal fleet?' yelled our captain, adjusting the helm so that the wind spilled from our sail and our drakkar lost speed through the water.

'Watch out!' – a sudden roar from our fore deck. Most of our crew swung round to see Thrand standing there, waving an arm in warning. Those who did not look at Thrand saw one of the Danes on the aft deck stoop down and produce a javelin, hidden behind the bulwark, and hand it up to their skipper. He drew back his arm and threw the missile across the narrowing gap. Either it was a very lucky throw or the Dane was a champion spearsman, for the weapon flew across between the ships and struck our Jutish captain in his side. Even above the sound of the waves I heard the soft thump as the metal point of the weapon sank into his unprotected ribs. The Jute staggered and fell, knocking down the helmsman. There was a rush of feet, and

Thrand raced past us along the central walkway, his feet pounding the boards. He reached the aft deck, leaped to the helm and flung his weight on the bar, heaving it across so that our vessel sheered away downwind, and presented her stern to the attacking Danish ship.

'Ease the starboard sheet, square away,' he shouted.

The rest of us had been taken completely off guard. We were sitting or standing, numb with shock.

'Jump to it!' bellowed Thrand. He glanced back over his shoulder, judging the distance between our vessel and the hostile Danish longship. Our drakkar's sudden swerve had taken the Danes by surprise and for a moment they had overshot their quarry. There was confusion on their deck as they too adjusted sail to follow in our wake.

'I thought Ulf's people were king's men,' shouted the Wend beside me.

'Not all of them, it seems,' muttered the Sjaellander, as shocked as any of us by the sudden attack. 'There's treachery somewhere.'

Our entire crew was in turmoil. Some were searching for shields and weapons, others frantically donning their padded jackets, and opening the store chests to pull out their byrnies. Only a handful who were sensible enough to attend to the ship were checking that sheets and halyards were set up taut, and our venerable drakkar was sailing to best advantage.

Our consort, the second Jomsviking drakkar, had seen the ambush and was also adjusting sail. Our sudden swerve had taken them by surprise too, and we nearly collided with them as we changed course, passing within ten paces of the startled crew. That close encounter was nearly their undoing, for we were to windward and, as we passed, we took the wind from their sail and their drakkar lost speed. The pursuing Danes promptly switched their pursuit from us to our floundering consort. They swooped in close enough to launch a barrage of spears and stones, which rained down on the hapless Jomsvikings and we saw several men fall.

Now the Danes were roaring in triumph. One of them held up a red-painted shield, the sign of war. A warrior seated ahead of me cursed and left his oar bench to run aft to the stern deck, javelin in hand. He made ready to throw, but Thrand, without even looking round, reached out and held his arm.

'Don't waste the weapon,' he said. 'They are out of range. Keep your strength for rowing if it comes to that.'

By now our consort had managed to adjust her sail to the course and was beginning to pick up speed. The captain of the leading Danish longship was unwilling to close and board her in case we turned back to help and he found himself tackling two drakkars at the same time. We watched his crew delicately spill the wind from her huge sail with its red, green and white stripes, so she slowed in the water and allowed the two other Danish longships to catch up. The troop-carrying knorrs were left behind now that the trap was sprung. The Danes were intent on finishing off their prey, but they would do so in their own time.

The outcome of the chase was clear from the start. Our drakkars were built to an outmoded design. Old and worn-out, they could not match the speed of the Danish ships and the inexperience of our crews increased our handicap. The landsmen among us fumbled vital ropes and got in the way of those who knew what they were doing as they went about the delicate task of extracting the best possible speed from our drakkar. These novices were harshly commanded to sit still and shift position only when ordered to, and then to move smartly to the place indicated and stay there until instructed otherwise. They were movable ballast. The only time they were actively involved was when Thrand, who had assumed command, ordered every loose item on board, except our weapons and oars, to be thrown overboard to lighten the ship. Then the landsmen were set to prising up from the bilges the heavy stones which acted as our ballast and tossing them in our wake. But it made little difference to the pursuit. We watched the splashes as the pursuing Danes lightened their vessels too and slowly gained on us.

With the wind directly aft, our hope was that we could keep ahead of the chasing Danes long enough to evade them in the darkness or, better, meet friendly vessels from Knut's war fleet who would scare them off. Until then every member of our crew watched intently, trying to gage whether the gap between ourselves and the pursing longships was increasing or diminishing. Occasionally we glanced across at our consort, who copied our every manouevre and stratagem because it was vital that the two of us kept together. For when — not if — the Danes caught up with us, at least the odds would be no worse than three to two against us.

The Gods, whether Wendish or the Aesir, seemed to smile on us. The wind, which had continued to be erratic, picked up strength. This helped the older vessels because, in a strong wind, there was less difference in their speed against the newer Danish ships, and the more ground we covered the better were our chances of meeting Knut's fleet. So we kept up full sail, even though we could all hear the mast foot grinding in its wooden socket. The wind raised a succession of fast-moving swells which swept beneath us, heaving up the ancient hulls and making them twist and groan. The swell turned into long breaking waves, the spray flew back from the bows and as our craft began to swoop and sway the stress on the elderly hulls became more and more obvious.

That was when disaster struck. Perhaps it was the absence of ballast, or it might have been the clumsiness of her inexperienced crew which brought our companion, the second Jomsviking drakkar, to make a fatal error. The accident happened so suddenly that we did not know whether a main sheet snapped or the mast step slipped on the keelson, or whether it was just plain bad fortune that a larger swell lifted up our accompanying drakkar's stern at the very moment she dipped her bow to leeward and skidded sideways on the forward rush of water. The drakkar abruptly buried her nose in the back of a wave, tripped and slewed, and water began to pour into her open hull. Without her ballast to hold her steady, her sail was driving her forward at full tilt, and the inrush of water plunged her even further downwards. She ran herself underwater. One moment she was sailing at full speed on the surface, the next moment she was on her side, bow down and half submerged. The halt was so abrupt that most of her crew were flung headlong into the water, while the remainder were left clinging onto the stern deck, which was all that was left above the surface of the sea.

From the Danes came a roar of triumph and there were frantic signals from the leading longship, clearly the commander of their squadron. In answer the vessel nearest to the stricken drakkar swiftly dropped sail, put out oars and began to row, bearing down on her disabled victim. As our own boat fled on, we looked back, unnerved, and saw the Danes reach our comrades. They began spearing them like salmon trapped in a net, stabbing repeatedly downward on the swimmers. Those who were not massacred, had already drowned, pulled down by the weight of their mail. There would be no survivors.

Only Thrand seemed unmoved by the calamity. He stood on the aft deck, gaunt and intense, the helm still in his hand, his face showing no emotion as he kept his attention fixed on the set of our sail, the strength and direction of the wind and the balance of our vessel. Just twice he glanced back over his shoulder at the slaughter in our wake and then – without warning – he suddenly pushed across the helm so that our drakkar heeled over and came hard on the wind, heading for the distant shore. He gave no explanation for the sudden change of course, and once again the abruptness of the manoeuvre caught the Danes by surprise. We gained a few precious boat lengths on them. Along the oar benches we looked at one another, wondering what Thrand had in mind. Not one of us challenged his decision. From the moment he had seized the helm, he became our unquestioned leader. I swivelled in my seat and looked forward over the bows. Ahead the Sjaelland coast stretched away on either hand, low and flat without any sign of a harbour or a channel into which we might escape. Yet Thrand was aiming our vessel straight towards the distant shore as if he had a plan to save us.

The captains of the two Danish ships must have been equally perplexed because the furious pace of their pursuit slackened while they conferred, shouting across the gap between their vessels. Then they decided that, whatever we intended, they could still overhaul us before we reached the land. I saw their white bow waves surge up again and the slant of their masts increase as the two ships hardened up against the wind and resumed the chase. Aboard our drakkar the entire crew except for five sail handlers had scrambled to the windward side to improve the vessel's trim. Even the greenest of our recruits now knew that our lives depended on how well we coaxed our venerable vessel to her best performance.

Slowly and inexorably the Danish ships gained on us, while in the far distance the third of their vessels, having finished off our comrades, hoisted sail and set out to join in the hunt. We could only sit and watch the advancing enemy, and note how the best of their warriors had assembled in the bows, ready to hurl javelins at our helmsman the moment they were in range, hoping to strike him down and cripple our flight.

One of the Wends reached under his oar bench, pulled out his chain-mail shirt and began to tug it over his head.

'That'll drown you if we capsize,' warned his neighbour. 'Didn't you see what happened with our other drakkar?'

'Makes no difference,' the Wend replied. 'I don't know how to swim.'

The tension mounted as we watched the shoreline rush closer. It still appeared featureless, a low, sandy, yellow beach backed by dunes and sea grass. The place was uninhabited. There were no fishing skiffs drawn up on the beach, no houses, nothing – only gulls circling hungrily, squabbling amongst themselves over a shoal of sprats.

'No one lives here. It's too barren,' said the Sjaellander who had previously sailed this coast. 'There are only shallows, mud-banks and the occasional sand spit.'

The Danes very nearly caught us. Their leading ship was close enough for the first javelins to be thrown, and an arrow or two whizzed overhead, but without any harm. Judging his moment, Thrand again pushed over the rudder bar and altered course abruptly. Our drakkar swerved, and like two greyhounds which overshoot the hare as it jinks, the Danish vessels over-reached and had to check their onward rush before they picked up the hunt again. Thrand had managed his manoeuvre well. The leading Danish ship cut across the bows of its companion and for a few moments there was confusion as they adjusted sails to avoid a collision.

By then Thrand had turned our drakkar back onto her original course and once again we were heading straight for the shore at full pace. He was staring forward intently, ignoring the chasing ships behind him as we sped towards the strand. We were already in the outer surf before I understood what he intended. Ahead of us a long outer bank of sand ran parallel to the beach itself. Waves were breaking across the ridge of the sandbank, washing into the shallow lagoon which lay on the far side.

'We're going to smash to pieces when she hits,' muttered the man seated next to me. 'At this speed she'll burst her planks like a barrel loses staves when the hoops let go.'

'We've no choice,' I answered. 'It's either that or be run down by the longships.'

Our course did seem suicidal. In the last fifty paces approaching the sandbar our drakkar was picked up by each wave and flung forward bodily. We heard the surf hissing all around us. Our bellying sail continued to drive the vessel onward, the pace never slackening, until our progress had a wild, lurching motion. When the water shallowed and the waves became steeper, I saw Thrand suddenly snatch out the bar from the rudder. A moment later the rudder blade, projecting below our keel, struck the sand beneath us and the rudder head swung forward. Now we were completely out of control, without any steering. A sudden scraping shock ran through the hull as the keel hit the ridge of the sandbar. Then came a deeper hissing sound as the keel ploughed on through the sand, and we felt the hull scrape on the sandbank beneath our feet. The impact snapped the mast. It toppled forward, taking the sail with it and knocking the foredeck man into the water. Luckily he grabbed the side of the ship as he fell and managed to hang on, dangling there until he could heave himself back aboard. For a moment the drakkar floundered on the flat crest of the sandbank, her mast lying over the side, sail dragging in the water. But the sheer weight of her headlong rush had carried her to the crest of the submerged barrier, and a moment later a fortunate wave broke at just the right instant and washed her over the sandbar. With a grinding, slithering wrench our vessel scraped into the lagoon, more of a wreck than a ship.

The pursuing Danes promptly put up their helms and swerved away. Their captains had seen how close we had come to complete destruction. 'Reckon their keels draw maybe a span more water than we do,' commented one of our sailors. 'Reckless to try the bar and risk such fine new ships as theirs, not like our ramshackle old hull.'

'She did us well, didn't she?' enquired one of our landsmen.

'Yes' answered the sailor. 'For now.'

'What do you mean?' the man asked, but after a moment's thought he added, 'we're trapped, aren't we?'

Before anyone could reply, Thrand called for our attention. He stood on the stern deck looking down at us as our crippled vessel floated gently on the lagoon. After the hustle and panic of the chase everything had gone so quiet that he barely had to raise his voice. 'Brothers of the felag,' he began, 'now is the time we honour our oath to our fellowship. Even now our enemies are patrolling the sandbank, searching for a channel where they can safely enter the lagoon. When they find it, they will advance on us and we must prepare to fight and, if the Gods so decide, die as Jomsvikings.'

We had a respite before the Danes came at us again. We spent the interval cutting away the wreckage of the mast and disposing of the sail, and the tallest of our men waded ashore to collect large stones where a small stream washed into the lagoon and had exposed the bedrock. Then we put our drakkar in fighting trim, the decks cleared fore and aft, our sea chests arranged to make a fighting platform, and every man armed and wearing his byrnie and knowing his battle station. Thrand himself took up position once again on the bow platform, where the extra height of the upswept bow would give him best advantage. I went to join him, but he gently pushed me back. 'No,' he said, 'I need men here who are battle-tried,' and he beckoned to a Gothlander to join him. I was puzzled because the man seemed slightly mad. While we had been readying the ship for battle, he had stayed off to one side by himself, muttering and laughing into his beard, then suddenly scowling as if he saw an imaginary demon.

'Thorgils, there is something more important you must do,' Thrand said quietly. He was unwinding a cloth which had been tied around his waist like a sash. 'Go aft to the weathervane,' he continued. 'Remove the vane from its staff and in its place put this.' He handed me the cloth. The fabric was a dirty white, old and frayed. 'Go on,' Thrand said sharply, 'Hurry. It is Odinn's banner. It flew when we met Earl Haakon.'

Then I knew. Thrand had told me about the banner when I was his pupil in Iceland, but he had not mentioned that he was speaking from personal experience. Odinn's flag bears no emblem. But in battle all those who truly believe in the All-Father can read their fate upon it, for they see the figure of Odinn's bird, the raven, upon the cloth. If the raven struts and spreads its wings, then victory is assured. When it lowers its head and mopes, defeat is due. As I fastened the cloth to its staff, I tried my hardest to see the raven sign. But I could detect nothing, only a few creases and ancient stains on the fabric.

The banner hung limp from the staff, for the wind had died completely. I glanced up at the sky. It was the calm before a storm. Far to the north black clouds were gathering and the sky had an ominous, heavy overcast. In the distance I saw the flicker of a lightning strike and much later heard the faint and distant echo of thunder. Thor, not Odinn, seemed to be the God of that day.

I had barely lashed the banner in place when the Danes appeared, rowing along the length of the lagoon. They must have found a safe entry channel through the sandbar. Seeing that we made no move to escape and were helpless, they paused deliberately to lower their masts for fighting action. Then they set course to approach us, one from each side, forcing us to divide our defence. But to carry out the manoeuvre they had to row, and this cancelled out their advantage in numbers because a third of their men stayed seated as oarsmen. Also they failed to anticipate how well we had prepared. Their first over-confident approach was met with a hail of the stones and rocks we had gathered, which caught them completely off guard. The Danes could respond only with a few arrows and thrown spears which did little harm, while our barrage of well-directed missiles sent three of their men sprawling on top of their comrades at the oars. Our second barrage was even better aimed and the oarsmen on both Danish ships hurriedly backed water as their captains ordered a temporary withdrawal while they reassessed the situation. It was then that I heard a strange, wild howling burst out. Looking round to where Thrand stood on the foredeck, I saw that the Gothlander had thrown off his helmet and removed his byrnie. He was now standing on the foredeck, naked from the waist and baying like a wild animal as he faced the enemy. He was a hulking, hairy-chested man and his pelt of body hair made him look a gross animal or a troll. He was raving and grimacing, now leaping up on the top rail and dancing in derision as he hurled insults at the enemy, then jumping down to the deck and capering back and forth and waving his war axe so wildly that I thought he would accidentally strike Thrand, who stood beside him. Eventually the berserker quietened down, but then picked up his shield and began biting its top edge furiously.

The savage sight made our foes even more cautious and for their second attack they took their time. They circled our ancient drakkar like a pair of wolves despatching a lame stag. In unison they darted in, one from each side, and then quickly pulled back after the warriors on their bow platforms had thrown a javelin or two and drawn our response of stones and rocks. Three or four times they launched these brief attacks until they saw that our supply of missiles was exhausted, then they came again, this time to close and board us.

I was standing in the waist of our drakkar, facing the starboard side so all I saw was the onslaught from that direction. It was terrifying. Four heavily armed Danes stood in the bows, ready to leap down on us as their vessel struck us amidships. They were big men, and made even bigger by the fact that they had the advantage of height and towered over us. Remembering our war instruction, I stood upon a sea chest and overlapped my shield with the Wend beside me on my left, while the man on my right did the same for me, though it was difficult to find secure footing on the uneven platform. We tried to slant our spears upward, hoping to impale our enemies as they leaped down upon our deck, but our awkward stance made the shield wall ragged and unstable, and the spear points wavered. As it turned out, our preparations were ineffectual. We were braced for the shock of the oncoming bows when, behind us, the second Danish ship rammed our vessel amidships, and our drakkar gave a sudden lurch so that we stumbled and slipped, and our shields separated, leaving wide gaps between them. If our enemies had been alert they could have burst through the gaps, but instead they misjudged. The first of the Danes jumped for our vessel too soon, and only his right foot landed on the edge of our drakkar. He stood there momentarily off balance, and I had the presence of mind to step forward and thrust the metal rim of my shield in his face, so that he overbalanced backwards and fell into the sea. Out of the corner of my eye I saw a spear point come from behind me and pass over my left shoulder to thrust neatly into the unprotected groin of the second Danish boarder. The Dane doubled up in pain and grasped the spear shaft. 'Like sticking boar in a forest,' said my companion the Wend with a satisfied grin, as he wrenched the weapon free. He had little time to gloat any further. The Danish longship was well handled. Their oarsmen were already swinging the vessel so she lay alongside us and the rest of their fighting men could board. A moment later there was a thud as the two ships came together and there was a yelling, stampeding rush as our enemies leaped into our ship.

If the Danes had expected an easy victory, they were quickly disillusioned. The Jomsvikings may have been inept sailors, but they were dogged fighters. We held our own, against odds of two to one, and the first Danish onslaught was met with skill and discipline. We remembered our training and we fought as brothers. Shoulder to shoulder with the unknown Wend, I deliberately jabbed my spear point into the shield of the next Dane to charge us, and his onward rush drove the weapon deep into the wood. Then I twisted on the spear shaft so the shield was forced aside. At that instant the Wend stepped forward nimbly with his axe and struck the unprotected Dane at the base of the neck, felling him as neatly as an ox in a slaughterhouse. I heard the Wend give a grunt of satisfaction. I tugged my spear to retrieve it, but the weapon was stuck fast. I abandoned it, as I had been trained to do, and stepped back into line, reaching for the battleaxe that hung by my left shoulder. On all sides men were shouting and roaring, and there was the constant thud of blows and the ring of metal striking metal. Over the clamour I heard the shout of the Danish captain calling on his men to fall back and regroup. Suddenly the enemy were at arm's length, backing

away from us and then scrambling aboard their longship, which
was then pushed clear and drifted free.

In the breathing space which followed I turned to see what
had happened behind us. Here, too, the initial Danish attack had
been beaten off. Several bodies lay on the deck of the other vessel,
which had also pushed away from us. Our own losses had been
minimal. Half a dozen wounded and one man dead. The wounded
were slumped on the deck and their sea chests, moaning in pain.

'Close up! Stand fast! There'll be another attack,' came
Thrand's shout. He was still on the foredeck, the shield on his
left arm splintered and battered, and a bloodied battleaxe held
loosely in his right hand. Instantly recognisable, he alone of
all the Jomsvikings had chosen to wear the old-fashioned battle
helmet with its owl-like eye guards, while the rest of us wore
the armoury's conical helmets. Thrand's antiquated war gear
reminded me of our time-honoured battle standard and I squinted
aft at Odinn's banner. The flag was now flapping and snapping in
the wind. In the heat of battle I had failed to notice that the
leading edge of the storm was now upon us. The sky was black
from horizon to horizon. Gusts of wind tore the surface of the
sea. I felt the old drakkar swing as the wind buffeted her ancient
hull. We were drifting, all three ships, across the surface of the
lagoon and towards the shallows. I also caught a glimpse of the
third Danish longship. She was arriving with fresh men aboard
and soon the odds would be three to one. I knew then that we
had no hope. I glanced again at Odinn's banner, but still saw only
the plain white cloth slatting in the gathering gale.

The Danes were shrewd. The crew of the newly arrived
longship lashed their vessel to another one and the two ships
together formed a single fighting platform. Then they rowed
upwind of us, shipped their oars and began to drift down on our
drakkar. Now they had no need of oarsmen. Every one of their
men was free to fight. Their third vessel positioned herself to
attack, once again, on our opposite side.

The crunching impact of the rafted longships stove in our

drakkar's topmost plank. I heard the ancient wood crack as the vessels collided. Our boat heeled with the weight of the sudden rush of the main Danish fighting force as their warriors jumped aboard. Some tripped and stumbled, and these men were despatched with an axe blow to the back of the head. But the sheer weight of comrades piling aboard behind them pushed their vanguard forward and broke our line. We were forced to give way and in a pace or two found ourselves back to back with our comrades who were trying to defend themselves against the attack from the opposite side. We fought viciously, either in desperation or because we believed in our oath to felag. Certainly not a single Jomsviking broke ranks. Spears were useless at such close quarters so we hacked with axes and stabbed with daggers. It was impossible to draw or to swing a sword. Shields were thrown aside as they split or splintered, and soon we were relying on our helmets and byrnies to turn aside the weapons of our enemies.

Gradually we retreated, step by step, towards the stern of our drakkar, our dwindling band packed so tightly that when the Wend beside me took an axe blow in the neck, his body stayed upright for several moments before it eventually slipping down at my feet. My shield arm shook to the impact of blows from the Danish axes and clubs, and the leather-bound shield began to disintegrate. I gasped for breath through the chain-mail curtain which hung across my face. My whole body ran with sweat within the padded jacket under the byrnie. Rivers of sweat ran down from my helmet and stung my eyes. I felt desperately tired, scarcely able to swing a counter-blow with my own axe. From sheer exhaustion I longed to drop my shield arm and rest. My vision blurred with glimpses of open-mouthed, yelling Danes hacking and thrusting and slashing, sometimes the blows directed at me, sometimes at my comrades on each side. I began to stagger and sway with a strange lassitude. I felt as if I was wading through a swamp of mud that sucked at my feet and legs.

I was slipping away into oblivion and a great blackness began to gather around me when an icy stinging sensation flicked at my eyes. Peering past the noseguard, I realised that our battle was shrouded in a sudden summer hailstorm. A clatter of large hailstones struck my metal helmet and suddenly my feet were slipping and skidding on the crunching white surface that covered the deck. It became very cold. The hail was so intense that gusts of the squall blew ice grains under the rims of our helmets and into our faces. It was difficult to see the full length of the drakkar, yet in the distance I glimpsed Odinn's banner waving at the stern post. I blinked to clear my eyes, and it might have been my utter exhaustion or the roaring of the blood in my ears that affected my sight, but I saw the raven, black and bloodthirsty, and it turned to look towards me and slowly lowered its knowing, wise head. At that moment a great agony erupted in my throat. My breath stopped.

I woke to a terrible pain in my gullet every time I breathed. I was lying face downwards, wedged between two oar benches. My left arm was trapped underneath something heavy which proved to be the corpse of the Abdorite who had been our instructor at Jomsburg. In his death throes he had toppled across me, pinning me down. Cautiously and painfully, each breath drawn as gently as possible through my tormented windpipe, I wriggled clear and raised my head to look along the length of the vessel. I could hear nothing except the faint slap of waves against the hull. There was no movement, no one standing on the deck. Everything seemed very still, and dark. It was night-time and our drakkar was silent. Pain sliced through me as I shifted my weight and carefully eased myself along the thwart. I heard a groan, but could not tell where it came from. All around me the oar benches were littered with bodies, Danes and Jomsvikings together. Dizzy from the effort, I began to crawl towards the foredeck where I had last seen Thrand.

I found him slumped down on the deck, his back against the bulwark. Even in the dim light I could see the rent in his byrnie over his chest. He was still wearing his antiquated helmet and I thought he was dead until I saw the faint movement of his eyes behind eye guards.

He must have seen my crab-like approach for his voice said softly, 'Odinn must love you, Thorgils.'

'What happened? Where are we?' I croaked.

'Where we met our fate,' he replied.

'Where are the Danes?'

'Not far away,' he said. 'They withdrew to their ships when it became too dark. Nightfall came early in the storm and they dread killing anyone in the dark in case the victim returns to haunt them as undead. At dawn they will return to finish off the wounded and strip the corpses.'

'Is there no one left?' I asked.

We fought well,' he answered. 'None better. The Jomsvikings are finished.'

'Not all of them. I can help you get away from here.'

Thrand made a faint gesture and I looked down. His legs were stretched out flat on the deck before him and I saw that his right foot was missing.

'Always the weak point in a ship battle,' he said. 'You defend yourself with your shield and someone crouches beneath a thwart until you are close enough for him to hack at your leg.'

'But I can't abandon you,' I said.

'Leave me, Thorgils. I'm not afraid to die.' And he quoted the High One:

> 'The sluggard believes he shall live for ever
> If the fight he faces not
> But age shall not grant him the gift of peace,
> though spears may spare his life.'

Reaching forward, he grasped my forearm.

'Odinn sent that storm for a purpose. He brought the early darkness to preserve you from the final slaughter of the wounded. You must go now and find King Knut. Tell him that the Jomsvikings kept their word. He must not think we failed to honour our hire. Tell him also that Earl Ulf is a traitor, and inform Thorkel the Tall that the dishonour of Hjorunga Bay has been expunged, and that it was Thrand who led the felag to their duty.'

He sank back, exhausted. There was a long silence. I was so tired that, even had I wanted to, I felt I had no strength to leave the drakkar. I only wanted to lie down on the deck and rest. But Thrand would not let me. 'Go on, Thorgils, go,' he said softly, and then as if there was no doubt, he added, 'you saw the raven. Defeat was Odinn's will.'

Every movement was agony as I took off the heavy byrnie. Its chain-mail throat guard had stopped the sword slash from taking off my head but had left me choking. I dragged off the padded undercoat and pulled myself across to the gap in the bulwark where the Danes had smashed into us. I was too bruised and exhausted to do anything more than lower myself though the gap and into the lagoon. The shock of the cold water revived me for a moment and I tried to swim. But I was too tired. My legs sank downward and I resolved to let go of the boat and allow myself to drown. To my surprise my feet touched the ground. Our drakkar must have drifted far enough into the shallows for me to stand. Slowly, half swimming, half walking, I headed for the shore, until I was able to lurch up the beach. My feet sank into the drier sand, and I stumbled over the first clump of dune grass and fell. I picked myself up, knowing that I had to put as great a distance as possible between myself and the Danes.

As I crossed the first of the dunes I looked back towards the drakkar and saw a point of light. It was a tiny burst of flame. It died down and then flared up and grew brighter. I remembered the pitch which the shipwrights had used to revive our ancient vessel inside and out, and knew that she would burn well. But whether it was Thrand who set the fire, or some other survivor of the fight, it was impossible to tell. I only knew that by daylight the last warship of the Jomsvikings would have burned down to the waterline.

TWELVE

It took me nearly two weeks to walk or, rather, stumble to Knut's headquarters at the town of Roskilde. I was crossing the lands of Earl Ulf, whom I knew to be a traitor, so I avoided human contact, skirting around villages and sleeping under hedges or in the lee of earth banks. I have no clear memory of how each day of that grim journey was spent, only that my nights were filled with terrible visions of violence and death. When it rained, I awoke shivering with cold and fear, the rain drops on my face reviving images of grotesquely swirling storm clouds, the vanquished raven and an image which at the time had seemed so malevolent that I had buried it deep in my thoughts – a black hag riding on the wind. Once or twice I could have sworn that Thrand sat somewhere close to me in the shadows, a pool of black blood leaking from his leg. I lay numb with despair, wondering if my second sight had summoned his ghost from the dead, only to realise that I was alone and close to madness. When hunger drove me to knock on the doors of cottages along my path to beg for charity, my throat was so badly bruised that the inhabitants thought I was a mute. I had to gesture with my hands to make myself understood. They gave me scraps of food occasionally. More often they drove me away with kicks and curses, or set their dogs on me.

In the end it was Odinn who relieved my plight. I crept into Roskilde like a vagrant, filthy and wild-eyed, and was promptly arrested by a sentry. Odinn had arranged that Kjartan, the one-handed huscarl, was commander of the guard that day, and when I was brought before him, he looked at me with astonishment.

'Thorgils, you look as though you have been chewed over by Nidhoggr, the corpse-tearer!' he said. 'What in Thor's name has happened to you?'

I glanced towards my captor, and Kjartan took the hint. He sent the sentry back to his post, then made me sit down and eat a meal before he heard my story. My battered throat allowed me only to swallow a bowl of lukewarm gruel before I told him of the ambush and destruction of the Jomsviking expedition sent to join Knut.

When I finished, Kjartan sat silent for a moment. 'This is the first I've heard of it,' he said. 'Your battle with the Danes was fought at a place so remote that no one knows about it. I presume the victors put to sea after binding up their wounds and, if they were Earl Ulf's men acting treacherously, then they would have kept quiet because events overtook them.'

'What do you mean?' I asked hoarsely.

'While you and the Jomsvikings were waylaid off Sjaeland, the king and his fleet caught up with his enemies off the coast of Skane. There was a great battle in the estuary of Holy River. Both sides are claiming the victory, and frankly I think we were lucky that we did not suffer a major defeat. But at least the Swedes and Norwegians have been thwarted for the time being.' Then he paused and asked, 'I need to be sure about this — when did you say the Jomsvikings were ambushed?'

'I lost track of time during my journey here,' I said, 'but it was about two weeks ago.'

'You had better tell your story to the king in person. I can arrange that. But don't say a word to anyone else until you've had your audience with him.'

'I would like to tell Thorkel the Tall,' I said. 'Thrand's last words to me were that I was to inform Thorkel that the dishonour of Hjorunga Bay had been wiped away.'

Kjartan looked at me. 'So you don't know about the changes at Knut's court.'

'What's happened?' I asked.

'You can't speak to Thorkel, that's for sure. He's dead. Died in his bed, amazingly enough. Never expected it from such an inveterate warrior. So he'll never get Thrand's message unless the two of them exchange news in Valholl, if that's where they have both gone. Thorkel's death was a setback for Knut. The king had appointed him regent here in Denmark, and when he died Earl Ulf took his place.'

'But it was Earl Ulf's men who attacked us,' I blurted.

'Precisely. That is why it would be wise if you did not tell anyone else about the Jomsvikings' ambush.'

Kjartan must have had considerable influence with the royal secretariat because my interview with the king took place that same evening. It was held in secret, away from the king's official residence. Only the three of us were present – Kjartan, myself and the husband of the woman I still loved.

For the first time I was able to see Knut close to, and of course I judged him jealously. The king was on his way to an official banquet, for he was wearing a brilliant blue cloak held at the right shoulder by a gold buckle, a tunic of fine linen with a thread of gold running through it, gold-embroidered bands at the hem and cuffs, scarlet leggings and cross gaiters. Even his soft leather shoes had lines of gold stitched in square patterns. He radiated authority, privilege and virility. What impressed me most was that he was almost my own age, perhaps three or four years older. I did a quick mental calculation. He would have been leading an army while he was in his teens and I was still a youngster in Vinland. I felt inadequate by comparison. I doubted that Aelfgifu had found me a satisfactory substitute. Knut had a magnificent physique, well proportioned and robust. Only his nose marred his good looks. It was prominent, thin and slightly hooked.

But that deficit was more than made up for by his eyes, which were large and wide-set and gave him a level, confident gaze as he stared at me while I stumbled huskily through my account.

When I had finished, Knut looked at Kjartan and asked bluntly, 'Is this true?'

'Yes, my lord, I've known the young man for some time and I can vouch for his honesty as well as his bravery.'

'He's not to tell his story to anyone else?'

'I've told him not to, my lord.'

'Well, he's certainly earned his pay. How much did we promise the Jomsvikings?'

'Fifteen marks of silver each man, my lord. Half in advance. Final payment to be made after they had fought for you.'

'Well, that's a bargain! They fought, it seems, and now there's only one of them to collect his pay. I'll double it. See to it that the paymaster gives him thirty marks. And make sure, also, that he's kept out of sight. Better yet, arrange to have him sent away, somewhere far off.'

The king turned on his heel, and was gone. Knut's brusque dismissal left me wondering whether he knew about my affair with Aelfgifu.

As Kjartan escorted me back to his own lodgings, I dared to ask, 'Is the queen, Aelfgifu, I mean, is she here with the king?'

Kjartan stopped. He turned to me in the darkness, and I could not see his expression but his voice sounded more serious than I had ever heard him. 'Thorgils,' he said, 'let me give you some advice, though I know it is not what you want to hear. You must forget Aelfgifu. Forget her completely, for your own safety. You do not understand about life at court. People act differently when they are close to the seat of power. They have particular reasons and motives and they pursue them ruthlessly. Aelfgifu's son, Svein, is now ten years old. He takes after his father in looks and manner, and she is ambitious for him to be Knut's heir rather than the children of Queen Emma. She will do anything to further his chances.'

I tried to interrupt. 'I never knew she had a son; she never told me.'

Kjartan's voice ground on remorselessly, overriding my half-hearted objection. 'She has two sons, in fact. If she failed to mention them to you, that makes my point. They were fostered out at an early age. They grew up in Denmark while Aelfgifu was in England. Right now she's playing for very high stakes — no less than the throne of England. If she thinks that you are a threat because of anything that happened at Northampton . . . I'm not accusing you of anything, Thorgils. I just want you to realise that Aelfgifu could be a danger to you. She has a ruthless streak, believe me.'

I was stunned. First I had lost Thrand and now my cherished vision of Aelfgifu was smashed. Mother of two, ambitious royal consort, deceitful, conniving — this was not the sweet, high-spirited woman whose memory I had cherished these two years past.

Kjartan's voice softened. 'Thorgils, give thanks to Odinn that you are still alive. You could be a corpse along with your ship-mates on the drakkars. You are young, you are free of restraints and from tomorrow you'll have money to spare. Tomorrow I'll take you to see the king's paymaster and you'll have your royal bounty. Look upon Knut's wish to be rid of you as another sign that Odinn protects you. The court is a snake pit of intrigue and you are best away from it. You may think that the king was generous in his payment to you, but if the Danish vessels which attacked you had reached Holy River in time for the battle, King Knut might have lost his crown. And monarchs do not like to know that they are in another's debt.'

His last observation made no sense. 'I don't understand how the defeat of the Jomsvikings could have saved the king. We never reached the rendezvous. We were no use to him,' I said.

'Think of it this way,' Kjartan replied. 'Recently Knut has been increasingly mistrustful of Ulf. He fears that the earl is plotting against him and your story of the ambush of the Jomsvikings confirms Ulf's double dealing. His ships attacked the

Jomsvikings, knowing them to be reinforcements for the king. They did not expect any survivors to live to tell the tale. But as it turned out, the ambush delayed Ulf's ships so they missed the vital engagement at Holy River. Had they been there, Ulf might have felt strong enough to switch sides and join the Swedes. And that would have been the end for King Knut.'

I thought that Kjartan was being overly cynical, but he was proved right. Soon afterwards matters came to a head between the king and Earl Ulf. They were playing a game of chess when Knut, a chess fanatic, made a wrong move on the board. Ulf promptly took one of his knights. Knut insisted in replaying the move, and this so angered Ulf that he got up from his seat, tipped over the chessboard and stalked out of the room. Knut called after him that he was running away. Ulf flung back the jibe that it was Knut who would have run away from Holy River if Ulf's force had not fought on his side.

That night the earl fled for sanctuary in Roskilde's White Christ church. It did him little good. At dawn Knut sent a huscarl to the church with orders to kill Ulf. There was uproar among the Christians that murder had been committed in one of their churches. But when I heard the story, I felt a more immediate chill. Ulf was married to Knut's sister. If a brother-in-law could be assassinated in the struggle for the throne, how much more likely a victim would be the queen's illicit lover.

'I NEED THE DETAILS!' said Herfid excitedly. 'It's perfect material for a saga – "The Last Fight of the Jomsvikings!" Can you describe to me the leader of the Danes? Was there any exchange of insults between him and Thrand? Hand-to-hand combat between the two of them? That would be a nice touch, to catch an audience's imagination.'

'No, Herfid, it was just as I described it. Chaotic and savage. I didn't see who chopped off Thrand's foot and I don't even know who led the Danes. At first we thought they were on our side, on their way to join the king. But then they attacked us.' My throat hurt. Sometimes, when I was tired, my voice suddenly changed pitch like a boy in his puberty.

By a happy coincidence Herfid was travelling on the ship that Kjartan had found to take me clear of court intrigue. Herfid had finally given up his attempts to find a permanent job as a royal skald, and was heading back to Orkney where the new earl might have work for him. 'Knut's got too many skalds as it is,' Herfid lamented. 'Sighvatr Thordarsson, Hallvardr Hareksblesi and Thorarin Loftunga, not to mention Ottar the Black, who is his favourite. They didn't welcome more competition.' He looked woebegone. 'But if I could compose a really good saga about the Jomsvikings, that might get me some attention.'

'I think not, Herfid,' I said. 'Knut may not want to be reminded of the episode.'

'Oh well ... if you ever change your mind. Meanwhile perhaps you could tell me some of the Irish sagas you heard when you were in that country, maybe I could work parts of them into my own compositions. In exchange I'll give you a few more lessons on style and structure. They could prove useful should you ever decide to make a living by story telling. Besides, it will help pass the hours at sea.'

The captain taking us towards Orkney was in a hurry. It was late in the season to be attempting the trip, but he was a man with weather luck and his crew trusted his judgement and sea skill. Herfid, by contrast, probably knew at least a hundred poetic phrases for the sea and its ships, but had no practical knowledge. He made a singular impression on our hard-bitten crew as he walked about the deck referring to the little vessel as a 'surge horse' and a 'twisted rope bear', even 'a fore-sheets snake'. When we cleared the Roskilde anchorage the waves became 'the whale's housetops', and the jagged rocks were 'the water's teeth'. I noticed several crew members raise their eyebrows in astonishment when he referred to our hard-driving skipper as a 'brig elf', and I feared the captain had overheard.

Fortunately, just when I was thinking that Herfid was going to get himself tossed overboard for his presumption, we ran into the sea race off the tip of Caithness. It was an intimidating experience, as unnerving as anything I had yet experienced at sea, except perhaps for being wrecked on the Greenland skerries, but I was too young to remember that. The west-going tide ripped past the headland, creating overfalls and strange, swirling patches of water, until it seemed we were riding a huge river in full spate rather than the ocean. I could see why his men trusted our captain so implicitly. He timed his vessel's entry into the race with perfection. He thrust boldly into the torrent just as the tide was gathering, and we were swept along like a wood chip on the spring flood. Our vessel began to make a strange swooping motion, lifting up, then sliding forward and down as if we would be sucked to the bottom of the sea, only to rise again, check, and begin the next plunge. It required prime seamanship to keep the vessel straight. The captain himself manipulated the side rudder, which Herfid had called 'the broad-blade ocean sword', and by some smart handling of the sheets the crew made sure that we did not broach and roll. We hurtled through the race, our ears filled with the grumbling roar of the tide.

Poor Herfid fell silent as the motion of the ship increased. Soon he had found his way to the rail and was hanging on to a mast stay, then in a sudden lurch he was doubled over the rail, throwing up the contents of his stomach. He was bent in that position for some time, retching and heaving miserably. When we were clear of the waves, and the motion had subsided enough for the skipper to be able to relinquish the helm, he sauntered over to Herfid and asked innocently, 'And what do you call the sea — "breakfast swallower" or "vomit taker?"' Herfid raised his green-white face and gave him a look of pure loathing.

BIRSAY, THE HOME of the Earl of Orkney, was just as I remembered it — a modest settlement of a few houses huddling behind tussock-covered sand dunes. As a port of call, Birsay only existed because it was on the crossroads of the shipping lanes between the seas of England, Ireland and Iceland. The anchorage was so exposed to the fierce winter gales raging in from the west that the local boats had been hauled ashore and secured in half-sunk sheds or bedded behind barriers of rock and sand. Our captain had no intention of staying a moment longer than necessary in such a dangerous place, and he paused only long enough for us to visit the long hall to pay our respects to the earl, and for Herfid to ask permission to stay.

Like Knut, the new Earl of Orkney was of the coming generation – energetic, ambitious and completely without qualms. His name was Thorfinn, and Herfid was in luck. The young earl was looking for a skald to enhance his reputation and Herfid was given the job, initially on approval. Afterwards – as I learned – his post was made permanent when Thorfinn heard that he was becoming known as 'the Mighty', a phrase that Herfid had used to describe him.

To my astonishment, the earl's grandmother Eithne was still alive. I had not seen her for almost eight years, yet she seemed to have changed hardly at all. Perhaps she was a little more stooped, and even more of her hair had fallen out, so that she kept her headscarf knotted securely under her chin. But her mind was as alert as ever.

'So another battle nearly killed you,' she wheezed at me by way of greeting. I was not surprised. Eithne was acknowledged to be a volva, a seeress, and there was little that she did not know or divine. She was the one who had told me that I was a spirit mirror, my second sight occurring most frequently when I was with someone else who had the gift.

'There's something I want to ask you about,' I said. 'There was a vision which I do not understand, and I have not mentioned to anyone as yet.'

'Tell me about it.'

'It was during a sea fight. In the midst of the battle a hailstorm suddenly lashed us, chilling us to the bone. The wind which brought the hailstones always seemed to be in our faces, never to hamper our enemies. It blew so powerfully that it turned our arrows, nor could we hurl our spears against it. It was unearthly. Everyone thought so. Some of our men from Wendland and Witland cried out that magic was being used against us.'

'What did you think?' the old woman asked.

'I think our enemies had a supernatural ally. I saw her – it was a woman – she appeared in the hailstorm. At first I thought she was a Valkyrie come to carry away our dead, for she seemed unearthly and she rode the wind. But this woman was different. She had a cruel face, a cold eye and was in a frenzy, shrieking and raging at us, and pointing at us with a clawlike hand. Whenever she appeared, the hail flew thicker and the wind came in stronger gusts.'

Eithne gave a snort of derision at my ignorance. 'A Valkyrie indeed. Have you never heard of Thorgerd Holgabrud? That's who you saw.'

'Who's she?' I asked.

'Thrand could have told you,' she replied. 'She appeared at Hrojunga Bay, the first time the Jomsvikings were defeated. She is the patron Goddess of the northern Norwegians. Earl Haakon, who led the battle against the Jomsvikings, sacrificed his own seven-year-old son to her to obtain the victory. That sacrifice was so powerful that, even now, Thorgerd Holgabrud returns to ensure the extinction of the Jomsvikings. She is a blood drinker, a war witch.'

I must have looked sceptical because Eithne reached out and gripped me by the arm. 'Listen to me: signs appeared in Caithness and Farroes soon after the great slaughter at Clontarf. There the Valkyries did appear to Old Believers – twelve Valkyries, riding horses. They set up a loom in each place, using the entrails of dead men as weft and warp, fresh skulls as the loom weights and a sword as the beater. An arrow was their shuttle. As they wove, they sang of the men who had fallen. You may never have heard

of Thorgerd Holgabrud, or her sister Irpa, but those Wends and
Witlanders were right. A volva was working against you that day,
someone invoking the hailstorm and the gale and inciting Thorgerd to fight against you. Learn from this event. Be on your
guard against those who use the occult to defeat you.'

I forgot her words over the next few months and paid the
price.

I ARRIVED BACK IN Iceland to find that Grettir was now a legend.
Against all odds he was still at large and evading every attempt to
hunt him down. What made his survival all the more remarkable
was that no outlaw had ever had such a high bounty put on his
head. Thorir of Gard had redoubled the reward he and his family
would pay to anyone who killed or captured Grettir, and several
bounty hunters had tried and failed to collect the prize money.
I heard a great deal of chuckling about the fate of one of them.
Grettir had overpowered him and forced him to undress and
return home in only his underclothes. Other stories were more
far-fetched and reminded me of when Grettir and I had robbed
the barrow grave together. It was claimed that Grettir had thrown
an evil troll-woman to her death over a cliff, that he had swum
under a waterfall and found a giant living in a cave carpeted with
men's bones, that he had shared a remote cave with a half-giant.
On one point, everyone was agreed: Grettir was now living on an
island in the north-west fiords.

'Why doesn't someone get together a group of like-minded
fellows to go and capture him?' I asked.

My informant, a farmer from Reykholt with whom I was
staying overnight, shook his head. 'You should see the island he's
chosen for his retreat,' he said. 'Sheer cliffs that are near impossible to climb. The only way to the summit is by ladders and
Grettir hauls them up whenever he sees a strange boat approaching. And he is not alone. His younger brother Illugi is living there
with him and there's said to be a servant as well. A man called

Glaum or some name like that. There may be others, too. It's difficult to be sure. Grettir has allowed no one on the island since he took it over, though I've heard that the local farmers are furious. Previously they grazed a few sheep on the flat top of the island. Someone would go ashore, lower down a rope and the sheep would be hauled up one by one. After you got the sheep on the summit, you could go away and leave them there without a shepherd. There was no way the animals could get off.'

He said the island was called Drang, meaning 'sea cliff', and it was in the mouth of Skagafiord.

'Is there any way of getting out there?' I asked.

'There's a story that Grettir occasionally swims ashore, but that's impossible,' the farmer said. 'The island is too far out in the entrance to the fiord, and there are powerful currents that would sweep away a man and drown him. I think that tale is pure fantasy.'

It was odd, I thought to myself, how a farmer would believe in trolls and giants living under waterfalls, but not in a man's ability to swim long distances. Yet I had seen Grettir do just that in Norway.

When I stood on the shore of Skagafiord a few days later, I understood why the farmer had been so sceptical. Drang Island was far in the distance. Its shape reminded me of the massive blocks of ice which occasionally drifted into harbour at Eiriksfiord in Greenland when I was a boy. These ice mountains had stayed in the channel for weeks at a time, slowly melting. But the ice blocks had been a cheerful, sparkling white tinged with blue, and Drang Island was a dark, square, brooding oblong. It gave me the shivers. The thought of swimming across the intervening expanse of sea – I could see the tide swirl – was daunting. Someone on the mainland must be acting as a go-between, occasionally rowing out to the island to bring supplies and news.

I made a circuit of the fiord's shoreline, staying at one farmhouse after another, claiming to be looking for land to buy. Already I was travelling under an assumed name as I had no wish for Gunnhildr and her father to learn that I was back in Iceland. The only man to know of my return was Snorri Godi, that wily old chieftain, on whom I had called in order to discuss the redemption of my fire ruby. He still held the gem in safe keeping, and I had left with him the bulk of my silver hoard, asking that he wait before handing on the cash to Gunnhildr's family so that I had time to meet Grettir. I kept only enough silver with me to show the farmers of Skagafiord that I could afford their land prices.

I quickly identified the farmer most likely to be Grettir's contact. He owned the farm closest to Drang and there was a landing beach and boatshed on his property. More important, he was not a member of the group taking its lead from Thorbjorn Ongul, the chief landholder in the region. Thorbjorn Ongul I judged to be a hard man. Everything about him was off-putting. He had a scarred eye socket. He had lost the eyeball in his youth when his stepmother had struck him in the face for being disobedient and had half-blinded him. Now he was surly and belligerent, and obviously a bully. 'We'll get that bastard off our island, if it's the last thing I do,' he assured me when I raised the subject of Grettir on the island. 'Half the men around here are too faint-hearted to take any action. But I've been buying out their shares of the island – we used to own it jointly – so that whoever takes the decision about its future, it'll be me.' He paused, and looked at me suspiciously. 'Anyway, what's your interest in the place?'

'I just wondered: if I get a farm around here would I be able to purchase a share in the island and put some sheep on it?'

'Not without my permission, you couldn't,' he said rudely. 'By the time you finalise any land deal, I'll have seen to it that I hold the majority share in the island. Grettir is dead meat. He's due for a surprise, the murderous son of a bitch.'

I returned to the farmer whom I had guessed was supplying Grettir on Drang. Sure enough, when I offered him enough silver, he agreed to row me over to the island after dark. He warned me, however, that Grettir was dangerous and unpredictable. 'You want to be careful,' he said. 'When the mood is on him, the outlaw turns violent. He swam over from the island last autumn and broke into my farm building. He was looking for supplies, but I wasn't at home at the time. So he stripped off his wet clothes, lay down by the fire and went to sleep. Two of the women servants walked in on him and found him stark naked. One woman made some sort of giggling remark about his penis being rather small for such a powerfully built man. Grettir had been half-asleep and heard the remark. He jumped up in a rage and grabbed for her. The other woman fled and Grettir proceeded to rape the woman he got his hands on. I know that he's been out on that island for a long time, but it was a brutal thing to do.'

The farmer's story depressed me. I had known that Grettir was moody and unpredictable. I had seen enough examples of his loutish behaviour for myself. But he had never before been violent towards women. According to rumour, he had even been saved from capture several times by women who had taken pity on him and hidden him in their houses. I was appalled that he should use rape to punish what was nothing more than impudence. I began to fear that prolonged outlawry had unhinged Grettir, and he had become half-savage. It made me wonder what reception my sworn brother would give me.

I paid the farmer handsomely to deliver me out to Drang under cover of darkness on the next windless night, and to keep my presence secret. He landed me on the small shelf of beach below the sheer cliff face, and I heard the splash of his oars receding in the distance as I felt my way to the foot of the wooden ladder he had told me I would find. All around me in the darkness I could hear the rustlings and scratchings of roosting seabirds, and my nostrils were filled with the acrid smell of their droppings. Cautiously I felt my way up the rickety wooden rungs, pulling myself up step by step. The first ladder brought me to a ledge on the cliff face. Groping around I found the foot of a second ladder leading even further upward. I wondered at Grettir's confidence that he should leave the ladders in position at night, not fearing the approach of an enemy.

It was when I had reached the flat crest of the island and was stumbling my way forward through tussock grass that I tripped over the body of his lookout. The man was sound asleep, wrapped in a heavy cloak and half buried in a shallow trench. He gave a startled grunt as I trod accidentally on his legs, and I sensed, rather than saw, him sit up and peer in my direction.

'Is that you, Illugi?' he asked.

'No, it's a friend,' I replied. 'Where's Grettir?'

The half-seen figure merely grunted and said, 'Well, that's all right then,' and sank back into his hole to return to sleep.

Fearful of stumbling over the cliff edge in the darkness, I sat down on the ground and waited for the dawn.

Daylight showed me that the summit of the island was covered with pasture, closely cropped by sheep. I could see at least a score of animals. In every direction the surface of the island stopped abruptly, ending in thin air where the cliff edge began. Only behind me, where the wooden ladder reached the summit, was there any access. And between me and the ladder I could see the little hump of cloth which marked the location of Grettir's watchman. He was still asleep.

I rose to my feet and went in search of Grettir. I could see nothing except for the sheep grazing quietly. There was no hut, no cabin, no sign of habitation. I walked across to the west side of the island. It took just a couple of hundred paces and I was at the cliff edge, looking straight down several hundred feet to the sea. I could see the white shapes of gulls circling and wheeling far beneath me in the updraughts. Puzzled by Grettir's absence, I turned back, retraced my steps, and searched towards the south end of the island. I had almost reached the lip of the furthest cliff when, coming round a large boulder jutting up from the soil, I came upon my sworn brother's home. It was a dug-out shelter, more like a bear's den than a human dwng. He had scraped out the soil to make an underground chamber roofed with three or four tree trunks he must have salvaged from the beach, for there were no trees on the island, not even a bush. Over the tree trunks was laid a layer of turf sods. A smoke hole at the back of the dugout provided a vent for the smoke from his cooking fire. It was a bleak, miserable place.

Grettir must have sensed my presence. I was still taking in the depressing scene when he emerged from the shelter. I was shocked by his appearance. He looked haggard and worn, his hair grey and streaked, and his skin was grimed with soil and smoke. His eyes were red-rimmed from the foul air in the dugout and his clothes were tattered and squalid. I realised that I had not seen a freshwater spring on the island, and wondered how he and his companions found their drinking water. Washing clothes did not seem possible. Despite his grotesque and shabby appearance, I felt a surge of pride. There was no mistaking the self-assurance in the look my sworn brother directed at me as, for a moment, he failed to recognise who I was.

'Thorgils! By the Gods, it's Thorgils!' he exclaimed and, stepping forward, gave me a great hug of affection. He stank, but it did not matter.

A moment later, he pulled back. 'How did you get here?' he asked in astonishment, which for a moment turned to suspicion. 'Who brought you? And how did you get past Glaum?' Glaum must have been the lazy sentinel I had stumbled on.

'All of Iceland knows that you are living on this island,' I replied, 'and it wasn't difficult to work out who your ferryman is. He dropped me off last night. As for Glaum, he doesn't take his duties very seriously.'

At that point, a second figure emerged from the dugout behind Grettir. It had to be his younger brother Illugi. He was at least ten years younger than Grettir, thin and undernourished looking, with black hair and a pale skin. He too was dressed in little better than rags. He said nothing, even when Grettir introduced me as his sworn brother, and I wondered if he was mistrustful of my intentions.

'Well, what do you think of my kingdom?' said Grettir, waving his arm expansively towards the southern horizon. The entrance to the dugout looked down the length of Skagafiord to the distant uplands on the mainland. To left and right extended the shores of the fiord, and rising behind them were the snow-streaked flanks of the mountains. 'Wonderful view, don't you agree, Thorgils? And practical too. From this spot I can see anyone approaching by boat down the length of the fiord, long before they reach the landing beach. It's impossible for anyone to sneak up on me.'

'At least in daylight,' I murmured.

'Yes,' said Grettir. 'No one has been bold enough to try a night landing previously, and in future I'll not trust that lazy servant Glaum to keep a look out. He's idle, but he amuses me with his chatter, and the Gods know, one needs a bit of humour and light-heartedness out here, especially in winter.'

'What do you live on?' I asked. 'Food must be very scarce.'

Grettir showed yellow teeth through his dirty tangle of beard. 'My neighbours kindly donate a sheep every couple of weeks,' he said. 'We ration ourselves, of course. There were about eighty animals on the island when we took over, and now we are down to about half that number.'

I did a quick mental calculation. Grettir had been living on Drang for at least a year, probably longer.

'There's one old ram who'll be the last one to be eaten. He's quite tame now. Visits the dugout every day and rubs his horns on the doorway, waiting to be petted.'

'What about water?' I asked.

'We gather rain, of which there is plenty, and when we get really short, there's a freshwater seep over on the east, in an over-hang. It oozes a few cupfuls of water every day, enough to keep us alive.'

'Enough to keep four people alive?' I asked.

Grettir took my meaning at once. 'You mean you want to stay?' he asked.

'Yes,' I said. 'If you and Illugi have no objection.'

So it was that I became the fourth member of the outlaw community and for almost a year Drang Island was my home.

THIRTEEN

GRETTIR WAS RIGHT: there was no shortage of food on the island, even with an extra mouth to feed. We were able to fish from the beach whenever the winter storms abated, and Grettir and Illugi had already saved an ample store of dried fish and the smoked carcasses of seabirds. For vegetables we ate a dark green weed which grew luxuriantly on the slopes too steep for the sheep to graze. The succulent leaves of this weed – I do not know its name – had a pleasant salty taste, and gave welcome variety to our diet. We had neither bread nor whey, the staple of the farmers on the mainland, but we never went hungry.

Our real struggle was how to keep warm and dry. The roof of the dugout kept out the rain, but the interior was constantly damp from the wetness rising up through the soil and we found it impossible to keep our garments dry. The fireplace was at the back of the dugout against the great boulder so that the stone reflected every bit of precious heat. But the ever-present problem was the scarcity of firewood. We depended on the chance discovery of driftwood. Each day one or other of us would descend the ladders and make a circuit of the island's narrow beach, hoping that the sea had brought us its bounty. Salvaging a good-sized log suitable for firewood was a greater cause for satisfaction than bringing back a string of freshly caught fish. When we found a log or dead branch, however small, we used ropes to hoist it back up the cliff and put it to dry in a sheltered spot. Then we would use an axe to chop the driftwood into kindling or shape a log to keep the fire at a gentle glow all night.

Grettir and I spent many hours in conversation, sometimes seated in the dugout, but more usually out in the open air where our discussions could not be overheard. He confessed to me that he was feeling more and more worn down by his long period of outlawry. 'I've lived over two-thirds of my life as an outlaw,' he said. 'I've scarcely known any other condition. I've never married, never been able to drop my guard in case there is someone ready to kill me.'

'But you've also become the most famous man in Iceland,' I said, trying to cheer him up. 'Everyone knows of Grettir the Strong. Long ago you told me that your reputation was all that mattered to you and that you wanted to be remembered. You've certainly achieved that. The Icelanders will never forget you.'

'Yes, but at what cost?' he replied. 'I've become a victim of my own pride. You'll remember how I swore no one would ever drive me away from Iceland by sending me into exile. Looking back, I see that was a mistake. I trapped myself here with those words. I often regret that I have travelled no further than Norway. How I would have loved to see the foreign lands you have known – Vinland, Greenland, Ireland, London, the shores of the Baltic Sea. I envy you. If I were to travel abroad now, people would say that I am running away. I have to stay here for ever, and that means until someone catches up with me when I am weak or old and kills me.'

Grettir looked out across the fiord. 'I have a premonition that this view is the one I will live and die with. That I will finish out my time on this small island.' Disconsolately he threw a pebble over the cliff edge. 'I feel cursed,' he went on. 'Everything I do seems to have the reverse effect of what I intend. If I start something for the best of reasons, it usually turns out quite differently. People are hurt or harmed by my actions. I never intended to kill that young man who insulted me in the church in Norway, and when I burned those unfortunates in that shore house it was largely their fault. If they had not been so drunk, they would have escaped the fire, which they themselves started.'

'What about that woman over at the farm? I'm told you raped her.'

Grettir looked down at the ground and mumbled his answer. 'I don't know what came over me. It was a black rage, not something I'm proud of. Sometimes I think that living like a hunted animal makes you into an animal. If you live too long away from normal company, you lose the habits of normal behaviour.'

'What about your brother Illugi? Why don't you send him away from here? He doesn't have to be bound to your fate.'

'I've tried a dozen times to persuade Illugi to go back home,' Grettir replied, 'but he is too much like me. He's stubborn. He sees my outlawry as a matter of personal pride. No one is going to dictate to him or his family what they should do and he has a strong sense of family. That's how we were brought up. Not even my mother wants me to surrender. When Illugi and I said goodbye to her before coming here, she said that she never expected to see either of us alive again, but she was pleased we were protecting the family's good name.'

'Then what about Glaum?' I said. 'What part does he play in all this? To me he seems nothing more than a lazy lout, a jester.'

'We met Glaum on our way to the island,' Grettir said. 'It was pure chance. Glaum is a nobody. He has no home, no land, nothing. But he's amusing, and his company can be entertaining. He volunteered to come to the island with us and until he decides to leave I'm willing to let him stay. He tries to make himself useful, collecting firewood, helping haul up the ladders, doing some fishing, generally being about the place.'

'You're not concerned that Glaum might try to attack you, like Redbeard, hoping to gain the bounty money?'

'No. Glaum's not like that. He's too lazy, too weak. He's not a bounty hunter.'

'But there's something foreboding about Glaum,' I said. 'I can't define what it is, but I have a feeling that he represents misfortune. I would be happier if you sent him away.'

'Maybe I will,' said Grettir, 'but not yet.'

'Perhaps matters will improve,' I suggested. 'I've heard it said that if a man survives outlawry for a span of twenty years then the sentence is complete. In a couple of years that will be the case for you.'

'I think not,' Grettir answered gloomily. 'Something is bound to go wrong before then. My luck is dire and my enemies will never give up. My reputation and the reward for my death or capture means that any young hothead will have a try at killing me or taking me prisoner.'

His forebodings came true in the early spring. This was the season when the farmers would normally bring out their sheep to Drang and leave them there for the summer grazing. Doubtless this prompted them, under Thorbjorn Ongul's leadership, to launch a plan to retake the island. A young man from Norway, Haering by name, had arrived in the area. Like everyone else, he soon heard about Grettir living on Drang Island and of the huge reward being offered for his death. He contacted Thorbjorn Ongul and told him that he was an expert climber of cliffs. Haering boasted that there was no cliff which he could not scale single-handed and without ropes. He suggested that if he could be landed on Drang without Grettir knowing, he would surprise the outlaw and either kill or wound him so severely that the others would be able to storm the island. Thorbjorn Ongul was shrewd. He decided that the best way to approach Drang without alerting Grettir's suspicions would be in a large, ten-oared boat with a cargo of live sheep. From his boat he would call up to Grettir, asking for permission to land the animals. Ongul calculated that Grettir would agree because he had already depleted the flock on the island. Meanwhile Haering would climb the cliffs on the opposite side of Drang and creep up on Grettir from behind.

Grettir and I worked out Ongul's stratagem only after it had failed and it was a narrow escape. We saw the ten-oared boat approaching from a great distance down the fiord, and watched as it slowly drew closer. Soon we could see the four or five men aboard and the dozen or so sheep. Haering himself was not visible. He must have crouched down and hidden among the animals. Ongul was at the helm and steered for the landing place at the foot of the ladder leading up to the summit. But he took a slightly unusual course and, at the time, we failed to understand why. There was a short interval when the boat was so close under the cliffs and passing round the end of the island that it was lost to sight from anyone standing at the cliff top. This was the moment when Haering must have slipped overboard and swum ashore. Moments later Ongul and his boat reappeared in view, the oarsmen rested on their oars, and Ongul shouted up to Grettir, asking him to agree to let more sheep graze on the island. Grettir called back down, and the negotiations began. Grettir, usually so alert, was hoodwinked. He warned Ongul that the moment anyone tried to climb the ladders, the upper ladder would be withdrawn. Meanwhile, with a great deal of deliberate fumbling, the men in the boat began to get the sheep ready to be hoisted.

Unknown to us up on the summit, Haering had begun to climb. The young man was inching his way up the cliff face by a route which no one had attempted or even imagined possible. It was, by any standards, an extraordinary feat of agility. Unaided, the young man managed to find one handhold after another. He hauled himself upward past the ledges of nesting seabirds. Sometimes the rock face leaned out so far that Haering was obliged to cling on, hanging by his fingers as he searched for a grip, then clambered upwards like a spider. His feet, to prevent them slipping, were clad only in thick woollen socks, which he had wetted to give them a better grip.

I know about the wet socks because it was I who first saw Haering after he had hauled himself over the topmost rim of the cliff. It was the old grey ram which alerted me. Grettir, Illugi and Glaum were clustered at the top of the ladder, looking down at

Ongul and his farmer colleagues as they discussed the landing of the sheep. Their attention was completely distracted. By contrast, I had deliberately stayed back from the cliff edge so I could not be seen from below. No one apart from the farmer who had brought me to Drang knew that I was on the island, and it seemed a good idea to keep my presence a secret. So I noticed the sudden movement among the sheep grazing near the cliff edge opposite where Grettir was standing. The animals raised their heads from grazing, and stood stock still, staring out into space. They were alarmed and I saw them tense as if to flee. The old grey ram, however, trotted confidently forward as though he expected to be petted. A moment later I saw a hand rise over the cliff edge, as if from the void, and feel around until it found a grip. Then Haering's head appeared. Slowly, very slowly, he eased himself over the rim of the cliff until he was lying face down flat on the grass. That was when I saw the wet socks and noted that, to lighten himself for the climb, his only weapon was a small axe tied with a leather thong to his back.

I gave a low whistle to warn the others. Grettir and Illugi both looked round and immediately saw the danger. As Haering got to his feet, Grettir said something to Illugi, and it was the younger man who turned and advanced on a now-exhausted Haering. His older brother stayed behind in case his great strength was needed, with Glaum's help, to haul up the wooden ladder.

Poor Haering, I felt sorry for him. He was utterly spent by the spectacular climb, and instead of finding Grettir and Illugi alone on the island, he now found himself confronted by four men, and without any advantage of surprise. He unslung the axe. He may have been a superb mountaineer, but he was an inexpert warrior. He held the axe loosely in from of him, and when Illugi struck at him with a sword the axe was knocked spinning out of his grasp.

Haering offered no further resistance. There was something manic about Illugi's headlong rush at the unarmed young man. Illugi may have felt that his refuge had been violated, or maybe he had never killed a man before and was desperate to finish the job. He ran at Haering wildly, swinging his sword. Unnerved, the Norwegian turned and fled, running in his socks over the turf. But there was nowhere to go. Illugi chased his prey grimly, still cutting and slashing with his sword as Haering dodged and turned. He ran towards the boulder which masked the entrance to the dugout. Perhaps he was seeking to shelter behind it, but he did not know the lie of the land. Beyond the rock the ground suddenly fell in a steep slope at the far end of which was the edge of the cliff. From there to the sea was a sheer drop of four hundred feet. Haering ran headlong down the slope towards the precipice. Perhaps he thought his speed would carry him far enough out. Perhaps he panicked. Maybe he wanted to die by his own hand and not on Illugi's sword. Whatever his intention was, he ran straight to the edge of the cliff and without hesitating flung himself outward . . . and continued running, as though still on solid ground. His legs and arms flailed as he dropped from view.

I joined Illugi at the cliff edge, crouching cautiously on the ground and then crawling forward on my belly, so that my head looked out over the vast drop. Far below, the cliff climber's body lay broken and twisted on the beach. To my right Ongul's people had seen the tragedy and were already rowing to the spot to retrieve the corpse.

No other attempt was made to dislodge us from Drang during the next three months. Probably Haering's death had shocked the farmers who supported Ongul and anyhow they had their summer chores to do. Grettir, Illugi, Glaum and I stayed on the island. The friendly farmer visited us only twice, bringing us news from the mainland. The main event was the death of Snorri Godi that winter, full of years and honour, and his son Thorodd – the man whom Grettir had spared – had succeeded to the chieftainship. I wondered if Thorodd had also inherited charge of my fire ruby which I had left in his father's safe keeping and if Snorri had told him of its history.

My sworn brother reacted glumly to the news of Snorri Godi's

death. 'So vanishes my last hope of obtaining justice,' he said to
me as we sat in our favourite spot near the cliff edge. 'I know
that Snorri refused to take up my case at the Althing when we
first arrived back in Iceland and you went to see him on my
behalf. But as long as Snorri was alive, I nursed a secret hope that
he would change his mind. After all, I spared his son Thorodd
when he tried to kill me and win his father's approval. But now it
is too late. Snorri was the only man in Iceland who had the
prestige and law skill to have my sentence of skogarmadur
annulled.'

After a short pause Grettir turned to face me and said
earnestly, 'Thorgils, I want you to promise me something: I want
you to give me your word that you will make something
exceptional of your own life. If my life is cut short at the hands
of my enemies, I don't want you to mourn me uselessly. I want
you to go out and do the things that my ill luck has never allowed
me to do. Imagine that my fylgja, my other spirit, has attached
itself to you, my sworn brother, and is at your shoulder, always
present, seeing what you see, experiencing what you experience.
A man should live his life seeking out his opportunities and
fulfilling them. Not like me, cornered here on this island and
becoming famous for surviving in the face of adversity.'

As Grettir spoke, a memory came back. It was of the day
when Grettir and I were leaving Norway, and Grettir's half-
brother, Thorstein Galleon, had said goodbye. He had promised
to avenge Grettir's death if he was killed unjustly. Now, sitting
on a cliff top on Drang, Grettir had taken me one step further.
He was asking me to continue his life for him, in remembrance of
our sworn brotherhood. And behind the request was an unspoken
understanding between us: neither Grettir nor I expected that he
would live out the full twenty years of outlawry and reach the
end of the sentence imposed upon him.

The conversation had a remarkable effect on me. It changed
my perception of life on Drang. Previously I had been despondent
about the future, fearing the outcome of Grettir's seemingly

endless difficulties. Now I saw that it was better to enjoy whatever time there was left for us together. The change of season helped my pessimism to lift. The arrival of the brief Icelandic summer wiped away the memory of a dank and melancholy winter. I watched the tiny island change from a remote, desolate outpost to a place full of life and movement. It was the birds that did it. They arrived in their thousands, perhaps from those distant lands which Grettir dreamed of. Flock after flock came in until the sky was filled with their wings and their constant mewing and screaming mingled with the sounds of the sea and the wind. They came to breed, and they settled on the ledges, crevices and tiny outcrops of the cliffs until it seemed that there was not a single hand's breadth that was not occupied by some seabird busily building a new nest or refurbishing an old one. Even in Greenland I had not seen so many seabirds clustered together. Their droppings ran down the cliff faces like streaks of wax when a candle gutters in the draught, and there was a constant movement of fluttering and flight. Of course, we took their eggs, or rather we took a minuscule portion of them. This was when Grettir was at his best. With his huge strength he lowered Illugi on a rope over the cliff edge so that his young brother could gather the eggs from the ledges while the angry gulls beat their wings around his head, or if they stayed on their nests, shot green slime from their throats into the face of the thief. Perhaps the proudest moment of all my relationship with Grettir was when he turned to me and asked if I would go down the precipice on the rope and I agreed. As I dangled there, high above the sea, swinging in space, with only my sworn brother's strength to prevent me falling to my death like Haering, I felt the satisfaction of utter trust in another.

So the summer weeks passed by: sudden rain showers were interspersed with spells of brilliant sunshine when we stood on the cliff tops and watched the whales feeding in the waters around the island; or we traced the evening spread of white mist over the high moors on the mainland. Occasionally I would go by myself to a little niche on the very lip of the precipice and lie on the turf, deliberately gazing across the void and imagining I was no longer in contact with the solid ground. I hoped to achieve something my seidr mentors had long ago described to me: spirit flying. Like a small bird beginning to take wing, I wanted to send my spirit out over the sea and distant mountains and away from my physical body. For brief moments I succeeded. The earth fell away beneath me, and I felt a rush of wind on my face and saw the ground far beneath. But I never travelled far or stayed out of my body for long. I had brief glimpses of dense forest, a white landscape and felt a piercing cold. Then, like the fledgling which flutters uncertainly back to the branch, my spirit would return to where I lay, and the rush of air on my cheeks often proved to be no more than the rising wind.

The intrusion of awful dread into this pleasant life was shocking. The day was bright and fresh, and the waters of Skagafiord had that intense dark blue into which one could look for ever. Grettir and I were at a spot where the small black and white seabirds which nested in their millions regularly flew towards their nests, a row of tiny fish neatly arranged in their rainbow beaks. As they skimmed low over the cliff, riding up-draughts, we would rise from ambush and with woven nets on sticks pull them down from the sky and break their necks. Smoked over our fire, their dark brown flesh was delicious, a cross between lamb's liver and the finest venison. We had netted perhaps a dozen of the birds when we heard Illugi call out that a small boat was coming down the fiord. We gathered at the cliff edge and saw a little skiff rowed by just one man heading our way. Soon we could make out Thorbjorn Ongul at the oars.

'I wonder what he wants this time,' said Grettir.

'He can't be coming to negotiate,' Illugi commented. 'By now he must know that we can't be shifted, whatever he offers us, whether threats or payment.'

I, too, had been watching the boat, and as it drew nearer, I began to feel uncomfortable. A chill came over me, a cold queasi-ness. At first I thought it was an expression of my mistrust of

Thorbjorn Ongul. I knew that he was the man from whom Grettir had the most to fear. But as the little boat came closer, I knew that there was something else, something more powerful and sinister. I broke out in a cold sweat and felt the hairs on the back of my neck rise. It seemed ridiculous. In front of me was a small boat, rowed by an aggressive farmer who could not climb the cliffs, floating on a pleasant summer sea. There could be no menace there.

I glanced at Grettir. He was pale and trembling slightly. Not since our shared vision of fire emerging from the tomb of old Kar on the headland had we both been touched by the second sight simultaneously. But this time the vision was blurred and indistinct.

'What is it?' I asked Grettir. I did not have to explain my question.

'I don't know,' he answered throatily. 'Something's not right.'

The fool Glaum broke our concentration. Suddenly he began capering on the cliff edge, where he could be seen by Ongul in the boat. He shouted obscenities and taunts, and went so far as to turn his back, drop his breeches to his ankles and expose his buttocks at the Ongul.

'Stop that!' ordered Grettir brusquely. He went across to Glaum and cuffed him so hard that the vagrant was knocked backwards. Glaum scrambled to his feet, pulling up his breeches, and shambled off, muttering crossly. Grettir turned back to face Ongul. He had stopped rowing and was keeping the little skiff a safe distance away from the beach.

'Clear off!' Grettir bellowed. 'There's nothing you can say that I want to hear.'

'I'll leave when I feel like it,' Ongul yelled back. 'I want to tell you what I think of you. You're a coward and a trespasser. You're touched in the head, a murderer, and the sooner you're dealt with the better it will be for all decent men.'

'Clear off!' repeated Grettir, shouting at the top of his lungs. 'Go back to minding your farm, you miserable one-eye. You're the one who is responsible for bringing death. That young man would never have tried to climb up here if you hadn't encouraged him. Now he's dead, and with your scheme unstuck so badly you've been made to look a fool.'

As the exchange of insults continued, I felt shooting pains in my head. Grettir did not seem affected. Perhaps he was distracted by his anger at Ongul. But I began to feel feverish. The day which had begun with such promise was turning heavy with menace. The sky was clouding over. I felt unsteady and sat down on the ground to stop myself retching. The shouting match between the two men echoed off the cliffs, but then I heard something else: a growing clatter of wings and a swelling volume of bird calls, rising in pitch. I looked back towards the north. Huge numbers of seabirds were taking to the sky. They were launching themselves in droves from the cliff ledges, gliding down towards the sea and then flapping briskly to gain height as they began to group together. They reminded me of bees about to swarm. The main flock spiralled upward as more and more birds joined in, flying up to meet their companions. Soon the flock was so immense it had to divide into ranks and squadrons. There were thousands upon thousands of them, too many to count or even guess their numbers. Many birds still stayed on the ledges, but most were on the move. Section by section, breed by breed, the great mass of flying creatures circled higher and higher like a storm cloud, until smaller groups began to break away and head out towards the sea. At first it seemed that their departure was random, in all directions. But then I realised there was one direction which all the birds avoided: none of them was returning to Drang. The birds were abandoning the island.

I dragged myself upright and walked unsteadily to where Grettir stood. My head and muscles ached. I felt terrible. 'The birds,' I said, 'they're leaving.'

'Of course they are,' he answered crossly over his shoulder, 'they leave every year about this time. It is the end of their breeding season. They go now, and come back in the spring.'

He searched around in the grass until he found a rounded

stone, about the size of a loaf. Plucking it from the grass, he heaved it above his head with both hands and let fly, aiming at Ongul in the boat far below. Ongul had imagined he was safely out of range. But he had not reckoned with Grettir the Strong who, since boyhood, had amazed everyone with just how far he could pitch a rock. The stone flew far out, its arc greater than I had imagined possible. Grettir's aim was true. The stone plummeted down, straight at the little skiff. It missed Ongul by inches. He was standing amidships, working the oars. The stone landed with a thump on a bundle of black rags on the stern thwart. As the stone struck, I saw the bundle shiver and flinch, and over the crying of the myriad departing birds, I heard distinctly a hideous cry of pain. At that moment I remembered where I had felt that same chill, the same sense of evil, and heard the same vile cry. It was when Thrand and I had fought the Danes in the sea ambush and I had had a vision of Thorgerd Holgabrud, the blood drinker and witch.

As Ongul rowed away, I was swaying on my feet.

'You've got a bad attack of some sort of fever,' said Grettir and put his arm around me to stop me falling. 'Here, Illugi, give me a hand to carry Thorgils inside.' The two of them lifted me down into the dugout and made me comfortable on some sheepskins on the earth floor.

I had just enough strength to ask, 'Who was in the boat with Ongul? Why didn't they show themselves?'

Grettir frowned. 'I don't know,' he said, 'but whoever it was is nursing a very bad bruise or a broken bone and won't forget this day in a hurry.'

Perhaps the birds began their migration because they knew that the weather was about to change, or perhaps – and this was my own private explanation – they were disturbed from their roosts by the evil that visited us that day. At any rate that was the last day of summer we enjoyed. By evening the rain had set in and the temperature began to fall. We did not see the sun again for a fortnight, and by then the first of the autumn gales had mauled the island unseasonably early. The ledges on the cliffs were empty of all but a handful of seabirds, and Drang had settled back prematurely into its gloomy routine though the autumn equinox had barely passed.

I continued very ill and weak with fever and from my sick bed I could see that Grettir was more subdued than usual. There was despondency in his face, perhaps at the thought of another winter spent in the raw, cramped isolation of Drang. He took to leaving the dugout at first light and often did not reappear until dusk. Illugi told me that his brother was spending much of his time alone, sitting staring out towards the mainland, saying nothing, refusing to be drawn into conversation. At other times Grettir would descend the ladders and, when the low tide permitted, walk around the island, furiously splashing through the shallows, always by himself. It was from one of these excursions that he returned with that look I had never seen before: a look of dismay.

'What's worrying you?' I asked.

'Down on the beach, I had that same feeling we both sensed the day that Ongul came to visit us and I threw the stone. I felt it mildly at first, but as I walked around the island it came on me more strongly. Oddly, I also had a stroke of luck. On the far side of the island I came across a fine piece of driftwood. The current must have brought it there from the east side of the fiord. It was a good, thick log, an entire tree trunk, roots and all, ideal for firewood. I was bending down to drag it further up the beach when I felt ill – I thought I was going down with your fever. But then it occurred to me that my feeling might have something to do with that particular spot on the beach – it faces across to that ruffian Ongul's farm – or perhaps it was to do with the log. I don't know. Anyhow, I took the wave of nausea to be a warning. So instead of salvaging the log, I shoved it out to sea again. I didn't want to have anything further to do with it.'

The very next day Glaum appeared with a smug expression at the door of the dugout. 'I've done well,' he said. 'Better than the lot of you, though you treat me as if I'm useless.'

'What is it, Glaum?' asked Grettir sourly.

We had all become weary of Glaum's endless vulgarities – his favourite amusement was to let out controlled farts, which did not help the fug of the dugout, and he snored so much that, unless the night was wild, we made him sleep outside. He had made a noxious lair for himself in the hollow by the ladders where I had first stumbled across him. There he pretended to play sentry, though there was little likelihood of any surprise attack now that the weather was so bad.

'I've salvaged a fine log,' said Glaum. 'Took me enough trouble too. Found it on the beach by the foot of the ladders and I've managed to hoist it up with ropes. There's enough timber to burn for three or four nights at least.'

It was one of those days when there was a brief break in the dreary weather and Grettir had half-carried me out of the fetid dugout so I could sit in the open air and enjoy the watery sunshine.

Glaum went on, 'Better cut up the log now. Before it rains again.'

Grettir picked up our axe. It was a fine, heavy tool, the only axe we had, too important for our well-being to let Glaum handle in case he lost it or damaged the blade. Grettir walked to where Glaum had dragged the log. I was lying on the ground so I could not see the log itself because it was concealed in the grass. But I heard Grettir say, 'That's strange, it's the same log I threw back into the water the other day. The current must have carried it right around the island and brought it back in the opposite beach.'

'Well, it's a good log wherever it came from. Well seasoned and tough,' said Glaum, 'and it took me enough trouble to get it up here. So this time it's not going to waste.'

I saw Grettir raise the axe with both hands and take a hefty swing. A moment later I heard the sound of a blow that has been mis-aimed – the false echo – as Grettir fell.

Illugi had been idling nearby. He rushed over to his brother, and was kneeling on the ground. I saw him rip off a piece of his own shirt and guessed that he was applying a bandage. Then Grettir's arm came up and took a hold around his brother's neck, and as Illugi strained back, the two men rose, Grettir with one leg bent up. Blood drenched the bandage. Slowly and painfully, Grettir hobbled past me into the dugout. Too fever-racked to move, I lay there worrying about how badly Grettir had hurt himself. Eventually, when Illugi and Glaum helped me inside, I found Grettir sitting on the ground with his back against the earth wall of the dugout. Instantly I was reminded of the last time I had seen Thrand, sitting in the same position when he had lost his foot to a Danish axe. But at least Grettir had both legs, though the injured one was leaking what seemed a huge amount of blood through the makeshift bandage.

'A fine lot we are,' said Grettir, his face twisted with pain, 'We've got two invalids now. I don't know what came over me. The axe bounced off that tough old log and twisted in my hand.'

'It's cut very deep,' said Illugi. 'Any deeper and you would have chopped off your leg. You'll be out of action for months.'

'That's all I need,' said Grettir, 'plain bad luck again.'

Illugi busied himself in rearranging the interior of the dugout to give Grettir more space. 'I'll light the fire,' he said to his brother. 'It'll be cold tonight, and you need to keep warm.' He called to Glaum to bring in some firewood, and there were sounds of grunting and mumbling as Glaum slowly backed into the dugout, dragging the unlucky log which had been the cause of Grettir's accident.

'That's too big to fit into the hearth. Get something smaller,' said Illugi.

'No, it isn't,' replied Glaum argumentatively. 'I can make it fit. You've seen for yourself that it's too tough to chop up into pieces.'

Illugi, I realised, lacked Grettir's authority over Glaum and I knew that the balance within our tight little community had gone. Glaum was wrestling the log into position in the hearth and turning it over so that it rested against the stone. As he did so, I

saw something on the underside of the wood and called, 'Stop!'
I crawled over to take a closer look. Part of the underside of the
log had been cut smooth. Somebody had deliberately shaved down
the surface, leaving a flat area as long as my forearm. On the
surface were a series of marks cut deep into the wood. I knew
what the marks were even before I saw the faint red stain in their
grooves. Thrand, my mentor in the Old Ways, had warned me
against them. They were curse runes, cut to invoke harm against
a victim, then smeared with the blood of the volva or seidrmann
to make the evil in the runes more effective. I knew then that
Grettir was the victim of black seidr.

For the next three days Grettir's injury appeared to be on the
mend. The gash began to close and the edges of the wound were
pink and healthy. Then, on the third night, he started to suffer
from a deep-seated throbbing pain and by dawn he was in agony.
Illugi unwrapped the bandage and we saw the reason. The flesh
around the wound was puffed and swollen. Fluid was seeping
from the gash. The next morning the flesh was beginning to
discolour, and as the days passed the area around the wound
turned dark blue, then a greenish-black, and we could smell the
putrefication. Grettir could not sleep – the pain was too bad. Nor
could he get to his feet. He lost weight and looked drained. By
the end of the week he knew that he was dying from the poison
in his leg.

That was when they unleashed their assault. How they knew
that Grettir was in a coma, I have no way of knowing.

The end was swift and bloody. More than a dozen farmers
came up the ladders, which had been left in place now that we no
longer had Grettir's strength to pull them clear. They came at
dusk, armed with axes and heavy spears, and overpowered Glaum
as he lay half asleep. They prodded him in front of them as he
led them to our dugout, though they would have found the place
soon enough for themselves. I heard them coming first, for they
were working themselves up into a battle rage. Illugi, in an
exhausted sleep, was slow to wake and scarcely had time to jam

shut the makeshift door. But the door was not designed to withstand a siege – it was nothing more than a few sticks of wood covered with sheepskins – and it burst open after the first few blows. By then Illugi was in position, sword in one hand, axe in the other. The first farmer who ventured in lost his right arm to a terrific blow from the same weapon that had been Grettir's bane.

For an hour or more the attack continued. I could hear Ongul's voice urging on his men. But they found it was deadly work. Two more farmers were badly wounded and another killed, all trying to rush the door. Our attackers were like men who corner a badger in its sett and try to take the prey alive. When Ilugi held them off with sword and axe, they began to dig down through the earth roof of our refuge. From inside we heard the sounds of digging and soon the roof began to shake. I was as weak as water and unable to intervene, only to observe. From where I lay on the floor I saw the earth rain down from the ceiling and then the point of a spear poked through. I knew the end could not be long in coming.

Another rush at the door and the frame split. Our defence was collapsing around us. A spear thrust through the doorway caught Illugi in the shoulder. Grettir struggled to his knees to face the attack. In his hand was the short sword that he and I had robbed from old Kar's burial mound. At that moment a section of the roof fell in close to the hearth. Amid the shower of earth, a farmer jumped down. Grettir turned to meet the new threat, stabbed with the sword and impaled the intruder, killing him. But the man fell forward so that Grettir's sword arm was trapped. As he struggled to withdraw the blade a second man dropped through the hole and stabbed Grettir in the back. I heard Grettir call out and Illugi turned to help, throwing up his shield to protect his brother. This left the door unguarded and suddenly the dugout was filled with armed men. In moments they had knocked Illugi to the ground and were hacking and stabbing him to death. One man, seeing me, stepped forward and planted the point of his spear against my blankets. He had only to press down his weight and I too was dead. But he made no move, and I watched as Ongul darted behind Grettir to avoid the outlaw's sword and knifed him several times in quick succession. Grettir did not even turn to look at his killer. He was already so weak that he slumped to the ground without a sound. I lay there, unable to move, as Ongul leaned down and roughly tried to prise Grettir's fingers from Kar's sword. But the death grip was too strong and Ongul pulled aside my sworn brother's hand until it lay across the fatal fire log. Then, like a skilful butcher, he severed the fingers so that the sword fell free.

Picking up the sword, Ongul cut Grettir's head from his shoulders. It took four blows. I counted every one as Ongul hacked down on the corpse. By then the blood-splattered remains of the ruined dugout were crammed with sweating, jubilant farmers, all shouting and talking and congratulating themselves on their victory.

FOURTEEN

I BOUGHT MY life for five and a half marks. That was the sum the farmers found on me, and I gave them a promise of ten marks more if they delivered me, alive, to Snorri Godi's son Thorodd for judgement. They accepted the bargain because, after the slaughter of Grettir and Illugi, some of them had had enough of bloodshed. They buried the corpses of Illugi and Grettir in the ruins of our dugout, then lowered my sick and aching body down the cliff face on a rope and placed me in the stern of the ten-oar boat they had come in. Destitute Glaum was not so lucky. On the way back to the mainland, they told him he had betrayed his master, cut his throat and threw his body overboard. Grettir's head they kept, wrapped in a bag, so Ongul could present the gruesome evidence to Thorir of Gard and claim his reward. Eavesdropping, I learned how we had been defeated: Ongul had gone to his aged foster-mother Thurid for help in evicting Grettir from Drang. Thurid was a volva, rumoured to use black arts. It was she who had lain concealed beneath the pile of rags when Ongul rowed out to quarrel with Grettir. She needed to hear and judge the quality of her victim before she chose her curse runes. She then cut the marks, stained them with her own blood and selected the hour on which Ongul should launch the cursed tree on the tide. My only consolation, as I listened to the boastful farmers, was to learn that the old crone was hobbling and in dreadful pain. The rock that Grettir threw had smashed her thigh bone and crippled her for life.

Ongul, as it turned out, never received his head money. Thorir of Gard refused to pay up. He said that, as a Christian, he would not reward the use of witchcraft. Ongul took this as a weasel excuse and sued Thorir before the next assembly of the Althing. To his rage the assembled godars supported Thorir's view – he may have bribed them – and went so far as to banish Ongul. They ruled that there had been enough bloodshed and, to forestall revenge by Grettir's friends, it was better that Ongul left Iceland for a while. I was to meet Ongul later, as I will relate, but in the meantime the Gods provided me with a way to honour the memory of my sworn brother.

Thorodd was lenient in his judgement, as I had anticipated. When I was brought before him, he remembered that Grettir had spared his own life when he had challenged the outlaw on the road, and now repaid his debt by declaring that I should be set free after I had paid my captors the ten marks I had promised. This done, Thorodd returned to me my fire ruby, saying that this was what his father had instructed him to do, and undertook to settle my affairs with Gunnhildr's family. He also surprised me by handing over Thrand's old hoard chest. Apparently Thrand had left instructions that if he failed to come back from Jomsburg, I was to be his heir. I donated the entire contents of the chest to Thor. Half the silver paid for a temple mound to be erected in the God's honour on the spot where Thrand's old cabin had stood, and the remainder I buried deep in its earth.

At the feast which followed the temple dedication, I found myself seated next to one of Snorri Godi's sons-in-law, an intelligent and well-to-do farmer by the name of Bolli Bollason. It turned out that Bolli was suffering from that itch for travel which is so characteristic of the northern peoples. 'I can hardly wait for the day when my oldest son can take over my farm, Thorgils,' he confessed. 'I'm going to put it in his care, pack and head off.

I want to see other countries, meet foreign peoples and see how they live while I am still fit and active. Iceland is too small and remote. I feel cooped up here.'

Naturally his words recalled Grettir's words, begging me to travel.

'If you had your choice, Bolli,' I asked, 'which of all the places in the world would you most want to see?'

'Miklagard, the great city,' he responded without a moment's hesitation. 'It's said that there is nowhere else on earth like it – immense palaces, public baths, statues which move of their own accord. Streets paved with marble and you can stroll along them after dark because the emperor who rules there decrees that blazing torches be set up at every corner and kept lit throughout the night.'

'And how does one get to Miklagard?' I asked.

'Across the land of the Rus,' he answered. 'Each year Rus traders bring furs to sell at the imperial court. They have special permits to enter the emperor's territories. If you took a load of furs yourself, you would make a profit from the venture.'

Bolli fingered the collar of his cloak. It was an expensive garment, worn specially for the feast, and the collar was trimmed with some glossy fur.

'The trader who sold me this cloak told me that the Rus get their furs from the northern peoples who trap the animals. I haven't seen it for myself, but it is said the Rus go to certain known places on the edge of the wilderness and lay out their trade goods on the ground. Then they go away and wait. In the night, or at dawn, the natives come out secretly from the woods, pick up the trade goods and replace them with the amount of furs that they think is a fair bargain. They are a strange lot, those fur hunters. They don't like intruders on their territory. If you trespass, they're likely to put a spell on you. No one else is more skilled in seidr, men and women both.'

This last remark decided me. Thor may have put the words

in Bolli's mouth as a reward for my offerings to him, but it was Odinn who determined the outcome. A journey to Miklagard would not only carry out Grettir's wish, it would also bring me closer to my God's mysteries.

So it was that, less than a month later, I had a trader's pack on my back and was plodding through the vast forests of Permia, wondering if Odinn had been in his role as the Deceiver when he lured me there. After a week in the wilderness I had yet to glimpse a single native. I was not even sure what they were called. Bolli Bollason had called them the Skridfinni, and said that the name meant 'the Finni who run on wooden boards'. Others referred to them as Lopar or Lapu and told me, variously, that the name meant 'the runners', 'witches' or 'the banished'. All my informants agreed that the territory they occupied was barren beyond belief. 'Nothing except trees grows up in their land. It's all rock and no soil,' Bolli had warned. 'No crops at all, not even hay. So you won't find cows. Therefore neither milk nor cheese. It's impossible to grow grain . . . so no beer. And as for vines to grow grapes, forget it. Not even sheep can survive. So the Gods alone know what the natives do for clothing to keep out the cold when they haven't any wool to weave. They must do something. There's snow and ice for eight months in the year, and the winter night lasts for two months.'

No one at the trading post where I had bought my trade stock had thrown more light on these mysteries. All they could say was that I should fill my pack with coloured ribbons, brass rings, copper figurines, fish hooks and knife blades. They thought I was mad. Winter was coming on, they pointed out, and this was not the time to trade. Better wait until the spring when the natives emerged from the forest with the winter pelts of their prey. Stubbornly I ignored their advice. I had no intention of spending several months in a remote settlement on the fringes of a wasteland. So I had slung my pack on my back and walked away. Now, with the chill wind beginning to numb my fingers and face,

I was wondering – and that not for the first time – if I had been incredibly foolish. The footpath I had been following through the forest was more and more difficult to trace. Soon I would be lost.

I blundered on. Everything around me was featureless. Each tree looked like the last one I had passed and identical to the trees that I had seen an hour earlier. Very occasionally I heard the sound of a wild animal fleeing from me, the sounds of its alarmed progress fading into the distance. I never saw the animals themselves. They were too wary. The straps of my pack were cutting into my shoulders, and I decided that I would set up camp early and start afresh in the morning. Casting around for a sheltered spot where I could light a fire and eat a meal of dried fish from my pack, I left the faint trace of the path and searched to my left. After fifty paces or so I came across such a dense thicket that I was forced to turn back. I tried in the opposite direction. Again I was thwarted by the thick undergrowth. I returned to the path and walked forward a little further, then tried again. This time I got only twenty paces – I counted them because I did not want to lose my track – before I was again forced to a halt. Once more I returned to the path and moved forward. The bushes were crowding closer. I limped on. There was a raw blister on my right heel where the shoe was rubbing and my foot hurt. I was concentrating on this pain when I noticed that the path led to an obvious gap between the dense thickets. Gratefully I quickened my pace and walked forward, then tripped. Looking down, I saw my foot was entangled in a net laid out on the ground. I was bending down to untangle the restraint when I heard a sharp, angry intake of breath. Straightening up, I saw a man step from behind a tree. He was carrying a hunting bow, its arrow set to the string and he drew it back deliberately and quietly, aiming at my chest. I stood absolutely still, trying to look innocent and harmless.

The stranger stood no higher than my chest. He was wearing the skin of an animal, some sort of deer, which he wore like a loose blouse. His head poked through a slit cut in the skin and the garment was gathered in at his waist by a broad belt made from the skin of the same animal. This blouse reached down to his knees and his lower legs were clad in leather leggings, which extended down to strange-looking leather slippers with turned-up toes. On his head was a conical cap, also of deerskin. For a moment he reminded me of a land wight. He had appeared just as silently and magically.

He made no further move towards me, but clicked his tongue softly. From behind other trees and out of the thickets emerged half a dozen of his companions. They ranged from one youngster who could only have been about twelve years old, to a much older man, whose scraggly beard was turning grey. Their precise ages were difficult to tell because their faces were unusually wrinkled and lined, and they were all dressed in identical deerskin garments. Not one of them was tall enough to come up to my shoulder, and they all had similar features – broad foreheads and pronounced cheekbones over wide mouths and narrow chins, which gave their faces a strangely triangular shape. Several of the men, I noted, had watery eyes as if they had been staring too long into the sun. Then I remembered what Olaf had told me about the long months of snow and ice, and recognised what I had seen in my childhood in Greenland – the lingering effects of snow blindness.

They were not aggressive. All of them were carrying long hunting bows, but only the first man kept an arrow aimed at me, and after a few moments he lowered his bow and let the tension relax. Then followed a brief discussion in a language that I could not understand. There seemed to be no leader – everyone including the youngster had an opinion to express. Suddenly they turned to leave and one of them jerked his head at me, indicating that I was to follow. Mystified, I set out, walking behind them along the trail. They did not even look over their shoulders to see if I was there and I found that, despite their small size, the Lopar – as I knew they must be – travelled remarkably quickly through the forest.

A brisk march brought us to where they lived. A cluster of
tents stood on the bank of a small river. At first I thought this
was a hunters' camp, but then I saw women, children and dogs
and even a baby's cradle hanging from a tree, and realised that
this was a nomad home. Tethered at a little distance were five
unusual-looking animals. That they were deer was evident because
they had antlers which would have done justice to the forest stags
I had hunted with Edgar in England. Yet their bodies were less
than half the size. Somehow their smallness seemed appropriate
among a people who – by Norse standards – were diminutive.

The man who had first revealed himself to me in the forest led
me to his tent, indicated that I should wait and ducked inside. I
eased the pack from my shoulders, lowered it to the ground and
sat down beside it. The man reappeared and silently handed me a
wooden bowl. It contained pieces of a cake. I tasted it and recognised fish and wild berries mashed together.

As I ate the fish cake, everyone in the camp continued about
their normal business, fetching water from the river in small
wooden buckets, bringing in sticks of firewood, moving between
the tents, all the while politely ignoring me. I wondered what
would happen next. After an interval, during which I finished
my meal and drank from a wooden cup of water brought to me
by one of the Lopar women, my guardian – which was how I
thought of him – again emerged from his tent. In his hand was
what I thought was a large sieve with a wooden rim. Then I saw
it was a drum, broad, flat and no deeper than the span of my
hand, an irregular oval in shape. He placed the drum carefully
upon the ground and squatted down beside it. Several of the other
men strolled over. They sat in a circle and another quiet discussion
followed. Again I could not understand what they were saying,
though several times I heard the word vuobman. Eventually my
guardian reached inside his deerskin tunic and produced a small
wedge of horn, no bigger than a gaming counter, which he placed
gently on the surface of his drum. From the folds of his blouse he
next pulled out a short hammer-shaped drumstick and began to

tap gently on the drum skin. All the onlookers leaned forward, watching intently.

I guessed what was happening and rose to my feet. Walking over to the group, I joined the circle, my neighbour politely shifting aside to give me space. I was reminded of the Saxon wands. The surface of the drum was painted with dozens of figures and symbols. Some I recognised: fish, deer, a dancing, stick-like man, a bow and arrow, half a dozen of the Elder runes. Many symbols were new to me and I could only guess their meaning – lozenges, zigzag lines, irregular star patterns, curves and ripples. I supposed that one of them must represent the sun, another the moon and perhaps a third depicted a forest of trees. I said nothing as the little horn counter hopped and skipped on the drum skin as it vibrated to the regular tapping of the drummer. The counter moved here and there, then seemed to find its own position, remaining on one spot – over the drawing of a man who seemed to have antlers on his head. Abruptly my guardian stopped his drumming. The counter stayed where it was. He picked it up, placed it on the centre of the drum and began again, tapping a slow, repeated rhythm. Again the counter advanced across the drum and came to the same position. A third time my guardian cast the lot, this time starting the counter at the edge of the drum skin before he began to urge it into life. Once more the wedge of horn moved to the figure of the antlered man, but then moved on until it came to rest on the symbol of a triangle. I guessed it was a tent.

My guardian slipped the drumstick back inside his blouse, and there was complete silence in the assembled group. Something had changed. Where the Lopar had previously been courteous, almost aloof, now they seemed a little nervous. Whatever the drum had told them, its message had been clear.

My guardian returned the drum to his tent and beckoned to me to follow him. He led me to a tent set slightly apart from the others. Like them it was an array of long thin poles propped together and neatly covered with sheets of birch bark. Pausing outside the tent flap, he called, 'Rassa!' The man who came out from the tent was the ugliest Lopar I had yet seen. He was of the same height and build as all the others in the camp, but every feature of his face was out of true. His nose was askew and bulbous. Eyes, bulging under bushy eyebrows, gave him a perpetually startled expression. His lips failed to close over slightly protruding teeth, and his mouth was definitely lopsided. Compared to the neat foxy-faced Lopars around him, he looked grotesque.

'You are welcome among us. I am glad you have arrived.' said this odd-looking native. I was startled. Not just by what he said, but that he had spoken in Norse, heavily accented and carefully phrased but clearly understandable.

'Your name is Rassa?' I asked hesitantly.

'Yes.' he replied. 'I told the hunters that the vuodman would provide an unusual catch today and they should not harm it, but bring it back to camp.'

'The vuodman?' I asked. 'I don't know what you mean.'

'The vuodman is where they lie in wait for the boazo.' He saw that I was looking even more mystified. 'You must excuse me. I don't know how to say boazo in your tongue. Those animals over there are boazo.' He nodded towards the five small tethered deer. 'Those are tame ones. We place them in the forest to attract their wild kind into the trap. Now is the season when the wild boazo leave the open ground and come into the forest to seek food and find shelter from the coming blizzards.'

'And the voudman?'

'That was the thicket that kept turning you back when you were walking. Our hunters were watching you. I hear you tried to leave the trail several times. You made much noise. In fact they nearly lost our prize boazo who was frightened by your approach and ran off. Luckily they recaptured it before it had gone too far.'

I recalled the hunting technique Edgar had showed me in the forest of Northamptonshire, how he had placed me where the deer would be directed towards the arrows of the waiting hunters. It seemed that the Lopar did the same, building thickets of brush to funnel the wild deer in the place where the hunters lay in ambush.

'I apologise for spoiling the hunt,' I said. 'I had no idea that I was in Lopar hunting grounds.'

'Our name is not Lopar,' said Rassa gently. 'That word I heard when I visited the settled peoples — at the time when I learned to speak some words of your language — we are Sabme. To call us Lopar would be the same as if we called you cavemen.'

'Cavemen? We don't live in caves.'

Rassa smiled his crooked smile.

'Sabme children learn how Ibmal the Creator made the first men. They were two brothers. Ibmal set the brothers on the earth and they flourished, hunting and fishing. Then Ibmal sent a great howling blizzard with gales and driving snow and ice. One of the brothers ran off and found a cave, and hid himself in it. He survived. But the other brother chose to stay outside and fight the blizzard. He went on hunting and fishing and learning how to keep alive. After the blizzard had passed over, one brother emerged from the cave and from him are descended all the settled peoples. From the other brother came the Sabme.'

I was beginning to take a liking to this forthright, homely little man. 'Come,' he said, 'as you are to be my guest, we should find out a little more about you and the days that lie ahead.'

With no more ceremony than Thrand consulting the rune tablets, Rassa produced his own prophecy drum. It was much bigger and more intricately decorated than the one I had seen before. Rassa's drum had many, many more symbols. They were drawn, he told me, with the red juice from the alder tree, and he had hung coloured ribbons, small amulets and charms of copper, horn and a few in silver round the drum's edge. I carried copies of the same charms in my trade pack.

Rassa dropped a small marker on the drum skin. This time the marker was a brass ring. Before he began to tap on the drum, I intervened.

'What do the symbols mean?' I asked.

He gave me a shrewd glance. 'I think you already know some of them,' he replied.

'I can see some runes,' I said.

'Yes, I learned those signs among the settled peoples.'

'What about that one? What does that signify?' I pointed to a wavy triple line. There were several similar symbols painted at different places on the drum skin.

'They are the mountains, the places where our ancestors dwell.'

'And that one?' I indicated the drawing of a man wearing antlers on his head.

'That is the noaide's own sign. You call him a seidrmann.'

'And if the marker goes there what does it mean?'

'It tells of the presence of a noaide, or that the noaide must be consulted. Every Sabme tent has a drum of prophecy, and some-one to use it. But only a noaide can read the deeper message of the arpa, the moving marker.'

Abruptly he closed his eyes and began to sing. It was a thin, quavering chant, the same short phrase repeated over and over and over again, rising in pitch until the words suddenly stopped, cut off mid-phrase as if the refrain had fallen into a pool of silence. After a short pause, Rassa began the chant again, once more raising the pitch of his voice until coming to the same abrupt halt. As he chanted, he tapped on his drum. Watching the ugly little man, his eyes closed, his body swaying back and forth very slightly, I knew that I was in the presence of a highly accom-plished seidrmann. Rassa was able to enter the spirit world as easily as I could strike sparks from a flint.

After the fourth repetition of his chant, Rassa opened his eyes and looked down at the drum. I was not surprised to see that the arpa was resting once again on the antlered man. Rassa grunted, as if it merely confirmed what he had expected. Then he closed his eyes and resumed tapping, more urgently this time. I watched the track of the brass ring as it skittered across the face of the drum. It visited symbol after symbol without pausing, hesitated and then retraced a slightly different track. Rassa's drumming ended and this time he did not look down at the drum but straight at me. 'Tell me,' he said.

Strangely, I had anticipated the question. It was as if a bond, an understanding, existed between the noiade and myself. We both took it for granted that I possessed seidr skill and had come to Rassa for enlightenment.

'Movement,' I said. 'There will be movement. Towards the mountains, though which mountains I do not know. Then the drum spoke of something I do not understand, something mysterious, obscure, a little dangerous. Also of a union, a meeting.'

Rassa now looked down at the drum himself. The brass ring had come to rest on a drawing of a man seated on horseback. 'Is that what you meant by movement?' he asked.

The answer seemed obvious, but I answered, 'No, not that sign. I can't be sure how to interpret it, but whatever it is, it concerns me closely. When the ring approached the symbol and then came to rest, my spirit felt strengthened.'

'Look again and tell me what you see,' the noiade replied.

I examined the figure more closely. It was almost the smallest symbol on the drum, squeezed into a narrow space between older, more faded figures. It was unique. Nowhere else could I see this mark repeated. The horse rider was carrying a round shield. That was odd, I thought. Nowhere among the Sabme had I seen a shield. Besides, a horse would never survive in this bleak cold land. I looked again, and noticed that the horse, drawn in simple outline, had eight legs.

I looked up at Rassa. He was gazing at me questioningly with his bulging eyes. 'That is Odinn,' I said. 'Odinn riding Sleipnir.'

'Is it? I copied that sign from something I saw among the settled folk. I saw it carved on a rock and knew that it had power.'

'Odinn is my God,' I said. 'I am his devotee. It was Odinn who brought me to your land.'

'Later you can tell me who is this Odinn,' Rassa answered, 'but among my people that symbol has another meaning. For us it is the symbol of approaching death.'

WITH THIS ENIGMATIC forecast I began my time among the forest Sabme. My days with them were to be some of the most remarkable, and satisfactory, of my life, thanks almost entirely to Rassa and his family. Rassa was no ordinary noaide. He was acknowledged as maybe the greatest noaide of his time. His unusual appearance had marked him out from his earliest childhood. Ungainly and clumsy, he had differed from other boys. Trying to play their games, he would sometimes fall down on the ground and choke or lose his senses entirely. Norse children would have mocked and teased him, but the Sabme treated him with special gentleness. No one had been surprised when, at the age of eight, he began to have strange and disturbing dreams. It was the proof to the Sabme that the sacred ancestors had sent Rassa as their intermediary, and Rassa's parents unhesitatingly handed over their son to the local shaman for instruction. Thirty years later his reputation extended from the forest margins where his own people lived as far as the distant coast, to those Sabme who fished for seal and small whale. Among all the Sabme bands, the siida, it was known that Rassa was a great noaide, and from time to time he would come to visit them in his spirit travels. So high was his reputation when I arrived among them that no one questioned why he decided to take a lumbering stranger into his tent and instruct him in the sacred ways. His own siida believed that their great noaide had summoned me. Their drums told them so. For my part, I believed sometimes that Rassa was Odinn's agent. At other times I thought he might be the All-Father himself, in human guise.

Our siida (as I soon came to think of it) shifted camp the morning after my arrival. They did not trouble to dismantle their birch-bark tents. They merely gathered up their few belongings, wrapped them in bundles, which they slung on rawhide cords over their shoulders or tied to their backs, and set off along the trail that followed the river bank. The fishing had been disappointing, Rassa explained. The local water spirit and the Fish Gods were displeased. The reason for their anger he did not know. There was a hole in the bottom of the river, leading to a subterranean spirit river, and the fish had all fled there. It would be wise for the siida to move to another spot, where the spirits were more friendly. There was no time to waste. Soon the river would be frozen over and fishing – on which the siida depended at least as much as hunting – would become impossible. Our straggle of twenty families, together with their dogs and the six haltered boazo, walked for half a day before we came to our destination, further downstream. Clearly the siida had occupied the site pre- viously. There were tent frames already standing, which the Sabme quickly covered with deerskins.

'Birch bark is not strong enough to withstand the snows and gales, nor warm enough,' Rassa explained. 'For the next few weeks we will use a single layer of deerskin. Later, when it gets really cold, we'll add extra layers to keep in the warmth.'

His own family consisted of his wife, a married daughter with her husband and their small baby, and a second daughter who seemed vaguely familiar. Then I realised that she had been with the hunting party at the vuodman. With all the Sabme dressed in their deerskin blouses, leggings and caps, it was difficult to tell men from women, and I had not expected a girl to be among the hunters. Nor, during the previous night spent in Rassa's tent, had I noticed that he had a second daughter because the Sabme removed only their shoes before they lay down and they slept almost fully clothed. I had crawled into Rassa's tent to find the place half filled with smoke. There was a fireplace in the centre, and the chimney hole in the apex of the tent had been partly covered over because several fish were hanging to cure from a pole projecting over the fire. Staying close to the ground was the only place where it was possible to breathe freely. Arranged

around the outer edge of the tent were the family possessions and
these became our pillows when we all lay down to sleep on
deerskins over a carpet of fresh birch twigs. There was no
furniture of any kind.

Rassa asked me to walk with him to the river bank. I noticed
that all the other Sabme stayed well back, watching us. The water
was shallow, fast flowing over gravel and rocks. Rassa had a fish
spear in one hand and a birch-bark fish basket in the other.
Without pausing, he waded out to a large, slick boulder which
projected above the water. Rassa scanned the surface of the river
for a few moments, then stabbed with his fish spear, successfully
spiking a small fish about the length of my hand. He carefully
removed the fish from the barbs, knocked its head against the
rock and laid the dead fish on the rock. Next he placed the fish
basket on his head, and spoke some words in the Sabme tongue,
apparently addressing the rock itself. Scooping up water in the
palm of his hand, he poured it onto the rock, and bowed three
times. With the curved knife which every Sabme wore dangling
from his belt, he scraped some scales from the fish. Cradling the
scales in the palm of his hand he returned to the camp, where he
distributed them to the man of each family. Only then did the
siida begin to prepare their nets and fishing lines and approach the
water. 'The rock is a sieidde,' Rassa explained to me, 'the spirit of
the river. I asked fishing luck for every family. I promised that
each family that catches fish will make an offering to the sieidde.
They will do this at the end of every day that we stay here, and
will do so whenever we return to this place in the future.'

'Why did you give fish scales only to the men?' I asked.

'It is bad luck for a woman to approach the sieidde of the
river. Ill luck for the siida and dangerous for the woman herself.
It can harm her future children.'

'But didn't I see your daughter with the hunters at the
vuodman. If the women can hunt, why can't they fish?'

'That is the way it has always been. My daughter Allba hunts because she's as good as many of the men when it comes to the chase, if not better. They can hardly keep up with her. She's quick and nimble even in dense forest. She was always like that, from when she was a little child. Her only fault is that she likes to talk all the time, a constant chatter. That's why my wife and I named her after the little bird that hops around in summer in the bushes and never stops saying "tik-a-tik".'

With every sentence, Rassa was strengthening my desire to stay among the Sabme if they would allow it. I wanted to learn more of Rassa's seidr and to honour my promise to Grettir by sharing in their way of life. Remembering the store of fish hooks in my trade pack, I went to fetch them and handed my entire stock to Rassa. He accepted the gift almost casually, as if it was the most natural thing in the world. 'We make our own fish hooks of wood or bone. But metal ones are far better,' he said as he began to distribute them among the different families.

'Do you share out everything?' I asked.

He shook his head. 'Not everything. Each person and each family knows what is theirs – clothes, dogs, knives, cooking gear. But they will lend or give that item to someone else if it meets a need. Not to do so would be selfish. We have learned that only by helping one another can we survive as a siida.'

'Then what about the other siida? What happens if you both want to fish on the same river or hunt boazo in the same area of forest?'

'Each siida knows its own territory,' he answered. 'Its members have hunted or fished in certain places down through the generations. We respect that custom.'

'But if you do have a dispute over, say, a good fishing place when there is a famine, do you fight for your rights?'

Rassa looked mildly shocked. 'We never fight. We use all our energy in finding food and shelter, making sure that our children grow up healthy, honouring our ancestors. If another siida is starving and needs a particular fishing spot or hunting ground, then they ask us and if possible we agree to lend it to them until their lives have improved. Besides, our land is so broad that there is room enough for all.'

'I find that strange,' I told him. 'Where I come from, a man will fight to defend what he owns. If a neighbour tries to take his land, or a stranger comes to seize his property, we fight and try to drive him away.'

'For the Sabme that's not necessary,' said the noaide. 'If someone invades our territory, we hide or we run away. We wait until the winter comes and the foreigners have to leave. We know that they are not fit to stay.'

He gestured towards the clothes I was wearing – woollen shirt and loose trousers, a thick travelling cloak and the same ill-fitting leather shoes which had given me blisters earlier. 'The foreigners dress like you. They don't know any better. That is why I've asked my wife and Allba to prepare clothes more suitable for the winter. They've never made clothes so big before, but they will have them ready for you in a few days.'

The unexpected benefit of Rassa's request for clothes that would fit me was that it silenced, temporarily, the constant chatter of his daughter Allba. She talked without pause, mostly to her mother, who went about her work quietly, scarcely bothering to reply. I had no idea what Allba was saying, but did not doubt that I was often the topic of her conversation. Now, as she sat with her mother stitching my winter wardrobe, Allba's mouth was too full of deer sinew for her to keep up her constant chatter. Every thread in the garment had to be ripped with teeth from dried sinew taken from a deer's back or legs, then chewed to soften the fibre and rolled into thread. While the women chewed and stitched, I helped Rassa prepare the family meals. One of the novel features of life among the Sabme was that the men did the cooking.

It must have been in about my fourth week with the siide that two events occurred which changed my situation. The first event was anticipated, but the second was a complete surprise. I woke

up one morning at the usual time, just after first light, and as
I lay on my deerskin rug I noticed that the interior of the tent
was much lighter than usual. I rolled over and peered at the small
gap between the edge of the tent and the ground. The daylight
was shining through the gap so brightly that it made me squint.
Quietly I got up, pushed aside the door flap, and stepped out. The
entire camp was shrouded in a covering of heavy snow. The first
great snowfall had come upon us in the night. Everything we had
left outside the tents – firewood, fish baskets, the nets, the sleeping
dogs – were humps in the snow. Even the six boazo had snowy
coats. Winter had arrived.

That was the day that Rassa's wife and daughter finished my
deerskin garments. There was much mirth among the Sabme as
they came to our tent to see me being shown how to put them
on. First came a deerskin shirt, worn with the fur against my skin,
then close-fitting deerskin trousers, which were awkward to pull
on though they had slits at the ankles, and a pair of hand-sewn
shoes. These had the characteristic turned-up toes but no heels.
'For when you wear skis,' Rassa explained. He was teasing out
some dried sedge grass by separating the strands, then arranging
them into two soft padded squares. 'Here put these in your shoes,'
he said, 'You'll find them better than any woollen socks. They'll
keep your feet warmer, and when they get wet they'll dry out in
moments if you hold them near the fire.' Finally he helped me
into the long Sabme deerskin blouse. It reached down to my
knees. A broad belt held the garment tight around my waist.
When I took a few experimental steps, the sensation was quite
different from any other clothes I had ever worn before – my
body warm and protected, my legs free.

The second event took place on the night after the snowfall.
When I entered the family tent, I found a second deerskin had
been left on my usual sleeping place. As the weather had turned
much colder, I pulled the deerskin over me as a blanket when I
lay down. I was on the verge of falling asleep, when I felt the
edge of the deerskin lift and someone crawl in beside me. There

was enough light from the fire's embers to see that my visitor was Rassa's daughter, Allba. I could see the gleam of the firelight in her eyes and her face had a mischievous look. She placed her mouth against my ear and said softly, 'Tik-a-tik,' then giggled and snuggled down beside me. I did not know what to do. Close by slept her father and mother, her sister and brother-in-law. I feared Rassa's reaction should he wake up. For several moments I lay there, pretending to be asleep. Then Allba's hand began to explore. Very quietly she loosened my Sabme belt and removed my leggings. Then she slid inside my Sabme blouse and nestled against me. She was naked.

I woke up to find that I had overslept. Allba lay curled up within my outstretched arm and the tent was empty. Rassa and the other members of his family had already begun their day. I could hear them moving about outside. Hurriedly I began to pull on my clothes, and this woke Allba. Her eyes were pale blue-grey, a colour sometimes found among the Sabme, and she gazed up at me without the slightest trace of embarrassment. She looked utterly content. She wriggled across to where her clothes lay and, a moment later, she was dressed and ducking out of the tent flap to join her parents. Slowly I followed, wondering what reception I would receive.

Rassa looked up at me as I emerged, and seemed utterly unconcerned. 'You know how to use these, I hope,' was all he said. He was wiping the snow off two long flat lathes of wood.

'I rode on a ski when I was a child, but only a few times, and mostly as a game,' I answered.

'You'll need to know more than that. Allba can show you.'

It dawned on me that Rassa was taking my relationship with his second daughter as normal. Later I was to discover that he actively approved of it. The Sabme thought it natural for a man and woman to sleep together if both were willing. They considered it a sensible arrangement if it is satisfactory for both partners. For a while I worried that Allba was anticipating that our relationship would become a permanent bond. But later, after she had instructed me in a few words of the Sabme language and I had taught her to speak some Norse, she laughed at me when I expressed my concern.

'How can one expect something like that to go on for ever? That's how the settled people think. It would be like staying in one spot permanently. The Sabme believe that in life, the seasons change and it is better to travel than to stay.' I began to say something more, but she laid a finger on my lips and added, 'I could have come to your bed as an act of kindness, as you are the guest in my tent. But that is not why I joined you. I did so because I wanted you and you have not disappointed me.'

Allba was the remedy for an ailment that I scarcely knew I suffered. My shabby treatment at the hands of Gunnhildr, my disenchantment with Aelfgifu, and my youthful heartbreaks had left me disillusioned with the opposite sex. I viewed women with caution, fearing either disappointment or some unforeseen calamity. Allba cured all that. She was so full of life, so active, so natural and uncomplicated. In love-making she was skilled as well as lustful, and I would have been a dullard not to have revelled in my good fortune. Beneath those layers of deerskin clothes, she was very seductive. She had small, fine bones which made her seem as fragile and lightweight as the little snow bird after which she had been named. Constant exercise while hunting and skiing meant that her body was in perfect condition, with slim shoulders and hips. Tiny, high, arched feet gave her a quick, graceful step, and I was roused to discover that the skin of her body and limbs was a smooth dark ivory in contrast to the dark tanned elfin face, its lines etched by snow glare and the wind. Although neither of us became hostage to the other, I think Allba relished our relationship. She was proud of my role as a foreign noaide. For my part I was entranced by her. In short, I fell in love with Allba and my love was unfettered and free.

She taught me how to travel on skis. Not as well as any Sabme, of course. The Sabme learn the skill of travelling across the country on wooden boards as soon as they learn to walk, and no one can really acquire their expertise. Just as the Norse are the finest ship handlers and shipbuilders, so the Sabme excel at snow travel. Nature seems to have designed them for it. Their light weight ensures that they glide across snow that would crack beneath a heavier burden, and their agility means they can thread their way across broken terrain that would thwart a clumsier man. They do not use the ski as the Norse do, riding a single board, with a stick to steer and propel themselves downhill or across a frozen surface. The Sabme attach a board to each foot and can stride at the speed of a running man. They keep up the pace for as long as daylight will allow them. Where Norse craftsmen know how to shape a hull or cut and stitch a sail to best advantage, the Sabme know how to select and shape the skis that bear them, birch wood when the snow is soft, pine when the surface hardens; every ski – they are unequal in length – is hand-crafted to suit the style and size of the user. In the end I learned to travel on the wooden lathes well enough to keep up with siida when we moved, or to travel slowly alongside when Rassa wanted to show me some remote sacred place. But I could never match Allba and the other hunters. They moved so confidently across the snow that they could run down a wolf and get its pelt. For hour after hour they would pursue their prey across the snow, the animal tiring as it leaped through the drifts over which the hunters glided effortlessly. Finally, when the exhausted wolf turned snarling on its pursuers, the leading Sabme would ski close enough to spear or knife the beast to death.

FIFTEEN

ALLBA WORE AROUND her neck an amulet in the shape of a bird. She never took it off, even when we were making love. The bird was her companion, she said, and she asked why I did not wear my own. As a man I should carry it on a cord looped round from my neck and under my arm, so that the talisman hung within my armpit. 'Are you so brave that you risk travelling alone?' she asked. 'Even my father does not do that.' I thought she was talking of a good-luck charm and I made a joke of it, telling her that I had a dozen talismans in my trade pack and was well guarded. It was one of the few times I saw Allba angry. She told me not to play the fool.

When I asked Rassa why his daughter had reacted with such intensity, he asked if I remembered where I had first joined the siida. 'The fishing had been very bad in that place,' he reminded me. 'The fish had gone away. They were still there, but they were not there. We had to move to where another sieidde would accept our sacrifices.'

'How could the fish be there and not there?'

'They had gone away to their own saivo river. I could have followed them, or sent my companion to plead with the water spirit who sent them there. But if the water spirit was still angry, the fish might not have returned.'

The saivo, according to Rassa, is a world which lies alongside our own. It is a mirror of our world, yet more substantial and in it live the spirits of the departed and the companions of the living. These companions come into our world to join us as wraiths and sometimes we can visit the saivo ourselves, but we need our guardian wraiths to guide and protect us.

'Our companions are animals, not people,' Rassa said, putting aside the wooden bowl he had been carving. 'Every Sabme has one – whether it is a fox, a lynx, a bird or some other animal. When we are very young the drum tells our parents which creature is to be our saivo companion through life. Occasionally the wrong choice is made and then the child gets sick or has an accident. So we ask the drum again and it indicates a new companion, one that will be more suitable. Since Allba was a baby her saivo wraith is the bird whose image she wears.'

'Among my people,' I said, 'there are fylga, the fetches. I have seen them myself at times of death. They are our other-persons from another world. When they appear, they resemble us directly. Do you mean that I have an animal companion as well?'

Rassa reached across to where his drum lay on the ground. It was always close to his hand. He placed the arpa on the taut drum skin, and without even closing his eyes or singing his chant, he gave a single hard rap on the drum with his forefinger. The arpa leaped, struck the wooden rim and bounced back. It landed on the outline figure of a bear.

I chose to doubt him. 'How do I know that my companion is a bear?'

'It was decided for you at the time of your birth.'

'But I was born on an island in the ocean where there are no bears.'

'Perhaps a bear entered the lives of your parents.'

I thought for a moment. 'I was told that when my father first met my mother, he was on his way back from a voyage to Norway to deliver a captive polar bear. But he had handed over the bear many weeks before he met my mother, and anyhow the bear died soon afterwards.'

'You will find that the bear died about the time you were born,' said Rassa firmly. 'The bear's spirit has protected you since then. That is your good fortune. The bear is the most powerful of all creatures. It has the intelligence of one man and the strength of nine.'

Before the sun vanished below the horizon for winter, Rassa suggested that if I wanted to know more about the saivo I should enter it myself. I hesitated. I told him that my experience of the other world had been in brief glimpses, through second sight, usually in the company of others who also possessed the ability, and that sometimes the experience had been disturbing and unpleasant. I said I was doubtful that I had the courage to enter the spirit world deliberately and alone. He assured me that my spirit companion would protect me, and that he himself could assist me to pass through the barrier that separated us from the saivo. 'Your second sight shows that you already live close enough to the saivo to see through the veil that divides it from us. I am only proposing that you pass through the veil entirely and discover what lies on the other side.'

'How do I know that I will be able to return?' I asked.

'That, too, I can arrange with Allba's help,' he answered.

He woke Allba and me long before dawn the next day. He had already lit a small fire in the central hearth and cleared a space at the back of the tent. There was enough room for me to sit cross-legged on a square of deerskin. The hide was placed fur side down, and its surface had been painted with the four white lines in the pattern that I had known from throwing the rune counters and the Saxon wands. Rassa indicated that I should sit within the central square and that Allba would squat facing me. 'As my daughter, she has inherited some of my powers,' he said. 'If she is near at hand, you may meet her in the saivo.'

Allba's presence gave me more confidence, for I was feeling

very nervous. She untied the small leather pouch she wore on her belt when she went on her hunting trips and shook out the contents onto the deerskin in front of me. The red caps with their white spots were faded to a dull, mottled pink, but I could still recognise the dried and shrivelled mushrooms. Allba picked them over carefully, running her small fingers over them delicately, feeling their rough surface. Then she selected three of the smallest. Carefully putting the others back into the pouch, she left two of the mushrooms on the deerskin, placed the third in her mouth and began to chew deliberately. She kept her eyes on me, her gaze never wavering. After a little time, she put her hand to her mouth and spat out the contents. She held out her palm to me. 'Eat,' she said. I took the warm moist pellet from her, placed it on my tongue and swallowed. Twice more she softened the mushrooms and twice more I swallowed.

Then I sat quietly facing her, observing the firelight play across her features. Her eyes were in shadow.

Time passed. I had no way of judging how long I sat there. Rassa stayed in the background and added several dry sticks to the fire to keep it alight.

Slowly, very slowly, I began to lose touch with my body. As I separated from its physical presence, I felt my body trembling. Once or twice I knew I twitched. But there was nothing I could do about it and I felt unconcerned. A hazy contentment was settling over me. My body seemed to grow lighter as my thoughts relaxed. Everything except for Allba's face became indistinct. She did not move, yet her face came closer and closer. I saw every tiny detail with extraordinary clarity. The lobe of her right ear filled my vision. I detected the gentle blush of blood beneath the skin, the soft fuzz of hair. I wanted to reach out and nibble it in my teeth.

Suddenly there was no ground beneath me. I was suspended in a comfortable space. I knew that my body was there with me, but it had no importance. Without any sensation of movement I was in an endless landscape of trees, snow and rock, but I felt no cold. I glided over the surface without contact. It was as if I was riding on a gentle air current. The trees were a vivid green and I could examine every leaf and wrinkle of the bark in minute detail. The snow reflected the colours of the rainbow, the crystals shifted, merged and rippled. A small bird flew up from a bush and I knew that it was Allba's companion. Between two trees I glimpsed the upright form of a white bear, close, yet not close. It was standing upright, its two eyes gazing at me with a human expression and motionless. I heard someone speaking to me. I recognised my own voice and replied. The conversation was reassuring. I felt peaceful. A bear, dark brown this time, appeared to one side of my path, head down, lumbering and swaying as it walked along and our tracks were converging. When the animal was in touching distance, we both halted. I felt the brush of a bird's wing against my cheek. The bear slowly turned to face me and its muzzle beneath the eyes seemed to smile.

The eyes were grey-blue, and I realised that I was looking into Allba's face. I was back on the deerskin, still seated.

'You have come back from the saivo,' said Rassa. 'You were there only a short time, but long enough to know how to return there if you wish.'

'It seemed very like our own world,' I said, 'only much larger and always just beyond reach, as though it withheld itself.'

'That is appearance only,' said the noaide. 'The saivo is full of spirits, the spirts of the dead as well as the spirits who rule our lives. By comparison our world is temporary and fragile. Our world is in the present, while the saivo is eternal. Those who travel into the saivo glimpse the forces that determine our existence, but only when those spirits wish to be seen. Those who visit the saivo regularly become accepted there and then the spirits reveal themselves.'

'Why should a bear smile?' I asked.

Opposite me Allba suddenly got to her feet and left the tent. Rassa did not answer. Without warning I felt dizzy and my stomach heaved. More than anything else, I wanted to lie down and close my eyes again. I could barely drag myself back to my sleeping place and the last thing I remembered was Rassa throwing a deerskin over me.

Snow fell almost daily now, heavy flakes drifting down through the trees and settling on the ground. Our hunters made repeated sweeps of the forest to lay out their wooden traps because the fur-bearing animals had grown their winter coats and were in their prime. The siida made one final move. It was laborious because our tents were now double- or triple-layered to keep out the cold and difficult to dismantle and we were hampered by our heavy winter clothing. We went to ground, quite literally. The siida had its midwinter camp in the lee of a low ridge, which gave shelter from the blizzards. Over the generations each family had dug itself a refuge, excavating the soft earthen side of the ridge, then covering the crater with a thick roof of logs and earth. The entrance to Rassa's cabin was little more than a tunnel, through which I crawled on hands and knees, but the place was surprisingly spacious once inside. I could stand upright and though the place was smoky from the small fire in the central hearth it was cosy. I admitted to myself that the thought of spending the next few months here with Allba was appealing. Rassa's wife had spread the floor with the usual carpet of fresh spruce twigs covered with deerskins, and had divided the interior into small cubicles by hanging up sheets of light cotton obtained from the springtime traders. The contrast with the squalid dugout where Grettir had died could not have been greater. I said so to Rassa and described how my sworn brother had met his end through a volva's malign intervention, with curse runes cut on a log.

'Had your sworn brother met with such an accident among the Sabme, injuring himself with that axe,' commented Rassa, 'we would have known that it was surely a staallu's doing. The staallu can disguise himself as an animal, a deer perhaps, and allows himself to be hunted down and killed. But when the hunter begins to cut up the animal to take its flesh and hide, the staallu turns the knife blade on the bone, so that the hunter cuts himself badly. If the hunter is far from his siida, he bleeds to death beside the carcass of his kill. Then the staallu returns to his normal shape, drinks the blood and feasts on the corpse of his victim.'

Allba, who was listening, gave a little scornful hiss. 'If I ever meet the staallu, he will regret the day. That's just a story to frighten children.'

'Don't be so sure, Allba. Just hope you never meet him,' her father murmured, then turning to me said, 'The staallu roams the forest. He's big and a bit simple and clumsy. We say he's like those coarse traders who come to acquire our furs in the spring-time, though the staallu's appetite is even more gross. He eats human flesh when times are hard, and has been known to carry off Sabme girls.'

That same week I gave away the rest of the contents of my trader's pack. I had lost any ambition to barter with the members of the siida for furs and I was ashamed to hold back items which could be useful to the band. The Sabme were so generous and hospitable to me that it seemed wrong not to contribute my share to their well-being. Apart from mending nets and doing some primitive metalwork, I was useless to them, so I handed the pack over to Rassa and asked that he distribute the contents to who-ever needed it most. The only item I kept back was the fire ruby – and that I gave to Allba as a love token. The jewel delighted her. She spent hours in the cabin, sitting by the fire with the ruby in her fingers and turning the gem this way and that so that the red light flickered within the gem. 'There is a spirit dancing inside the stone,' she would say. 'It is the spirit which brought you to me.'

The effect of giving away all my trade goods was the reverse of what I had expected – instead of ending my chances of obtain-ing furs to take to Miklagard, I was deluged with them. Nearly every day a hunter left outside Rassa's cabin the frost-stiffened carcass of an ermine, a sable, a squirrel or a white fox, whose luxurious pelt Allba would skin and prepare for me. There was no way of knowing which hunter was responsible for the gift. They came and went silently on their skis. Only the blizzards stopped them. When the blizzard spirit raged the entire siida would disappear inside their underground shelters and wait for the terrible wind and driving snow to end. Then, cautiously, the Sabme dug themselves out of the snow-covered lairs and, like the animals they hunted, sniffed the wind and set out to forage.

Of course we ate the flesh of the animals we skinned. Some were rank and disagreeable – marten and otter were particularly unpleasant. But squirrel was tasty and so too was beaver. Whatever meat was left over we placed in the little larders each Sabme family had built close to their cabin, a small hutch on a pole or set on top of a rock, so as it was out of reach of animals. The food never spoiled in the bitter cold. If a hunter was lucky enough to kill a wild boaz, he stored wooden bowls of the fresh deer's blood in the same place. Within hours it had frozen hard and could be chopped in pieces with an axe and brought within the cabin as required.

Rassa was called away by the spirits from time to time, though not always when he wanted. Without warning he would begin to twitch and writhe, then lose his balance and fall to the ground. If the spirit call was urgent, he foamed at the mouth. He had told us to press a rag into his mouth if his tongue lolled out, but not to restrain him if he was in spasms because, as his body writhed, his spirit was entering the saivo, and soon all would be calm. Rassa's family were accustomed to these sudden departures. They would lay the unconscious noaide comfortably on his face, place his drum beneath his outstretched right hand in case he had need of it in the saivo, and then await his return to our world. When Rassa did rejoin us, his mood depended on what he had experienced in his absence. Sometimes, if he had been fighting evil spirits, he would come back exhausted. At other times he was elated, telling us of the great spirits that he had encountered. Ibmal the Sky God was untouchable and unknowable, but Rassa sometimes met Biegg-Olbmai, the God of Wind, and wrestled with him to prevent a three-day blizzard. On another occasion he had asked the God responsible for hunting, a spirit he called 'Blood Man', that the siida's hunters should be rewarded. Two days later they tracked and killed an elk. The Gods and spirits whom Rassa revered were new to me, but his words aroused a faint recollection of a spirit world far older than the Elder Faith. I sensed that my own Gods, Odinn, Frey, Thor and the others, had all emerged from Rassa's saivo to take the shapes in which I knew them.

It was when Bolive, the Sabme Sun God, had begun to appear regularly over the southern horizon that one of our neighbours came to the entrance of Rassa's cabin and called excitedly down the tunnel. He gabbled his words so fast that I could not understand what he was saying, though Allba had spent many hours teaching me a working knowledge of her language. Whatever the hunter's message, Rassa immediately put aside the drum he was repainting and rose to his feet. Reaching for his heavy wolfskin cloak, he gestured for me to follow, and the two of us emerged from the cabin to find a group of eight Sabme hunters, looking towards him, impatient for instructions. One of the Sabme said something about 'honey paws', and when Rassa replied, the hunters began to disperse towards their cabins, calling out to their families excitedly.

'What's happening?' I asked Rassa.

'The time has come to leave our cabins and live in our tents again, though this is much earlier in the season than is usual,' he said, 'but the Old One wants it to be that way.'

'The Old One? Who's he?'

Rassa would not answer directly. He asked his wife and Allba to get ready to leave the cabin. So uncomplicated was the Sabme life that our entire siida was on the move within the time it took for the men, women and children to load our belongings onto light sledges, strap infants to their mothers' backs in tiny boat-shaped cradles lined with moss, and fasten on skis. I had no sledge to pull as I was so clumsy on skis, nor was I given a pack because I was already heavier than the Sabme and would have broken through the crust of snow.

We returned to the camp that we had left before we went into the cabins, and once again triple-covered the standing tent frames with deer hides. Everyone seemed in great good humour, leaving me confused as to what was going on.

'What is it?' I asked Allba, 'Why did we leave the cabins so quickly?'

'It's time for the most important hunt of the entire year,' she replied. 'The hunt that will ensure our siida's future.'

'Are you going on the hunt?'

'That is forbidden.'

'But you're almost our best hunter,' I objected. 'You will be needed.'

'Brothers are needed, not women,' she replied enigmatically as she tugged the final layer of the tent's deerskin into position.

I was still bemused the next morning when I woke up to find myself covered with a layer of snow a hand's breadth deep. The smoke hole in the top of the tent had been left open, and a late heavy fall of snow had half-buried the camp. No one seemed perturbed.

'Here, wear these,' said Allba, handing me a pair of shoes she had been working on all winter.

I turned them over in my hand. 'Can't I wear my usual shoes?'

'No,' she said. 'I stitched those with the seams inside so that the snow does not gather on them and I made them from the skin from a boaz head. The thickest and strongest hide, it is fitting that you should wear them today.' She also insisted that I put on my best winter garment – a heavy wolfskin cape – though it looked strange on me because the cape had previously belonged to Rassa, and Allba had lengthened it with a skirt of reindeer hide to make it fit my extra height. Rassa himself was donning his noaide's belt hung with the jawbones of the various fur-bearing animals we hunted, a cap sewn with sacred amulets and a heavy bearskin cloak. I had never seen him wear all these items at the same time, nor the short staff wound with red and blue ribbons and its cluster of small hawk's bells. When I offered to carry his sacred drum for him, Rassa shook his head and gestured for me to leave the tent ahead of him. Outside I found every hunter in our siida already waiting and dressed as if for a festival. Some had put on dark blue surcoats made of cloth acquired from the traders, and their wives had sewn the hems with strips of red and yellow ribbon. Others wore the familiar deerskin hunting garments, but had added colourful hats and belts and tied sprigs of spruce to their sleeves. They all looked excited and eager, and it took me several moments to realise that they were not equipped with their usual hunting bows and arrows, throwing sticks and wooden traps. Each man was armed with a stout spear, its shaft of rough wood, the tip a broad metal head.

I had no time to ask the hunters why they had changed their equipment because Rassa now made his formal appearance. He emerged from the tent and tramped through the snow to the flat boulder at the centre of our camp. With each step he softly jingled the bells on his noaide's wand and chanted a song I had never heard before. The words were very strange. They came from a language which bore no relation to that I had learned over the winter. When Rassa reached the rock he placed his magic drum on it, then faced towards the south. He raised the wand three times and called out what I took to be an invocation. Then he reached inside his cloak with his right hand and pulled something out from under his left armpit. He held it up for all to see. It was an arpa ring, but not of brass. From where I stood, I guessed that it was of gold and was sure of it when Rassa tossed the ring onto the drum skin. It fell with a dull and heavier thud than a token made of baser metal.

Rassa struck the drum's wooden rim with the end of his noaide's wand. The golden arpa skidded across the taut deerskin and came to a halt. Everyone craned forward to see the symbol where it rested. It lay on the serpent sign of the mountains. A shiver of delight ran through the crowd. The small, nimble men glanced at one another and nodded happily. The ancestors were observing and approving. Again the noiade rapped the drum with his staff and this time the golden ring came to rest on the figure of a bear. Now I detected that the onlookers were puzzled, almost doubtful. Rassa sensed their hesitation. Instead of striking the drum a third time with his wand, he snatched up the golden arpa and with a cry like a heron's angry croak he tossed it in the air so that it landed on the drum skin. By chance the ring landed on its edge, and began to roll, first to the edge of the drum, then rebounding it began to trace its path erratically. It wobbled along as if uncertain until it finally slowed, remained for a heartbeat on its edge, then toppled gently to one side and settled with the gentle reverberation that a coin makes as it falls upon a gaming table. Again all the spectators leaned forward to see where it had come to rest. This time the arpa lay upon the sign of my saivo companion – the bear.

Rassa did not hesitate. He picked up the ring, walked across to the nearest hunter and took away his heavy spear. Next he placed the golden ring over the spear tip. Finally he turned to where I stood and, with a formal gesture, placed the spear in my hand.

The drum had decided. The hunters dispersed to their tents to collect their skis and Rassa led me to where his wife and Allba were standing by our tent, watching. Allba knelt down in the snow to tie on my skis and, as she rose to her feet, I made a movement as if to embrace her. To my chagrin, she leaped back as if I had struck her and moved away from me, making it plain that she wanted nothing to do with me. Puzzled and a little hurt, I accompanied her father to where a little procession was forming up. It was led by the man who had first called Rassa from our cabin. I recognised his voice. He was the only one without a heavy spear in his hand. Instead he carried a long hunting bow of willow bound with birch bark. The bow was unstrung and a spruce twig was fastened to the tip. Behind him came Rassa in his bearskin cape, then myself, and finally the remainder of the brightly dressed hunters in single file. In complete silence we left the camp and began to ski through the forest, following the man with the bow. How he picked his way I could not tell, for the snowfall had obliterated all tracks. But he did not falter and I was hard put to it to keep up with the pace. From time to time he slowed so that I could catch my breath, and I marvelled at the patience of the Sabme hunters behind me who must have thought me half-crippled on my skis.

At mid-morning our leader abruptly came to a stop. I looked around, trying to see what had made him halt. There was nothing different. The forest trees stretched away on all sides. The snow lay thick on the ground and clung in little piles to the branches. I could hear no sound. There was utter stillness apart from the sound of my own breathing.

Our leader bent down and unfastened his skis. Still holding his bow, he stepped to one side and began to walk in a wide circle, sinking deep into the snow with each step. The rest of us waited, watching him, not saying a word. I looked across at Rassa, hoping for some guidance, but he was standing with his eyes closed, his lips moving as if in prayer. Slowly the bowman walked on, leaving his footmarks in the snow and finally coming back to his starting point. Again I tried to understand the significance of his actions. Everything was done so quietly and deliberately that I knew it had to be a ritual. I scanned the circle of footprints he had made. I still saw nothing. The circle enclosed a small rise in the ground, not even large enough to be called a knoll. For want of any other explanation, I presumed that it was a sieidde place. We had come to pay homage to the nature spirit.

I waited for Rassa to begin his incantation to the spirit. But the noaide was now removing his own skis and so too were the other Sabme. I did the same. My hands were stiff with cold and it took me several attempts to undo the knots in the thongs holding the skis to the new shoes Allba had made for me. I was pleased to see that, as she had promised, the snow had not stuck to them. I laid down the heavy spear to use both hands to undo the knots, and fearing that the gold ring would slip off and be lost in the snow, I pushed it more firmly in place. I put my skis to one side and straightened up. Glancing round, I saw that the other hunters had spread out to either side of me. Rassa was standing slightly aside. The only person directly ahead of me was the bowman and he was walking to the middle of the circle he had made with his footprints. He still had his bow in his right hand, but it was not yet strung. Coming almost to the centre of the circle, the hunter took three or four steps to one side, then another five or six steps forward, and turned to face me. Some instinct warned me, and made me grasp the heavy spear more firmly. I wondered if he would string the bow and attack me. Instead he raised the bow with both hands, and plunged it into the snow at his feet. Nothing happened. Two or three times more he repeated the same action. Then, shockingly, the snow directly in front of him cracked open, and a massive shape came bursting out. In the next instant I recognised the snow-covered form of an angry bear charging straight towards me.

To this day I do not know whether I was saved by my natural sense of self-preservation or by following Edgar's hunting instructions given long ago in an English forest. I had no time to turn and flee. The snow would have hampered my flight and the bear would have caught and ripped me in an instant. So I stood my ground, rammed the butt of the crude spear into the snow behind me and felt it strike solid, frozen earth. Scattering snow in all directions, the bear came careering towards me. When it saw the obstacle in its path, its angry warning growl rose to a full threatening roar and it rose on its back legs, its paws ready to strike. If the bear had stayed on all fours, I would not have known where to aim the spear. Now I was confronted with the hairy belly, the small eyes glaring down at me in rage, the open mouth and pink gullet, and I guided the spear point into the open and inviting chest. The bear impaled itself and I did nothing more than hold the shaft firm. It gave a deep coughing grunt as the broad metal spear head entered its chest, and then it began to sink down onto all fours, shaking its head as if in surprise. The end was swift. For a moment the bear looked incredulous. Even as it tried to turn and lumber away and my spear was wrenched from my grasp, the Sabme were closing in from either side. I looked on, shaking with shock, as they ran up and with cool precision speared the bear in its heart.

Rassa approached the carcass where it lay on the blood-smeared snow. The hunters reverentially stepped back several paces to give him space. The noiade leaned down and felt the bear's body. I saw him reach behind the bear's left front leg, against the chest. A moment later the noiade stood up and gave a thin wailing shout of jubilation. Holding up his right hand, he showed what he had retrieved. It was the golden ring arpa.

Pandemonium broke out among the hunters. I thought they had lost their senses. Those with sprigs of spruce on their garments snatched them free and ran up to the bear and began to flog the carcass. Others picked up their skis and laid them across the dead animal. All of them were yelling and shouting with joy, and I heard cries of thanks, praise and congratulation. Some of the men kept chanting phrases from the arcane song that Rassa had sung in camp before we began the hunt, but still I could not understand a word. When the hunters had capered and danced themselves to exhaustion, Rassa knelt in the snow, facing the bear and called out solemnly to the dead animal, 'We thank you for the gift. May your spirit now roam happily in the saivo, and be born again in the spring, refreshed and in full health.'

Very soon it would be dark. Leaving the dead animal where it lay, we began to make our way back towards the camp. This time instead of skiing through the forest in solemn silence, the Sabme called out to one another, laughed and joked, and while still some distance from home they sent out long whooping calls that echoed far ahead of us among the trees to announce our return.

I shall never forget the sight which greeted us when we

entered the camp. The women had lit a blazing fire on the flat-topped rock, and were standing where the light from the flames flickered across their faces. Every one of their faces was stained a bloody red. For a moment I thought there had been a terrible atrocity. Then I saw the movements of a dance, the gestures of welcome and recognised a song of praise for our hunting skill. I was exhausted. All I wanted to do was lie down and rest, preferably with Allba beside me. But when I headed towards our tent, Rassa took me by the arm and led me away from the entrance flap and around to the back. There he made me drop on all fours, and crawl under the hem of the tent. As I entered I found Allba standing facing me across the hearth. Her face too was stained red, and she was looking at me through a brass ring held up to one eye. As I crawled into view, she backed away from me and disappeared. Too tired to care, I crawled fully dressed to our sleeping place and fell into a deep sleep.

Rassa prodded me awake at first light. Neither Allba nor his wife were anywhere to be seen. 'We go to fetch the Old One now,' he said. 'I thank you for what you have done for the siida. Now it is the time to celebrate.'

'Why do you keep on calling him the Old One?' I asked, feeling peevish. 'You might have warned me we were hunting for bear.'

'We can call him a bear now that he has given his life for us,' he replied cheerfully, 'but if we had spoken directly of him before the hunt, he would have been insulted. It removes respect if we call him by his earth name before the hunt.'

'But my saivo companion is a bear? Surely it is not right that I killed his kind?'

'Your saivo companion protected you from the Old One's charge when he emerged from his long winter sleep. You see, the Old One you killed was killed many times before. Yet he always comes again, for he wishes to give himself to the siida, to strengthen us because he is our own ancestor. That is why we returned the gold ring under his arm, for that is where our great-

great-grandfathers first found the golden arpa, and knew that he was the original father of our siida.'

We skiied back to the dead bear, taking a light sledge with us, and hauled its carcass to the encampment. Under Rassa's watchful gaze the hunters removed the large pelt – the bear was a full-grown male – and then with their curved knives separated the flesh from the bones, taking exquisite care. Not a bone was broken or even nicked with a knife blade, and each part of the skeleton was carefully put on one side. 'Later,' said Rassa, 'we will bury the skeleton intact, every bone of it, so that when the Old One comes again to life he will be as well and strong as he was this year.'

'Like Thor's goats,' I said.

Rassa looked at me questioningly. 'Thor is a God of my people,' I said. 'Each evening he feasts on the two goats which draw his chariot through the sky – the thunder is the sound of his passing – and after the meal he sets aside their bones and skins. In the morning, when he awakes, the goats are whole again. Unfortunately one of Thor's dinner guests broke open a hind leg to get at the marrowbone, and ever since that goat has walked with a limp.'

The siida made a great fuss of me for the three days of feasting it took to consume every last morsel of the animal I had killed. 'Scut of boaz, paw of bear,' was Rassa's recommendation as he helped me to the delicacy, explaining that to set aside or keep any portion of the dead animal would be an insult to the generosity of its death. 'The Old One made sure that the blizzard did not destroy us, and that the spring will come and the snow will melt. Already he is roaming the hills ahead of us, calling upon the grass and the tree shoots to appear and for the birds that left to return.'

My only regret was that Allba still kept her distance from me. 'If she comes to your bed within three days of the hunt,' her father enlightened me, 'she will turn barren. Such is the power of our father-ancestor whose presence came so close to you. Even as you set off to hunt the Old One, his power was already reaching out towards you.' This seemed to explain why Allba had been behaving so strangely, and only when Rassa wore on his face the muzzle we had flayed from the Old One and every hunter – myself included – had danced around the central rock in imitation of Old Honey Paws on the final night of feasting, did she once again snuggle against my shoulder.

She also made me a fine cloak from the pelt, long enough for my height. 'You are wearing the presence of the Old One, a sign that he himself gave you,' Rassa said. 'Even a Sabme from another band would know that and treat you with respect.' He was anxious to press ahead with my instruction, and as the days grew longer he took me on trips into the forest to show me strange-shaped rocks, trees split by lightning or bent by the wind into human shapes, and ancient wooden statues hidden deep in the forest. They were all places where the spirits resided, he explained, and on one special occasion he brought me to a long, low rock face shielded from the snow by an overhanging cliff. The grey rock was painted with many pictures and I recognised the images that appeared on the siida's magic drums, as well as some I had not seen before – outlines of whales, boats and sledges. Others were too old and faded to decipher.

'Who painted these?' I asked Rassa.

'I do not know,' he said. 'They have always been here for as long as our siida has existed. I believe they were left for our instruction, to remind us who has gone before and to guide us when we are in need of help.'

'And where are they now, the painters?' I asked.

'In the saivo, of course,' he replied. 'And they are happy. In the winter nights when the curtains of light hang and twist and mingle in the sky, the spirits of the dead are dancing with joy.'

With each day came more signs of spring. Our footprints in the snow, once clear and distinct, now had softer edges, and I heard the sound of running water from small rivulets hidden beneath the icy crust and the patter of drips falling from the forest branches. A few early flowers emerged through the snow and flocks of birds began to pass overhead in increasing numbers. Their calls heralded their arrival, then faded into the distance as they flew onward to their nesting grounds. Rassa took the chance to teach me how to interpret the meanings hidden in their numbers, the directions which they appeared from or vanished to, even the messages in the manner of their calls. 'Birds in flight or smoke rising from the fire. It is the same,' he said. 'For those who can read them, they are signs and portents.' Then he added 'though in your case it requires no such skill.' He had noted how my gaze lingered towards the south even after the birds had gone. 'Soon the siida will be heading north for our spring hunting grounds and you will be going in the opposite direction and leaving us,' he said. I was about to deny it, when his crooked smile stopped me. 'I have known this since the very first day you arrived among us, and so has every member of our siida, including my wife and Allba. You are a wanderer just as we are, but we retrace the paths laid down by our ancestors, while you are restless in a deeper way. You told me that the spirit God you serve was a seeker after knowledge. I have seen how he sent you among us, just as I know that he now wishes you to continue onward. It is my duty to assist and there is little time left. You must leave before the melting snow makes it impossible to travel easily on skis. Soon the staallu men will be arriving to trade for furs. For fear of them, we will retreat deeper into our forests. But before that happens, three of our best hunters will take our winter furs to the special place for the trading. You must go with them.'

As usual, the Sabme, once they came to a decision, carried it out quickly. The next morning there was every sign that they were breaking camp. Deerskin coverings were being stripped from the tent poles and the three designated hunters were stacking two sledges with tight-packed bundles of furs. Everything was done with such bewildering speed that I had no time to think what I should say to Allba, how best to say goodbye. I need not have worried. She left her mother to attend to the dismantling of our

tent and led me a little way from the camp. Stepping behind the
shelter of a spruce tree, she took my hand, and pressed something
small and hard into my palm. I knew that she was returning to
me the fire ruby. It was still warm from where it had lain against
her flesh.

'You must keep it,' I objected. 'It is yours, a token of my love
for you.'

'You don't understand,' she said. 'For me it is much more
important that the spirit that flickers within the stone continues to
guard and guide you. Then I know you will be safe wherever you
are. Besides, you have left with me something just as precious. It
stirs inside me.'

I took her meaning. 'How can you be sure?'

'Now is the season that all creatures can feel the stirrings of
their young. The Sabme are no different. Madder Acce, who lives
beneath the hearth, has placed within me a daughter. I knew she
would, from that day that we both visited the saivo.'

'How can you be sure that our child will be a girl?'

'Do you remember the bear you met on your saivo journey?'
she answered. 'I was there with you as my companion bird,
though you did not see me.'

'I felt your wings brush my cheek.'

'And the bear? Don't you remember the bear you met at that
time?'

'Of course, I do. It smiled at me.'

'If it had growled, that would have meant my child would be
a boy. But when the bear smiles then a girl child is promised. All
Sabme know that.'

'Don't you want me to stay, to help you with our child?'

'Everyone in the siida will know that she is the child of a
foreign noiade and the grandchild of a great noiade. So everyone
will help me because they will expect the girl will become a great
noiade too, and help our siida to survive. If you stayed among us
for my sake, it would make me sad. I told you when you first
arrived among us that the Sabme believe it is far, far better to

travel onward than to remain in one place. By staying you imprison your spirit, just as the fire is held within that magic stone you lent me. Please listen to me, travel onward and know that you have left me happy.'

She turned her face up towards me for one last kiss, and I took the opportunity to close her fingers once more around the fire ruby. 'Give it to our daughter when she is grown, in memory of her father.' There was a tiny moment of hesitation and then Allba acquiesced. She turned and walked back towards her family. Rassa was beckoning to me. The men with the fur sledges were anxious to leave. They had already strapped on their skis and were adjusting the leather hauling straps of the sledges more comfortably across their shoulders. I went across to thank Rassa for all he had done for me. But, strangely for him, he looked worried.

'Don't trust the staallu men,' he warned me. 'Last night I visited the saivo to consult your saivo companion about what will happen. My journey was shadowy and disturbed, and I sensed death and deceit. But I could not see from where it came, though a voice told me that already you knew the danger.'

I had no idea what he was talking about, but I respected him too much to doubt his sincerity. 'Rassa, I will remember what you have said. I can look after myself, and it is you who have the greater task – to look after the siida. I hope that the spirits guard and protect your people, for they are in my memory always.'

'Go now' said the stunted little man. 'your companions are good men and they will bring you to the staallu place safely. After that you must guard yourself. Goodbye.'

It took four days of steady skiing, always southward, to reach the place where my siida traded with the outsiders. At night the four of us wrapped ourselves in furs and slept beside our sledges. We ate dried food or, on the second evening, a ptarmigan which one of the hunters knocked down with his throwing stick. As we drew closer to the meeting place, I sensed my comrades' growing nervousness. They feared the foreign traders and the last day we

travelled in complete silence, as if we were on our way to hunt a
dangerous wild beast. We detected the staallu men from a great
distance. In that pristine, quiet forest we heard them and smelled
the smoke from their cooking fire. My companions halted at once,
and one of them slipped out of the hauling harness and glided off
quietly to scout. The others pulled the sledges out of sight and
we waited. Our scout returned to say that two staallu men were
camped in the place where they usually waited for the silent trade.
With them were four more men, boaz men. For a moment I was
puzzled. Then I understood that he was talking about the slaves
who would act as porters for the traders.

The foreign traders had already displayed their trade goods in
a deserted clearing, the bundles hung like fruit from the trees.
That night our little group furtively approached, and in the first
light of dawn my companions examined what was on offer –
cloth, salt, metal items. Apparently they were satisfied, for we
hurriedly unloaded the sledges of the furs, replaced them with the
trade goods, and soon the Sabme were ready to depart. They
embraced me and skiied away as silently as they had arrived,
leaving me among their furs.

This is how the traders found me, to their amazement: seated
on a bundle of prime furs in a deserted forest glade, as if I had
appeared by magic, and wearing my noiade's heavy bearskin
cloak.

SIXTEEN

THEY SPOKE CRUDE Norse.

'Frey's prick! What have we got here?' the first one called out to his companion. The two men were clumsily pushing themselves forward across the snow with stout poles, each on a single ski in the Norse fashion. I thought how ungainly they looked compared with the agile Sabme. Both men were bundled up in heavy coats, felt hats and thick loose trousers gathered into stout boots.

'Nice cape he's got on,' said the other. 'A bearskin that size would fetch a good price.'

'So would he,' replied his companion. 'Go up to him slowly. I'll see if I can get behind him. They say that once those Skridfinni get going, there's no hope of catching up with them. Act friendly.'

They sidled closer, the leader wearing a false smile which only emphasised that his bulbous nose was dripping a slimy trail down his heavy moustache and beard.

I waited until they were within a few paces and then said clearly, 'Greetings. The bearskin is not for sale.'

The pair of them stopped in their tracks. They were too astonished to speak.

'Nor are the furs in the pack I am sitting on,' I continued. 'Your furs are lying over there. They are fair exchange for the goods you left.'

The two men recovered from their shock that I had spoken in their language.

'Where did you drop from?' the leader asked belligerently, mistaking me for a rival. 'This is our patch. No one trespasses.'

'I came with the furs,' I said.

For a moment they did not believe me. Then they read the ski tracks of my Sabme companions. They clearly came from the rim of the silent forest and then returned again. Then the traders noted my Sabme fur hat, and the deerskin shoes that Allba had sewn for me.

'I want to get to the coast,' I said. 'I would pay you well.'

The two men looked at one another. 'How much?' asked the snot-nosed individual bluntly.

'A pair of marten skins, perfectly matched,' I suggested.

It must have been a generous offer because both men nodded at once. Then the leader turned to his companion and said, 'Here, let's see what they've left for us,' and began to grub among the furs that the Sabme hunters had left behind. Apparently satisfied, he turned back towards his camp and let out a huge bellow. Out of the thickets appeared a sad little procession. Four men bundled up against the cold in ragged and dirty clothes trudged along on small square boards attached to their feet, dragging crude sledges. They were what my Sabme companions had called the boaz people, porters and hauliers for the fur traders. As they loaded the sledges, I saw they had the beaten air of thralls and did not understand more than a few words of their masters' language. Every command was accompanied by kicks and blows as well as simple gestures to show what needed to be done.

The two fur traders, Vermundr and Angantyr, told me they were collecting the furs on behalf of their felag. It was the same word the Jomsvikings had used to describe their military fellowship, but in the mouths of the fur traders the meaning was much debased. Their felag was a group of merchants who swore to help one another and share profits and expenses. But it was soon apparent to me that Vermundr and Angantyr were both prepared to cheat their colleagues. They demanded my marten skins in advance, hid them in their personal belongings, and when we reached the rendezvous with the felag at the trading town of Aldeigjuborg they failed to mention the extra pelts.

I had never seen so much mud in my life as I found at Aldeigjuborg. Everywhere you walked you sank almost ankle deep, and within a day I had lost both of Allba's shoes and had to buy a pair of heavy boots. Built on a swampy riverside, Aldeigjuborg lies in that region the Norse call Gardariki, the land of forts, and is the gateway to an area stretching for an unimaginable distance to the east. The place is surrounded by endless forest, so all the houses are made of wood. The logs are cut, squared and laid to make walls, the roofs are wooden shingles, and a tall fence of wooden stakes encloses each house's yard. The houses have been erected at random so there is no single main street, and barely any attempt is made to keep the roadways passable. Occasionally a layer of tree trunks is laid down on the earth to provide a surface, but in the spring these trees sink into the soft soil and are soon slippery with rain. Everywhere the puddles are fed by the filth seeping out from the house yards. There is no drainage and, when I was there, each householder used his yard as a latrine and rubbish dump, never clearing away the squalor. As a result the place stank and rotted at the same time.

Yet Aldeigjuborg was thriving. Flotillas of small boats were constantly coming and going at the landing staithes along the river. They were laden with the commercial products of the northern woodlands – furs, honey, beeswax, either obtained cheaply by silent barter such as I had witnessed or, more usually, by straightforward extortion. Gangs of heavily armed traders travelled into the remoter regions and demanded tribute from the forest-dwelling peoples. Often they obliged the natives to provide them with porters and oarsmen as well, so the muddy lanes of Aldeigjuborg were thronged with Polians, Krivichi, Berendeis, Severyane,

Pechenegs and Chuds, as well as people from tribes so obscure
that they had no known name. A few were traders in their own
right, but the majority were kholops – slaves.

With such a rapacious and mixed population, Aldeigjuborg
was a turbulent place. The town was nominally subject to the
overlord of Kiev, a great city several days' journey to the south,
and he appointed a member of his family as regent. But real
power lay in the hands of the merchants, particularly the better
armed ones. They were commonly known as Varangians, a name
by which I was proud to call myself in later days, but when I first
met them I was appalled by their behaviour. They were out-and-
out ruffians. Mostly of Swedish descent, they came to Gardariki
to make their fortunes. They took the var – the oath which
formed them into felags – and became a law unto themselves.
Some hired themselves out as mercenaries to whoever would pay
the highest price; others joined felags which masqueraded as
trading groups, though they were little more than pirate bands.
The most notorious of all the felags when I arrived was the one
to which Vermundr and Angantyr belonged, and no Varangian
was more feared than its leader, Ivarr known as the Pitiless.
Vermundr and Angantyr were so terrified of him that the moment
we arrived in Aldeigjuborg they took me straight to see their
leader to report on their mission and seek his approval of what
they had done.

Ivarr held court – that is the only phrase – in a large
warehouse close to the landing place. Like all the other buildings
of Aldeigjuborg, it was single-storey though far bigger than most.
Two scruffy guards lounged at the entrance gate and checked
everyone who entered, removing any weapons they found and
demanding a bribe to let visitors past. Led across the filthy yard,
I was taken into Ivarr's living quarters – a scene of barbaric
squalor. The single main room was decorated in what I learned
was a style favoured by tribal rulers in the east. Rich brocades
and carpets, mostly patterned in red, black and blue, hung from
the walls. Cushions and couches provided the only furniture and

the room was lit by heavy brass lamps on chains. Even though it was midday, these were burning and the place smelled of candle wax and stale food. Half-eaten meals lay on trays on the floor, and the rugs were stained with spilled wine and kvas, the local beer. Half a dozen Varangs, dressed in their characteristic baggy trousers and loose, belted shirts, stood or squatted around the edge of the room. Some were playing dice, others were talking idly among themselves, but all took care to show that they were there in attendance upon their leader.

Ivarr was one of those remarkable men whose physical presence arouses immediate fear. I have met much bigger men in my life of travel, and I have observed men who make it their style to inspire dread with threatening gestures or a cruel manner of speech. Ivarr imposed his will by exuding sheer brute menace, and he did so naturally without conscious effort. Between forty and fifty years old, he was short and so thick-set that he could have been a wrestler, albeit a dandified one, for he was wearing a rust-coloured velvet tunic, and silk pantaloons, and his feet were encased in soft yellow leather boots trimmed with fur. His short, powerful arms had small hands, and his stubby fingers were decorated with expensive rings. The most striking feature about him was his head. Like his body, it was round and compact. The skin was the colour of antique walrus ivory and hinted of mixed ancestry, maybe part-Norse and part-Asiatic. His eyes were dark brown, and he had greased and perfumed his ample beard so that it lay on the front of his tunic like a glossy black animal. By contrast his scalp was shaved clean except for a single lock of hair, which hung from the side of his head in a long curl and touched his left shoulder. This, it seemed, was regarded as a sign of royalty, which Ivarr claimed to be. But for the moment my attention was caught by his right ear. It was decorated with three studs – two pearls and between them a large single diamond.

'So you are the poacher,' he said, thrusting his head forward pugnaciously, as if he was about to spring up from his couch and knock me to the ground. I tore my gaze away from the ear studs.

'I don't know what you're talking about,' I said calmly. There was a tremor of surprise from the Varangs in the room behind me. They were not accustomed to hearing their master addressed in this way.

'My men tell me that you were collecting furs from the Skridfinni in an area where my felag alone deals with them.'

'I did not collect the furs,' I answered. 'They were given to me.'

The truculent brown eyes regarded me. I noted that they held a look of quick intelligence.

'Given to you? For nothing?'

'That's correct.'

'How did that happen?'

'I lived the winter among them.'

'Impossible. Their magicians make their people vanish if any strangers approach.'

'A magician invited me to stay.'

'Prove it.'

I glanced around the room. The other Varangs were like a pack of hungry dogs awaiting a treat. They expected their leader to quash me. Two stopped the game of dice that they had been playing and another filled the pause before I gave my answer, by spitting noisily onto the carpet.

'Give me some dice and a tray,' I said, trying to sound disdainful.

The remnants of a meal were swept from a heavy brass tray, and I indicated that it should be placed on the carpet in front of me. I held out my hand to the dice players and they gave me the dice they had been using. Seated on his couch Ivarr adopted a bored look as if already unimpressed. I was sure he expected me to claim magical assistance in throwing the dice. Instead I asked for five more pairs of dice. This brought a stir of interest. Each of the Varangs carried his own set and I laid the twelve dice down on the tray, arranging them in the pattern of nine squares, three by three. In the first square I placed a single dice so that the number four showed. In the next square I put two dice whose combined total was nine. In the third square I again laid a single dice showing two. In the second row, the numbers were three, five and seven. The last row was eight, one and six.

The pattern looked thus:

$$4 \quad 9 \quad 2$$
$$3 \quad 5 \quad 7$$
$$8 \quad 1 \quad 6$$

I stepped back and said nothing. There was a long, long silence. My audience was puzzled. Perhaps they expected that the dice would move on their own, or that they would burst into flames. They looked long and hard at the dice, then at me, and nothing whatsoever happened. I gazed straight at Ivarr, challenging him. It was for him to see the magic. He looked down at the dice and frowned. Then he looked a second time and I could see the sudden light of understanding. He glanced up at me and we shared the knowledge. My gamble had paid off. I had flattered his raw intelligence.

His lackeys still looked puzzled. None of them dared question their master. They were too frightened of him.

'You learned well,' said Ivarr. He had seen the magic of the pattern: whichever way you read the lines, across, sideways, downwards, or on both diagonals, the total that they gave was always fifteen.

'I am told that you will soon be going to Miklagard,' I said. 'I would like to accompany your boats.'

'If you are as good at trading as you are at numbers, you would be a useful addition,' Ivarr replied, 'but you still have to convince my men.'

The Varangians, still puzzled, were collecting up their dice from the tray. I stopped one of them as he was picking up his two gaming pieces. 'I'll gamble on it. Highest wins.' I said. The Varang smirked, then threw his dice. I was not surprised that they fell showing double six. The dice were almost certainly loaded and I wondered how many games he had won by cheating. His score was unbeatable. I picked up his two dice, made as if to throw them on the tray, then checked myself. I set one of the dice aside and picked up a replacement from the pile. It was a dice that had seen much use. Made of bone, it was old and cracked. Now it was not Rassa's magic that I used, but something that I had learned among the Jomsvikings. As I held the two dice in my hand, I pressed them together hard and felt the older dice begin to split. With a silent prayer to Odinn, I flung the two dice down upon the tray with all my strength. Odinn, who invented dice for man's amusement, heard my plea. As the two dice struck the metal tray, one of them broke apart. My opponent's dice still read its false six, while the other gave a six and a two. 'I win, I think,' I said and the other Varangs broke into guffaws of laughter.

The Varang I had beaten scowled and would have struck me if Ivarr had not said sharply, 'Froygeir! That's enough!' Froygeir snatched up his dice and stalked away, furious and humiliated, and I knew that I had made a dangerous enemy.

The felag had been waiting for the return of Vermundr and Angantyr, and was now ready to depart for Miklagard. I counted nine Varangians of the felag, including Ivarr, and about thirty kholops, whose task was to row the flotilla of light river boats they loaded with our bales of furs. Several of the Varangians also brought along their women as cooks and servants, and it was clear these unfortunates were part slave, part concubine. Ivarr, as befitted his rank, was accompanied by three of his women and also two of his sons, lads no more than seven or eight years old of whom he seemed extremely fond. So our expedition totalled rather more than fifty.

The way to Miklagard lay upriver through Kiev, so I was surprised when our flotilla pushed off from the river landing place and headed downstream in the opposite direction. I thought it best not to ask the reason. I was well aware that I was still unwelcome in Ivarr's felag. It was not just Froygeir who disliked me. His colleagues resented the ease with which I seemed to have won

Ivarr's favour and they envied the rich stock of furs that I had brought with me. I had not taken the var, the oath of fellowship, so I was a private trader taking advantage of their journey and this meant that my profit would not be shared. The Varangians grumbled among themselves and pointedly left me to fend for myself when it came to preparing meals or finding a place to sleep. So, by default, I spent most of my time on Ivarr's boat as we travelled the waterways across Gardariki, and I slept in his tent when we stopped at night and pitched camp on the river bank. This only made matters worse because the other Varangs soon saw me as Ivarr's favourite, and sometimes I wondered if it was our leader's deliberate policy to provide his followers with a focus for their malcontent. My travelling companions were a ferocious lot and, like the pack of wild dogs they resembled, they were only partly tamed. They held together only as long as they submitted to Ivarr's savage rule, and the moment that was lifted they would fight amongst themselves to divide the spoils and decide upon their next leader.

Ivarr himself was an unpredictable mixture of viciousness, pride and shrewdness. Twice I saw him stamp his authority on the group by brute violence. He liked to carry a short thick-handled whip, whose strands were weighted with thin strips of lead and the butt decorated with silver. I thought it was a badge of office or perhaps an instrument for striking lazy kholops. But the first time I saw him use it was when a Varangian hesitated in carrying out one of his orders. The man paused for the briefest moment, but it was enough for Ivarr to lash out – the blow was all the more shocking because Ivarr did not give the slightest warning – and the weighted thongs caught the man full across the face. He fell to his knees, clutching his face for fear that he had been blinded. He got back to his feet and stumbled away to carry out his orders, and for a week afterwards a crust of dried blood marked the welts across his cheeks.

On the second occasion the challenge to Ivarr's authority was more serious. One of the Varangians, drunk on too much kvas,

openly contested Ivarr's right to lead the group. It happened as
we sat around a cooking fire on the river bank eating our evening meal. The Varangian was a head taller than Ivarr and he drew
his sword as he rose to his feet and shouted across the fire, calling on Ivarr to fight. The man stood there, swaying slightly,
as Ivarr calmly wiped his hands on a towel held out to him by
his favourite concubine, then turned as if to reach for his own
weapon. In the next instant he had uncoiled from the ground and
in a blur of movement ran across the burning fire, scattering
the blazing sticks in all directions. Head down, he charged his
challenger, who was too drunk and too surprised to save himself.
Ivarr butted the man in the chest and the shock threw him flat on
his back. Scorning even to remove the contender's sword, Ivarr
grabbed his opponent's arm and hauled him across the ground
back to the fire. There, in front of the watching Varangians, he
thrust the man's arm into the embers and held it there as his
enemy howled with pain and we smelled the burning flesh. Only
then did Ivarr release his grip and his victim crawled away, his
hand a blackened mess. Ivarr calmly returned to his place and
beckoned to his slave girl to bring him another plate of food.

The following day I made the mistake of calling Ivarr a
Varangian, and he bridled at the name. 'I am a Rus,' he said. 'My
father was a Varangian. He came across the western sea with the
rops-karlar, the river rowers, to trade or raid, it did not matter
which. He liked the country so much that he decided to stay and
took a job as captain of the guard at Kiev. He married my mother,
who was from Karelia, of royal blood, though she had the
misfortune of being taken captive by the Kievans. My father
bought her for eighty grivna, a colossal sum which goes to show
how beautiful she was. I was their only child.'

'And where's your father now?' I enquired.

'My father abandoned me when my mother died. I was eight
years old. So I grew up in the company of whoever would have
me, peasants mostly, who saw me as a useful pair of hands to help
them gather crops or cut firewood. You know what the Kievans

call their peasants? Smerdi. It means "stinkers". They deserve the name. I ran away often.'

'Do you know what happened to your father?'

'Most likely he's dead,' Ivarr answered casually. He was seated on a carpet inside his tent – he liked to travel in style – and was playing some complicated child's game with his younger son. 'He left Kiev with a company of his soldiers who thought they would get better pay from the great emperor in Miklagard. Rumour came back that the entire group was wiped out on their journey by Pechenegs.'

'Are we likely to meet Pechenegs too?'

'I doubt it,' he replied. 'We go a different way.' But he would not say where.

By the fifth day after leaving Aldeigjuborg, we had rowed and sailed our boats around the shores of two lakes, along the river connecting them and turned into yet another river mouth. Now we were heading upstream and progress became more difficult. As the river narrowed we were obliged to get out of the boats and push them across the shallows. Finally we reached a point when we could go no further. There was not enough water to float our craft. We unloaded the boats and set our kholops to cutting down small trees to make rollers. The larger boats and those which leaked badly we deliberately set on fire to destroy them and then searched the ashes to retrieve any rivets or other metal fastenings. To me it seemed a prodigious waste because I had grown up in Iceland and Greenland, countries where no large trees grow. But Ivarr and the felag thought nothing of it. Timber in abundance was all they had known. Their main concern was that we had enough kholops to manhandle our remaining boats across the portage.

There was a track, overgrown with grass and bushes but still discernible, leading eastward through dense forest. Our axemen went ahead to clear the path. The kholops were harnessed like oxen, ten in a team, to ropes attached to the keels of our three remaining boats. The rest of us steadied the boats to keep them

level on the rollers, or worked in pairs, picking up the rollers as
they passed beneath the hulls and throwing them down ahead of
the advancing keels. It took us four days of sweating labour,
plagued by flying insects, to drag our boats to the headwaters of
a stream that flowed to the east. There we rested for another week
while our shipwright – a Varangian originally from Norway –
directed the building of four replacement craft. He found what he
needed less than an arrow-shot from our camp – four massive
trees, which were promptly felled. Then he directed the kholops
in hollowing out the trunks with axe and fire to make the keels
and lower hulls of our boats. Other kholops split the planks which
were attached to the sides of these dugouts, building up the hulls
until I recognised the familiar curves of our Norse vessels. I complimented the shipwright on his skill.

He grimaced. 'Call these boats?' he said. 'More like cattle
troughs. You need time and care to build proper boats, and skilled
carpenters, not these clumsy oafs. Most of them would be better
off chopping firewood.'

I pointed out that two of the kholops from the far north had
proved useful when the supply of metal rivets for fastening the
planks had run out. The men had used lengths of pine-tree root
to lash the planks in place, a practice in their own country.

The Norse shipwright was still unimpressed. 'Where I come
from, you get only knife and needle.'

'What do you mean?' I asked.

'When you think you are good enough to call yourself a
boatbuilder, the master shipwright who taught you gives you a
knife and a needle and tells you to make and rig a boat, using no
other tools. Until you can do that, you're considered a wood
butcher, like this lot here.'

The Norwegian seemed the least vicious of our company. He
spoke the best Norse, while all the others mixed so many local
words into their sentences that it was often hard to understand
them. I asked him how it was that, as a skilled shipwright, he
found himself a Varangian. 'I killed a couple of men back home,'

he said, 'and the local earl took offence. It turned out that they were his followers, so I had to make myself scarce. Maybe I'll go back home one day, but I doubt it. This life suits me – no need to break your back hauling logs or lose a finger carving planks when there are slaves to do the work, and you can have as many women as you want without marrying them.'

As we recommenced our journey, we saw only the occasional trace of human habitation, a footpath leading from the water's edge into the forest, a tree stump that had been cut with an axe, the faint smell of a fire from somewhere deep in the forest, which stretched without a break along both banks. But we did not meet the natives themselves, though once or twice I thought I saw far in the distance the outline of a small boat disappearing into the reeds as we approached. By the time we reached the spot there was nothing to show, the reeds had sprung back into position and I wondered if I had been imagining it. 'Where are all the people who live here?' I asked Vermundr. He gave a coarse laugh and looked at me as if I was weak in the head.

We did eventually come to a couple of trading posts and a sizeable town. The latter, situated on a river junction, was very like Aldeigjuborg, a cluster of log-built houses sheltering behind a wooden palisade, and protected on at least two sides by the river and a marsh. We did not stop. The inhabitants shut their gates and regarded us warily as we drifted past. I guessed that the reputation of Ivarr's felag had preceded us.

The river was much wider now, and we steered our course in midstream so I saw little of the countryside except the monotonous vista of green forest moving slowly past on either hand. I thought, naively, that we stayed in midstream to take best advantage of the current. Then I began to see plumes of smoke rising from the forest cover. The smoke arose ahead of us or from some vantage point, usually a high bluff overlooking the river. It did not require much intelligence to guess that unseen inhabitants were signalling our progress to one another, keeping track of our flotilla. Now whenever we came ashore for the night we set guards around our camp and, on one occasion when the smoke signals were very frequent, Ivarr refused to let us go ashore at all. We spent the night anchored in the shallows and ate a cold supper.

Finally we left behind the area of watchful natives and the land around us became more level. Here we turned aside into a small river that flowed into the main stream from the north, and began to steer much closer to the left-hand bank. I noticed that Ivarr scanned the shore intently, as if he was searching for a particular sign. He must have seen what he was looking for because at the next suitable landing place he beached our boat. All the other vessels followed.

'Empty the two lightest boats and set up camp here,' Ivarr ordered.

I saw the Varangians glance at one another in anticipation as the kholops unloaded the goods and carried them up to a patch of level ground. Ivarr spoke to the Varangian whose burned hand was still wrapped in rags soaked in bear's grease. 'You stay here till we get back. See to it that no one lights a cooking fire or uses an axe.' The man had learned his lesson well. He dropped his gaze submissively as he accepted his assignment.

'You, you and you.' Ivarr walked amongst the kholops and touched about a dozen of them on the shoulder with the silver butt of his whip. They were the tallest and strongest of our slaves. He pointed to where Vermundr and Angantyr were unwrapping one of the cargo bales. I saw that it contained weapons – cheap swords and a heap of light chain. For a moment I thought it was anchor chain, but then I saw that the links were longer and thinner than any ship's chain, and that it came in sections about an arm's span long. There was a large metal loop at the end of each length and I recognised what they were: fetters.

Ivarr handed each kholop a sword. This was taking a risk, I thought to myself. What if the kholops decided to rebel? Yet Ivarr seemed unconcerned as several of the kholops began to swing their swords through the air to test their weight. He was confident enough to turn his back on them.

'Here, Thorgils,' he said, 'you'd better come with us. You can make yourself useful, if necessary, by making us all disappear.' The rest of the Varangians laughed sycophantically.

With five Varangians and half a dozen kholops aboard each boat, we set off to row upstream. Again, Ivarr was watching the river bank closely. The oarsmen took care to make as little noise as possible, dipping their blades gently into the water as we glided forward. Both Vermundr and Angantyr were with me in Ivarr's vessel and seemed tense. 'We should have waited until dawn,' said Vermundr under his breath to his companion. Ivarr must have overheard his comment because he turned round from where he stood in the bow and looked at Vermundr. His glance was enough to make Vermundr cringe.

Late in the afternoon Ivarr held up his hand to attract our attention, then silently gestured towards the bank. The slope was marked with footprints leading down to the water's edge. A large, half-submerged log was worn and smooth. Its upper surface had been used as a surface for washing clothes. A broken wooden scoop lay discarded close by. Ivarr made a circular gesture and waved on the second boat, indicating that it was to row further upstream. He pointed to the sun, then brought his arm down towards the horizon and made a chopping motion. The Varangians in the second boat waved in acknowledgement and they and the kholops rowed onwards silently. Very soon they were out of sight round a bend in the river.

Aboard our own vessel, the current carried us gently back back downstream until we were out of sight of the washing place. A few oar strokes and the boat slid under the shelter of some overhanging branches, where we hung on and waited. We sat in silence and listened to the pluck and gurgle of the water on the hull. Occasionally there was the splash of a fish jumping. A heron glided down to settle in the shallows a few paces away from us. It began its fishing, stalking cautiously through the water, step by step until suddenly it noticed our vessel and its human cargo. It gave a sudden twitch of panic, leaped up into the air and flew off,

releasing a loud and angry croak once it was safely clear. Beside
me Angantyr muttered angrily at the heron's alarm call. Another
glance from Ivarr quietened him instantly. Ivarr himself sat
motionless. With his glistening shaven head and his squat body,
he reminded me of a waterside toad waiting in ambush.

Finally Ivarr rose to his feet and nodded. The sun was about
to dip below the treeline. The oarsmen eased their blades into
the water and our boat emerged from its hiding place. Within
moments we were back at the washing place and this time we
landed. The boat was drawn up on the mud and the men formed
up into a column, Ivarr at its head, Angantyr right behind him.
Vermundr and I brought up the rear, behind the kholops. All of
us were armed with swords or axes, and each Varangian carried a
set of manacles, wrapped around his waist like an iron sash.

We walked briskly along the track, which led inland. The path
was sufficiently well worn for us to make quick progress and we
made scarcely any noise. Very soon I heard the shouts of children
at play and a sudden burst of barking, indicating that dogs had
detected us. Within moments there came the urgent clamour of a
horn sounding the alarm. Ivarr broke into a run. We burst out of
the forest and found ourselves in open ground where the trees
had been cleared to provide space for small plots of farmland and
vegetable gardens. A hundred paces away was a native village of
forty or fifty log huts. The place was defenceless – it did not even
have a palisade. The inhabitants must have thought they were too
isolated and well hidden to take any precautions.

In the next few moments they learned their error. Ivarr and
the Varangians swept into the settlement, waving their weapons
and yelling at the top of their voices to terrorise the villagers. To
my surprise the kholops joined in the charge with just as much
relish. They ran forward, howling and bellowing and swinging
their swords. A man who had been working in his vegetable patch
tried to delay our onslaught. He swung his spade at Angantyr,
who cut him down with a back-handed swing, barely pausing in

his stride. Women and children appeared in the doorways. They took one look at our attack and ran screaming. An old woman hobbled out of a house to see what was the matter. One of our kholops smashed her in the face with the hilt of his sword and she dropped to the ground. A child, no more than three years old, wandered into our path. Dirty and dishevelled, probably woken from sleep, the child gazed at us wonderingly as we raced past. An arrow whizzed past me and struck one of the kholops in the back. He sprawled on the ground. The arrow had come from behind. Vermundr and I turned to see a man armed with a hunting bow setting a second arrow to his bowstring. Vermundr may have been an uncouth brute, but he had his full share of courage. Though he had no shield to protect himself, he gave a blood-curdling roar as he charged straight at the archer. The sight of the raging Varangian running towards him unnerved the bowman. He missed his second shot and a few strides later Vermundr was on him. The Varangian had chosen an axe for his weapon and now he swung the blade so hard that I heard the thud as he chopped his opponent in the waist. His victim was lifted off his feet and fell sideways in a heap.

'Come on, Thorgils, you arse-licker,' Vermundr yelled in my face as he rushed back past me to continue the sweep through the village. I ran after him, trying to make out what was happening. One or two corpses were lying on the ground. They looked like bundles of abandoned rags until you saw a battered head, a bloody outflung arm, or dirty, shoeless feet. Somewhere in front of me were more shouts and yells and out from a side alley burst the figure of an older man, running for his life. I recognised the short bearskin cape. It must have been the village shaman. He was unarmed and must have doubled back through our cordon. At that moment Ivarr stepped into view. He had a throwing axe in his hand. As smoothly as a boy throws flat pebbles to skip across a pond, he skimmed the axe towards the fugitive. The weapon went whirling across the gap as if the target was standing still.

The axe struck the shaman in the back of his skull and he sprawled forward and lay still. Ivarr saw me standing there, looking appalled. 'Friend of yours, I suppose,' he said.

There was no further resistance from the villagers. The shocking swiftness of our attack had taken them by surprise and they lacked the weapons or skill to defend themselves. We herded those still alive into the central square of their little settlement, where they stood in a huddled and dejected group. They were an unremarkable people, typical of those who scratch a living from the forest. In appearance they were of medium height, with pale skin but dark hair, almost black. They were poorly dressed in homespun clothes of wool and none of them wore any form of jewellery apart from simple amulets on leather thongs around their necks. We knew this because the Varangians promptly searched everyone, looking for valuables, and found nothing.

'Miserable lot of shitheads. Hardly worth the trouble,' complained Vermundr.

I looked at our prisoners. They gazed at the ground dully, knowing what was coming next.

Angmantyr and my particular enemy, Froygeir, whom I had humiliated at dice, strode over to the prisoners and began to divide them into two groups. To one side they shoved the older men and women, the smaller children and anyone who was deformed or blemished in some way. These formed the larger group since many of the villagers had badly pock-marked faces. This left the younger, fitter men and children over the age of eight or nine standing where they were. Except for one mother weeping bitterly at being separated from her small child, who had been sent to join the others, this second group contained almost no women. I was puzzling about the reason for this, when the crew of our second raiding boat strode into the square. In front of them they were herding, like a flock of geese, the women of the village. I realised that Vermundr, Froygeir and the rest of us in the first boat had been the beaters. The second boat's crew had been given enough time to circle around behind the village and wait for us to flush out the game. The real prey in our manhunt had fled straight into the trap, as Ivarr had intended.

There were about twenty women in the group. Their faces and arms were scratched and torn from branches, several of them had raw bruises on their faces and all of them had their wrists bound together with leather thongs. With their straggly hair and grimy faces they looked a sorry lot. However, Vermundr, standing next to me, disagreed. 'Not a bad catch,' he said. 'Give them a good scrub and they'll be worth a tidy sum.' He went forward to inspect them more closely. The women huddled together, several looking piteously across towards their children, who had been set aside. Others kept their heads down so that their tangled hair concealed their features. Vermundr was clearly a veteran slave catcher for he now went from one woman to the next, seizing each by the chin, and forcing back her head so that he could look into the woman's face and judge her worth. Suddenly he let out a whoop of delight. 'Ivarr's Luck!' he called, 'Look at this.' He seized two women by their wrists, dragged them out from the group, and made them stand side by side in front of us. Judging by their bodies the girls were aged about sixteen, though with their shapeless gowns it was difficult to tell precisely, and they kept their heads bowed forward so it was impossible to see their faces. Vermundr changed that. He went behind the girls, gathered up their hair in his hands, and like a trader in a market who flaunts his best produce with a flourish, pulled back their heads so we could see straight into their faces. They were identical twins, and even with their tear-streaked faces it was clear that they were astonishingly beautiful. I remembered how I had bribed Vermundr and Angantyr with a pair of marten skins, perfectly matched. Now I saw in front of me the human equivalent: two slave girls of perfect quality, a matching pair. Ivarr's felag had found riches.

We did not linger. The light was fading. 'Back to the boats!' Ivarr ordered. 'These people may have friends, and I want us well

clear by the time they get together to launch an attack.' The last
rivets were hammered tight on the fetters of the male slaves, and
the felag began to withdraw to the sounds of wailing and sobbing
from the despairing villagers. Several of the women captives fell
to the ground, either because they fainted or because their limbs
simply would not carry them away from their children. They
were picked up and carried by the kholops. One male captive who
refused to budge received a savage blow from the flat of a sword,
which sent him stumbling forward. The majority of our captives
meekly began to shuffle out of the village.

Ivarr beckoned to me. 'Come with me, Thorgils,' he said.
'Here's where you might be useful.'

He led me back through the empty village to where the corpse
of the shaman lay. I thought he had only gone to retrieve his
throwing axe.

'That's the same sort of cloak that you wear, isn't it?' he
asked.

'Yes,' I said. 'It's a noiade's cloak. What you call a magician.
Though I don't know anything about this tribe. They are completely different from the Skridfinni among whom I lived.'

'But if these people had a magician, then that means they had
a God. Isn't that so?'

'Very likely,' I said.

'And if they had a god and a magician, that means they probably had a shrine to worship at,' Ivarr looked about us, then
asked, 'And as you know so much about these noiades or whatever you call them, where would you guess that shrine is to be
found?'

I was at a loss. I genuinely wanted to answer Ivarr's question
because, like everyone else, I was frightened of him. But the
village we had raided bore no resemblance to a Skridfinni camp.
These people were settled forest dwellers, while the Sabme had
been nomads. The village shrine could be anywhere nearby,
hidden in the forest. 'I really have no idea,' I said, 'but if I were

to guess, I would say that the noiade was running towards it, either to seek sanctuary there or to plead to his God for help.'

'That's just what I was thinking,' said Ivarr and set off at a brisk walk towards the edge of the dark forest in the direction that the shaman had been fleeing.

The shrine was less than an arrow flight away once we had left the open, cultivated ground and entered the forest. A tall fence of wooden planks, grey with age, concealed the sacred mystery. We walked around the fence – it was no more than thirty paces in circumference – looking for a gateway, but did not find one. I expected Ivarr simply to batter open a gap, but he was cautious. 'Don't want to make too much noise,' he said. 'We've not much time, and the villagers will soon be gathering their forces. Here, I'll help you over.' I found myself hoisted up to the top of the fence and I dropped down on the other side. As I had expected, the shrine was a simple place, suitable for such a modest settlement. The circular area inside the fence was plain beaten earth. In the centre stood what I first took to be a heavy wooden post set in the ground. Then I saw that the villagers had worshipped what Rassa would have called a sieidde. It was the stump of a tree struck by lightning and left with the vague resemblance to a seated man. The villagers had enhanced the similarity, carving out the shape of knees, and folded arms, and whittling back the neck to emphasise the head. The image was very, very old.

I spotted the latch that allowed a section of the surrounding fence to swing open, and went to let Ivarr in. He approached to within touching distance of the effigy and halted. 'Not as poor a village as it seemed, Thorgils,' he said. He was looking into the plain wooden bowl which the effigy held on its knees. It was where the villagers placed their offerings to their God. I stepped up beside Ivarr and glanced down into the bowl to see what they had given. Abruptly the breath had left my lungs. I felt giddy, not because I saw some gruesome offering, but because a poignant

memory came surging into my mind and left me reeling. The
bowl was half full of silver coins. Many of them were old and
worn and indecipherable. They must have lain there for generations. But several coins on the surface were not yet tarnished and
their patterns were instantly readable. All of them bore that
strange rippling writing that I had seen during my days in London
– a time I would never forget. It was when I had first made love
with Aelfgifu and she had worn a necklace of those coins around
her graceful neck.

Ivarr ripped the sleeve from his shirt, and knotted the end to
create a makeshift sack. 'Here, Thorgils, hold this open,' he said
as he lifted the wooden bowl from its place and poured in the
cascade of coins. Then he tossed the bowl aside. He looked up at
the roughly carved head of the wooden statue. Around its neck
was a torc. The neck ring was so weatherbeaten that it was
impossible to tell whether it was plain iron or blackened silver.
Clearly Ivarr thought it was precious metal because he reached up
to tug it free. But the torc remained fast. Ivarr was reaching for
his throwing axe when I intervened.

'Don't do it, Ivarr,' I said, trying to sound calm and reasonable. I feared his violent reaction to anyone who thwarted him.

He turned to face me, and scowled. 'Why not?'

'It is a sacred thing,' I said. 'It belongs to the sieidde. To steal
it will call down his anger. It will bring bad luck.'

'Don't waste my time. What's a sieidde?' he growled, beginning to look angry.

'A God, the local God who controls this place.'

'Their God, not mine,' Ivarr retorted and swung his axe. I
was glad the blow was directed at the statue not me, for it
decapitated the wooden effigy with a single blow. Ivarr lifted off
the torc and slid it up his naked arm. 'You're too timid, Thorgils,'
he said. 'Look, it even fits.' Then he ran for the gate.

It was dark by the time we arrived back at the river bank.
The crews were already on board the two boats and waiting.
They had made the captives lie in the bilges and the moment

Ivarr and I took our places the oarsmen began to row. We fled from that place as fast as we could travel and the darkness hid our withdrawal. No natives intercepted us and as soon as we reached our camp Ivarr stormed up the beach, insisting that everyone make ready to depart at once. By dawn we were already well on our way back to the great river highway.

SEVENTEEN

THE SUCCESS OF the slave raid greatly improved the temper of the felag. The underlying feeling of ferocity was still there, but the Varangians showed Ivarr a respect which bordered on admiration. Apparently it was very rare to find girl twins among the tribes, let alone a pair as exquisite as the ones we had captured. There was much talk of 'Ivarr's Luck', and a mood of self-congratulation spread among the Varangians as they preened themselves on their decision to join his felag. Only I was morose, troubled by the desecration of the shrine. Rassa had taught me to respect such places and I had a sense of foreboding.

'Still worrying about that piddling little village idol, Thorgils?' said Ivarr that evening, sitting down beside me on the thwart.

'Don't you respect any God?' I asked.

'How could I?' he answered. 'Look at that lot there.' He nodded towards the Varangians in the nearest accompanying boat. 'Those who don't worship Perun venerate their ancestors. I don't even know who my mother's ancestors were, and certainly not my father's.'

'Why not Perun? From what I've heard he's the same God we call Thor in the Norse country. He is the God of warriors. Couldn't you venerate him?'

'I've no need of Perun's help,' Ivarr said confidently. 'He

didn't assist me when I was a youngster. I made my own way. Let others believe in forest hags with iron teeth and claws, or that Crnobog the black God of death seizes us when we die. When I meet my end, if my body is available for burial and not hacked to pieces, it will be enough for my companions to treat my corpse as they wish. I will no longer be there to be concerned with their superstitions.'

For a brief moment I thought to tell him about my devotion to Odinn the All-Father, but the intensity of his fatalism held me back and I changed the subject.

'How was it,' I asked, 'that our kholops took part in the raid for slaves with such enthusiasm when they themselves are slaves?'

Ivarr shrugged. 'Kholops are prepared to inflict on others what they themselves suffer. It makes them accept their own condition more easily. Of course I took back their weapons once they had completed the task and now they are kholops once again.'

'Aren't you afraid that they, or our new captives, will attempt to escape?'

Ivarr gave a grim laugh. 'Where would they find themselves if they did? They are far from home, they don't know which way to turn, and if they did run away, the first people to find them would merely turn them back into slaves again. So they accept their lot.'

In that opinion, Ivarr was wrong. Two days later he gave our male captives a little more space. The prisoners' wrist and ankle fetters had been fastened to the boats' timbers, so they were forced to crouch in the bilges. Ivarr ordered that the shackles be eased so they could stand and move about. As a precaution he kept them chained in pairs. This did not prevent two of our male captives from taking their chance to leap overboard. They flung themselves into the water and made no attempt to save their lives. They deliberately raised their arms and sank beneath the water, dragged down by the weight of their manacles, so there was no chance that our cursing oarsmen could turn and retrieve them.

The great river was now so wide that it was as if we were

floating on an inland sea, and we were able to raise sail and greatly increase the distance we travelled each day. A full cargo of slaves and furs meant we had no reason to halt except to revictual the flotilla at the riverside towns which began to appear with increasing frequency. The townsfolk recognised us from a distance because only the Varangian craft had those curved profiles from the northern lands and the local traders were waiting with what we required.

We bought food for our slaves, mostly salted and dried fish, and cheap jewellery to prettify them. 'A well-turned-out slave girl gets ten times the price than one looking like a slut,' Ivarr told me, 'and if she has a pretty voice and can sing and play an instrument, then there's almost no limit to the money a rich man will pay.' He had taken me to the market in the largest of the river cities where he had a commercial arrangement with a local merchant. This man, a Jewish Khazar, specialised in the slave trade. In exchange for our least favoured slave, a male, he provided us with lengths of brightly coloured fabric for women's clothes, necklaces of green glass, beads and bangles, and an interpreter who knew the languages spoken along the lower river.

'What about the men and children we've captured?' I asked Ivarr as we waited in the Khazar's shop for the goods to be delivered.

'The children, that depends. If they are sprightly and show promise, they are easy to sell. Girls are usually more saleable than boys, though if you have a really intelligent male you can sometimes be lucky in Miklagard, the great city, particularly if the lad has fair skin and blue eyes.'

'You mean for men who like that sort or for their wives?'

'Neither. Their masters arrange to have their stones removed, then educate them. They become trusted servants, secretaries and bookkeepers and such like. Some have been bought for the imperial staff and have risen to power and responsibility. At the highest levels of the emperor's government are men who have been gelded.'

I wondered what was in store for the twins we had captured. The Khazar Jew had offered to buy them, but Ivarr would not hear of it. 'The Jews rival us for mastery of the slave trade,' he said, 'but they are middle men. They don't take the risks of raiding among the tribes. If I can sell the twins direct to a client, the felag will make a far greater profit.'

He had given the two girls into the care of his favourite concubine. She was gentle with them, showing them how best to wash and braid their hair, how to apply unguents to their faces and wear the clothes and jewellery we supplied. When the sun shone brightly, she insisted that the girls wear heavy veils to protect their fair complexions. There was no possibility that the girls would be molested by any of our men. Everyone knew that untarnished twins were far too valuable.

The weather was very much warmer now. We set aside our heavy clothes and took to wearing loose shirts and baggy trousers made of many folds of cotton. The loose trousers meant that we could scramble unhampered about the boat, yet remain cool in the increasing heat of summer. At dusk we landed on sandbanks and slept in the light tents we had purchased so we could take advantage of the night breeze. The river had left behind the dense forests, and now flowed through flat, open country grazed by the cattle of the local tribes whose language, according our interpreter, was spoken by the horse-riding peoples further east. Whenever we encountered the boats of other river travellers, they sheered off like frightened minnows. It did not matter whether people thought of us as Varangian or Rus, it was clear that we had an unsavoury reputation.

'Ivarr! On the river bank! Serklanders!' Vermundr called out one hot afternoon. The excitement in his voice made me look round to see what had made him so eager. In the distance was a small riverside village and beside it a cluster of long, low tents made of dark material. In front of the tents half a dozen river boats were drawn up on the shore.

Ivarr squinted across the glare of the river's surface. 'Thorgils, you bring good fortune with you yet again,' he said. 'I've never known Serklanders so far north.' He ordered the helmsman to steer for land. With our slave raid fresh in my mind, I wondered if Ivarr planned to swoop down on the strangers and rob them like a common pirate.

I said as much to Vermundr, and he sneered back at me. 'Perun knows why Ivarr thinks so much of you. Serklanders travel well protected, by Black Hoods usually.'

As we came closer to the landing place, I saw what he meant. A squad of men, wearing long dark hooded gowns, emerged from the tents and took up positions on the river bank, facing us. They deployed with the discipline of trained fighting men and were armed with powerful-looking double-curved bows, which they trained on us. Ivarr stood up in the bow of our boat, his brawny arms held well away from his body to show that he was unarmed.

'Tell them we come to talk of trade,' he told our interpreter, who shouted the message across the gap. The leader of the Black Hoods brusquely gestured that we were not to land close to the tents, but a little further downriver. To my surprise, Ivarr meekly obeyed. It was the first time I had seen him accept an order.

He then sent our interpreter to talk with the strangers while we set up our camp. On Ivarr's instructions, we took more care than usual. 'Expect to be here for a few days,' he said. 'We need to make a good impression.' By the time the interpreter returned, we had pitched our tents in a neat row and Ivarr's favourite concubine had shepherded our batch of slave girls to their own accommodation, a separate tent set beside our leader's pavilion with its array of rugs and cushions.

'The Serklander says he will visit you tomorrow after his prayers,' our interpreter reported. 'He asks that you prepare your wares for his inspection.'

'The land of silk, that's Serkland.' Ivarr said to me, wiping the beads of sweat from his scalp. He was sweating more than usual. 'I've never been there. It's beyond the mountains, far to the south. Their rulers like to buy slave girls, particularly if they are beautiful and accomplished. And they pay in honest silver.'

Thinking back to my time with Brithmaer the royal moneyer and his clever forgeries, I hoped that Ivarr was right. 'If it's called the land of silk why do they pay in silver?'

Ivarr shrugged. 'We'll be paid in silk when we sell our furs in the great city but the Serklanders prefer to use silver. Sometimes they exchange for gems which they bring from their country, like these.' He tugged at his pearl ear studs and the diamond.

I wondered if, yet again, my life was turning back upon itself. It was Brithmaer who had told me the rumour that fire rubies came from lands beyond the mountains.

So I awaited the arrival of the mysterious Serklander with great interest to see what he was like.

I do not know what I had been expecting, perhaps a giant clad in glistening silks or a gaunt bearded sage. Instead the Serklander proved to be a small, jovial, tubby man with a pale brown skin and dark eyes. He was dressed in a simple white cotton gown, with a cloth of the same material wrapped around his head, and plain leather sandals. To my disappointment he wore no jewellery of any kind. His affable manner was emphasised by the dourness of his escort of Black Hoods, who looked every bit as suspicious as when they had warned us off. By contrast the Serklander smiled at everyone. He trotted round our camp on his short legs, beaming at everyone, kholops and Rus alike. He patted Ivarr's two children on the head in a fatherly way, and even laughed at himself when he tripped over a tent rope and almost went headlong. But I noticed that his alert gaze missed nothing.

Finally Ivarr brought him to where the slave girls were waiting. Their tent was like a market booth and Ivarr had ordered that the front flap should be hanging down as we approached. Our little procession consisted of Ivarr, the Serklander and his guards, the Serklander's interpreter and our own, and myself as Ivarr's lucky mascot. Everyone else was kept well back by the

Black Hoods. We came to a halt, facing the curtain. There was a
pause and I saw two of the Black Hoods exchange a quick glance.
They suspected an ambush and made a move as if to step forward
and check. But the little Serklander was too quick for them. He
was enjoying Ivarr's showmanship. He made a small restraining
gesture and waited expectantly, a cheery smile on his face. Ivarr
stepped forward, took hold of the edge of the tent curtain and
threw it open, revealing the tableau inside. The slave girls had
been arranged so that they stood in a line, hands demurely clasped
in front of them. They were dressed in all the finery that Ivarr's
concubine had been able to muster – flowing gowns, bright belts,
coloured necklaces. Their hair had been washed and combed and
arranged to best advantage. Some had flowers braided in their
hair.

I watched the Serklander's face. His glance swept along the
line of the dozen women on offer and the cheerful smile remained
on his lips as if he was highly amused. Then I saw his gaze halt
and – just for an instant – his eyes widened a fraction. He was
looking at the far end of the line of slave girls where Ivarr's
woman had positioned the twins, so that the sunshine filtering
through the tent cloth bathed them in a luminous light. Daringly
she had decided not to decorate the two girls at all. They wore
only plain, cotton gowns, belted with a simple pale blue cord.
Their feet were bare. The twins looked virginal and pure.

I knew instantly that Ivarr had made the sale.

Nevertheless, it took a week to settle a price for the girls.
Neither the Serklander nor Ivarr were involved directly. The
trading custom was that the two interpreters proposed bid and
counter-bid, though of course their masters were the ones who
dictated the value of their offers. Ivarr mistrusted the man whom
the Khazar Jew had provided, so instructed me to accompany our
interpreter whenever he visited the Serklander camp to negotiate,
to keep an eye on him. I found this difficult because the two men
carried on their negotiation entirely by touch, not word. After the
usual formalities and a glass of some sweet drink, they would sit

down on the ground facing one another and clasp their right hands. A cloth was then placed over the hands to shield them from the gaze of onlookers and the bargaining began. It must have been done by the varying pressures and positions of fingers and palms in a code to signal the offers and responses. All I could do was sit and watch, and try to read their faces.

'It's impossible,' I said to Ivarr after returning back to his camp after one session. 'I can't tell you if the trading is fair and honest, or if the two of them are making a private deal and you are being cheated.'

'Never mind, Thorgils,' he said. 'I still want you to be there. You are my good luck.'

So I continued with my visits to the Serklander's camp, and thus I came to his attention. His name was Salim ibn Hauk, and he was both merchant and diplomat. He was returning from an embassy to the Bolgars of the river on behalf of his master, whom he referred to as Caliph al-Qadir. Meeting with our felag had been as much a stroke of good fortune for him as it had been for us. He had been charged with collecting information about the foreign lands, and wished to know more about the Rus.

A Black Hood was sent to fetch me to ibn Hauk's tent.

'Greetings,' said the cheerful little man, speaking through his interpreter. Ibn Hauk was seated cross-legged on a carpet in his tent, a light airy canopy spread over slender supports which allowed the maximum of breeze. In front of him was a low wooden desk and he held a metal stylus in his hand. 'I would be very grateful if you could tell me something about your people.'

'Your excellency, I'm not sure that I can tell you very much,' I answered.

He looked at me quizzically. 'Don't be alarmed,' he said, 'I only want to learn about your customs. Nothing that would be considered as spying.'

'It's not that, your excellency. I have only lived among the Rus for a few months. I am not one of them.'

He looked disappointed. 'You are a freed slave?'

'No, I joined them of my own wish. I wanted to travel.'

'For profit?'

'To fulfil a vow I made to a friend before his death. They are on their way to the great city, to Miklagard.'

'How remarkable.' He made a note with his stylus on the page in front of him and I saw that he wrote from right to left. Also he used a version of the curving script which had haunted me since I had seen it on Aelfgifu's necklace coins.

'Excuse me, your excellency,' I asked. 'What is it that you write?'

'Just a few notes,' he said. 'Never worry. There's nothing magical in making marks on paper. It does not steal away the knowledge.'

He thought me illiterate like most members of the felag.

'No, your excellency. I was wondering just how your script conveys the spoken word. You write in the opposite direction from us, yet you begin at the top of the page just as we do. If there is more than one page of writing, which page is the first? I mean, do you turn the pages from left to right, or in the other direction? Or is there perhaps another system?'

He looked astonished. 'You mean to say that you can read and write!'

'Yes, your excellency, I have been taught the Roman script and the Greek. I know also the rune letters.'

He laid down his stylus with an expression of delight. 'And I thought that I had found only two gems for my master. Now I discover that I have a treasure of my own.' He paused, 'And just for your information, yes, I do write letters from right to left, but numbers in the opposite direction.'

The Serklander summoned me several times to his tent to question me, and he detained me for many hours so I could supply the information he required. That might have been one reason why he did not hurry the negotiations over the sale of the twins, and this meant, in turn, that our felag stayed camped on the river bank for longer than was wise. The Varangians had not troubled to dig latrines, and our original neat encampment grew dirty and foul. As I have noticed in my travels, pestilence soon appears in such conditions, and this time the first victim was Ivarr himself.

His guts turned to water. One day he was healthy, the next he was staggering in his walk and vomiting incessantly. There were small white flecks in his bile and in the liquid that began to pour from his bowels. He retreated to his tent and, despite his bull-like strength, collapsed. His concubines hurried to minister to him, but there was little they could do. Ivarr shrivelled. His cheeks fell in, his skin took on a dull grey pallor and his eyes sank back in their sockets. It was like watching the contents of a full wine skin drain away. Occasionally he groaned and writhed with cramp and his skin was cold to the touch. His breath came in short, shallow gasps and by the third day ceased altogether. I knew that it was the vengeance of the village sieidde he had defiled, but the felag thought otherwise. They blamed the Serkander or his servants for poisoning Ivarr and they may have had a point. When I reported the signs of Ivarr's illness to ibn Hauk, he immediately asked me to leave his presence and the Black Hoods struck camp that same evening. Before sunset the Serklander and his people were embarking on their boats and heading downstream, taking the twins with them. The felag took their hasty departure as evidence of their guilt.

Sudden death was commonplace for the felag. Their first response to Ivarr's death was to calculate how much extra profit would accrue to each member of the felag now that he was gone. Then, from respect to his memory or perhaps because it gave an excuse for much drinking, they resolved to celebrate his funeral rites. What followed is scarred into my memory.

They found themselves a gand volva – a black witch – in the nearby village. Who she was or from whom she had learned her seidr I do not know. But her knowledge was partly of things that I had learned from Thrand and Rassa, and partly of other elements more evil and malign. She was a woman perhaps in her sixtieth

year, emaciated but still active and possessed of a sinewy strength.
When she arrived at our camp I looked for her noiade emblems –
such as a sacred staff, a girdle of dried fungi, gloves of fur worn
inside out or a string of amulets. But I saw nothing that might
signify her calling, except a single large pendant, a polished green
and white stone dangling from her belt. But there was no doubting
who she was. I felt the presence radiate from her as powerfully as
I could smell a rotting carcass and the sensation made me queasy.

She ordered the materials for a scaffold. It was to be built on
the shore, and as she drew the outline of the structure in the sand
with the point of a stick my fears were calmed. It was to be a
wooden platform similar to one Rassa had shown me when he
took me through the northern forests. The height of a man, the
scaffold was where a noiade often chose to keep vigil when
seeking to enter the saivo world, sitting above the earth in the
cold air until the spirit chose to leave the body. When the kholops
had brought timber for the structure, the volva called for Ivarr's
favourite knife. She used it to cut runes on the main cross timber
and as I watched her I shivered. I had seen those runes only once
before: on the log which had been the cause of Grettir's death,
the log that turned the axe to wound him. They were curse runes.
Of course the volva sensed my dismay. She turned to look straight
at me and the venom in her glance was like a blow to the head.
She knew that I possessed the second sight and she dared me to
intervene. I was helpless and afraid. Her power, I knew, was far
greater than mine.

Ivarr's funeral began an hour before dusk. By then the
members of the felag were already well and truly drunk. They
had supervised the kholops as they dragged the leakiest of our
boats from the river bank up to the scaffold and placed firewood
under and around the hull. The crone had then taken charge. She
ordered Ivarr's tent to be taken down, then reassembled amidships
on the boat. In it the kholops placed his carpets, rugs and cushions.
Finally Ivarr's corpse, dressed in a gown of brocade, was carried
aboard and laid upon the cushions. When all had been arranged

to her satisfaction, the volva went to fetch Ivarr's favourite
concubine. She was a plump, obedient girl with long, black braids
which she wore coiled round her head. I guessed that she was the
mother of at least one of Ivarr's boys, for she wore a heavy neck
ring of gold, a sign of her master's favour. I liked her because she
had shown kindness when she supervised the preparation of the
twins for sale. Now I feared that she would fall into the hands of
owners as vicious as Vermundr or Froygeir. When the volva
arrived to collect her, she was standing on the patch of bare earth
where Ivarr's tent had stood and looking bereft. I saw the volva
whisper something in her ear and take her by the wrist.

Walking as if in a dream, the girl was led towards the scaffold.
From her wavering steps it seemed to me that she had been
drugged or was intoxicated. Certainly every member of the felag
was tipsy and I confess I was far from sober myself. Overwhelmed
with dread, I had taken several cups of mead to repel the sense of
doom.

'You should go with her. You were just as much his favourite,'
Vermundr jeered, his drunken breath in my face as we watched
the concubine approach the scaffold. Two hefty Varangians took
her by the waist and lifted her to the platform. Three times they
raised and lowered the girl in some sort of ceremony, and I saw
her lips move as she mumbled an incantation or maybe a plea for
help. On the third occasion the volva handed her a living cockerel.
For a moment, the girl hesitated and I heard the volva scream
urgently at her. What language was used I do not know, but the
girl put the head of the cockerel in her mouth and bit it off, then
flung its corpse, still fluttering, so that it landed upon the funeral
ship. I saw the spray of chicken blood scatter through the air.

The girl was lifted from the scaffold one more time and,
weaving and stumbling, brought to her master's ship. She slipped
and fell as she tried to climb the stacked firewood and the volva
had to help her. Four members of the felag, including Vermundr,
followed her and so did the volva. The light was fading, which
made it difficult to see the details, but the girl lost her balance and

toppled into the open door of the tent. Perhaps the volva had deliberately tripped her. She slumped on the cushions and one of the four Varangians began to fumble drunkenly at his trousers. Then he advanced on the girl and raped her. The volva stood to one side, looking on dispassionately. Each of the Varangians took the girl, then stood up and, turning towards us where we were clustered around the campfire, shouted, 'That I have done in honour of Ivarr.' Afterwards he descended from the boat and allowed the next man to take his turn.

When all four men were back on the ground, the volva reached down, seized the girl by the hair and dragged her further into the tent. By that stage the concubine was completely limp. The flickering light of the campfire illuminated the final death rite. I saw the volva make a noose with the cord to which the blue and green stone was attached, and slip it over her victim's head. Next she placed one foot on the girl's face, and leaning back, pulled tight the noose with a powerful jerk. Lastly she took Ivarr's knife from her belt, and repeatedly stabbed down on the human sacrifice.

Only then did the volva descend and, selecting a brand from the camp fire, thrust it into the kindling heaped around the boat. The wood was dry from the summer heat and immediately caught fire. The breeze fanned the flames and within moments the funeral pyre was burning fiercely. As the blaze sucked in more air, I threw up my arm to protect my face from the heat. Flames roared and crackled, sending columns of blazing sparks into the air. In the heart of the conflagration, great holes suddenly appeared in the fabric of the tent sheltering Ivarr's corpse. The holes spread their burning edges, eating away the cloth so rapidly that for an instant the frame of the tent stood alone as if to defy the inferno. Then the tent poles collapsed inwards across the bodies of Ivarr and his murdered concubine.

That night I drank myself into oblivion. The heat radiating from the blaze had brought on a powerful thirst, but I drank to forget what I had just seen. All around me the Varangians caroused and celebrated. They drank until they threw up, wiped their beards and then went back to drink. Two of them came to blows over an imagined insult. They groped for their swords and daggers and made futile stabs and slashes at one another until too weak to continue the dispute. Others guzzled mead and ale until they fell senseless on the ground. Those who could still stand, staggered off to the tent where our slave girls slept, and molested them drunkenly. The volva was nowhere to be seen. She had vanished, gone back to her village, no doubt. Nauseous with too much drink, I crept away to a quiet corner behind some cargo bales and fell asleep.

I awoke with a racking headache, a queasy stomach and a foul taste in my mouth. It was well past daybreak and the sun was already high above the horizon. It promised to be another scorching day. Holding onto the cargo bale for support, I pulled myself to my feet and looked across to where Ivarr's funeral pyre had stood. There was nothing but a heap of charred wood and ash. Only the volva's scaffold remained. Beside it a chicken feather stirred in the breeze on the scorched ground.

A few kholops were moving about the camp in an aimless way, lacking orders. Their masters, those I could see, lay snoring on the ground, motionless after their debauch.

Gingerly I made my way slowly across the camp, then down the river bank to the water's edge. I felt defiled and in desperate need of a wash even if the river water looked far from clean. It was a dark brown, almost black. I pulled off my soiled shirt and wrapped it around my waist as a loincloth, and removed my loose Varangian trousers. Slowly and carefully I waded out into the river until the tepid water reached the middle of my thighs. I stopped there for a moment, letting the sun warm my back, feeling the mud ooze up between my toes. I was in a back eddy. The water was barely moving. Cautiously I leaned forward, fearing that a sudden movement would bring on an attack of nausea. Gradually I brought my face closer to the dark water, and got ready to splash water in my face. Just before I plunged my cupped hands into the river, I paused and looked at my reflection. The sun was at such an angle that I saw my head and shoulders as a vague outline. Suddenly I was assailed by a violent swaying sickness. My head spun. A chill washed over me, and I was about to faint. I thought it was the result of my debauchery, but then realised that I had seen the very same reflection before. It was the image I had seen when I peered into the well of prophecy that Edgar the royal huntsman had shown me in the forest at Northampton. Even as I came to that understanding, I saw the flash of something bright in the mirror of the river. For a heartbeat I mistook it for the silver flicker of a fish, then I recognised the reflection of a knife blade and the upraised arm that held it as I fell to one side and the assassin struck.

There was an agonising pain high up in my left shoulder. The blow aimed at my back had missed. A swirl of water, a growl of rage and I felt a hand grab for me, slip on wet skin and then another slash of pain as a second knife stroke sliced my left side. I flung myself forward, desperate to avoid the dagger. Again a hand tried to hold me and this time seized the shirt wrapped around my waist. I ducked underwater, twisted and pushed down with my feet. The ooze gave no grip and I panicked. My flailing feet touched the legs of my attacker. Even without seeing his face, I knew who it was. It had to be Froygeir. He had hated me since the day I humiliated him at dice in front of the other Varangians. Now, with Ivarr dead, the time for his revenge had come.

I wriggled like a salmon trying to avoid the barbs of a fishing spear. Froygeir was a big, agile man, well used to fighting at close quarters with a knife. Normally he would have finished me off with ease. Perhaps he was feeling the effects of his night's debauch or maybe he wanted to haul me out of the water, turn me so I could see my killer and then cut my throat. So, instead of stabbing again, he made the mistake of trying to pull me close by heaving on my loincloth. Its knot came undone and I squirmed free.

As Froygeir stumbled backwards, I seized my chance to swim

clear. The pain in my wounded left shoulder was so excruciating that I forgot the cut to my ribs. Terror drove me as I found the strength to move my arms and legs and swim a dozen frenzied strokes. I had no idea in which direction I was going. All I knew was that I had to get away from Froygeir. I thrashed forward blindly, expecting at any moment to feel his hand grasp my ankle and pull me back.

My nakedness saved me. I can think of no other explanation. Froygeir was a river man. He knew how to swim and should have overhauled his wounded prey with no difficulty, but he was wearing Varangian trousers with their many folds of material and, waterlogged, they hampered him. I heard him surge after me, wading at first, then forced to swim in my wake. As my initial panic receded, I took a quick look to see where I was heading – directly away from shore, out into the broad river. I forced myself to breathe deeply and move through the muddy water in some sort of rhythm. Only when I had swum at least two hundred strokes did I risk glancing back. Froygeir had abandoned the chase. I could see the back of his head as he returned towards the shore. There, I knew, he would be waiting for me if I was so foolish as to return to the camp.

Utterly exhausted, I stopped swimming and trod water. A red stain was spreading from my shoulder all around me. I had heard of giant fish in the river – it was said they were longer than a man – and wondered if they fed on flesh and would be attracted by blood. I prayed to Odinn for help.

Slimy and ancient, the log was floating so low in the water that I did not see my salvation until it nuzzled against me and I flinched, thinking of those meat-eating fish. Then I wrapped my arms gratefully around the slippery wood and let the timber take my weight. Another circle of my life was closing, I thought to myself. Driftwood had caused the death of my sworn brother and now another floating log would prolong my life if only I could hang on. Bleeding to death would be better than drowning. I

clenched my teeth against the pain from my shoulder, squeezed
my eyes tight shut, and deliberately sought the relief of darkness.

I KNEW NOTHING MORE until a sour smell roused me. Fumes stung
my nose and brought tears in my eyes. A trickle of liquid, sharp
and astringent, ran into my throat and made me cough. Someone
was bathing my face with a sponge. I opened my eyes. I must have
fainted while clinging to the log – I had no idea how I came to be
lying on my back on a carpet and looking up into the chubby face
of ibn Hauk. For once, his expression was sombre. He said something in his own language and I heard the voice of his interpreter.

'Why were you floating in the river?'

I licked my lips and tasted vinegar.

'They tried to kill me.'

The Serklander did not even bother to ask who had made the
attempt. He knew.

'Then it was lucky that one of my Black Hoods spotted you.'

'You must get away,' I said urgently. 'The man who sold you
the slaves, Ivarr, is dead. His comrades think you poisoned him.
Now the Varangians are leaderless they are very dangerous and
will try to catch up with you to get back the twin girls.'

'No more than I would expect of those savages,' he answered.
'We are already on our way downriver.'

I tried to sit up.

'My master asks you to lie still,' said the interpreter. 'You will
disturb the dressing.'

I turned my head and saw that my left shoulder was bandaged.
Again I smelled vinegar and wondered why.

Ibn Hauk answered before I had time to enquire.

'The vinegar is against the pestilence,' he said. 'It is to cleanse
you from the sickness that killed Ivarr. Rest now. We will not be
stopping, but will travel through the darkness. I do not think that
your Rus will catch up with us. And if they do the Black Hoods
will deal with them.'

I relaxed and thought about this turn of events. Everything I owned – my precious furs, my clothes, even the knife that Thrand had given me and which I treasured – was lost irretrievably. They were in the hands of the Varangians, who would already have divided the spoils amongst themselves. I was glad that I had given away the fire ruby to Allba. I was destitute and now I did not even have clothes to wear. Under the loose cotton sheet which covered me I was naked.

Ibn Hauk personally attended to me as we sailed downriver. He carried a stock of healing drugs from his own country and prepared the poultices of herbs and spices which were applied to my knife wounds. Certainly he was very skilled in their use, for eventually the wounds closed up so cleanly that they left barely the faintest scars. Each time he came to change the dressings he took the chance to question me about the customs of the Varangians and the countries where I had travelled. He had never heard of Iceland or Greenland, and of course he knew nothing of Vinland. But he had heard of King Knut of England and had some vague information about the northern lands.

When I told him how Ivarr's corpse had been burned, he was shocked. 'That is utter barbarism,' he said. 'No wonder the pestilence spreads among those river pirates. My religion demands that we wash before our prayers, but I observed that your former travelling companions are more filthy in their habits than donkeys.'

'Not all are so uncouth,' I said. 'There are men who know the use of herbs and simples just as you do, and the true Varangians, the men who come from the northern lands, are strict about their personal cleanliness. They bathe regularly, keep their hair and fingernails clean and take a pride in their appearance. I know because I have had to wield the heavy stones they use to press their clothes.'

'But burning a corpse to ashes,' ibn Hauk observed, 'that is abominable.'

'In your country what do they do?' I asked.

'We bury our dead,' he answered. 'Often the grave must be

shallow because the soil is rocky, but we put the dead into the ground as quickly as possible before putrefaction sets in. Our climate is very hot.'

'That is what the Christians also do – bury the dead,' I said, and found myself repeating what Thrand had said long ago. 'You see, for those who follow the Old Ways that is an insult to the deceased. We – for I am an Old Believer – find it repugnant to let a man's corpse decompose or be eaten by worms. We prefer that it is destroyed neatly and cleanly, so that the soul rises to Valholl.'

Then, of course I had to explain what I meant by Valholl, while ibn Hauk busily made notes. 'Your Valholl sounds very much like the valley that some of our believers, a strange sect, think they will achieve if they die in battle sacrificing their lives for their leader.'

He was so amiable and outgoing that I took the chance to ask him if he had ever seen precious stones that were the colour of pigeon's blood and had a burning fire within them.

He recognised the description instantly.

'Of course. We call them laal. My master owns several – they are among the pride of his royal jewels. The best ones he received as gifts from other great potentates.'

'Do you know where they come from?'

'That's not an easy question to answer. The gem dealers refer to these jewels as badakshi, and this may have something to do with the name of the country where they are found,' he said. 'It is said that the mines lie in high mountains, close to the borders of the country we call al-Hind. Their precise location is kept a secret, but there are rumours. It is reported that the rubies are found encased in lumps of white rock, which are broken open with great care by the miners, using chisels, to reveal the jewel within. If they find a small jewel of poor quality, they call it a foot soldier. A better jewel is known as a horse soldier, and so on up through an amir jewel, a vizier jewel, until the very best – the emperor jewel – which is reserved for royalty.'

In such intelligent and informative company the journey south passed rapidly, and it was with genuine regret that I heard ibn Hauk announce one afternoon that our paths were about to separate.

'Tomorrow we reach the outer frontiers of Rumiyah,' he said. 'I expect we will meet with a border patrol. The great river curves away to the east and the way to Rumiyah, where you want to go, is south and west. You have to cross from this river to another, which takes you to a port from where you take ship and finally, after a passage of two or three weeks, you will arrive at its capital, Constantinople, or Miklagard as you call it.'

I must have looked dejected because he added, 'Don't worry. One traveller should always help another and my religion tells me that acts of charity will be rewarded. I promise that I will see to it that you reach your Miklagard.'

Only when the commander of the frontier guard came to interview ibn Hauk did I fully appreciate how influential was my modest travelling companion. The commander was a Pecheneg mercenary, hired with his troop of tribal cavalry to patrol the buffer zone between the empire and the wilder region to the north. The Pecheneg was either arrogant or looking for a bribe. He spoke to ibn Hauk rudely, demanding proof of his claim that he was an ambassador. Quietly ibn Hauk produced a small metal tablet. It was about the length of my hand and three fingers broad. There were lines of Greek script engraved on it, though I doubted that the Pecheneg could read them. However, the soldier had no need of literacy. The tablet was solid gold. He blenched when he saw it and became very obsequious. Was there anything the ambassador wanted? He asked. He would be happy to oblige.

'Allow myself and my retinue to continue downriver,' answered the Arab gently, 'and provide an escort, if you would be so kind, for this young man. He is carrying a message to his majesty the emperor.'

I had the presence of mind not to gape with astonishment.

The moment the Pecheneg had left the tent, I asked, 'Your excellency, what was meant about a message for Constantinople?'

'Oh, that.' Ibn Hauk waved his hand dismissively. 'It will do no harm if I send the compliments of the caliph to the emperor of Rumiyah. Indeed it would be much appreciated. The imperial court positively relishes the niceties of diplomacy, and the protocol department might take it as an insult if they heard that I had visited a corner of imperial territory without sending a few flattering words to the great emperor of the Romans, for that is how he styles himself. You can carry the note for me. In fact you can help write it out in Greek letters.'

'But I don't understand why the Pecheneg should go to the trouble of arranging my journey.'

'He has little choice,' said ibn Hauk. 'The imperial office only issues gold passport tablets to the representatives of the most important fellow rulers. Each tablet carries the authority of the emperor himself. If the Pecheneg failed in his duty, he would be lucky to hold onto his job, if not thrown into gaol. The bureaucrats of Constantinople are corrupt and conceited, but they hate disobedience. To smooth your passage, I will give you enough silver to sweeten them on arrival. Here, let us compose the message you will carry.'

So it was that I had my first and only lesson in transcribing from Serkland script to Greek. I found the task not that difficult because many of the letters had their close equivalents, and with the help of the interpreter I made what I think was a reasonable translation of ibn Hauk's flowery congratulations and compliments to the basileus, as the Byzantines call their emperor.

'I doubt he will ever see the letter, anyhow,' commented ibn Hauk. 'It will probably get filed away somewhere in the palace archives, and be forgotten. A pity as I'm rather proud of my calligraphy.'

He had taken great care with his penmanship, delicately inking in the lines of script on a fresh, smooth parchment. He reminded me of the monks whom I had seen at work in the scriptorium of the monastery where I had served a brief novitiate. His hand-writing was a work of art. I said as much and he looked even more cheerful than usual.

'You will have noted,' he said, 'that I used a different script from the one I wrote when I was making my notes about your travels. That was my everyday working hand. This letter I have penned in our formal lettering, which is reserved for important documents and inscriptions, copies of our holy book and anything which bears my master's name. Which reminds me: you will need money to cover your travelling expenses on the way to Constantinople.'

Which is how I came to travel the final stage of my journey to Miklagard dressed in a cotton Arab gown and carrying coins which I had first seen around the neck of the queen of England, and which I now knew were struck in the name of the great caliph of Baghdad.

EIGHTEEN

MUCH HAS BEEN written of the splendours of Constantinople, the city we northerners know as Miklagard and others call Metropolis, the queen or – simply – the great city. Yet nowhere have I read of the phenomenon which intrigued me as I arrived at the mouth of the narrow strait on which Constantinople stands. The phenomenon is this: the sea water runs only one way through the strait. This is against nature. As every sailor knows, if a sea is tidal, there is a regular ebb and flow in such a constricted place. If there is no tide or very little, as at Constantinople, there should be no movement of the water at all. Yet the captain of the cargo vessel which had brought me to the strait, assured me that a sea always flows through in the same direction.

'You can count on it running from north to south,' he said, watching my expression of disbelief, 'and sometimes the current is as swift as a powerful river.' We were passing between the two rocky headlands which mark the northern entrance to the channel. 'In ancient times,' he continued, 'it was said that those rocks could clash together, smashing to splinters any vessel that tried to slip through. That is mere fable, but it is certain that the current always goes one way.'

I watched our speed increase as we came into the current. On the beach a gang of men were man-hauling a vessel upstream, so to speak, with tow ropes tied to their bodies. They reminded me of our kholops dragging our light boats in the land of the Rus.

'Now I will show you something still more remarkable,' said the captain, pleased to teach an ignorant foreigner the wonders of his home port. 'That vessel over there, the one that looks as if it is anchored in midstream.' He pointed to a tubby little trading ship, which appeared to have dropped anchor far from shore, though quite why its crew were rowing when the ship was at anchor, was a mystery. 'That ship is not anchored at all. You couldn't reach the bottom with the longest line. The skipper is dangling a big basket of stones overboard. He's done it to catch a current deep down. It flows the other way, from south to north, and is helping to drag his vessel in the way he wants.'

I was too astonished to comment, for the strait ahead of us was widening. Its banks, with their villas and country houses, were opening out to frame a spectacle which was nothing like anything I had imagined could be possible. Constantinople had come full into view.

The city was immense. I had seen Dublin from the Black Pool and I had sailed up the Thames to arrive in London's port, but Constantinople far exceeded anything I had ever witnessed. There was no comparison. Constantinople's population was said to number more than half a million citizens, ten times the size of the next largest city in the known world. Judging by the immense number of palaces, public buildings and houses covering the entire width of the peninsula ahead of me, this was no exaggeration. To my right a capacious harbour opened out, an entire gulf crowded with merchant shipping of every shape and description. Looming over the wharves were buildings which I identified as warehouses and arsenals and I could see the outlines of shipyards and dry docks. Beyond the waterfront rose an imposing city wall, whose ramparts encircled the city as far as the eye could see. Yet even this tall city wall was dwarfed by the structures behind it. There was a skyline of lofty towers, columns, high roofs and domes, all built of marble and stone, brick and tile, not of wood, plaster and thatch like the cities with which I was familiar. But it was not the magnitude of the place that silenced me, nor its air of solid permanence, for I had carried a wondrous vision of the city in my head ever since Bolli Bollason had sung the praises of Miklagard, and I had promised Grettir to travel in his memory. The reason for my stunned amazement came from something else: the panorama of the city was dominated by a vast assembly of churches and oratories and monasteries, most of them built to a design that I had never seen before – clusters of domes surmounted by the cross-shaped symbol of the White Christ. Many of the domes were covered with gold leaf and glittered in the sunshine. I had totally failed to realise that my destination was the greatest stronghold of the White Christ faith on earth.

Despite all this magnificence I had little time to gaze. The current rapidly brought our ship into the anchorage, which my captain proudly informed me was known throughout the civilised – and he emphasised the word civilised – world as the Golden Horn for its prosperity and wealth. 'There'll be a customs man waiting on the dock to check my cargo and charge me taxes. Ten per cent for those grasping rogues in the state treasury. I'll ask him to arrange for a clerk to escort you to the imperial chancery, where you can hand over that letter you are carrying.' Then he added meaningfully, 'If you have to deal with the officials there, I wish you luck.'

My monastery-learned Greek, I rapidly discovered, either made people smile or wince. The latter was the reaction of the palace functionary who accepted ibn Hauk's letter on behalf of the court protocol department. He made me wait for an hour in a bleak antechamber before I was ushered into his presence. As ibn Hauk had anticipated, I was greeted with supreme bureaucratic indifference.

'This will be placed before the memoriales in due course,' the functionary said, using only his fingertips to touch ibn Hauk's exquisitely written letter, as if it was tainted.

'Will the memoriales want to send a reply?' I asked politely.

The civil servant curled his lip. 'The memoriales,' he said, 'are the secretaries of the imperial records department. They will study the document and decide if the letter should be placed on file or if it merits onward transmission to the charturalius –' he saw my puzzlement – 'the chief clerk. He in turn will decide whether it should be forwarded to the office of the dromos, the foreign minister, or to the basilikoi, who heads the office of special emissaries. In either case it will require the secretariat's approval and, of course, the consent of the minister himself, before the matter of a response is brought forward for consideration. ' His reply convinced me that my duty towards ibn Hauk had been amply discharged. His letter would be mired in the imperial bureaucracy for months.

'Perhaps you could tell me where I might find the Varangians,' I ventured.

The secretary raised a disdainful eyebrow at my antiquated Greek.

'The Varangians,' I repeated. 'The imperial guardsmen.'

There was a pause as he deliberated over my question, it was as if he was smelling a bad odour. 'Oh, you mean the emperor's wineskins,' he answered. 'That drunken lot of barbarians. I haven't the least idea. You'd better ask someone else.' It was quite plain that he knew the answer to my question, but was not prepared to help.

I had better luck with a passer-by in the street. 'Follow this main avenue,' he said, 'past the porticos and arcades of shops until you come to the Milion – that's a pillar with a heavy iron chain round the base. There's a dome over it, held up on four columns, rather like an upside-down soup bowl. You can't miss it. It's where all the official measurements for distances in the empire start from. Go past the Milion and take the first right. In front of you you'll see a large building, looks like a prison, which is not surprising because that is what it used to be. That's now the barracks for the imperial guard. Ask for the Numera if you get lost.'

I followed his directions. It seemed natural to seek out the Varangians. I knew no one in this immense city. In my purse I had a few silver coins left over from ibn Hauk's generosity, but they would soon be spent. The only northerners whom I knew for certain lived in Miklagard were the soldiers of the emperor's bodyguard. They came from Denmark, Norway, Sweden and some from England. Many, like Ivarr's father, had once served in Kiev before deciding to come on to Constantinople and apply to join the imperial bodyguard. It occurred to me that I might even ask if I could join. After all, I had served with the Jomsvikings.

My scheme, had I known it, was as clumsy and whimsical as my knowledge of spoken Greek, but even in the city of churches Odinn still watched over me.

As I reached the Numera, a man emerged from the doorway to the barracks and started to walk across the large square away from me. He was obviously a guardsman. His height and breadth of shoulder made that much clear. He was a head taller than the majority of the citizens around him. They were small and neat, dark haired and olive skinned, and dressed in the typical Greek costume, loose shirt and trousers for the men, long flowing gowns and veils for the women. By contrast, the guardsman was wearing a tunic of red, and I could see the hilt of a heavy sword hanging from his right shoulder. I noticed too that his long blond hair hung in three plaits down his neck. I was staring at the back of his head as he moved through the crowd, when I recognised something about him. It was the way he walked. He moved like a ship rolling and cresting over the swell of the sea. The faster-moving civilians had to step aside to get past him. They were like a river flowing around a rock. Then I remembered where I had seen that gait before. There was only one man that tall, who walked in that measured way — Grettir's half-brother, Thorstein Galleon.

I broke into a run and chased after him. The coincidence seemed so far-fetched that I did not yet dare say a prayer of thanks to Odinn in case I was deluded. I was still wearing an

Arab gown that ibn Hauk had given me and to the pedestrians I
must have looked a strange sight indeed, a fair-haired barbarian
in a flapping cotton robe pushing rudely through the crowd in
pursuit of one of the imperial guard.

'Thorstein!' I shouted.

He stopped, and turned. I saw his face and knew I would
make a sacrifice to Odinn in gratitude.

'Thorstein!' I repeated, coming closer. 'It's me Thorgils,
Thorgils Leifsson. I haven't seen you since Grettir and I were at
your farmhouse in Tonsberg, on our way to Iceland.'

For a moment Thorstein looked puzzled. My Arab dress must
have confused him, and my face was tanned by the sun. 'By Thor
and his goats,' he rumbled, 'it is indeed Thorgils. What on earth
are you doing here and how did you find your way to Miklagard?'
He clapped me on the shoulder and I flinched. His hand had
touched the wound left by Froygeir's knife.

'I only arrived today,' I answered. 'It's a long story but I
came here through Gardariki and along the rivers with the fur
traders.'

'But how is it that you are alone and inside the city itself?'
Thorstein asked. 'River traders are not allowed inside the city
walls unless they are accompanied by an official.'

'I came as an ambassadorial courier,' I said. 'It's so good to
see you.'

'You too,' answered Thorstein heartily. 'I heard that you
became Grettir's sworn brother after you got back to Iceland.
Which makes a bond between us.' Abruptly he checked himself,
as though his initial enthusiasm was misplaced. 'I was on my way
to report for duty at the palace guardroom, but there's time for us
to go and share a glass of wine in a tavern,' and, strangely, he
took me by the arm, and almost pushed me away from the open
square and into the shelter of one of the arcades. We turned into
the first tavern we came to and he led me to the back of the
room. Here he sat us down where we could not be observed from
the street.

'I'm sorry to seem so brusque, Thorgils,' he said, 'but no one else knows that Grettir was my half-brother and I want it to stay that way.'

For a moment I was scandalised. I had never imagined that Thorstein would conceal his relationship to Grettir, even though his half-brother had earned such an unsavoury reputation as a brigand and outlaw. But I was misjudging Thorstein badly.

'Thorgils, you remember the promise I made to Grettir at my farm in Norway. On the day that you and he were about to set sail for Iceland?'

'You promised to avenge him if ever he was killed unjustly.'

'That's why I'm here in Constantinople, because of Grettir,' Thorstein went on. His voice had a new intensity. 'I've come here in pursuit of the man who killed him. It's taken a long time to track him down and now I'm very close. In fact I don't want him to know just how close. It's not that I think he will make a run for it, he's come too far for that. What I want is to pick the right moment. When I'm to take my revenge, it won't be a hole-in-the-corner deed. It will be out in the open, something to make men remember.'

'That's exactly what Grettir would have said,' I replied. 'But tell me, how does Thorbjorn Ongul come to be here in Miklagard?'

'So you know it was that one-eyed bastard who caused the deaths of Grettir and Illugi,' said Thorstein. 'That's common knowledge in Iceland but nowhere else. He was condemned to exile by the Althing for employing the help of a black witch to cause Grettir's death. Since then he's taken care to keep out of sight. He went to Norway, then came here to Miklagard, where there's little chance of running into any other Icelanders or being recognised. In fact the other members of the guard know nothing about his background. He applied to the service about a year ago, met the entry requirements, greased a few palms and has established himself as a reliable soldier. That's another reason why I have to strike at the right moment. The regiment won't like it.'

He paused for a moment and then said quietly, 'Thorgils, your arrival has complicated matters for me. I cannot allow anything which might interfere with my promise or risk its outcome. I would prefer if you stayed out of Constantinople, at least until I have settled matters with Thorbjorn Ongul.'

'There's another way, Thorstein,' I said. 'Both of us are honour bound to Grettir's memory, whether as half-brother or sworn brother. As witness to your oath to Grettir I have a duty to support you, should you ever need my help. I am utterly certain that it was Odinn who brought about this meeting between us and that he did it for a purpose. Until that purpose becomes clear, I ask you to reconsider. Try to think how I might remain in Constantinople and be close at hand. For instance, why don't I join the guard as a recruit? Anonymously of course.'

Thorstein shook his head. 'Out of the question. Right now there are many more volunteers than vacancies and a long waiting list. I paid a hefty bribe to get in. Four pounds of gold is the going rate for the greedy officials who maintain the army list. Of course the pay scales are so good that you earn the money back in three or four years. The emperor knows enough to keep his guardsmen happy. They're the only troops he can trust in this city of intrigues and plots.' He thought for a moment, then added, 'Maybe there is a way of arranging for you to be close at hand, but you will have to be very discreet. Each guardsman has the right to have one valet on regimental strength. It's a menial job, but it provides you with a billet in the main barracks. I have not yet exercised my nomination.'

'Won't there be a risk that Ongul will see and recognise me?' I asked.

'Not if you keep in the background,' Thorstein answered. 'The Varangian guard has grown in size. There are nearly five hundred of us nowadays and we no longer all fit into the Numera Barracks. Two or three platoons are quartered in the former barracks of the excubitors – they are the palace regiment of Greek guardsmen. Their regimental strength is in decline, while ours is growing. That's where Thorbjorn Ongul has his room – another reason why it's been difficult for me to find the right moment to challenge him over Grettir's death.'

So it was that I became Thorstein Galleon's valet, not a very demanding task as it turned out. At least not for someone who, as a youngster, had been on the palace staff of that great dandy, King Sigtryggr of Dublin. I had learned a long time ago how to comb and plait hair, wash and press clothes, and polish armour and weapons till they gleamed. And it turned out to be the Varangians' pride in their weapons which provided Thorstein with the opportunity to take revenge, far earlier than he or I had expected.

The Byzantines love pomp. More than any other nation I have seen, they adore pageantry and outward show. I can scarcely recall a single day when they did not have some sort of parade or ceremony in which the basileus took a prominent part. It might be a procession from the palace to attend a service in one of the many churches, a formal parade to commemorate a victory of the army, or a trip to the harbour to inspect the fleet and the arsenal. Even a local excursion to the horse races at the Hippodrome – less than a bow shot from the palace outer wall – was organised by the master of ceremonies and his multitude of officious staff. They kept an immensely long list of precedence, detailing who held what rank in the palace hierarchy, what their precise title was, who was senior to whom, how they must be addressed, and so forth. When an imperial procession formed up to leave the palace grounds, these busybodies could be seen rushing around, making sure that everyone was in their correct place in the column and carried the proper emblem of rank – a jewelled whip, a gold chain, inscribed ivory tablets, a rolled-up diploma, a sword with a golden hilt, a jewelled gold collar, and so forth. For onlookers it was easy to identify the imperial family: only they were allowed to wear the colour purple, and immediately in front and behind of them marched the guards, just in case of trouble.

The Varangians carried the symbols of their trade: battleaxe and sword. The axe had a single blade, often inlaid with expensive silver scrollwork. The haft was waxed as far as the two-handed grip with its fancy, hand-stitched leatherwork. Both blade and shaft were polished until they gleamed. The heavy sword was worn, as I have mentioned, dangling from the right shoulder, but there was a problem when it came to its embellishment because a sword with a gold hilt was the emblem of a spartharios, a court official of middle rank whose rights and privileges were jealously preserved. So the guardsmen found other ways to ornament their weapons. In my time in Constantinople silver sword handles were popular, and some soldiers had their swords fitted with grips made of exotic wood. Nearly all the men had paid the scabbard makers to have their sword sheaths covered in scarlet silk to match their tunics.

Less than a week after I had taken up my duties as Thorstein's valet, a message arrived at the Numera barracks from the logothete, a high official of the chancery. The basileus and his entourage were to process to a service of thanksgiving in the church of Hagia Sophia, and the guard was to provide the usual imperial escort. However, the logothete – he was far too grand to speak for himself but sent a deputy – stressed that the occasion was sufficiently important for the entire guard to be on parade in full regalia. The procession was scheduled to take place in three days' time.

Typically, the first response of the senior officers was to order a dress rehearsal, which took place in the great square before the Numera barracks. I watched from an upper window and had to admit that I was impressed. The Varangian guard looked awe-inspiring, rank upon rank of burly, heavily bearded axemen, fierce enough in appearance to terrify any opposition. Even Thorstein, with his great height, was overtopped by several colleagues, and I spotted Thorbjorn Ongul with his villainous one-eyed look.

The moment the dress rehearsal ended, I and the other orderlies hurried out into the square to collect up the tunics, sword belts and other accoutrements which we would have to keep clean and neat until the procession itself. Naturally a number of the soldiers gathered in groups to gossip and at that point I saw Thorstein walk across and join the group which included Thorbjorn Ongul.

Rashly, I followed.

Taking up my position on the edge of the circle, I took care to keep out of Thorbjorn Ongul's sight, but moved close enough to see what was going on. As I had noted with the Jomsvikings, soldiers love nothing better than to compare their weaponry and this is precisely what the guardsmen were doing. They were showing off their swords, axes and daggers to one another and making claims, mostly exaggerated, about the merits of each item – its excellent balance, its sharpness, how it kept an edge when hacking at a wooden shield, the number of enemies the weapon had despatched, and so on. When it came to Ongul's turn, he unhitched his scabbard, withdrew his sword and flourished it proudly.

My mouth went dry. The sword which Ongul held up for all to see was the very same sword which Grettir had looted from the barrow mound in my company. I recognised it at once. It was a unique weapon, beautifully made with that wavy pattern in the metal of the blade that denotes the finest workmanship of the Frankish swordsmiths. It was the sword Ongul had wrenched from Grettir's hand, chopping off his fingers to release his grip as my sworn brother lay dying on the squalid floor of his hideout on Drang. I made a mental note to tell Thorstein how the sword came to be in Ongul's possession, but Grettir's killer did it for me. The guardsman standing next to Ongul asked if he might look more closely at the weapon and Ongul proudly handed over the sword. The guardsman sighted along the blade and pointed out to Ongul that there were two nicks on the cutting edge.

'You should get those attended to. It's a shame that such a fine blade has such marks,' he said.

'Oh no,' announced Ongul boastfully as he took back the sword. 'I made those nicks myself. They come from the day that

I used this sword to put an end to the perverted outlaw, Grettir the Strong. This was his sword. I took it from him and those two nicks were made when I hacked off his head. Grettir the Strong was like no other man. Even his neck bones were like iron. It took four good blows to cut through his neck and that was when the sword edge was chipped. I wouldn't grind out those marks even if the commander-in-chief himself asked me to.'

'Can I see the weapon?' asked a voice. I recognised the deep tones of Thorstein Galleon, and saw Ongul hand over the weapon. Thorstein swung the sword from side to side experimentally to find what a true swordsman calls the sweet spot, the balance point where the edge carries the most impact and a blade should meet its target. The sweep of Thorstein's swing made the crowd move back to give him more space and, to my horror, the man standing in front of me stepped aside and left me exposed to Ongul's view. He glanced round the circle and the gaze of his single eye settled on my face. I knew that he recognised me immediately as the man who had been carried off Drang after Grettir's death. I saw him frown as he tried to understand why I was there. But it was too late.

'This is to avenge Grettir Asmundarson, the man you foully murdered,' Thorstein called out as he stepped across the watching circle of men, raised the nicked sword and from his great height brought it slicing down directly on Ongul's unprotected skull. Thorstein had found the sweet spot. The sword bit through Ongul's skull and split his head like a melon. The man who had killed my closest friend died instantly.

For a moment there was stunned silence. The onlookers gazed down at Ongul's corpse, sprawled on the flagstones of the parade ground. Thorstein made no move to escape. He stood with bloody sword in his grasp, an expression of profound satisfaction on his face. Then he calmly wiped the blood from the sword, walked across to where I stood and handed it to me with the words, 'In Grettir's memory.'

As soon as word of the killing reached the excubitors, who

were responsible for police duties, a Greek officer arrived to place
Thorstein under arrest. He offered no resistance but allowed
himself to be led quietly away. He was at peace with himself. He
had done what he had set out to do.

'He hasn't got a hope,' said Thorstein's platoon commander,
looking on. He was a tough veteran from Jutland with ten years'
service in the guard. 'To kill within the palace precincts is a
capital offence. The pen pushers in the imperial secretariat dislike
us so much that they will lose no opportunity to damage the
regiment. They will say that Ongul's death was just another
squalid brawl amongst bloodthirsty barbarians. Thorstein's as
good as dead.'

'Isn't there anything that can be done to help him?' I asked
from the edge of the little group of onlookers. The Jutlander
turned to look at me, standing there with Grettir's sword in my
hand.

'Not unless you can oil the wheels of justice,' he said.

Grettir's sword felt like a living thing in my grasp.

'What happens when a guardsman dies on active service?' I
asked.'

'His possessions are divided among his comrades. That's our
custom. If he leaves a widow or children, we auction off his
personal effects and the money goes to them, along with any back
pay that is outstanding.'

'You say that Thorstein is as good as dead. Could you
organise an auction of his possessions in the barracks, including
the sale of this sword? Ongul told you how he looted it from
Grettir the Strong, even used it for his death blow, and you've
seen how Thorstein took it back.'

The Jutlander looked at me in surprise. 'That sword's worth
two years' salary,' he said.

'I know, but Thorstein presented me with the weapon and I
would gladly put it up for auction.'

The platoon commander looked intrigued. He knew me only
as Thorstein's valet and was probably curious to know what role

I had played in this affair. Perhaps he was wondering if he could acquire the sword for himself. 'It's irregular, but I will see what I can do,' he said. It'll be better if the auction is held without the Greeks knowing. They would only claim that we were so avaricious that we sold off Thorstein's effects before he was even dead. Not that they can accuse others of avarice. They're the past masters.'

'There's one more thing I would ask,' I continued. 'A lot of people heard Thorstein shout out the name of Grettir the Strong just before he cut down Thorbjorn Ongul. No one really knows why he did so, though there's a lot of speculation. If the auction could be held tonight, just when interest is at its height, it would attract the largest number. More than just his platoon.'

In fact nearly half the regiment crowded into the courtyard of the Numera barracks to attend the auction that evening, cramming themselves into the porticos that surrounded the yard. It was precisely what I had wanted.

Thorstein's platoon commander, Ragnvald, called them to silence. 'All of you know what happened this afternoon. Thorstein, nicknamed the Galleon, took the life of his fellow countryman, Thorbjorn Ongul, and none of us know why. Thorbjorn can't tell us because he's dead and Thorstein is in solitary confinement awaiting trial. But this man, Thorgils Leifsson, claims he can answer your questions, and he wants to auction the sword that Thorstein gave him.' He turned to me. 'Now it's your turn.'

I climbed up on a block of stone and faced my audience. Then I held up the sword so all could see it and waited until I had their complete attention. 'Let me tell you where this sword comes from, how it was found among the dead, where it travelled, and the story of the remarkable man who owned it.' And then I proceeded to tell the tale of Grettir the Strong and his remarkable career, from the night we had robbed the barrow grave, through all our times together, both good and bad: how he had twice saved my life, first in a tavern brawl and then aboard a foundering ship. I told them about the man: how perverse and stubborn he could be, how often his best intentions had led to tragedy, how he could be violent and brutal, how he did not know his own strength and yet had struggled to remain honest to himself in the face of adversity. I went on to describe his life as an outlaw in the wilderness, his victories in hand-to-hand combat over those who had been sent to kill him and how, finally, he had been defeated by black seidr invoked by Thorbjorn Ongul's volva foster-mother, and had died on Drang.

It was Grettir's saga and, as I told it, I knew that the men who heard it would remember and repeat the tale so that Grettir's name would live on in honoured memory. I was fulfilling my final promise to my sworn brother.

When I had finished my tale, the Jutlander stood up. 'Time to auction the sword of Grettir the Strong,' he called out. 'From what we have just heard, Ongul's death was not murder, but an act of honourable revenge, justified under our own laws and customs. I suggest that the money raised from the sale of this sword is put towards the expense of defending Thorstein Galleon in the law courts of Constantinople. I call upon you to be generous.'

Then something remarkable happened. The bidding for the sword began, but it was not in the manner I had anticipated. Each of the Guardsmen shouted out a price far less than I had expected. One after another they called out a number and the Jutlander carved marks on a tally stick. Finally the bidding stopped. The Jutlander looked down at the marks. 'Seven pounds in gold, and five numisma. That's the total,' he announced. 'That should be enough to see that Thorstein avoids the hangman's rope, and receives instead a prison sentence.'

He looked round the circle of watching faces. 'My platoon has a vacancy,' he called. 'I propose that it is filled, not by purchase, but by acclamation of our general gathering. I propose to you that the place of Thorstein Galleon is taken by the sworn brother to Grettir Asmundarsson. Do you agree?'

A general mutter of agreement came back. One or two

guardsmen banged their sword hilts on the stones. The Jutlander turned to me. 'Thorgils, you may keep the sword. Use it as a member of the guard.'

And that is how I, Thorgils Leifsson, was recruited into the imperial guard of the basileus in Metropolis, and was on hand to pledge my allegiance to the man called the 'thunderbolt of the north' or, to some, the last of the Vikings. In his service I would travel to the very hub of the world, win spoils of war sufficient to rig a ship with sails of silk, and – as his spy and diplomat – come within an arrow's length of placing him on the throne of England.

AFTERWORD

THORSTEIN GALLEON DID take his revenge on the murderer of Grettir his half-brother, according to Grettir's Saga written *c.* AD 1325. That saga traces the celebrated events in Grettir's life, from his rebellious childhood, through the plundering of a barrow grave and his many escapades as a notorious outlaw, to his eventual death on Drang Island at the hands of Thorbjorn Ongul and a posse of local farmers. Thorstein Galleon is said to have tracked down Thorbjorn Ongul to Constantinople and confronted him at a weapons inspection of the Varangian guard. Ongul was boasting how he had killed the outlaw with Grettir's own sword, taken from him as he lay dying. The weapon was passed from hand to hand among the guardsmen and when it came to Thorstein, in the words of the saga, 'Thorstein took the short sword, and at once raised it up and struck at Ongul. The blow landed on his head, and it was so powerful that the sword went right down to his jaws. Thorbjorn Ongul fell dead to the ground. Everyone was speechless . . .'

from *Grettir's Saga*, translated by Denton Fox and Hermann Palsson, University of Toronto Press, 1998

VIKING
King's Man

MAPS

ICELAND

FAEROES

Orkney

Clontarf

Dublin

SCOTLAND

IRELAND

ENGLAND

York

ENGLISH
SEA

NORWAY

Nidaros/
Trondheim

Uppsala

DENMARK

BALTIC SEA

Bremen

Rouen
Normandy

Lotharingia

Burgundy

FRANKIA

Aquitaine
Auvergne

Rome

GREAT

Traina

Catania
Augusta
Syracuse

SICILY

Kairouan

LIBYA

Thorgil's Journeys

------- Norway – Scotland

———— Norway – Duke William's court

.... Normandy – Harald's last battle

ICELAND

FAEROES

NORWAY

Orkney
Caithness
Firth of Moray
The Mounth
Birnam

SCOTLAND

Nidaros/
Trondheim

Upplands

Vaner
Lake

Uppsala

Clontarf

IRELAND

Dublin

Northumbria

ENGLISH
SEA

Väster
Gotland

DENMARK

York
Stamford Bridge

BALTIC SEA

ENGLAND

London

Hastings

Bremen

St Valéry
Fécamp

Flanders
Boulogne
Ponthieu

Dives

Rouen
Jumièges

Auxerre

Normandy

Burgundy

Cluny

FRANKIA

❊

To my holy and blessed master, Abbot Geraldus, in humble obedience to your wish, I send this, the third and last packet of the writings of the false monk Thangbrand. Inauspicious was the day when I first found these pages in our library! May I be forgiven for reading them with my sinful eyes, for I was urged on by my imagination and impatience.

Here I have found false witness artfully woven into a tale intended to beguile the credulous. This serpent in our bosom levels vile and wicked allegations against our brothers in Christ, and shamelessly admits piracy and the desecration of hallowed relic. Even when among the schismatics of the East he cannot restrain his viper's tongue.

Nothing has grieved me more than to learn that this false monk made a journey to the Holy Land, a pilgrimage which is the greatest desire of those who are as poor and unworthy as I. Yet he besmirches his witness with profane mistrust, and thereby seeks to undermine the faith of all those who believe in the Incarnation of the Word. As scripture avers, to an evil, unbelieving man, the truth becomes a lie.

His spew of corruption is the more disturbing, for it touches on high matters of state. Questioned is the very ascent to the throne of England itself, and his words must surely be judged treasonable by those who have competence in these matters.

We will speak no further of this matter, but will leave the pious labours of the faithful to be rewarded and paid for by the Just Judge.

Will there ever be an end to the deceit and mendacity of this impostor? I pray for his salvation in the fear of God, for is it not said that even one sparrow cannot fall into a snare without his providence, and that when God wills the end may be good?

Aethelred
Sacristan and Librarian
Written in the month of January in the Year of our Lord One Thousand and Seventy-two

ONE

THE EMPEROR WAS pretending to be a whale. He put his head under water and filled his mouth, then came back up to the surface and squirted little spouts across the palace plunge pool. I watched him out of the corner of my eye, not knowing whether to feel disdainful or sympathetic. He was, after all, an old man. Past seventy years of age, he would be relishing the touch of warm water on his blotchy skin as well as the feeling of weightlessness. He was afflicted with a bloating disease which had puffed up his body and limbs so grossly that he found walking very painful. Only the week before I had seen him return to the palace so exhausted after one of the endless ceremonials that he had collapsed into the arms of an attendant the moment the great bronze doors closed behind him. Today was the festival the Christians call Good Friday, so in the afternoon there was to be yet another imperial ceremony and it would last for hours. I decided that the emperor deserved his moment of relaxation, though his whalelike antics in the pool might have surprised his subjects as the majority of them considered him to be their God's representative on earth.

I shifted the heavy axe on my shoulder. There was a damp patch where the haft had rested on my scarlet tunic. Beads of sweat were trickling down under the rim of my iron helmet with

5

its elaborate gold inlay, and the heat in the pool room was making me drowsy. I struggled to stay alert. As a member of the Hetaira, the imperial household troops, my duty was to protect the life of the Basileus Romanus III, ruler of Byzantium, and Equal of the Apostles. With five hundred fellow members of his personal Life Guard, the palace Varangians, I had sworn to keep the emperor safe from his enemies, and he paid us handsomely to do so. He trusted us more than his fellow countrymen, and with good reason.

At the far end of the baths were clustered a group of the emperor's staff, five or six of them. Sensibly they were maintaining their distance from their master, not just to give him privacy, but also because his advancing illness made him very tetchy. The Basileus had become notoriously short-tempered. The slightest wrong word or gesture could make him fly into a rage. During the three years I had served at the palace, I had seen him change from being even-handed and generous to waspish and mean. Men accustomed to receiving rich gifts in appreciation from the imperial bounty were now ignored or sharply criticised. Fortunately the Basileus did not yet treat his Life Guard in a similar fashion, and we still gave him our complete loyalty. We played no part in the courtiers' constant plotting and scheming as various factions sought to gain advantage. The ordinary members of the guard did not even speak their language. Our senior officers were patrician Greeks, but the rank and file were recruited from the northern lands and we continued to speak Norse among ourselves. A court official with the title of the Grand Interpreter for the Hetaira was supposed to translate for the guardsmen, but the post was in name only, another high-sounding title in a court mesmerised by precedence and ceremonial.

'Guardsman!' The shout broke into my thoughts. One man in the group was beckoning to me. I recognised the Keeper of the Imperial Inkwell. The post, despite its pompous name, was one of real importance. Officially the keeper proffered the bottle of purple ink whenever the Basileus was ready to sign an official document. In reality he acted as secretary of the emperor's private office. The post gave him open access to the imperial presence, a privilege denied even to the highest ministers, who had to make a formal appointment before being brought before the Basileus.

The keeper repeated his gesture. I glanced across at the Basileus. Romanus was still wallowing and spouting in the pool, eyes closed, happy in his warm and watery world. The pool had recently been deepened in its centre, yet was still shallow enough for a man to stand upright and keep his head above the surface. There seemed no danger there. I strode over towards the keeper, who held out a parchment. I caught a glimpse of the imperial signature in purple ink even as the keeper indicated that I was to take the document to the adjacent room, a small office where the notaries waited.

It was not unusual for a guardsman to act as a footman. The palace officials were so preoccupied with their own dignity that they found it demeaning to carry out the simplest tasks like opening a door or carrying a scroll. So I took the parchment, cast another quick look over my shoulder and walked to the door. The Basileus was still blissfully enjoying his swim.

IN THE NEXT room I found the Orphanotrophus waiting. He was in charge of the city orphanage, an institution financed from the royal purse. Once again the title was no reflection of his real importance. John the Orphanotrophus was the most powerful man in the empire, excluding only the Basileus. Thanks to a combination of raw intellect and shrewd application, John had worked his way up through the various grades of the imperial hierarchy and was prime minister of the empire in all but name. Feared by all, he was a thin man who had a gaunt face with deep-sunk eyes under startlingly black eyebrows. He was also a beardless one, a eunuch.

I came to attention in front of him, but did not salute. Only the Basileus and the immediate members of the imperial family

warranted a guardsman's salute, and John the Orphanotrophus
was certainly not born to the purple. His family came from
Paphalagonia on the Black Sea coast, and it was rumoured that
the family's first profession when they came to Constantinople
was to run a money exchange. Some said that they had been
forgers.

When I handed over the parchment, the Orphanotrophus
glanced through it, and then said to me slowly, pronouncing each
word with exaggerated care, 'Take this to the logothete of
finance.'

I stood my ground and replied in Greek, 'My apologies, your
excellency. I am on duty. I cannot leave the imperial presence.'

The Orphanotrophus raised an eyebrow. 'Well, well, a guardsman who speaks Greek,' he murmured. 'The palace is finally
becoming civilised.'

'Perhaps someone could call a dekanos, ' I suggested. 'That is
their duty, to carry messages.' I saw I had made a mistake.

'Yes, and you should do yours,' the Orphanotrophus retorted
acidly.

Smarting at the rebuff, I turned on my heel and marched back
to the baths. As I entered the long chamber with its high, domed
ceiling and walls patterned with mosaics of dolphins and waves, I
knew immediately that something was terribly wrong. The Basileus was still in the water, but now he was lying on his back,
waving feebly with his arms. Only his corpulence was keeping
him from sinking. The attendants who had previously been in the
room were nowhere to be seen. I dropped my axe to the marble
floor, wrenched off my helmet and sprinted for the pool. 'Alarm!
Alarm!' I bellowed as I ran. 'Guardsmen to me!' In a few strides
I was at the edge of the pool and, fully clothed, dived in and
swam as fast as I could manage towards the Basileus. Silently I
thanked my own God, Odinn, that we Norse learn how to swim
when we are still young.

The Basileus seemed unaware of my presence as I reached
him. He was barely moving and occasionally his head slipped

underwater. I put one hand under his chin, lowered my legs until I could touch the bottom of the pool, and began to tow him towards the edge, taking care to keep his head on my shoulder, clear of the water. He was limp in my arms, and his scalp against my chin was bald except for a few straggly hairs.

'Guardsmen to me!' I shouted again. Then in Greek I called out, 'Fetch a doctor!'

This time my calls were answered. Several staff members — scribes, attendants, courtiers — came running into the room and clustered at the edge of the pool. Someone knelt down to grab the Basileus under the armpits and haul him dripping out of the water. But the rescue was clumsy and slow. The Basileus lay on the marble edge of the pool, looking more than ever like a whale, a beached and dying one this time. I clambered out and pushed aside the courtiers.

'Help me lift him,' I said.

'In Thor's name what's going on?' said a voice.

A decurion, the petty officer of my watch, had finally arrived. He glowered so fiercely at the gawking courtiers that they fell back. The two of us picked up the emperor's limp body and carried him towards a marble bench. One of the bath attendants had the wit to spread a layer of towels over it before we laid down the old man, who was moving feebly. The decurion looked round and ripped a brocaded silk gown off the shoulders of a courtier and laid it over the emperor's nakedness.

'Let me through, please'.

This was one of the palace physicians. A short, paunchy man, he lifted up the emperor's eyelids with his stubby fingers. I could see that he was nervous. He pulled his hands back as if he had been scalded. He was probably frightened that the Basileus would expire under his touch. But the emperor's eyes stayed open and he shifted his head slightly to look around him.

At that moment there was a stir among the watching courtiers, and their circle parted to allow a woman through. It was Zoë, the empress. She must have been summoned from the gynaeceum, the

women's quarters of the palace. It was the first time I had seen
her close to, and I was struck by her poise. Despite her age she
held herself with great dignity. She must have been at least fifty
years old and had probably never been a beauty, but her face
retained that fine-boned structure which hinted at aristocratic
descent. She was the daughter and granddaughter of emperors,
and had the haughty manners to prove it.

Zoë swept through the crowd, and stepped up to within an
arm's length of her husband where he lay on the marble slab. Her
face showed no emotion as she gazed down at the emperor, who
was ashen pale and breathing with difficulty. For a brief moment
she just stared. Then, without a word, she turned and walked out
of the room.

The courtiers avoided looking at one another. Everyone,
including myself, knew that there was no love between the
emperor and his wife. The previous Basileus, Constantine, had
insisted that they marry. Zoë was Constantine's favoured daughter, and in the last days of his reign he had searched for a suitable
husband for her from among the ranks of Constantinople's
aristocracy. Father and daughter had both wanted to ensure the
family succession, though Zoë was past childbearing age. That
had not prevented her and Romanus when they ascended the
throne together from attempting to found their own dynasty.
Romanus had dosed himself with huge amounts of aphrodisiacs –
the reason for his hair loss, it was claimed – while his elderly
consort hung herself with fertility charms and consulted quacks
and charlatans who proposed more and more grotesque ways of
ensuring pregnancy. When all their efforts failed, the couple slid
into a mutual dislike. Romanus had taken a mistress and Zoë had
been bundled off to the gynaeceum, frustrated and resentful.

But that was not the whole story. Zoë had also acquired a
lover, not two years since. Several members of the guard had
come across the two of them coupling together and turned a blind
eye. Their tact had not been out of respect for the empress – she
conducted her affair openly – but because her consort was the

younger brother of John the Orphanotrophus. Here was an area where high politics mingled with ambition and lust, and it was better left alone.

'Stand back!' ordered the decurion.

He took up his position a spear's length from the Basileus's bald head, and as a reflex I stationed myself by the emperor's feet and also came to attention. My axe was still lying somewhere on the marble floor, but I was wearing a dagger at my belt and I dropped my hand to its hilt. The doctor paced nervously up and down, wringing his hands with worry. Suddenly Romanus gave a deep moan. He raised his head a fraction from the towel that was his pillow and made a slight gesture with his right hand. It was as if he was beckoning someone closer. Not knowing whom he gestured to, no one dared move. The awe and majesty of the imperial presence still had a grip on the spectators. The emperor's gaze shifted slowly, passing across the faces of his watching courtiers. He seemed to be trying to say something, to be pleading. His throat moved but no sounds emerged. Then his eyes closed and his head fell back and rolled to one side. He began to pant, his breath coming in short shallow gasps. Suddenly, the breathing paused, and his mouth fell open. Out flowed a thick, dark brown substance, and after two more choking breaths, he expired.

I stood rigidly to attention. There were the sounds of running feet, of tumult, and in the distance a wailing and crying as news of the emperor's death spread among the palace staff. I took no notice. Until a new Basileus was crowned, the duty of the guard was to protect the body of the dead emperor.

'Thorgils, you look like the village idiot standing there in your soaking uniform. Get back to the guardroom and report to the duty officer.'

The instructions were delivered in Norse and I recognised the voice of Halfdan, my company commander. A beefy veteran, Halfdan had served in the Life Guard for close on ten years. He should have retired by now, after amassing a small fortune from his salary, but he liked the life of a guardsman and had cut his ties with his Danish homeland, so he had nowhere else to go.

'Tell him that everything is under control in the imperial presence. You might suggest that he places a curfew on the palace.'

I squelched away, pausing to collect my helmet and the spiked axe which someone had obligingly picked up off the floor and leaned against the wall. My route to the guardroom lay through a labyrinth of passages, reception rooms and courtyards. Romanus III could have died in any one of his palaces – they all had swimming pools – but he had chosen to expire in the largest and most sprawling of them, the Great Palace. Standing close to the tip of the peninsula of Constantinople, the Great Palace had been extended and remodelled so many times by its imperial occupants that it had turned into a bewildering maze of chambers and anterooms. Erecting ever grander buildings was a fascination bordering on mania for each occupant of the purple throne. Every Basileus wanted to immortalise his rule by leaving at least one extravagant structure, whether a new church, a monastery, a huge palace, or some ostentatious public building. Romanus had been busily squandering millions of gold pieces on an immense new church to the mother of his God, though it seemed to me that she already had more than enough churches and monasteries to her name. Romanus's new church was to be dedicated to her as Mary the Celebrated, and what with its surrounding gardens and walkways and fountains – and the constant changes of design, which meant pulling down half-finished buildings – the project had run so far over budget that Romanus had been obliged to raise a special tax to pay for the construction. The church was not yet finished and I suspected it never would be. I surprised myself by realising how easily I was already thinking of Romanus in the past tense.

'Change into a dry uniform and join the detail on the main gate,' the duty officer ordered when I reported to him. No more than twenty years old, he was almost as edgy as the physician who had attended the dying emperor. A Greek from one of Constantinople's leading families, his family would have paid handsomely to buy his commission in the Life Guard. Merely by placing him inside the walls of the palace, they hoped he might attract the attention of the Basileus and gain preferment. Now their investment would be wasted if a new Basileus decided, out of concern for his own safety, to replace all the Greek officers. It was another deception so characteristic of palace life. Byzantine society still pretended that the Hetaira was Greek. Their sons prided themselves on being officers of the guard, and they dressed up in uniforms which denoted the old palace regiments – the Excubia, the Numeri, the Scholae and others – but when it came to real work our Basileus had trusted only us, the foreigners, his palace Varangians.

I joined twenty of my comrades at the main gate. They had already slammed the doors shut without asking permission of the keeper of the gate, whose duty it was to supervise the opening of the main gate at dawn, close it again at noon, and then reopen it for a few hours in the early evening. But today the death of the emperor had removed his authority and the keeper was at a loss to know what to do. The decurion decided the matter for him. He was refusing to let anyone in or out.

Even as I arrived, there was a great hubbub outside the gate, and I could hear thunderous knocking and loud, impatient shouts.

'Glad you've got here, Thorgils,' said the guard commander. 'Maybe you can tell me what those wild men out there want.'

I listened carefully. 'I think you had better let them in,' I said. 'It sounds as though you've got the Great Patriarch outside, and he's demanding admittance.'

'The Great Patriarch? That black-clad old goat,' grumbled the guard commander, who was a staunch Old Believer. 'Lads, open the side door and allow the monks through. But hold your breath. They don't wash very often.'

A moment later a very angry group of monks, all with chest-length beards and black gowns, stormed through the gap between

the doors, glared at us, and hurried off down the corridor with a
righteous-sounding slap of sandals and the clatter of their wooden
staffs on the marble floor slabs. In their midst I saw the white-
bearded figure of Alexis of the Studius, the supreme religious
authority of the empire.

'Wonder what's brought them down from their monastery in
such a hurry,' muttered a Varangian as he pushed shut the door
and dropped the bar back in place.

His question was answered later, when we came off duty and
returned to the guardroom. Half a dozen of my colleagues were
lounging there, smirking.

'The old bitch has already got herself a new husband. The
moment she was sure that old Romanus was definitely on his way
out, she sent someone to fetch the high priest.'

'I know, we let him and his crows in.'

'Well, she certainly didn't summon them to give her beloved
husband the last rites. Even while the priests were on their way,
the old lady called an emergency meeting of her advisers,
including that foxy creep, the Orphanotrophus. She told them that
she wanted her fancy-boy to be the new Basileus.'

'Not the handsome rattle-brain!'

'She had it all worked out. She said that, by right of imperial
descent, she represented the continuity of the state, and that it was
in the best interests of the empire if "my darling Michael", as she
called him, took the throne with her.'

'You must be joking! How do you know all this?'

The guardsman gave a snort of derision. 'The Orphanotrophus
had ordered four of us to act as close escort for the empress in
case there was an attempt on her life. It was a ruse, of course.
When the other courtiers showed up to dispute the idea of
Michael's succession, they saw the guard standing there, and came
to the conclusion that the matter had already been settled.'

'So what happened when the high priest arrived?'

'He plunged straight into the wedding ceremony for the old

woman and her lover-boy. She paid him a fat bribe, of course, and within the hour they were man and wife.'

This bizarre story was interrupted by the arrival of another of our Greek officers, who scuttled into the room, anxiously demanding a full sovereign's escort. We were to don our formal uniforms and accompany him to the Triklinium, the grand audience chamber. He insisted that there was not a moment to be lost.

Thirty of us formed up and marched through the passageways to the enormous hall, floored with mosaics, hung with silk banners and decorated with rich icons, where the Basileus formally received his ministers, foreign ambassadors and other dignitaries. Two ornate thrones stood on a dais at the far end of the hall and our officer led us straight to our positions – to stand in a semicircle at the back of the dais, looking out across the audience chamber. A dozen equerries and the marshal of the Triklinium were busily making sure that everything was in order for the arrival of their majesties. Within moments the Empress Zoë and Michael, her new husband, entered the room and hurried up to the thrones. Close behind came the Orphanotrophus, some high-ranking priests, and a gaggle of courtiers associated with the empress's faction at court. Zoë and Michael stepped up on the dais, our Greek officer hissed a command, and we, the members of the Life Guard, obediently raised our axes vertically in front of us in a formal salute. The empress and emperor turned to face down the hall. Just as they were about to sit down there came a tense moment. By custom the guard acknowledges the presence of the Basileus as he takes his seat upon the throne. As the emperor lowers himself on to his seat, the guards transfer their axes from the salute to their right shoulders. It is a signal that all is well and that the business of the empire is continuing as normal. Now, as Zoë and Michael were about to settle on their throne cushions, my comrades and I glanced at one another questioningly. For the space of a heartbeat nothing happened. I sensed our Greek officer stiffen with anxiety, and then, raggedly, the guard placed their axes on their shoulders. I could almost hear the sigh of relief from Zoë's retinue.

That crisis safely past, the proceedings quickly took on an air of farce. Zoë's people must have sent word throughout the palace, summoning the senior ministers and their staff, who came in one by one. Many, I suspected, arrived thinking that they would be paying their respects to the body of their dead emperor. Instead they were confronted with the astonishing spectacle of his widow already remarried and seated beside a new husband nearly young enough to be her grandson. No wonder several of the new arrivals faltered on the threshold, dumbfounded. The matronly empress and her youthful consort were clutching the emblems of state in their jewelled hands, their glittering robes had been carefully arranged by their pages, and on Zoë's face was an expression which showed that she expected full homage. From the back of the dais I watched the courtiers' eyes take in the scene – the aloof empress, her boyish husband, the waiting cluster of high officials, and the sinister, brooding figure of John the Orphanotrophus, Michael's brother, noting how each new arrival responded. After a brief moment of hesitation and calculation, the high ministers and courtiers came forward to the twin thrones, bowed deeply to the empress, then knelt and kissed the ring of her bright-eyed husband, who, less than six hours earlier, had been known as nothing more than her illicit lover.

The next day we buried Romanus. Overnight someone – it must have been the supremely efficient Orphanotrophus – arranged for his swollen corpse to be dressed in official robes of purple silk and laid out on a bier. Within an hour of sunrise the funeral procession had already assembled with everyone in their correct place according to rank, and the palace's main gates were thrown open. I was one of the one hundred guards who marched, according to tradition, immediately before and after the dead Basileus as we emerged on to the Mese, the broad main avenue which bisects the city. I was surprised to see how many of the citizens of Constantinople had left their beds this early. Word of the Basileus's sudden death must have spread very fast. Those who stood at the front of the dense crowd lining the route could see for themselves the waxen skin and swollen face of the dead emperor, for his head and hands had been left uncovered. Once or twice I heard someone shout out, 'Poisoned!', but for the most part the crowd remained eerily silent. I did not hear a single expression of sorrow or regret for his passing. Romanus III, I realised, had not been popular in Constantinople.

At the great Forum of Amastration we wheeled left, and half a mile further on the cortège entered the Via Triumphalis. Normally an emperor processed along this broad avenue to the cheers of the crowd, at the head of his victorious troops, as he displayed captured booty and files of defeated enemy in chains. Now Romanus was carried in the opposite direction in a gloomy silence broken only by the creaking wheels of the carriage which carried his bier, the sound of the horses' hooves and the muted footfalls of hundreds upon hundreds of the ordinary citizens of Constantinople, who, simply out of morbid curiosity, joined in behind our procession. They went with us all the way to the enormous unfinished church of Mary the Celebrated that was Romanus's great project, and where he was now the first person to benefit from his own extravagance. Here the priests hurriedly placed him into the green and white sarcophagus which Romanus had selected for himself, following another curious imperial custom that the Basileus should choose his own tomb on the day of his accession.

Then, as the crowd was dispersing in a mood of sombre apathy, our cortège briskly retraced its steps to the palace, for there was no a moment to be lost.

'Two parades in one day, but it will be worth it,' said Halfdan cheerfully as he shrugged off the dark sash he had worn during the funeral and replaced it with one that glittered with gold thread. 'Thank Christ it's only a short march this afternoon, and anyhow we would have to be doing it anyway as it's Palm Sunday.'

Halfdan, like several members of the guard, was part-Christian and part-pagan. Superficially he subscribed to the religion of the White Christ — and swore by him — and he attended services at the new church to St Olaf recently built near our regimental headquarters down by the Golden Horn, Constantinople's main harbour. But he also wore Thor's hammer as an amulet on a leather strap around his neck, and when he was in his cups he often announced that when he died he would much prefer to feast and fight in Odinn's Valholl than finish up as a bloodless being with wings like a fluffy dove in the Christians' heaven.

'Thorgils, how come you speak Greek so well?' The question came from one of the Varangians who had been at the palace gate the previous day. He was a recent recruit into the guard.

'He licked up a drop of Fafnir's blood, that's how,' Halfdan interjected. 'Give Thorgils a couple of weeks and he could learn any language, even if it's bird talk.'

I ignored his ponderous attempt at humour. 'I was made to study Greek when I was a youngster,' I said, 'in a monastery in Ireland.'

'You were once a monk?' the man asked, surprised. 'I thought you were a devotee of Odinn. At least that is what I've heard.'

'I am,' I told him. 'Odinn watched over me when I was among the monks and got me away from them.'

'Then you understand this stuff with the holy pictures they carry about whenever we're on parade, the relics and bits of saints and all the rest of it.'

'Some of it. But the Christianity I was made to study is different from the one here in Constantinople. It's the same God, of course, but a different way of worshipping him. I must admit that until I came here, I had never even heard of half of the saints they honour.'

'Not surprising,' grumbled the Varangian. 'Down in the market last week a huckster tried to sell me a human bone. Said it came from the right arm of St Demetrios, and I should buy it because I was a soldier and St Demetrios was a fighting man. He claimed the relic would bring me victory in any fight.'

'I hope you didn't buy it.'

'Not a chance. Someone in the crowd warned me that the huckster had sold so many arm and leg bones from St Demetrios that the holy martyr must have had more limbs than a centipede.' He gave a wry laugh.

Later that afternoon I sympathised with the soldier as we marched off for the acclamation of our young new Basileus, who was to be pronounced as Michael IV before a congregation of city dignitaries in the church of Hagia Sophia. We shuffled rather than marched towards the church because there were so many slow-moving priests in the column, all holding up pictures of their saints painted on wooden boards, tottering under heavy banners and pennants embroidered with holy symbols, or carrying precious relics of their faith sealed in gold and silver caskets. Just in front of me was their most venerated memento, a fragment from the wooden cross on which their Christ had hung at the time of his death, and I wondered if perhaps Odinn, the master of disguise, had impersonated their Jesus. The Father of the Gods had also hung on a wooden tree, his side pierced with a spear as he sought to gain world knowledge. It was a pity, I thought to myself, that the Christians were so certain that theirs was the only true faith. If they were a little more tolerant, they would have admitted that other religions had their merits, too. Old Believers were perfectly willing to let people follow their own gods, and we did not seek to impose our ideas on others. But at least the Christians of Constantinople were not as bigoted as their brethren further north, who were busy stamping out what they considered pagan practices. In Constantinople life was tolerant enough for there to be a mosque in the sixth district where the Saracens could worship and several synagogues for the Jews.

A hundred paces from the doors of Hagia Sophia, we, the members of the guard, came to a halt while the rest of the procession solemnly walked on and entered the church. The priests had no love for the Varangians, and it was customary for us to wait outside until the service was concluded. Presumably it was thought that no one would make an attempt on the life of the Basileus inside such a sacred building, but I had my doubts.

Halfdan let my company stand at ease, and we stood and chatted idly among ourselves, waiting for the service to end and to escort the acclaimed Basileus back to the palace. It was then that I noticed a young man dressed in the characteristic hooded gown of a middle-class citizen, a junior clerk by the look of him. He was approaching various members of the guard to try to speak to them. He must have been asking his questions in Greek, for they either shook their heads uncomprehendingly or ignored him. Eventually someone pointed in my direction and he came over towards me. He introduced himself as Constantine Psellus, and said he was a student in the city, studying to enter the imperial service. I judged him to be no more than sixteen or seventeen years old, about half my age.

'I am planning to write a history of the empire,' he told me, 'a chapter for each emperor, and I would very much appreciate any details of the last days of Basileus Romanus.'

I liked his formal politeness and was impressed by his air of quick intelligence, so decided to help him out.

'I was present when he drowned,' I said, and briefly sketched what I had witnessed.

'You say he drowned?' commented the young man gently.

'Yes, that seems to have been the case. Though he actually expired when he was laid out on the bench. Maybe he had a heart attack. He was old enough, after all.'

'I saw his corpse yesterday when it was being carried in the funeral procession, and I thought it looked very strange, so puffed up and grey.'

'Oh, he had had that appearance for quite some time.'

'You don't think he died from some other cause, the effects of a slow-acting poison maybe?' the young man suggested as calmly as if he had been discussing a change in the weather. 'Or perhaps you were deliberately called away from the baths so someone could hold the emperor underwater for a few moments to bring on a heart attack.'

The theory of poisoning had been discussed in the guardroom ever since the emperor's death, and some of us had gone as far as debating whether it was hellebore or some other poison which was being fed to Romanus. But it was not our job to enquire further: our responsibility was to defend him from violent physical attack, the sort you block with a shield or deflect with a shrewd axe blow, not the insidious assault of a lethal drug in his food or drink. The Basileus employed food-tasters for that work, though they could be bribed to act a sham, and any astute assassin would make sure that the poison was slow-acting enough for its effect not to be detected until too late.

But the young man's other suggestion, that I had been lured away to leave Romanus unguarded, alarmed me. If that was the case, then the Keeper of the Inkwell was certainly implicated in the Basileus's death, and perhaps the Orphanotrophus as well. I remembered how he had tried to send me on to the logothete of finance with the parchment. That would have delayed me even more. The thought that I might have been a dupe in the assassination of the Basileus brought a chill to my spine. If true, I was in real danger. Any guardsman found to be negligent in his duty to protect the Basileus was executed by his company commander, usually by public beheading. More than that, if Romanus had indeed been murdered, I was still a potential witness, and that meant I was a likely target for elimination by the culprits. Someone as powerful as the Orphanotrophus could easily have me killed, in a tavern brawl, for example.

Suddenly I was very frightened.

'I think I hear the chanting of the priests,' said Psellus, interrupting my thoughts and fidgeting slightly. Maybe he realised he had gone too far in his theorising, and was close to treason. 'They must have opened the doors of Hagia Sophia, getting ready for the emergence of our new Basileus. It's time for me to let you

go. Thank you for your information. You have been most helpful.'
And he slipped away into the crowd.

We took up our positions around Michael IV, who was
mounted on a superb sorrel horse, one of the best in the royal
stables. I remembered how Romanus had been a great judge of
horseflesh and had built up a magnificent stud farm, though he
had been too sick to enjoy riding. Now I had to admit that the
youthful Michael, though he came from a very plebeian background, looked truly imperial in the saddle. Perhaps that was
what Zoë had seen in him from the beginning. Halfdan had told
me how he had been on duty when Zoë had first gazed on her
future lover. 'You would have been an utter dolt not to have
noticed her reaction. She couldn't take her eyes off him. It was
the Orphanotrophus who introduced him to her. He brought
Michael into the audience chamber when Zoë and Romanus were
holding an imperial reception, and led him right up to the twin
thrones. Old Romanus was gracious enough, but Zoë looked at
the young man as if she wanted to eat him on the spot. He was
good looking, all right, fresh-faced and ruddy-cheeked, likely to
blush like a girl. I reckon the Orphanotrophus knew what he was
doing. Set it all up.'

'Didn't Romanus notice, if it was that obvious?' I asked.

'No. The old boy barely used to look at the empress by then.
Kept looking anywhere except in her direction, as though her
presence gave him a pain.'

I mulled over the conversation as we marched back to the
Grand Palace, entered the great courtyard and the gates were
closed behind us. Our new Basileus dismounted, paused for a
moment while his courtiers and officials formed up in two lines,
and then walked down between them to the applause and smiles
of his retinue before entering the palace. I noted that the Basileus
was unescorted, which seemed very unusual. Even stranger was
the fact that the courtiers broke ranks and began to hurry into the
palace behind the Basileus, almost like a mob. Halfdan astonished
me by rushing off in their wake, all discipline gone. So did the

guardsmen around me, and I joined them in pushing and jostling as if we were a crowd of spectators leaving the hippodrome at the end of the games.

It was unimaginable. All the stiffness and formality of court life had evaporated. The crowd of us, ministers, courtiers, advisers, even priests, all flooded into the great Trikilinium. There, seated up on the dais, was our young new emperor, smiling down at us. On each side were two slaves holding small strongboxes. As I watched, one of the slaves tilted the coffer he held and a stream of gold coins poured out, falling into the emperor's lap. Michael reached down, seized a fistful of the coins, and flung them high into the air above the crowd. I gaped in surprise. The shower of gold coins, each one of them worth six months' wages for a skilled man, glittered and flashed before plummeting towards the upstretched hands. A few coins were caught as they fell, but most tumbled on to the marble floor, landing with a distinct ringing sound. Men dropped to their hands and knees to pick up the coins, even as the emperor dipped his hand into his lap and flung another golden cascade over our heads. Now I understood why Halfdan had been so quick off the mark. My company commander had shrewdly elbowed his way to a spot where the arc of bullion was thickest, and was clawing up the golden bounty.

I, too, crouched down and began to gather up the coins. But at the very moment that my fingers closed around the first gold coin, I was thinking to myself that I would be wise to find some way of resigning from the Life Guard without attracting attention before it was too late.

TWO

THE THOUGHT THAT Romanus had been murdered nagged at me in the weeks that followed. I brooded on the possible consequences of my unwitting participation in a regicide and began to take precautions for my personal safety. I only ate mess food prepared by the army cooks, and I did not leave the barracks unless I was on duty or in the company of two or three of my colleagues, and then I only visited places I knew to be safe. Had my companions realised my fears, they would have scoffed at my timidity. Compared with the other cities I had known – London for example – Constantinople was remarkably peaceful and well run. Its governor, the city eparch, maintained an efficient police force, while a host of civic employees patrolled the marketplaces, checking on fair trade, cleanliness and orderly behaviour. Only at night, when the streets were given over to prostitutes and thieves, would my colleagues have bothered to carry weapons to defend themselves. But I was not reassured. If I was to be silenced for what I had witnessed in the imperial swimming pool, then the attack would come when I was least expecting it.

The one person to whom I confessed my fears was my friend Pelagia. She ran a bread stall on the Mese, and I had been seeing her twice a week to practise my conversational Greek because the language I had learned in the Irish monastery was antiquated and closer, coincidentally, to the language spoken in the imperial court than koine, the language of the common people. An energetic, shrewd woman with the characteristic dark hair and sallow skin of someone native to the city, Pelagia had already provided me with a lesson in the tortuous ways of Byzantine thinking, which often succeeded in extracting advantage from calamity. She had started her business just days after her husband, a baker, had burned to death in a blaze which had started when the bread oven cracked. A city ordinance banned bakeries from operating in close proximity to town houses, otherwise the accident would have sent the entire district up in flames. The ashes of the fire were barely cold before Pelagia had gone to her husband's former business competitors and worked on their sympathy. She coaxed them into agreeing to supply her stall at a favourable discount, and by the time I met her she was well on her way to being a wealthy woman. Pelagia kept me up to date with all the latest city rumours about palace politics – a favourite topic among her many clients – and, more important, she had a sister who worked as a seamstress for the empress Zoë.

'No one doubts that Zoë had a hand in Romanus's death, though it's less certain that she actively organised what happened in the bathhouse,' Pelagia told me. We had met in the spacious rooms of her third-floor apartment. Astonishing to people like myself from lands where a two-storeyed building is unusual, many of Constantinople's houses had four or even five floors. 'My sister tells me that poisons of every sort are readily available in the empress's quarters. They are not even kept locked up for safety. Zoë has a mania for creating new perfumes and unguents. Some say it's a hangover from the days when she was trying to rejuvenate herself and bear a child. She keeps a small army of women servants grinding, mixing and distilling different concoctions, and several of the ingredients are decidedly poisonous. One young girl fainted the other day merely from inhaling the fumes from one of the brews.'

'So you think Zoë was the poisoner, but not the person who

arranged for Romanus to have an accident during his swim,' I asked.

'It's hard to say. If the empress did plot with her lover to do away with Romanus and rule the empire through him, she's been disappointed. Michael, my sister tells me, has been acting as if he alone is in charge. She is not consulted on matters of state – they are all taken care of by his brother, the Orphanotrophus. So if Zoë had nothing to do with the murder, she may well bring an accusation against the new Basileus in order to overthrow him. Either way, you are in real danger. If there is an enquiry, the investigating tribunal will call witnesses to Romanus's death, and their usual way of interrogating witnesses is to torture them.'

'I don't follow you,' I said. 'Surely if there was a conspiracy between Zoë and Michael, neither party would want to risk it being discovered. And if only Michael is guilty, and perhaps the Orphanotrophus as well, then Zoë would be unlikely to harm the man with whom she is infatuated.'

'You don't know what a silly and capricious woman Zoë can be, despite her age and position,' Pelagia replied witheringly. 'My sister has been talking to some of the people who look after Zoë's wardrobe. Apparently Zoë feels that she is a woman scorned. Michael has banished her to the gynaeceum, and doesn't even visit her bedchamber as often as when she was still married to Romanus. Now there is even a rumour that Michael has some sort of incurable sickness and that the Orphanotrophus deliberately hid that fact from Zoë when he first introduced him to her.'

The intrigues of the court were beyond normal comprehension, I thought to myself. Never would I be able to untangle the subterfuges of those who seek or wield absolute power. It would be better for me to make myself as unobtrusive as possible and place my trust in the protection of Odinn, the arch-deceiver. I promised myself that next time my Christianised comrades in the guard went off to pray in the new church to St Olaf, I would find a quiet spot and make an offering to the All Wise. Perhaps the God of Cargoes would show me a way out of my predicament.

It turned out that Odinn answered even before I made the sacrifice. But first he gave me a fright I was to remember for the rest of my days in the service of the Basileus.

Early in June Pelagia told me that a report was sweeping the city that a force of Rus were about to attack Constantinople. A war fleet had been sighted making its way down the great river which leads from the kingdom of Kiev.

'Of course you know that route yourself, Thorgils. That's the way you came to Constantinople,' Pelagia said. She was standing in the shade of the portico behind her bread stall, chatting with a group of her fellow traders while her assistant sold the loaves off the counter.

'No, I came by a different route, along another river further east. But it's much the same thing: all paths lead to Constantinople.'

'Just as all Rus are much the same thing – violent, hairy barbarians who worship idols.' The jibe came from one of Pelagia's fellow stallholders, another bread-seller who had the chirpy swagger of a true city-dweller. Over his stall hung a crudely sketched picture of the White Christ issuing loaves and fishes to the multitude, so I knew him to be a vehement Christian.

'Well, not exactly,' I corrected him mildly. 'The people you lump together as Rus are all sorts and types – those who come from Kiev are Christians and acknowledge your own Great Patriarch. Others like myself are from the lands of the northmen and, while we follow our own gods, we come to trade not to fight. Half your churches would be in darkness if those so-called barbarians didn't bring beeswax from the northern forests for you to turn into candles to illuminate your painted saints while you adore them.'

The stallholder was not to be placated. 'This city can defend itself whatever that scum throws at it. You would have thought they had learned their lesson last time.' He saw I had missed his point. 'My grandfather loved telling me how we dealt with those ignorant savages the last time they dared to assault the Queen of

Cities. They showed up with their fleet expecting to swarm in and put the place to the sack. But Blessed Mary and our Basileus protected us. The enemy never even got past the city walls – much too strong for them. So they muddled about, went here and there in their stupid, mindless way, raiding and raping in small settlements along the coast. But all the while our Basileus was biding his time. He waited until the Rus were off guard, and then sent out our ships and caught them fair and square. We burned them to cinders with the Fire. They never knew what hit them. Less than a hundred of them returned home. It was a massacre. My grandfather told me that burned bodies were washing up on the shore, and you could smell the stench of burned flesh . . .' At that moment he must have remembered how Pelagia's husband had died, for his voice trailed away in embarrassment and he looked down at his feet before finding an excuse to turn away and attend to the display on his stall.

I was about to ask Pelagia what the man had meant by 'the Fire', when I heard my name called out, and turned to see Halfdan pushing through the crowd towards me. Close behind him was a palace messenger.

'There you are, Thorgils. Thought I might find you here with Pelagia,' Halfdan exclaimed, though without the innuendo that normally accompanied his mention of Pelagia's name. 'There's some sort of flap on at the palace, and it involves you. You are to report at once to the office of the Orphanotrophus. It's urgent.'

Panic gripped me as I glanced across at Pelagia. There was no mistaking the alarm in her expression too.

I quickly followed the messenger to the palace. He brought me to the office of the Orphanotrophus, where I noticed that the emperor's eunuch brother had appropriated for himself the chambers immediately beside the staterooms of the Basileus. My colleagues who were on duty glanced at me curiously as I passed them. Never before had any of them seen a mere guardsman summoned in this way.

A moment later my stomach was churning with anxiety as I

stood in front of John. He was sitting at an ornate desk, reading through a document, and when he raised his head to look at me, I thought how very tired he seemed. His eyes were sunk even deeper than usual. Perhaps the cares of state were weighing more heavily than he had expected, or maybe the rumours in the marketplace were true: that the Orphanotrophus never slept, but in the night dressed up as a monk and walked the streets of the city, eavesdropping on conversations, questioning ordinary citizens and learning the mood of the people. It was little wonder that people feared him. Certainly I felt sick with apprehension as I waited for him to speak. And his first words told me that he remembered exactly who I was.

'I have summoned you because you speak excellent Greek as well as Varangian,' he said. 'I have a mission for you.'

The tight knot in my stomach began to relax, but only for a moment. Was this another court deceit? Was the Orphanotrophus putting me at ease before revealing his true intention?

'My agents tell me that a large force of Rus is approaching. It appears that there are about five hundred of them travelling in monocylon, the vessels which traders from Rus normally use, and they are coming by the same route.'

Five hundred Rus did not amount to an invading force, I thought to myself. The market rumour was greatly exaggerated. It would take at least ten times that number to pose a threat to Constantinople's well-tried defences.

As though reading my mind, the Orphanotrophus added, 'I'm not concerned about the safety of the city. What does interest me is that my informants tell me these men are not merchants. They do not carry trade goods, they are heavily armed and there is a report that their leader is some sort of prince or nobleman. His name is Araltes, or something like that. Do you know anyone by this name?'

'No, your excellency,' I replied. 'It's not a name that I am familiar with.'

'You soon will be,' the Orphanotrophus replied dryly. 'I have given orders that the foreigners are to be intercepted at the entrance to the straits. They will be escorted to the district of St Mamas on the opposite side of the Golden Horn and held there, well away from the city, pending an investigation of their intentions. That is where you come in. I want to know who they are and why they have come here. If they are Rus, you will understand their language when they speak among themselves, and you seem to be an intelligent man who can make his own judgements and ask the right questions. Afterwards you come back to me and report your impressions in person.'

'Yes, your excellency,' I answered, beginning to think that I had been unnecessarily suspicious of John. 'When do you expect the foreigners to arrive?'

'In three days' time,' he answered. 'Now go and report to my chief chartularius. He will write out your instructions. Officially you will be serving as escort to the deputation from the office of dromos.' He paused, and then said something which – as intended – reminded me of the words I had used when delivering the message that lured me from my duty to guard the Basileus. 'As I'm sure you are aware,' the eunuch continued softly, 'the logothete of the dromos is responsible for foreign relations, secret intelligence and embassies, as well as the imperial postal system – a curious mixture, don't you think? – while the dekanos are the palace messengers. So the men from the dromos will manage the official contact with these five hundred barbarians, but you are my eyes and ears. I want you to eavesdrop on the foreigners for me.'

My interview was at an end. I looked into the hooded eyes of the Orphanotrophus and, with numbing certainty, understood why he was so confident that I would act as his spy, even against my own people. It was just as Pelagia had said: it did not matter whether John had plotted to put his brother Michael on the throne. Basileus Romanus had died during my watch, when I had been responsible for his safety. John had witnessed my dereliction of duty and he could bring me to account at any time he chose. I was at his mercy. Yet he was too subtle to mention that fact outright. He preferred to rely on my fear and make me his creature.

So it was that three days after my interview with the Basileus's sinister brother I was aboard a small ferry boat, being rowed across the choppy waters of the Golden Horn towards the landing place at Mamas. With me were two dour-looking officials from the secretariat of the dromos. To judge from their manner, they thought it was a vile imposition to be plucked from the calm shelter of their offices and sent to interview a gang of uncouth barbarians from the north. One of the officials wrinkled his nose with distaste as he clutched his robe so that the hem did not get soaked by the slop of bilge water. Since they were on official business, both he and his colleague were wearing formal costumes which denoted their bureaucratic rank. His cloak had a green border, so I knew he was a high-ranking civil servant, and I wondered whether he too spoke Norse. The office of the dromos maintained a college of trained interpreters and it would be typical of the Orphanotrophus to send not one but two spies so he could cross-check their impressions.

As our little boat approached the landing stage, the sight of the moored flotilla of a dozen or so boats suddenly made me homesick for the northern lands. The monocylon, as John had called them, were a smaller version of the curved seagoing ships I had known all my life. The boats docked at Mamas were less well built than genuine ocean-going vessels, but they were handy enough for short sea crossings and very different from the tubby hulls favoured by the Greeks. My nostalgia grew as I scrambled up on to the quay and walked across the open ground where the foreigners had been given permission to pitch their tents. There were piles of flax sails, wooden kegs, spars, coils of rope, anchors and other ship's gear, all so familiar to me. I could smell the tar on the ropes and the grease on the leather straps of the steering blades. Even the stacked oars were of the same pattern I had used when I was a youngster.

The encampment, with its neat rows of tents, had a vaguely

military feeling, and I understood why the imperial spies had
reported their unease. This large assembly of travellers had
definitely not come to Constantinople to buy and sell goods. The
men strolling around the camp, hovering over the cooking pots,
or simply lazing in the sun, all had the look of warriors. They
were big and self-confident and they were Norse – that was sure.
They had the blond colouring of the Norse, the long hair and
luxuriant beards, and they wore the characteristic heavy leggings
and cross-garters, though their tunics were a motley of colours
and cloths, ranging from linen to leather. One or two even wore
sheepskin jerkins, which were highly unsuitable in Constantinople's sunshine.

I scarcely attracted a glance from these burly strangers as
I headed for a tent, larger than the others, which stood apart. I
recognised it at once as a command tent, and did not need to be
told that this was where we would find the leaders of this unknown
group.

Gesturing to my two companions that they should wait outside, I pushed open the door flap. As I entered, it took a moment
for my eyes to adjust to the subdued light. Around a trestle table
stood a group of four or five men. Observing that I was a stranger
and dressed in a foreign uniform – for I wore the guards' scarlet
tunic – they waited impassively for me to explain what I wanted.
But one man, thickset, with bushy grey hair and a heavy beard,
reacted differently. He stared hard at me.

There was an awkward silence while I wondered how I should
introduce myself, and what tone I should adopt. Then the silence
was broken. 'Thorgils Leifsson! By all the Gods, if it isn't
Thorgils!' the grey-haired man exclaimed loudly. He spoke with
an unmistakable Icelandic accent, and I could even pick out which
region of Iceland he came from: he was a man from the west
fjords. His voice also gave me the clue to his identity, and a
moment later I placed him. He was Halldor Snorrason, fifth son
of Snorri Godi, with whose family I had stayed in Iceland as a

young man. In fact, Halldor's sister Hallbera had been the first girl with whom I had fallen in love, and Halldor's father had played a crucial role in my teenage years.

'What's that fancy uniform you're wearing?' Halldor asked, striding across to clap me on the shoulder. 'The last we heard, you were headed off into Permia to buy furs from the ski-runners. Don't tell me that Thorgils, former associate of that outlaw Grettir the Strong, is now a member of the imperial Life Guard.'

'Yes, I'll have been a guardsman three years this autumn,' I said, and here I dropped my voice in case the men from the dromos could hear me through the tent cloth. 'I've been sent to find out what you and your comrades are doing, and why you have come to Constantinople.'

'Oh, that's no secret. You can go back to your chief and tell him that we've come to offer our services as fighting men to the Emperor of Miklagard,' Halldor replied cheerfully. 'We hear that he pays very well and the chances of loot are excellent. We want to go home as rich men!' He laughed.

I had to smile at his enthusiasm. 'What? All of you want to join the Life Guard? I'm told that there are five hundred of you. A recruit only joins when there is a vacancy and there is a long waiting list.'

'No,' said Halldor. 'We don't want to join the guard. Our plan is to stay together as a single fighting unit.'

The idea was so unexpected that for a moment I was silenced. Norsemen did not usually form themselves into disciplined warrior brigades, particularly when they were roving freebooters hoping to loot and plunder. They were far too independent-minded. There had to be another factor.

Halldor saw my puzzlement. 'Every one of us has already pledged allegiance to one man, a single leader. If he finds service with the Basileus, then we follow him.'

'Who is that man?' I asked.

'I am,' said a deep voice, and I turned to see a tall, soldierly figure stooping in under the door flap at the far end of the tent. He straightened up to his full height, and in that instant I knew that Odinn had answered my profoundest hope.

Harald Sigurdsson – as I soon knew him to be and that was long before he became known as Hardrada, 'Hard Ruler' – stood a little under six and a half feet tall, and in the half light of the tent he was like a hero emerging from the shadowy world of the earliest sagas. Broad-shouldered and muscular, he moved with an athletic grace, towering over the other men. When he came closer, I imagined for a moment that I was looking up into the face of someone I had heard described in a fireside tale when I was a child. He had the fierce look of a sea eagle. His prominent nose was like a beak, while his close-set bright blue eyes had an intense, almost unblinking stare. His thick yellow hair, too, resembled the ruff of long feathers around a sea eagle's neck, for it hung down to his shoulders, and he had a quick way of turning his head, like a bird of prey seeking a victim, so that the hair shifted on his shoulders like an eagle's ruff. His moustache was even more spectacular. It was dressed in a style long out of fashion: two thick strands of moustache hung down on either side of his mouth, like blond silk cords, and dangled against his chest.

'And who are you?' he demanded.

I was so stunned by his appearance that I faltered in my reply, and Halldor had to fill the gap for me.

'He is Thorgils, son of Leif the Lucky,' said the Icelander. 'He used to stay at my father's place in Iceland when he was a teenager.'

'He's your foster brother?'

'No – my father took an interest in him because he was what you might call gifted. He has, or had, the second sight.'

The giant Norseman turned towards me, and his eyes searched my face, judging me. I sensed that he was calculating whether I could be useful to him.

'Is that the uniform of an imperial Life Guard?'

'Yes, my lord,' I replied. Calling him 'my lord' seemed utterly

natural. If ever I had seen a born aristocrat, it was this tall, proud
stranger. I guessed he was about fifteen years younger than me,
but there was no question who was owed respect.

'I suppose they've sent you as a spy,' he said bluntly. 'Tell
your master that we are exactly what we seem to be – a war band
– and that its leader is Harald Sigurdsson of Norway, half-brother
of St Olaf. Tell him that I have come to place my myself and my
men at his disposal. Tell him also that we are veteran fighters.
Most of us have already seen service in the household of King
Jaroslav of Kiev.'

Now I knew exactly who he was: scion of one of the most
powerful families in Norway. His half-brother Olaf had ruled
Norway for a dozen years before being toppled by jealous
chieftains. 'I'm only a duty escort, my lord,' I said meekly. 'You
need to talk to the two officials waiting outside. They are from
the seketron – from the office which looks after foreign envoys.
They will handle the arrangements.'

'Then don't let's waste time,' Harald said briskly. 'Introduce
me.' And he turned on his heel and left the tent. I hurried after
him just in time to see the expressions on the faces of the two
bureaucrats as this imperious giant of a man bore down on them.
They looked alarmed.

'This is the leader of the, er, barbarians,' I said in Greek. 'He
is very high-born. In his own country he's a nobelissimus. He has
spent some time in the court of Kiev and now wishes that he and
his men enter the service of the great Basileus.'

The two civil servants had regained their composure. They
produced parchment and reed pens from the small ivory work
cases they carried and waited expectantly.

'Please repeat the name of the nobelissimus,' said the man
whom I took to be the senior.

'Harald, son of Sigurd,' I answered.

'His rank and tribe?'

'No tribe,' I replied. 'From his family have come the kings of
a far northern country called Norway.'

The civil servant murmured something to his colleague. I could not hear what he said, but the man nodded.

'Is his father the current king of his people?'

This was becoming embarrassing. I had no idea of Harald's current status, and was too nervous to ask him directly, so I translated the question to Halldor, who had joined us. But it was Harald himself who replied.

'Tell him that my country was ruled by my half-brother until he was killed in battle by his enemies and that I am the rightful heir.'

Harald, I thought to myself, had a very clear idea of his own worth. I translated his statement and the official wrote it down carefully. He was clearly feeling more comfortable now that he could reduce everything to the written word.

'I will need an exact roster of the people in his company – their names, ages, rank and places of origin. Also a full inventory of any goods they are carrying: type, size and description of their weapons; number and condition of the sea craft they have; whether there has been any sickness during the journey from Kiev . . .'

I sensed that Harald, beside me, was losing patience.

'Making lists, are they?' he interrupted.

'Yes, my lord. They have to report back to their office with a full description of your war band and all its equipment.'

'Excellent,' he said. 'Tell them to make a second copy for me. It could be useful for my quartermasters.' Then he turned on his heel and strode away.

Fortunately one of the Rus guides who had brought Harald and his men downriver from Kiev spoke adequate Greek and volunteered to relieve me of the chore of translating as the bureaucrats from the dromos patiently went about their task. I took the chance to draw Halldor to one side and ask him about Harald.

'What's this about him being the rightful heir to the throne of Norway?' I asked. 'And if he is the rightful heir, why has he been spending time at the court of King Jaroslav in Kiev?'

'He had to flee Norway when his half-brother was defeated and killed in battle while trying to regain the throne. He found refuge with King Jaroslav, as did many other Norwegians who backed the wrong side in the civil war. He spent three years in Kiev as a military commander and was so outstanding that he asked the king if he could marry his daughter Elizabeth.'

It seemed that there was no limit to the self-confidence of Harald Sigurdsson.

'So what was the king's answer?'

'He didn't need to say anything. The Princess Elizabeth told Harald to come back when he had riches and renown, and as Harald is not one to let the grass grow under his feet, he retorted that he would win his fortune in the service of the Basileus. Anyone who wanted to join him could do so if they were good warriors and swore allegiance to him. Then he left Kiev with his war band.'

'Well, what about you? Was Harald's boast enough to make you join up?'

'It's just as I said, Thorgils. I want to be rich. If there's anyone on this earth who's going to win plunder, it's Harald Sigurdsson. He's ambitious, he's energetic, and, above all, he's got battle luck.'

There was one more question which I had to ask, and I dreaded the reply.

'Is Harald a follower of the White Christ,' I asked, 'or does he follow the Old Ways?'

'That's the odd thing,' replied Halldor. 'You would have thought Harald would be as Christian as his half-brother King Olaf, whom many are now calling "St Olaf". Yet, I've never seen Harald go out of his way to attend a church service or say a prayer to Christ. He serves just one God – himself. He knows exactly what he wants: to win the throne of Norway, and he will follow any God or belief that will help him achieve his ambition.'

It was that statement which, in due course, convinced me to throw in my lot with Harald Sigurdsson. Later I was to join him, not for riches, but because I believed that I had finally met the one man capable of restoring the fortunes of the Old Ways. If I could help Harald to gain his throne and show that Odinn and the Old Gods had favoured him, then he might return his kingdom to the Elder Faith. My scheme was refined and shaped in my mind over the weeks and months to come, but it began on the day that Halldor Snorrason told me of Harald's ambition.

'You should know that Harald's more than just a bold warrior,' Halldor went on, unaware that his every word was adding to my certainty that Odinn himself had groomed Harald as his champion. 'He's a great patron to skalds. He can judge their poetry because he knows the ancient lore as well as any man alive, and gives a handsome reward to any skald who skilfully portrays the world of the Gods. And he's more than just a critic. He composes good verse himself. Most of us in his war band can quote the couplet he composed as he fled from the battle that killed his half-brother – ' Here Halldor paused. Then he took a breath and recited:

> 'Now I go creeping from forest
> To forest with little honour;
> Who knows, my name may yet become
> Renowned far and wide in the end.'

'Not bad for a fifteen-year-old wounded while fighting on the losing side of a battle that decides a throne,' he commented.

Yet again I felt that Odinn was pointing the way. I too had been fifteen years old when I fought and was wounded in a great battle that had decided a kingdom, the throne of Ireland. The Norns, who determine men's destiny, had woven the same patterns into the lives of Harald Sigurdsson and myself. Now Odinn had brought us to where our paths crossed.

The sound of a footfall behind me made me turn, and there was the man himself. With the sunshine falling full on his sea eagle's face, I saw something that I had not noticed before: his features were regular and well made, and he was a very handsome man, except in one strange detail – his left eyebrow was very much higher than the other. I took it to be a shadow of Odinn's lop-sided mark, Odinn the one-eyed.

'So what did you make of this Araltes?' asked John the Orphanotrophus when I reported back to him the following day. I noted a sheet of parchment on the desk in front of him, and guessed that it was the written report from the office of the dromos. It was widely acknowledged that the imperial bureaucracy had never operated so efficiently as when John had taken over the running of the state.

'He seems genuine, your excellency. In Norse his name is Harald, son of Sigurd,' I answered, standing to attention and staring fixedly at a semicircle of gold paint. It was a saint's halo in an icon fixed to the wall behind the Orphanotrophus's head. I was still frightened of the man and I did not want him looking into my eyes and reading my thoughts.

'What about this tale that he is some sort of nobleman?'

'It is correct, your excellency. He is related to the royal family of Norway. He and his men have come to offer their services to his majesty, the Basileus.'

'And what would you say is the status of their morale and equipment?'

'First-class morale, your excellency. Their weaponry is work-manlike and well maintained.'

'Their ships?'

'In need of some overhaul, but seaworthy.'

'Good. I see that you kept your wits about you. My pedantic colleagues in the dromos have taken care to remind me of the regulation that no foreign prince may serve in the imperial Life Guard. Too risky, it seems. In case he gets ideas above his station. But I believe I have a use for these barbarians. I am sending a note to the akolouthos, the commanding officer of the guard, telling him that you are detached for special duties. You are to be the liaison between my office and Araltes and his force. You will receive a bonus above your regular guard's pay and, unless you are employed otherwise by me, you will continue to perform your normal guard duties. That is all.'

I left the room and was immediately intercepted by a secretary. He handed me a scroll and I opened it to see that it contained my written orders. It seemed that the Orphanotrophus had decided on his course of action before I even reported to his office. I read that I was to prepare 'the visitor Araltes' for an audience with his imperial majesty, the Basileus, at a date yet to be decided. Until that time I was to assist in familiarising Araltes with the organis- ation and operational structure of the imperial navy. I reread this sentence, as it was not what I had anticipated. The imperial navy was very much the junior branch of the imperial forces, though it possessed the most powerful fleet in the Great Sea. I had expected Harald and his men to be recruited into the Varangians-without- the-walls, the brigade of foreign mercenaries which included Armenians, Georgians, Vlachs and the like. But instead Harald and his men were to be marines.

When I next visited the camp at Mamas, I explained these orders to Halldor, who merely grunted. 'Makes sense,' he said. 'We're used to sea fights. But what's all this about preparing us for reception by the Basileus?'

'You've got to get the details absolutely right,' I told him. 'Nothing angers the emperor's councillors more than mistakes in court etiquette. It reinforces their view that anyone unfamiliar with court procedures is an ignorant savage, utterly uncouth and not worth dealing with. They've been known to turn down the requests of foreign ambassadors simply because of some minor transgression of court protocol. For example, a visiting ambassa- dor who uses the wrong title to address the Basileus will be refused further audiences with the emperor, have his ambassa- dorial privileges withdrawn, and so on.'

'So what should Harald call the Basileus?'

'Emperor of the Romans.'

Halldor looked puzzled. 'How's that? This is Constantinople, not Rome, and anyhow isn't there a German ruler who calls himself the Holy Roman Emperor?'

'That's what I mean. The Basileus and his entire court are convinced that they are the true heirs of the Roman empire, that they represent its true ideals and continue its glory. They are prepared to grant that the German is the "the king" of the Romans, but not "the emperor". Just the same way that their own holy men claim that their Great Patriarch is the high priest of White Christ worship, not the person in Rome who calls himself the pope. It also explains why there's such a confusing mix of Latin and Greek in their military ranks – they speak of decurions and centurions as if they were soldiers in a Roman army, but the higher ranks nearly all have Greek titles.'

Halldor sighed. 'Well, I just hope you can persuade Harald to use the right phrases and do the right thing. I'm not sure he will like grovelling to the Basileus. He's not that sort.'

Halldor's worries were needless. I found that Harald Sigurdsson was fully prepared to rein in his usually arrogant behaviour if it was to be to his advantage, and because I desperately wanted the Norwegian prince to succeed, I worked hard at tutoring him in exactly how to behave during his visit to the Great Palace. The emperor's subjects, I told him first, thought it such a great privilege to be allowed to meet the Basileus in person that they would wait for years to be granted an audience. For them it was the equivalent of meeting their God's representative on earth, and everything inside the palace was regulated to enhance this impression.

'Think of it, my lord, like a service in the most lavish White Christ church,' I said. 'Everything is ceremony and pomp. The courtiers wear special silken robes, each man knows his exact duties, the spot where he must stand, the exact gestures to use, the correct words to say. Everything focuses on the emperor himself. He sits on his golden throne, wearing the jewel-encrusted costume they call the chlamys. Across his shoulders is the loros, the long stole that only the emperor may wear, and on his feet are the tzangia, the purple boots exclusive to his rank. He will be motionless, gazing down the hall towards the door where you enter. You will be ushered in and then must advance down the hall and perform proskynesis.'

'What's proskynesis?' Harald asked, leaning forward on his stool.

I realised that I had got carried away with the splendour of the ceremony, and hesitated because I did not know how Harald would react to my explanation.

'Proskynesis is the act of homage,' I said.

'Go on.'

I swallowed nervously. 'It means lying prostrate on the floor, face down, and staying there until the word comes from a courtier for you to rise.'

There was a long pause as Harald thought this over. I feared that he was about to refuse to debase himself this way, but instead he asked, 'How far am I from the throne when I have to do this lying-down performance?'

I had been holding my breath, and let it out gently. 'As you walk down the hall towards the Basileus, look downward and you will see that there is a purple disc set in the marble floor. That marks the spot where you should lie down.'

Harald asked promptly, 'How do you know all this?'

'Because a detail of the guard stands behind the emperor's throne during the ceremony, and I have watched it happen many times. The guardsmen get to know the little tricks which make the ceremony seem more impressive. In fact sometimes it is difficult to keep a straight face.'

'Like when?'

'If the court chamberlain thinks the visitor is impressionable enough, the Basileus's throne is made to elevate during the proskynesis. While the supplicant is face down on the floor, a team of operators winds a lifting jack hidden behind the throne so that when the supplicant lifts his head he sees the emperor seated higher than before. The look of astonishment on the supplicant's face can be very entertaining. But,' I added hurriedly, 'I don't think they will try that ruse on the day you have an imperial audience.'

Recalling my first conversations with Harald, it occurs to me now that I was possibly making a mistake. I thought I was merely preparing him for his meeting with the Basileus, but I fear that Harald was in fact learning a very different lesson: the importance of establishing dominion over others, how to dazzle them. If so, in my enthusiasm for Harald's success I was preparing the seeds for my own later disappointment.

The Orphanotrophus had also instructed me to familiarise the Norwegian prince with the imperial navy, so I took Harald to the naval arsenal on the Golden Horn. There the eparch of the dockyard, fearing espionage, received us coolly and insisted that an official from the dromos as well as his own deputy accompany us on our tour. I showed Harald rank upon rank of slipways, where the warships were built and repaired, warehouses filled with naval stores, mast sheds and sail lofts, and I explained how most of the seamen were recruited from the coastal peoples across the straits in Asia Minor. Harald, who had an expert eye for ship-wright's skills, asked such probing questions of the master carpenters that I was sometimes at a loss for the right words as I translated into Greek. Then he demanded to inspect a warship in commission. When the eparch's deputy hesitated, Harald insisted. If his men were to serve on the imperial ships, then at least they should know what to expect. He pointed at a dromon of the largest size, a three-masted fleet battleship which lay at anchor in the Golden Horn, awaiting orders. He would like to inspect that vessel, he said. As I was to notice many times later, when Harald Sigurdsson put a request, it sounded more like a command.

A naval pinnace rowed us out. Close up, the dromon was even larger than I had expected. I had never been aboard one before, and she was immense, at least half as long again as the largest longship that I had seen in the past and two or three times as broad. But what really made her seem imposing was her height above the water. Our Norse warships are low and sleek, but the imperial battleships are built upwards from the waterline. The intention is to overawe the enemy and give a superior platform from which archers can shoot downwards. So the dromon loomed over us as we approached, her height increased by a castle-like structure built amidship. We clambered up her side and on her deck immediately came face to face with her kentarchos, her sailing master. Angrily he demanded to know who this strange-looking foreigner with the long moustaches was who came climbing aboard his ship as though he owned her. When the man from the dromos explained that Harald had a letter from the sekreton of the Orphanotrophus, the kentarchos glowered, then accompanied us at every pace around her deck, watching us suspiciously.

Harald missed nothing. Fascinated by this unknown design of war vessel, he asked how the dromon handled in a seaway, how her sails were set and reefed, how nimbly she could alter course, how fast she went when all two hundred oarsmen were at the benches and for how long they could keep up a cruising pace. The kentarchos answered reluctantly. To him a bearded Norseman was a natural foe. Time and again I had to remind our guide that it was the Orphanotrophus's order that Harald should be familiar with the imperial war fleet, and one day Harald's men might be aboard as his marines. The kentarchos looked as if he would prefer to scuttle his vessel.

Finally we reached the forecastle in the dromon's bows.

'And what is that?' asked Harald.

A bronze tube protruded through a metal plate, pointing forward like a single nostril. Close behind the tube stood two metal baths, joined by copper pipes to an apparatus that looked like a pump.

'That's the vessel's siphon,' said the man from the dromos.

The kentarchos glared at him, then rudely walked in front of Harald, deliberately blocking his view.

'Not even the emperor's direct command allows me to tell you more,' he growled. 'Now get off my ship.'

To my surprise, Harald obeyed.

Much later, when we were safely back outside the arsenal and no officials were in earshot, Harald muttered, 'So that's how they launch the Fire. But how do they create it?'

'I don't know,' I said. 'I'm not even sure what it is.'

'When I was in Kiev I heard people describe how it destroyed a war fleet in their grandfathers' time,' Harald said. 'People marvelled how the Fire ignites in the air, turning to cinders anything it touches. It even burns underwater. It's amazing.'

That evening, when I asked Pelagia about the Fire, my normally reliable source of information was little help. She told me that only a handful of technicians knew how to create it, and that the ingredients were among the most closely guarded state secrets. Rumour had it that the Fire was made of quicklime mixed with an oil that comes from the earth. I told her about the strange bronze tube aboard the dromon and she laughed. She said that there were foreign sailors who believed the imperial navy had a breeding programme of fire-breathing dragons, which they stowed below decks before setting out on a campaign and then let loose in the bows of their ships just before a fleet action.

Shortly after the feast day of the Transfiguration, one of Constantinople's major festivals, and two months after his arrival Harald finally had his audience with Michael. It took place in yet another of the splendid halls within the Great Palace, the Magnaura, which was often used for greeting foreign ambassadors, and as luck would have it I was a member of the imperial escort. As I took up my position behind the throne and rested my axe on my shoulder, I felt like a nervous schoolmaster who waits to see how his star pupil will perform. The interior of the hall was like a vast church, with columns and galleries and high windows glazed with coloured glass. The far end opened on to a wide courtyard planted with trees, and there the supplicants were assembled. Among them I could see Harald, standing a full head taller than his colleagues. In the foreground stood a host of court dignitaries waiting for the signal from the master of ceremonies. Even after witnessing dozens of such ceremonies, I still marvelled at the splendour of the occasion. The courtiers and dignitaries were dressed according to their seniority and the office they held. There were senators and patricians in blue and green, Greek officers of the Hetaira in white tunics with gold bands, magistrates and high officials dressed in shimmering patterned silk and holding their insignia – golden staffs, ivory wands, court swords in scabbards ornate with enamel plaques, jewelled whips, tablets and illuminated scrolls. Many of the costumes were so stiffly sewn with gold and silver embroidery, as well as precious stones and pearls, that their wearers could barely move. But that was also part of the ritual. All the assembly was expected to stay motionless, or at least nearly so. Any movement must be slow and dignified.

A trumpet blast announced that the ceremony was to begin, and the assembly, facing towards Michael on his throne (Zoë had not been invited), raised the customary paean in honour of the Basileus. After several minutes of praise and acclamation I saw in the distance the ostiarios, the palace eunuch whose duty was to introduce dignitaries to the emperor, approach Harald and indicate that he was to walk forward. The crowd had now parted, leaving an aisle which led towards the throne. On the marble floor, in the open space before the throne, I could see the purple disc where Harald was to lie face down and perform proskynesis. At that moment I suddenly realised that I had failed to warn Harald about the automata. I had told him of the elevating throne, but forgotten that in the Magnaura, on each side of the purple disc, stood the lifelike bronze statue of a lion. The statues were hollow and articulated; by an ingenious system of hidden air pumps the animals could be made to lash their tails, open their jaws and let out a roar. The operators of the automata, concealed in the crowd, were instructed to make the beasts roar at the very moment the supplicant was about to prostrate himself before the throne.

I watched Harald as he stalked down the great hall between the lines of watching courtiers. He was bare-headed and wearing a velvet tunic of dark green with loose silk pantaloons. His only jewellery was a plain gold torc on each arm. In such a glittering and flamboyant assembly he should have been inconspicuous, but his presence dominated those around him. It was not just his height and obvious physical strength which impressed the onlookers, it was that Harald of Norway walked the length of Magnaura as if the ceremonial hall belonged to him, not the Basileus.

He approached the purple disc and halted in the open space before the throne, clear of the watching crowd. There was a pause, a long moment of silence, as he faced the emperor. At that moment the hidden operators of the automata opened the valves and the mechanical beasts lashed their tails and roared. If the audience had been expecting Harald to flinch or look startled, they were disappointed. He turned his head to look into the open jaws, first of one beast, then the other. He seemed thoughtful, even curious. Then, nonchalantly, he lay down on the marble floor and performed proskynesis.

Much later he told me that it was as he stared into the open mouths of the bronze lions and heard the hiss of the air pumps that made them move and roar that he understood the Fire.

THREE

I DID NOT SEE Harald again for nearly four months. After his proskynesis to the Basileus, he and his men left Constantinople. The Orphanotrophus had given them the task of dealing with the growing menace from Arab pirates who regularly attacked ships sailing from Dyrrachium on the west coast of Greece. The port of Dyrrachium was a vital link in the empire's communications. Through its harbour passed imperial couriers, troops and merchandise on their way to and from Constantinople and the colonies in southern Italy. Recently the raiders had been so bold as to establish bases in the nearby Greek islands, from where their fast galleys pounced on passing ships. The Orphanotrophus's original plan was to send to the area additional units of the imperial navy with Harald's men aboard. But, according to my colleagues in the guard, the drungarios, the admiral of the fleet, refused. He baulked at taking so many barbarians on board his ships, and Harald had made matters worse by stating that he would not take orders from a Greek commander. The deadlock was resolved when Harald offered to use his own vessels, the light monocylon, and base them at Dyrrachium. From there he would send them out as escorts for the merchant ships and to patrol against the enemy.

With Harald gone, I returned to my previous duties with the guard and found that the whispers about Michael's ill health were true. The young emperor was afflicted by what the palace physicians tactfully called 'the holy sickness'.

I first noticed the symptoms when Michael was dressing for the festival which celebrates the birth of the White Christ. With five other members of the bodyguard, I had escorted Michael to the imperial robing chamber. There the vestitores, the officials who solemnly place the imperial regalia on the Basileus, ceremonially opened the chest containing the royal garb. The most junior of the officials took out the cloak, the chlamys, which he solemnly handed to the next most senior in rank. From hand to hand the garment was passed until finally it reached the senior vestitor, who reverently approached the waiting Basileus, intoned a prayer, and settled the cloak on the emperor's shoulders. There followed the pearl-encrusted stole, the jewelled gloves, the chest pendant. All the time the Basileus stood motionless until the crown was presented to him. At that moment, something went awry. Instead of leaning forward to kiss the cross on the crown, as ritual demanded, Michael began to tremble. It was only a slight movement, but standing behind him we, the members of the escort, could see that his right arm was shaking uncontrollably. The vestitor waited, still proffering the crown, but Michael was paralysed, unable to move except for the trembling of his arm. There was complete silence as the interval lengthened and everyone in the room stood still, as if frozen in place, the only movement the rapid shaking of Michael's right arm. Then, after the time it takes for a man to empty his lungs slowly seven or eight times, the arm slowly grew still, and Michael resumed full control of his body. Later that day, as if nothing had happened, he joined the procession along the garlanded streets to a service at the church of Hagia Sophia, then held several formal receptions in the Great Palace at which senior bureaucrats received their Nativity gifts, and in the evening appeared at a great banquet in the lausakios, the dining hall of the Great Palace. But the Orphanotrophus must have been advised of the emperor's brief moment of paralysis, because the normal seating arrangements had been modified. Michael was seated alone at a separate ivory table, on view to all his noble guests, but no one could come close to him.

'They say this kind of sickness is caused by demons in the brain,' Halfdan commented to me as we were removing our ceremonial armour later that evening in the guardroom.

'Maybe,' I replied. 'Yet some people see it as a gift.'

'Where's that?'

'Among the ski-runners in Permia,' I said. 'I spent the winter with the family of one of their wise men, who sometimes behaved in the same way as the emperor, only it was more than just his arm trembling. Often he would fall on the ground and lie without moving for as long as an hour. When he woke up again, he told us how his spirit had been visiting the otherworld. It could happen with the Basileus.'

'If it does, the Christians won't believe he visited any spirit world,' Halfdan grumbled. 'They don't hold with that sort of thing. Their saints show up on earth and perform miracles, but no one travels in the opposite direction and comes back.'

My analysis turned out to be correct. As the weeks passed, Michael's eccentric behaviour became more pronounced and the episodes lasted longer. Sometimes he would sit mumbling to himself, or begin chewing rhythmically though there was no food in his mouth. On other occasions he would suddenly start to wander about the palace in a state of confusion until, abruptly, he came to his senses and looked about him trying to identify where he stood. The duty guardsmen escorted him as best they could, walking behind the dazed Basileus while someone sent hastily for a palace physician. If there was an encounter with someone who did not know about the emperor's state of health, then the guardsmen had orders to form a circle around the Basileus and shield him from view. The handful of doctors who were privy to Michael's condition tried doses of opium and rose oil, and induced him to drink muddy concoctions of earth gathered in their Holy Land and dissolved in holy water from a sacred well in a church at Pege just outside the city walls. But the emperor's behaviour did not return to normal. Rather, it grew ever more extreme and unpredictable.

By contrast, as this crisis gradually developed, my own troubles seemed to recede. Having successfully obeyed the Orphanotrophus's instructions in dealing with Harald and his men, I calculated that John would keep me as a go-between as long as Harald proved loyal. Pelagia encouraged me in this thinking. I was spending more and more time with her, and in the evenings when off duty I would go to dine at her apartment – she always brought back fresh delicacies from the market where she kept her bread stall – and we would sit and chat together, ostensibly to practise my Greek but more and more because I found her company to be a pleasant change from regimental life and because I valued her shrewd commentary on the power play that I was observing in the palace.

'As long as you might prove useful to the Orphanotrophus,' she said, 'you should be safe. He's got much to worry him now that his brother is showing signs of ill health.'

'So news of the emperor's condition has leaked out?'

'Naturally,' she replied. 'There's not much that goes on in the palace that doesn't eventually become gossip in the marketplace. There are too many people employed in the palace for there to be secrets. Incidentally,' she added, 'your bearded northern friends who went off to Dyrrachium with their ships must be doing well. That cheese I served with the first course this evening comes from Italy, and until recently it was almost impossible to get. The Italian cheese-makers were reluctant to send their produce when so many of the merchant vessels were falling into the hands of the Arab pirates. Now the cheese has reappeared in the market. That's a good sign.'

I remembered our conversation when I received my next summons from the Orphanotrophus. This time I found he was not alone. The fleet admiral, the drungarios, was in his office, as well as a naval kentarchos, by coincidence the same man who had

turned Harald and myself off his dromon. Both men looked
surprised and resentful that I had been called to the meeting, and
I made sure I stood respectfully, eyes fixed once again on the
golden halo of the icon, but listening with close attention to what
the Orphanotrophus had to say.

'Guardsman, I've received an unusual request from war captain Araltes, now on anti-piracy patrol. He wants you to accompany the next pay shipment for our army in Italy.'

'As your excellency orders,' I answered crisply.

'It is not that straightforward,' said the Orphanotrophus,
'otherwise I would not have summoned you in person. This
shipment could be a little different from usual. Araltes – or Harald
as you told me your people call him – has been very effective.
His men have destroyed several pirate bases and captured or sunk
a number of the Saracen vessels, but not all of them. One
particularly dangerous vessel remains at large. Araltes reports that
the vessel's base is in Sicily and therefore beyond the operational
range of his monocylon. The drungarios here agrees with this
assessment. He also tells me that several of his warships have
attempted to hunt down this corsair but so far have failed.'

'The vessel has been too quick for them,' explained the
drungarios in self-defence. 'She is powerful and well manned and
she has been able to outrun my dromons.'

The Orphanotrophus ignored the interruption. 'It is vital that
our troops now on campaign in southern Italy receive their pay in
the next few weeks. If they do not, they will lose heart. They
have not been paid for half a year as both the last two pay
shipments were lost. We believe the vessels carrying the payments
were intercepted by the same cruising pirate, who has yet to be
accounted for. It was either a remarkably bad stroke of luck for
the raider or, as Araltes suggests, the pirate was informed in
advance when and where the shipments were being made.'

I waited impassively to hear what the Orphanotrophus would
say next. So far he had not mentioned anything which explained
why Harald wanted me to accompany the next shipment.

'War captain Araltes has suggested a ruse to ensure that the next payment does get through. He proposes that the army's pay is not sent in the usual way, by the imperial highway from the capital to Dyrrachium and there trans-shipped for Italy. He proposes that the money is delivered by sea all the way, aboard a fast ship sailing from Constantinople, around Greece and then directly across to Italy.'

'That plan is madness, your excellency. Typical of a barbarian,' protested the kentarchos, 'What is there to say that the merchant ship would not equally be intercepted by the pirate. Unarmed, the vessel would be helpless. It would be an even easier target.'

'There is a second part to the plan,' said the Orphanotrophus smoothly. 'Araltes suggests a fake pay shipment is also sent, at the same time and along the normal route, to distract the raider. This shipment is to be of lead bars instead of the usual gold bullion. It will be fully escorted as if it were the real consignment, taken to Dyrrachium, and loaded aboard a military transport carrying extra fighting men supplied by Araltes. This decoy vessel will then set sail for Italy. If the pirate's spies tell him about this vessel, he will intercept it, and this time he may be destroyed. Meanwhile the real shipment will have slipped through.'

'If it please your excellency,' the kentarchos interjected, 'the shipment can go all the way by sea, but why not aboard a dromon? No pirate would dare attack.'

'The drungarios assures me that this is impossible. He cannot spare a battleship,' replied the Orphanotrophus. 'Every dromon is already committed.'

Out of the corner of my eye I watched the drungarios. He looked towards his kentarchos and gave a shrug. The drungarios, I thought to myself, was as much a courtier as a seaman. He did not want the risk of the imperial navy losing another bullion shipment, nor did he want to contradict the Orphantrophus.

'Guardsman, what is your opinion?'

From the tone of his voice I knew the Orphanotrophus had

directed his question at me, but still I dared not look directly into his face, and kept my gaze fixed on the icon on the wall behind him.

'I am not an expert on naval matters, your excellency,' I said, choosing my words carefully, 'but I would suggest that, just as a precaution, two of the monocylon escort the bullion vessel through the zone where the pirate ship is most likely to be operating, at least to the limit of their range.'

'Strange you should mention that,' observed the Orphanotrophus. 'That is just what Araltes also proposes. He says he can send two of the monocylon to a rendezvous off the south cape of Greece. That is why he asks that you be aboard the bullion ship. So that there are no misunderstandings when the captain of the Greek ship meets up with the Varangian captains.'

'As your excellency wishes,' I replied. Harald's deception plan was the sort of strategy which would appeal to the Orphanotrophus.

'Araltes asks one more thing. He requests that we send him an engineer and materials for the Fire.'

Beside me the kentarchos almost choked with astonishment. John noted his reaction.

'Don't worry,' he said soothingly. 'I have no intention of allowing the Fire to be made available to barbarian vessels. At the same time I don't want to snub Araltes. He is evidently someone who takes offence easily. He says nothing about requiring a siphon to dispense the Fire. So I'll send him the engineer and the materials, but no siphon. It will be a genuine mistake.'

It took three weeks to prepare the plan. First the bureau of the logothete of the domestikos, the army's secretariat, had to draw up two sets of orders: the official one for the false shipment and a second, secret set of instructions for the genuine consignment. Then their colleagues in the office of the logothete of the dromos, responsible for the imperial highways, had to make their preparations for an escorted convoy to go overland from Constantinople to Dyrrachium. The managers of the way stations were warned to be ready with changes of pack mules for carrying the payment, as well as horses for the mounted troopers. The eparch of the palace treasury received his instructions direct from the Orphanotrophus: he was to cast eight hundred bars of lead to the same weight as the thousands of gold nomisma, the imperial coins with which the troops were paid. Last, but not least, the navy had to find a suitable merchant ship to carry the genuine shipment around the coast.

When I went to the Golden Horn to view the chosen vessel, I had to admit that the kentarchos, who had been given this responsibility, knew his job. He had picked a vessel known locally as a dorkon or 'gazelle'. Twenty paces in length, the vessel was light and fast for a cargo carrier. She had two masts for her triangular sails, a draught shallow enough to allow her to work close inshore, and extra oar benches for sixteen men so she could make progress in a calm as well as manoeuvre her way safely in and out of harbour. Her captain also inspired me with confidence. A short, sinewy Greek by the name of Theodore, he came from the island of Lemnos, and he kept his ship in good order. Once he had made it clear to me that he was in charge and I was to be only a supercargo, he was polite and friendly. He had been told only that he was to sail to Italy by the direct route and expect a rendezvous at sea with auxiliary ships of the imperial navy. He had not been told the nature of his cargo. Nor did he ask.

I next saw Theodore on the night we left harbour. In keeping with the secrecy of our mission, we sailed within hours of the chests of bullion being carried aboard. The water guard were expecting us. They patrolled the great iron chain strung across the entrance to the Golden Horn at dusk to hinder smugglers or enemy attack, and they opened a gap so that the dorkon could slip out and catch the favourable current to take us down towards the Propontis or inner sea. As I looked towards the towering black mass of Constantinople spread across its seven hills, I recalled the day when I had first arrived. Then I had been awed by the sheer scale and splendour of Miklagard. Now the city was defined by the pinprick lights of the apartment blocks where thousands upon thousands of ordinary working citizens were still awake. Closer to hand, the steady beam of Constantinople's lighthouse shone out across the water, its array of lanterns fuelled by olive oil and burning in great glass jars to protect the flames from the wind.

The dorkon performed even better than I had anticipated. We set course directly across the Propontis, and this in itself was a measure of our captain's competence. Greek mariners normally stopped each evening and anchored at some regular shelter or pulled into a local port, so they hugged the coast and were seldom out of sight of land. But Theodore headed directly for the lower straits which led into what he called the Great Sea. Nor did he divert into the harbour at Abydos, where the empire maintained a customs post and all commercial vessels were required to stop and pay a toll. A patrol boat, alerted by signals from the customs post, managed to intercept us but I showed the written authority that the Orphanotrophus's chief chartularius had given me, and they let us proceed. The document stated we were on urgent imperial business and not to be delayed. John, I noted, had even taken to signing his name in the purple ink.

I was rolling up the scroll with its lead seal and about to return it to my satchel when the wind plucked a folded sheet of parchment from the bag and blew it across the deck. Theodore deftly caught the paper before it disappeared overboard, and as he returned it to me he gave me a questioning glance. He had obviously recognised some sort of map. I had been planning to show it to him later, but now seemed an opportune moment.

'The commander of the vessels which will join us later as our escort provided me with this,' I said, spreading out the page. 'He sent it by courier from Dyrrachium to the office of the dromos in Constantinople to be passed on to me. It shows where we can expect to rendezvous with our escort.'

The Greek captain glanced down at the outline drawn on the

parchment and recognised the coastline immediately. 'Just beyond the Taenarum cape,' he said, then shrugged. 'Your commander need not have troubled himself. I know that coastline as well as my home port. Sailed past it more times than I can remember.'

'Well, it's best to be sure,' I said. 'He's marked where his ships will be waiting for us.' I placed my finger next to a runic letter drawn on the parchment. Recalling what Halldor had told me about Harald's knowledge of the ancient lore, I recognised it as a private code.

'What's that sign?' asked Theodore.

'The first letter of what might be described as the alphabet my people use. It's called fehu – it represents livestock or wealth.'

'And that one?' asked the captain. A vertical stave line with a single diagonal bar had been drawn near the coast a little further north.

'That's nauthiz, the letter which signifies need or distress.'

The Greek captain examined the map more closely and remarked, 'What's it put there for? There's nothing along that stretch of coast except sheer cliffs. Not a place to be caught in an onshore gale either. Deep water right up to the land and no holding ground. You'd be dashed to pieces in an instant. Wiser to give the place a wide berth.'

'I don't know the reason,' I said, for I was equally puzzled.

With each mile that our ship travelled, I noticed the difference between sailing in the Great Sea and the conditions I had experienced in colder northern waters. The water had a more intense blue, the wave crests were whiter and more crisp against the darker background, and the waves themselves more lively. They formed and re-formed in a rapid dance, and seemed never to acquire the height and majesty of ocean rollers. I commented on this to Theodore, and his reply was serious.

'You should see what it is like in a storm,' he warned. 'A sort of madness. Steep waves falling down on themselves, coming from more than one direction to confuse the helmsman. Each big enough to swamp the boat. And no hint before the tempest strikes. That's the worst. It sweeps in from a cloudless sky and churns the sea into a rage even before you've had time to shorten sail.'

'Have you ever been shipwrecked?' I asked.

'Never,' he said and made the sign of the cross. 'But don't be lulled into complacency – the Great Sea has seen more than its share of shipwrecks, from the blessed St Paul right back to the times of our earliest seafarers, to Odysseus himself.'

The dorkon was sailing close inshore at the time, passing beneath a tall headland, and he gestured up towards its crest. High up, I could see a double row of white columns, close spaced and crowned with a band of white stone. The structure gleamed, so brilliant was its whiteness.

'See that there. It's a temple to the old Gods. You'll likely find one on every major headland – either that or some sort of burial mound.'

For a moment I thought he was talking about my Gods and the Elder Way, but then realised he meant the Gods whom his people had worshipped before they believed in the White Christ.

'They were built where they could be seen by passing sailors,' the captain went on. 'I reckon that in former times the mariners prayed when they saw those temples, asking their heathen gods to give them safe passage, or thanking them for a voyage safely completed. Like today I lit a candle and said a prayer to St Nicholas of Myra, patron saint of mariners, before I embarked.'

'Who were those older Gods?' I asked.

'Don't know,' he answered. 'But they seem to have been some sort of family, ruled over by a father god, with other Gods responsible for the weather for crops, for war and such like.'

Much like my own Gods, I thought.

Our vessel was far ahead of the most optimistic schedule, and when we rounded Taenarum cape and reached the place where Harald's two ships were due to meet us, I was not surprised that the sea was empty. There was no sign yet of the two monocylon, and I had some difficulty in persuading Theodore that we should wait a few extra days. He was well aware that we were entering the area where piracy was rife, but he was also worried by the risk of dawdling off a dangerous shore.

'As I told you,' he said, gesturing towards the distant horizon where we could see the faint line of the coast, 'there's no harbour over there, and if the wind swings round and strengthens we could be in trouble.'

In the end he agreed to wait three days, and we spent them tacking back and forth, then drifting each night with sails furled. Each morning we hoisted our lookout, seated on a wooden cradle, to the masthead, and there he clung, gazing to the north, the direction from which we expected Harald's ships to arrive.

At dawn on the third day, as he was being hauled up to his vantage point and glancing around, the lookout let out a warning shout. A vessel was approaching from the south-west. Theodore jumped up on the rail, gazed in that direction, then leaped back on deck and came striding towards me. Any hint of his usual friendliness was gone. Fury was mingled with suspicion in his expression.

'Is that why you wanted us to wait?' he shouted, seizing me by the arm and bringing his face up close. His breath smelled overpoweringly of garum, the rotten fish sauce the sailors relished. For a moment I thought he was going to strike me.

'What do you mean?' I asked.

'Over there,' he shouted, waving towards the distant sail. 'Don't tell me you weren't expecting that. I should have known it all along. You treacherous savage. You lied about waiting for an escort. That's a Saracen ship twice our size, and you're the reason why she turned up here so conveniently.'

'How can you be so sure she's an Arab vessel? No one can tell at this distance,' I defended myself.

'Oh, yes I can,' the captain snarled, his fingers digging deeper into my arm. 'See how she's rigged. Three triangular sails on three masts. She's an Arab galea out of Sicily or—'

'Keep calm,' I interrupted. 'I've no idea how that ship happens to be here just now. Even if you don't believe me, we're wasting time. Set all sail, get your oarsmen to stand by, steer north. I'm sure our escort ships are well on their way, and we should meet up with them before the Saracens catch us.'

The Greek captain laughed bitterly. 'No chance. If that Saracen ship is the one I think she is, we won't get far. You know what "galea" means. It's our word for a swordfish, and if you've ever seen a swordfish racing in for the attack, you'd know she'll catch us. Probably by noon, and there's no way out. There isn't even a friendly harbour where we can seek refuge.'

His words reminded me of the map Harald had sent. I fumbled in my satchel and pulled out his chart. 'Here, what about this?' I tapped the nauthiz rune. 'Isn't that the reason for this mark. It's a place to go if we're in distress.'

The captain looked at me with dislike. 'Why should I trust you now?' he said grimly.

'You don't need to,' I replied, 'but if you're right, and that Arab vessel is as fast and dangerous as you say, you've no other choice.'

He thought about it for a moment, then angrily spun on his heel and began yelling at his crew to set all sail, then get themselves to the oar benches. Taking the helm, he steered the dorkon on a slanting course towards the distant coast. He didn't even look at me, but set his jaw and concentrated on getting the best speed from his ship.

Even the most ignorant sailor would have seen that our vessel was no match for the Arab galea. We were light and quick for a merchant vessel, but the Arab had been designed as a pure seagoing hunter. She carried far more sail than we did and was expertly handled. Worse, the southerly breeze suited her to perfection and she began to overhaul us so rapidly, her bow slicing through the sea and sending up a curl of white foam, that I wondered if we would even get as far as the coast. I had been in a sea chase years earlier, pursued by longships, and we had gained temporary advantage by running across a sandbar into waters too shallow for our enemies. But this was not an option now. As the coast ahead drew nearer, I saw that it was utterly forbidding, a rampart of cliffs directly ahead of us.

The Arab ship was undoubtedly a pirate. As she closed on us we could make out that she carried at least eighty men, far more than any trading ship would require, and they were chillingly professional in the way they went about their duties. They adjusted the three huge sails to perfection, then moved across the deck and lined the windward side to trim their vessel and waited there. They did not shout or cheer, but remained poised and silent, certain of the outcome of the pursuit. Up in her bows I saw the archers, sitting quietly with their weapons, waiting until we were in range.

Theodore knew our situation was hopeless, yet he passed from panic to a sense of defiance. Every time he turned and saw how much the gap between the ships had closed, he did not change expression but merely looked up to see that our sails were at their best, then turned back to face towards the cliffs as they drew closer. After three hours' chase we were no more than a mile from the coast, and I could see that Theodore had been right. The sheer rock face extended in each direction for mile after mile, yellow-brown in colour, sun-baked and utterly desolate. The dark sea heaved against the boulders along their base. Either the pursuing galley would overtake and its crew board us, or we would simply crunch against the rocks. Fifty paces from the cliff, our captain pushed across the helm and our vessel turned and began to run parallel to the precipice, so close that I could hear the cries of the sea birds nesting on the high ledges. Here the wind was fluky, bouncing off the rock face so that our sails began to flap and we lost speed.

'Get out your oars and row!' bellowed Theodore.

The crew stabbed at the water and did their best, but it was almost impossible to get a grip on the choppy water and they were not professional galley rowers. They looked shocked and frightened, but to their credit they remained almost as silent as the chasing pirates. Only occasionally did I hear a sob of effort or despair as they tugged on the looms of the oars.

Of course I joined them on the oar bench. I had rowed a longship and knew how to handle an oar, but it was only a gesture. Our sole hope was that Harald's two monocylon would suddenly appear, sweeping down from the north. But each time I looked over my shoulder the sea remained empty. To one side of us, and almost level now, the Arab galea kept pace. Her captain had reduced sail so he did not overshoot his victim. Half his oarsmen, perhaps forty men, were rowing to hold their position steady. He was, I realised, worried that he might come too close to the cliffs, and did not want to risk damaging his vessel. I judged that he would bide his time until we were in more open water, then close in for the kill.

We were approaching a low headland which jutted from the line of cliffs, obscuring what lay further up the coast.

'Listen, men,' shouted our captain. 'I'm going to beach the ship if I see a suitable spot. When I do that, it's every man for himself. Drop your oars, leap out and make a run for it. So keep up the pressure now, row as best you can, and wait until I give the word.'

Soon the dorkon was lurching past the headland, so near that I could have thrown a pebble on to the rocks. Now the pirate galley closed the range. One or two arrows flew. The archers were hoping for a lucky strike, to maim a few of our oarsmen. Not too many, of course, because crippled slaves fetched a lower price.

Past the headland the coastline opened up ahead. To our right was a wide, shallow bay, but the beach itself was a mass of stones and rock. There was no place where we could run ashore. Theodore jerked his head at me and I left my oar to join him at the helm. He seemed almost calm, resigned to his fate.

'This is the spot marked on your map where we should be in case of need. But I don't see anything.'

I looked around the sweep of the bay. Ahead of us, perhaps

half a mile, I saw a narrow break in the cliffs which rose again on the far side. 'Over there,' I said, pointing. 'Perhaps in there we will find a landing place. And maybe the entrance is too narrow for the Arab ship to follow us. If we can squeeze in, we might have a few moments to abandon ship and run clear.'

'It's worth a try,' grunted the captain, and altered course.

We laboured ever closer, heading for the cleft. But as we approached, I saw that I had misjudged it. The gap was wider than I had supposed, which meant our dorkon could slip in, but so too could the pirate ship if her steersman was bold enough. The skipper of the Arab craft must have thought the same, for he did not harry us as we crept closer to where two low reefs reached out, leaving a narrow gap between. Our pursuer even had the confidence to stop rowing: I saw the regular beat of the sweeps come to a halt. They waited and watched.

Sails flapping, our dorkon glided through the gap. As we entered, I knew we were doomed. We found ourselves in a natural harbour, a small cove, almost totally landlocked. Sheer cliffs of yellow rock rose on each side, banded with ledges. They enclosed a circular sea pool, some forty paces across. Here the colour of the water was the palest blue, so clear that I could see the sandy bottom, no more than ten feet below our keel. Despairingly I realised that the water was deep enough for the Arab galley to float. There was not a breath of wind. The cove was so tightly surrounded that the cliffs overhung the water in places, and if the lip of the precipice crumbled, the rocks would fall straight on to our deck. We had found the refuge marked on the map, and had we reached it earlier, even by a day, we could have concealed ourselves here and waited in safety for Harald's monocylon to appear. I had failed.

'We're trapped,' said Theodore quietly.

In the distance I heard a shout. It must have been the voice of the Arab captain prowling outside, ordering his men to furl sail and prepare to row their larger ship through the entrance. Then I heard the creak of ropes in wooden blocks and supposed that the

Arabs were lowering the spars as well. They were taking their time, knowing that they had us at their mercy.

'Every man for himself!' called Theodore, and his crew needed no urging. They began to jump into the clear water – it was no more than a few strokes for them to swim ashore. At the back of the cove was a ledge of rock where a man could haul himself out. From there the faint line of a goat path meandered up the cliff face. If we scrambled up fast enough, maybe we could get clear before the slave-catchers arrived.

'I'm sorry—' I began to say, but Theodore interrupted.

'It's too late for that now. Get going.'

I threw myself overboard and he jumped a moment later. We were the last to abandon the ship, leaving her bobbing quietly in the placid water.

I hauled myself out on to the rock ledge, reached down and gave Theodore a hand, pulling him ashore. He followed the line of wet footprints where his crew had scrambled for the goat path. Up above me I heard the clattering of falling stones as they clambered upwards as fast as possible.

Glancing back, I saw the Arab ship was nosing in cautiously through the gap between the rocks. Her hull almost filled the entrance, and her oarsmen had scarcely enough room to row. Several of the pirates stood on deck and were using the long sweeps to push the vessel into the cove.

I turned and climbed for my life. I had kicked off my boots before I swam, so I felt the sharp rocks cut and bruise my bare feet. I slipped and grabbed for handholds while I looked upwards trying to locate the path. Dirt and small pebbles dislodged by the Greek captain rained down on me. I was less than halfway up the cliff face when I caught up with Theodore. There was no room to overtake him, so I paused, panting with exhaustion, the blood roaring in my ears, and stared back down into the cove.

The Arab galea now lay alongside our abandoned ship, with about a dozen looters already on the dorkon's deck. They were levering up the hatch cover, and soon they would reach the bullion chests lying in the hold. Shouts from below told me that the Arab captain – I could clearly identify him by his red and white striped turban – was ordering some of his men to pursue and capture us. Two or three of them were already swimming ashore.

Suddenly, a speck dropped past the cliff face on the far side of the cove. At first I thought it was a fault in my eyesight, a grain of dirt in my eye or one of those black spots which sometimes swims across one's vision when one is panting for breath. Then two more dark specks followed, and I saw the splashes where they hit the water. Something was falling from the lip of the cliff. I looked across and glimpsed a sudden movement in the fringe of scrub and bushes. It was an arm, throwing some sort of object. The projectile travelled through the air, curving far out and gathering speed until it struck the deck of the galea. It burst on impact. I watched in amazement. Several more of the missiles sped through the air. Whoever was throwing them had found their range. One or two of the missiles splashed into the water, but another four or five landed on the pirate vessel.

From below me came shouts of alarm. The men who had boarded the dorkon began to scramble back aboard their own ship, while their captain raced towards the stern of his vessel. He was shouting at his crew and waving urgently. One of the Arabs picked up from the deck a missile which had failed to burst and threw it overboard. I saw it was some sort of round clay pot, the size of a man's head. The Saracens kept their discipline, even though they had been taken totally by surprise. Now, those who had been swimming ashore turned back towards their vessel. Others hacked through the ropes binding the galea to the captured dorkon and began to push clear. Most of the crew found their places on the benches again and set their oars in place, but they were hampered by the confines of the little cove. There was little room to row and not enough space to turn the galley. The Arab captain yelled another command and the oarsmen changed their stroke. They were backing water, now attempting to reverse the galea out through the narrow gap.

Meanwhile the clay pots continued to rain down. From several came spouts of flame as they struck. Fire broke out on the galea's cotton sails, neatly furled on their spars. The rolled-up cloth served as enormous candle wicks, and I watched the flames run along the spars, then catch the tarred rigging and race up the masts. More fire pots struck. As they burst, they spilled a dark liquid which splashed across the wooden deck. Sometimes the liquid was already ablaze as it spread. At other times it oozed sideways until it touched a living flame and then burst into fire. Within moments the deck of the galea was ablaze with pools of fire expanding towards one another, joining and growing fiercer.

The Saracens began to panic. Rivulets of flaming liquid spilled down and ran below the galley benches. An oarsman leapt up, frantically beating at his gown, which had caught fire. His companions on the bench abandoned their task and tried to help put out the flames. They failed, and I saw the desperate oarsman fling himself overboard to douse himself.

Then I saw something else which I would not have believed was possible. The burning liquid from the fire pots dripped from the galea's scuppers and ran down the hull, then spread across the surface of the pool and *the liquid continued to blaze*, even on the water. Now I knew I was witnessing the same terrible weapon that had destroyed the Rus fleet when it attacked the Queen of Cities two generations earlier. This was the Fire.

As the Fire took hold, there was no stopping or extinguishing or diverting it. The blazing liquid spread across the galea's deck, sought out her hold, ran along the oar benches and surrounded the vessel in flickering tongues of flame. The expanding fire licked the sides of the abandoned dorkon, and soon that vessel too was alight. Smoke was pouring up from the two burning vessels. The column of smoke twisted and roiled. Its base expanded and shifted, enveloping the wretched Saracens. Some wrapped their turbans around their faces to protect themselves, and tried uselessly to beat back the flames. The majority jumped into the fiery water. I watched them try to duck beneath the floating skin of Fire. But when they surfaced for air they sucked the Fire down into their lungs and sank back down, not to rise again. A handful managed to swim towards the open sea, heading towards the gap between the reefs. They must have dived down and swum underwater to get beyond the reach of the floating Fire. But their escape was blocked. Now their attackers showed themselves.

Along the arms of the two reefs scrambled armed warriors. Big and heavily bearded, wearing cross-gartered leggings and jerkins, I recognised them at once: they were Harald of Norway's men. They carried long spears and took up their positions on the rocks where their weapons could reach the swimmers. I was reminded of the fishermen in the northern lands who wait on riverbanks, on shingle spits, or at weirs, ready to spear the migrating salmon. Only this time it was men they speared. Not a single swimmer escaped through the gap.

Just five of the pirates managed to reach the rocky ledge below me and haul themselves ashore. Suddenly I was knocked aside by a Norseman leading ten of his fellows down the goat track to the ledge. This time they did not kill their enemy, because the Arabs sank down on their knees and begged to be spared.

'Hey, Thorgils, time to come on up!' It was Halldor's voice, shouting cheerfully. I saw him on the far lip of the cliff waving to me. I turned away from the massacre, a picture of those dying men seared into my mind. Weeks earlier, in Constantinople, I had come across one of the White Christ fanatics haranguing a crowd in the marketplace. To me he had seemed half mad as he threatened his listeners with terrible punishment if they did not repent of their sins. They would fall into an abyss, he screamed at them, and suffer terrible horrors, burning in torment. That image came very close to the scene I had just witnessed.

'You used us as bait!' I accused Halldor after I had climbed to the top of the cliff and found some forty Norsemen gathered, looking very pleased with themselves. Concealed in a fold in the ground some distance away was their camp, a cluster of tents where they had established themselves as they waited to spring the trap.

'And very good bait you made,' answered Halldor, a grin of triumph showing his teeth through his beard.

'You could at least have warned me,' I said, still disgruntled.

'That was part of the plan. Harald calculated that you would understand the meanings of the rune symbols on the map, and be so pleased with yourself for having worked them out, that you wouldn't think of anything else but carrying out the message. That would make the scheme all the more effective.'

His answer made me feel even worse. I, as well as the Arab pirate, had been hoodwinked.

'And what would have happened if our ship had got here earlier, or the Arab pirate had showed up later? Your elaborate scheme would have collapsed.'

Halldor was not in the least contrite. 'If the Arab had shown up late, then the bullion shipment would have got through safely. If you were very early and tucked yourselves away in the cove, he would have come looking for you. Naturally we would then have helped him, sending up smoke from a cooking fire or some other way of guiding him to the spot.'

I looked round the group of Norsemen. There were very few of them to have destroyed the most powerful Saracen vessel in the region.

'Don't you see the genius of it?' Halldor went on, unable to conceal his satisfaction. 'Both the pirate and that eunuch minister in Constantinople thought this was a double deception. The minister believed we would lure in the pirate to the fake shipment and the real bullion would get through. The pirate thought he had seen through that plot and would pounce upon an easy prize. But Harald was playing a triple game. He reckoned on using the real shipment as the genuine bait, and look how well it turned out.'

'And if the galea had overhauled us at sea, and captured us and the gold?'

Halldor shrugged dismissively. 'That was a risk Harald was prepared to take. As I told you, he has battle luck.'

I looked around. 'Where's Harald now?'

'He entrusted the ambush to me,' said Halldor. 'We stumbled on the cove when we were searching for pirate bases along the coast. Harald immediately saw how it could provide the perfect location for an ambush. But he thinks the imperial bureaucracy is so riddled with spies and traitors that he had to take every precaution. He sent only a handful of men to set up the ambush so their absence would not be noticed in Dyrrachium, while he himself stayed with our ships. They should be here in a day or two, and Harald will be aboard.'

I must still have looked resentful because Halldor added, 'There's another benefit. Harald's cunning has exposed the source of the pirates' information. It must be the office of the dromos. Someone there who makes the practical arrangements for the bullion shipments was informing the Saracens where and when to strike. Harald suspected this, so when he sent that map with the rune signs he set another trap.'

I remembered the officials from the dromos who had accompanied me on my first visit to Harald's camp at Mamas. Even then I had wondered if one of them had learned to speak Norse in the dromos's college of interpreters.

'You mean the spy had to be able to read rune signs if he was to understand the significance of the map,' I said. 'And only someone in the dromos office would have that skill.'

Halldor nodded. 'Tell that to your castrated minister when you get back to Constantinople.'

Harald himself arrived with his patrol ships just as Halldor and his men were beginning the task of salvaging the cargoes of the two burned-out wrecks. The water in the cove was so shallow that it was easy to recover the bullion chests from the dorkon.

Their contents were unharmed. Halldor's divers then turned their attention to seeing what had sunk with the galea. To everyone's delight it turned out that the ship was packed with booty the pirates had taken earlier. Many of the valuables had been damaged by the Fire and seawater had ruined much of what remained, but there was still a good deal worth salvaging. The finest items were church ornaments, presumably looted from raids on Christian towns. They included dishes and bowls of silver as well as altar cloths. The fabric was a blackened mass, but the pearls and semi-precious stones which had once been stitched to the cloth were unharmed. They too were added to the growing pile of valuables.

'One-sixth goes to the imperial treasury as the emperor's share, the rest is for us. That's the rule,' gloated Halldor as another dripping mass of plunder was brought to the surface.

Harald, I noticed, kept a very close eye on what was being recovered. He trusted his men to carry out an ambush unsuper-vised, but when it came to division of the spoils he made sure that every single item was precisely accounted for. He stood beside the makeshift table on which each piece of salvage was examined, and watched as its value was calculated. When a mass of silver Arab dinars was brought up, the coins melted together as a lump of metal by the Fire's heat, he ordered it to be weighed three times for value before he was satisfied.

Watching him, I could not help but wonder about his inner thoughts. I had seen him lie full length on the marble floor before the Basileus, who claimed to be the White Christ's representative on earth, and I feared that this lucky outcome for his allegiance might prove a step along the path that would lead Harald to favour the Christian faith. It would be easy for him to be seduced by the wealth and luxury. Standing with a group – Harald, Halldor, and several of his councillors – I was on hand when the most precious of all the objects recovered from the galea was laid upon the table. A Christian cross, it had no doubt been stolen from some rich monastery or church. Each arm was at least three spans in length, as thick as a man's finger, and embellished with patterns moulded on its surface. I knew from my days as a novice in an Irish monastery that to create such an exquisite piece was itself an act of great devotion. The magnificent cross lay upon the bare wood, giving off the dull sheen that only pure gold will give.

Halldor ran his fingers over the workmanship with admiration. 'What's that worth?' he wondered aloud.

'Weigh it and we'll find out,' came Harald's blunt instruction. 'There are seventy-two nomisma to every pound of gold.'

If Harald was naturally inclined to follow any god, I thought to myself, it was not the White Christ but Gullveig from my own Elder Faith. Thrown into the fire to be destroyed, Gullveig, whose name meant 'gold draught', always emerged more radiant than before, the very personification of thrice-smelted gold. But she was also a treacherous and malignant witch-goddess, and suddenly I felt a twinge of foreboding that Harald's gold thirst would lead to his downfall.

FOUR

'YOUR EXCELLENCY, HARALD plans to return to Constantinople now that the pirate menace is dealt with,' I reported to John the Orphanotrophus when I got back to the capital. 'He has already transferred the bullion shipment to Dyrrachium, where he intends to purchase a replacement ship for the Greek captain Theodore so that he can continue on to Italy with the army's pay. They may even have received it by now.'

'This Araltes acts without waiting for orders,' commented the Orphanotrophus.

'It is his nature, your excellency.'

The Orphanotrophus was silent for several moments. 'Corruption is everywhere in the bureaucracy,' he said, 'so the information that the pirate had a spy in the office of dromos is useful, though hardly surprising.'

His words had an undertone which made me wonder if the discovered spy was to be added to the minister's schemes. John was as likely to blackmail the informant into working for him as to punish the man. I felt sympathy for the victim. His position was not so different from my own.

'Does Araltes trust you?' the eunuch asked abruptly.

'I don't know, your excellency. He is not someone who gives trust easily.'

'Then I want you to win his trust. When he arrives back here, you are to assist him in any way you think will earn his confidence.'

When I told Pelagia about my new assignment that evening, she was apprehensive.

'Thorgils, it looks as if you can't untangle yourself from affairs of state, however much you try. From what you've told me about Harald, he is a remarkable man, but dangerous also. In any conflict of interest between him and the Orphanotrophus, you will be caught in the middle. Not an enviable position. If I were you I would pray to your Gods for help.'

Her remark prompted me to ask if she knew anything about the older Gods who were worshipped by the Greeks before they began to follow the ways of the White Christ.

'Theodore, the Greek captain I sailed with,' I told her, 'pointed out to me a ruined temple up on one of the headlands. He said the old Gods were like a family. So I'm wondering if they were the same Gods we worship in the northern lands.'

Pelagia shrugged dismissively. 'I'm not the right person to answer that. I'm not devout. Why would I be when I am named after a reformed prostitute?' She saw she had to explain herself and continued wryly. 'St Pelagia was a streetwalker who took the faith and became a nun. She dressed up as a eunuch and lived in a cave on the Mount of Olives in the Holy Land. She's not the only harlot to have done her bit for the Christians. The mother of Constantine, who founded this city, previously ran a tavern where she provided her clients with more than cheap wine and stale bread. Yet she was the one who found the True Cross and Christ's tomb in the Holy Land.'

Seeing that I genuinely wanted to know more about the older beliefs, Pelagia relented.

'There's a building called the Basilike on the Mese, close to the Milion. It's stuffed full of old statues which no one knows what to do with. Some of them have been stored there for centuries, and among them you may be able to find a few statues

of the old Gods. Though whether anyone can identify them for
you is another matter.'

The following day I located the Basilike without difficulty and
gave the elderly doorkeeper a few coins to let me look around.
My intention, of course, was to discover who the old Gods were
and why they had been replaced. I hoped to learn something
which might save my Gods of the North from the same fate.

The interior of the Basilike was dark and depressing. Hall
after hall was filled with dusty statues, placed with no sense of
order. Some were damaged, others lay on their sides or had been
leaned casually against one another by the workmen who had
brought them there. The only sunlight was in the central courtyard, where the larger pieces had been dumped. All were crammed
so close together that it was difficult to squeeze through between
them. I saw busts of former emperors, sections of triumphal
columns, and all manner of marble odds and ends. There were
heads which lacked bodies, faces with broken noses, riders without
horses, warriors missing shields or holding broken swords and
spears. Every few paces I came across inscribed marble panels
which had been prised from their original locations. Cut in
different sizes and thicknesses, the panels had once identified the
statues to which they had been fixed. I read the names of long-
dead emperors, forgotten victories, unknown triumphs. Somewhere in the jumble of statuary, I imagined, were many of the
originals to which the inscriptions had once belonged. To reunite
them would be impossible.

I was standing in front of a marble panel trying to decipher
the worn letters when a wheezing voice said, 'What size are you
looking for?'

I turned to see an old man who had shuffled out from the
maze of figures. He was wearing a shapeless woollen mantle with
a frayed hem.

'The best pieces go quite quickly, but there are some large
ones at the back which have cracks in them. If you cut away the
damaged areas, they're still usable.'

I realised that the old man had mistaken me for someone searching for scrap marble. Pelagia had mentioned that marble-work in the city was now made mostly from pieces of salvaged material.

'I had no idea there was so much derelict statuary in store,' I said.

The old man sniffled; the dust was getting in his nose as well as his eyes.

'The city authorities need the display space,' he explained. 'Every time there's a new monument, the sponsors want to put it in the city centre where most people will see it. But the city centre is full up. Not surprising when they've been erecting public monuments there for seven hundred years. So they tear something down and, if they're trying to save money, reuse the plinth. Half the time no one can remember who or what the original statue commemorated. And that's not to mention the statues and monuments which get pulled down when someone wants to build a new apartment block, or which topple over due to neglect or during an earthquake. The city council doesn't want to spend money on putting statues back on their feet.'

'I came here to look at the older statues,' I said cautiously. I did not want to arouse any suspicions that I was a heathen. 'Maybe I can find a representation of one of the ancient Gods.'

'You're not the first person to do that ' said the old man, 'though I doubt if you'll have much luck. Difficult to turn an old God into a new man.' He cackled. He still believed that I was a monumental sculptor looking for a cheap and quick way to carry out a commission by remodelling an earlier statue.

'Can you tell me the best place to look?'

The old man shrugged. 'Can't help you there,' he replied curtly. 'Could be anywhere.' As he turned away with complete lack of interest, I reflected that when the old Gods were discarded, they fell into oblivion.

I spent the next few hours nosing around the Basilike. Nowhere did I find a statue that resembled the Gods I believed in, though I did find what was obviously a sea god, for he had a fishy tail and carried a seashell in one hand. But he was not Njord, my own God of the Sea, so I presumed he belonged to a different faith. In one corner I saw a well-muscled statue sporting a bushy beard, and thought I had stumbled across Thor. But, looking more closely, I changed my mind. The unknown God carried a club, not a hammer. No True Believer would have failed to show Mjollnir, or Thor's iron gloves and strength-giving belt. The other effigy which raised my hopes was the contorted figure of a man pinioned to a rock. The writhing figure was obviously in torment, and I thought it might be Loki the trickster whom the Gods punished by tying him to a rock, using the entrails of his own son as his bonds. But I could see no trace of the serpent whose venom would fall on Loki's face if it was not collected in a bowl by his faithful wife Sigyn, nor a statue of Sigyn herself. The carving remained a mystery, and I was disappointed that I found no trace whatever of the God whom I expected to be there – Odinn. And among all the inscriptions I saw not a single rune letter.

I had reached the very back of the last storage hall when I finally came across one image that I could identify for certain. The carving was done on a panel, and there were holes drilled for the attachment points where it had been fixed on public display. It was a picture of the three Norns, the women who weave the fate of all beings. One of them was spinning, another measuring, and the third held scissors. As I gazed at the panel, it occurred to me that here, perhaps, was a message that I should heed. Not even the Gods themselves can alter the destiny that the Norns have woven, so there was nothing that I could do to change the ultimate fate of the Elder Way. It was better that I should try to understand what was replacing it.

Perhaps Odinn put that thought into my head, because he soon arranged for me to fulfil my wish. On my return to the guards barracks, a message was waiting for me from John's sekreton. It informed me that I had been seconded to the staff of

Araltes, and my duty was to act as his interpreter with proto-maistor Trdat on a mission of great importance. When I showed the message to Pelagia and asked her if she knew about this Trdat, what he did or where he was going, she seemed baffled.

'A lot of citizens would know the name of Trdat,' she said, 'but it can't be the same man. He was the protomaistor, the master builder, who repaired the church of Hagia Sophia, the Holy Wisdom, after it had been damaged in an earthquake. But that was in my grandparents' time. That Trdat must be long dead by now. He was an Armenian, a genius as an architect. It is said that no one else had the talent to make such an elegant repair. Maybe this Trdat is his grandson, or his great-nephew. The role of protomaistor passes down through families.'

'And what about this mysterious mission of great importance the Orphanotrophus mentions? Does the gossip in the marketplace have any clues as to what that might be?'

'No doubt it has something to do with the Basileus,' she answered. 'His sickness – even though you still don't want to call it that – isn't getting any better. In fact it has been growing worse. It now affects him almost daily. The doctors are unable to halt the progress of the illness, so Michael has turned to the priests. He's becoming more and more religious, some would say morbid. He thinks that he can obtain a cure from God by prayer and religious works.'

'There's something else I need to ask you before Harald gets back to Constantinople,' I said. 'I didn't mention this to the Orphanotrophus, but Harald asked me to find out the best way of converting his booty from the pirate ambush into cash or bullion. And he would like to make the arrangement discreetly so that the authorities do not know.'

Pelagia gave a thin smile. 'Your Harald is already acquiring some of the habits of this city. But, as I said, you had better be careful. If the Orphanotrophus gets to hear that you are acting for Harald in the conversion of loot into cash on the black market, and not keeping him informed, you will suffer for it.'

'I will say that I was carrying out his instructions to win Harald's confidence. What could be more helpful than acting as his money agent?'

'What sort of loot does Harald have on offer?' Pelagia asked bluntly, and I reminded myself that she was a woman of business.

'Silver and gold items mostly,' I replied. 'Plate, cups, jugs, that sort of thing, foreign coins of various countries, some jewellery, a few pearls. The pirate was making shore raids as well as seizing merchant ships before he was caught. His galea had a very mixed haul of booty. Our divers brought up a small clay jar from the burned-out wreck. It was packed in straw and carefully crated so it had survived unbroken. Our Greek captain was most excited when he saw it. He read the marks and told us that it was a dye shipment on its way to the imperial silk factory.'

'If that was a jar of purple dye, then he had every reason to be excited,' Pelagia told me. 'The dye comes from seashells, and the extract of twelve thousand shells is needed to colour a single imperial robe. By weight that dye is far more precious than fine gold.'

'Where could Harald dispose of such things without attracting attention?'

Pelagia thought for a moment, then said, 'He should deal with a man called Simeon. Officially he's an argyroprates, a seller of silver. But he also handles gold and precious stones. In fact he has another string to his bow as a moneylender. He's not supposed to be in that business, but he can't resist the eight per cent interest. The bankers' guild probably knows what he is up to, but they let Simeon operate because they find it useful to have someone who can do the occasional deal for them off the books. But it would be best if I contact Simeon first. He has a money changer's table on the Milion, not so far from the bread market, and we know each other by sight. If I make the connection successfully between Simeon and Araltes, I will want an introduction fee of, say, half a per cent.'

Pelagia was as good as her word, and it turned out that the half per cent was a bargain for the services that Simeon was to provide Harald with. The argyroprates always contrived to find someone willing to pay silver or gold for brocades, silks, boxes of spices, holy artefacts, even on one occasion a pair of lion cubs. In that particular transaction the keeper of the Basileus's menagerie in the Great Palace paid a premium price.

Harald came back to Constantinople shortly before Ascension Day, and barely had time for one private meeting with Simeon – at which I acted as the interpreter – before he received the details of his new assignment. His war band was to be sworn in as a unit of the Varangians-without-the-walls and receive regular army pay and accommodation. Harald himself was to select twenty of his best men and report aboard a warship loading stores and materials in the harbour of Bucephalon.

A copy of his orders had been sent to me, with a note penned in the margin by the chief secretary to the Orphanotrophus telling me that I was to accompany Araltes. I had lived long enough in Constantinople to know that Bucephalon harbour was reserved for vessels used by the imperial family. The only warship stationed, as far as I was aware, was the fast dromon assigned for the use of the Basileus himself. I had no idea why Harald and his men should be on board.

The intelligent-looking young man who greeted me on the dromon's deck quickly explained the situation. A civilian, he was slightly chubby with a glossy mass of curly black hair, and he had the look of a man always ready to find an excuse to smile or make a joke.

'I'm Trdat,' he said genially. 'Welcome aboard. I gather that you are to be the interpreter for my military escort. Though why I need one is beyond me.' He spoke with such lack of formality that I wondered what he was doing on board the Basileus's personal dromon.

Trdat waved his hand casually at the taut rigging of the

immaculate warship, the scrubbed decks and gilded detailing, the
smartly dressed officers. Even the blades of the thirty-foot rowing
sweeps were picked out in imperial purple and gold.

'Quite a ship, don't you think? Couldn't imagine anything
finer for a gentle sea voyage in the best season of the year.'

'Where are we going?' I asked. 'And why?'

'Those stuffy bureaucrats haven't told you? Just like them.
Always priding themselves on their discretion when there's no
need for secrecy, yet willing to sell classified information if it
swells their purses. We are bound for the Holy Land to see what
can be done about the state of Golgotha. It's a mission for His
Majesty the Basileus. By the way, I'm an architect, a protomaistor.'

'But I was told that protomaistor Trdat restored the Church
of Holy Wisdom more than forty years ago.'

'That would be my grandfather,' the architect replied cheerfully. 'And he did a very good job too. That's why I've been
picked for this commission. The Basileus hopes I can do as well
as my grandfather. This is to be another restoration project.'

'Perhaps you could tell me exactly what is involved so I could
explain it to your escort when they arrive.'

'I don't want to bore you with the details, and I can hear by
your accent that you are a northerner – don't be offended, I'm
Armenian by origin – so you may not even be a Christian. But
the spot where the Christ died and was buried is one of the truly
sacred places of our faith. A magnificent basilica was erected there
not long after the blessed Augusta Helena discovered the True
Cross and her people identified the cave where the Christ's body
was interred. For centuries the sanctity of the sepulchre was
respected, even when it fell into the hands of the Muslims.
Unfortunately times have changed. In my father's day a Caliph,
who justly earned the title of Murad the Mad, gave orders for
both the basilica and the sepulchre to be destroyed. He told the
local governor that no stone was to be left upon another. The
governor was also ordered to close all the other Christian churches
in the province and turn away Christian visitors. Since then we

have had no reliable information as to how bad was the destruction
of the sepulchre – the Anastasis or Resurrection, as it is known –
nor what the ruins look like today. Murad the Mad went to meet
his maker sixteen years ago. He was assassinated by a religious
zealot – rather appropriate, don't you think? – and our Basileus is
currently negotiating with his successors for permission to rebuild
the basilica and repair the sanctuary. That's where I come in. I
have been commissioned to assess the present condition of the
buildings and make on-the-spot repairs. Those civil servants may
be venal idlers, but they are good at keeping archives, and I've
managed to locate the plans of the original basilica. But if the
shrine is so badly wrecked that it cannot be restored, then I am to
design an entirely new building worthy of the site.'

'That's quite a responsibility,' I observed.

'Yes, the emperor sets great store by the scheme. He believes
it will show the depth and extent of his devotion, and he hopes he
will be rewarded with an improvement in his health. I presume
you are familiar with the problems he has been having in that
regard. That's also why he placed the imperial dromon at my
disposal. It shows his level of concern.'

To my surprise Trdat had not bothered to lower his voice
when he spoke of the state of Michael's health.

He breezed on. 'Perhaps you could pass word to your military
friends that we will be ready to sail as soon as I've loaded the last
of the paints and tesserae – those are the little cubes we use for
making mosaics. It should be no later than the day after tomorrow.
My own staff – the mosaicists, plasterworkers, painters and the
rest – are already on standby. Though whether they will actually
have any work to do when we get to the Holy Land remains to
be seen.'

When I relayed all this information to Harald, he seemed
pleased. I supposed he thought that the personal vessel of the
Basileus was exactly the sort of transport that he merited. Certainly when Harald and his men, including Halldor, whom I was
glad to see, arrived at the Bucephalon, the Norwegian prince

walked up the gangplank as though he was the owner of the vessel, not just the escort commander for an architect.

'Tell your Varangians that we'll be making just one stop en route,' Trdat said to me. 'We need to put in to the island of Prokonnesos to pick up some marble in case we can patch up the place of resurrection.'

Already the dromon was moving out to sea under oars, every stroke closely supervised by the protokarabos, the officer responsible for the rowing. He was very conscious that people were watching from the windows of the Great Palace, and he wanted as smart a departure as possible.

It occurred to me that the protomaistor might well know something about the derelict statues in the Basilike, and I asked him if he had ever visited the place.

'Of course,' he answered. 'My father and grandfather, while he was alive, put me through all the hoops. They made me study everything an architect needs to know and more – geometry, arithmetic, astronomy, physics, building construction, hydraulics, carpentry, metalwork, painting. There seemed no end to it. Luckily I enjoyed the work, particularly drawing. I still get satisfaction from preparing diagrams and elevations. They positively encouraged me to visit the old temple sites, took me round the Basilike, and never lost the chance to point out the remnants of the old statuary on display in Constantinople. It's still there if you know what you are looking at. That tall bronze statue of a woman in the Forum of Constantine, for example. Everyone thinks it's a former empress or perhaps a saint. In fact, it's an early Greek goddess. And have you ever noticed the figure on top of the Anemodoulion?'

'The monument near the Forum Tauri, the pyramid with a bronze figure of a woman at the top, which turns and points with the slightest breath of wind? We have similar wind vanes on our ships and houses in the north lands, but they are much smaller and simpler in design.'

'Yes, that's right,' said Trdat, 'But how many people know

that when they look up at the Anemodoulion to check the wind direction, they are actually consulting a bygone pagan goddess? But we'll talk more about this during the voyage. I expect it will take us at least three weeks to reach the Holy Land, even aboard the fastest dromon in the fleet.'

Trdat's company turned our trip into one of the most informative sea journeys I have ever undertaken. The Armenian loved to talk and he was free with his knowledge. He pointed out details about coastlines, described his upbringing in a family of famous architects, and introduced me to some of the techniques of his profession. He took me down into the hold to open up sacks of tesserae and showed me the little cubes of marble, terracotta, different-coloured glass and mother-of-pearl. He demonstrated how they would be stuck into a bed of soft mortar to make portraits or patterns on a wall or on the floor, and told me that a skilled mosaicist, working flat out, could complete in one day an area as wide as a man could spread his arms in each direction.

'Imagine how long it took to decorate the inside of the apse in the church of the Holy Wisdom. Grandfather Trdat calculated that it required two and a half million tesserae.'

When we reached the marble island of Prokonnesos halfway across the Propontis Sea, he also invited me to go ashore with him as he visited the quarries where miners were cracking open the rock and splitting away sheets of marble ready to be sawn and carved to shape.

'Prokonnesos marble is so widely used that I find it rather boring,' he confessed. 'You see it everywhere – the same white stone with blue-grey veining. But it's readily available, and the supply seems inexhaustible.'

'I thought that most of the new marblework was made from salvage.'

'True. Yet many of those salvaged pieces came from Prokonnesos in the first place, and the quarry owners have been shrewd enough to pander to the builders' laziness. They prepare the marble pieces here on the island, carving out the shapes and patterns, and have them ready and waiting on the quay. You simply pick up ready-made segments for columns, and capitals and pediments in stock designs, but it restricts an architect's creative skill if he has to work with such stuff just because his client wants to save money. I know of at least nineteen different varieties of marble, yet if you were to walk around Constantinople you would think there was only one – Prokonessos. I love it when I have the chance to work with dark red porphyry from Egypt, serpentine from Sparta, green from Thessaly, or rose red from Syria. There's even a black and white marble that can be brought from the far end of the Great Sea.'

In the end my new-found friend selected only a few plain slabs of the Prokonnesos marble which, as he put it, 'were good enough to put down as paving around Christ's tomb if the flooring has been ripped up at Mad Murad's command'.

Harald, Halldor and the other Varangians kept to themselves throughout the trip, though I sensed they were itching to take the helm or adjust the dromon's sails. Her captain was a palace appointee with no apparent seafaring skills, and he had the good sense to leave the running of the vessel to the protokarabos and his assistants. Navigation presented few challenges as they could set the course from one island to the next, watching for each new sea mark to come up over the horizon ahead even as the last island peak dropped out of sight behind us.

As we were steering toward the distant loom of an island, Trdat made a comment which caused a jolt of memory. Squinting at the high ground taking shape ahead, he remarked, 'That must be the lame smith's favourite haunt.'

His words brought back an image of my first tutor in the Old Ways, Tyrkyr the German. He had been heating and shaping iron in his forge when he told me how Volund the master metalworker had been deliberately crippled by the evil King Nidud and left on an island where he was forced to work for his captor.

'A lame smith on that island. What was his name?' I asked Trdat. 'Hephestus the smith God,' he replied. 'That island over there is Lemnos. Legend says that it was the place where Hephestus resided. There's a shrine to him there and a cult still flourishes, so I'm told, though it operates in secret.'

'Why was Hephestus lame? Was he mutilated deliberately?'

'No,' Trdat replied. 'As far as I know, he was born lame, and he was ugly enough as well. But he was a magnificent metal-worker, the finest ever known. He could make anything. He even fashioned a metal net, which he hung over his bed when he suspected his wife of adultery with another God. He pretended to leave home, then crept back, and when his wife and her lover were in action, Hephestus dropped the net on them as they lay stark naked. Then he called the other Gods to visit him and have a laugh at their embarrassment. It's said to have happened over on that island, inside a burning mountain.'

'Strange,' I said. 'We also have the story of a lame metal-worker who took his revenge on his enemy. Though it was by murdering his sons and making drinking cups of their skulls and jewels from their eyes and teeth, which he presented to their unknowing parents.'

Trdat grimaced. 'Bloodthirsty lot, your Gods,' he said.

'I suppose so,' I replied. 'They could be cruel, but only when it was deserved. Like Loki, whom they punished for his endless deceit by tying him to a rock with the entrails of his own son. The earth shakes when Loki struggles to free himself. I saw Loki's statue in the Basilike.'

Trdat laughed out loud. 'That wasn't Loki or whatever you call him. I remember that statue. It used to be in the Forum of Constantine until someone needed the space and it was taken away and dumped in the Basilike. It's one of the earlier Gods – well, he was the son of what they called a Titan – by the name of Prometheus. He was a trickster who angered Zeus, the chief of the Gods, once too often. Zeus punished him by telling Hephestus to nail him to a rock. Then Zeus sent an eagle each day to eat Prometheus's liver, which grew again during the night. So he was in endless torment.'

'Sounds as if your old Gods were just as cruel as mine,' I said.

'Equally human, I would say,' was Trdat's response. 'Or perhaps inhuman, if you want to put it that way. Depends how you look at it.'

'Was I also mistaken in thinking that there's a marble panel in the Basilike which shows the Norns?'

'Never heard of them. Who are they?'

'The women who decide our destiny when we are born,' I said. 'They know the past, present and future, and they weave the pattern of our lives.'

'I can't remember seeing that panel, but you must be talking about the three Fates,' Trdat answered after a moment's thought. 'One spins the thread of a man's life, another measures it and the third cuts it. Norns or Fates, the message is the same.'

We reached our destination, the port of Joppa on the coast of Palestine, to find that the local governor knew nothing about our mission. For three days we sweltered in the summer heat, confined aboard the dromon while the governor checked with his superiors in the capital at Ramla if we could be allowed to land.

Finally Harald, rather than the easy-going Trdat, took command of the situation. He stormed ashore and I went with him to the governor's residence, where the anger of the towering northerner with his long moustaches and strange lopsided eyebrows cowed the governor into agreeing that a small advance party could go ahead to inspect the Anastasis while the majority of Trdat's technicians and workmen stayed behind. As we left the governor's office, we were surrounded by a clamouring crowd of elderly men, each offering to act as our guide. For years they had made their living by taking devout Christians up to see their holy places, but the prohibitions of Murad the Mad had destroyed their trade. Now they offered to hire us carts, tents, donkeys, and all at a special price. Brusquely Harald told me to inform them that he did not ride on carts and certainly not donkeys. The first person to come to the dockside with two dozen horses would be employed.

The horses that were brought were so small and scrawny that I thought for a moment Harald would take it as an insult. But their owner, as lean and malnourished-looking as his animals, assured me that the creatures were adequate to the task, and it was only two days' easy ride to our destination. Yet when Harald got into the saddle, his feet almost touched the ground on either side, and the other Varangians looked equally out of proportion to their mounts. So it was an undignified cavalcade that rode out of the town, crossed a narrow, waterless, coastal plain, and began to climb into the rocky hills of what our guide enthusiastically called the Promised Land.

I have to admit that I had expected something better. The landscape was bleached and bare with an occasional small field scratched out of the hillside. The few settlements were meagre clusters of small, square, mud-walled houses, and the inn where we stayed that night was crumbling and badly run-down. It offered only a dirty courtyard where we could stable the horses, a dreary meal of pea soup and flat bread, and flea-infested bed mats. Yet if we were to believe our guide, who was very garrulous and spoke Latin and Greek with equal ease, the sere brown land we were crossing was fortunate beyond all others. He reeled off lists of the holy men or miraculous events associated with each spot we passed, beginning with Joppa, on whose beach, he claimed, a great fish had vomited up a prophet.

When I translated this yarn to Harald and the Varangians they looked utterly incredulous.

'And the Christians revile us for believing that the Midgard serpent lies at the bottom of the World Ocean,' was Halldor's comment. 'Thorgils, don't waste your breath translating that old fool's prattle unless he says something believable.'

In mid-afternoon on the second day we rode across a ridge and there, spreading up the slope of the next hill, was our goal: the holy city of the Christians, known to them as Jerusalem. No larger than a single suburb of Constantinople, the place was totally enclosed within a high city wall studded with at least a dozen watchtowers. What caught our attention was a huge dome. It dominated the skyline of the city. Built on rising ground, it dwarfed the buildings all around it. Most astonishing of all, it appeared to be of solid gold.

'Is that the Anastasis, the place where the White Christ was buried?' I asked our guide.

He was taken aback at my ignorance. 'No,' he said. 'It is the Holy of Holies, sacred to the followers of Muhammad and those of the Jewish faith. The Anastasis is over there,' and he pointed to the right. I looked in that direction, but saw nothing except a nondescript jumble of roofs.

We rode through the city gate, crossed a large open forum with a tall column in its centre and proceeded along a colonnaded avenue which led to the area the guide had indicated. Our exotic appearance drew curious and sometimes hostile glances from the crowds. They were an amazing mix – Saracen officials in loose white gowns and turbans, merchants dressed in black cloaks and brick-coloured sandals, veiled women, half-naked urchins.

Midway along the avenue we came to a great gap in the line of buildings, and the guide announced, 'Here is the place.'

Trdat looked aghast. The space ahead of us was a scene of utter devastation. Massive building blocks, broken and dislodged, marked the lines of former walls. Heaps of smashed tiles were all that remained of roofs. Charred beams showed where the destruction had been hastened by fire. Everywhere was rubble and filth. Without a word, Trdat leaned down and picked up a small stone from among the weeds that were growing over the rubbish. Sadly he turned it over in his fingers. It was a single tessera, dark blue. It must once have graced a mosaic in the basilica that had sheltered worshippers who came to this spot. Of the church itself, nothing remained.

Our guide hitched up his loose gown and scrambled over the heaps of rubbish, beckoning us to follow. Harald and the others stayed behind. Even the hardened Norsemen were silenced by the sight of so much destruction.

I joined Trdat and the guide, just as the latter was saying, 'It was here,' as he pointed downward towards marks on the bare rock. To me it looked like the ragged scars left on Prokonnesos when the marbleworkers had prised away what they needed, only the marks of the chisels and pickaxes were random, and the spoil – the stone they had broken – was tossed to one side in a haphazard pile.

'What was here?' asked Trdat in a hushed voice.

'The tomb, the sepulchre itself. Murad's people hacked it to pieces.'

Trdat seemed numb with shock as the guide led us back through the lanes to find an inn where we could stay. The protomaistor said nothing for several hours, except to ask me to send word back to Joppa that the craftsmen waiting on the dromon should stay where they were. There was no point in them coming inland. The splendid buildings which had once stood around the Anastasis were utterly beyond repair.

'Thorgils, I never thought that I would face a challenge like this,' the architect confessed to me. 'The task is even more daunting than when my grandfather had to repair the Church of Holy Wisdom after the earthquake. At least he had something to work with. Here I have to start from scratch. I'm going to need your help.'

So it was that I, Thorgils, the devotee of Odinn, came to assist in the recreation of what our guide called the Holy Sepulchre. Partly my work was practical: I held the end of the tape as Trdat took the measurements of the area he had to work in, and I took down notes of the angles he measured. I helped him uncover the lines of the damaged walls, so that he could trace the ground plan of the earlier buildings and compare them with the architectural plans he had brought from the archives in Constantinople. I also made lists of the materials on site that might be reused – the surviving sections of columns, the larger building stones and so forth. But by far my most important contribution was assisting him in interviewing all those who had known the holy place before it was razed on the orders of Murad the Mad.

Our talkative guide was our primary source, but rumours of our enquiries spread throughout the city, and furtive figures appeared, followers of the White Christ, who were able to tell us what the shrine had looked like before its demolition. In the light of what those Christians told us, we cleared away some of the rubble and chalked out on the ground the dimensions of the tomb as they indicated. It had been a small, free-standing building, chiselled from the living rock, sheathed in marble and surmounted by a golden cross. The cave inside had been large enough for nine men to stand inside as they prayed, and at the back was the shelf on which the White Christ's body had been laid.

Trdat wanted measurements and practical details. He was told that the cave had been high enough for there to be a space of one and a half feet between the top of a man's head and the roof; the shelf was seven feet long; the entrance to the cave had faced east according to some, south according to others. Our informants told us that it had taken seven men to move the large rock rolled in front of the cave at the time of the Christ's burial, but that it had broken in half. Its two parts had been squared off and turned into altars, which had been set up within the great circular church that once covered the entire site. The man who told us that particular detail took us on a search through the rubble to see if we could find either altar, but without success.

Trdat was unperturbed. He drew a quick sketch of a squared-off stone, and showed it to the Christian. 'Is that how it looked?' he asked.

The man looked at the drawing. 'Yes, just like that,' he agreed readily.

Trdat gave me a quizzical glance and drew another altar stone, a slightly different shape this time. 'And the other one. Was it like this?'

'Oh yes, you have it perfectly,' his informant replied, so eager to please that he barely glanced at the drawing.

In our inn later that evening I asked Trdat if he really believed our informants.

He shrugged. 'It's not important if I do. People will believe what they want to. Of course I will do my best and try to reproduce the original details when I do the designs for a restoration. But as the years pass, I'm sure that those who are devout will come to believe that what they are seeing is the original, not my copy.'

All this time Harald and the other Varangians had been remarkably patient. They spent most of their hours in the inn, playing at dice, or they came to where Trdat and I were at work. The presence of these bearded warriors was useful as it kept onlookers at bay and discouraged those Saracens who shouted curses at us or threw stones. In the evenings Trdat sat at a table, ceaselessly drawing his plans or scratching out diagrams and calculations. Occasionally a Varangian might saunter over and peer over his shoulder at the work, then return to his place. But I was aware that their patience would not last for ever. I felt that without some sort of distraction, Harald and his men would want to leave.

It was our guide who proposed an excursion. He offered to show us the Christian sights in and around the city, then take us on a short trip to the nearby river, where, he said, the White Christ had undergone a ceremony of immersion. Trdat was at the stage when he was working on perspective drawings and wanted to be left alone in the inn in peace and quiet, so he readily agreed that Harald, Halldor and the others should take up the guide's suggestion, and that I should go as their interpreter.

To me that tour of the Holy Places was astonishing. There was hardly an item, a building or street corner that was not in some way associated with the White Christ or his followers. Here was Golgotha, where the White Christ was crucified, and our guide pointed to a bloodstain on the rock, which, if you were to believe him, had never been washed away. Nearby was a crack in the stone, and he assured us that if anyone put his ear to it he would hear running water, and that if an apple was dropped into the crack it would reappear in a pool outside the city wall a mile away. Eighty paces in that direction, so he claimed, was the very centre of the world. At that point rose four great underground rivers.

Next, with many backward glances to see that we were not being followed, he took us to a storeroom where he showed us a cup that the White Christ had blessed at his final meal, as well as a reed that apparently had been used to offer up a sponge of water to the Christ as he hung on the Cross, and the sponge itself, all withered and dry. The item of most interest to me was a rusty spear propped in a corner. According to our guide, it was the very lance that had been used to stab the Christ in the side as he hung on the Cross, and had been rescued from the Anastasis before Murad's men smashed up the place. I handled the spear – it seemed very well preserved to be so ancient – and I thought it strange that the followers of the White Christ would claim to find such relics, while we, the followers of the Elder Faith, never imagined we could possess the spear which pierced Odinn as he hung upon the tree of knowledge. For us, what belonged to the Gods was their own.

The catalogue of marvels outside the city walls was just as wide ranging. Here were the marks of the White Christ's knees as he knelt to pray, the stone receiving the impression as if it had been molten wax. There was the same fig tree from which a traitor by the name of Judas had hanged himself; earlier the guide had showed us the iron chain he had used for the suicide. On the Mount of Olives were more marks in the rock. This time they were footprints left behind when the White Christ was taken up to the place which was the equivalent of Valholl for his followers. Remembering my conversation with Pelagia back in Constantinople, I asked if I could see the cave where her namesake had lived, disguised as a eunuch. Without hesitation I was led to a small, dank grotto on the side of the mountain. I peered inside, but not for long. Someone had been using it as an animal pen. It smelled of goat.

The more I saw, the more baffled I became that the faith of the White Christ was so successful. Everything associated with it seemed so ordinary. I asked myself how people could believe in such obvious fictions as the suicide's fig tree, and I put the question to Harald, picking a moment when he seemed to be in good humour, because I wanted to know if he was susceptible to the White Christ's teaching.

He turned that great predatory look upon me, the sea eagle's stare, and said, 'Thorgils, you miss the point. It is not the physical things that matter: not the lance nor the sponge nor any of the other things we have been shown. The strength lies in the ideas the Christians preach. They offer hope to the ordinary people. That is their reward.'

'And for someone who is above the ordinary, my lord?' I ventured to ask.

Harald thought for a moment and then said, 'There is something there, too. Have you not noticed how obedient the Christians are to their one God. They talk about following him, and no other. That is what any ruler would want of his subjects.'

I was still thinking about Harold's reply as we collected our horses from the inn's stable and rode out of the city behind Cosmas, our guide. We left through the eastern gate, and Cosmas asked me to warn Harald and the others that some of the people we would meet along our road could prove unfriendly. The most hostile were Samaritans. They had a horror of unbelievers, whether Christian or Jew. If we wished to buy anything from a Samaritan we would have to place the coins in a bowl of water because they would receive nothing direct from our hands, considering us unclean. And after we left, they would burn straw over the hoof prints left by our horses to purify all traces of us.

I suspect that our guide was secretly pleased when, close to the river, we did encounter a group of them. The Samaritans

behaved exactly as predicted, blocking our path, spitting and
cursing, shaking their fists and working themselves into a frenzy
of hatred. Then they searched the roadside for stones which they
began to hurl at us, very accurately. At that stage Harald and the
Varangians were provoked into action. They spurred their small
horses into a canter and charged at their tormentors, smacking
them with the flat of their swords and scattering the shrieking
zealots, who fled up the hillside, surprised at such brisk treatment.

The countryside became even more desolate than before. After
crossing the plateau, our road descended through a steep-sided
gorge where the only building was a distant monastery clinging
to the rock face like a swallow's nest. A few monks still lived
there, our guide told us, because the semi-derelict building was so
difficult to access that the Saracens left it alone. Emerging from
the gorge we found ourselves riding through a wilderness of sand
and scrub completely devoid of people, except for a single party
of nomads who had set up their brown tents among the dunes.
They were burning thorn bushes for their campfire, and had
tethered their animals. I had previously seen such creatures in
the imperial menagerie – camels – and I wondered that these
beasts, which attracted so much attention in Constantinople, were
regarded here as no more unusual than an ass or donkey.

We camped on the outskirts of a ruined town. The place had
been completely levelled four years earlier by a great earthquake,
and the sight of the tumbled ruins prompted Cosmas to claim
that, long ago, its defences had similarly collapsed when an army
of besiegers had played trumpets and marched around the walls,
calling on their God to aid them.

'The din probably woke up Loki, and he squirmed in his
bonds,' muttered Halldor sarcastically. He was finding the guide's
stories more and more outrageous.

It was another disappointment when we reached the river
which we had been promised would be a marvel to behold. It was
no larger than the streams beside which I had played as a child
in Greenland. A muddy creek, it ran through reed beds, and the

water when we tasted it was gritty and unpleasant. Yet this was the river, the guide assured us, in which the White Christ had been immersed, affirming his faith. The guide showed us a set of stone steps leading down from the bank. Several of the steps were missing, others were unstable, and there was a half-rotten rope to serve as a handhold. The steps, he said, were where the faithful had come in former times to imitate the example of the White Christ.

As if on cue – indeed I suspected that Cosmas may have arranged it – a ragged priest of the White Christ appeared from a small shelter of reeds nearby. He offered to conduct just such a ceremony for a small fee, promising that anyone who did so would store up 'riches in heaven'. I translated his offer, and to my consternation Harald accepted. He removed his clothes, piled them on the river bank and, wearing only a loose gown, descended the steps and waded in. There Harald allowed the priest to splash water over him and chant a prayer. I was dismayed. Until that moment I was sure that I could sway Harald towards the Elder Faith.

Halldor saw my expression. 'Don't take it too seriously, Thorgils,' he said, 'When you've known Harald as long as I have, you'll understand that the only riches he is interested in are those on this earth. He will do anything that will help him gain them, even if it means taking a dip in a muddy river. Right now, he's probably thinking that the White Christ is fortunate to have him as a recruit.'

My consternation lasted all the way back to Aelia, as the Greeks called the Holy City, and it took Trdat's air of suppressed excitement to dispel my disappointment. The architect was positively quivering with happy anticipation.

'You can't guess what occurred in your absence, ' he said as he welcomed me. 'It's unheard of, at least since my grandfather's time.'

'What's unheard of? You look as though you've found a fortune,' I said.

'Better than that. While you were away, I went back to the site of the Anastasis to check some details on my drawings, and an elderly Saracen came over to see what I was doing. He was very distinguished looking and well dressed. Of course I showed him my work, made gestures trying to explain what I was doing, and so forth. It turned out that he spoke a few words of Armenian and enough Greek to tell me that he is one of the dignitaries responsible for the upkeep of the Holy of Holies, the Golden Dome. He has invited me to visit the place if I promise to be discreet. Can you imagine! No Christian has been allowed to look inside the Dome and see its wonders for years.'

'Don't talk to me about the wonders of local religion,' I said. 'I've been disappointed enough in the last few days.'

'Come on, Thorgils. This is an opportunity that won't come again. Of course you must accompany me to visit the Dome. My visit is scheduled for tomorrow.'

A servant collected us when the last echoes of the Saracens' prayer call had died away, and I had to admit a sense of excitement as Trdat and I, both wearing Saracen gowns, set off. Ahead of us the great shining Dome glowed in the early morning sunshine, seeming to float above the rooftops of the city. At an outer gate to the sacred area the servant asked us to change our footwear, providing us with slippers, then brought us across a broad platform paved with granite slabs to where Trdat's acquaintance was already waiting. Trdat introduced me as his architectural assistant and then, even before our host could speak, the proto-maistor had grabbed my arm and was blurting out 'the Tower of the Winds!' To my surprise he was not staring at the magnificent building soaring up ahead of us, but at a much smaller structure built beside it.

'That is the Dome of the Chain,' explained our host, whose name I gathered was Nasir. 'It's the model of the main building, made by the original architects. They produced it so that the caliph Abd-al-Malik, who ordered the construction, could approve the design before building began. Nowadays we use it for storing valuables.'

But Trdat was already out of earshot, hurrying towards the smaller structure.

'Thorgils, that eight-sided base on which the Dome rests,' he called over his shoulder, 'there was one in ancient Athens just like that. That's why my grandfather made me study the classic buildings, to learn from their skills. Just as the men who designed the Dome must have done. How I wish my grandfather could have seen this.'

Trdat circled the small building excitedly. 'Do you mind if I take some rough measurements?' he asked Nasir.

The Saracen hesitated for a moment, then said, 'I suppose it can't do any harm. It will not be allowed inside the Kubbat as-Sakhra, the Dome itself. There you can only take a quick look.'

Trdat walked around the Dome of the Chain, counting his paces. Then he measured its diameter by reckoning the number of paving slabs across its width.

'Brilliant,' he breathed admiringly as he stood back to judge its height. 'It's the geometry, Thorgils. The height of the eight-sided base is the same as its width, and the height of the Dome is the same again. The result: perfect proportion and harmony. Whoever designed the structure was a genius.'

'Two of them,' said Nasir. 'A local man from the city by the name of Yazid-ibn-Sallam, and a great scholar called Abdul-ibn-Hayah.'

Trdat was squatting down and drawing with his finger across a paving slab, attempting make an outline in the dust. 'I wish I had brought wax and stylus,' he said, 'but I think I know what we will find inside the main building.'

Nasir looked at the Armenian as if he was touched in the head. 'We should not be loitering here. Just a quick glance inside is all that is permitted,' he warned, escorting us to the Golden Dome.

To me it was like a triumph of the jeweller's art, a diadem. Swathes of glittering mosaics covered the outer sides of the octagon, while the cupola above it gleamed as if solid bullion.

'How do you keep the Dome so clean?' I asked.

'In winter, when there is snow or rain, we cover it with animal skins and felt.' Nasir replied. 'The caliph had not intended that the Dome should be gilded, but the work went so well and so swiftly – it took just four years to build – that a hundred thousand gold dinars were left over from the money allocated to the architects. It was decided to melt down the coins and use them to cover the Dome in gold leaf.'

We had reached the entrance to the building, and he held up his arm to prevent us going any further, but we were close enough to see inside. At the centre, right beneath the Dome, was a honey-coloured area of bare rock which, Nasir explained, was the spot from which their prophet ascended to a Seventh Heaven. This Holy of Holies was surrounded by a circuit of marble columns which supported the great vault soaring overhead. Looking upward into the bowl of the Dome, I gasped in astonishment. Its interior was covered with gold mosaic work, and from the very centre dangled a chain on which was suspended a gigantic chandelier. The light from hundreds upon hundreds of lamps reflected and glittered off the golden surface.

'Now breathe deeply,' Nasir advised us. The air was heavy with the smell of saffron, ambergris and attar of roses. 'That's my task,' said our host proudly. 'I supervise the preparation of the perfumes which the attendants sprinkle on the sacred rock and burn in the censers. But it is time we left.'

'Double squares,' mused Trdat thoughtfully as we walked back to the inn. 'Just as I thought. That is what I was trying to work out when I was scratching in the dust. The interior of the building is based on a design of two sets of squares interlocking. The inner ones determine the circumference of the Dome itself, the outer ones provide the dimensions for the octagon. Best of all, I now know the size and shape of the dome which I will propose for the shape of the new basilica at Golgotha. I will model it on what I saw today, placing twelve pillars below, one for each of the apostles. I have all the information I need to work up my designs for the restoration of the Anastasis and the buildings around it. It is time we returned to Constantinople.'

Harald and the Varangians, when I told them the news, looked very pleased.

'Is the great Dome really solid gold?' Halldor asked.

'No, it's a hundred thousand dinars turned into gold leaf,' I answered.

'Who would have so much money to spare?' he marvelled.

'Saracen rulers are prepared to pay enormous sums for what they hold most dear,' I said casually, not realising that my comment would help Harald achieve his life's ambition – the throne of Norway.

FIVE

THE DROMON PICKED up her moorings in Bucephalon harbour after a frustrating homeward voyage. Headwinds meant that our passage back to Constantinople took much longer than anticipated, and already there was a wintry feel to the city when I said goodbye to Trdat, then accompanied Harald, Halldor and the others to the barracks of the Varangians-without-the-Walls.

We arrived in time to intervene in an angry confrontation between the Norsemen of Harald's war band and a senior Greek staff officer. The professional army, the tagmata, was soon to deploy to Italy for a campaign in the west, and the Armamenton, the imperial arsenal, had been working at full stretch to prepare weapons and supplies. Now the clerks who issued horses and weapons to the soldiers had drawn up a timetable for the troops to collect their requirements. Harald's five hundred Varangians were flatly refusing to re-equip with standard weaponry, preferring to retain their own axes and shields. Harald curtly informed the Greek staff officer that his men were a special force, recruited under his personal command, and he took instructions only from the palace or direct from the army commander, the strategos. The Greek glared at the Norwegian and snapped, 'So be it. You will find that the new strategos expects instant obedience, especially from barbarians.' Then he stalked off, seething with indignation.

'Why all this fuss about our weapons?' Halldor asked me. 'Why wouldn't they be good enough for the Greeks?'

'They are fiercely proud of their history,' I told him, 'They've been running an empire for seven hundred years and so feel they've learned how to organise things properly, whether a tax system or a military campaign. They like to do everything by the book – quite literally. During my time in the Palace Guard, our young Greek officers would arrive with their heads stuffed full of military information. They'd learned it by reading army manuals written by retired generals. Much of the advice was very helpful – how to load pack mules or scout an enemy position, for instance – but the trouble was that it was all book-learned, not practical.'

'Fighting is fighting,' grumbled Halldor. 'You don't have to read books to learn how to do it. Practising how to form up in a battle line or how to use a battle axe left-handed, that sort of thing helps. But in the end it is valour and strength that win the day.'

'Not as far as the imperial army is concerned,' I countered. 'They call themselves "Rhomai", the Romans, because their military tradition goes back to the Caesars and they've been fighting on the frontiers of empire for centuries, often against huge odds. They've won most of their battles through superior generalship or because they are better equipped or better organised or . . .' and here I thought about the scheming Orphanotrophus . . . 'because they've been able to bribe the opposing generals or create some sort of disarray in the enemy ranks with rumours and plots.'

'Too clever by half,' muttered Halldor. 'No wonder they have to hire foreigners to protect the emperor himself. They're so busy scheming that it's become a habit and they forget who their real enemies are. They finish up by stabbing one another in the back, and no longer trust their own people.'

Harald, who had been listening to us, said nothing. Maybe he already knew what I was talking about, though years later I was to remember that conversation with Halldor and wonder if, once again, I had helped to shape the course of Harald's life. If so, then I was an unwitting agent, if not of Odinn, then of the Norns, or – as Trdat would have said – the Fates.

Leaving Harald and his men at the barracks, I lost no time in going to visit Pelagia, for I had been missing her while I was away in the Holy Land. Until now we had been friends, not lovers, but I was coming to sense that if our relationship continued to develop she might soon mean more to me than agreeable companionship and wise advice. Hoping to find her at home, I felt a pang of disappointment to discover that she was no longer living at her old address. I was redirected to a luxurious apartment in a more fashionable part of the city. When I complimented her on the move as well as the expensive furnishings of her new home, she was typically down-to-earth in her response.

'I have the coming war to thank,' she said. 'It's amazing how much money can be made from army contracts. It's such a relief not having to chase creditors in private commerce. The government always pays up, provided you grease a few palms in the commissariat.'

'Surely the army can't be buying its bread already,' I said. 'I know that army bread is rock hard and stale, but the campaign is several months away. Nothing's going to happen until spring, and by then the army will be in Italy and will be able to obtain bread locally.'

'I'm not selling them bread,' said Pelagia. 'I've got the contract to supply them with emergency rations, the sort you use on a forced march. The department of the new strategos asked for tenders, and I located someone who could supply sea onions at a good price. It was simple enough for me to assemble the other ingredients.'

'What on earth's a sea onion?' I asked.

'A plant like a giant onion. The bulb can be the size of a man's head. It's boiled, washed in water, dried and then sliced very thin. The army contract stipulated that one part of sesame was to be added to five parts onion, and one part poppy seed to fifteen parts onion, the whole lot crushed and kneaded together with honey. Nothing that a competent baker can't organise easily.'

'What's it taste like?' I asked.

Pelagia grimaced. 'Pretty foul. But then it is only eaten in emergencies. The soldiers are issued with two olive-sized pills of it per day. The stuff is claimed to be sweet and filling, and doesn't make a man thirsty. Just the sort of thing which the new strategos would want for his troops. He's a stickler for detail.'

'That's the second time I've heard about this new strategos,' I said. 'Everyone seems to be in awe of him.'

'So they should be. Comes from somewhere on the eastern frontier where he used to be just a local town commander. He made a reputation for himself by wiping out a raiding column of Saracens when the imperial army was very low on morale. The Saracens laid siege to his town and demanded its surrender. He pretended to be scared and promised to hand over the place next morning without a fight, even sent supplies to the Saracens to show his good intentions. But he deliberately included plenty of wine in the shipment and the Saracens got themselves drunk. That night the city defenders rushed the Saracen camp and killed every one of them. He presented himself in front of the Basileus with a sack out of which he tipped a torrent of Saracen ears and noses. The emperor promoted him to corps commander on the spot. Since then he's never lost a battle. He's a brilliant tactician, and his troops would follow him anywhere.'

'He sounds very like Harald.' I said, 'Is this military paragon going to command the campaign in Italy?'

'Only the land forces,' said Pelagia. 'My sister, who's still got her job in the women's quarters at the palace, tells me that the naval contingent will be commanded by John's brother-in-law, Stephen. It's the usual set-up. The palace doesn't trust anyone enough to give them sole command, so they divide the leadership.'

'And what's the name of this general who'll command the land forces?'

'George Maniakes,' she told me.

RATHER TO MY surprise I heard nothing from the Orphanotrophus directly. I had been expecting a summons to his office to report on Harald's conduct in the Holy Land, but as my guardsman's salary continued to be paid – and I arranged for Pelagia to receive and hold the money – I presumed that I was to carry on the duties the Orphanotrophus had given me. Doubtless he had more important matters to occupy him, because the Basileus's health was showing no signs of improvement despite a frenzy of pious work. More and more of the civil administration had passed into the hands of the man the public referred to as John the Eunuch.

'You want to be even more cautious than before if you are called to his office,' Pelagia warned. 'The strain is telling on John. To relax, he organises debauches at which he and his friends get blind drunk and conduct bestial acts. But next morning his friends regret what they have done and said. The Orphanotrophus calls them in to explain any loose talk they have uttered the previous night. It's yet another of his methods of exercising control.'

'What does his brother, the Basileus, think of this behaviour?' I asked. 'I thought he was very religious.'

'More and more so. Besides sending Trdat to the Holy Sepulchre, Michael is lavishing money on monasteries and nunneries all over Constantinople. He's spending a huge sum on a church dedicated to St Cosmas and St Damian over on the east side of the city. The place is being remodelled. It's being given new chapels, an adjacent monastery, finest marble for the floors, walls covered with frescoes. You should go and see it some time. The Basileus hopes that his donations will result in his own cure because Cosmas and Damian were both physicians before they were martyred. They're known as the Anargyroi, "the Unpaid", because they never accepted any money for what they did, unlike some physicians in this city that I could think of. That's not all. The Basileus is paying for a new city hospice for beggars, and he's come up with a scheme to save all the prostitutes in the capital. He's having a splendid new nunnery built, and the public criers are circulating in the streets announcing that when the building is ready, any harlot who agrees to go and live there as a nun will be accepted. Doubtless the place will be dedicated to St Pelagia.'

The exodus of the tagmata began the week after we, the Old Believers in Harald's war band, celebrated our Jol feast, and the Christians observed the Nativity of their God. Watching the orderly departure of the troops, I had to admit that I was impressed by the efficiency of the army's organisation. First to leave the capital were the heavy weapons units, because they would move the slowest. Their petrobolla for firing rocks, the long-range arrow launchers and the cheiroballistra shaped like giant crossbows were dismantled and then loaded on to carts which ground their way out of the western gate of the city. From there they began the long overland plod to Dyrrachium, where they would be put on transports and ferried to Italy. When the column was halfway along the road, the army signallers flashed back the news along a chain of signal stations and the army despatchers released the light infantry battalions, the slingers and the archers to follow. Everything was tidy and methodical. The regiments of archers were accompanied by squads of sagittopoio, experts in repairing their bows, while the infantry had platoons of armourers who could mend or replace iron weapons. The squadron of Fire operators marched with a dedicated cavalry troop whose task was to protect the munitions wagons loaded with the mysterious ingredients for their secret weapon. Naturally each brigade also had its own field kitchen, and somewhere in the middle of the column was a team of army doctors with chests of surgical instruments and drugs.

The heavy infantry and the armoured cavalry were the last to

leave. For their departure the Basileus himself attended the
ceremony. It was a brilliant spectacle. The four palace regiments
collected their battle standards from the church of St Stephen and
the church of the Lord after the flags had been blessed by the
priests, then formed up to march along the Triumphal Way. In
front of them rode the heavy cavalry, coloured pennants fluttering
from the tips of their lances. Each trooper wore a padded surcoat
of heavy felt over his armour, and his horse was similarly
protected with a jacket of stiffened leather and a mail breastplate.
They looked formidable. Finally came my old regiment, the
Palace Guard, on foot and surrounding the Basileus on his
charger. They would proceed only as far as the Golden Gate,
where the emperor would say farewell to his troops, then the
Palace Guard would return with the Basileus to the Palace to
carry on their duties.

Michael himself looked sickly, his face grey with fatigue and
strangely bloated. I was reminded of the appearance of his predecessor, the murdered Romanus, at his funeral, which was the
last occasion on which the Guard had marched along the Triumphal Way. Then there had been near silence. Now, as the imperial
army set out for war, there was music. For the only time in my
life I heard an orchestra on the march – drums, pipes and lyres –
even as I wondered if I was seeing history repeat itself, and
Basileus Michael was being slowly poisoned in some sort of
labyrinthine court intrigue.

I left for Italy by sea a week later with Harald and his war
band. Once again Harald's Norsemen had been assigned to serve
as marines, perhaps because they had won fame for their actions
against the pirates, but also as a reprimand for their Norse
obstinacy about conforming to the army rule book. The result
was that for the next two years we were given only a peripheral
role in the campaign to regain a former jewel of the empire – the
great island of Sicily.

Our enemy were Saracens from North Africa. For more than
a century they had ruled the island after overrunning the Greek

garrison. They had established a thriving capital at Palermo, and from their Sicilian bases they raided the empire's province of southern Italy and, of course, their ships menaced the sea lanes. Now the Basileus was determined to drive back the Saracens and restore Sicily to his dominions. George Maniakes, promoted to the rank of autokrator, was the man to do it.

He began with an invasion across the straits at Messina. Harald's war band was there to protect the southern flank of the landing, so I was a witness to the expertise of the imperial troops. The light cavalry had been rehearsing for weeks, and the attack went flawlessly. They arrived off the landing beach soon after dawn in specially built barges. Ahead of them three shallow-draught dromons, packed with archers, cruised up and down the shallows, forcing back the Saracen cavalry which had assembled to deny the landing. When the imperial landing craft touched land, the sailors lowered the sides of their barges, and the light cavalry, already mounted, clattered down the ramps. They splashed through the shallows, formed up and charged up the beach. The Saracens turned and fled. For the next ten days a steady stream of transports, barges and warships shuttled back and forth across the straits, bringing more troops and supplies, and very soon an imperial army of ten thousand men stood on Sicilian soil.

Maniakes himself crossed over on the fourth day. It was a measure of his professionalism that he saw no need to indulge in heroics by leading the attack. He and his general staff went ashore only when his command headquarters had been set up, ready to receive him. It was there, when he called a war council of his senior officers, that I first laid eyes on him.

There are times, I believe, when the Gods play tricks on us. For their amusement they create situations which otherwise would seem to be impossible. Trdat had told me that the ancient Gods of the Greeks did the same, and relished the results. The meeting between Harald of Norway and George Maniakes was one of those moments which we ordinary humans describe as coincidences, but I believe are mischievously arranged by the Gods.

How else, I ask myself, could two men so similar have been brought together, yet each man be so unusual that he was unique. Harald, as I have described, was a giant, half a head taller than his colleagues, arrogant, fierce and predatory. He struck fear into those who aroused his anger, and was a natural leader. George Maniakes was identical. He too was enormously tall, almost an ogre with his massive frame, a huge voice, and a scowl that made men tremble. He also radiated absolute authority and dominated his surroundings. When the two men came face to face for the first time in the imperial command tent, it was as if no one else was in the room. They loomed over everyone else. Neither man could have imagined he would ever meet someone so like himself, though one was blond and the other dark. There was a long moment of surprise, followed by a pause of calculation as the two men took the measure of one another. Everyone saw it. We sensed that they made a temporary truce. It was like watching two great stags who encounter one another in the forest, stop and stare, and then cautiously pass one another by, neither challenging the other, yet neither giving ground.

Harald's war band, it was confirmed at the council, was to patrol the Sicilian coast and make diversionary attacks on Saracen settlements. Our task was to discourage the local Saracen commanders from sending reinforcements to their emir, who could be expected to mass his forces near Palermo and come westward, hoping to drive the imperial army back into the sea. To meet that attack, Maniakes and the tagmata would march inland and seize the highway which linked Palermo with the wealthy cities of the east coast. Once the highway was under imperial control, Maniakes would turn south and march on Catania, Augusta and the greatest prize: Syracuse.

The Gods arranged another coincidence that day which, in its way, was a foretaste of what was to come for me and for Harald. Harald, Halldor and I were leaving the council tent when we saw four or five men coming towards us on foot. From a distance they looked like Norsemen. Indeed at first we thought they must be

Varangians; they certainly seemed to be Varangian in size and manner. We took them to be volunteers who had recently arrived from Kiev or from the lands of the Rus. It was as they drew closer that we saw differences. For one thing they were clean-shaven, which was unusual. For another their weapons and armour were not quite what we ourselves would have chosen. They carried long swords rather than axes, and though their conical helmets were very like our own, their chain-mail shirts were longer, and the skirt of the mail was split in the middle. It took a moment to understand that these warriors were dressed for fighting from horseback, not from ships. Our two groups stared at one another in puzzlement.

'Greetings! To which company do you belong?' Halldor called out in Norse.

The strangers stopped and eyed us. Clearly they had not understood Halldor's question. One of them answered in a language which, by its tone and inflection, I recognised. Yet the accent was so strong that I had difficulty in understanding. Several words were familiar, though the meaning of the sentence was confused. I summoned up the Latin that I had learned as a lad in an Irish monastery and repeated Halldor's question. This time one of the strangers understood.

'We ride with Hervé,' he said in slow Latin. 'And you?'

'Our commander is Harald of Norway. We have taken service in the army of the Basileus.'

'We also serve the Basileus,' the warrior replied. 'They call us Frankoi.'

Then I knew. The men were mercenaries from Francia, but not from the central kingdom. They were speaking the Frankish tongue with the accent of the north. They were descendants of Vikings who had settled the lands of Normannia generations earlier, and that was why they looked so familiar to us. I had heard rumours about their prowess as horse warriors, and how they sold their swords to the highest bidder. While we Varangians arrived by sea and along the rivers, the Frankoi came overland, also seeking their fortunes in the service of the emperor. There was, however, a major difference between us: Varangians wanted to return home once we were rich; the men of Normannia – or Normandy, as they themselves called it – preferred to settle in the lands they conquered.

Maniakes took the Frankoi mercenaries with him when he marched inland, and they lived up to their warlike reputation when Maniakes rebuffed the emir's forces in their counter-attack. Then the autokrator began his long, grinding campaign to regain the east Sicilian cities. The tagmata steadily advanced along the coast, laying siege to one city after another, patiently waiting for them to fall before moving on. Maniakes took no risks, and Harald and his war band grew more and more frustrated. His Norsemen had enrolled in the army of the Basileus hoping for more than their annual pay of nine nomisma: they wanted plunder. But there was little to be had, and, worse, Harald's men received a lesser share when the army's accountants divided up the booty because the Norsemen were regarded as belonging to the fleet under Stephen, the brother-in-law of the Orphantrophus, and not part of Maniakes's main force. By the second spring of the campaign, Harald and his Varangians were very restless.

By then we were besieging Syracuse. The city fortifications were immensely strong, and the garrison was numerous and ably led. Harald's squadron of a dozen light galleys had the task of occupying the great harbour so that no more supplies reached the defenders from the sea, nor could messengers slip out to summon help. From the decks of our vessels we heard the clamour of the war trumpets as Maniakes manoeuvred his battalions on the landward side, and we saw boulders and fire arrows lobbed over the defences and into the city. We even glimpsed the top of a siege tower as it was inched forward. But the walls of Syracuse had withstood attacks for more than a thousand years, and we doubted that Maniakes would succeed in capturing such a powerful except after many months of siege.

An engineer visited our flotilla. He was rowed out in a small boat and came aboard Harald's vessel. As usual I was summoned to act as interpreter, and when the engineer scrambled up the side of our ship, I thought there was something familiar about the man.

'May I introduce myself,' he said. 'My name is Nikephorus, and I am with the army technites, the engineers. I'm a siege specialist and, with your permission, I would like to investigate the possibility of building a floating siege tower.'

'What does that involve?' I asked.

'I'd like to see if we could perhaps tie up two, or maybe three, of your galleys side by side to make a raft. We would then use the raft as a base on which to build a tower which could then be floated up against the city wall.'

I translated his request to Harald, and he gave his agreement. The engineer produced a wax tablet and began making his drawings and calculations, and then I knew whom he reminded me of.

'Do you know Trdat, the protomaistor, by any chance?'

The engineer gave a broad smile and nodded. 'All my life,' he said. 'In fact we are first cousins, and both of us were students together. He studied how to build things up, I learned how to knock them down.'

'I went with Trdat to the Holy Land,' I said.

'Ah, you must be Thorgils. Trdat called you "the educated Varangian". He spoke to me about you several times. I'm delighted to make your acquaintance. We should talk some more after I've finished my arithmetic.'

In the end Nikephorus calculated that the width and stability of the makeshift raft would not be sufficient for a floating siege tower. He feared the structure would capsize.

'A pity,' he said, 'I would love to have designed something novel and to have followed in the footsteps of the great Syracusan master.'

'Who's that?' I asked.

'Archimedes the great engineer and technician, of course. He created machines and devices to protect Syracuse when the Romans were attacking. Cranes lifted their ships out of the water and dashed them to pieces, weights plunged on to their decks and sank them, and even some sort of focusing mirror, like our signal mirrors, set them ablaze. To no avail, for he lost his life when the city fell. But Archimedes is a hero to anyone who studies siege craft and the application of science to fortifications, their assault and defence.'

'I had no idea that there was so much theory to your work.'

'If you've got time,' Nikephorus suggested, 'I'll show you just how much theory there is. If your commander can spare you for a few days, you could join me on the landward side of the city, and see how the army engineers function.'

Harald agreed to let me go, and for the next few days I was privileged to see Nikephorus in action. It turned out that he had been very modest about his qualifications. He was in fact the army's chief engineer and responsible for the creation and employment of all the heavy equipment against the walls of Syracuse.

'Note how those drills are angled slightly upward. It improves the final result,' he said as he showed me around a device like a very strong wooden shed on wheels. Inside were various cogs and pulleys connected to the sort of tool that ship carpenters use for drilling holes, only the instrument was far larger. 'The shed is pushed up against the base of the city wall, where the roof protects the operators from whatever missiles and unpleasantness the defenders drop down on them. The drill opens up holes in the city wall which are then stuffed with inflammable matter and set on fire. By quenching the hot rock – urine is the most effective liquid – the stone can be made to crack. If enough holes are drilled and enough fissures result, the wall will eventually collapse.'

'Wouldn't it be safer and easier to dig a tunnel under the wall foundations so it comes down?' I asked.

Nikephorus nodded. 'Trdat was right. You should have been an engineer. Yes, if the army technites were to have a motto, it should be "Dig, prop and burn". Excavate the tunnel under the wall, put in wooden props to hold everything in place, and just before you pull out, set fire to the props and then wait for the wall to tumble down. The trouble is that tunnelling takes time, and often the enemy digs counter-tunnels to ambush your miners, then kills them like rats in a drain.'

'Is that why you preferred to build a siege tower?' I asked. 'We saw the top of it from our ships. And heard the war trumpets.'

Nikephorus shook his head. 'That was just a ruse. That particular tower was a flimsy contraption, only for show. At the start of a siege, it's a good idea to create as much commotion as you can. Make it appear that you have more troops than is the case, launch fake attacks, allow the enemy as little rest as possible. That way you dishearten the defenders and, more important, you get to see how they respond to each feint, how well organised they are, which are the strong points in their defences, and which are the gaps.'

He then took me to see the proper siege tower he was building. The structure was already massive. Eventually it would be higher than the city walls, Nikephorus explained, and when the dropbridge on the topmost level was released, it would provide a gangway for the shock troops to rush across directly on to the battlements. 'Just the job for your axe-wielding Varangians,' he added with a grin, 'but it will be several weeks before the tower is ready. As you can see, we've only got as far as putting together the main framework of the structure. We still have to install the intermediate floor, where I intend to place a platoon of Fire throwers, and the exterior will need cladding with fresh ox hides. The Saracens are accomplished in countermeasures, and I expect they will try to set the tower alight with missiles of burning pitch or oil as we approach the wall. I'm designing a system of pipes and ducts to be fitted to the tower, so that if any portion catches alight, my men stationed on the topmost level with tubs of water will be able to direct the flow of water to extinguish the flames.'

'Won't that make the tower very heavy to move?' I objected.

'Yes, that's always a problem,' Nikephorus admitted. 'But with levers and enough manpower we should be able to roll the tower slowly forward. My main concern is that the Saracens will already have prepared the ground so that the tower topples before it is in place.'

We had clambered up a series of builders' ladders and were now standing precariously on the siege tower's highest cross-beam.

'See over there?' said Nikephorus pointing. 'That smooth, level approach to the city wall? It looks like the perfect spot for the tower when we launch our attack. But I am suspicious. It's too inviting. I think the defence has buried large clay pots deep in the soil at that point. The ground is firm enough to carry foot soldiers and cavalry, but if the tower rolls over them, the amphorae will collapse and the ground cave in. Then the tower will tilt and fall, and, in addition to the loss of life, we will have wasted weeks of work.'

But the Saracens did not wait for the operation of their sunken trap, if there ever was one. Even as Nikephorus and I stood on the half-built siege tower looking down on the suspect ground, a trumpet sounded the alarm. A sharp-eyed sentry had noticed the bronze gates of Syracuse were beginning to swing open. Moments later the gap was wide enough for a troop of Saracen cavalry to ride out. There were at least forty of them, and they must have hoped to catch the imperial troops by surprise with their sudden sortie. As they charged, they nearly succeeded.

There were more trumpet calls, each one more urgent, from the tagmata's lines. We heard shouts and orders from below us, and a squad of Greek heavy infantry came running towards the base of the tower. They were menaulatos, pikemen with long weapons specially designed to fend off a cavalry attack, and they must have been on standby for just such an emergency. They formed up around the base of the tower and lowered their pikes to make a defensive hedge, for it was now clear that the siege tower was the target of the Saracen sortie.

The raiders were led by a flamboyant figure. He wore a cloak of green and white patterns over his chain mail, and a scarf of the same colour wrapped around his helmet streamed out behind him as he galloped forward. The quality of his horse, a bay stallion, carried him well clear of his men, and he was shouting encouragement at them to follow him. Even the disciplined pikemen wavered in the face of such confidence. The rider swerved into a gap between the pikes. With a deft double swing of his scimitar, first forehand and then with a backward stroke, he hacked down two of our men before his horse spun round nimbly and carried him clear.

Seeing that the siege tower was now protected, the main raiding party changed the direction of their attack and rode towards the infantry lines, where lightly armoured troops were emerging from their tents, hastily pulling on their corselets and caps. The Saracens managed to get in among their victims long enough for them to cut down a dozen or so men before wheeling about and beginning to fall back towards the city gates.

Their entire sortie had been very quick. There had been no time for the imperial cavalry to respond, with the exception of just one man. As the Saracens were about to slip back through the city gates, a lone rider came out from the tagmata's lines. He was wearing mail and a helmet, and was mounted on a very ordinary horse which, even at a full gallop, would never have caught up with the retreating Saracens. He yelled defiance, and the green-clad leader must have heard his shout, for just as he was about to ride back in through the city gates, he glanced over his shoulder and turned his stallion. The Saracen then waited, motionless, facing his challenger. When he judged the distance to be right, he spurred his mount and the animal sprang forward.

Horse and rider were superb. The Saracen wore a small round shield on his left arm, and held his scimitar in his right hand.

Scorning the use of reins, he guided his mount with his knees and raced towards his opponent. At the last moment he bent forward in his saddle and leaned his body slightly to one side. The stallion responded by changing stride and flashed past the other horse, surprising the animal so that it checked and almost unseated its rider. At the same moment the Saracen slashed out with his scimitar at his enemy. Only by chance was the blow blocked by the long shield his opponent carried.

Belatedly I had made out that the Saracen's challenger was one of the Frankoi mercenaries. He appeared cumbersome and ungainly on his horse, and his weapon was a long iron sword instead of the heavy mace that an imperial cavalryman would have carried. Hardly had the Saracen ridden past his opponent than his agile stallion turned tightly and a moment later was galloping past the Frank, this time on the opposite side. Again the scimitar swept through the air, and it was all the Frank could do to raise his sword in time to deflect the blow.

By now the walls of Syracuse were lined with cheering spectators observing the unequal contest, while below them the troops of the tagmata stood watching and waiting for its inevitable outcome. The Saracen relished the audience. He played with the Frankish rider, galloping in, swerving, feinting with his scimitar, racing past, turning and coming again at a gallop. The heavily built Frank no longer attempted to urge his horse into action. All he could do was tug on the reins and try to turn his horse so that he faced the next attack.

Finally, it seemed that the Saracen had had enough of his amusement, and, riding a little further off than normal, he wheeled about and with a halloo of triumph came racing down on his victim. The scimitar was poised, ready to slice, when the Frank abruptly leaned back over the crupper of his horse. The Saracen's blow whipped through empty air, and at that moment the Frank swung his heavy sword. It was an ugly, inelegant blow. Delivered flat, and from a man almost lying on his horse's rump, it was an awkward scything motion requiring enormous strength of the arm. The long blade swept over the ears of the racing stallion and struck its rider full in the midriff, almost chopping the Saracen in half. The green and white striped cloak wrapped around the blade, the Saracen doubled forward even as he was swept out of the saddle by the force of the blow, and his corpse crashed to the ground and lay still. The helmet with its green and white scarf rolled off across the level ground.

For one moment there was a stunned silence, and then a great shout rose from the imperial lines. The stallion, puzzled by the sudden disappearance of his rider, whickered and turned to where his master's corpse lay, nuzzled the body for a moment, then trotted quietly back to the city gate, which was opened to let the creature in. The Frank ponderously rode back to the tagmata without a word or gesture.

He earned the name Iron Arm, Fer de Bras in his Frankish tongue, for his achievement. His adversary, we later learned, was a caid or nobleman of Syracuse. His defeat in single combat severely affected the morale of the city's defenders, while, on our side, the rank and file of the Greek army regarded the burly and taciturn mercenaries from Normannia with increased respect.

SIX

MANIAKES'S TROOPS HAD little time to celebrate. Word reached us that the Saracens were massing in the interior of Sicily, ready to march on Syracuse and relieve the siege. Their new army was commanded by another emir, and he was dangerous. Abdallah, son of the ruler of Kairouan on the Libyan coast, had brought several thousand seasoned warriors across the Great Sea, and our spies estimated that his force would soon increase to more than twenty thousand men, as more recruits were arriving every day.

Maniakes reacted with typical decisiveness. He ordered the tagmata to prepare to march, but not strike camp. Each unit was to leave behind a few men who would give the impression that the siege was still in place. They were to remain as visible as possible, keep the cooking fires burning, mount patrols and follow the normal routines. At the same time the engineers and heavy weapons units were to discourage further sorties from the city by keeping up a regular discharge of missiles, and the Frankish mercenaries from Normannia were to stay behind in case of emergencies. Our harbour flotilla was stripped of men. Skeleton crews, changing from one vessel to the next, would make it look as if the blockade was still operative. Harald gave command of this minimal force to Halldor, and then he and I, with about two

hundred fellow Varangians, joined the flying column that Maniakes led inland, leaving quietly by night.

A week of forced marches across a dry and dusty landscape
brought us to the west of a mountain whose subterranean fires
reminded me of my days in Iceland, where the Gods in anger
similarly cause hot rock to flow. Here the emir had established
and fortified his base camp. He must have had warning of our
approach, because when the tagmata arrived, the Saracens had
already withdrawn within their defences and shut the gates.

Abdallah had chosen his position well. Behind the emir's
camp, and on both sides, was broken terrain unsuitable for any
direct assault against the fortifications. In front, open ground led
down to a small stream shallow enough to be crossed on foot. On
the opposite bank the land rose gently upward again to the low
ridge where Maniakes set up his own headquarters, facing across
to the Saracens. And here I watched how Maniakes's military
genius turned Abdallah's apparent advantage against him.

Nikephorus explained to me what was going on. I had been
perplexed to find the engineer included in the flying column
because his heavy equipment was much too ponderous to be
brought along. When I said as much, Nikephorus had grinned at
me and said cheerfully, 'We'll find something on the spot to make
up what is needed.' Now, as I waited near Maniakes's command
post, I saw the engineer busy by a table and went over to see
what he was doing. He had prepared a model of Abdallah's camp
and its surrounding terrain set in a bed of soft clay.

'Hello, Thorgils,' he greeted me. 'As you can see, I don't
always knock things down. I can also build them, but usually in
miniature. This is where the strategos will fight his battle.'

'You and Trdat are just the same,' I said. 'In the Holy Land
Trdat spent more time examining a model of the Golden Dome
than looking at the real thing.'

'No, no, I mean it. Victory on the battlefield often depends on
observation and timing, particularly when the enemy is so obliging
as to shut himself up and let us take the initiative. See these little

coloured markers? They represent the tagmata's forces. The grey
markers are light infantry, orange for the archers and slingers,
yellow for the heavy infantry, and red for the kataphractos, our
armoured cavalry. Note that I've placed half of the red markers
in that dip behind this ridge where they're out of sight of the
Saracen lookouts. Later I'll add markers for the Saracen forces
when I know more about them.'

'How's that possible? The Saracen forces are hidden behind
their defences.'

Nikephorus winked at me. 'Not for long. That's just a wooden
palisade, not a high city wall. Look behind you.'

I turned round to see an extraordinary structure rising from
the ground. It was like the mast of a ship, but far, far taller than
any I could have imagined. It was being hauled upright by a
complex web of ropes and angled poles. 'It's a bit makeshift,'
admitted Nikephorus, 'You can see the joints where my men have
had to lash the sections together. But it will do. Think of it as a
giant fishing rod, and that we're fishing for information.'

'What do you call it?' I asked.

'A spy pole,' he said, 'and that's only the lower section. We'll
hoist an upper section later, and then steady it with guy ropes of
twisted horsehair. There'll be a pulley at the top, and we'll use it
to haul our observer into position. He'll not be the heaviest man
in the army, of course. But he'll know his signal book, and after
he's had a good look over into the Saracen camp, he'll signal
down the information. Our scouts have already told us that
Abdallah is expecting a frontal attack. His men have sewn the
ground in front of their main gate with spikes, intending to lame
our cavalry. They know that the kataphract is our main weapon.'

We spent the next four days waiting in front of the Saracen
camp while Nikephorus and his assistants added to the coloured
markers on the sand table according to the information from the
lookouts. Each time they did so, Maniakes and his staff would
come across to review their own tactics. They shifted the markers
back and forth, discussed various possible manoeuvres, and heard

additional reports from the scouts. Twice a day the officers of the tagmata were told the latest assessment of the enemy strength, and as I watched them cluster around the table I soon differentiated between them. Infantry men wore knee-length quilted cotton coats and greaves of iron to protect their shins, while the cavalry dressed in chain-mail body armour or the jacket they called a thorax, which was made of small iron plates stitched to a leather backing. Rank was denoted by a metal band of gold, silver or copper worn on each arm. The imperial troops were recruited from a dozen different countries and spoke at least as many languages, but all had been trained to the same army standard. They observed closely the little counters as they were moved about, and it was clear that every officer was learning precisely what was expected of him. I realised how chaotic and ill disciplined our Norse contingent must have seemed by comparison, and I understood why Harald and his men had been assigned a position where we would be directly under the eye of our general.

Abdallah brought us to battle on the fifth day. Perhaps he thought his advantage in numbers was overwhelming, or maybe he was still relying on the crippling effect of the iron spikes sewn on the battlefield. He did not know that our scouts had been picking up the iron spikes under cover of darkness, and that half of Maniakes's heavy cavalry had always remained hidden behind the ridge, where the army farriers had reshod all the cavalry horses with flat iron plates to protect their hooves. Nor had the emir any benefit of surprise. Hours before the Saracen army began to emerge from its defences, our observer on the spy pole had flagged a warning, and the imperial light cavalry were poised to disrupt the Saracens from forming ranks.

Standing next to Maniakes's command post, waiting to relay his orders to Harald and the Varangians, I watched as our scorpions, as Nikephorus called them, began to fling small rocks and iron bolts into the enemy ranks. These scorpions were the army's portable artillery — long-range crossbows mounted on tripods and light enough to be carried on the march. Between their salvoes the light cavalry unleashed wave upon wave of attack. One squadron after another they cantered deliberately forward to within range, then released a first and a second flight of arrows. Then each squadron wheeled about, and as it rode away the riders turned in their saddles and released a third volley.

'Our army learned that technique generations ago, on the eastern frontier, against the Persians. It triples their effective firepower,' Nikephorus commented.

Their assault looked to me more like a war game than a serious battle, yet men were falling in the Saracen ranks when each flight of arrows rained down, and I could see the disorder which resulted.

'If you watch carefully, Thorgils,' Nikephorus added, 'you'll note that one-third of the light cavalry is engaging the enemy, one-third is preparing the next attack, and one-third is regrouping, attending to their wounded, or resting.'

Fifty paces to the rear of each cavalry squadron rode eight men. They carried no offensive weapons apart from short swords. The moment they saw a cavalryman unhorsed, one of them came dashing forward at full gallop to retrieve the downed man who, reaching up, grabbed the rider's forearm, and at the same time placed his foot in a third stirrup dangling behind the rescuer's saddle. In one smooth movement the unhorsed cavalryman was plucked off the ground, and the two men were speeding away to the rear, where the cavalryman was provided with a remount. I estimated that for every five cavalry horses struck down by Saracen arrows, four riders were back in action by the time their squadron next moved forward. The exceptions, of course, were those men who were wounded. But they were not abandoned. They were taken to where Maniakes's medical teams had set up their field hospital behind the ridge and out of sight of the enemy.

All this time Maniakes never stirred from his position on the crest of the ridge, but stood watching the conflict. The tagmata was extended in a line along the slope of the hill, facing across the shallow valley towards Abdallah's forces. The Saracens were still clumped together in a disorganised mass as they flinched from the repeated attacks of the imperial cavalry. More and more of the Saracen troops were emerging from the gates of the camp, and now they filled the space in front of the palisade until they were too closely packed to be effective. Most of them were foot soldiers, as presumably Abdallah had not been able to ship much cavalry with him from North Africa, and many seemed to be peasant levies, for they were armed with only small swords and shields, and wore leather caps instead of helmets. I saw Saracen officers trying to cajole their men into orderly lines, pushing and shoving at the troops, hoping for some formation. Meanwhile the tagmata stood calmly, regiment by regiment, scarcely moving as their company commanders watched Maniakes's signallers for their orders. I had no idea of their battle plan, and counting the superior numbers of Saracen troops I wondered what Maniakes had in mind.

I never found out, because the Gods intervened. I have mentioned that our march to the battleground was across dry and dusty ground baked under the summer sun. The soil was very loose, almost sandy. As we waited for Maniakes's instructions, I felt a puff of wind, which stirred the dust around my feet. Looking behind me I saw that a windstorm was gathering, rolling down from the distant slopes of the fiery mountain and sweeping across the dry countryside. It drove before it a cloud of fine dust. In almost the same instant Maniakes must have noticed the approaching dust storm, because he said something to a staff officer who produced a wax tablet and scribbled a note on it. Then he handed the tablet to a rider, who galloped away to the rear towards the hidden heavy cavalry. Moments later Maniakes's signallers were flapping their flags and sending orders down the infantry line. Two regiments of the heavy infantry who had been facing the centre of the enemy position moved fifty paces farther apart, leaving a clear path between them.

Glancing back towards the Saracen forces I saw that Abdallah himself had now come out from the camp. A cluster of green and yellow banners rose above what seemed to be a group of his senior officers. They were positioned directly opposite the path that the infantry regiments had now left clear.

The wind ruffled the hair on the back of my neck. I heard the sudden slatting sound of the flap of the command tent. Small twigs and dry leaves tumbled past me, and the wind brought a strange noise to my ears: it was the metallic clatter of the horseshoes of the kataphract riding up the hill behind us, still out of sight of the enemy, but heading directly for the path that led to the heart of Abdallah's army.

Moments later the dust storm was over us. Grains of sand were falling down my collar, and the hot breath of the wind pressed my leggings against the backs of my legs. The enemy vanished from sight, obscured in a brown-grey cloud. A bugle sounded, and was answered by another, then a third. Through the gloom, over to my right, I could make out the shapes of heavy cavalry riding past in a dense mass.

Then, as suddenly as it arrived, the dust cloud swept on and the air cleared. Ahead of me on the far side of the shallow valley, the Saracens were still half blinded by the trailing edge of the swirling sand; many of them had turned away to shield their eyes, or stood with heads bowed, arms raised across their faces. Those with turbans had wrapped the cloth over their mouths and eyes. All of them must have heard the triple trumpet call of the imperial heavy cavalry as they sounded the charge, and looked up to see the kataphract descending down the slope towards them like those sand devils they fear, an evil spectre spawned by the dust.

The kataphract was the cutting edge of the tagamata. As a cavalry force it was unique. Hand-picked and rigorously trained, it was the ultimate shock weapon of the imperial army. Palace regiments could be relied to fight with great bravery, but they were comparatively unwieldy on the battlefield because they were on foot. Only the heavy cavalry of the kataphract could be rapidly directed with devastating effect at a weak point in the enemy lines. Maniakes was doing just this, ignoring the military manuals which advised a field commander to be cautious about committing the kataphract. Maniakes had seen his chance, and now sent it into action very early in the battle.

Five hundred troopers, Nikephorus later told me, made up the kataphract that day. Three hundred of them were heavy cavalry, the remainder were archers. They rode in a close-packed arrow-head formation, the troopers on the outer edges protecting the bowmen in the centre as they laid down a devastating rain of arrows directly ahead of them. The advancing horses moved at a deliberate trot for they were too heavily burdened to gallop or canter. Long padded blankets hung down on each horse's sides, shielding the animal's flanks and legs. Steel plates were strapped to the horses' faces, and across each charger's chest hung a guard of chain-mail. Their riders were equally well protected. They wore steel helmets and thick body armour. Heavy gauntlets covered hands and forearms, and their legs were encased in chain mail leggings under aprons of leather reaching to their heels. The lances they had carried on parade in Constantinople had been for show. Now they held the kataphract's weapon of choice: the heavy mace. Four feet long and made of iron with a six-sided head, it was an ideal instrument to smash any enemy.

The kataphract split the Saracen forces just as a butcher's chopper cleaves a chicken carcass on the block. They rode down the slope, splashed across the shallow stream, and drove their way into the enemy ranks. I saw the leading troopers wielding their maces as though beating on anvils. The kataphract's arrowhead formation thrust deeper and deeper into the mass of their opponents, and those Saracens who did not fall under the rain of blows were thrust aside by the armoured horses. They were too far away for me to hear their cries. Many slipped and were trampled under the hooves. A platoon of disciplined pikemen might have stopped the charge of the kataphract, but the Saracens had no such defence, and their foot soldiers were too lightly armed. The only real resistance came from the Saracen cavalry, who defended their emir. There was a confused struggle as their

riders fought back with swords and lances against the remorseless
advance of the mace-wielding shock troops. But the impetus of
the kataphract was too great. Their charge thrust far into the
Saracen position, and I saw the clump of battle standards around
the emir begin to waver.

Maniakes saw it, too. He growled an order, and the signallers
sounded the general advance. Drums began to beat, a war cymbal
clashed, its sound ringing clearly across the valley. To my right I
noticed the battle standards of the four palace regiments hoisted
in the air. Behind them the icons of the White Christ and his
saints were lifted up on poles to encourage the men. To the steady
clash of the cymbals, Maniakes's entire force, some seven thousand
men, swept down the slope towards the disorganised and leaderless
Saracens. They broke and ran. Within moments the battle became
a rout. A Greek staff officer shouted to me to tell Harald and his
Varangians that they too should join the fighting, but the Norsemen did not need me to translate. Yelling, they ran down the hill
towards the combat. I was about to join them when Nikephorus
held me by the arm and advised calmly, 'Stay back. Your place
is here. In case the situation changes.' I looked across towards
Maniakes. He still stood carefully watching the confusion and,
surprisingly, I could not detect any look of satisfaction on his
face. He seemed to be thinking, not of the battle just won, but of
what would happen next.

Four hours later the exhausted officers of the tagmata trudged
back up the slope to report total victory. In front of the palisade,
the emir's army had been crushed. The majority of the Saracens
had run away, throwing down their arms and fleeing into the
scrubland. The rest of them were either dead or sat meekly on the
ground, knowing that soon they would be sold as slaves. The
tagmata had lost less than a hundred men killed, and four times
that number wounded. Yet Maniakes scowled as he surveyed his
officers.

'Where is the emir?' he demanded sourly. 'The kataphract's
duty is to decapitate the enemy by killing or capturing their

commander. Otherwise victory is nothing. The Saracens will re-group around their leader, and we will face another battle.'

Abruptly Maniakes swung round and faced me. I quailed in front of his bad temper.

'You there,' he shouted at me, 'tell your northern colleagues that now they are going to earn their pay. As soon as we get back to Syracuse, I want every galley to put to sea and blockade the coasts. Abdallah must not be allowed to escape back to Libya. I want him taken.'

He turned again towards the officers.

'The palace regiments and the kataphract will return to Syracuse. Light infantry and cavalry are to go in pursuit of the emir. Track him down. He must be somewhere. I want this matter settled for good.'

Behind me I heard someone mutter in Norse, 'What about our loot?'

Maniakes must have heard and guessed the meaning of the remark, for he stared icily over my shoulder at the Norsemen, and said, 'All loot taken from the dead bodies or found in the enemy camp is to be brought to the quartermasters. They will assess its value, and it will not be shared out until the tagmata is back in Syracuse.'

Syracuse knew of our victory long before the tagmata reached the city walls. With no hope of relief from Abdallah, the citizens opened the city gates. The Greeks in the population greeted us ecstatically, the Saracens with resignation. Naturally Harald's Norsemen were eager to know just how much reward they would receive after the great battle of Traina, and we contrived to delay our departure for the coastal patrol until Maniakes's quartermas-ters had made their calculations. In the end each man in Harald's war band received a bonus of thirty nomisma, more than three years' pay. Certain items, however, were kept back for distribution to the senior officers, and this led to an open quarrel between Maniakes and Hervé, the leader of the Frankish mercenaries. The object of their dispute was the same bay stallion which had carried the nobleman that Iron Arm had killed in spectacular single combat, a superlative example of that breed of horse for which the Saracens were famous. When the stallion was led forward by a groom and shown off to Maniakes, there was not a man in the watching crowd who would not have wanted to own the creature.

Unwisely, Hervé, who spoke some Greek, ventured a suggestion. 'Autokrator,' he proposed, 'the horse should given to Iron Arm in recognition of his victory over the Saracen champion.'

Maniakes took this remark as an affront and an encroachment on his absolute authority. 'No,' he said harshly. 'That horse will be placed in my stables. I keep the animal for myself.'

Hervé blundered on, compounding his error. 'Surely that is unjust,' he said. 'Iron Arm defeated his opponent in fair combat, and by custom he should receive the weapons and horse of the vanquished.'

Maniakes glared at him, his scowl of anger deepening. The two men were facing one another in the main city square. With Maniakes were a few Greek staff officers, while Hervé was accompanied by half a dozen of his mercenaries. This was a very public squabble.

'The horse is mine,' Maniakes repeated. He was now so angry that his voice had deepened to an ugly growl.

Hervé opened his mouth as if to speak, and at that moment Maniakes stepped forward and struck the mercenary full in the face. Maniakes, as I have said, was a huge man, a giant. The force of the blow knocked Hervé off his feet, though he was tall and strong enough to be capable of standing up to a normal assault. As the mercenary started to get up from the ground, his mouth bloody from a cut lip, the Greek general unleashed a kick that sent Hervé sprawling once again. Maniakes was breathing heavily, his eyes filled with rage as he watched the humiliated mercenary slowly stand upright with the help of two of his men, who hurried forward to support him. Maniakes's staff officers stayed rooted to the spot, terrified by the fury of their leader. I remembered the warning of the Greek officer back in Constantinople that the new commander-in-chief demanded instant obedience, 'particularly from northern barbarians'.

No one said anything, and the stallion and his groom stood there until into this fraught moment entered one of Hervé's mercenaries, Iron Arm himself. He detached himself from the group of onlookers and strolled across to the horse. As he walked, Iron Arm was pulling on to his right hand his heavy metal-plated gauntlet. Coming up to the stallion, the mercenary began to pet the animal, stroking the magnificent head and neck, patting his flanks and fondling his ears. The stallion responded with pleasure, turning his fine head to nuzzle the man. Then Iron Arm moved to stand directly in front of the animal, put his left hand behind his back, and clicked his fingers. The stallion's head came up, the ears pricked in curiosity, the eyes bright and questioning, wondering at the sound. In that instant Iron Arm raised his gauntleted right hand and delivered a terrific blow with his clenched right fist, right between the stallion's eyes. The stallion collapsed, his legs folding up, killed outright. Iron Arm calmly turned and walked back to join his comrades.

Next day Hervé and his entire band of mercenaries left Syracuse and returned to Italy, refusing to serve under Maniakes again.

'WHAT A PUNCH that man has got!' commented Halldor. 'The Greek general is going to regret getting on the wrong side of the Frankish mercenaries.'

We were taking our galleys out of harbour to begin our patrol, and the death of the stallion was the sole topic of conversation.

'Maniakes has been in an evil temper ever since Abdallah escaped him. I doubt that the emir will be caught now. Abdallah has had plenty of time to make his escape back to Libya. Still, if we are cruising the coast, maybe we can make a few shore raids on our own account and pick up a little booty on the side.'

Halldor's Viking instincts were to be rewarded beyond his wildest dreams. Of the five galleys in our flotilla, Harald despatched two northwards to cruise towards Palermo in case the emir was still there. Two more galleys were sent to patrol the coast, facing across to Libya and the emir's most likely escape route. The fifth galley, Harald's own, had a more free-ranging task. We would search along the south-eastern coast, examining the bays and harbours for any trace of Saracen shipping capable of carrying the emir off the island. Now that Abdallah was on the run, we knew we could rely on receiving intelligence from the Greek-speaking population who lived along the coast.

For nearly a week, we made our way slowly along the rock-bound coast, looking into creeks and harbours, interrogating fishermen and finding nothing suspicious. It seemed that Sicily was quiet again now the emir was defeated, and the populace had returned to their normal peacetime lives. We were about halfway along the coast when we came to a long beach of white sand backed with low dunes covered with tussock grass. This itself was unusual, for most of the shore that we had seen was cliff and reef. I asked the Greek fisherman who was our pilot along this stretch of coast if this beach was ever used as a landing place, and he shook his head. Apparently the nearest village was far inland, and the fishermen had no reason to come there because the fishing in the area was bad. I translated his reply to Harald, and immediately the Norwegian's predatory instinct was aroused. He scanned the beach for several moments. We could see nothing. The beach looked quiet.

'Turn for shore,' Harald ordered the helmsman. 'This needs a closer look.'

Gently we ran the galley's bows on land, and a dozen of us jumped ashore. I could hear only the slight lap of the waves on the beach. Squinting against the glare of the white sand, for the sun was blazing down, we began to walk up along the beach.

'You four,' Harald ordered a group of men next to him,

'Search in that direction as far as those low bushes in the distance. The others come with me.'

He began to walk towards the dunes. I followed him, my feet sinking in the soft sand as I tried to keep up with his massive stride. We had gone perhaps fifty paces when, suddenly, four Saracens sprang up in front of us. They had been crouched down, hiding behind a dune, and now they sprinted away inland, feet flying so I could see the soles of their bare feet. They reminded me of hares who wait until the last moment before the hunter treads on them, then start away in panic. And they were as quick, for there was no hope of catching them. We stopped and watched them growing smaller in the distance. When they were out of range of even the most ambitious archer, one of the fugitives stopped and turned, then waited there, watching us.

Harald narrowed his eyes as he looked at the distant figure. 'What does that remind you of, Thorgils?' he asked.

'My lord? I was just thinking to myself that they ran as fast as hares.'

'Not hares,' he said. 'Think of nesting birds. What do they do?'

Immediately I understood. 'Leave the nest, run off as a distraction, hoping to divert the hunter.'

'So now we look for the nest.'

But for the boy's eyes we would never have found him. He had been buried in the sand beneath the overhang of a bush. The only part of him left on the surface was his face, and even that had been covered in a light cotton rag whose colour matched the sand around him. But in breathing the boy had caused the rag to slip slightly to one side. I was walking past the bush when I saw the glint of an eyeball. I beckoned quietly to Harald, who was searching the bushes a few paces from me, and he came over to look where I pointed. The boy knew he had been found. Harald reached down, brushed away the sand and seized him by the shoulder, pulling him from his hiding place. The boy was no more than six or seven years old, slim, with a skin that was fair for a Saracen, and fine features. He was trembling with fright.

'By all the saints!' exclaimed the Greek fisherman. He had come across to see what we had found. 'That's Abdallah's son!'

'How can you be sure?' I asked.

'He rode on his father's horse the day that the emir came to visit our village. Abdallah held him up to show him off to our people and present to us our future ruler. There's no mistaking the lad. Besides, look at those clothes he's wearing. That's no peasant brat.'

I translated the fisherman's words to Harald, and, as if he was picking up a doll, the Norwegian suddenly swung the boy up in the air and held him high over his head. Then he turned to face the distant watcher, and stood there, showing off our find. After a few moments, the Saracen began to walk towards us.

'I am his tutor,' he explained, speaking good Greek with the high, quick intonation of the Saracens. He was an older man, thin, grey-bearded and clearly anguished. 'Do not harm him, I beg you.'

'Where is Abdallah, the emir?' demanded Harald.

'I do not know,' the man answered miserably. 'I was only told to bring the boy to this beach and wait for us to be picked up. But when a ship would come I had no idea. At first we thought it was your vessel. And when we realised our mistake it was too late to get away, so we tried to conceal the boy, hoping you would go away.'

'Thorgils, a word with you in private,' said Harald. 'Halldor, here, you take a hold of the lad.' Then he led me a few paces to one side and said bluntly, 'What's the boy worth?'

I was searching for an answer when Harald went on fiercely, 'Come on, think! Abdallah cannot be too far away to receive our message. What's the boy worth?'

I was so taken aback by the fierceness of his questioning that I began to stammer. 'M-m-my lord, I have no idea.'

Harald cut across me. 'What was it you said when we saw

that golden dome in the Holy Land? That the Saracens pay huge sums for those things which are most dear to them?'

'But that was a holy shrine,'

'And is not a son and heir equally precious, to a father? We don't have any time to waste, Thorgils. How much was it that the caliph or whatever he was called set aside for the gilding of the dome?'

'The sum was a hundred thousand dinars, our guide said.'

'Right. Tell the boy's tutor that if the emir pays a hundred thousand dinars, he'll see his son again, unharmed. Otherwise we hand the boy over to Maniakes. That's my message.'

'But how can the emir raise that amount of money now?' I said. 'He's a fugitive.'

'I've never heard of a ruler who doesn't take his treasure with him when he flees, provided he has the transport. And you can add a second message as a sweetener. If the hundred thousand is paid, not only will the emir get his son back, but I will make sure that my flotilla does not hinder his escape to Libya.'

I suppose I should have been shocked by Harald's double-dealing, but I was not. Perhaps the years I had spent in Constantinople had hardened me to intrigue and treachery. Certainly every Norseman in Harald's war band would have expected him to exact a price for the boy, and not one of them would want to share the ransom with the autokrator if Harald could somehow arrange it. But, even as Harald spoke, his blatant perfidy made me acknowledge to myself that my ultimate loyalty had never been to the palace in Constantinople or its appointees, but to my own people. Faced with the stark choice of serving either the Basileus or Harald, I did not hesitate.

'I will see what I can arrange, my lord,' I answered, even as I remembered just how hard-headed Pelagia could be in matters of business profit. She would certainly have advised me to extract the greatest advantage from our lucky catch.

'Good, Thorgils, do that. And be quick. If this is to succeed it must be done quickly. Three days at the most.'

The boy's tutor winced slightly when I mentioned the enormous sum, but, like a good negotiator, he avoided direct haggling.
'And how is such a large quantity of money to be delivered and
the boy's well-being guaranteed?' he enquired, his eyes flicking
nervously to Halldor, who still had the youngster in his grip.

'As regards the boy's safety, you will have to trust us on that,'
I said. 'It's in our interest to keep him safe and well. He's not our
enemy, nor is his father if he accepts this proposal. We'll keep the
boy aboard ship until the ransom is paid.'

'And the payment itself? How is that transaction to be made?
When so much gold is on view, men tend to lose their heads and
seek more. They break their word.'

For a moment I was silent. I had never organised the paying
of a ransom, and did not know how it was done so that the
interests of both sides were protected. Then, perhaps with Odinn's
help, I recalled my time among the ski-runners of Permia. They
were a fur-trading people who mistrusted all outsiders, so they
conducted any barter at arm's length. They left their furs for
inspection in a deserted open place, and their customers left a
similar value in payment at the same spot. Perhaps I could modify
that arrangement for Harald's purposes.

'The ransom is to be brought to this end of the beach at noon
on the third day from now,' I said. 'Our vessel will be in the bay
close enough to watch your men place the ransom on the sand
and withdraw a safe distance to a point on the dunes where they
can still be seen. The only people on the beach will be the boy
and myself, waiting for you at the opposite end of the beach. You
will be able to see for yourselves that he is alive and well. But
you are not to come any nearer. If you do so, the galley will
immediately come and retrieve the boy. I will walk along the
beach to inspect the ransom, and if everything is satisfactory, I
will signal the galley to come and pick up the money. At that
moment your people can advance and collect the boy. Neither
side will be close enough to the trade to be able to take both the
boy and the ransom.'

The old man looked at me and said softly, 'You I trust. But not that tall pirate who is your leader. It will be up to you to make him respect these rules. Otherwise there will be a tragedy.'

When the Saracens had left to take our message to the emir, I explained the ransom arrangement to Harald. I had never seen him so deep in thought. He chewed on his moustache as he reflected on my device, and scowled at me.

'Thorgils,' he said, 'you've lived too long among these people. You are beginning to scheme like them. Of course, if anything goes wrong, it will be you left sitting on the beach, not us.'

'I think the handover will work,' I reassured him with a confidence that I did not feel, 'though whether the emir will find so much money is another matter.'

As it turned out, the handover of the ransom went exactly as I had hoped, except for one flaw which, if I had foreseen it, might have prevented me from setting up the plan.

Shortly before noon on the third day, as our galley lay out in the bay, a file of fifteen mules approached over the sand dunes. I was seated on the far end of the beach with the young Saracen boy, who had not said a word all the time he had been with us. He was still in a state of shock. When he saw the approaching mules, his face lit up with hope, for he must have known what was going on. If I had been sensible, I should have tied his arms and legs so he could not run away when I went to examine the panniers that the muleteers dumped on the beach before they withdrew, but I did not have the heart to do so. Instead, after he had stood up and waved to his tutor, who was watching from a distance, I gestured for the boy to sit down and wait quietly, which he did. Then I walked along the sand to the pile of mule bags, unfastened the thongs that tied one or two of them, and lifted up the flaps. I had never seen so much gold coin in one place in all my life. Certainly not when I had worked for the king's moneyer in London, for he had minted silver coin, nor even when the Basileus had flung gold bounty to his courtiers in the audience hall of the Great Palace. Here were riches that were

beyond my comprehension. Surprisingly, the entire payment was
in coin, mostly Arab dinars, but also nomisma from the imperial
mint. I could not see a single item like a gold necklace or a
jewelled band whose value would have to be assessed. I had no
idea what a hundred thousand dinars looked like, and there was
no time to count, so I turned round and waved to the boy,
gesturing for him to go. The last I saw of him he was racing up
across the sand dunes to join his father's deputation.

'Thorgils, you are a genius!' exulted Harald as he came ashore,
opened one of the panniers and scooped up a handful of coins. I
had never seen him look so pleased. His normally harsh expression
was replaced with a look of utter pleasure.

'You have the Gods to thank,' I said, seizing my chance.
'They clearly favour you.'

'Yes, the Gods,' he said. 'Freya must have wept for many
nights and days.'

For a moment I did not know what he was talking about, as I
had been away from my homeland for so long that my Old Beliefs
were growing dim. Then I remembered that Freya, goddess of
wealth, had cried tears of gold when she lost her husband.

'There's only one detail you have overlooked,' said Harald.
His cautionary tone brought a sudden chill to our conversation.
'The Greek sailor who identified the emir's son for us. My own
men will keep their mouths shut about this treasure when we get
back to Syracuse, because they will get their share. But Greeks
never hold their tongues. Even if the fisherman were handsomely
rewarded, he would boast if he got back home, and Maniakes
would get to hear what happened. Thorgils, I tidied up your plan
a little. The Greek is dead.'

SEVEN

MANIAKES NEVER LEARNED the truth. As our vessel entered Syracuse harbour, we passed an imperial dromon beating out to sea. Twenty-four hours earlier she had arrived with an order signed in purple ink, stripping Maniakes of his command. Now the dromon was carrying the former autokrator to Constantinople to face the Basileus and his eunuch brother John. Maniakes had made the error of shaming their brother-in-law, Stephen, commander of the imperial fleet, by accusing him of allowing the emir to escape by sea. The rebuke had been made in public, Maniakes once again losing his temper and shouting at Stephen that he was useless and effeminate while he beat him about the head with a whip. Stephen had reacted like the true palace politician he was: he secretly sent word to the Orphanotrophus that Maniakes had grown overbearing with his military success and was plotting to seize the throne. Nothing was calculated to arouse the Orphanotrophus's hostility more, because John the Eunuch would do anything to maintain his family's grip on power.

We could scarcely believe our good fortune. With Stephen censured for allowing the emir's escape, our own treason was unlikely to be discovered, and Maniakes's disgrace gave Harald his excuse to declare that he too was withdrawing from the Sicilian expedition. Our flotilla, as soon as it reassembled, also set sail for

Constantinople, and from there three of our vessels continued onward for the Pontic Sea, and eventually for Kiev. In their bilges lay hidden the bulk of the emir's ransom: their crews were returning home as rich as they had dreamed of. Their departure suited Harald, as it left fewer men to let slip the truth about our faithlessness. Only a hundred of his original war band remained, and the army secretariat in Constantinople judged the number insufficient for an independent unit. So, in recognition of our contribution to the Sicilian campaign, they removed us from the Varangians-without-the-walls and attached us directly to the imperial Life Guard. To add to the irony, Harald was decorated for his services to the empire, and elevated to the rank of spatharokandidatos. This entitled him to wear a cloak of white silk and carry a jewelled court sword at ceremonials. I, of course, found myself once again an imperial guardsman.

Pelagia was dismissive of my military career. I returned to find her just as energetic and self-confident, and even more successful. She now had commercial interests in shipping and olive production as well as owning an entire chain of bakeries and bread stalls. With her newly acquired wealth she had bought a brand new substantial villa in a pleasant suburb on the Galata side of the Golden Horn, with its own garden and overlooking the straits. It was there that I found her in the main reception room, reading through bills and documents relating to her business.

'Thorgils, you come back from Sicily with a suntan but little else,' she said after I had briefly sketched in the details of my time on campaign. 'You're looking thinner, and you've got several grey hairs, but no promotion. Fortunately I've been investing your salary for you, and you'll find that you've returned to a nest egg.'

I decided it would be wiser not to tell Pelagia that I would eventually be receiving a portion of the emir's ransom money, nor that I had placed my share from the salvage from the pirate ship with Halldor to look after.

'You'll find little changed in the palace when you get back to the guardroom,' Pelagia went on. 'John is still running the government, and Michael has less and less to do with affairs of state. He's become more pious than ever. A couple of soothsayers – charlatans the pair of them – managed to convince him that he sold his soul to the devil before he married the empress Zoë in return for a glorious future, and now he punishes himself for this lapse. I'm beginning to feel sorry for the poor man. His suffering comes in waves. When it is at its worst the pain nearly drives him out of his mind, and he makes matters worse by humiliating himself.'

My colleagues in the guardroom confirmed Pelagia's sombre description.

'You'll need a strong stomach for guard duty outside the royal apartment nowadays,' I was warned by my company commander, the same Halfdan who had taken charge of the detail when the Basileus Romanus drowned. 'You should see the diseased creatures who are brought up to the imperial bedchamber – tramps picked up from the street by the nightwatch, or invalids from the hospitals. It's said Michael washes their clothes, cleans their wounds, even kisses their open sores, in emulation of his own God. He insists that they sleep in the royal bed while he lies down on the cold marble floor with a stone as a pillow so he suffers mortification. I looked in the bedchamber one morning when the Basileus and his attendants had left, and there was a stinking pile of old rags by the bed. Looked like a beggars' nest.'

My summons to the office of John the Orphanotrophus was not long in arriving, and as usual the eunuch came straight to the point.

'What's your impression of Araltes now?' he demanded. 'After two years in his company, I trust that you have won his confidence as I required.'

'I believe so, your excellency,' I replied. I was as wary of the Orphanotrophus as on the first day he had sent me to spy on Harald, but I was bold enough to add, 'He has served the Basileus well. He has been created spatharokandidatos.'

'I know, I know. But the administration of the empire rests on two pillars: honours and cash,' retorted the Orphanotrophus irritably. 'Your Araltes benefits from the honours, but what about the cash? I've been told he is gold-hungry.'

'I know nothing about that, your excellency,' I answered evasively.

'Strange that he hasn't complained about the division of booty after the fall of Syracuse, like those Frankoi mercenaries who made such an issue of it. Over a horse, I believe.'

I began to wonder if there was any limit to the eunuch's network of spies. Careful to avoid an outright lie, I told him, 'Araltes gives the impression of being content with his booty from Sicily.'

The Orphanotrophus's next words made me feel as if I had fallen through the ice of a frozen lake.

'I'm hearing that certain bullion transactions are going unreported to the city archon. One of the money changers seems to be making unusually high profits. What's his name . . .' and the eunuch made a pretence of looking down at the note on his desk, though I was sure he had no need to refresh his memory. 'A certain argyroprates named Simeon. Mention has been made that he is dealing with Varangians.'

'It could be any of the Varangian units, your excellency,' I said, trying to keep panic out of my voice, 'not necessarily those who serve Araltes.'

'Guardsman,' said the eunuch slowly and deliberately, 'if anything is going on, I want to know it.'

HARALD HAD BEEN living in his own quarters away from the Life Guard's barracks, and after the interview with John I had to restrain myself from going straight there to warn him. I suspected that I was being watched by the Orphanotrophus's agents, so I went instead to seek Pelagia's advice, and she was not reassuring.

'Simeon has been looking particularly smug these past few

months. He dresses in the latest fashions, wears expensive jewellery, and generally likes to show off how well he's doing.'

'Can't he be persuaded to be less conspicuous? If he keeps this up, sooner or later John's people will call him in for questioning.'

'I doubt it. Simeon thinks too highly of himself.'

'Couldn't Harald switch to using someone else on the Mese, a more discreet money changer, to handle the booty?'

'Simeon's the only man who would take the risk of Harald's monetary affairs.'

'What about those shifty-looking characters I sometimes see walking up and down the Mese in the financial zone, offering better rates for foreign exchange.'

Pelagia snorted with derision. 'I wouldn't advise Harald to deal with them. They're unlicensed traders. They're likely to run off with any valuables entrusted to them, or give back dud coins. And they don't have the resources to deal in the amounts that Harald brings in. Their working capital is in those grubby bags they carry about. At least Simeon has the iron table. That's what it symbolises: a metal surface on which you can bang suspect coins to hear whether they ring true. You had better tell your tall friend with the lopsided eyebrows to be very, very discreet whenever he brings any valuables to Simeon for exchanging into cash.'

My daily life, now that I was back with the Hetaira, reverted to its former pattern. There were the familiar drills and kit inspections, the regular rotation of guard duty – one week inside the Great Palace, the next week in barracks – and of course the endless parades. I found it truly tedious to spend hour after hour solemnly marching out from the palace to some great church, waiting outside for the service to finish, going back along the same route, and then having to clean up my equipment and prepare for the next ceremonial outing, which could be the next day.

Harald avoided most of this mind-numbing routine because he, Halldor and a few of his immediate followers were assigned to assist the exaktors. These were, as their name implies, the tax gatherers. How Harald got in with them is something I never learned, but later I came to realise that it was part of his own grand plan. There was certainly nothing unusual about a detachment of guards accompanying the exaktors. In fact it was a necessity. When the tax collectors set out from the capital to visit some area in the countryside that had been assessed, naturally the local inhabitants would be reluctant to pay up, so the exaktors took along an armed escort to bully the taxpayers into compliance. Few things were more terrifying to a local farmer than the menacing sight of foreign barbarians who were prepared to smash up his property if he did not pay his dues to the emperor – the arrival of a squad of Varangians was usually sufficient to loosen the purse strings. Harald, with his ferocious appearance, must have been particularly daunting, nor was he reluctant to resort to force, and that may be why he and his men were picked for the work.

Thus Harald and the others missed the bizarre event which surprised even someone as well informed as Pelagia: the proclamation that the Basileus and Empress Zoë were to have a son. Physically, of course, this was impossible. Zoë was now at least sixty years old, though as vain as ever, and Michael the Basileus was much too ill to procreate. Their son was to be by adoption. But what really stunned everyone was his identity. His only previous official role had been as commander of the Palace Guard, a purely nominal post for which he did nothing more than wear a gaudy uniform at palace ceremonials. Named Michael, just like the emperor, his father was that same Stephen who had plotted to have Maniakes recalled in disgrace, and his mother was the Basileus's sister. He was to be known by the title of Caesar, to signify that he was the heir to the imperial throne, and naturally John the Eunuch had made the choice. The Orphanotrophus knew that the sickly Basileus could die at any moment, and he was determined that the succession should stay within the family.

The actual ceremony of adoption was even more grotesque

than when the youthful Basileus had married Zoë, who was old enough to be his mother. This time the ritual took place in the church of the Blachernae Palace and culminated with the new Caesar symbolically sitting down on the ageing Zoë's lap, so he could be acclaimed by the congregation of dignitaries and high officials as her 'son'.

A few days later I was crossing a courtyard on my way to the guardroom when I passed a middle-ranking official of the chancellery. His face seemed familiar, but I would have walked right past him if he had not stopped suddenly and said, 'Excuse me, aren't you the Greek-speaking Varangian who told me how Romanus drowned?'

'That's right,' I answered, recognising the young man who had interviewed me on the day of the funeral parade. 'You're Constantine Psellus. You seem to have come a long way since you were a young student watching a funeral parade. I congratulate you.'

'You're beginning to sound like a courtier yourself. This time you must tell me your name.'

'Thorgils Leifsson.'

'Obviously you're still with the Palace Guard.'

'Back with the guard, more correctly, after service in Sicily.'

'So you know what this new Caesar is like? After all, he is, or was, your commanding officer.'

I hesitated, and Psellus said softly, 'You may speak freely. This is an opinion for posterity. I'm still compiling notes for my history of the rulers of the empire.'

Once again his frank approach won my confidence. 'Well,' I admitted, 'from the little I've seen of him, the Caesar is vindictive and shallow. His one true talent is that he is superlative at hiding his true feelings.'

'Sounds as though he was an excellent choice for the throne,' said Psellus with irony. 'I'll make a bargain with you, Thorgils. As a guardsman you sometimes see things which we outsiders never get to witness. If you'll be so kind as to keep me informed about what is going on behind the scenes, I won't forget you when the time comes — as it surely will — that you need a friend within the bureaucracy.' And he hurried on his way.

Over the next few months, there was little I could tell Psellus that he would not have observed for himself. Michael's health was in rapid decline. His limbs swelled, bloating so that his fingers became as thick as sausages. To hide his physical deterioration from public gaze, the Basileus spent less time in the city, and withdrew to his country residence. He left behind the usual intrigues inside the palace, which grew more viperish as it became evident that he did not have long to live. John the Eunuch still held the real power, but some courtiers began to pander to the young Caesar, preparing for the day when he mounted the throne. Other sycophants coalesced around his favourite uncle, Constantine, another of the Orphanotrophus's brothers. A few diehards again paid attention to the empress Zoë, though she was still confined to the gynaeceum, the women's quarters, and the Basileus had cut off her allowance so she was living in near poverty. No one trusted anyone else, and there was a growing sense that the whole structure of government was on the verge of collapse.

I came to appreciate how far the decay had spread when an official arrived in the guardroom late one December evening. He was out of breath and flustered.

'I'm looking for the guardsman Thorgils,' he announced.

'What can I do for you?' I asked.

The man looked nervously at the other off-duty guardsmen, who were watching him with open curiosity.

'You are to select one reliable colleague,' he said. 'Bring heavy cloaks, and accompany me.'

I glanced at Halfdan. 'Take Lars with you,' he ordered.

Lars was a stolid guardsman who had been with the Hetaira almost as long as Halfdan himself. Lars and I gathered up our weapons, and the official took us, half running, to the office of John the Eunuch. We found him dressed in his monk's clothes and ready to leave the palace.

'You are to accompany me as an escort in case of trouble,' said John. 'Be discreet, conceal your uniforms, and you may leave your axes behind. Swords hidden under your cloaks will be sufficient.'

We slipped out of the palace through one of the minor gates, where the doorkeepers were clearly expecting us, and hurried through the streets of the city. We kept to alleys and side streets, but I recognised the direction we were taking. It was towards the area known as the Venetian quarter because of the number of foreign merchants, mostly Italians, residing there. It was also the district of several of Constantinople's most important monasteries, and when we stopped and knocked on the wooden doors to one of them, I knew that we stood before the gate of the monastery known locally as the Kosmidion. It was the same monastery which the Basileus had funded so generously because it was dedicated to the doctor saints, Cosmas and Damian.

A grim-looking monk let us in without a word and ushered us along several stone-flagged corridors. In the background I heard chanting, and, as we turned a corner, I detected the hurried withdrawal of some cowled figures who had been waiting in the shadows, curious to see who the visitors were at such a late hour. Finally we came to the door of an ordinary monk's cell. The door stood open. Inside, on a simple cot, lay the Basileus.

I recognised him by his gross and swollen hands, for he was wearing not the clothes of an emperor, but the simple black tunic of a monk. Also, his head had been shaved in a tonsure: I could still see the nicks and cuts where the work had been done hurriedly and very recently. The Basileus looked truly ghastly, and I had no doubt that he had only a few hours left to live.

'Watch the door and passage,' snapped the Orphanotrophus. 'Let no one in.'

He appeared genuinely distressed at the sight of his sickly brother. He stepped into the room, and I had a glimpse of him dropping to his knees beside the bed and embracing the invalid before I turned my back and stared down the passageway. Behind me I heard John croon comforting words to the man whom he had manoeuvred on to the throne of the empire. I found it difficult to believe that the young and handsome courtier who had married Zoë was now the bloated and sweating wreck who lay on the cot behind me.

Nothing could be kept secret in the palace, least of all the disappearance of the emperor. At dawn we had our first visitors: the new Caesar Michael and his uncle Constantine arrived. By then the Basileus was in great pain, and the Orphanotrophus allowed them to stay only for a short time before ordering them to leave. Two physicans, one from the monastery infirmary, the other from the palace, came and attempted to relieve the patient's suffering with pain-killing drugs. Then I heard the Basileus shout aloud that he wanted to die like his Lord, in agony, and the Orphanotrophus ordered me to no longer let the physicians pass. One monk at a time was to be allowed into the cell, where he could pray for the invalid's soul. The rest of the brethren were to say their prayers for him in their chapel.

Lars and I guarded the dreary corridor for twenty hours without a break, cooped up in the heart of the monastery complex, hearing only the shuffle of feet, the moaning of the Basileus, and the muttered prayers for the sick and dying. The strangest interlude was when the empress herself appeared in the passage-way, demanding to see her husband. The doorkeepers of the monastery had let Zoë in – she was, after all, the emperor's wife – but Lars and I obeyed orders and blocked her path until John the Eunuch heard her protests and came out to see what was going on.

'Tell my husband that I want to see him,' begged Zoë.

The Orphanotrophus went back inside for a few moments, then reappeared.

'He does not wish to see you,' he said to Zoë in a flat tone. 'He asks that you go away.'

Zoë clenched her hands and looked miserable.

'Go away,' John repeated, 'otherwise I'll have the guards throw you out.'

Fortunately, for I would not have relished bundling the old woman down the corridor, Zoë turned and left. As I watched her walk away, the smell of the aged empress's musk perfume lingered in the still air of the passageway, and I remembered how she had looked upon the corpse of her first husband as he lay cold on the marble bench by the swimming pool, and wondered if she could have known that events would come to this gruesome conclusion.

At about noon the Basileus must have recovered his strength, for I heard him ask whether it was time for the midday service. He announced that, as a monk, it was his duty to attend. Then came an outburst of petulance. Trying to get up from the cot, he found that no one had provided him with the suitable monk's sandals; beside his cot were the purple boots that only the reigning emperor might wear, and he refused to put them on. Two of the monks came to fetch him, and physically carried him to the chapel, barefoot. When they brought him back an hour later, hanging between them, Michael was scarcely breathing. They took him into the cell, laid him on the bed, then left. After that there was a long silence, and then I heard nothing more. Basileus Michael had died.

John the Eunuch stayed in that cell for two more days, sitting beside his brother's corpse, mourning. It was the one truly human act I remember of a man whom, until then, I had thought of as the most cold-hearted, calculating person I had ever met. Monks came and went, washed and put new clothes on the dead emperor, and mounted a vigil in relays. The Orphanotrophus barely stirred. Officials arrived from the palace seeking instructions, and he told them that he would return to his office only when he was ready; until then they should consult the Caesar.

Finally, on the third day after his brother's death, John came out of the cell. He looked haggard.

'Guardsman,' he said as he looked straight into my eyes, 'for the second time, you've been present at the passing of a Basileus. On the last occasion you showed great discretion. That is why I chose you. These are matters of state, and the personal details are rarely dignified. They must be kept from public knowledge. A seamless transfer of power is needed; appearance is all.'

He brushed past me, and as I followed him along the passageway I promised myself that the next time I saw Psellus, I would make him swear never to reveal the source of his information.

In fact, Psellus was among the cluster of officials waiting anxiously in the outer courtyard of the palace as we came back from the monastery. Standing at the back of the group, he caught my eye. I kept my face expressionless. Now, I was just another member of the guard.

Halfdan had been hovering at the palace gate with a squad of men waiting to escort the returning Orphanotrophus to a meeting in the grand audience chamber.

'Thank the Gods you brought him back,' Halfdan hissed at me. 'The place is all in a heap. Nobody knows what's going on, or who's in charge. Everyone was waiting for the Eunuch to make decisions. What kept you?'

Before I could reply, Michael the Caesar approached. With him was his uncle, Constantine. The two men began to fawn over the Orphantrophus as we headed towards the audience chamber. They commented how tired he looked, and asked repeatedly how they might assist. It occurred to me that the two men were frightened out of their wits. They wanted to know what the Eunuch had decided for their futures, and were relying on him to guide them through the next few days until the succession of power was established. As we entered the packed Trikilinium it was evident that everyone, including the palace officials, was on edge and overwrought. Even the empress Zoë had appeared from the women's quarters. She stood there, looking at the Orphan-otrophus. She too was waiting for his decision. The atmosphere was thick with fear, ambition and duplicity.

'Now is the time to stand together, to assist one another. We should carry out the wishes of the deceased,' announced the Orphanotrophus, raising his voice so he could be heard by everyone in the waiting audience. He had recovered his composure, and his words had their usual quality of slight menace. 'We proceed with the arrangements envisaged at the time when our dear nephew, Michael –' here he gave a thin, insincere smile – 'became Caesar. It is appropriate that he is acclaimed as Basileus at the earliest opportunity. He will, I know, value and accept the advice and support of his family.'

There was a general easing of tension in the chamber at this. The Orphanotrophus's statement was interpreted as meaning that the various factions were to share the power between them. The young Caesar would occupy the throne, but his family – John himself, his brother Constantine, and the empress Zoë – would be his silent partners. It was to be a web of alliances.

The spider at the centre of the web now stepped forward. The Caesar was a slender, sallow-complexioned young man going prematurely bald. Turning to the assembled officials, he announced that he would only accept the imperial mantle if he could share its burden and privilege with his 'revered guide and mentor the Orphanotrophus'. Here he kissed his uncle's hand. Then he walked across to his elderly adoptive mother and embraced her theatrically. 'I want all of you to bear witness,' he called out to the assembly. 'When I am crowned, there will be a second throne beside mine, occupied by my mother and mistress. I will be her slave-emperor, obedient to her commands.'

'This makes you want to puke,' muttered Halfdan near me. 'I wonder just how long that little shit will keep his word.'

Michael was crowned as Basileus by the Patriarch in a glittering ceremony the very next day. As promised, there was a second throne for the aged empress. Psellus, who watched the coronation, came away with the same opinion of the new Basileus as my company commander.

'That man reeks of hypocrisy,' he said. 'I was at a meeting of the family council taking notes, and you should have heard the way he speaks to her. Always asking her opinion, saying that he defers to her judgement, that he "is hers to command" and on and on in similar vein. He's got her quite addled. She seems to believe him.'

'It does seem odd that he should crawl to her so blatantly,' I commented. 'He's the emperor, not her.'

'Thorgils, the citizens of Constantinople are calling their new ruler "Michael the Caulker" or "The Little Twister". You may not be aware that at one time his father Stephen worked in the shipyards as a humble labourer. His job was to caulk the seams of planks with spun yarn and slop pine tar on the hulls. His family are base born, not from the sort of background that the mob respects or forgets. To the ordinary people, Zoë is the only one who has a genuine claim to wear the purple. She and her sister Theodora are true aristocrats. There's a dangerous feeling in the city that the antics of John the Eunuch and his jumped-up family have soiled the status of the Basileus, that they've gone too far with their ambitions.'

'I didn't know Zoë has a sister.'

'Hardly surprising. The two women hate one another. Zoë arranged for her sibling to be shut away in a nunnery years ago. What a pair,' the bureaucrat sighed. 'Sometimes I think the palace is like a large rock. When you roll it aside you find all sorts of unpleasant creatures creeping and crawling around underneath. At least Zoë is open in her dislike of her sister, whereas with John the Eunuch and his brother Constantine, I get the feeling that they are a pair of scorpions, tails up and circling one another warily, each always ready to deliver a fatal sting. God help us when that happens.'

Pelagia was equally alert to the impending clash. The Orphanotrophus owned a large estate very close to her villa in Galata, and he often came there to relax. Pelagia was worried that the more vicious aspects of palace politics might accompany him.

'John the Eunuch always brings an escort with him, at least

twenty soldiers. He must be expecting trouble. You couldn't arrange for some private security guards for me, Thorgils, could you? Perhaps half a dozen of your colleagues might like to spend their free days here in Galata. I would pay them well, and they would have as much wine to drink as they liked.'

'Nothing could be easier,' I replied. 'The new Basileus appointed an entirely new batch of bodyguards just last week. They are loyal only to him. We Varangians are kept on, but we don't have much to do. Besides, the Basileus's new Life Guards are an odd lot, and clannish. They're Pechenegs from the north. Michael purchased them, and every one of them is a eunuch. I'm sure that many of my colleagues would like to get away from the atmosphere in the palace. It's becoming more and more freakish.'

IN FEBRUARY MY world came crashing down around my ears. Harald and Halldor were arrested, as were Simeon the money changer and three of the exaktors. All of them were accused of swindling the state treasury. It was a simple enough fraud: they had terrorised their victims into paying more than the official tax assessment and pocketed the difference. One of their victims had complained to the chancellery, and when a clerk checked the ledgers it was clear that the tax collectors had been under-reporting their receipts.

'What idiots,' said Pelagia when I told her. 'It's no good stealing from the state unless you can cover your tracks properly. All those files and written reports pile up in the archives. They may seem a waste of effort, but if someone has the motivation they can be used to bring down even the most powerful person.'

'What's going to happen to them?'

'The tax collectors will be dismissed from their posts, all their private property will be seized to pay the massive fines levied on them, and they will be lucky not to be sent to jail. As for your Varangian friends, I don't know. They might be able to bribe their way out of trouble and flee the country, or they might be made an example of. Depends who their friends are. I'm sure you remember that Bulgarian who was paraded through the streets last autumn.'

Indeed I did. Like Harald, the unfortunate man had been a foreigner at court. He had decided to raise a rebellion in his native country, slipped out of the capital and gathered an army. The tagmata had crushed him, and he had been brought back to Constantinople, where he was paraded through the streets on a leading chain, his nose cut off, then strangled.

'My best guess,' Pelagia continued, 'is that the authorities will hold Harald and his associates in jail and interrogate them until they reveal where they've put the stolen money so that the treasury can try to recover it. The interrogation will be a nasty business. The interrogators pride themselves on being able to extract information without spilling blood. It's not that they're squeamish – it's a matter of having pride in their work.'

Pelagia and I were standing in her garden, overlooking the straits. The moment I had heard about Harald's arrest I had fled the city, crossing the Golden Horn on one of the public ferries to Galata. I knew very well that the Orphanotrophus would want to question me. He would ask why I had not alerted his office to Harald's conspiracy, and I was sure that Simeon would soon reveal that Harald had extorted a ransom for the emir's son. Then my failure to report truthfully to John the Eunuch would concern not theft from the state, but an act of treason.

'I can hide you here in Galata for a few days,' Pelagia offered. 'Long enough for you to find some way of escaping from the reach of the Orphanotrophus, though that will be difficult. Luckily the Eunuch has troubles of his own, and may be distracted from your case. Matters are coming to a head between him and his nephew. The Basileus has been scheming – he's fed up with doing whatever John says – and he's been playing John off against his other uncle, Constantine. No one knows who's going to win. My guess is that it will be the Orphanotrophus.'

Pelagia was wrong, and spectacularly so. The young Basileus

delivered his masterstroke right before our eyes. Several days had passed, and we were once again in the garden, overlooking the straits, when we saw a state barge about to put out from our side of the harbour and return to the city. We recognised the vessel at once: it was the boat reserved for the personal use of the Orphanotrophus, and the pennant showed that John himself was aboard.

'I wonder why he's going back so soon?' Pelagia mused. 'My servants tell me that the Eunuch only came here last night, and in a towering rage. The Basileus had publicly snubbed him at court, refused to grant him an audience, and went to consult with Constantine instead. If the Orphanotrophus is being summoned back to the Great Palace, it must be to arrange some sort of truce between the family factions.'

We watched the barge cast off from the landing stage below us. A small cluster of brilliantly dressed officials stood amidships, among them the soberly dressed figure of the Eunuch himself. It was a bright sunny day, with a gentle breeze, and the personal standard of the Orphanotrophus rippled prettily. Everything seemed peaceful and normal. A few fishing boats had their nets down in the bay, a couple of merchant ships were on passage down the straits, and an imperial dromon was heading into the Golden Horn. I guessed she was on her way to the naval arsenal to pick up stores.

We saw the gap widening between the dock and the departing barge. Down on the quayside the bodyguard of Varangians which had accompanied the Orphanotrophus to his embarkation turned and began to march back up the hill to his residence.

'I wonder what the Basileus has got to say to him, and whether he'll manage to patch up his quarrel with his brother Constantine,' Pelagia mused.

Even as she spoke, a bright flash came from high up on the walls of the Great Palace. At first I thought it was the sunlight reflecting off a polished metal shield or a pane of glass in one of the palace rooms, but then the flash was repeated, and I knew it was a signal mirror. Someone in the palace was sending a message across the water. Even as the mirror stopped flickering I saw the dromon, inbound to the arsenal, suddenly change course. Her oars began to thrash the water as her rowers were urged into action, and their blades left a line of small whirlpools in her wake as the warship accelerated. Her target was the Orphanotrophus's barge which was making its way sedately across the harbour. Capture was inevitable. Within moments, the dromon had laid alongside the slow-moving barge and grappled with her. A boarding party from the dromon – I guessed it must be a squad of the Basileus's Pechenegs – rushed across the barge's deck. In a few strides they had surrounded the Orphantrophus and his entourage, who were so astonished that they offered no resistance. For ten years no one had dared challenge the Eunuch's authority, let alone lay hands on him.

I could just make out that the Pechenegs had seized the Orphanotrophus and were carrying him back aboard the dromon, then saw that the warship cast off her lines. She pulled away rapidly from her victim and set course out of the bay, southwards towards the horizon, carrying John with her. The entire operation had lasted less time than the Orphanotrophus's bodyguards took to return back up the hill to his house. The most powerful man in the empire until now had been kidnapped.

'His eyes have almost certainly been put out,' said Psellus with a grimace when I managed to get an appointment with him at his office in the chancellery a week later. 'He may even have been executed. The rumour in the palace is that the Basileus himself stood on the battlements and gave the signal for the Orphanotrophus to be carried off.'

His remark made me realise how lucky I was. I could have been similarly maimed if the Eunuch had set his interrogators on me.

'I've come to ask for your assistance,' I told Psellus. 'Can anything be done to extricate the spatharokandidatos Harald and his colleagues from jail, now that the Orphanotrophus is out of the way? They were put there on his orders.'

To my disappointment, Psellus shook his head. 'I can't risk anything at this time. Not until I know who really holds the reins of power now. Is it the Basileus or is it his uncle Constantine? And what's going to happen to Zoë? Is she still going to be treated as the Empress Mother, as her "son" promised? It's better to wait for things to settle down. There's no need to be distressed about the prison conditions for your friends. I've heard that Araltes has been very generous, spreading his money around, so that he and his companions are living very comfortably. No dark dungeons, heavy chains and that sort of thing. They're being held in the Prandiara prison, and have their own suite of rooms. He has even hired his own staff. Your Araltes lives like a prince.'

'That's what he is, in his own country.'

'My advice to you is to act normally, as if nothing has happened. Carry on with whatever duties are allocated to the Varangians, and not to those Pecheneg ruffians whom Michael brought in as his enforcers. I'll contact you as soon as I see an opportunity to get Araltes's case reviewed by the officials in the Treasury. However, I must warn you that there's no way of knowing when that will be. The civil administration is in paralysis. Everyone believes that the arrest of the Orphanotrophus heralds the start of the power struggle. It has shown that our new Basileus Michael is capable of lashing out suddenly. Who the next victim will be is anyone's guess. Yet as fast as he cuts down his rivals, he makes enemies for himself, not least among the priests. Our religion tells us that the Basileus is Christ's divine appointment, so the Church thinks that it should have a say in how the emperor conducts himself. If Michael alienates the Patriarch, he will have a dangerous foe.'

I did as Psellus recommended and spent the next month as a dutiful member of the Hetaira. Apart from the usual round of ceremonies, there was really very little work to do now that the Pechenegs were responsible for the emperor's personal safety. Former Life Guards gave a wide berth to the Pechenegs, whom we judged to be little more than professional cut-throats unworthy of the tradition of the Hetaira. Their loyalty was only to Michael himself, while our Varangian tradition had been to serve whoever was the legally recognised emperor. In consequence I had ample time to spend with Pelagia, and I must admit that I was finding her style of life increasingly agreeable. Like many people who have worked their way from humble beginnings, she knew how to run an efficient household. As a former baker's wife, she had clear ideas about what should be served at her table, whether it was the quality of the ingredients or the way the food should be cooked. Never in all my life had I eaten so well. Her kitchen staff prepared poultry marinated in wine and stuffed with almonds, served caviar followed by fresh cuts of sturgeon, wild game cooked in olive and garlic, and rich casseroles of pigeon. Most meals concluded with something sweet flavoured with cinnamon, Pelagia's particular favourite. After such banquets I found it necessary to stroll in the garden to aid my digestion, as my stomach was protesting so noisily. One afternoon Pelagia made a joke of it.

'You should make a living in the market. Set up your pitch among the snake charmers and the showmen with their performing dogs, and tell fortunes as a stomach talker. They claim that their rumbling guts speak of the future in the same way the brontologists say that they can interpret the meaning of the thunder claps. Mind you, with the din your stomach makes, I'm not sure to which group you should belong.'

'Where I come from,' I answered huffily, 'we believe that thunder is nothing more than the sound of one of our Gods driving his chariot through the sky. It doesn't signify anything.' I belched as discreetly as possible. 'But we do believe it is possible to read the future in dreams or by reading signs in the sky, the movements of birds and smoke, or by casting certain sticks carved with mystic signs.'

'Civilised or barbarian, everyone believes in the significance of dreams,' observed Pelagia, trying to placate me. 'Entire books have been written about how to do it, though I've never read any of them.'

'There was a time when I used to dream a lot,' I told her. 'And I had the occasional vision which foretold the future, though this was difficult to interpret. Yet since I arrived in Constantinople, I've not had a single prophetic vision, and it's only after a particularly rich meal like that roast peacock with pistachio sauce we had yesterday that I have even dreamed.'

'And what was in that peacock dream?' Pelagia enquired, grinning.

'More a nightmare, really,' I said. 'The Varangians were back on duty as the Life Guard, instead of the Pechenegs, and we were escorting Michael to the throne room. They were all there – the empress Zoë, his uncle Constantine, even the Orphanotrophus. They all stood around and stared at us. They were looking at the state of the Basileus's robes. I remember thinking to myself that the vestitores who dressed him were playing a joke. They had given him to wear a chlamys, the imperial cloak, which was in rags. It also needed a good wash—'

I stopped in mid-sentence because Pelagia had laid her hand on my arm. 'Don't go on,' she said quietly but firmly, 'I don't want to hear any more.'

'Nothing much happened after that in my dream.'

'I know next to nothing about oneirokritika, the science of interpreting dreams,' Pelagia murmured, 'but I do know that the appearance of the Basileus wearing a dirty or threadbare chlamys means the end of his reign is at hand.' She paused. 'Perhaps even the collapse of his dynasty.'

EIGHT

FIVE WEEKS AFTER the elimination of the Orphanotrophus, Michael lashed out once more. A platoon of his eunuch guards burst into the gynaeceum, sheared off Zoë's hair, and forced the empress to put on a nun's black habit. Then they bustled the old lady out of the palace and hurried her down to the Bucephalon harbour where a ship was waiting to carry her to the Prinkipio Islands, half a day's sail away and a traditional place of exile for unwanted members of the royal family. There the Pechenegs handed Zoë over to a nunnery.

The kidnap would have been successful if Michael had not over-reached himself. Alexis the Patriarch had long dabbled in politics and was known to be a supporter of Zoë, whose marriage to the previous emperor he had solemnised. Michael, intending to remove any potential source of dissent, sent four Pechenegs to lure Alexis from the monastery of the Studius. They took a gift of gold and an invitation for Alexis to attend a meeting with the Basileus. The intention was that the gold would lull the Patriarch's suspicions that he might be the next victim of Michael's megalomania, but it had the opposite effect. Alexis fled the monastery, and instead of going to the rendezvous, where Michael had an assassination squad of eunuchs waiting, he went to the church of Hagia Sophia, summoned the senior officials of the administration, and denounced the Basileus as unworthy of the throne.

The first that I and the other Varangians idling in our guardroom knew of these events was when we heard the bells. It began with the great bell of Hagia Sophia sounding out an urgent alarm. Then, as the news spread across the capital, dozens of monasteries and churches joined in. The noise was extraordinary, a massive, constant tolling that reverberated through the city, rolled out across the suburbs, and grew louder and more insistent. The walls of the guardroom seemed to vibrate with the noise. Such a signal was given only when Constantinople was under dire threat, and the citizens poured out into the streets to demand what was happening. The Basileus, they were told by their priests, had tried to kill the Patriarch, and had banished Zoë, representative of the true line of emperors. The Basileus was wickedness personified, and unless he was curbed, he would bring ruin on the city.

The citizenry were puzzled and anxious, not knowing whether to believe the priests or stay loyal to Michael. Some went to the churches to enquire further and to pray; others flocked towards the Great Palace to demand an explanation from the emperor. He sent his most senior representative, the sebastokrator, to address them in the Forum of Constantine and, because the Pechenegs were held back to protect the emperor himself, the sebastokrator took with him a Varangian escort. Halfdan, myself and twenty others marched along the Mese to the Forum with the sebastokrator in our midst and the clamour of the bells pounding in our ears.

The great square of Constantine was packed when we arrived. I saw shopkeepers, ironworkers, beggars, cutlers, carpenters, tilers, masons, stevedores and fishermen. There were also a surprisingly large number of women and children.

The sebastokrator stood on a mounting block and began to address the crowd, shouting to make himself heard over the noise of the bells. His listeners were attentive, though sullen. Zoë the empress had been banished, he shouted, because she was a poisoner. It was better that she was placed where she could do no further harm. Listening, I thought to myself that it was possible that Zoë had poisoned poor bloated Romanus, whom I had seen drown, and that she had done away with her second husband, Michael, whom I had also witnessed dying agonised in the monastery. But claiming that Zoë was involved in a plot to poison the present Basileus seemed highly unlikely.

The sebastokrator ended his announcement and was met with silence. This was more worrying than if the crowd had jeered or scoffed. Only the clanging of the bells sounded.

Beside me Halfdan said quietly, 'Tell him to get down from the mounting block and begin walking back to the palace. He must move calmly and without haste and make it seem as if he has completed his assignment. If he does that, we can protect him. But if he shows any panic, the crowd may turn nasty. There are not enough of us to hold them off.'

I translated Halfdan's instructions and the sebastokrator followed them scrupulously. It was only a short distance back to the palace, but at any moment I expected to feel the thud of thrown stones on our unprotected backs. For the first time I regretted that the Varangians did not carry shields, and I began to appreciate just how menacing a crowd can be. The main gate of the palace, the Bronze Gate, opened a fraction to allow us in, and Halfdan let out a sigh of relief as we slipped inside.

'The Basileus had better do something, and quickly or we'll have a full-scale riot on our hands,' he said.

Michael's response was to reverse his policy towards Zoë. No sooner had the sebastokrator reported the crowd's mood than a squad of Varangians was detailed to accompany a high official of the chancellery to the Bucephalon harbour. A guard boat rushed them to the Prinkipio Islands, where the grovelling official explained to Zoë that her 'son' desired her to return to the city as he needed her advice.

As we waited for Zoë's return, we became aware of increasing disturbances in the city. Frightened messengers arrived with reports of gangs of looters on the prowl: the marauders were selecting the town houses of those who were most closely associated with the Basileus. The largest mob had laid siege to the palace of the emperor's uncle and confidant, Constantine, who had been elevated to the rank of nobelissimus, second in seniority only to the Basileus himself. This worried us because a detachment of Varangians had been assigned to guard Constantine, and we wondered what was happening to our comrades. In mid-morning they joined us, several with cuts and bruises. Constantine had decided to abandon his palace, they said, and had asked his Varangians to escort him through the streets to the Grand Palace where he could join his nephew.

'What's it like out there?' asked one of my colleagues.

A weary-looking guardsman, with a deep gash over one eye where a stone had hit, shrugged. 'No one seems to know what's going on. The crowds are still disorganised. The only thing they do agree on is that the Basileus should not have mistreated Zoë. They're shouting that she is the true imperial line, and that Michael and his family are upstarts. The women in the mob are the worst. They scream and yell abuse. Apparently the staff from the gynaeceum has been spreading rumours that Zoë was beaten up by the Pechenegs. The crowd can't tell the difference between Pechenegs and Varangians. It was a woman who flung the stone that caught me in the face.'

'Is Zoë really the true imperial line?' someone asked. 'What should we do now? Seems to me that we don't owe any loyalty to the new emperor. He ditched us in favour of those beardless Pechenegs. Let them look after him.'

'Enough of that!' snapped Halfdan. 'The guard is always loyal to the emperor. As long as Michael is Basileus, we serve him. That is our oath.'

'And what happens if the mob decides someone else is the emperor? Whom do we follow then?'

'You follow orders,' said Halfdan. But I could see that many of my colleagues were uneasy.

That night we mounted double patrols on the ramparts and gates of the palace. It was an awkward place to protect because, having been expanded and altered over the centuries, it lacked a single defensive perimeter. The best defence, according to the Basileus's councillors, who hurriedly convened, was somehow to deflect the anger of the citizenry and prevent the mob from attacking. So when Zoë arrived back in the palace the following morning, Michael apologised to her for his earlier behaviour and then took her to show her to the crowd.

Crossing the footbridge which joined the palace to the hippodrome, Michael made his entrance in the imperial box with Zoë at his side. But if he thought this display would reassure the mob, he was mistaken.

The hippodrome could hold forty thousand people to watch the parades and spectacles held there. That day not a single seat was empty, and even the sandy arena where the chariots normally raced was packed. The crowd had waited since dawn for Michael to show himself, and the long delay had increased their discontent. When he finally appeared on the balcony, many in the crowd were too far away to recognise that it was Zoë at his side. Others, suspicious of the duplicity of the palace, believed that the old woman beside the Basileus was not the empress at all, but an impostor dressed up in the imperial regalia. Listening from the parapet above the Bronze Gate where Halfdan's company was stationed – the Pechenegs were on Life Guard duty and the bells were silent at last – I heard something which previously I had associated with a bungled circus act in the hippodrome: the sound of jeering interspersed with insults and cries of anger.

As the heckling continued, a movement in the courtyard below me caught my eye. A small group of gatekeepers, the manglabites, was heading towards the palace entrance. Something about their furtive manner told me that they were about to desert their posts. Halfdan noticed it too.

There was a confused shouting in the distance. The Basileus must have left the hippodrome and returned across the footbridge.

'Here they come,' warned Halfdan. 'Lars, take ten men and get down to the gate, make sure it is bolted and barred. Thorgils, you stay close by me. I may need a Greek speaker.'

When I next peered over the parapet, the front ranks of the mob were already milling about in the open space before the Bronze Gate. Most of them were armed with rocks and stones, crowbars and torches. Several, however, carried swords and pikes. These were soldiers, not civilians. The palace was facing a military mutiny as well as a popular uprising of the citizenry.

'We need archers, slingers and javelin men up here, not a squad of axemen,' muttered Halfdan. Once again, the veteran guardsman seemed to be taking charge in a palace crisis. 'Thorgils, go and find me someone in authority who can explain to us the overall plan of defence. Not a tablet scribbler, but a trained soldier.'

I hurried through the corridors and hallways of the palace. All around me there were signs of panic. Officials, still dressed in their formal costumes, were scurrying about, some of them carrying their personal possessions as they anxiously sought to find some way of leaving the building. Once or twice I passed a detachment of Excubitors, the Greek household regiment, and I was relieved that at least some of the local garrison were still loyal to the throne. Eventually I caught up with one of their Greek officers. Saluting him, I asked if he could send archers to the parapet above the Bronze Gate as the mob was getting dangerously close to breaking in.

'Of course,' he snapped. 'I'll send bowmen. Anything else you need?'

'Two or three scorpions would be helpful. If they could be positioned high up on the wall, they would have a good field of fire and prevent the crowd from massing in front of the gate.'

'Can't help you there,' answered the officer. 'There are no ballistae operators in the Palace Guard. Nobody ever thought they would be needed. Try the Armamenton. Maybe someone there can assist. I know they've got some scorpions stored there.'

I had forgotten about the armoury. The rambling Great Palace was like a city in miniature. It had its royal apartments, formal state rooms, chancellery, treasury, tax office, kitchens, silk-weaving workshops, and of course a major arms store. I raced back to the Bronze Gate, where Halfdan was now standing cautiously behind a battlement, looking down at the mob, which had doubled in size and grown much more belligerent

'Stand well back, Thorgils,' he warned. 'They've got archers down there, and some slingers.' An arrow clattered against the stone buttress.

'Can you let me have a dozen men?' I asked. 'I want to get to the armoury and see if I can bring up a scorpion or two.'

Halfdan looked at me quizzically. 'Since when did you become an artillery man?'

'I had a few lessons in Sicily,' I said.

'Well then, take as many men as you need. The mob has not yet got itself sufficiently worked up to launch a concerted attack.'

With a squad of a dozen Varangians at my heels, I headed towards the armoury. I hammered on the heavy double doors until a storekeeper pulled one of them open cautiously. He looked decidedly peevish. Doubtless he had hoped that he was in a safe retreat, well away from any trouble.

'I need weapons,' I blurted, out of breath.

'Where's your written order? You must have a signed author-ity from the archon strategos before I can issue any weapons.'

'Where can I find him?'

'Can't tell you. Haven't seen him all day,' said the storekeeper with an air of smug finality.

'This is an emergency,' I insisted.

'No paperwork, no weapons. That's my orders,' was the short answer I got.

I put my hand on his chest and pushed him aside.

'Here, you can't do that,' he objected, but I was already inside and looking around.

The armoury was generously equipped. I could see everything

from parade equipment with gilded hilts and coloured silk tassels to workaday swords and pikes. Against one wall was a stack of the small round shields used by light infantry.

'Grab as many of those as you can carry,' I told my men, 'and take them back up to the ramparts, and get some of those bows from that rack over there and as many arrows as you can handle. Tell Halfdan that there are plenty more bows and arrows if he needs them.'

Meanwhile I had spotted the heavier weapons in the far corner of the store. I recognised the wooden stocks, the iron winding handles, and the thick stubby arms of the bows of at least a dozen scorpions neatly arranged. Looped around a wooden frame were the special bowstrings made of animal sinew. Trying to recall exactly what I had seen in Syracuse when Nikephorus had shown me round his siege tower, and again during the battle at Traina, I began to select enough items to assemble three scorpions. To the strongest man in my squad, an ox-like Swede, I gave all three tripods to carry. To the others I handed out the remainder of the parts as well as two large bags full of iron bolts. I personally took charge of the trigger mechanisms, as they looked fragile and easily damaged.

'Hail to the new technicians,' joked Lars as my men laid out the items on the walkway behind the parapet and I began to experiment how they would fit together.

As it turned out, the scorpions were easy to assemble. Anyone who knew how to lock together the complicated joints in ship-wright's carpentry could do it, and several of my Varangians had that skill. Only the trigger mechanisms were puzzling, and it took one or two false attempts before I finally got them correctly installed and the scorpions were ready for use.

'Here, Thorgils, you get to release the first bolt,' offered Halfdan as he hoisted the completed weapon up on its tripod.

'No thanks,' I said. 'You wind up and pull the trigger. I want to watch and make sure that I have the tension right.'

Halfdan cranked the handle, drawing back the arms of the

bow, placed a metal bolt in its groove, took aim, and squeezed the trigger. To my satisfaction the bolt flew straight, though Halfdan had overcompensated for the angle and the metal bolt whizzed over the heads of the crowd and smacked into the facade of the buildings opposite.

'Powerful stuff, eh?' commented Halfdan contentedly. 'Still, if I was going to kill someone, I would prefer to do it from close-up, where I can see exactly whom I despatch.'

My satisfaction at assembling the ballistae was replaced by dismay. Looking down into the crowd, I saw Harald. Standing a full head taller than those around him, his long hair and moustaches were unmistakable. Then I identified Halldor and several others of Harald's war band right behind their leader, pushing their way through the crowd to reach the front rank. All of them were wearing helmets and carrying their axes. Obviously the mob had broken into the jails and released all the prisoners. The insurrection had also found a common scapegoat. The mob was chanting, 'Give us the Caulker! Give us the Caulker!'

'Don't fire into the crowd,' I begged Halfdan.

'Are you crazy?' he demanded. 'Why go to the trouble of providing these weapons and not use them?' He reloaded, swivelled the scorpion on its mounting and took aim. The chances that he would hit Harald were remote, but I removed his hand from the trigger.

'Over there to the left,' I said. 'That's Harald of Norway, and behind him, Varangians.'

'So they've broken their oath and joined the rebels,' grunted Halfdan.

'You can't shoot down your own people.'

'No,' said Halfdan. 'That would be cowardly. Hand to hand is the only way. They're traitors.'

He abandoned the scorpion and unslung his axe. 'Time for a sortie, men. Show them that we mean business,' he announced.

I watched the reaction of my comrades. They looked as if they were in two minds whether to follow Halfdan or ignore him.

There was an awkward pause, which was interrupted by the sound of feet on the stone steps leading to the parapet. A Greek officer appeared, a man I recognised vaguely from the siege of Syracuse. He seemed competent, and there was no doubt about what he intended. He gestured for us to leave the parapet.

'We're taking over now,' he said in Greek, and I translated for Halfdan's benefit.

'Ask him what he wants us to do,' Halfdan asked.

The Greek muttered something about the Varangians being held as a strategic reserve, and that we were to wait in the open courtyard behind the Bronze Gate in case a frontal attack was launched. Halfdan seemed disappointed, but obediently he led our platoon down into the courtyard.

'That does it,' said one of our men as we watched a file of Greek heavy infantry mount the stairway to take up the positions we had just left. 'That was a lie about needing a strategic reserve. They don't trust us. They think we will join up with our countrymen outside the palace and throw in our lot with the rebels.' Angrily he stumped over to a bench, dropped his axe on the paving slabs and sat down. 'I don't know about the rest of you, but I'm going to wait here until the Greeks sort out among themselves who is really running this place.'

I knew that the platoon agreed with him, and that in a few moments Halfdan would entirely lose his authority. I had always judged Halfdan to be a decent type, if unimaginative; to save his dignity, I said, 'Maybe I could locate someone in charge who can decide where we can be most useful. It will save time if Halfdan comes with me so that he can explain the tactical situation.'

Without waiting for a response, I set off for Psellus's office in the chancellery. He was the only person in the palace whom I trusted to give me an honest answer: something odd was going on. The mob outside the walls was hanging back, as if waiting for something, and I did not know what it was. The Greek infantry who had replaced us on the parapet had appeared strangely complacent. They were not as bellicose as I had expected, and I did not know why. Perhaps Psellus could explain.

Halfdan and I met him in the corridor long before we reached his office, and to my astonishment he greeted us as his saviours. 'The blessed Demetrios himself must have sent you,' he exclaimed. 'The Pechenegs have abandoned their posts and fled, every last one of them, just when the Basileus needed them most. Are there any more of you Varangians?'

'There are,' I said, 'but they are back near the Bronze Gate, awaiting orders, and frankly I'm not sure that they will obey them. Please tell me what is going on. Why aren't the household troops defending the palace more actively, and why hasn't the mob launched an all-out attack?'

'The emperor has renounced his title,' said Psellus urbanely. 'He wishes to retire to a life of peaceful contemplation. He is to become a monk.'

I must have looked dumbfounded, because Psellus went on, 'he has abdicated in favour of his "mother", the empress Zoë, and her sister, the empress Theodora.'

'But I thought that Theodora was in a nunnery.'

'Until yesterday evening,' said Psellus. 'The Patriarch Alexis suggested that she should renounce her vows and enter political life. She is, after all, born to the purple. To Theodora's credit she resisted the idea at first, but was eventually persuaded. The Patriarch crowned her empress a few minutes after midnight. I expect that she and her sister Zoë will be co-rulers of the empire of the Romans as soon as they can come to a suitable arrangement.'

'What about Michael? Where is he now?' My mind was in a whirl as I tried to grasp the sudden change in the politics of imperial rule.

'Close by, and that is why I am so pleased to see you and your colleague. Michael and his uncle, the Nobelissimus, are awaiting immediate departure to the monastery of the Studius.'

By this stage my mind was reeling. 'But isn't the Studius

monastery the residence of the Patriarch Alexis? And wasn't he the man who led the uprising against the Basileus?'

'Thorgils, for a barbarian you are unusually well informed. However, the Studius monastery is the only one which the former Basileus can reach without being molested by the mob, which, as you have observed, is baying for his blood. From the Bucephalon harbour he can reach the monastery by boat before the crowd knows that he has departed. I presume that you can handle a small boat.'

'Of course.'

'There will be only three passengers: Michael, his uncle Constantine, and a chamberlain. The rest of his staff will go on foot to the monastery, discreetly and in small groups, so that they can arrange Michael's reception. In recent weeks I have been privileged to act as the Basileus's private secretary, so I see it as my duty to intercede on his behalf with the new empresses and organise a smooth handover of the imperial government. As soon as I have their majesties' decision, I will come to the monastery with the news. In the meantime I know that I can trust you and your colleague to transport their highnesses safely to the Studius.'

So that is how it came about that I, Thorgils Leifsson, and my company commander, Halfdan, became a boat crew for the former Basileus, Michael V, as he evaded capture by the mob of Constantinople. It felt strange to be rowing a man who, only the previous day, had been considered semi-divine, so that even his closest attendants were obliged to wear gloves when approaching his presence in case they touched his consecrated flesh. Now he and his uncle, disguised as simple monks, sat an arm's length away in the stern of the small rowing boat we commandeered for the short journey. Their chamberlain was in the bows, directing our course as we picked our way between the mass of fishing boats and the cargo ships at anchor off the city. It seemed that all their crews were ashore, joining the insurrection.

Throughout our brief journey Michael kept his head down, staring silently into the bilge of the boat, and I noticed that water was soaking into his purple boots, which he had not yet removed. His uncle, by contrast, took a more intelligent interest in our surroundings. Surreptitiously I watched him as I heaved on the loom of the oar. There was no mistaking his resemblance to his brother, the Orphanotrophus. They both had the same deep-sunk eyes and shrewd gaze, and they shared an aura of knowing exactly how to set about obtaining what they wanted. What a remarkably talented family, I thought to myself. It had supplied an emperor, a Nobelissimus, and, in the Orphanotrophus, a gifted civil admin-istrator. The mob was wrong to dismiss them as nobodies. The family were adventurers, certainly, but no more so than the giant Maniakes whom the citizenry adored. Only Michael the nephew, sitting in a fog of self-pity, had let them down. He had thrown away his inheritance through inexperience in the wielding of power and his unbridled ambition.

The chamberlain called out that we were to steer for shore. Glancing over my shoulder I saw that we were level with the Studius monastery. Its massive walls of red and grey brick loomed over the landing place, a complex of chapels and cloisters crowned by an array of tiled domes, each topped by a cross. The monas-tery had its own landing steps, and Halfdan and I grabbed on to the mooring chains as our passengers disembarked. By force of habit I refrained from reaching out and touching the ex-Basileus, even when he slipped on the weed-covered steps and nearly fell.

A reception party of monks and courtiers was waiting, and they ushered the two men away.

'Tie up the boat,' the chamberlain ordered, 'and accompany their highnesses. You may be needed.'

Halfdan and I followed the little group into the monastery and then on to the great chapel, entering through a side door half hidden within an angle of the wall.

I gazed around me with interest. The main worship hall was certainly impressive. Above my head rose a great dome, lined with mosaics. Staring down at me from within the vault was a gigantic image of the White Christ, gaunt and stern, with great dark eyes. He looked stiff and sad. In one hand he held his holy book; the other hand was held up in what I supposed was a gesture of blessing or admonition. The light from hundreds of candles in iron holders suspended by chains flickered across his severe expression. The dome rested on great pillars from which hung wooden boards painted with images of the White Christ's most famous followers. The windows were small and set high up in the building, and the shafts of light reached only the upper part of the huge chamber. At ground level illumination depended on many more candles set in huge candlesticks, some as tall as a man, some arranged in banks of at least a hundred at a time. The general impression was of darkness and shadow interspersed with pools of radiant light. The air smelled strongly of incense. At the far end of the church stood the altar, and on each side were yet more masses of candles, as well as two carved and gilded wooden platforms where I supposed the priests of the White Christ stood during their devotions. These two platforms were now occupied by several dozen courtiers, monks, and various bureaucrats. I was reminded of the audience who, in a market square, clamber up on carts to get a better view when jugglers or hucksters perform. They were all looking at Michael and his uncle Constantine as they crossed the floor of the church towards the altar itself.

'I claim the sanctuary of the monastery!' Michael cried out shrilly. He reached the altar and turned towards a monk standing a little in advance of his fellows. The man was, I presumed, the chief priest.

'I claim sanctuary,' Michael repeated, 'and wish to offer myself humbly to the service of our Lord.'

There was a long, long silence, and then the shadows all around the sides of the chapel moved. The walls, I realised, were lined with men. They had been standing there waiting silently, whether in respect or in ambush I could not tell. They stood three or four deep, and now they produced an exasperated sound, a collective, angry muttering. Peering into the shadows I saw that several hundred of the citizens of Constantinople were already in the chapel. They must have been told, or guessed, where the ex-Basileus and his uncle had been heading when they left the palace, and they had got here before us.

Hearing the sound, Michael gave a frightened glance and edged closer to the altar.

'Sanctuary,' he cried again, almost shrieking. 'I have a right to sanctuary.'

Again came angry muttering, and Michael sank to his knees in supplication and seized hold of the cloth that covered the altar. His uncle moved to be beside him, but remained standing.

'Respect the Church!' cried Michael.

Then a man stepped out from the crowd. He appeared to be a minor official, a city employee perhaps. Evidently he was a spokesman.

'You are to stand trial for your crimes—' he began, but Michael interrupted frantically, 'How dare you address me in this fashion?'

Clearly he had forgotten that he was now meant to be a humble monk. He looked round and saw Halfdan and myself standing there.

'Guardsmen,' he ordered, his voice cracking with fear, 'protect me from this lunatic.'

Halfdan took several paces forward and placed himself between the cringing ex-Basileus and the leader of the crowd. I followed him, thinking to myself how ridiculous it was for just two men to attempt to serve as a shield. But for the moment, at least, our presence was effective. The crowd held back, and to my relief I saw Psellus enter the chapel by the main door and come hurrying towards us. With him was a delegation of officials.

'With the authority of the empress Zoë,' he announced loudly so all could hear, 'I bring an order for the detention of His Highness Michael and the Nobelissimus. They are to be brought to the palace for due judgement of their actions. They must not be harmed.'

'He'll only smooth-talk his way out of trouble. Let's deal with him now, our own justice,' an angry voice shouted from the back of the crowd. The onlookers stirred, closing in. Behind us I heard Michael's yelp of fear, and I sensed that the two groups of onlookers on each side of the altar were spellbound by the scene being played out before them.

Psellus was soothing. 'I assure you, your highness, no harm will come to you if you accompany us,' he told him. Then, addressing the crowd's spokesman, he said, 'I promise you that the people will have justice. The empress Zoë is discussing with her sister Theodora how best to restore peace to the city. The people, through their representatives, will be consulted before any decision is reached. For the moment it would be prudent for His Highness Michael and the Nobelissimus to be held within the palace.'

After some hesitation the crowd began to move aside so that the group of officials with Psellus could approach the altar. Michael was still petrified. 'They'll kill me if I leave the church,' he sobbed. 'I refuse to go with you. I won't get a fair trial.' Watching his craven response, I remembered how little mercy he had shown his uncle the Orphanotrophus, and thought to myself that though John the Eunuch might have been ruthless and menacing, he at least had had courage. His nephew was a coward.

'These two guardsmen will accompany us,' said Psellus. 'They will see you safely back to the palace. Just as they brought you here.' He glanced across at me. 'Thorgils, perhaps you and your colleague would be so good as to accompany us on the way to the palace.'

Reluctantly Michael released his grip on the altar cloth and rose to his feet. Then he and his uncle walked down the length of the chapel, surrounded by Psellus's delegation. I noted that several courtiers descended from their vantage point and joined our little procession. I guessed that they were loyal members of Michael's faction.

We emerged from the gloom of the chapel and into daylight, and I realised that it was mid-afternoon. The overthrow of the Basileus had taken less than three days from the moment he had unwisely sent his eunuchs to arrest Zoë until his desperate plea for sanctuary in the monastery.

We started along the broad avenue of the Triumphal Way leading to the heart of the city. I remembered how I had marched the route with the Hetaira, escorting the corpse of Romanus, and later to bid farewell to Maniakes's army as it left for the Sicilian campaign. On the first occasion the crowd had been silent; the second time they had been cheering and shouting encouragement. Now, the crowd was resentful. They pushed in on us from each side, shouting abuse and spitting. We had to thrust our way forward.

We had got as far as the open space called the Sigma, named because it had the same shape as the Greek letter, when I became aware of another agitated group elbowing its way through the crowd towards us. A few steps later I recognised its leader: Harald. With him were at least a dozen of his men, including Halldor. He was escorting a high official of the court, dressed in his formal silk robe of blue and white and carrying his badge of office, an ivory baton. He made a vivid contrast to the shabby figures of Michael and his uncle in their rumpled monks' gowns.

Harald and his men barred our path. We halted, and the crowd drew back to give us a little space. The brilliantly clad official stepped forward and opened a scroll. A silver and purple seal dangled from the lower edge.

'By the authority of their joint Augustae, Zoë and Theodora,' he began. 'Punishment is to be carried out on the former Basileus Michael and the Nobelissimus Constantine.'

Michael let out a shout of protest. 'You have no right. I was promised safe conduct,' he screamed.

From the crowd came a muted growl of approval.

'The punishment is to be carried out with immediate effect,' concluded the official, rolling up his scroll and nodding to his Varangian escort.

Four of Harald's men stepped forward and took hold of Michael and his uncle by their arms. Halfdan and I did not interfere. We were outnumbered, and besides, I felt exhausted. Events had moved beyond anything I could have imagined, and I was tired of the whole business. I no longer cared who held the reins of power in the Queen of Cities. As far as I was concerned, this was a matter for the Greeks to sort out among themselves.

Michael continued pleading and sobbing. He was writhing in the grasp of the two Varangians, begging to be spared. 'Let me go! Let me go! I was promised safe conduct,' he repeated over and over again. He knew what would happen next.

Later it would be said that Harald of Norway carried out the mutilation, but that was not so. The little group had brought their own specialist with them, and he had with him the tools of his trade. A small, rather effeminate-looking man came forward and asked for a brazier.

We waited for a short while before someone came back with a brazier of the common household sort normally used for cooking. Its embers were glowing and it was placed on the ground. The executioner, for that was his role, I now realised, placed the tip of a long thin iron bar in the centre of the fire and blew delicately on the embers. The crowd pushed around so closely that he had to ask them to move back to allow him space to work. When the tip of the rod was glowing red-hot, the little man looked up at his victims. He was expressionless. I remembered Pelagia's warning that the torturers and interrogators of the palace took a pride in their work.

Michael was in hysterics, thrashing from side to side, begging to be spared. His uncle Constantine, the Nobelissimus, calmly took a pace forward.

'Let me go first,' he said quietly. Then, turning towards the crowd, he said firmly: 'I ask you to step back a little further still, so that there may be sufficient witnesses to the fact that I met my fate with courage.' Then he calmly lay down on the paving slabs, flat on his back, face to the sky, eyes wide open.

I wanted to look away, but found that I was too appalled. The executioner came forward with his iron rod and deftly pressed the tip into Constantine's right eye. The man's body arched back in agony, and at almost the same moment the iron rod was dipped into the left eye. A little hiss of steam came with each movement. Constantine rolled over on to his front, his hands pressed against his sightless eyes. He let out a deep, agonised groan. Hands reached down to help him back on his feet. Someone had produced a silk scarf, which was quickly bound around his head, and I saw two courtiers, themselves weeping, support the Nobelissimus, who was unable to stand unaided.

The executioner now turned towards Michael. He was squirming in the grip of the two Varangians and blubbering with terror. His gown was wet where he had soiled himself. The executioner nodded, indicating that the ex-Basileus was to be forced to the ground and held there, face up. The two Varangians pressed Michael to his knees, then pulled him over backwards. Michael still flailed about, twisting and turning, trying to escape. Two more of Harald's men knelt down and took a grip of his legs, pinning them to the paving stones. The Varangians who held his arms pulled them out straight, then pressed down on his wrists so that he was pinioned in the shape of a cross.

Michael's howls had risen to a desperate pitch, and he whipped his head from side to side. The executioner was reheating the iron, blowing gently on the charcoal. When he was ready, he sidled softly across to the spread-eagled ex-Basileus, and, without bothering to clamp the head steady, he again made a double dart with the burning spit. A sound rose from deep within Michael's throat and burst out in a terrible howl.

The executioner stepped back, his face still expressionless, and the Varangians released their grip. Michael curled up in a sobbing ball, his arms wrapped around his head. Mercifully, his courtiers picked him up. Then they turned and carried him away, as the crowd, silenced by the terrible punishment, parted to let them through.

NINE

LIKE A SHIP BUFFETED by a sudden great wave, the empire of the Romans heeled, almost capsized, then began to right itself when the ballast of centuries of obedience to the throne made itself felt. During the days which followed the blinding of Michael and his uncle, there was widespread disquiet in Constantinople. The citizens asked themselves whether it was possible that two elderly women could run an empire. Surely the machinery of the administration would stutter and come to a halt. Foreign foes would then take the chance to attack the imperial frontiers. There would be civil war. But as day followed day and nothing dire occurred, tensions eased. In the chancellery, in the tribunals, and in the myriad offices of state, the bureaucrats returned to their records and ledgers, and the government of the empire resumed its normal course. Yet not everything was quite as it had been before. During the insurrection the mob had broken into the Great Palace. Most of the crowd had hunted for valuables to loot, but a small and determined band had headed for the archives and burned the tax records, as those officials who came back to the treasury discovered.

'Simeon the money changer suggested that we torch the files,' Halldor told me in the guardroom where the Varangians had once again taken up their duties. 'I doubt that Harald himself would have thought of it, but Simeon sought us out during the uproar. He too had been released from jail by the mob, and he gave us directions as to where to find the archives.' And with a chuckle he added, 'It means, of course, that now there is no evidence against those accused of collusion with the tax collectors.'

'I'm surprised that you found time to destroy tax records when you were also carrying out the instructions to arrest Michael and the Nobelissimus.'

'There was time enough,' said Halldor. 'The sister empresses argued for hours over what should be done with the former Basileus. Zoë wanted him imprisoned, awaiting trial. But Theodora was all for having his eyes put out, and as quick as possible.'

'Surely it was the other way round? Theodora was a nun, or at least had been.'

'No,' said Halldor. 'Theodora was the bloodthirsty one.'

I murmured something about the idea that the Christians, especially the nuns and monks, were meant to practise forgiveness and charity, but that evening, when I crossed over to Galata to spend the evening at Pelagia's villa, my friend soon set me straight.

'You still don't understand, do you, Thorgils? When it comes to the pursuit of power, nothing matters to those who are really ambitious. Take the example of Araltes. You think so highly of him and you assist in every way you can. Yet he will stop at nothing to achieve his ambitions, and one day you may regret being so loyal to him.'

I was thinking to myself that Pelagia probably resented my allegiance to Harald, when abruptly she changed the subject: 'Next time you are on ceremonial guard duty, take a good look at the two empresses for me, will you? I'd be interested to hear what you make of them.'

I did as she asked, and at the next meeting of the supreme state council in the Golden Hall I made sure that my position in the circle of Life Guards was right beside the imperial throne. In fact there were now two thrones, one for each of the empresses, and Theodora's throne was set back a fraction, signifying that Theodora was very slightly junior to her sister. I could see that court protocol had adapted remarkably smoothly to the novel arrangement of twin female rulers. All the usual high functionaries were present, dressed in their official robes of silk brocade and holding their emblems of office. Standing nearest to the empresses were their special favourites, and behind them were the most senior ministers. Then came an outer ring of senators and patricians, and finally, in the background, a group of ranking civil servants. Among them, I identified Psellus who, judging by his green and gold robe, was now a senior official of the chancery.

I took careful note of details to tell Pelagia. Zoë was more plump than her sister, and had managed to retain a remarkable youthfulness, perhaps as a result of all those ointments and perfumes I had heard about. Her skin was smooth and unlined, and it was difficult to equate the harassed supplicant whom I had turned away from her husband's deathbed with the poised and immaculately manicured woman who now sat on the throne in front of me. Interestingly, when Zoë was bored she amused herself by eyeing the more handsome men in the room, and so I judged that she was still man-hungry. Theodora, by contrast, fidgeted as she sat. Taller than her sister, she was rather scrawny, with a head that seemed too small for her body, and I had the impression that she was unintelligent and frivolous.

While I was wondering which of the two sisters was dominant in their partnership, I heard Harald's name mentioned. The akolouthos, the commander of the Hetaira, was making a formal request on behalf of spatharokandidatus Araltes. He had asked permission to leave the imperial service. The logothete of the dromos who was hearing the petition turned to consult Zoë, bowed obsequiously and asked for her decision. Zoë had been gazing at a handsome young senator, and I doubt that she even knew what the subject was. 'Denied,' she said absently. The logothete bowed a second time and turned back to face the akolouthos. 'Denied,' he repeated. The business of the day moved on.

'Harald won't like that at all,' said Halldor when I told him the decision that evening. 'He's heard that his nephew Magnus has been declared King of Norway.'

'What difference does that make?'

Halldor looked at me as though I was a dimwit. 'Harald has as good a claim to the throne as his nephew, probably better. That's what all this has been about – the amassing of loot, the gathering in of valuables. The money will be his war chest if he has to fight for what he considers rightfully his. Sooner or later he will seek his inheritance, and the longer he delays, the more difficult it will be to press his case. My guess is that he will ignore the government's decision and leave.'

'But where will he find the ships to take him back up the straits to the Pontic Sea and along the rivers to Gardariki? ' I objected. 'It is not like when he sent those three ships back with the emir's ransom from Sicily. What's left of his war band is now a land force, without ships. If he tries to leave without permission, he'll be arrested again. Then he'll never get to claim the throne.'

'They'll have to catch him first,' said Halldor stubbornly, but I could see that he lacked a solution to the problem.

'Let me see what I can come up with,' I said, for something told me that this was my chance to make myself indispensable to Harald and win his trust for the future.

Psellus was so swamped with work that I had to sweeten the chartularius of his office with a small bribe to give me an appointment.

'It's all very well having two empresses,' Psellus complained when I finally got to see him, 'but it doubles the workload of the officials. Everything must be prepared in duplicate. Every document has to be written out twice so that a copy can be sent to the staff of each empress, but frankly neither woman seems much interested in dealing with the chores of government when the papers do arrive. They prefer the more frivolous aspects of their role. It's very pleasant having so many banquets, receptions, pageants and the like, but the administration moves very slowly, mired in honey, you might say.' He sighed and shifted the pile of paperwork on his desk. 'How's your friend the spatharokandidatos doing?'

'You've guessed correctly,' I said. 'My visit is about Araltes.' I lowered my voice. There was no one else in the room, but I knew that very little was truly private in the Great Palace. 'Araltes urgently needs to resign his post and leave Constantinople. It is very important that he does so. But he has been forbidden permission by Zoë.'

Psellus got up from his seat and went over to check that there was no one loitering outside.

'Thorgils,' he said seriously, 'it was one thing to suggest how Araltes might be cleared of charges for tax fraud. That could have been arranged with some judicious bribes. It is entirely another matter to connive at the direct disobedience of an imperial decision. It could lead to my impeachment and – at worst – the death penalty. I have no wish to be scourged, tied up in a sack and thrown into the sea.'

'I know,' I said. 'It gets worse. It's not just Araltes who should be allowed to leave. The surviving members of his war band – there are about eighty men – will want to depart with him. They've got what they came for. They've made their fortunes.'

Psellus sighed. 'That's outright desertion. Army regulations call for punishment by mutilation or death.'

'I know,' I said. 'But don't you have any suggestions as to how Araltes and his men can get away?'

Psellus thought for a while. 'Right now I don't have any idea,' he said, 'but I can assure you that if Araltes does succeed in leaving without permission, there will be a violent hue and cry. There will be a hunt for those who might have helped him. His close associates will be picked up and interrogated. You have worked with Araltes for several years now, and you would be the first to fall under suspicion. I suggest that if Araltes does leave the city, you make sure that you leave with him.'

'That's something that I've already been thinking about,' I said.

Psellus came to a decision. 'Thorgils, I promised that I would assist you. But this request of yours goes beyond anything I had expected. I have to protect myself. If the scheme fails and you, Araltes and the others are caught, I must not be traceable. If an opportunity for Harald's departure with his men presents itself, I will contact you, but not in person. That would be too dangerous. Even your visit here today is now a risk to me. I do not want you to come to this office again. Instead I will write to you, and that message will be the last you will hear from me.'

'I understand,' I said. 'I'll wait for your contact.'

'It may never arrive,' Psellus warned. 'Anything could happen. I may get transferred out of this office, or I may never see the opportunity for Araltes to slip away. And if the letter falls into the wrong hands, that would be a disaster for all of us.'

By now I had guessed what Psellus was leading up to. I remembered how Harald had used rune symbols as a private code to set up the ambush of the Arab pirate, anticipating that his letter would be intercepted.

'You will use code?' I asked.

Psellus blinked in surprise. 'As I've noted before, Thorgils, for a barbarian you are remarkably astute. Here, let me show you.' He reached for a sheet of paper and wrote out the Greek alphabet, arranging the twenty-seven letters in three equal lines. 'The principle is simple,' he said. 'One letter substitutes for another that falls on the same line but in the mirror position. Thus, the second letter on the first line, beta, is substituted with the second to last letter on the same line, eta. Similarly with the other letters. It's a very basic code, and any senior bureaucrat would recognise it immediately. But it would baffle a mere messenger who might open the letter and read it out of curiosity.'

'I understand,' I said. 'I'm very grateful.'

I HAD TO WAIT nearly five weeks for Psellus's coded message to arrive, and it was a bitter-sweet interval. As Psellus had remarked, the reign of the Augustae, the two empresses, was characterised by frivolity. It was as if the terrible events of the fall of the Basileus Michael had to be followed by a period of gaiety so that the people could expunge the memory of the rebellion. Apparently, when Halfdan and I had been taking the Basileus to the Studius monastery, hundreds had died in the streets during skirmishes between the rebels and the troops loyal to the Basileus, as well as among the bands of looters fighting over the spoils. Now the populace wanted to be distracted, and Zoë and Theodora dipped into the treasury reserves to pay for parades and spectacles in the hippodrome. They gave lavish banquets, and even allowed selected members of the public to visit the Great Palace and see its marvels.

This gave me the opportunity to repay Pelagia for her kindness and hospitality, and I showed her as much of the Great Palace as was permitted. As a commoner she was banned from the great apartments of state, of course, but I took her to see the private zoo with its collection of exotic animals, including a hippopotamus and a long-necked African cameleopard, and in the Tzykanisterion sports ground we watched a horseback tournament. Young patricians were playing a game which involved using long-handled mallets to hit a leather ball the size of an apple into a goal. The game bored Pelagia, but she was fascinated by the horologion, a Saracen-made contraption which calculated hours by measuring water draining from a bowl and opened and closed small doors from which carved figures emerged according to the time of day.

'Isn't it strange,' she commented 'that the palace tries to make sure that everything endures and remains the same as it has always been. Yet it is also the place that measures how time is passing. It is almost as if the palace believes that one day they will discover how time could be stopped.'

At that moment I should have told Pelagia that my own time

in that city might soon be coming to an end, that I would be leaving Constantinople. But I shirked the opportunity, and we went instead to visit the gynaeceum, where Pelagia's sister was waiting to show her around. I was forbidden from entering. As I stood in the courtyard of the beardless ones, the guardian eunuchs, I agonised that perhaps I had been too hasty in seeking Psellus's help in extricating Harald and the others from their service to the emperor. Maybe, instead, I should make my life in the Queen of Cities, just as Halfdan had done. I was now forty-two years of age, past the prime of life, and the attractions of Constantinople with its luxurious lifestyle and pleasant climate had a strong appeal. Pelagia had never remarried since the death of her husband, and the two of us had become very close, so there was every chance that she would accept me as her partner, if that was what I proposed. There was no doubt that life with Pelagia, whom I respected deeply, would be very agreeable. I would retire from the Life Guard, live harmoniously with her in the villa in Galata, and give up my ambition to restore the Old Gods in the northern lands. All I had to do was ignore Psellus's message, if it ever came.

I was on the verge of making this decision when Pelagia emerged from the gynaeceum. She was marvelling at the luxury with which Zoë had surrounded herself, yet dismayed by the tedium of life within the women's quarters. 'They eat their meals with golden forks in there,' she said, 'but the food must taste like the ashes of the living dead.' Her remark, following so closely on my thoughts about my dilemma, made me wonder if, by taking the more comfortable path, my life would become a hollow shell; and whether, should Pelagia ever learn that I had abandoned my deeply held ambition, she would blame herself.

Even so, perhaps I would have stayed in Constantinople had not Loki strained at his bonds. There was a shaking of the ground on the evening after Pelagia and I visited the Great Palace. It was only a minor tremor, scarcely felt in the Varangian barracks. A few statues fell from their plinths along the Mese, several apartment blocks were damaged, and the city engineers had to come with ladders and hooks the next day to pull down the structures that were too dangerous. But on the Galata side of the Golden Horn the damage was far more severe. Several of the new houses collapsed as a result of shoddy workmanship. One of them was Pelagia's villa. She had just returned to her house, and she and several of her servants were crushed. I heard of her death from her sister Maria, who came to fetch me the next morning, and the two of us crossed the Golden Horn to visit the scene of the calamity. As I looked on the tumbled ruins of her house, I felt as desolate as if I was standing on the edge of a great void into which Pelagia had disappeared and from which she would never return. Numbed, I was overcome by a profound sadness that someone so full of spirit had gone, and I wondered whether Pelagia, who had believed neither in the salvation promised by the White Christ nor in my Old Gods, now existed in some other world.

Her death broke the only real link that I had with the Great City, and persuaded me that Odinn had other plans for the remaining years of my life.

Pelagia's family gathered to settle her affairs, and from them I learned that she had been very astute in investing my guardsman's salary for me. Thanks to her I was now reasonably wealthy, even without my secret share of the emir's ransom and the salvage of the Arab pirate galea, most of which had already been carried northward in Harald's ships returning from the Sicilian campaign. The following week I went discreetly to see the financier, a member of the banker's guild, to whom Pelagia had entrusted the safekeeping of my funds and asked him if I could withdraw the money as I was thinking of travelling abroad.

'No need to do that,' he replied. 'If you carry too much coin, you might be waylaid and robbed. I can arrange for you to collect your money at your destination from my fellow bankers, if the place is not too distant.'

'Would the city of Kiev be too far?' I asked.

'Not at all. I could manage to have your funds made available to you in Kiev. We have been doing an increasing amount of business there these past few years, transferring money for the Rus traders who come annually to this city. Not all of them want to travel back burdened with trade goods, struggling to haul them back upstream over the portages. They get notes of credit from me, which they redeem in Kiev.'

The banker's assurance removed my worry that Harald's departure from Constantinople might be hampered by financial complications. He too could use the bankers to move his assets from Constantinople. Now everything depended on Psellus to come up with some scheme whereby we could escape.

His cryptogram, when it finally arrived in late May, was so terse that there were just six words. It read, 'Two ousiai, Neiron, peach silk, Nativity.'

The first part was clear to me. Ousiai are small dromons, about the size of our Norse ships. Each normally carries a crew of about fifty men and they serve as fast escort vessels. The Neiron was the naval arsenal on the Golden Horn, so presumably the two ousiai would be docked there at the time of the feast of the Nativity. But I was puzzled and disappointed by Psellus's mention of the Nativity. If this was the date when he thought Harald and his men would have their chance to leave Constantinople, then my friend was more of a cloistered bureaucrat than I thought. The Nativity, the birth of the White Christ, occurs in mid-winter, and surely, I told myself, Psellus knew that December was far too late for a departure from Constantinople. The sailing weather was atrocious, and by the time we reached the river leading towards Kiev it would be in flood or frozen over. We had to leave in the summer or early autumn at the latest.

The reference to peach silk was a complete enigma. I could see no connection with warships at the arsenal.

So I went to the House of Lights. This was the most luxurious shopping emporium in the capital. Occupying a prime site on the most fashionable stretch of the Mese, it stayed open day and night,

its arcades lit by hundreds upon hundreds of candles. Only one
item was on sale – silk. The precious fabric was available in every
grade and style and colour, whether as lengths of cloth, as
complete garments, or cut and part-finished ready to be sewn
together. In all the known world the House of Lights was the
largest single market for silk, and the market dealers there were
among the wealthiest merchants in the city, as well as the most
rigorously controlled. They were obliged to report every single
transaction over ten nomisma in value to the eparch of the city so
that his officials knew exactly where each length of material came
from and to whom it went. If a foreigner wished to buy silk, the
dealer was only allowed to offer the lower grades of fabric, and
he was obliged to report his customer's departure from Constantinople so that his baggage could be searched for contraband.
Failure to do so would mean that the silk merchant was flogged,
his head shaved in public humiliation, and all his goods confiscated.

Mindful of this strict regime, I chose the most discreet of the
silk merchants' shops in the House of Lights and asked to speak
with the owner. A white-haired man with a sleek, prosperous
appearance came out from a back room, and the moment he saw
I was a foreigner suggested that we discuss our business in private,
in a back alcove.

'I'm enquiring about the price and availability of good quality
silks for export,' I explained.

He complimented me on my excellent Greek and asked where
I had learned to speak the language with such fluency.

'In trade,' I answered evasively. 'Mostly the shipping business.'

'Then you will already be familiar with the restrictions
forbidding me to sell certain categories of silk to those who are
not resident in this city,' he murmured, 'but alternative arrangements can sometimes be made. Did you have any particular goods
in mind?'

'Highly coloured silks make more profit for me when I sell
them on. It depends what is available.'

'At this moment I have good stocks of dark green and yellow in half-tint.'

'What about other colours? Orange, for example? That's popular where I come from.'

'It depends on the depth of the hue. I can probably find a pale lemon orange, close to the yellow I have. But the more dye stuff used in colouring the material, the more difficult it is to obtain. And, of course, more expensive.'

'If I placed an order for a specific colour, could you prepare it for me?'

He shook his head. 'The law forbids silk dealers from exercising the craft of dyeing silk. That is a separate craft. Nor can I handle raw silk. That too is a separate profession.'

I adopted a disappointed look. 'I had particularly hoped to find peach-coloured silk, for a very special client. And I could pay a premium price.'

'Let me send someone to check.'

He called a servant, gave him his instructions, and while we waited for the man to return from his errand, he showed me various samples of his stock.

'I'm sorry to say,' reported the silk merchant when his servant came back with the information he needed, 'that peach-coloured silk will be impossible to obtain, at least for some time.' He looked knowing, and continued, 'There's a rumour that the Augusta Zoë is due to get married again . . . for the third time, can you imagine! The royal workshops are working at full stretch to produce all the garments and hangings needed for the ceremony, and peach-coloured silk is a major item on their list of requirements.'

'But I thought purple was the imperial colour?'

'It is,' said the silk merchant, 'and so too is deep red and those shades of violet which border on purple. All those hues are strictly reserved for the palace. Anyone making or selling such material would be in serious trouble. Peach-coloured silk is made with the same dyestuff that produces the forbidden shades. It is a matter of precisely how much of the dye is mixed with certain tinting herbs, the temperature in the dyer's vat, and other craft secrets. Because of this association, peach is considered to be very exclusive and is customarily sent as a present to foreign rulers to inform them of important palace events such as weddings or coronations.'

I sighed. 'How very disappointing. I don't suppose it is worth my waiting in the city for peach-coloured silk to become available again?'

'Preparing the gifts for the foreign potentates will not be a high priority,' the silk dealer said. 'The royal workshops will want to get all the ceremonial material out of the way first, then use up the last stocks of dye to make the peach silk for shipment.'

'And when might that be? I need to leave well before the celebration of the Nativity.'

'It depends which Nativity you mean,' he replied. 'I presume you are from Venice, or Genoa perhaps. In the west you celebrate the Nativity of our Lord, and so do we. But this city celebrates another very special Nativity, that of Mary, our protectress. And her Nativity falls in September.'

My sudden intake of breath must have puzzled the silk merchant, for I saw that I had given Psellus too little credit for his secret intelligence, and even as I hurried away from the House of Lights, I was busy recalculating how much time I had to prepare Harald's escape from Constantinople. If Psellus's information about the two galleys was correct, then I had three months to get everything ready.

IT COST ME five nomisma to bribe a clerk working in the dromos to keep me supplied with further details of the silk shipment as they emerged. Psellus must have had an excellent contact in the royal silk factory, because on June the eleventh Zoë did get married again – to a patrician by the name of Constantine who was acclaimed as the new Basileus the next day – and it was a little less than three months later that the corrupt clerk in the dromos informed me that the thirty bolts of peach-coloured silk were ready for despatch as gifts to the Caliph of Egypt. The silk was to be taken there by the imperial envoy carrying the official news of the acclamation of a new Basileus.

'According to my information,' I told Harald, 'two ousiai have been ordered to the Neiron to pick up the silk and other gifts. They are on standby to receive the imperial ambassador. He will come aboard as soon as the chancery has prepared the official letters announcing the coronation of the new Basileus.'

'You suggest that we seize the vessels?'

'Yes, my lord. They would suit your purpose. Ousiai are fast and manoeuvrable, and they can carry you and your men up to the Pontic Sea.'

'And how do you propose that we acquire these vessels? The arsenal is heavily guarded.'

'My lord, you remember your mission to the Holy Land as an escort for the architect Trdat?'

'Of course.'

'I suggest that you and your men present yourselves at the gates of the Neiron as the escort for this new ambassador.'

I could see that Harald immediately liked the idea of this deception. 'And what makes you think that the authorities in the dockyard will be tricked?'

'Leave that to me, my lord. All I ask is that you and your men act like a formal escort, and that you are ready to seize the two dromons when the time is right.'

'That part of the plan will not be a problem.'

Never before had I forged an official document, but I had retained the official orders I received when we had accompanied Trdat, and now I used them as my model. I found myself thanking the Irish monks who had taught me penmanship in my youth as I drew up an official-looking document stating that Harald and his men were to escort the envoy bearing gifts to the Caliph of Egypt. For paper I used a sheet of parchment which I purchased from my contact in the dromos. I paid him another two nomisma extra for the right colour ink — black for the text, red for the invocation to the Holy Trinity which is placed at the beginning of every official order. The ministerial signature I copied from my genuine original, and the seal with its grey silk ribbon I merely cut off and transferred. Finally I carefully folded the fake document with exactly the same creases, as I had heard that this was a secret method by which the clerks guaranteed the authenticity of a document.

Then, on the day before the feast of the Nativity of Mary, Harald, the remainder of his war band and I arrived at the main gate of the Neiron and requested permission to stow our gear aboard the two dromons. Fortunately the archon, the director of the dockyard, was absent as he was preparing for the feast day, and his deputy was too nervous to question why so many men were needed as an embassy escort. Also, Harald's imperious manner cowed him. The official barely glanced at the forged orders before handing us over to a junior assistant to take us to the dromons. We made our way past the shipwrights, riggers and painters, who glanced at us curiously, surprised to see so many foreigners within the arsenal, and eventually came to a short wooden pier where the two ousiai were moored. As I had anticipated, their crews had been given leave to prepare for the festival, and they had left their vessels in care of the dockyard. There was no one aboard.

'Sweeps and sails left on deck, thank the Gods,' muttered Halldor, looking around the vessels, and I realised that in my enthusiasm as a forger I had forgotten that the dromons might not be fully ready for sea.

'We'll stow our gear on board and stay the night,' I told the archon's assistant.

He looked surprised. 'Are you not attending the festivities tomorrow?' he asked.

'No,' I said. 'These men are unbelievers. Also the sekreton of the dromos informs me that the ambassador himself may arrive tomorrow evening, and we could be getting under way without delay.'

'But the regular crews are on shore leave,' the man objected.

'And if they are found to have neglected their duty, they will be reprimanded,' I added.

The dockyard assistant took the hint. 'Very well. I will make arrangements for additional fresh water and stores to be brought aboard tomorrow. But as it is a feast day, I cannot guarantee that it will be possible to provide all that is needed. I was not made aware that the ambassador would have such a numerous escort.'

'Do your best,' I assured him. 'We've brought enough rations with us to last the next few days.'

By mid-afternoon the activity of the dockyard was already subsiding. The sounds of hammering and sawing and the shouts of workers faded as the shipwrights left their tasks and went home early to prepare for the festival. Soon the only people left in the Neiron were the members of the fire watch, whose duty was to keep an eye on the highly combustible stores, and a night guard of about a dozen men who patrolled the slipways and quays.

Harald's men made pretence of settling down for the night aboard the two ousiai, but many of us were too nervous to sleep, and I worried that the night guard would become suspicious. Their patrol was random, and there was no way of anticipating their visits, so I told the young officer in charge that we would post our own sentries, as this was our custom, and persuaded him that his own men needed to come no closer than the foot of the jetty.

Everything now depended on the timing of our next move.

At the first glimmer of dawn, Harald quietly gave the order to unmoor our vessel from the quay. Astern of us, the second ousiai followed us. As silently as possible we pushed off from the pier and began to row out into the Golden Horn. We could feel the ripples slapping against the thin wooden hulls of the lightly built dromons. A fresh breeze from the north was raising waves in the straits outside, but in the sheltered waters of the great harbour the waves had little effect.

We were a long bowshot from the shore when a trumpet sounded the alarm from the Neiron behind us. The nightwatch had discovered we were missing.

'Put your backs into it!' roared Halldor, who was at the helm. 'Show those Greeks what real rowing is like.'

Each ousiai had a single bank of oars, identical to a longship, and Harald's Norsemen, two men to each oar handle, were relishing the return to their old ways. Harald himself was not too proud to seat himself on the oar bench nearest to the helm and row alongside his men.

'Row your guts out, men!' urged Halldor. From astern we could hear the shouts of the helmsman of the second ousiai following in our wake. Further in the distance was the clamour of alarm bells and more trumpet calls.

We picked up speed. The light was strengthening, and soon we would be in full view of anyone watching from the harbour walls. If the alarm was passed quickly enough, the signal mirrors on the harbour wall would begin to flash a message to the guard boats in the bay.

Halldor grabbed my arm and pointed ahead. 'Look!' he said. 'The chain is still in place.'

I squinted forward through the grey light of dawn and knew that my plan was in ruins. Directly across our path stretched a line of wooden rafts, evenly spaced, about fifteen paces apart. Low in the water, so that even the smallest wave broke across them, they bobbed and gleamed blackly. Hanging below them was the chain which closed off the Golden Horn each night and turned it into a lake. It was supposed to be removed at first light so that the harbour was open to traffic, and our way to the straits should have been clear, but I had failed to anticipate that, on the feast day of the Nativity, the chain-keepers would be slow in carrying out their duties. We were trapped.

Seeing my dismay, Harald left his oar handle to his neighbour on the bench and stepped up to the stern deck. 'What's the trouble?' he demanded.

There was no need to explain, I pointed at the line of rafts.

Coolly he surveyed the obstacle. 'How deep does the chain hang?' he asked.

'I don't know. The shoreward end is fastened to land, and it is floated out with the rafts each sunset.' In the days when I had stayed in Pelagia's house overlooking the bay, I had often seen the teams of workboats struggling out with the chain at dusk and closing off the harbour.

Harald looked up at the sky. There was enough light for us to see the links of the chain where they crossed each raft. 'What do you think, Halldor?' he said, turning to the Icelander.

'Can't say to be sure,' Halldor replied. 'Must sag a bit between each raft. Stands to reason.'

Again we heard alarm signals from the shore. A fire gong was being beaten, its clangour carrying unmistakably across the water.

Harald stepped to the edge of the steersman's platform and looked down the length of our ousiai. Ahead of him forty or more Norsemen were rowing steadily. They had the vessel moving sweetly through the water, so they had dropped the rhythm of the oar strokes to a measured beat. To an observer it might have looked as if they were relaxing their effort, but every man aboard knew that it was a waste of effort to tug dramatically at the oar handles. What was needed now was disciplined, powerful rowing to keep our vessel cruising forward.

'When I give the word,' called Harald, 'every man takes twenty oar strokes with all his strength. When I shout a second time, the oarsmen on the first five benches drop their oars, leave their benches and run to the stern. The others are to keep rowing. Is that understood?'

The labouring oarsmen looked up at their leader standing on the deck above them and nodded. Every last one of them knew what Harald had in mind.

The line of rafts was very close now. 'Get ready,' Harald
warned.

I jumped down from the stern deck and took the place at the
oar bench that Harald had vacated. Next to me sat a Swede, a
scarred veteran from the Sicilian campaign. 'So they've finally got
you at an oar handle, rowing and not scheming,' he grunted at
me. 'That's a change worth waiting for.'

'Now!' shouted Harald, and we began to count our twenty
strokes, roaring out the numbers before Harald shouted out again,
and behind me I heard the clatter of oar handles as the men in the
forward benches dropped their oars and ran back down the length
of the galley. I felt the angle of the vessel alter, the bow rising as
the weight of the extra men came on the stern. Three strokes later
there was a grinding, slithering wrench as the keel of our little
dromon struck the chain with a crash. In a few paces we came to
a complete stop. The force of our collision had sent the galley
sliding up on the hidden links; we hung there, stranded on the
chain.

'Now! Every man forward!' yelled Harald, and all of us left
our benches and scrambled into the bows. Slowly, very slowly,
the galley tilted forward. For a moment I feared the vessel would
capsize, as she teetered half out of the water. Then the added
weight in her bows pulled her forward, and with a creaking groan
the ousiai slid forward over the chain and into the open water on
the far side. We all lost our balance, trod on one another, and
grabbed for oars that were sliding overboard as we cheered with
relief. We had forced the barrier, and now the open sea lay ahead.

As we settled again to the oar benches, we looked back to see
our second galley approaching the chain. She followed the same
technique. We watched the ousiai accelerate, heard the shout of
her helmsman and saw the men jump up from the forward benches
and run towards the stern. We could clearly see the bow lift, then
the sudden tilt as the vessel struck the hidden chain and come to
a halt, straddled across the links. Like us, the crew then ran

forward and we held our breath as the vessel rocked forward, only this time the ousiai did not slip clear; she was too firmly stuck. Another command, and the crew, forty or more men, scrambled back towards the stern, then turned and threw their weight forward, striving to break the grip of the chain. The ousiai rocked again, but still stayed fast.

'Guard boats!' Halldor shouted, and pointed. Close to the shore where the chain was attached to the land, five or six harbour guard boats were putting out to intercept us.

Once more our comrades on the stranded ousiai tried to rock their vessel clear. This time their frantic effort brought disaster. As the crew applied their weight, first in the bow and then at the stern, the strain proved too great. Like a stick which breaks when overloaded, the keel of the ousiai snapped. Perhaps the vessel was older and weaker than ours, or less well built, or maybe by ill fortune the chain lay directly under a joint in her main timbers where the shipwrights had scarfed the keel. The result was that the ousiai cracked in half. The long narrow hull broke apart, her planks sprang open, and her men fell into the sea.

'Backwater with your blades,' called Halldor. 'We must save those we can.'

We reversed our vessel, and began hauling men from the water. Dragging them aboard was easy – our ousiai was built low to the water – but there was nothing we could do to reach those unfortunates from the stern of the shattered vessel; they had slipped into the sea on the far side of the chain. A few of them managed to swim and reach us. Others clung to the wooden rafts, and we collected as many as we could, but the guard boats were closing in and there was no time to save them all.

'Row on!' ordered Harald, and we began to pull away from the approaching guard boats.

'Poor bastards,' muttered the Swede next to me. 'I don't fancy their chances as prisoners . . .'

His voice died away as I glanced up.

Harald was standing on the stern deck, hard-faced and glaring down at us. The flash of anger in his eyes told us that it was time we shut our mouths, concentrated at the oar handles, and carried him towards his destiny.

TEN

WE ENTERED KIEV in great style. Harald led our column on horseback, dressed in his finest court robes from Constantinople and wearing the ceremonial sword with its gold handle and enamelled scabbard which marked his rank as spatharokandidatos. Behind him marched his war band, all in their best costumes and adorned with their silver and gold jewellery. A column of porters and slaves, loaded with the bales of peach silk and the other valuables we had stripped from the ousiai, brought up the rear. I too was on horseback, riding with Halldor and the other members of Harald's inner council. After our escape from the Queen of Cities, Harald had formally appointed me as his adviser. In return I promised to be his liegeman, to serve and support him as my superior lord, even to the day he took his rightful place upon the Norwegian throne.

'Cheer up!' Halldor said to me as we clattered through the city gate and King Jaroslav's guards cheered us. News of Harald's prowess had gone ahead, and the guards, many of them Norse mercenaries, were eager to lay eyes on the man who had been sending back such a mass of treasure for safe keeping.

I gestured towards the red-tiled domes of a large monastery on the hill ahead of us. 'I hadn't expected to see so much of the White Christ here,' I said morosely, for I was in low spirits.

'You'll have to get used to it,' said Halldor. 'I expect Harald will soon be getting married in a place just like that.'

His remark took me aback.

'Thorgils, you've forgotten that on his way to Constantinople, Harald asked for the hand in marriage of the king's second daughter, Elizabeth. He was sent away with a flea in his ear. Told to come back when he had riches and renown. Well, now he's got just that, and more. Elizabeth and her family are devout Christians. They'll insist on a wedding in the White Christ manner.'

I listened without enthusiasm. I had been congratulating myself that my appointment as councillor to Harald would give me the chance to shape his policies in favour of the Old Ways. Now, it appeared, I would find myself competing with the views of his wife and the retinue of advisers she would surely bring with her. The thought made me more depressed than I was already. Pelagia's death had hit me hard, depriving me of both a friend and a confidante, and on the way to Kiev I had been feeling more and more isolated amidst the often ribald company of Harald's followers.

'Then this is not the sort of place where I'll be comfortable,' I concluded. 'If I'm to serve Harald, I can be of more use to him in the northlands. I'll ask his permission to go ahead and prepare for his arrival in Norway. I can try to find out which of the powerful nobles might support him, and who would be against him when he makes his claim for the throne.'

'You'll be a spy again?' asked Halldor, to whom I had related my role as an informant for John the Eunuch. 'Harald will like that. He's always in favour of subterfuge and trickery.'

'Part spy, part envoy,' I answered.

Harald agreed to my proposal, and as soon as I had collected the money arranged for me by the banker in Constantinople, I headed onward with those of Harald's ex-Varangians who had asked to go home early. By the time Halldor and the others were celebrating the glittering wedding of the Prince of Norway to King Yaroslav's second daughter, I was back in the northlands where my own Gods belonged.

My first impression was how little had changed in the twelve years I had been away. Among the three main kingdoms, Norway and Denmark still regarded one another with suspicion, while Sweden stood aside and quietly fanned the flames of rivalry between her neighbours. Norwegian raided Dane and was raided in return. Alliances shifted. Leading families squabbled, and wherever Norsemen had seized land across the sea – in England, Scotland or Ireland – there were great magnates who nominally owed allegiance to an overlord in the homeland, but acted independently. Through these turbulent waters I had to plot a course for Harald when he returned.

I made a start by visiting the court of Harald's nephew, Magnus. He held the Norwegian throne, and also claimed the kingship of Denmark. I found him to be personable, energetic, proud, and shrewd beyond his years. He was only twenty-five years old, yet had won the affection of his people by his fairness and his habit of winning his battles against the Danes. Harald, I concluded, would find it difficult to dislodge the man his people called Magnus the Good.

I came to Magnus's court posing as an Icelander returning after service in Constantinople and wealthy enough to dawdle on the way. It was near enough to the truth, and no one questioned me too closely about my background. The only time I nearly dropped my guard was when I heard that the dowager queen Aelfgifu had died. She was the woman who had first taken me to bed. 'Good riddance, for all that she was the great Knut's first wife,' commented the man who told me of her death. 'Her husband sent her to us as co-regent, along with that callous son of hers. They weren't popular, and we drove them out. Can't say I'm sorry that she's gone.' His remark made me feel old. No one likes to think that their first lover is in the grave. Not when you remember their warmth and beauty.

IT WAS TO be nearly two years before I was able to tell Harald of my impression of Magnus, because King Jaroslav insisted that his new son-in-law stay on in Kiev for longer than Harald had intended. But I scarcely noticed the delay, for I had at last found a place where the Old Gods were revered, and I was happy.

I was travelling from Magnus's capital at Nidaros on my way to Denmark to assess the strength and character of Earl Svein Estrithson, who ruled there, and it was autumn. I had taken the land route over the mountain passes and reached the area known as Vaster Gotland. It lies on the border between Norway and Sweden, but is such a bleak and unforgiving region that no one really cares about the exact position of the frontier. It is a place of rock and forest, small lakes and shallow streams, and a large expanse of inland water – the Vaner Lake – which, like everything else, freezes over in winter because the climate is very harsh. I was on foot because the trail is difficult for horses and there is no fodder to be found. Nor did I have a servant to accompany me, but was travelling alone. Vaster Gotland has a reputation for outlawry, so I was beginning to wonder whether I was wise to carry so much gold and silver with me when I came across a memorial stone beside the track. On the rock was carved an epitaph to a lost warrior who, according to the runes, had ended his life in Serkland, 'the land of silk'. The mason who had cut the inscription was no rune master, for the gouges left by the chisel were plain to see, and the lettering was crudely done. Nor could I tell who was commemorated, for the rock had split away where the dead man's name had been written, and I could not find the broken piece. But I took it as a sign from Odinn, and after clearing away the undergrowth I buried half my hoard.

There were no villages along the trail, only an occasional farmhouse set well back from the path. The land was so poor and grudging that these dwellings were no more than small log cabins with roofs of wooden shingles and perhaps a shed or two. I was

expecting to encounter the farmers returning home, as it would
soon be dusk. But I saw no one. Whenever I passed a house, and
that was rare enough, the door was shut tight and nothing stirred.
It was as if the plague had struck, and everyone had retreated
indoors or died.

The chill in the evening air warned of a cold night to come,
and I had already caught a glimpse of a wolf in the forest, so
I left the track when I saw the next house and went towards
it, intending to ask for shelter for the night. I knocked on the
heavy wooden door planks and called out. For a moment there
was no response. Then, from deep within the house, a low voice
said urgently, 'Go away! You disturb us! Go away!' I was as
shocked as if someone had struck me in the face. The country
folk had always been hospitable. That was their tradition. They
enjoyed hearing a traveller's news and they appreciated the small
coins paid for food and lodging. To turn away a stranger on a
cold evening seemed unthinkable. I knocked again, more insis-
tently, and called out that I was a traveller, on my own, hungry,
and would pay for my lodging. This time I heard the shuffle
of feet, and very slowly the door opened, just enough for me
to see that the interior of the cabin was in darkness. Someone
had covered over the small windows. From the gloom within, a
voice said, 'Go away, please leave. This is not the right time to
visit us.'

Something about the atmosphere of the place made me say,
'In the name of Odinn the Roadwise I ask for shelter.'

There was a long pause, and then the door pulled back a
hand's breadth and the voice asked softly, 'Tell me, stranger, what
is the name of the steed who westward draws night over the
glorious Gods?'

The accent was local and strong, but the rhythm of the words
was unmistakable. The man, whoever he was, was reciting lines
of poetry. Long ago my tutors in the Old Ways had taught me
the next verse, so I answered:

'Hrimfaxi's his name who draws the nights
Over the glorious gods
Each morning he dribbles down the flakes of foam
That brings dew upon the dales.'

The heavy door eased back, just wide enough to allow me to
step inside, and the moment I had entered, it was closed behind
me. I found myself in total darkness.

A hand took my wrist, and I felt myself carefully guided
forward. Then the pressure of the hand indicated that I was to
stop where I stood. I felt something touch the back of my knees,
and knew that someone had placed a stool behind me. I sat down
quietly. Not a word had been said, and still I could see only
blackness.

There were people in the room: not many of them, though I
could sense their presence. The floor beneath my boots was plain
beaten earth. This was a humble home. I heard the rustle of
clothing, light breathing. Then a point of dull red appeared a few
feet away, close to the ground. Someone had uncovered an ember.
I guessed that it lay in the family hearth. The glow vanished as
a shadow moved between me and the fireplace. There was the
sound of a person blowing gently on the ember, and then the
shadow moved aside and I could see the hearth again. Now there
was a small dance of flame in the fireplace, which gave just
enough light for me to make out that there were half a dozen
people in the room, three adults and three children, all dressed in
the plain dun and brown garments of farming people. It was
difficult to distinguish whether the children were girls or boys,
but the adults were two women and a man. I guessed he was the
person who had brought me into the house.

One of the women was moving towards the fireplace. She
placed something on the ground in front of the hearth. It was a
small bowl. She tilted a jug and I heard the splash of liquid. I sat
completely still. Now I knew what was happening. This was the
alfablot, the household's annual sacrifice to honour the spirits

which live in every home. As landvaettir, they also exist among
the trees and rocks and underground. They are the spirits of
place, the ancient inhabitants who were there before men came,
and they will be there long after men have gone. Their approval
helps men prosper, their hostility brings ruin.

There were soft footfalls as the woman moved away from the
fire, and her dark shape moved around the room, pausing in each
corner. She held something. I guessed it was a small offering of
food for the alfar.

I felt a nudge on my fingers. It was the rough crust of a hunk
of bread. Then I was passed a wooden cup of beer. I tasted the
bread. It was peasant's rye bread, coarse but wholesome. The beer
was thin and watery. I ate and drank, taking care to move gently
and carefully. Alfar are easily frightened away. I left a few dregs
of beer in the cup, leaned forward when I had finished, and tipped
the last few drops on the earthen floor. I knew that my offering
had been observed by my hosts.

Not a word had been said from the moment that I had entered
the house, and I knew that, out of respect for the spirits, all would
be silent until daylight came. When the family completed their
offerings, they retired to their communal bed, a wooden box
against one wall, like a large manger. I wrapped myself in my
travelling cloak and quietly lay down on the floor to sleep.

'WE ARE ALL pagans here,' were the first words of the farmer
next morning. He spoke apologetically. 'Otherwise you would
have had a kinder welcome.'

'Old Believers,' I corrected him gently.

He was a middle-aged man, unremarkable except for the
bright blue eyes in his weather-beaten face and an unruly fringe
of almost pure white hair around his bald scalp. He had the care-
worn look of someone who laboured hard to support his family.
Behind him his wife, a handsome woman who also showed signs
of an exacting life, was washing the children's faces. The second

woman appeared to be her sister, for she had the same thick reddish-brown hair and fine bone structure, as well as a gracefulness in the way she was collecting up the small offerings that had been set out during the night. The milk that had been left in the bowl for the alfr, I noticed, was poured back into the jug after a few drops had been sprinkled on the hearth. There was no surplus food in this household.

'You are a devotee of Odinn?' the farmer asked in a deep, quiet voice. He was probing, wanting to know more about me and to establish some sort of common ground between us. I liked him.

'From childhood. I have followed Odinn since I was a boy. And you?'

'Here we worship Frey. We are farmers, not warriors or sailors. We need Frey's generosity.' I knew what he spoke of. Frey is the God of fertility. He multiplies the seed that is planted in the soil, brings the rain and warmth which ripens crops, and makes good harvests. With Frey's help the cattle thrive, lambs and calves are plentiful, sows farrow generously. Even the milk we were drinking we owed ultimately to Frey's bounty.

'Last evening you invoked Odinn Vegtamr,' the farmer continued. 'Do you travel far?'

'Only as far as the Danish lands, if the rain holds off for another week or so. I don't like squelching through mud.'

'Many berries on the bushes this year,' the man said. 'And the swallows left early. Snow will come sooner than rain, I'd say. Not that it means much to us in these parts. We don't travel except to the great Hof, and it's a three-day walk to reach anywhere worth visiting.'

'Yet I saw a memorial back along the road to a man who died in Serkland. That's a great distance.'

There was a sudden tension in the room. The farmer looked uneasy.

'Have you been to Serkland?' he enquired.

'I have, or at least close to it,' I said. 'I served with the emperor's guard in Miklagard, and he sent me to their Holy Land. That's close by. It's the place where the White Christ God lived.'

'Don't know about this Holy Land. We're too remote to see the White Christ priests. One of them did visit a few years back, but found us too set in our ways. He left and never came back.'

'Perhaps you were fortunate,' I commented.

The farmer seemed to reach a decision. 'It was I who cut that memorial stone,' he acknowledged. 'Did my best, though the work is rough. Should have picked a better rock. A corner broke off in the winter frost two years later. We wanted to have something to remember him by. He was married to my wife's sister.'

He glanced across the room towards the woman who had been cleaning up the hearth. She was standing still, staring at me, hanging on every word.

'News reached us, third or fourth hand, that he had died in Serkland. But there were no details. He had set out from here to make his fortune, and never came back. Vanished. We don't know anything of the place where he met his end, or how it happened. His name was Thorald.'

'I didn't know anyone by that name when I was in Miklagard,' I said, 'but if it will repay your hospitality, perhaps I could tell you what I know of Serkland.'

The farmer nodded to his sister-in-law, and she stepped closer. Her eyes were still fixed on me as I began to describe my time in the Hetaira, my visit to the Holy Land, and how I had met Saracens both as friends and enemies. It was a lengthy tale, and I tried to tell it briefly. But the farmer soon detected that I was leaving much unsaid, and he interrupted.

'There is so much we want to know. Would you not stay with us a few days and tell us your tale more fully? It would help Runa here.'

I hesitated. The family lived in such straitened circumstances that I was reluctant to impose myself on their kindness. But then the farmer, whose name was Folkmar, insisted, and I agreed to stay one more day.

It was among the best decisions of my life. That one day became a week, and by the end of it I knew that Folkmar's home was my haven. Nothing could have been a greater contrast to the sophistication and luxury of Constantinople with its broad avenues, well-stocked markets, and teeming crowds. There I had enjoyed the comforts of fine food, public bathhouses, and lavish entertainment on a scale unimaginable to my hosts in the harsh barrens of Vaster Gotland, where much of each day was spent in routine labour to achieve the basics of everyday life, whether drawing water, mending farm tools or grinding grain. Yet Folkmar and his wife were content to place their trust in the Gods, and in consequence there was nothing fearful in their lives. They were deeply fond of one another and their children; they lived simply and frugally, and they were sure of where they stood in relation to the land and the seasons of the year. Every time I accompanied Folkmar to his work in one of his small fields or to gather firewood in the forest, I saw how he respected the unseen spirits around him. He laid small tokens, even if they were no more than a broken twig or a leaf, on the isolated boulders which we passed, and if the children were with us he would insist they hushed their voices, and he forbade them to play games close by the sacred rocks. To him the deep forest was home to skogsra, female woodland deities who, if respected, would return a cow or calf that wandered from the meadow. If insulted, they would feed the stray to the wolves.

Folkmar's devotion to his main Gods, Frey and his sister Freyja, was uncomplicated. He kept their statuettes in his home, Frey with his enormous phallus, and Freyja voluptuous and sensual, but he knew little of their lore other than the popular tales.

'Cats,' he said. 'Freyja's chariot is drawn by cats. Just like a woman to be able to harness cats. That would be something to see. Hereabouts in mid-summer a man and woman dress up as

Frey and his sister and travel from farm to farm in a cart to
collect offerings, but they are drawn along by a working nag.' He
paused before saying, 'I'll be bringing those offerings to the Great
Hof next week. Care to come with me? It means delaying your
trip to Denmark, but Odinn has his own place in the Hof as well.
It would be a chance for you to honour him.'

'How far is it to the Hof?' I asked.

'About ten days. Lots of people will be going. The king
himself could be there.'

This time I did not hesitate. My trip to Denmark could wait.
I had heard about the Great Hof from the Swedish Varangians I
had met in Miklagard, who had told me about the festivals held
near a place they called Uppsala where, since time out of mind,
there had been a temple to the Old Gods. Here, in spring and just
before the onset of winter, appeared great gatherings of Old
Believers, who came in multitudes to make their sacrifices and
pray for all the blessings that the Old Gods can bestow: health,
prosperity, victory, a good life. The Swedish king himself often
attended, because his ancestors traced their line back to Frey
himself. I decided that after many years of living among the
followers of the White Christ, now, at last, I could immerse
myself again in the celebration of the Old Ways.

Folkmar was delighted when I agreed to accompany him, and
our journey proved to be what the Christians would have called
a pilgrimage. We were like a master and disciple as we trudged
along and I answered his questions about the Gods, for he was
keen to learn more and I was slowly coming to realise that my
knowledge of the Old Ways was more profound than most
possessed. I told him how Frey and Freyja belonged to the Vanir,
the primal Gods who had at first resisted the Aesir under Odinn
and fought against them. When peace was agreed, they had gone
to join the Aesir as hostages and had been with them ever since.

'Pity the Norwegians and the Danes can't do the same. Make
peace with one another, I mean,' Folkmar observed. 'It would put
an end to this constant warring between them which does no one

any good. I often think how fortunate it is that my people live so
far out of the way. The quarrels of the outer world usually pass
us by.'

'Perhaps that is why Frey and his sister chose not to live
under Odinn's roof in Valhol. They have a space to themselves,'
I answered. 'Frey has his own hall in Alfheim where the light
elves live. And he and his sister have their special privileges. Frey
is near equal to Odinn, and his sister in some ways is superior.
After battle she takes half of those who have died honourably and
brings them back to her hall, Sessrumnir, leaving Odinn and the
Valkyries to select the rest. Freyja gets to make the first choice
among the dead.'

'You would need to be a God to share power like that, never
quarrelling over precedence,' observed Folkmar.

'I saw it done back in the Great City,' I said. 'Two empresses
sharing the same throne. But I admit, it was unusual.'

'It's against nature. Sooner or later, there must be a contest
for power,' said Folkmar. With his native shrewdness he had
forecast what was to follow.

THE GREAT TEMPLE at Uppsala was worth our ten-day walk. It
was the largest hof I had ever seen, an enormous hall of timber
built close beside three large barrow graves which contained the
bodies of the early kings. In front of the hof grew a huge tree,
the very symbol of Yggdrasil, the world tree where the Aesir
meet. This giant was even more remarkable because its leaves
never faded, but remained green throughout even the hardest
winter. To one side, clustering like attendants, smaller trees
formed a sacred grove. These trees too were very ancient, and
each was hallowed. On them were displayed the sacrifices made
to the Gods whose images were within the Hof itself. Folkmar
told me that at the great spring festival, the temple priests
celebrated nine successive days of ritual, nine being their sacred
number. Each day they emerged from the Hof and hung on the

branches of the sacred trees the heads of the nine animals they had sacrificed to the Gods as proof of their devotion. Ritual demanded that each animal was a male, and that there was one from each type of living creature.

'Does that include human sacrifice as well?' I asked.

'In earlier times, that was so,' explained Folkmar, 'But no longer.'

He led me inside the Hof. Even though the autumn festival was of less importance than the spring celebration, the dark interior of the temple was crowded with worshippers bringing gifts. The builders of the temple had left openings in the high roof so that the daylight fell in shafts, illuminating the statues of the Gods. And today, despite the fact that it was cloudy, the three Gods seemed to loom over the congregation. Thor was in the centre – powerful, bearded, and holding his hammer aloft. To his right stood my own God, Odinn. Carved from a single enormous block of wood, and black with the smoke of centuries of sacrifices, Odinn squinted down with his single eye. To Thor's left stood Frey's image. This statue too was of wood, but brightly painted with the colours of the bountiful earth – ochre, red, brown, gold and green. Frey was seated cross-legged, a conical helmet on his head, one hand clutching his pointed beard, which jutted forward, the other hand on his knee. His eyes bulged. He was stark naked, and from his loins rose the gigantic phallus that was the symbol of the fertility he controlled, and also of physical joy.

Folkmar approached one of the Frey priests and handed over the package he had carried on his back all the way during our walk. I had no idea what the package contained, but knowing the poverty of Folkmar and his neighbours I doubted it was anything more than a few items of farmer's produce, yet the priest took the package as if it was of great value and thanked the farmer graciously. He beckoned to an assistant, and a moment later a small pig was dragged out from the shadows, and with a quick movement the priest cut its throat. The assistant already had a bowl in place, and as the blood drained into it, the priest took a whisk of twigs and, dipping it into the blood, flicked the drops towards the image of the God, then over Folkmar, who stood with bowed head.

I had expected the priest to set the pig's carcass aside, but instead he handed it to Folkmar and said, 'Feast well tonight.'

His duty done, Folkmar turned and began to leave when he remembered that I had not yet honoured Odinn. 'I am sorry, Thorgils, I did not think to keep something back that you could offer to your God.'

'Your people collected for Frey's honour,' I said as we moved through the crowd towards the soot-black image of the father of the Gods. 'It would not have been right to divert the slightest morsel of it elsewhere.'

We had reached the foot of Odinn's statue. It towered above us, twice the height of a man. The image was so old that the timber from which it had been carved was split and dry, and I wondered how many centuries it had stood there. Apart from the closed eye, the details of the God's face were blurred with age. I reached inside my shirt where my money pouch hung on a leather thong around my neck, then laid my offering at the God's feet. Folkmar's eyes opened wide in surprise. I had set down a solid gold coin, an imperial nomisma, worth more than all the farmer's worldly possessions. To me, it was a small token of my gratitude to Odinn for having brought me to Folkmar and his home.

'YOU SAY THAT you follow Harald Sigurdsson and are sworn to serve him,' said Folkmar to me that evening as we roasted the sacrificial pig, 'but it is too late in the season for Harald to arrive. The earliest he can be expected is in the spring. Why don't you spend the winter with us. I know that would please my wife and her sister.'

'First I must visit Svein Estrithson in Denmark so that later I can tell Harald what the man is like,' I answered cautiously, though Folkmar's invitation had forced me to acknowledge that perhaps I was not as solitary and self-possessed as I had always imagined myself to be. During the days I had spent with him and his family, I had experienced a sense of quiet harmony that I had never expected. Gazing into the flames of our cooking fire, I found myself wondering if my advancing years were having their effect, and whether the time had come when I should consider forsaking my rootless life and, if not settling down, at least having a place where I could stay and rest. So I allowed myself the luxury of calculating just how quickly I could complete my mission to Denmark and get back to Vaster Gotland.

Odinn must have favoured me because snow fell the very next morning and the ground froze hard. Travelling across a frozen landscape is far easier and quicker than in spring or autumn mud, and I made the journey to Denmark in less than two weeks' travel. I found that I neither liked nor trusted Svein Estrithson. He was stout, foul-mouthed and a great womaniser. He was also a powerful advocate for the White Christ, whose priests over-looked his lewd behaviour. For some reason, the Danes were very loyal to him, and rallied to his cause whenever Magnus's Norwegians threatened. I judged that Harald would find it almost as hard to dislodge Svein as to replace Magnus.

It was no hardship to cut short my visit and retrace my steps to Vaster Gotland. On the way there I stopped in a trading station to make some purchases and hire a carter. The man demanded a substantial sum to make such a long journey, but I was wealthy and his payment barely touched my store of ready funds. Thus, soon after I was once again back with Folkmar's family, a shout brought them to the door. Outside stood two small and sturdy horses with shaggy winter coats, their breath steaming in the cold air. Fitted to their hooves were the spiked shoes that had allowed them to traverse the icy ground as they dragged the sled that contained the furs, cloth, utensils and extra food that I now presented to Folkmar and his family as my guest offering.

Runa and I were joined as man and wife soon after the Jol festival, and no one in that remote community was in the least surprised. Runa and I had discovered that we were quietly suited, as if we had known one another for many years. We shared a mutual understanding, which neither of us mentioned because we already knew that the other was equally sensitive to it. In the confines of the little cabin our harmony occasionally revealed itself in a shared glance, or a half smile that passed between us. But more often it was simply that Runa and I were gladdened by each other's presence, and savoured the contentment that flowed from being together. Naturally Folkmar and his wife had noticed what was happening, and took care not to intrude.

Our wedding was not, of course, a marriage in the Christian rite, all priest and prayers. As a young man I had married that way in Iceland, and the union had been a humiliating failure. This time Folkmar himself performed the ceremony, because Runa and her sister had been orphaned at an early age and this left him as her senior male relative. Folkmar made a simple declaration to the Gods, and then, standing before the images of Frey and Freyja, took steel and flint, and, striking one against the other, produced a trail of sparks. It was to show that within each substance, stone and metal, as in man and woman, lived a vital element which, when brought together, provided life.

Next day he hosted a feast for our immediate neighbours, at which they consumed the smoked and salted delicacies that I had earlier provided, and toasted our happiness in mead made from forest honey and shoots of bog myrtle in place of hops. During their toasts, several guests gave praise to Frey and Freyja, saying that the Gods had surely arranged for Runa to marry me. The Gods had taken her first husband when he was far away in Serkland, they said, and from Serkland they had sent his successor. They were fulsome in their congratulations, and during the winter months several of them came to help to construct the small extension that was built on Folkmar's cabin where Runa and I had our bedchamber. I could have told them to wait until the spring, when I could hire professional builders and purchase costly materials because I was rich. But I desisted. I liked my haven and I feared to disturb its equilibrium.

From the outset Runa herself took great comfort from her sister's open approval of our union, and she went on to make me very happy. She was to prove to be an ideal wife, loving and supportive. On our wedding night she told me that when she heard of her first husband's death, she had prayed to Freyja, pleading that she did not wish to spend the rest of her life as a widow. 'Freyja heard my prayers,' she said quietly, looking down at the earthen floor.

'But I'm fifteen years older than you,' I pointed out. 'Don't you worry that you will again be a widow one day?'

'That is for the Gods to decide. Some men they bless with health and allow to live. To others they give a life of drudgery which brings them to an early death. To me you seem no older than men of my own age, for already they are half worn out by toil.' Then she snuggled down against me, and proved that Freyja was indeed the goddess of sensual joy.

I was so utterly content all that winter and the following spring that I might have set aside my promise to serve Harald had not Odinn reminded me of my duty. He did so with a dream that was both shocking and, as it turned out much later, a deception. In my sleep I saw a fleet of ships coming across the sea and disembarking an army whose commander sought to seize a throne. The leader's face was never visible but always turned away from me, and I took him to be my liege lord Harald, for the man was uncommonly tall. He boldly led his army inland, his troops marching across baked and barren fields until they were brought to battle by their enemy. The fighting was intense, but gradually the invaders were gaining the upper hand. Then, just on the point of victory, an arrow flew out from nowhere and struck the tall commander in the throat. I saw his hands go up – his face was still turned away – and I heard the breath whistle in his torn windpipe. Then he fell, dying.

I woke in a cold sweat of alarm. Beside me Runa reached out to comfort me. 'What is the matter?' she asked.

'I have just seen my lord Harald die,' I said, still shivering. 'Perhaps I can avert catastrophe. I must warn him.'

'Of course you must,' she agreed soothingly. 'That is your duty. But sleep now and rest, so that in the morning you have a clearer head.'

Next day she was just as sensible and made me repeat the details of the dream, then asked, 'Is this the first time that you have seen omens in your dreams?'

'No, there was a time when I had many dreams that hinted at the future if they were correctly understood. It's something that I have inherited from my mother. I hardly knew her, but she was a volva, a seeress gifted with the second sight. When I was in Miklagard among the Christians, such dreams were very rare, and certainly there was nothing so disturbing as what I saw last night.'

'Maybe your dreaming has returned because you are among people who still hold to the Old Ways. The Gods reveal themselves more readily in such places.'

'A wise woman once told me something similar. She herself possessed second sight and said I was a spirit mirror, and that I was more likely to have visions when I was in the company of others who also possessed the same ability. I suppose that being among Old Believers has the same effect.'

'Then you already know that we would want you to heed what the Gods are trying to tell you. You should seek Harald out and try to warn him. I am content to wait here for your return. I don't have to have second sight to know that you will surely come back to me. The sooner you set out, the sooner you will return.'

I left that same afternoon, taking the same eastward path that Folkmar and I had followed when we went to the Great Hof. On the third day I found someone to sell me a horse, and within a week I had reached the coast, and just in time. A fisherman mending his nets on the beach told me there was a rumour that a remarkable warship was under construction somewhere in the north, the like of which had never been seen before. The builders had been told to use only the finest timber and to install the best fittings, and that no imperfection would be tolerated. 'Must be costing someone a fortune,' said the fisherman, spitting towards his grubby little skiff as if to emphasise his point. 'Don't know who the client is, but he must be made of money.'

'Is the vessel launched yet, do you know?'

'Can't say as I do,' he replied, 'but it will be a sight to see.'

'I'll pay you to take me to see it.'

'Beats hauling on lines and baiting hooks,' he answered readily. 'Give me a couple of hours to pick up some extra gear and a bit of food and water, and off we go. Mind if my lad accompanies us? He's handy in a boat, and could come in useful. Breeze is in the north so it'll be rowing to start with.'

WE HAD BARELY cleared the bay when Harald's ship came into view, sailing southward and less than a mile offshore, and silently I thanked Runa for insisting that I hurried. Another couple of hours and I would have missed him.

There was no mistaking that it was Harald's ship. No one else would have required that his vessel be so extravagant and colourful. In later years, during frontier raids on the Danes, I was to sail aboard the largest vessel Harald ever commissioned, his *Great Dragon*, which had thirty-five oar benches, making her one of the biggest longships ever known. But that giant still does not compare in my memory with the vessel I saw that pleasant summer afternoon as Harald sailed to claim his inheritance. His longship was a blaze of colour. Immaculate display shields of red and white were slotted in the shield rack. The snarling serpent's head on the prow was gilded bronze, and flashed back the sun as the ship eased across the swells. A long scarlet pennant floated from her masthead, her rigging had been whitened, and the upper plank along her entire length had been decorated with gold leaf.

But that was not the reason why I knew for sure that she was Harald's ship. Who else would have ordered his sailmakers to use a cloth that, weight for weight, was as expensive as gold: every third panel of the mainsail had been cut and stitched from peach silk.

I stood up on the thwart of the fishing skiff and waved an oar. An alert lookout on the longship saw me, and a moment later the vessel altered course. Soon I was scrambling over the side and making my way to the stern deck where Harald stood with his councillors. I knew all of them – Halldor, his marshal Ulf Ospaksson, and the others.

'Welcome aboard, councillor. What do you have to report?' Harald demanded as if I had seen him only yesterday.

'I have visited both Magnus of Norway and Earl Estrithson, my lord,' I began, when Harald interrupted me.

'We have already met the Danish earl. He came north to ask help from the Swedes in his conflict with Magnus, and by chance we encountered him. How did he impress you?'

I paused, not wanting to sound pessimistic. But there was no getting round my opinion. 'He's not to be trusted,' I said bluntly.

'And my nephew Magnus?'

'My lord, he seems to be well regarded by his people.'

It was a tactless thing to say, and Harald rudely turned to look out across the sea, ignoring me. I suppose he felt that I was hinting he might not be so popular. Meekly I crossed the deck to join the other councillors.

Halldor commiserated. 'He needs someone to tell him the true facts from time to time.'

'There's more,' I said. 'I wanted to give him a warning, but now is not the moment.'

'What's the warning?'

'A dream I had recently, a portent.'

'You were always an odd one, Thorgils. Even when you first came to my father's house, my brothers and I wondered why he took you in and gave you such special treatment. Is it to do with your second sight? What have you seen?'

'Harald's death,' I answered.

Halldor shot me a sideways glance. 'How will it happen?'

'An arrow in the throat during a great battle.'

'When?'

'I don't know. The dreams are never precise. It could happen soon, or many years from now.'

'You had better tell me the details. Together we might be able to persuade Harald to avoid an open battle, if not now then at least for some time.'

So I told Halldor what I had dreamed. I described the fleet, the invading army, the tall man, the march across a dry land under a blazing sun, and his death.

When I finished, Halldor was looking at me with a mixture of relief and awe.

'Thorgils,' he said, 'my father was right. You really do have the second sight. But this time you have misinterpreted your vision. Harald is safe.'

'What do you mean?'

'It was not Harald you saw die. It was Maniakes, the tall Greek general who led us in the campaign in Sicily.'

'But that's not possible. I haven't seen Maniakes for years, and in all that time I've never given him a thought.'

'Why should you,' said the Icelander. 'You've been in the northlands these two years past and you could not know the news. A year ago Maniakes rebelled against the new Basileus. That man-eating old empress Zoë had got herself married for a third time and handed over most of the power to her new husband, and Maniakes tried to seize the throne for himself. He was commanding the imperial army in Italy at the time, and he led an invasion into Greece. That's the parched landscape you saw. The Basileus assembled all the troops he could muster, including the garrison of Constantinople, and marched out to confront him. The two armies met — and it was on a hot sunny day on a barren plain — and there was a great battle which was to decide the fate of the empire. Maniakes had victory within his grasp, his troops had the enemy soundly beaten when a chance arrow struck him in the throat, killing him. It was all over. His army fled, and there was a great slaughter. This took place just a few months ago. We heard the news in Kiev just before we left to come here. Maniakes, not Harald, was the man in your vision.'

I was dumbfounded and relieved at the same time. I remembered how very alike the two men had been in height and manner, and that I had never seen the face of the dead commander in my dream. It had all been a mistake: I had been spirit-flying. At various times in my life I had been in the presence of certain seidrmanna, the seers of the northlands who were capable of leaving their bodies while in a trance and flying to other regions far away. That was what had happened in my dream. I had been transported to another place and another time, and there I had seen Maniakes die. It had never happened to me before. I felt bewildered and a little dizzy. But at least I had not made a fool of myself in Harald's eyes by telling him of my fears.

Yet I failed to ask myself why Odinn had brought me to Harald's ship, if indeed it was Maniakes's death I had seen. Had I posed myself that simple question, matters might have turned out differently. But then, deception was always Odinn's way.

ELEVEN

WHAT WAS IT like to be councillor to the wealthiest ruler in the northlands? For that is what Harald became in less than three years.

Initially he had to accept his nephew's offer to share the throne of Norway, but it was an uneasy arrangement and would certainly have ended in civil war, had Magnus not been killed in a freak accident when he was out hunting. A hare leaped up in front of his horse, the horse bolted, and a low branch swept Magnus out of his saddle. He broke his neck. The hare, like her cats, is another familiar of Freyja, so I thought at the time that the king's accident was a sign that the Old Gods were acting in my favour, because Magnus's death left Harald as the sole ruler of Norway. But I soon had my doubts when Harald's elevation to the undisputed kingship changed him. He became even more difficult and high-handed.

I measured his change through his treatment of Halldor. The bluff Icelander had been at Harald's side throughout his foreign travels, and in Sicily had received a face wound which had left him badly scarred, yet his record of loyalty did not protect him from Harald's vainglory. Halldor had always been outspoken. He gave his opinions without mincing his words, and the more powerful Harald became, the less he liked to hear blunt speaking, even from a favoured adviser. One example will suffice: during one of Harald's frequent seaborne raids on Earl Svein's Danish lands, Halldor was the lookout on the foredeck of Harald's longship, a position of honour and great responsibility. As the vessel sailed along the coast, Halldor called out that there were rocks ahead. Harald, standing near the helmsman, chose to ignore the warning. Minutes later the longship crashed upon the rocks and was badly damaged. Exasperated, Halldor informed Harald that there was little point in serving as a lookout if his advice was ignored. Angrily Harald retorted that he had no need of men like Halldor.

There had been countless incidents of a similar nature, but from that time forward relations between them cooled, and I was sorry to see how Harald took pleasure in baiting Halldor. It was a rule at Harald's court that every member of his entourage had to be dressed and ready for attendance upon the king by the time the royal herald sounded the trumpet announcing that the king was about to emerge from his bedchamber. One morning, to make mischief, Harald paid the herald to sound the trumpet at the crack of dawn, much earlier than usual. Halldor and his friends had been carousing the night before and were caught unprepared. Harald then made Halldor and the others sit on the floor of the banqueting hall, in the foul straw, and gulp down full horns of ale while the other courtiers mocked them. Another royal rule was that at meals no one should continue to eat after the king himself had finished eating. To mark that moment, Harald would rap on the table with the handle of his knife. One day Halldor ignored the signal and continued to chew on his food. Harald called out down the length of the hall that Halldor was growing fat from too much food and too little exercise, and once again insisted that the Icelander pay a drinking forfeit.

Matters came to a head on the day of Harald's coinage. This was the occasion each year on the eighth day after Jol festival when the king gave his retainers their annual bounty. Though his wealth was still vast – it took ten strong men to lift Harald's treasure chests – Harald paid Halldor, myself and his other sworn men with copper coin instead of the usual silver. Only Halldor was bold enough to complain. He announced that he could no longer serve such a penny-pinching lord and preferred to return home to Iceland. He sold off all his possessions in Norway and had an ugly confrontation with Harald, when he demanded that the king pay the proper price for a ship he had agreed to buy from Halldor. The whole sorry affair ended with Halldor storming into the king's private chambers and, at sword point, demanding that Harald hand over one of his wife's gold rings to settle the debt. Then Halldor sailed off for Iceland, never to return.

His departure saddened me. He had been a friend from the first, and I valued his good sense. But I did not follow his example and leave Harald's service because I was still hoping that Harald would champion the Old Ways, and, in some matters, Harald was living up to my expectations. He married again, without divorcing Elizabeth, his first wife. His new bride, Thora, the daughter of a Norwegian magnate, was a robust Old Believer. When the Christian priests at court objected, claiming that Harald was committing bigamy, Harald bluntly told them to mind their own business. Equally, when a brace of new bishops arrived in Norway sent by the Archbishop of Bremen in the German lands, Harald promptly despatched them back to the Archbishop with a curt message that the king alone decided Church appointments. Unfortunately for me, Harald also displayed Christian tendencies whenever it suited him. He refurbished the church where the bodies of his half-brother 'Saint' Olaf and his nephew Magnus lay, and whenever he dealt with the followers of the White Christ he made a point of reminding them that St Olaf was his close relative. It was to be several years before I had finally to admit to myself that Halldor had been right from the beginning. Harald was serving only one God – himself.

Yet I persevered. Life at Harald's court was the closest to the ideals that I had heard about when I was a child growing up in Greenland, and I reassured myself that Harald genuinely respected the traditions of the north. He surrounded himself with royal skalds and paid them handsomely for verses which celebrated past glories. His chief skald was another Icelander, Thjodolf, but his other poets – Valgard, Illugi, Bolverk, Halli, known as the Sarcastic, and Stuf the Blind – were almost as deft at producing intricate poems in the courtly style, whose quality Harald himself was capable of judging for he was a competent versifier himself. For lighter moments he employed a court dwarf, a Frisian by the name of Tuta, who had a long broad back and very stumpy legs and who made us laugh by parading around the great hall of the palace dressed in Harald's full-length coat of mail. This armour had been specially made for him in Constantinople and was so famous that it even had its own name – 'Emma'. Harald himself always dressed stylishly, sporting a red and gold headband when not wearing his crown, and on formal occasions the glittering sword that he had been awarded as a spatharokandidatos in Miklagard.

Regrettably, the sword and mail coat were not the only reminders of his days at the Basileus's court. In Miklagard Harald had observed how to wield power pitilessly and to remove rivals without warning. Now I watched as Harald eliminated one potential threat after another, suddenly and without mercy. A nobleman who grew too powerful was summoned to a conference and rashly entered the council hall without his own bodyguard in attendance. He found the hall in darkness – Harald had ordered the shutters closed – and was murdered in the dark. Another rival was promoted to command of Harald's army vanguard and sent to lead an attack on a strong enemy position. Harald then delayed his own arrival on the battlefield so the vanguard and its commander were slaughtered. Before very long those who called Harald a 'hard ruler' were outnumbered by those who knew him more plainly as 'Harald the Bad'.

This, then, was the man I continued to serve faithfully, and to whom I acknowledged myself as 'king's man' while I clung stubbornly to the hope that he would stem the steady advance of the White Christ faith and lead his people back to the happier days of the Elder Way. Had I been more honest with myself, I might have admitted that my dream was unlikely ever to be realised. Yet I lacked the courage to change my way of thinking. The truth was that my own life had reached a plateau and I was set in my ways. I was forty-six when Harald ascended the Norwegian throne, but instead of accepting that I was at a time of life when most men would have been considered to have entered old age, I still felt I might have a hand in shaping events.

And Runa was keeping me young.

For six months of every year, I put Harald's court behind me and went back to my beloved Vaster Gotland. I timed my arrival for mid-autumn when it was time to harvest the meagre crops grown in the rocky fields wrested from the forest around our settlement, and my return soon acquired its own small ritual. I would come home on foot and dressed in sombre travelling clothes, not my expensive court dress, and in a leather pouch I carried a special gift for Runa — a pair of gilt brooches worked with interlaced patterns to fasten the straps of her outer tunic, a silver belt, a necklace of amber beads, a bracelet of black jet cunningly carved in the likeness of a snake. The two of us would go inside the small wooden house that I had built for us close beside her sister's home, and, the moment we were away from curious onlookers, her eyes would sparkle with anticipation. Handing her the present, I would stand back and watch with delight as she unwrapped the item I had folded inside a length of coloured silk which later she would sew into trimmings for her best garments. After she had admired the gift, Runa would reach up and give me a long and tender kiss, then she would carefully put the item into the treasure casket that she kept hidden in a cavity in the wall.

Only after that reassuring welcome would I report to Folkmar and ask what farm work needed to be done. He would set me to cutting grain, helping slaughter and skin cattle for which we would have no winter feed, or salting down the meat. Then there

was firewood to be cut, gathered and stacked, and the roofs of
our houses had to be checked for wooden shingles that had come
loose or needed replacing. As a young man I had detested the
repetition and stern rigour of this country life, but now I found
the physical labour to be reinvigorating, and I enjoyed testing just
how much of my youthful strength remained, pacing myself as I
worked, and finding satisfaction in completing the tasks allocated
to me. In the evenings as I prepared to go to bed beside Runa, I
would say a prayer of thanks to Odinn for having brought me
from an orphaned childhood through battle, slavery and near
death to the arms and warmth of a woman that I deeply loved.

To my surprise I found that my neighbours regarded me as
some sort of sage, a man deeply learned in the ancient wisdom,
and they would come to me for instruction. I responded readily
because I was beginning to understand that the future for the
Old Ways might not lie with great princes like Harald, but
among the ordinary country folk. I reminded myself that 'pagan',
the word the Christian priests used disparagingly to describe non-
believers, meant no more than someone who was of the countryside, so I taught the villagers what I had learned in my own
youth: about the Gods, how to observe the Elder Way, how to
live in harmony with the unseen world. In return my neighbours
made me a sort of priest, and one year I came back to find that
they had constructed a small hof for me. It was no more than a
little circular hut set in a grove of trees, a short walk from the
house where Runa and I lived. Here I could sacrifice and pray
to Odinn undisturbed. And once again Odinn heard me, for in
the eighth year of Harald's kingship, Runa delighted me by
informing that she was with child, and in due course she gave
birth to a boy and a girl, both healthy and strong. We named
them Freyvid and Freygerd in honour of the Gods who were
also twins.

BEFORE THE TWINS had learned to walk, Harald sent me on a mission which was a foretaste of his grand ambition — nothing less than to become a second Knut by achieving mastery over all the Norse lands. He summoned me, alone, to his council room, and stated bluntly, 'Thorgils, you speak the language of the Scots.'

'No, my lord,' I answered. 'As a youth I learned the language of the Irish when I was a slave among them.'

'But the Irish language is close enough to the Scots tongue for you to conduct secret negotiations without the need for interpreters?'

'Probably, my lord, though I have never put it to the test.'

'Then you are to travel to Scotland on my behalf, to visit the King of the Scots, and sound out whether he would be willing to make an alliance with me.'

'An alliance for what purpose?' I dared to enquire.

Harald watched me closely for my response as he said, 'To conquer England. He has no love for his southern neighbours.'

I said nothing, but waited for Harald to go on.

'The king's name is Magbjothr, and he has held the throne of Scotland for fourteen years. By all accounts he's skilled in warfare. He would make a powerful ally. There's only one problem: he mistrusts the Norse. His father fought our Norse cousins in the Orkneys, when Sigurd the Stout was earl there.'

Harald's mention of Sigurd the Stout brought a twinge of pain to my left hand. It was an involuntary response to the familiar stiffness of an old wound.

'I fought at Earl Sigurd's side in the great battle of Clontarf in Ireland, where he died trying to overthrow the Irish High King,' I said, choosing my words carefully. I refrained from adding that I was the last man to hold aloft Sigurd's famous raven banner, and had received a smashing blow to my hand when the banner's pole was wrenched from my grasp.

'It's England's High King I plan to overthrow this time, with

Magbjothr's support,' Harald declared. 'Your task is to persuade
him to make common cause with us. There's a vessel ready to
take you to Scotland. It's only a two-day sail.'

I arrived in Scotland expecting to find Magbjothr at his
stronghold on the southern shore of what the Scots call the Firth
of Moray, but when I got there, his steward told me that the king
was on a royal progress around his domains, and not expected
back for several weeks. He added, 'The queen has gone with him.
May the Lord preserve her.' I must have looked blank because
the steward went on, 'She's been getting worse these past few
months, and no one seems able to help. And such a fine lady, too.
I'm not sure she's fit to travel.'

Finding that my spoken Irish was readily understood, I made
discreet enquiries and learned that the queen, whose name was
Gruoch, was suffering from some sort of mysterious illness. 'Elf
shot,' was how one informant put it, and another said flatly,
'Demons have entered her head.' Everyone I spoke to made it
clear that Gruoch was highly esteemed. Apparently she was a
direct descendant of Scots kings, and by marrying Magbjothr had
greatly strengthened his claim to the throne. Magbjothr was also
of royal blood, but had held the lesser rank of Mormaer of Moray,
a title equivalent to Earl, before he came to the throne by
deposing the previous king in circumstances that my informants
were reluctant to describe. Some said he had defeated the king in
open battle, others claimed that he killed him in a man-to-man
duel, while a third account hinted that Magbjothr had treacherously assassinated his king while he was his guest. Listening to
their conflicting stories, one thing became clear: Magbjothr was a
man to be reckoned with. Not only had he won the throne of
Scotland through violence, but he had also acquired his wife by
force of arms. Gruoch had been married to the previous Mormaer
of Moray, who was burned to death along with his retinue of fifty
men in a dispute with Magbjothr. What made the outcome all the
more remarkable was that Magbjothr had married the widow, and
then agreed that her son by her previous husband was to be his

heir. The King and Queen of the Scots, I thought to myself, must be a very unusual pair.

My route southward to find Magbjothr took me across a wild landscape of moor and rocky highland. Called the Mounth, the region was often swathed in mist and cut through with narrow valleys choked with dense brush and woodland. It was perfect country for an ambush, and I understood why so much of what I had heard about the quarrels of the Scots involved surprise attacks and sudden raids. When I finally caught up with the king, I thought he was wise to have installed himself and his entourage in an easily defended fortress. Sited on a hilltop with a clear view on all sides, the building was protected by a triple ring of earth banks topped with wooden palisades which, even as I plodded up the slope, were being reinforced by his soldiers.

I was greeted with suspicion. A sentry stopped me at the outer gate and searched me for hidden weapons before demanding to know my business. I told him that I had come on an embassy from Harald of Norway and sought an audience with the king. The soldier looked doubtful. No strangers were allowed into the inner citadel, he said. These were his standing orders now that the Northumbrians were threatening to invade across the border. I might be a spy for them. I pointed out that the Northumbrians' traditional allies were the Danes, and that King Harald and his Norwegians had been fighting the Danes ever since Harald came to the throne. 'That's as may be,' retorted the sentry, as he escorted me to see his captain, 'but as far as I'm concerned, all you Norsemen are alike. Bandits, best kept out of places where you don't belong.'

His captain cross-examined me before leaving me to wait in an antechamber, and it was only after a delay of several hours that I was finally ushered into the presence of a tall, soldierly looking man, perhaps a decade younger than myself, with a ruddy wind-scoured complexion and long yellow hair. It was the King of the Scots, known to the Norsemen as Magbjothr, but to his own people as Mac Bethad mac Findlaech.

'Where did you learn to speak our language?' he asked, tapping the table in front of him with the naked blade of a dagger. I guessed that the weapon was not just there for show. The king mistrusted strangers.

'In Ireland, your majesty. In a monastery.'

The king frowned. 'You don't look like a Christian.'

'I'm not. I entered the monastery under duress. Initially as a slave. But I never accepted the faith.'

'A pity,' said Mac Bethad. 'I myself am a Christian. How come you were a slave?'

'I was taken prisoner in battle.'

'And where was that?'

'At a place called Clontarf, your majesty.'

The rhythmic tapping of the dagger suddenly slowed.

'At Clontarf? That was a long time ago. You don't look old enough to have been there.'

'I was only a lad, not more than fifteen years old.'

'Then you would have known the Mormaer of Mar. He fought and died in that battle.'

'No, your majesty. I did not know him. I was in the company of Earl Sigurd.'

Mac Bethad looked at me, trying to judge whether I was telling the truth. Pensively, he continued to tap the knife blade on the pitted surface of the wooden table.

'I'm surprised,' he said, 'that Harald of Norway should send me as his spokesman someone who served Fat Sigurd. The Earl of Orkney was a mortal enemy to my father all his life. They fought at least three battles, and thanks to that magic banner of his, Sigurd always came out best. Then the Orkney men stole our lands.'

My first meeting with Mac Bethad had got off to a very poor start, I thought to myself. I would never make a successful diplomat.

'The banner was useless to Sigurd at Clontarf,' I observed,

trying to sound conciliatory. 'He died with it tied around his waist.'

'And how do you know that?' This time the question was aggressive.

'He took the banner from me when the fight was going against us, and no one else would carry it. He wrapped it around him, saying that the beggar must carry his own purse. Then he walked into the thick of the fight. To certain death. I did not see the moment when he fell.'

Yet again Mac Bethad was looking at me with disbelief.

'Are you telling me that you were Sigurd's standard-bearer, and yet you survived?'

'Yes, your majesty.'

'And you did not know the prophecy that whoever flew the raven banner in battle would be victorious, but the man who actually held the raven banner would die in the moment of victory?'

'I had heard that prophecy, your majesty. But at Clontarf it turned out to be wrong. My fate was different. The Norns decreed that I should survive and that the earl would be defeated.'

When I mentioned the Norns, Mac Bethad grew very still. The tip of the dagger slowed its rhythm and stopped. There was a silence. 'You believe in the Norns?' he asked softly.

'I do, your majesty. I am an Old Believer. The Norns decide our fate when we are born.'

'And at other times? Do they decide our fate in later years?'

'That I do not know. But whatever the Norns decree for us will eventually come about. We can delay the outcome of their decision, but we cannot escape it.'

Mac Bethad laid the weapon gently on the table. 'I was about to send you away without hearing the message you bring from Harald of Norway. But maybe your arrival here was also decided by Fate. This evening I would like you to meet with my wife and me in private. Maybe you can help us. You have probably heard that my wife is ill.'

'I am not a physician, your majesty,' I warned.

'It is not a physician that she needs,' said the king. 'Perhaps it is someone who can explain what seems to be against all reason. I am a devout Christian. Yet I have seen the Norns.'

This time it was I who fell silent.

THE ROYAL CHAMBERLAIN found a place for me to sleep, a small alcove scarcely more than a cupboard, close to the king's apartments, and left me to eat my midday meal with the garrison of the fortress. Listening to their conversation, I gathered that they were all members of Mac Bethad's personal retinue and that they had a high opinion of their leader's generalship. The only time I heard any doubt expressed was in reference to the queen. One veteran complained that Mac Bethad was so distracted by the queen's illness that he was paying insufficient attention to preparing his defence against the expected invasion. The Earl of Northumbria, Siward, had given sanctuary to two sons of the previous Scottish king, the man Mac Bethad had killed, and was using their claim to the throne to justify his attack.

When the chamberlain fetched me that evening and brought me to the king's private apartments, I was shown into a small room furnished only with a table and several plain wooden chairs. The light came from a single candle on the table, positioned well away from the woman in a long dark cloak seated at the far end of the room. She sat in the shadows, her hands in her lap, and she was twisting her fingers together nervously. The only other person in the room was Mac Bethad, and he was looking troubled.

'You must excuse the darkness,' he began, after the chamberlain had withdrawn and closed the door behind him. 'The queen finds too much light to be painful.'

I glanced towards the woman. Her cloak had a hood which she had drawn up over her head, almost concealing her face. Just at that moment the candle flared briefly, and I caught a glimpse of a taut, strained face, dark-rimmed eyes peering out, a pale skin

and high cheek bones. Even in that brief instant the cheek nearest
to me gave a small, distinct twitch. Simultaneously I felt a tingling
shock as though I had accidentally knocked the point of my elbow
against a rock, the sort of impact that leaves the arm numb. But
the shock was not to my arm, it was to my mind. I knew that I
was in the presence of someone with otherworldly powers.

It was a familiar sensation. I had experienced it whenever I
encountered men and women skilled in seidr, the art of magic.
Usually I reacted strongly, because there were times when I too
was gifted with what the Norse call ofreskir, second sight. But
this occasion was different. The power emanating from the woman
in the cloak was unmistakably that of a volva, a woman with seidr
ability, but it was disturbed and irregular. It came at me in waves
in the same way that a distant horizon shimmers on a summer's
evening with lightning. Not the harsh and shattering flash when
Thor hurls his hammer Mjollnir, but the insistent and irregular
flicker that country folk who live far inland say is the silver
reflection of great shoals of fish in the ocean rising to the surface
and reflecting off the belly of the clouds.

Again I noticed the woman's hands. She was twisting and
rubbing them together as if she was washing them in water, not
the empty air.

'People here know them as the three Wyrds,' Mac Bethad
suddenly blurted out. There was anguish in his voice. 'As a
Christian I thought it was just a heathen belief, a superstition.
Until I met the three of them, dressed in their rags. It was in
Moray, when I was still the Mormaer there, not yet king.'

The king was speaking of the Norns, launching directly upon
the subject without any introduction. Obviously the topic had
been preying on his mind.

'They appeared as three hags, clustered by the roadside. I
would have ridden on if they had not called out for my attention.
Perhaps if I had not stopped to listen, my wife would have been
spared.'

'You saw the Norns in Moray?' I asked, filling the awkward

gap. 'They were seen nearby, in Caithness, at the time of Clontarf. Weaving a shroud and using the entrails of men as the threads. They were celebrating the battle's slaughter. When you saw them, what did they say?'

'Their words were garbled and indistinct. They were short of teeth and mumbled. But one of them was prophesying. Said I would become the king of the Scots, and warned me of treachery among my nobles. At the time I thought it was all nonsense. Trite stuff that any fool would dream up.'

'If they were indeed the Norns, that would be Verdhandi who spoke to you. She is that-which-is-becoming. Her two sisters, Urhr and Skuld, concern themselves with what is and what should be.'

'As a Christian I know nothing of their names or attributes. Indeed I would have paid no heed to their words, if Gruoch had not encouraged me.'

I looked again towards the hooded woman. Now she was rocking back and forth in her seat, her hands still twisting together ceaselessly. She must have heard everything we had said, but she had not uttered a word since I had entered the room.

'Gruoch is as good a Christian as I am,' Mac Bethad went on, speaking more gently. 'A better one, in fact. She is charitable and kind. No one could ask for a better consort.'

I realised, a little belatedly, that Mac Bethad truly loved his queen. It was an unexpected revelation, and it explained his present concern for her, even as his next words revealed how his love for his wife had ensnared them both.

'When I told Gruoch what the Wyrds had said, she too dismissed their prophecies as heathen babbling. But she did point out that I had a better right to the throne of Scotland than the weakling who held it — I mean my cousin, Duncan. She left unsaid that she herself is equally well born. Maybe that was not what she was thinking, but I imagined it was so. Her words made me determined to overthrow the king. Not for my own sake, though everyone knows that the stronger the king, the happier will be his realm. That's "the king's truth". For the sake of my wife I made up my mind that one day I would be seated on the sacred stone and acclaimed as the King of Scots. Then Gruoch would be a queen. It was her birthright, which was to be my gift to her.'

'And did it turn out as the Norns predicted?'

'I challenged King Duncan and defeated him in open battle. I was not alone in wanting him gone. More than half the other Mormaers and thegns supported me.'

'I have heard it said that the king was murdered while he was your guest.'

Mac Bethad grimaced. 'That's a well-rehearsed tale, a black rumour spread by those who would like to see one of Duncan's sons on the throne. They would be puppets of the Northumbrians, of course. Duncan was not murdered. He died because he was a poor tactician and a careless commander. He led his men into Moray to attack me, and his scouts were incompetent. They failed to detect the ambush we had set. After the battle I had the scouts executed for failing in their duty. If anyone was responsible for Duncan's death it was them.'

'And was it then that your wife fell ill?'

Mac Bethad shook his head. 'No. She is a king's granddaughter, and she knows the price that must be paid for gaining or maintaining power. Her sickness began less than three years ago. But it is getting worse, slowly and inexorably, and that is what I hope you may be able to explain, for I fear it has something to do with your Elder Ways.'

He turned to face his wife. She had raised her head, and the look which passed between them made it clear that Gruoch loved her husband as much as he loved her.

'I was too occupied with my duties as king to appreciate what was happening,' explained Mac Bethad slowly. 'After I gained the throne, she began to question why the Wyrds had appeared, and if they were no more than a heathen superstition, how it was that what they said had come true. The doubts preyed on her mind.

Our Christian priests told us that it was the work of the devil. They persuaded her that she had unknowingly become an agent of the dark one. She began to think of herself as unclean. That is why she constantly washes her hands, as you must have noted.'

'And did the priests suggest a cure?' I asked, unable to resist adding, 'They seem to think they have the answers to every human condition.'

Mac Bethad stood up and went across to where his wife sat. He bent and kissed her gently, then eased back her hood so he could reach down and remove an amulet hanging on a leather thong around her neck. As the hood fell back, I saw that Queen Gruoch must have once possessed a striking beauty. Her hair was unkempt and wild, but it was still thick and luxuriant and shot through with glints of reddish gold, though most of it was faded to a dull bronze. From her left temple a strange white streak extended back through her hair, giving her a strange and unsettling appearance.

Mac Bethad laid the amulet upon the table in front of me. It was a small tube of brass. I teased out the tightly rolled scrap of paper and smoothed it on the table so that I could read the words written there. They were penned in a combination of three scripts – runes, Greek and Roman lettering. '*In nomine domini summi sit benedictum*, thine hand vexeth, thine hand troubles thee, Veronica aid thee,' I read.

'The priest who prepared this note said that my wife should wear this close to her left breast,' explained Mac Bethad, 'and for it to be effective she must remain silent. But as you observe, it has had little effect. At least it is less harmful than the other cures that have been suggested. A different priest claimed that my wife's affliction could be controlled if I used a whip made of porpoise skin to beat her every day and expel the demons that have possessed her.' He grimaced with distaste.

I recalled the twitch that had passed across the queen's cheek, and remembered how the young Basileus Michael in Miklagard had trembled uncontrollably in the moments before his spirit had strayed. In Miklagard, too, ignorant priests had diagnosed devilish intervention. Other physicians, however, had been more practical. Long ago, in Ireland, I had seen a drui use herbs and potions to treat convulsions among his patients.

'There are no devils, nor dark elves in possession of your queen,' I assured the king. 'What is written on that paper is worse than foolishness. If you wish to ease your queen's suffering, throw away the amulet, let her speak when she wishes, and if she is distressed, give her potions to drink of warm vinegar in which henbane or cowbane has been soaked, or a light infusion of the plant called deadly nightshade.'

Mac Bethad paled. 'But those are plants known to be favoured by witches and warlocks – and the Wyrds,' he said accusingly. 'You are leading her towards that dark world, not away from it.'

I shrugged. 'I am an Old Believer,' I reminded him, 'and I find no fault in using them if they are effective.' As I spoke, I found myself wondering if Gruoch knew that she had seidr powers. And if she did know, whether she had suppressed or denied them because she was a Christian. If that was the case, the tension within her must have become insupportable.

'Will the medicine cure my wife, as well as ease her suffering?' he asked.

'That I cannot say,' I warned him. 'I believe that her spirit is in turmoil. Divided between the White Christ and the Elder Way.'

'The White Christ has been no help,' said Mac Bethad. 'Four years ago, when I was really worried about the queen's condition, I took her to Rome on pilgrimage. Sought out all the holy men, prayed, gave alms in abundance, but with no result. Maybe I should now turn to the Elder Way. If it cured my wife, I would give up my Christian faith, knowing that no harm can ever come to me.'

His words sent an alarm signal. I knew there was something not quite right.

'What do you mean by "that no harm will come to you"?'

'The final prophecy of the Wyrds was that I could not be killed by mortal man, and that my throne was secure.'

'And did they offer some sort of guarantee or proof?'

'They stated that I would not lose a battle until the wood of Birnam came to this stronghold. But Birnam is half a day's travel away. That is impossible.'

But I knew that it was possible. Even as Mac Bethad told me the prophecy, I understood that his kingship was doomed. Perhaps the country folk back in Vaster Gotland were right and I was some sort of sage, because I already knew that a prophecy of a moving wood had proved to be a sure sign of defeat to come. Travelling in Denmark some years earlier, I had come to a place known locally as the Spring of Carnage. Intrigued, I had enquired the reason for the name. I was told it was the spot where a king of Denmark lost his final battle to an enemy who advanced into their attack carrying the leaves and shrubs of trees to hide their numbers. The place where they had cut the fronds was still called the Deadly Marsh.

Composing my features to hide my consternation, I looked at the king of the Scots in the half darkness. There was no doubt in my mind that the prophecy of the Norns was an augury for Mac Bethad, not a surety. Odinn had allowed me a glimpse into Mac Bethad's future, but had denied it to the king. There was nothing that I could do to alter Mac Bethad's fate. It was his orlog, his destiny. I wondered what to say to him. I chose the coward's course.

'Be careful,' I cautioned Mac Bethad, rising to my feet. 'A single tree can destroy a king. Magnus of Norway who shared the throne with my liege lord Harald was killed by a single branch which swept him from the saddle. He too was a Christian.'

Then, burdened with a sense of foreboding, I said I was tired, asked Mac Bethad for permission to return to my chamber, and left the room.

Next morning I did not trouble to request for a second audience with the king, because I knew that any alliance I made between Mac Bethad and King Harald would prove futile. Instead I asked for permission to return to Norway for further consultations with my liege lord, and even as I was waiting on the coast for the ship that would carry me back to Nidaros, I heard that Siward and his Northumbrians had made a sudden strike across the border and overrun Mac Bethad's stronghold on the hill. I did not doubt that the advancing troops had carried branches from the wood of Birnam. Mac Bethad himself escaped the battle, and was to survive for two more years before he was hunted down and killed in the glens of the Mounth. How he was killed when he had been assured that no man born of a woman could kill him, I never found out. Nor did I hear what happened to his Queen Gruoch and whether she converted to the Old Ways or remained torn between the two faiths, tormented by her doubts.

'YOU COULD ALSO have warned Magbjothr that even the divine Baldr, whom the Gods thought was unassailable, was killed by a branch of mistletoe,' Harald observed shrewdly when I reported the failure of my mission to him.

His remark was typical of his familiarity with the Old Gods. Baldr was the most handsome of all of them. When he was born his mother asked all potential sources of harm that they would never hurt him. She obtained the promise from all things that might harm him – fire, water, disease, all animals, including snakes. She even asked the trees to give her their pledge. But she made an exception of the mistletoe, which she considered to be a plant too young and slender to be a risk. Confident of this protection, the other Gods amused themselves at banquets by pelting Baldr with rocks and stones, throwing spears at him and shooting arrows. Always the missiles fell short or were turned aside, until the trickster Loki made an arrow from mistletoe and gave it to Baldr's brother, Hod. Unthinkingly, Hod, who was blind, shot the arrow and killed his brother.

'Odinn the Wise One told us that it is better that men do

not know their fate,' I answered, and quoted a verse from the
Havamal, the Song of Odinn:

> 'Medium wise should a man be
> Never too wise
> No man should know his fate in advance
> His heart will be freer of care.'

Harald grunted his approval of the verse, then dismissed me.
'Go back to your family in Vaster Gotland, Thorgils, and enjoy
the rest of your days with them. You have more than discharged
all your duties to me as a king's man, and I release you from that
obligation. I will only send for you again if I can turn to no
other.'

TWELVE

HARALD NEVER NEEDED to summon me again. When I did come back to his court a full ten years later, it was of my own free will and burdened with a sense of impending doom. I was in the sixty-sixth year of my life, and I felt I had nothing left to live for.

The unthinkable had happened: I had lost Runa. She died of disease when our peaceful corner of Vaster Gotland fell victim to one of those petty but vicious squabbles which plagued the northern lands. I was away from home on a trip to the coast to buy a winter supply of dried fish when a band of marauders crossed our previously tranquil territory, and of course they burned and pillaged as they went. My brother-in-law fled with his own family and Runa and the twins into the recesses of the surrounding forest, so they all survived unscathed. But when they crept out of their shelter and returned to our houses, they found the carefully hoarded stocks of food had been looted. There was no time to plant a second crop so they sought to lay in emergency supplies. I returned home with my purchases to find my family anxiously scouring the forest for edible roots and late-season berries.

We might have come through the crisis if the winter that followed had not been so harsh. The snow came earlier than usual and fell more heavily. For weeks we were trapped in our cabins, unable to emerge or seek assistance, though our neighbours would have been of little help for they too were suffering equal distress. The fish I had brought back was soon eaten, and I cursed myself for not purchasing more. All my hoarded wealth was useless if we could not reach the outside world.

Gradually we sank into a numbed apathy caused by near starvation. Runa, as was her nature, put the well-being of our children ahead of her own needs. Secretly she fed them from her own share of our dwindling rations and concealed her own increasing weakness. When spring finally came and the snows began to melt and the days lengthened, it seemed that all of us would survive. But then, cruelly, the fever struck. Initially it was no more than a soreness in Runa's throat, and she found difficulty in swallowing. But then my wife began to cough and spit blood, and to suffer pains in her chest and shortness of breath. In her already weakened condition, her body offered no resistance to the raging of the illness. I tried all the remedies I knew, but the speed of her decline defeated me. Then came the dreadful night – it was only three days after she showed the first symptoms – when I lay awake beside her and listened to her rapid breathing grow more and more desperate and shallow. By dawn she could no longer lift her head, nor hear me when I sought to comfort her, and her skin was dry and hot to the touch, yet she was shivering.

I went to fetch a bowl of fresh water in which to soak the cloth I laid on her brow, and returned to find she was no longer breathing. She lay as still and quiet as a leaf which, after trembling in the breeze, finally departs from the bough and drifts silently downwards to settle, lifeless, on the earth.

Folkmar and I buried her in a shallow grave scraped from the rocky soil. A half-dozen of our neighbours came to join us. They were little more than walking skeletons themselves, their clothes hanging loose on their bodies, and they stood in silence as I knelt down and laid a few mementoes of Runa's life beside the corpse in its simple homespun gown. There were a pair of scissors, the little strongbox in which she had kept her jewellery, and her favourite embroidered ribbon which she had used to hold back her auburn hair. Looking up at the faces of the mourners and the heart-broken twins, I felt totally bereft, and the tears were streaming down my cheeks.

It was Folkmar who comforted me in his down-to-earth peasant way. 'She never expected so much happiness as you and the children brought her in her final years,' he said. 'If she could speak, she would tell you that.' Then, solemn-faced, he began to cover the corpse with earth and gravel.

It was another week before Folkmar gently stated what he and his wife had decided even as they stood at Runa's graveside. 'We'll take care of the twins,' he said. 'We will treat them as our own until you can arrange something better for them.'

'Better?' I said dully, for I was still too grief-stricken to consider any course of action.

'Yes, better. You should return to Harald's court, where you have influence and command respect. There you can do more for the twins than anything which can be found here. When the time is ripe, maybe you can arrange for them to be taken into royal service, or perhaps fostered to a rich and powerful family.'

Folkmar's trust in my competence touched me deeply, though I doubted that I could achieve half of what he expected. Yet he and his wife were so insistent that I could not bear to disappoint them, and when the weather improved sufficiently I took the twins for a long and melancholy walk in the forest until we came to a dank clearing, surrounded by dark pine trees. There, as the melting snow dripped from the branches, I told my children the details of my own life that they had never heard before. I described how I had been abandoned as an infant and brought up by kindly strangers, and made my own way in the world. As intelligent youngsters do, they already knew where my talk was leading, and looked at me calmly. Both of them had inherited Runa's light brown eyes, and also her way of waiting patiently for me to reach the conclusion of my little speeches. As I groped to find the right words, I thought to myself how strange it must be for them to have for their parent a man who was old enough to

be their grandfather. That wide gap in our ages was one reason
why I felt I hardly knew them, and I found myself wondering
what they really thought of me. Their mother had been the link
between us, and once again the sorrow of her death nearly overwhelmed me.

'Both of you – and I as well – must learn how best to live
now that your mother is gone,' I ended lamely, trying to keep my
voice steady and not show my grief, 'so tomorrow I'm going to
travel to the king to ask for his help. I will send for you as soon
as our future becomes clear.'

They were the last words I ever spoke to them.

I arrived in Harald's new capital at Trondheim just in time to
attend what was to prove the most important council meeting of
Harald's reign. A sea-stained merchant ship had put in to Trondheim with news from London. On the fifth day of January the
king of England, Edward, had died without leaving a direct male
heir. The English kingdom was in turmoil. The English council,
the witan, had elected the most powerful of their number to the
vacant throne, but he was not of royal blood and there was much
dissent. There were other claimants to the kingship, chief among
them the Duke of Normandy, as well as the brother of the newly
appointed king, who felt himself overlooked.

'I have as good a claim as any,' Harald stated flatly as his
council gathered in an emergency session to discuss the situation.
Out of respect for my grey hairs and my long service to the king,
I had been asked to attend the meeting. 'My nephew Magnus was
promised the kingdom of England by Knut's son and heir. When
Magnus died, his claim passed to me as his co-ruler.' There was a
silence. There were those among us who were thinking privately
that Svein Estrithson in Denmark had an equal or even better
claim because he was the great Knut's nephew. 'I intend to press
for what is mine by right,' Harald went on, 'as I did for the
throne of Norway.'

The silence deepened. All of us knew that the only way

Harald could pursue his claim was by force of arms. He was talking about waging full-scale war.

'Who holds the English throne now?' someone enquired tactfully. The questioner knew that it would give Harald a chance to tell us what he had in mind.

'Harold Godwinsson,' said Harald. 'He maintains that Edward named him as his heir while on his deathbed. But there is no proof.'

'That would be the same Harold who defeated the combined Welsh and Irish army last year,' observed one of Harald's captains, a veteran who had family connections among the Norse in Dublin. 'He's a capable field commander. Any campaign against him will need careful planning if it is to be successful.'

'There can be no delay,' declared Harald. 'With each month that passes, Harold Godwinsson makes himself more secure on the throne. I intend to attack this summer.'

'Impossible,' interrupted a voice, and I turned to see who was so bold as to contradict Harald so directly. The speaker was Harald's own marshal, Ulf Ospaksson. I had known him since our campaigns in the service of the Basileus, and he was the most experienced and canny of the king's military advisers. 'Impossible,' Ulf repeated. 'We cannot assemble a sufficiently large invasion fleet in that short time. We need at least a year in which to recruit and train our troops.'

'No one doubts your skill and experience,' answered Harald, 'but it can be done. I have the resources.' He was adamant.

Ulf was equally stubborn. 'Harold Godwinsson has resources too. He rules the wealthiest and largest kingdom in the west. He can raise an army and pay to keep it in the field. And he has his huscarls.'

'We will smash the huscarls to pieces,' boasted a young man, intervening. He was Skule Konfrostre, a close friend of Harald's son, Olaf, and one of the council's hotheads.

The marshal gave a weary sigh. He had heard enough of such

bravado in his days as a soldier. 'According to their reputation, one English huscarl is worth two of the best of Norway's fighting men. Think of that when you come up against their axes.'

'Enough!' broke in Harald. 'We may never need to face their axes. There is a better way.'

Everyone was straining to hear what the king had decided. It was another of Harald's rules that everyone had to stand while in the royal presence, unless given permission to be seated. Harald was sitting on a low stool while we stood in a circle around him. It did not make it any easier to hear what was being said.

Deliberately Harald turned his head and looked straight at me. I felt again the power of his stare, and in that moment I realised that Harald of Norway would never settle down to the quiet enjoyment of his realm nor abandon his grand design of being a second Knut. The death of the English king had been something that Harald had been waiting for. To the very last, the king was a predator at heart.

'Thorgils here can help,' he said.

I had no idea what he was talking about.

'If two claimants to the throne act together, we can depose Godwinsson and divide England between ourselves.'

'Like in Forkbeard's time,' said a sycophant. 'Half of England ruled by the Norsemen, the other half in Saxon hands.'

'Something like that,' said Harald dryly, though looking at him I knew him well enough to know that he was lying. Harald of Norway would never share the throne of England for long. It would be like his arrangement with Magnus for the Norwegian throne all over again. If Magnus had not died in an accident, Harald would have dispossessed him when the time was right.

Harald waited for a few moments, then continued. 'My information is that William the Bastard, Duke of Normandy, is convinced that Edward left the throne of England to him and that Harold Godwinsson is a usurper. My spies also tell me that William intends to press his claim, just as I will, by invading England. With Thorgils's help we can make sure that the two invasions are coordinated, and that Harold Godwinsson is crushed between the hammer of Norway and the anvil of Duke William's Normans.'

A glint of humour came into my liege lord's eyes.

'William the Bastard is a devout Christian. He surrounds himself with priests and bishops and listens to their advice. I propose to send Thorgils to his court as my emissary to suggest a coordination of our plans. Nothing would be more appropriate than to send Thorgils disguised as a priest.'

There was an amused murmur from the councillors. All of them knew my reputation as a staunch adherent to the Elder Faith.

'What do you have to say to this scheme, Thorgils?' Harald asked. He was baiting me.

'Of course I will carry out your wishes, my lord,' I said. 'But I am not sure that I will be able to pass myself off as a Christian priest.'

'And why not?'

'Though I had some training in a monastery when I was young,' I said, 'that was long ago, and in Ireland the monks followed a different version of the White Christ belief. Their way of worship has fallen into disuse. It has been supplanted by teachings from the All Father of the Christians in Rome, and by the new generation of reformers in the Frankish lands.'

'Then you must learn their ways and how to think like them so that you are mistaken for one of them. I want you to get close enough to William the Bastard so that you can form an opinion of him before you reveal your true identity as my ambassador. You must satisfy yourself that the Duke of Normandy will make a worthy ally. Only if you think that he will carry out his invasion are you to propose that he coordinate his attack with mine. Otherwise you are to maintain your disguise, and withdraw quietly.'

'And if I judge the duke to be a serious contender, what date should I suggest he launches his invasion?'

Harald chewed his lip, then glanced across at Ulf Ospaksson. 'Marshal, what do you recommend?'

Ospaksson still looked doubtful. Clearly he was uneasy at the idea of launching a major onslaught with so little preparation. I heard the reluctance in his voice as he set out his advice.

'We will need as much time as possible to raise an army, gather our ships and equip the fleet. Yet we cannot risk crossing the English Sea too late in the season when the autumn gales are due. So I would say that early September is as late as we dare leave it. But it will be cutting matters very short, and it will be impossible to supply the army once it is ashore in England. The distance from Norway is too great.'

'Our army will live off the land, just as it always has,' said Harald.

An image came into my mind of the dreadful famine that ravaged my home in the wake of the warriors. I took a deep breath and risked Harald's anger by asking, in front of the councillors, 'My lord, when I go on this mission for you I will be leaving my family and neighbours behind.'

Harald drew his eyebrows down in a scowl. I knew that he hated to be asked favours, and he had detected that I was about to ask for one.

'What are you trying to say? All of us will be leaving families behind.'

'The district where I spent the last four months is wracked by famine,' I explained. 'It would be a kingly act if you could send some assistance.'

'Anything else?'

'I have two children, my lord, a boy and a girl. Their mother died only a few weeks ago. I would be glad if they could benefit from royal favour.'

Harald grunted – whether in agreement I could not tell – before turning back to the matter of raising his army. Half of the levies of Norway were to assemble at Trondheim as soon as the harvest was in, every available warship was to be pressed into

service, a bounty would be paid to the smithies for extra production of arrowheads and axe blades and so forth. Only later did
I learn that, to his credit, he had arranged for three shiploads of
flour to be sent to Vaster Gotland, but that when his messengers
reached my home they found they had been mistaken for raiders,
and that Folkmar had disappeared. Last seen, he was heading in
the direction of the Thor temple at Uppsala, taking my twins with
him.

I spent the next two weeks trying to learn as much as possible
about the man on whom I was being sent to spy, and the more I
learned, the more I feared that Harald was overreaching himself
if he thought such a wily ally would cooperate. William the
Bastard attracted gossip like rotting meat attracts flies. His mother,
it was said, was a tanner's daughter whose heart-stopping beauty
had caught the eye of the Duke of Normandy, and their illegitimate child was only seven when he had inherited the ducal title.
Against all expectations the youngster had survived the power
struggles over his inheritance because he possessed what the
Christians liked to call 'the devil's luck'. On one occasion a hired
murderer got as far as the boy's bedroom, and he awoke to see
his would-be killer struggling with his guardian, who had taken
the precaution of sleeping in the same room. The murderer cut
his guardian's throat but made such a commotion that he was
forced to flee before he completed his mission. Even William's
marriage was the subject of lurid description. Apparently he had
married a cousin, although his own priests had forbidden the
union as too close to incest, and, to add spice to the gossip, it was
rumoured that his bride was a dwarf who had borne him at least
half a dozen children. On one point, however, all the rumours
and speculation met: William of Normandy had shown himself to
be a master of statecraft. He had connived and fought until he
had secured his grip on the dukedom he had inherited, and now
he was the most feared warlord in France, as powerful as the king
of France himself.

This, then, was the man that my lord had sent me to evaluate and perhaps ensnare within Harald's grand design. It would be a dangerous assignment, and I was not at all sure that I still had the mental agility or the subtlety to act the spy. If I was to carry it off, it would only be with the help of Odinn, himself the great dissembler. It would be my last effort, and a distraction from the pain of losing Runa.

I began by acquiring my own disguise. I decided to wear the simple brown robe which would mark me as a humble monk. At Harald's court there were enough Christian priests for me to observe and copy their mannerisms, while the Latin I had learned in Ireland was more than good enough to mimic their prayers and incantations. The only dilemma I had was about my tonsure. Discreet enquiry among the priests revealed that the shape and manner of my haircut could be significant. Apparently the area of the scalp that was shaved, the length of remaining hair and the way it hung could indicate a White Christ devotee's background in the same way that the painted pattern on a shield indicates a warrior's allegiance. So I chose to have my head shaved completely of its last few remaining white hairs. If questioned, I would say that it was in honour of St Paul who was, according to the priest I interviewed, completely bald.

A cog took me from Norway south to its home port of Bremen and then towards the coast of Normandy, where I intended to disembark. This cog was a vessel that I had never experienced before, and I was ill at ease throughout the voyage. Designed for cargo carrying, the sides of the ship rose rather too high out of the water for my liking, and the bow and stern were made yet more clumsy by high wooden platforms. I thought the cog resembled a large barn that had somehow floated out to sea, though I had to admit that she was uncommonly capacious. The cog on which I sailed carried twice as much cargo as any ship I had ever travelled on, and as she waddled down from port to port I watched her hold fill up with stores that was clearly war material. There were bundles of shields, bales of sword blades, flax cloth for tent making, large quantities of ship-building nails

as well as more humdrum gear such as boots, spades and bill
hooks. Our ultimate destination was Rouen, Duke William's
capital.

Njord the sea God, however, imposed a different outcome on
our voyage. The cog loaded her final batch of cargo in Boulogne
– a mixed consignment of metal helmets, tanned hides and
pickaxes – and was working along the coast when, in the early
afternoon, the weather turned against us. It was a typical spring
gale when the sky swiftly darkens, clouds come scudding up from
the west, and heavy bursts of cold rain spatter the sea with
exploding raindrops. The sea, which had been a neutral blue-grey,
turned a greenish black, and as the wind gathered in strength the
swells began to mount and grow more violent until they toppled
and broke. At first the cog's size and weight made her seem
impervious to the deteriorating conditions, but eventually the
waves which are Njord's servants gradually took control. Our
Bremen skipper did his best to find shelter from the storm, but as
luck would have it the gale had caught him at a point where he
had no safe harbour to run to. So he ordered the sailors to shorten
sail and tried to ride out the worsening conditions. Our deep-
laden ship wallowed sickeningly as the waves rolled under her
keel, and the wind buffeted the high bow and stern. It required
all the steersman's skill to keep her riding to the seas, and it was
impossible to prevent her drifting downwind as her slab sides
acted as an unwelcome sail. As the wind shifted further into the
north, I saw the skipper begin to look alarmed. He sent his crew
below decks to fetch up the spare anchors from the bilges and get
them ready on the heaving deck.

By now the rain was so heavy that it was impossible to see
more than an arrow's flight in any direction, yet it was clear that
the cog was being driven towards the unseen coast and into
danger. I took care to conceal my own unease – priests are not
supposed to be experienced mariners – but I noted how the waves
were becoming shorter and steeper, and I suspected we were
passing over shoals. That suspicion became a certainty when the

churning of the waves began to throw up a yellow tinge of sand and mud. Once or twice I thought I heard the sound of distant breakers.

Then, abruptly, the rain stopped and the air around us cleared as if a hood had been lifted from our eyes. We turned to look over the lee rail to see where the wind had brought us. The sight brought an urgent command from our skipper. 'Let go all anchors,' he yelled.

Away to our port side, less than half a mile away, was a low shoreline. A beach of grey sand, glistening with the recent rain, sloped gently towards a ridge of dunes, and behind them rose a barrier of bone-white cliffs. To a landsman's eye it might have looked as if our cog was still far enough from land to be in deep water and safely clear of danger, but our skipper knew better. The gradual slope of the beach and the white crests of the waves between us and the shoreline told him that we had entered shoal ground. At any moment our vessel's keel might touch bottom.

The crew scrambled to carry out their captain's orders. Their greased leather sea boots slithered on the slippery deck as they wrestled the largest of our anchors, a great iron grapnel weighted with bands of lead, across to the side rail and heaved it overboard. The anchor rope flew after it, the first few coils disappearing quickly, but then suddenly slowing as the anchor hit the sea floor close beneath the surface.

'Jump to it!' bellowed the captain. 'Get the second anchor down.'

This time the anchor was smaller, a wooden shaft with a metal crossbar, easier to manage but less effective. It too was flung overboard, and by now the skipper had run forward and laid his hand on the main anchor rope. He was feeling its tremor, trying to sense whether the anchor itself had dug into the sea floor and was holding firm. His conclusion was evident as he shouted at the crew to throw out more anchors. 'Everything!' he yelled. 'She's dragging!' Desperately the crew obeyed. Four more anchors were tossed into the sea and their anchor lines made fast to strong points on the deck. But these emergency anchors were feeble affairs, the last one no more than a heavy rock with a wooden bar thrust through it, intended as a fang to bite into the sand.

All this time the cog was heaving up and down as each wave rolled under her hull, the anchor ropes went taut and then grew slack as the vessel worked her tethers, and the motion tugged the anchors treacherously across the soft sea floor.

There was nothing we could do but wait and hope that one or more anchors might take a firmer grip and halt our slithering progress. But we were disappointed. There came the deeper trough of a large wave, and we felt the keel of the cog thump down on the sand. Several moments passed, and then the vessel shuddered again, though the wave trough had been less obvious. Even the most inexperienced novice on our crew knew that our ship was being pushed farther into the shallows. Inexorably the gale drove the cog onward, and soon the shocks of the hull striking sea floor became a steady pounding. The cog was a credit to her shipwrights. Her stout hull stayed watertight, but no vessel could withstand such a battering for ever. The gale was showing no sign of easing, and each wave carried our ship a few inches farther towards her tomb.

Before long she was tilting over, the deck at so steep an angle that we had to cling to the rigging to prevent ourselves slipping into the sea. The cog was halfway towards her death. Even if her hull stayed intact, she would be mired in the shifting sands until she was buried and her timbers rotted. Her skipper, whose livelihood depended on his vessel, finally recognised that the sand would never let her escape.

'Abandon ship,' he called despondently, shouting to make himself heard above the grumbling of the waves which tumbled all around us.

When the gale had first hit us, our vessel's main tender – a ten-oared rowing boat – had been towing astern on a heavy cable, but when the cog struck the sands, the lighter boat had been carried ahead by the waves, the cable had parted, and our tender had been swept away. The remaining boat was a square-ended skiff, clumsy and heavy, suitable only for sheltered waters. The crew took axes and hacked away the low bulwarks to open a gap through which they pushed her into the seas. Even as the skiff slid overboard and hit the water, the breaking crest of a wave rose up and half filled her. The sailors shoved and jostled as they began to climb over the rail.

The skipper held back; probably he could not bear to abandon his ship. He saw me hesitating at the spot I had chosen. I was clinging to a shroud at the highest point on the vessel so that I did not tumble down the sloping deck. He must have thought that I was too frightened to move, and was hanging there, frozen with in terror.

'Come on, father,' he shouted, beckoning me. 'The boat is your only hope.'

I took a second look at the squabbling boat crew and doubted what he said. Gathering up the hem of my brown priest's gown, I tucked the material into the rope belt around my waist, waited for the next wave to crest, and the last the skipper saw of me was my flailing arms and naked legs as I launched myself out into the air and flung myself into the sea.

The water was surprisingly warm. I felt myself plunging down, then rolled and turned by the waves. I gasped for air and gulped down seawater, gritty to the taste. I spat out a mouthful as I came to the surface, looked around to locate the shoreline, and began to swim towards it. Waves broke over my head again and thrust me downward so that I was swimming underwater. I struggled to keep my direction. Another wave tumbled me head over heels, and I lost my bearings. As I came back to the surface, I squeezed my eyelids together to clear my vision, and my eyes stung with the salt. Once more I looked around, trying to realign myself with the shore, and caught a glimpse of the ship's small boat and its desperate crew. Four of the sailors were rowing raggedly, while the others bailed frantically, but their craft was dangerously low in the water. Even as I watched, a breaking wave lifted up the skiff, held the little boat there for a moment, and then casually overturned it, stern over bow, and flung the crew into the water. Most of them, I was sure, did not know how to swim.

Grimly I battled on, remembering my days in Iceland when I had taken part in the water games when the young men competed at wrestling as they swam, the winner attempting to hold his opponent underwater until he gasped for mercy. I recalled how to hold my breath, and so I kept my nerve as the waves crashed over me, trying to smother me, but also washing me closer to the shore. I was an old man, I cautioned myself, and I should dole out my last remaining strength like a miser. If I could stay afloat, the sea might deliver me to land. Had Niord and his handmaidens, the waves, wanted to drown me, they would have done so long ago.

I was on the point of abandoning the struggle when suddenly a pair of hands gripped me painfully under the shoulders and I found myself being hauled ashore, up the sloping beach. Then the hands abruptly released their grip, and I flopped face down on wet sand, while my rescuer, speaking in thickly accented Frankish, said, 'What shitty luck. All I've got is a useless priest.' At that moment I closed my eyes and passed into a haze of exhaustion.

A kinder voice awoke me. Someone was turning me on my back, and I could feel the clinging wetness of my monk's gown against my skin. 'We must find some dry clothing for you, brother. The good Lord did not spare you from the sea just to let you die of ague.'

I was looking up into the anxious face of a small, wiry man kneeling beside me. He wore a monk's habit of black cloth over a white gown, and was tonsured. Even in my exhausted condition I wondered to which monastic order he belonged, and how he came to be on a windswept beach, the scene of a shipwreck.

'Here, try to stand,' he was saying. 'Someone nearby will provide shelter.'

He slipped one arm under me and helped me rise to a sitting position. Then he coaxed me to my feet. I stood there, swaying.

My body felt as though it had been thrashed with a thick leather strap. I looked around. Behind me the waves still rumbled and crashed upon the sand, and some distance away I could see the wreck of our cog. She was well and truly aground now, lying askew. Her single mast had snapped and fallen overboard. Closer, in the shallows, the upturned hull of the ship's skiff was washing back and forth in the surge and return of the breakers. Occasionally, a large crest half rolled the little boat, and she gyrated helplessly. A group of about a dozen men was standing knee-deep in the sea, their backs turned towards me. Some were staring intently at the little skiff, others were watching the waves as they came sweeping towards the shore.

'No use asking them for help,' said my companion.

Then I noticed the two bodies lying on the sand, just a few yards away from the watchers. I guessed they were corpses of sailors from the cog who had drowned when the skiff capsized. When last I saw them, they were fully dressed. Now they were stripped naked.

'Wreckers and scavengers. Heartless men,' lamented my companion. 'This is a dangerous part of the coast. Yours is not the first ship to have come to grief here.' Gently he turned me around, and helped me stumble towards the distant line of cliffs.

A fisherman took pity on us. He had a small lean-to against the foot of the cliffs, where he kept his nets and other fishing gear. Over a small charcoal fire he heated a broth of half-cured fish and onions, which he gave us to eat while I sat shivering on a pile of sacks. A cart would be coming shortly, he said. The driver was his cousin, who passed by at the same time each day, and he would carry us into town. There the church priest would assist us. Listening to him, I found I was able to follow his words as they were mainly of the Frankish tongue, though mixed with a few words I recognised from my own Norse, as well as phrases I had heard when I lived in England. With my companion, I conversed in Latin.

'Where am I?' I asked the fisherman.

He looked surprised. 'In Ponthieu, of course. In the lands of
Duke Guy. By rights, I should take you to his castle at Beaurain
and deliver you as sea flotsam. Everything which is washed up
by the sea is the duke's by right. That's the law of lagan. But I
wouldn't be thanked for that, not since that business with the
Englishman. The one who's now scrambled on to the throne over
there, though he has no right. '

Odinn had a hand in my shipwreck, I thought to myself. The
broth was warming me and I could feel the strength beginning to
seep back through my limbs. 'What's his name, this Englishman?'
I continued to enquire through lips that were painfully cracked
and tasted salty.

'Harold Godwinsson,' answered the fisherman. 'He was cast
up on the shore, just like you, along with half a dozen of his
attendants. We get a dozen or so ships wrecked here every year,
always on a north-west gale. He was a nobleman all right, anyone
could see that from his fancy clothes. Even those plunderers, the
wreckers, knew that they would have to take a care. No knowing
what would happen if they messed about with the castaway. Too
rich a fish altogether. Might stick in their gullets. So straightaway
they took him to the duke, expecting a reward, though little good
it did them. The duke stowed the man and his attendants in his
dungeon while he made some enquiries as to who he was, and
when he found out how important and wealthy he really was, he
sent a ship over to England – my oldest brother was the first mate
on her – asking for a good fat ransom. But our duke got no more
profit out of it than the wreckers. Word of the castaway reached
William the Bastard, and before you know it, a gang of his men-
at-arms is on our doorstep telling our duke that he has to hand
over the captive, or his castle will be torched and his head will be
on a pole. Not a threat you ignore if Bastard William is behind it.
Also he's Duke Guy's overlord, so he had a right to tell him what
to do. So this captive is released from the dungeons, dressed up

in a new set of finery, and the last we saw of him he was being escorted off to Rouen as though he was William's long-lost brother.'

The fisherman hawked to clear his throat, turned his head and spat a gob of phlegm accurately through the door of his shack. 'That's my cousin now, coming along with the ass and cart. You better get moving.'

'Bless you,' said my companion. 'Thrice bless you. You have done a Christian act today, for which God will reward you.'

'More than the duke would. He's a mean sod,' commented the fisherman sourly.

The little cart made slow progress. Its ill-shaped wheels wobbled on a single axle, and the vehicle lurched and slewed as it bumped across the tussocks of sea grass. I felt so sorry for the struggling donkey that I slid down from the pile of damp and smelly nets and walked beside the tailgate, holding on to the cart for support. I must have given the impression that I had recovered from my near drowning, because my companion could no longer restrain his curiosity.

'How came you to be upon that ship, and what is your name, brother?' he asked.

I had been expecting the question and had prepared what I hoped was a satisfactory reply.

'My name is Thangbrand. I have been preaching in the northern lands on behalf of our community in Bremen, though I fear that the word fell on stony ground.'

'Bremen indeed. I have heard that the bishop there holds authority over the northern kingdoms. But you are the first of his people that I have met.'

I relaxed. I doubted there were any survivors from the ship-wreck who could throw doubt on my story.

'But you did not say why you were aboard the boat that wrecked.'

'The bishop sent me to seek out more recruits for our mission.

The northerners are a stubborn people, and we need help if we are to succeed in spreading the word of our Redeemer.'

My companion sighed. 'How true. Minds and ears are often closed to the magnificent and awesome mystery. Truly it is said that Christ was facing westward when he hung from the cross. All can see how in that direction the word of God has spread most easily. His almighty right arm pointed to the north which was to be mellowed by the holy word of the faith, and his left hand was for the barbaric peoples of the south. Only the peoples of the east are condemned, for they were hidden behind his head.

'And you, brother, how came you to be on the beach in my hour of need?' I asked, anxious to turn the conversation away from my own background and learn more about my pious companion.

'My name is Maurus and I am named for the assistant to the teacher of the Rule. I come from the region of Burgundy where its governance has long flourished.'

Baffled by his reply, I remained silent and hoped that he would provide a few clues as to what he was talking about.

'I was on my way to the Holy and Undivided Trinity to present to Abbot John a chronicle which celebrates the life of his predecessor, the saintly Lord Abbot William. I do this on behalf of the chronicler himself as he is no longer able to travel due to advancing years and ill health.'

'And this chronicler?'

'My mentor and friend, Rudolfus Glaber. Like myself he is from Burgundy. For years he has laboured compiling and writing a Life of Lord Abbot William. In addition he has written five books of Histories to relate the lives of the other important men of our time. Even now he is engaged in writing a sixth book, for he is determined to leave a written record for posterity of the many events which have occurred with unusual frequency since the millennium of the Incarnation of Christ our Saviour.'

I took a closer look at Maurus. He was, I guessed, somewhere between forty and fifty years old, small and sinewy, with a brick-red complexion that was either scorched by long exposure to the sun and wind or was the result of too much strong drink.

'Forgive me for my ignorance, brother,' I said, 'but this Rule you mentioned. What is that?'

He looked mildly shocked by my ignorance. 'That the brethren of a monastery obey one common will, are equal in agreement, and work and follow a uniform way of prayer and psalmody, eating and dress.'

'That makes them sound like soldiers,' I commented,

He beamed with approval. 'Exactly, servant soldiers of Christ.'

'That is something I would like to see.'

'You shall!' Maurus said enthusiastically. 'Why don't you travel with me to the Holy and Undivided Trinity? The monastery is second only to my own monastery of Cluny for the renown of its strict rule and discretion, the mother of virtues.'

It was precisely what I hoped he would say, because to travel in the company of a genuine priest would be excellent camouflage. His next words were even more encouraging.

'The monastery is at Fécamp, in Duke William's lands.'

THIRTEEN

IT TOOK US a week to reach Fécamp, walking by day and taking rides on farm carts when they were offered. At night we stayed with village priests, and twice we slept under hedges as it was now early summer and the night was mild. Throughout our journey I looked about me, trying to assess the resources which might allow Duke William to launch an invasion of England. What I saw impressed me. The countryside was fertile and well farmed. Rolling hills were cultivated for large fields of wheat, and every village was surrounded by carefully tended orchards. There were also large tracts of forest, mainly oak trees, and frequently we passed groups of men carrying saws and ropes, or we heard the sound of axes in the distance and encountered timber wagons drawn by oxen and piled high with raw logs, sawn baulks of wood, and the crooks and roots of large trees. I could recognise boat-building timber when I saw it, and I noted that the timber cargoes were all heading north, towards the coast of what the local people called 'the sleeve', the narrow sea separating Frankia from England.

Several times small groups of heavily armed men passed us. The weapons they carried looked well cared for, and I guessed them to be mercenary soldiers. Eavesdropping on their conversation as they passed, I identified men who came from Lotharingia,

Flanders, and even Schwabia. All of them were seeking hire by Duke William. When I commented on this to Maurus, he grimaced and said, 'Just as long as they keep their swords sheathed while they are among us. With the Duke you never know. He has brought peace to this land, but at a cost.'

We had reached the crest of a low hill and were beginning our descent into the far valley. In the distance a small walled town straddled the banks of a river.

'I once passed through a town just like that one over there,' Maurus recalled sombrely. 'It was border country, and the towns-folk had made the mistake of denying the duke's authority. They gave their allegiance to one of his rivals, and quickly found themselves under siege from the duke's men. They thought their walls could not be breached and compounded their error by insulting the duke himself. Some of the bolder citizens stood on the town walls, jeering and calling out that the tanner's daughter was a whore. The duke tightened the siege, and when food within the town ran out and a delegation of burghers came to beg for clemency, he had their hands cut off, then had them hanged from a row of gibbets erected opposite the main gate. The town surrendered, of course, but he showed no mercy even then. He gave his soldiers leave to put the place to the sack, then to set it on fire. There were only ashes and blackened house frames when I passed through.'

Duke William the Bastard, I thought to myself, was a match for my lord Harald when it came to being ruthless.

'Did not the town priests intervene, asking for their flock to be spared?' I asked.

'There is God's mercy, and the duke's mercy,' stated Maurus bleakly, 'and the sins of the earth can rise even to the heavens. The calamities we have suffered since the millennium of the Incarnation of Christ our Saviour are a sign that we have strayed from the path of righteousness.'

'It is true that there has been famine in the northern lands,' I commented, thinking of Runa's pitiful death.

'Famine, and worse, is our punishment,' said Maurus gloomily. 'My friend Glaber has written of it. For three years the weather was so unseasonable that it was impossible to furrow the land and sow crops. Then the harvest was destroyed by floods. So many died of hunger that the corpses could not be shrived in church, but were thrown into pits, twenty or thirty at a time. In their desperation men and women began to dig up and eat a certain white earth like potter's clay which they mixed with whatever they had by way of flour or bran to make bread, but it failed to allay their hunger cravings. Others turned to eating carrion, and to feasting on human flesh. Travellers like ourselves became victims of brigands who killed us in order to sell our meat in the markets. One trader even sold human flesh ready cooked. When arrested, he did not deny the shameful charge. He was bound and burned to death. The meat was buried in the ground, but another fellow dug it up and ate it.'

Maurus paused, and for a moment I wondered if he was imagining what human flesh tasted like, for I had noted that he paid the closest attention to his food and drink. Even in the humblest home he would encourage the housewife to improve her dishes with sauces, and he was constantly complaining about the standard of cooking in Normandy which, if he was to be believed, compared unfavourably with what he was accustomed to in Burgundy.

'But that is all in the past,' I ventured. 'Today the people look well fed and content.'

'We must not ignore portents which foretell a great tragedy,' Maurus responded. 'In a certain town in Auxerre, the wooden statue of Christ in the marketplace began to weep tears, and a wolf entered the church, seized the bell rope with his teeth, and began to toll the bell. And you can see for yourself the blazing star which appeared in the night sky in late April, and now burns every night, moving slowly across the heavens.'

Years earlier my teacher, a learned drui in Ireland, had told me about this wandering star and predicted its appearance. But to have told that to Maurus would have made it seem that I had learned witchcraft, so I said nothing.

'The world is tainted with blind cupidity, extreme abominations, thefts and adulteries,' he continued. 'The devil's assistants show themselves boldly. I myself have seen one. In my own monastery in Burgundy, he appeared to me in the form of a mannikin. He had a scrawny neck, jet-black eyes and a lined and wrinkled forehead. He had a wide mouth and blubbery lips, and pointed hairy ears under a shaggy mop of dirty hair. His lower legs were covered with coarse brown fur and he dribbled. He shrieked and gibbered at me, pointing and cursing. I was so terrified that I ran into the chapel, flung myself face down in front of the altar and prayed for protection. Truly it is said that the Antichrist will soon be set free, because this foul mannikin was one of his harbingers.'

But when we reached Fécamp and the monastery of the Holy and Undivided Trinity, it seemed to me that Maurus's fellow monks did not share his pessimistic view of the future. They were busy refurbishing their church in a manner clearly intended to last for years to come. The huge building swarmed with stoneworkers, labourers, carpenters, glaziers and scaffolders. The central feature was the tomb of the Lord Abbot William, whose Life had been written by Rudolfus Glaber. It was the scene of miracles, so a monk told me in hushed whispers. A ten-year-old boy, gravely ill, had been brought there by his despairing mother and left before the tomb. The child, looking around, had seen a small dove sitting upon the tomb, and after watching it for some time had fallen asleep. 'When he awoke,' the monk told me, 'he found himself perfectly cured.'

His pious tale was of less interest to me than the cloister gossip. The monks of the Holy Trinity were remarkably knowledgeable about what was going on in the duchy. They had their informants everywhere, from the smallest hamlets to the ducal court itself, and they discussed avidly the war preparations that Duke William was making – how many ships each of his great lords was expected to supply, the number of men-at-arms needed if the venture was to be a success, the quantity of wine and grain being hoarded in great bins, and so forth. The monks were very enthusiastic about the forthcoming campaign, and listening closely I discovered why: the monastery of the Trinity owned rich farmlands in England, and after Harold Godwinsson took the throne, they had ceased to receive any income from their property. Now they wanted Duke William to restore what was theirs, once he had supplanted Harold as king of England. The monastery had even pledged to supply Duke William with a warship for his fleet, paid for from the monastery's ample funds.

I commented to Maurus that some might see it as a contradiction for the house of God to be providing instruments of warfare, and he laughed.

'Let me show you something which is an even more useful contribution to his campaign. Come with me; it is only a short walk.'

He led me out of a side gate to the monastery and down a rutted lane until we came to an orchard. Unusually, the orchard was surrounded by a strongly built stone wall.

'There!' he said, pointing.

I peered over the wall. Grazing under apple trees were three extraordinary animals. I recognised that they were horses, but they did not look like any horses that I had ever seen before. Each animal was broad and heavy, with short muscular legs like thick pillars, and a back as broad as a refectory table.

'Stallions, all three of them,' explained Maurus approvingly. 'The monastery will donate them to William's army.'

'As pack animals?' I queried.

'No, no, as destriers, as battle chargers. Each can carry a knight in full armour. There is not a foot soldier in the world who can withstand the shock of a knight mounted on a beast like that. Our monastery specialises in the breeding of these animals.'

I thought back to the incident outside the walls of Syracuse when I had witnessed Iron Arm, the sword-wielding Frankish knight, use his brute strength to destroy a skilful Arab rider mounted on an agile steed, and I had a vivid picture of William's heavy cavalry mounted on their destriers, smashing down a shield wall of infantry.

'But how will William manage to transport such heavy animals on his ships and land them safely on the English shore?' I asked.

'I have no idea,' admitted Maurus, 'but there will be a means, that's for sure. William leaves nothing to chance when he wages war, and he has expert advisers, even from this abbey.' I must have looked sceptical, for he added, 'Do you remember meeting the monastery's almoner yesterday? He sat near us during the evening meal in the refectory, the gaunt-looking man with three fingers missing from his left hand. That's a war wound. Before he entered the monastery, he was a mercenary soldier. He's a member of Duke William's council and helps in planning the invasion. The monastery owns a parcel of land on the coast of England, just opposite the shortest sea crossing. It will be an ideal spot for William's troops to come ashore, and the almoner – his name is Regimus – will accompany the fleet so he can point out the best place to beach the boats carrying our troops and, of course, the heavy horses.

I was thoughtful as I walked back to the monastery. Everything I had heard about the Duke of Normandy indicated that he was serious about invading England, and that he was preparing his campaign with close attention to detail. I had the impression that when William the Bastard decided on a course of action, he followed it through and made sure that it was a success. It was not 'devil's luck' which had brought him this far; it was his determination and shrewdness, coupled with his ruthlessness. My earlier misgivings that Harald might be foolhardy in seeking an alliance with William came seeping back. And this time I also had to ask myself whether I too was being rash in involving myself so closely with these Christians who seemed so self-confident and pugnacious.

I made my excuses to Maurus, telling him that I intended to

travel onward to Rome carrying the bishop of Bremen's request for more priests to be sent to the northern lands. Maurus was content to remain at Fécamp, and now that I had had the experience of travelling with him, I was more confident in my disguise as an itinerant preacher for the White Christ. However, when I left the monastery early on a bright summer morning, I did make one important adjustment to my costume. I stole a black habit and a white gown from the laundry, leaving in their place my travel-stained robe of brown. From now on, I would pretend that I was a follower of the Rule.

Looking back on that theft, I realise that it was perhaps another sign that I was now too old to be a successful spy, and that I was becoming careless.

I needed a private audience with the duke at which I could propose the alliance with Harald of Norway, but I had failed to take into account how difficult it would be to gain access to him. William would be fully occupied with his invasion plans, and far too busy to listen to a humble priest, and his bodyguards would be suspicious of strangers, fearing that they were hired killers sent by the duke's enemies or even by Harold Godwinsson in England. So, recklessly, I had devised a stratagem which I hoped would lead to a meeting with the duke and only a handful of his closest advisers. This hare-brained scheme arose from a remark made by one of the monks at Fécamp. When Maurus had described how he found me half-drowned on the beach, the monks had told us that Harold Godwinsson had spent several months at the duke's court after a similar accident had befallen him. There Harold had been treated generously, and, in return, he had sworn allegiance to the duke and promised to support William's candidacy for the English throne. 'Godwinsson treacherously broke his oath by seizing the throne for himself. He is a usurper and needs to be exposed,' asserted one of the monks. 'There is a brother at the monastery in Jumieges who is writing a full account of this act of perfidy, and he will soon be presenting it to Duke William, just as brother Maurus here has brought to us the Life of Lord Abbot

William, lovingly prepared by his friend Rudolfus Glaber in Burgundy. Duke William keenly appreciates those who write the truth.'

Thus, when I reached the duke's palace at Rouen, I pretended I was on my way to its chapel, but then swerved aside and found my way to the anteroom where his secretaries were hard at work. Standing there in my black habit, I said that I wished to meet the duke privately on a matter of importance.

'And what is the subject that you wish to discuss?' asked a junior secretary cautiously. From his expression I judged that, but for my priestly dress, I would have been turned away on the spot.

'For many years I have been compiling a history of the deeds of great men,' I answered, allowing a sanctimonious tone to creep into my voice, 'and Duke William's fame is such that I have already included much about him. Now, if the Duke would be so gracious, I would like to record how he came to inherit the throne of England, despite the false claims of his liegeman Harold Godwinsson. Then posterity can judge the matter correctly.'

'Who should I say is presenting this request?' said the secretary, making a note.

'My name,' I said, unblushingly, 'is Rudolfus Glaber. I come from Burgundy.'

It took three days for my request to filter through the levels of bureaucracy which surrounded the duke. I spent the interval observing the preparations for the forthcoming campaign. Not since my days in Constantinople had I seen such a well-managed military machine. A space had been cleared in front of the city wall where, in the mornings, a company of bowmen practised their archery. Their task would be to pin down the enemy formations under a rain of arrows until the mounted knights could deliver their charge. In the afternoons the same practice ground was used for infantry drill.

A little to the north of the city was a grassy field where I watched the manoeuvres of a large conroy, a cavalry unit contributed to the duke's army by the Count of Mortagne. The Convoy numbered about a dozen knights accompanied by an equal number of squires or assistants. All wore chain mail, but only six of the knights were mounted on the heavy destriers. The others rode horses of a more normal size, and so they were practising how best to coordinate their attack. The lighter cavalry cantered their horses up to a line of straw targets and threw their lances, using them as javelins. Then they wheeled away, leaving their comrades on the heavy horses to advance at a ponderous trot so that their riders could run the targets through with their thicker, weightier lances or slash them to shreds with long swords. When this part of the exercise was over, the light cavalry dismounted, laid aside their metal swords and were given practice weapons with wooden blades. The conroy then divided in two and fought a mock battle, cutting and hacking at one another under the gaze of their leaders, who from time to time shouted out an order. At that moment one side or the other would turn and pretend to flee, drawing opponents forward. Then, at another shouted command, the fugitives would halt their pretended flight and the heavy cavalry, who were still on horseback and waited in reserve, lumbered forward to deliver the counter-blow.

While this was going on, I quietly sauntered forward to take a closer look at one of the battle swords that had been laid aside. It was heavier and longer than the weapons I had seen when in the emperor's Life Guard in Constantinople, and it had a groove down the length of the long straight blade. There was also an inscription worked in bronze lettering. I read INNOMINIDOMINI.

'Very appropriate, don't you think, father?' said a voice, and I looked up to meet the gaze of a heavily muscled man wearing a leather apron. No doubt he was the armourer for the conroy.

'Yes,' I agreed. 'In the Lord's name. It seems to be a fine blade.'

'Made in the Rhine countries, like most of our swords,' continued the armourer. 'Quality depends on which smithy makes them. The Germans turn them out by the dozen. If the blade snaps, it's not worth repairing. You only have to prise off the handle grips and fit a new blade.'

I remembered the consignment of sword blades taken aboard the cog before she wrecked. 'Can't be easy finding a replacement blade.'

'Not this time,' said the armourer. 'I've served the count for the best part of twenty years, making mail and repairing weapons on his campaigns, and I've never seen anything like the amount of spare gear that is being provided – not just sword blades, but helmets, lance heads, arrow shafts, the lot. Cartloads and cartloads of it. I'm beginning to wonder how it will all fit on the transports – if the transports are ready in time, that is. There's a rumour that some of us will be sent to Dives to help the shipwrights.'

'Dives? Where's that?' I asked.

'West along. The gear that's coming in to Rouen is being shipped downriver. The boats themselves are being built all up and down the coast. Dives is where the fleet is assembling. From there it will strike at England.'

It occurred to me that Harold Godwinsson must know what was going on, and that the English could put a stop to the invasion by raiding across the sea and destroying the Norman fleet while it was still at anchor. William's transports would make easy targets. By contrast, Harald's Norwegian ships, now gathering at Trondheim, were too far distant to be intercepted.

I was just about to ask the armourer if Duke William was taking any precautions against an English raid when a pageboy arrived with an urgent summons to the ducal palace. My request for a meeting with the duke had been granted, and I was to go there at once.

I followed the lad through the streets and along a series of corridors into the heart of the palace, where Duke William had his audience chamber. My suspicions should have been aroused by the swiftness of my reception. The pageboy handed me over to a knight who acted as the doorkeeper, and within moments I was ushered into the council chamber itself, the doorkeeper at my heels. I found myself in a large, rather dark room, poorly lit by narrow window slits in the thick stone walls. Seated on a carved wooden chair in the centre of the room was a burly man of about my own height but running to fat, with a close-cropped head and a bad-tempered look on his face. I guessed him to be in his mid-forties. I knew he must be Duke William of Normandy, but to me he looked more like a truculent farm bailiff accustomed to bullying his peasants. He was eyeing me with dislike.

Five other men were in the room. Three of them were obviously high-ranking nobles. They were dressed, like the duke, in belted costumes of expensive fabric, tight hose, and laced leather shoes. They had the bearing and manner of fighting men, yet they were strangely dandified because they wore their hair close-shaved from halfway down their heads in pudding-bowl style, a foppish fashion which, I later learned, had been copied from the southern lands of Auvergne and Aquitaine. They too were regarding me with hostility. The other two occupants of the room were churchmen. In stark contrast to my plain black and white costume, they wore long white robes with embroidered silk borders at the neck and sleeves, and the crosses suspended on their chests were studded with semi-precious stones. The crosses looked more like jewellery than symbols of their faith.

'I hear you want to write about me,' stated the duke. His voice was harsh and guttural, in keeping with his coarse appearance.

'Yes, my lord. With your permission. I am a chronicler and I have already completed five books of history, and – with God's grace – I am embarking on a sixth. My name is Rudolfus Glaber, and I have travelled here from my monastery in Burgundy.'

'I think not,' said a voice behind me.

I turned. Stepping out of the shadows was a man wearing the same plain black and white costume as myself. My glance dropped to his left hand, which lacked three fingers. It was Regimus, the almoner of the monastery of the Holy Trinity at Fécamp. In the same instant the doorkeeper, standing directly behind me, clasped his arms around me, pinioning my arms to my sides.

'Brother Maurus never mentioned that you came from Bur-

gundy, and you do not speak with a Burgundian accent,' said the
almoner. 'The brother in charge of our laundry also reported that
a gown and habit were missing from his inventory, but not until
I heard about a mysterious black-clad monk here in Rouen did I
deduce that you must be the same man. I had not expected you to
be so bold as to claim you were Rudolf Glaber himself.'

'Who are you, old man?' interrupted William, his voice even
harsher than before. 'A spy for Harold? I did not know he
employed dotards.'

'Not a spy for Harold, my lord,' I wheezed. I could scarcely
breathe. The doorkeeper was gripping me so hard that I thought
he would break my ribs. 'I am sent by Harald, Harald of Norway.'

'Let him speak,' ordered William.

The painful grip eased. I took several deep breaths.

'My lord, my name is Thorgils, and I am the envoy of King
Harald of Norway.'

'If you are his ambassador, why did you not come openly
rather than creeping about in disguise.'

I thought quickly. It would be disastrous to confess that
Harald had asked me to evaluate William's invasion plans before
offering an alliance. That was true espionage.

'The message I bring is so confidential that my lord instructed
me to deliver it privately. I adopted this disguise for that purpose.'

'You soil the cloth you wear,' sneered one of the exquisitely
dressed priests.

The duke silenced him with an impatient wave of his hand. I
could see that William demanded, and received, instant obedience
from his entourage. He seemed more than ever like a bullying
bailiff.

'What is this message that you bring from Norway?'

I had recovered my confidence enough to glance at William's
attendants, then say, 'It is for your ears only.'

William was beginning to get angry. A small vein on the right
side of his forehead had started to throb.

'State your message before I have you hanged as a spy or put to torture to learn the truth.'

'My lord Harald of Norway suggests an alliance,' I began quickly. 'He is assembling a fleet to invade the north of England, and knows that you are planning to land forces in the south of the country. You both fight the same enemy, so he proposes that the two armies coordinate their attack. Harold Godwinsson will be obliged to fight on two fronts, and will be crushed.'

'And what then?' There was disdain in William's voice.

'After Godwinsson has been defeated, England is to be divided. The south ruled by Normandy, the north by Norway.'

The duke narrowed his eyes. 'And where will the dividing line be drawn?'

'That I do not know, my lord. But the division would be based on mutual agreement, once Godwinsson has been disposed of.'

William gave a grunt of dismissal. 'I'll think about it,' he said, 'but first I need to know the timing. When does Harald plan to land his forces.'

'His advisers are pressing him to invade England no later than September.'

'Take him away,' said William to the doorkeeper, who was still standing behind me. 'Make sure he is kept in safe custody.'

I passed that night in a cell in the ducal prison, sleeping on damp straw, and in the morning I was encouraged when the same pageboy who had brought me to the palace reappeared to tell the guard to release me. Once again, I was led to the duke's audience chamber, where I found William and the same advisers already gathered. The duke came straight to the point.

'You may inform your lord that I agree to his proposal. My army will land on the south coast of England in the first or second week of September. The precise date will depend on the weather. My transport barges need calm conditions and a favourable wind to make the crossing. According to my information, Harold

Godwinsson has called out the English levies, and is presently
holding his forces on the south coast, so it is likely that he will
dispute our landing. Therefore it is important that King Harald
keeps to his programme and opens a second front no later than
mid-September.'

'I understand, my lord.'

'One more detail. You are to remain here with me. It may be
necessary to communicate with your king as the campaign gets
under way. You will act as our intermediary.'

'As you wish, my lord. I will prepare a despatch for King
Harald confirming the details. If you can provide a vessel, I will
send the message to Norway.'

That same day, feeling quietly satisfied that my mission had
been accomplished so easily, I wrote out a summary of what had
happened. To prevent William's secretaries tampering with my
report, I hid my meanings in phrases that only those who knew
the ways of skaldic verse would understand. Harald became 'the
feeder of eagle of sea of carrion vulture' and the Norman invasion
fleet was 'the gull's wake horses'. And when I came to write about
William himself, I buried my meaning even deeper, because I was
not complimentary about his character. He became the 'horse of
wife of Yggr' because Harold would know that Yggr's wife was a
giantess, and that she rode a wolf. Finally, to make doubly sure
that the letter was treated as genuine, I folded the parchment,
using the same system of secret folds which, in Constantinople,
would prove that the despatch was authentic and which was
known to Harald, and gave the letter to a mounted courier, who
took it to the Norman coast. From there a ship would carry the
despatch to Trondheim.

For the next five weeks my status at William's court was
ambiguous. I was neither a prisoner nor a free man. I was treated
as if I was a minor retainer in the service of William, yet
everywhere I was accompanied by an armed guard. All around
me the preparations for the invasion continued apace, and in early

August, when William moved with his retinue to Dives to begin the embarkation of his troops, I went with him.

The scene at Dives was the culmination of the months of preparation. The port lay at the mouth of a small river, and by the time I arrived almost the entire invasion fleet had mustered in the roadstead. I counted at least six hundred vessels, many of them simple barges specially designed to carry troops. Lines of tents had been erected on the beach, and the army engineers had built cookhouses, latrines and stables. Squads of shipwrights were putting the finishing touches to the transports, and there was a constant coming and going of messengers and despatch riders as the infantry and conroys mustered for their embarkation. I had wondered how the destriers, the heavy horses, would be loaded, and now I saw the method. The cavalry transports were brought up on to the gently sloping beaches at high tide, and anchored. The ebbing tide left the flat-bottomed barges stranded, and the carpenters then placed low ramps up which the horses were led – sometimes with difficulty – and then stabled in the barges with their feed and water. There the massive animals seemed content to stand and eat as the incoming tide refloated the vessels and they were warped out into the roadstead.

On the eleventh day of September the duke did have his 'devil's luck', because, just at the time he had promised his invasion, the wind turned into the south-west as a gentle breeze, and held. At dusk William summoned me to his command tent, and, in the presence of his commanders, gestured towards the northern horizon.

'Now you can tell your master,' he said, 'that William of Normandy keeps his word. Tomorrow we complete our loading and sail for England. You will be staying behind to make your final report.'

The following morning I watched the entire fleet raise anchor and, taking advantage of the flood tide, set out to sea. As I trudged back up the beach to where my guardian man-at-arms stood waiting, I felt I had served my liege lord well, and for the last time. When the opportunity came I would be king's man for Harald no longer, and I would return to Sweden and seek out my twins. I was feeling old.

The man-at-arms was content to dawdle. It was pleasant on the coast, and he was in no hurry to return to his barracks at Rouen, so we spent the next few days at Dives. The place, now that the fleet had sailed, had a slightly desolate atmosphere. The beach where the barges had loaded still showed signs of the departure, and there were traces where the tents had stood, piles of horse droppings, grooves left by the carts that had brought the stores, and charred marks where cooking fires had burned. There was an air of finality. The roadstead was empty. Time was suspended while we waited to hear what was happening with the invasion.

The weather continued fair, with bright sunshine and a light south-west breeze, and to pass the time I arranged with a local fisherman to go out on his boat each morning when he checked his nets. There, ten days after I had watched the Norman fleet depart, we were bobbing gently on the sea when I identified a familiar profile. A small vessel was beating down towards us. Hard on the wind, she was making slow progress, but there was no mistaking her origin. She was a small trading ship, Danish- or Norwegian-built. As she tacked her way into the roadstead at Dives, I was sure that she had come to collect me, and that Harald must have received my letter.

I asked the fisherman to row me across so that we intercepted the vessel before she made her landfall. Standing up in the fishing boat, I called out a greeting, glad to speak Norse once again. I was still wearing my stolen monkish gown, so the vessel's skipper must have thought it odd that a Christian priest spoke his language, but he spilled the wind from his sail and the vessel turned up into the wind so I could scramble aboard. The first person whom I saw on deck was Skule Konfrostre, the same young hothead who had boasted that the Norwegians would smash the English huscarls. I was perturbed to see that he was very agitated.

'Is everything all right with Harald's campaign?' I asked, alarmed by his manner. 'Has he landed safely on the English coast?'

'Yes, yes, our fleet crossed from Norway in late August and safely reached the coast of Scotland. When I left him, Harald was advancing down the coast. He sent me to find out what was happening with the attack that Duke William promised. He has heard nothing further.'

'You need not worry about that,' I said complacently. 'I watched Duke William's fleet sail for England ten days ago. By now they should be well ashore and advancing inland. Godwinsson is caught in a trap.'

Skule looked at me as if I had lost my wits.

'How is it, then, that only yesterday, as we passed southward along the coast, we saw the Norman fleet lying quietly at anchor some distance up the coast. The skipper knows the place. He says it is a port called St Valery, in the lands of the Duke of Ponthieu. They have not even crossed to England yet.'

I felt as if the deck had shifted beneath my feet. I, who had thought to deceive Duke William, had been the victim of a much greater deceit. Too late I thought back to the day that I had first suggested Harald's plan for a coordinated attack. I recalled the armourer who had met me at the practice ground and how he had been so eager to tell me that Dives was the departure point for the invasion, and how, once I had that information, I had quickly been brought before the duke. To my chagrin I realised that my disguise as a monk had been penetrated far earlier than I knew, and that William and his advisers had thought up a scheme to turn my presence to their advantage: I was to be used to conceal the true direction and timing of the Norman attack. After I had revealed myself as King Harald's envoy and suggested the coordinated campaign, William and his advisers must scarcely have believed their good luck. They had duped the King of Norway into landing on English soil to face Harold Godwinsson's army, while the Normans hung back and waited to make their landing unopposed. It would not matter who won the first battle – Harald of Norway or Harold of England – because the victor would be weakened when he came to face Duke William and his conroys.

'We must warn King Harald that he faces the English army on his own,' I exclaimed, queasy with the knowledge of what a fool I had been. Then, to hide my humiliation, I added bitterly, 'So now, Skule, you will learn what it's like to face the huscarls and their axes.'

William, Duke of Normandy, had used me as a pawn.

FOURTEEN

THE VOYAGE NORTHWARD to warn Harald was a misery for me. I spent my time regretting how gullible I had been, then tormenting myself by imagining how I should have seen through William's subterfuge. Worse, now that I knew the extent of the duke's guile, his next move was clear to me: Godwinsson would have his spies in the duke's camp, and the duke would make it possible for them to relay to their master the news that, for the time being, the Norman invasion was at a standstill. Thus, as soon as Harold was confident that the Normans posed no immediate threat, the English king would head north to beat back the Norwegian invaders. The prospect of what might follow a Norwegian defeat filled me with despair. From the day I had first met Harald of Norway long ago in Miklagard I had imagined him as the last, best champion for the Old Ways of the north. Often he had disappointed me, but he still retained an enduring quality. Despite his arrogance and his despotism, he remained the symbol of my yearning that it might be possible to restore the glories of the past.

'Our fleet crossed from Norway to the Shetlands late in August,' Skule Konfrostre confirmed as we journeyed, adding to my discomfort. 'Two hundred longships we were, as well as smaller vessels, the largest fleet that Norway could muster. Such a spectacle! Harald has staked everything on this venture. Before we set sail, he went to the tomb of his ancestor St Olaf and prayed for success. Then he locked the door to the tomb and threw the keys into the River Nid, saying he would not return there until he had conquered England.'

'If you are a Christian, my friend, you may well find yourself fighting other Christians,' I retorted grumpily. 'If Harald overwhelms the English, then his next enemy in line will be Duke William and his Norman knights, and they are convinced that the White Christ is on their side. The duke himself constantly wears a holy relic around his neck, and his senior army commander is a bishop. Mind you, he's the duke's half-brother, so I don't suppose he was appointed for his religious qualities.'

'I'm not a Christian,' said Skule stubbornly. 'As I said, Harald left nothing to chance. He did not forget the Old Gods either. He made sacrifices to them for victory, and he cut his hair and nails before we sailed, so that Naglfar will not benefit if we fail.'

I shivered at the mention of Naglfar, because the young Norwegian had touched on my darkest premonition. Naglfar is the ship of corpses. At Ragnarok, the day of the final dread battle when the Old Gods are defeated, Naglfar will be launched on the floods created by the writhings of the Midgard Serpent lying deep within the ocean. Built from the fingernails of dead men, Naglfar is a monstrous vessel, the largest ever known, big enough to ferry all the enemies of the Old Gods to the battlefield where the world as we know it will be destroyed. If Harald the Hard Ruler had trimmed his nails before sailing for England, then perhaps he foresaw his own death.

Our grey-bearded skipper's opinion only added to my dejection. 'The king should never have sailed in the first place,' he interrupted. 'He should have heeded the omens. Christian or otherwise, they all point towards disaster.' The skipper, like many mariners, was swayed by omens and portents, and my silence only encouraged him to continue. 'Harald himself had a warning dream. St Olaf appeared to him and advised him not to proceed. Said it would result in his death, and that's not all.' He looked at me, still in my black and white gown. 'You're not a White Christ priest, are you?'

'No,' I replied. 'I am a follower of Odinn.'

'Then let me tell you what Gyrdir saw on the very day the fleet sailed. Gyrdir's a royal officer, and he was standing on the prow of the king's ship, looking back over the fleet. It seemed to him that on the prow of every vessel was perched a bird, either an eagle or a black raven. And when he looked towards the Solund Islands, there, looming over the islands, was the figure of a huge ogress. She had a knife in one hand and a slaughtering trough in the other, and she was chanting these lines:

> 'Norway's warrior sea king
> Has been enticed westward
> To fill England's graveyards
> It's all to my advantage
> Birds of carrion follow
> To feast on valiant seamen
> They know there will be plenty,
> And I'll be there to help them.'

I felt sick to my stomach. I remembered the words of the message that I had sent to Harald. I had referred to him as 'the feeder of eagle of sea of carrion vulture'. I had meant that Harald was the sea eagle, the image that I had held of him from the day I had first set eyes on him in Constantinople. Now I realised that the words in my letter could be interpreted to mean that he was the one who would deliver the carrion flesh of his own men to the ravens and eagles. If so, I was the one who had enticed him and his men to his doom with my letter from Normandy.

'You said there were other portents?' I asked shakily.

'Several,' the seaman replied, 'but I can remember the details of only one. Another of the king's men dreamed it. He saw our fleet sailing towards land. In the lead was King Harald's longship flying its banner, and he knew that the land they were approaching was England. On the shoreline waited a great host of warriors, and in front of them was an ogress – perhaps it was the same one, I don't know. This time she was riding a gigantic wolf, and the wolf held a bleeding human carcass in its jaws as easily as a terrier grips a rat. When Harald and his men came ashore, both sides joined battle, and the Norwegian warriors fell in swathes. The ogress collected up their corpses and hurled them, one by one, into the mouth of the great wolf until its jaws ran with blood as the beast gulped down its feast of victims.'

Now I knew for certain that my own power of second sight, dormant for so many years, had returned. When I had composed my report in Normandy, I had referred to Harald as a sea eagle and hidden Duke William's identity under the guise of the wolf which the ogress Yggr rides. In doing so, I had touched unwittingly upon the future: every death among Harald's men would be sustenance for the wolf, the name I had chosen for Duke William. Failing to recognise my own augury, I now quailed at the prospect that my premonition would prove correct. Should William emerge victorious, I would have helped put on the throne, not a possible champion of the Old Ways, but a voracious follower of the White Christ.

Even the weather conspired to depress me. The wind stayed as a gentle breeze from the south-west, so our ship ran speedily up the narrow sea between England and Frankia. I knew the same wind was ideal for William to launch his invasion, yet when we passed the port of St Valery and our skipper took the risk of sailing closer inshore to look into the roadstead, we saw the great assembly of William's ships still riding quietly at anchor or securely hauled up on the beach. Clearly, the Duke of Normandy had no intention of making the crossing until he heard that Harold Godwinsson had turned his attention to countering the threat from Norway.

Thanks to that favourable wind we made a near-record passage, and my hopes of averting disaster rose when we encountered one of King Harald's warships. It was patrolling off the river mouth into which Harald had led his fleet less than three days before. There were a few shouted exchanges between the two vessels, and Skule and I transferred hastily to the warship. Her captain, understanding the urgency of our mission, agreed to navigate the estuary at night and row up against the current. So it was that, a little after daybreak on the twenty-fifth of September, I came in sight of the muddy river foreshore where Norway's massive invasion fleet lay anchored. To my relief, I saw that the fleet was intact. The river bank swarmed with men. Harald's army, it seemed, was safe.

'Where do I find the king?' I demanded of the first soldier we met on landing. He was taken aback by the urgency in my tone, and looked at me in astonishment. I must have made a strange sight – an elderly bald priest, the hem of my white undergown spattered with river mud, and my sandals sinking in the ooze. 'The king!' I repeated. 'Where is he?'

The soldier pointed up the slope. 'Best ask one of his councillors,' he answered. 'You'll find them over there.'

I slipped and slithered up the muddy bank, and hurried in the direction he indicated. Behind me I could hear Skule say, 'Slow down, Thorgils, slow down. The king may be busy.' I ignored him, though I was short of breath and painfully aware that my advancing years had taken their toll. I may have made a dreadful error in supplying false information to Harald, but I still desperately wanted to undo the harm I had done.

I saw a tent, larger and grander than the others, and hastened towards it. Standing outside was a group talking among themselves, and I recognised several of Harald's councillors. They were in attendance on a young man, Harald's son Olaf. Rudely I interrupted.

'The king,' I said, 'I need to speak with him.'

Again the anxiety in my tone took my audience aback, until one of the councillors looked a little more closely.

'Thorgils Leifsson, isn't it? I didn't recognise you at first. I'm sorry.'

I brushed aside his apology. It seemed to me that everyone was being fatally obtuse. My voice was quivering with emotion as I repeated my demand. I had to speak with the king. It was a matter of the greatest urgency.

'Oh, the king,' said the councillor, whom I now remembered as one of Harald's sworn men from the Upplands. 'You won't find him here. He left at first light.'

I clenched my teeth in frustration. 'Where did he go?' I asked, trying unsuccessfully to keep my voice calm.

'Inland,' said the Norwegian casually, 'to the meeting place, to accept hostages and tribute from the English. Took nearly half the army with him. It's going to be a scorching day.' He turned back to his conversation.

I seized him by the arm. 'The meeting place, where's that?' I begged. 'I need to speak with him, or at least with Marshal Ulf.'

That brought a different reaction. The Norwegian shook his head.

'Ulf Ospaksson. Don't you know? He died in late spring. Great loss. At his burial ceremony the king described him as the most loyal and valiant soldier he had ever known. Styrkar is the marshal now.'

Another chill swept over me. Ulf Ospaksson had been Harald's marshal ever since Harald had come to the throne. Ulf was the most level-headed of the military advisers. It was Ulf who had opposed the idea of the invasion of England, and now that he was gone, there was no one to rein in Harald's reckless ambition to be another Knut.

The blood was pounding in my ears.

'Steady, Thorgils. Easy now.' It was Skule behind me.

'I must speak with Harald,' I repeated. It seemed to me that I was wading through a swamp of indifference. 'He has to reshape his campaign.'

'Why are you so agitated, Thorgils?' said one of the other councillors soothingly. 'You've only just got here and already you're wanting to change the king's mind. Everything has been working out just as planned. These English troops aren't as fearsome as their reputation. We gave them a thrashing just five days ago. We advanced on York as soon as we had got off our ships. The garrison came out to fight, led by a couple of their local earls. They blocked our road, and it was a fair fight, though perhaps we had a slight advantage in numbers. Harald led us brilliantly. Just as he always does. They came at us first. Hit us hard with a bold charge against our right wing. For a while it looked as if they might even overwhelm our men, but then Harald led the counter-attack and took them in the flank. Rolled up their line in double-quick time, and the next thing they knew we had them penned up against marshy ground, and nowhere to go. That was when we punished them. We killed so many that we walked on corpses as though the quagmire was solid ground. The city surrendered, of course, and now Harald's gone off to collect the tribute and stores the city fathers promised, as well as hostages for good behaviour in the future. He won't be long. You might as well stay here until he returns to camp. Or maybe you would prefer to give your information to Prince Olaf, who will tell his father when he gets back.'

'No,' I said firmly, 'my message is for Harald himself, and it cannot wait. Can someone arrange for me to have a horse so that I can try to overtake the army?'

The councillor shrugged. 'We didn't bring many horses with us on the fleet – we needed the ship space for men and weapons. But we've captured a few animals locally, and if you look around the camp, maybe you'll find one that suits. Harald can't have gone far.'

I lost more time trying to locate a horse, and succeeded only in finding a starveling pack pony. But the scrawny little creature was better than nothing, and before the troops had finished their breakfast I was riding away from the ships and along the trail that Harald and his army had taken as they marched north.

'Tell him we need some good juicy cattle,' a soldier yelled after me as I left the outskirts of the camp. 'Something to get our

teeth into instead of stale bread and mouldy cheese. And as much
beer as he can bring back. This weather makes a man thirsty.'

The soldier was right. The air had a dry, still feel. The sky
was cloudless, and soon the heat would be intense. Already the
ground was cracked in many places, baked hard by the sun, and I
could feel my pony's unshod hooves hammering down on the
unyielding surface.

It was easy to follow the army's trail. The dust was churned
up where the foot soldiers had tramped along, and occasionally
there were piles of dung left by the horses that Harald and his
leading men were riding. Their road followed the line of a small
river, the track keeping to the higher ground on its left bank, and
on both sides the low hills were desiccated and brown from the
summer drought. From time to time I could see the footmarks
where men had left the track and gone down to the water's edge
to slake their thirst. I saw nothing of the soldiery themselves,
except at one place where I came across a small detachment of
men guarding a pile of weapons and armour. At first I thought it
was captured material left behind by the enemy, but then I
recognised that the weaponry and shields and the thick leather
jerkins sewn with plates of metal belonged to our own men. They
must have taken them off and left them there, under guard, as it
was too hot to march in such heavy gear.

The soldiers told me that Harald and his army were not far
ahead, and sure enough I saw them in the distance when I topped
the next rise and found myself looking across a bend on the river.
The army was waiting on the far bank. Side tracks converged on
the main road shortly before it crossed a wooden bridge, and from
there the main road continued on up the far slope and over the
crest of the hill, leading directly to the city of York. It was a
natural crossroads and I could see why the place had been chosen
for the assembly point where the men of York would bring their
tribute.

I kicked my pony into one last effort, and came down into the

valley. A handful of Harald's troops had not yet crossed the
bridge, and my haste attracted their curious glances as I scurried
past. Most of the men were sprawling on the ground in the
sunshine. Many had stripped off their shirts and were bare-chested.
Swords, helmets and shields lay where they had casually put them
aside. A score of men were standing in the shallows of the river,
splashing water on themselves to keep cool.

I clattered across the worn grey planks of the bridge. For a
moment I thought of dismounting. The bridge was in poor repair,
and there were wide cracks between the planks, but the little pony
was sure-footed, and a moment later I was riding up the slope of
the far bank towards a knot of men gathered around the royal
standard. Even if the flag, Land Ravager, had not been flying
from its pole, I would have recognised the little group as Harald's
entourage. Harald himself was visible, towering above most men.
His long yellow hair and drooping moustaches were unmistakable.

I slid off the pony's back, stumbling as my feet touched
ground. It had taken me half the morning to reach Harald, and I
felt stiff and saddle sore. I brushed aside the bodyguard who tried
to intercept me as I approached Harald and his little group. They
too looked completely at ease. Doubtless they were contemplating
the pleasant task of how best to divide up the spoils. Among them
I saw Tostig, half-brother of the English king. Until recently he
had ruled these lands as its earl, but had been deposed. Now he
had thrown in his lot with Harald, anticipating that he would
regain his former title.

'My lord,' I called out as I approached the little group. 'I am
glad to see you well. I have news from Frankia.'

Everyone in the little group turned to look at me. I realised
that my voice had sounded cracked and harsh. My throat was dry
and dusty from my ride.

'Thorgils. What brings you here?' asked Harald. There was
an angry edge to his question. He was staring down at me from
his great height, obviously irritated. I knew that he was thinking

I had abandoned my responsibilities. He would have preferred me to stay in Normandy, to act as his intermediary in dealing with Duke William.

'I had no choice, my lord. There are developments which you must know at once. I could not trust anyone else to bring the news.'

'What news is that?' Harald was scowling.

I decided that I had to be blunt. I needed to shock Harald into changing his plans, even if it meant drawing down his wrath on me.

'Duke William has betrayed you, my lord,' I said, adding hastily, 'It was my error. He used me as a tool to deceive you. He made me believe that he had agreed to your offer, and that he would time his invasion to coincide with yours. But that was never his intention. His fleet has not yet sailed. He is deliberately hanging back, giving time for the English king to attack you.'

For a long moment Harald's expression did not change. He continued to scowl at me, and then – to my surprise – he threw back his head and laughed.

'So Bastard William deceived me, did he? Well, so be it. Now I know what he is like, and that knowledge will be useful when we meet face to face and decide who really takes the realm of England. I'll make him regret his treachery. But he has miscalculated. Whoever beats Harold Godwinsson will hold the advantage. There's nothing like a recent victory to put heart into one's troops, and the English will follow the first victor. As soon as I have disposed of Harold Godwinsson, I'll drive William of Normandy back into the sea if he is so bold as to make his invasion. When he hears of my victory he may even cancel his invasion plans altogether.'

Once more, I sensed that I was swimming against a tide of events, and there was little that I could do.

'Duke William will not set aside his invasion, my lord. He has planned it down to the last detail, trained his troops, rehearsed, and committed all his resources to it. He may have as many as eight thousand fighting men. For him, there is no going back.'

'Nor for me,' Harald snapped. 'I came to take the realm of England and that is what I'll do.'

I fell silent, not knowing what to say.

Tostig intervened. 'Harold is far away. He has to march the length of England if he is to meet us on the battlefield. In the meantime our army will grow stronger. As people hear about us they will join our cause. Many in this region have Norse blood in their veins and trace their line back to the time of great Knut. The English will prefer to throw in their lot with us than with a gang of plundering Normans.'

Somewhere near us, a horse neighed. It was one of the handful of small Norwegian horses which Harald had brought with him. They were sturdy animals, ideal for long journeys across bleak moorland, but by no means as powerful as the battle chargers that I had seen in Normandy. I was wondering how they would withstand a charge of Norman knights, when someone said, 'At last! The good burghers of York are finally showing up.'

Everyone in our little group looked westward, up the slope of the hill towards the unseen city. A faint cloud of dust could be seen beyond the distant crest. The horse neighed again.

The first figures to come over the brow of the hill were indistinct, no more than dark shapes. I wiped away the sweat that was trickling down into my eyes. The black and white costume of a follower of the Rule could be very hot on a warm day. I should find myself a light cotton shirt and loose trousers and get rid of the Christian costume.

'That's not a cattle herd,' commented Styrkar, Harald's new marshal. 'Looks more like troops.'

'Reinforcements from the fleet, sent up by Prince Olaf so as not to miss the division of the booty.' The speaker sounded a little resentful.

'Where did they get all those horses, I wonder?' asked a

veteran, a note of puzzlement in his voice as he stared into the distance. 'That's cavalry, and a lot of it.'

King Harald had turned and was facing up the hill. 'Styrkar,' he asked softly. 'Did we post any sentinels on the hill?'

'No, my lord. I did not consider it necessary. Our scouts reported only a few peasants in the area.'

'Those are not peasants.'

Tostig was also watching the new arrivals. More and more men, both mounted and on foot, were coming over the brow of the hill. The leading ranks were beginning to descend the slope, fanning out to make room for those behind them.

'If I didn't know otherwise, I would say those are royal huscarls,' said Tostig. 'But that's impossible. Harold Godwinsson would always keep his huscarls with him. They are pledged to serve the king and guard his person.' He turned to me. 'When did you say Harold would know that the Norman fleet was delayed and was staying on in Frankia?'

'I didn't say,' I replied, 'but my guess is that Duke William deliberately planted that information on Harold soon after he left Dives. That would be about twelve days ago.'

Styrkar was making his calculation. 'Let's say it was ten days ago, and then allow Godwinsson two days in which to consult his councillors and make his plans. That would give him a little more than a week to march north and get here. It's difficult but not impossible. Those troops could be led by Harold Godwinsson himself.'

'If it is Harold,' said Tostig, 'it might be wise to fall back to our ships and gather the rest of our forces.'

But Harald seemed unperturbed. 'Well, if it does prove to be Harold, then he's got here by forced marches, and his troops will be footsore and weary. That makes them ripe for slaughter.'

He gave a snort of confidence, and I could see how his faith in his own success as a military commander was unshakeable. In the past decade he had never lost a major fight, and now he was certain that his battle luck would hold. Godwinsson, as far as Harald was concerned, was offering himself for defeat. With growing dread, I knew differently. I recalled the details of my nightmare on the night before Harald returned from Kiev on his splendid ship with silken sails. I had dreamed of a great fleet and its tall commander struck down by an arrow at the moment of victory, and when I had voiced my fears, I had been told that I had seen the death of the Greek general Maniakes, Harald's near double. Now, far too late, the image sprang into my mind of the great assembly of Harald's longships drawn up on shore or lying at anchor in the shallows of the river just ten miles away. That spectacle, I knew with absolute certainty, was the true fulfilment of my dream. Yet again I had failed. Years ago I should have warned Harald about the macabre portent.

'If it is Harold Godwinsson, then we had better get the formalities concluded,' Harald continued. He looked about him, caught my eye, and said, 'Thorgils. You're just the man. You can be my herald in your black and white gown.' He smiled grimly. 'They won't attack a man of the cloth, even if he's a fraud. Ride out and ask for a parlay.'

Knowing that I was being swept along by events over which I had no control, I walked back to where my pack pony was hopefully nuzzling the earth, trying to find a few wisps of dried-up grass. I felt that I was no more than a puppet in some vast and cruel game being played out by unseen powers. My legs ached as I hauled myself back on to the wooden saddle and plucked on the rope reins. Reluctantly, the pony lifted its head and began to walk. Its legs, too, were stiff and painful. Slowly, almost apologet-ically, the little pony and I climbed up the slope. Ahead of us, more and more English foot soldiers and cavalry were appearing over the ridge and taking up their positions across the hillside. The Norwegians below me were no longer relaxing in the sunshine. They had scrambled to their feet and were searching for the weapons and shields they had laid aside. There was no sense of order or discipline. They looked towards Harald and his councillors, waiting for instructions, and they watched me on my pony slowly plod towards the hostile army.

I noted a cluster of banners among the English cavalry, and veered in that direction. As I rode along the front rank of the English line, the foot soldiers called out, asking what I wanted. I ignored them. Around the banners was a group of some twenty men. All were mounted. I made a mental note to tell Harald that many of the English troops now massing behind their leaders were also on horseback. That would explain how Harold Godwinsson had managed to travel so quickly and take us by surprise. At least a third of his force were cavalry, and I guessed that the remainder were levies that he had collected locally.

The gleam of a sword hilt caught my attention, a dull yellow glint among the riders. I looked again, and knew that the ranks of horsemen nearest the banners were royal huscarls, Godwinsson's personal force, the finest troops in England. Since Knut's time they had carried gold-hilted swords. Many of them also carried spears, while others had long-handled axes dangling from their saddles. I wondered whether they would choose to fight on horseback or on foot.

'King Harald of Norway wishes to talk with your leader,' I called out when I was close enough to the group around the banners for them to hear me distinctly. They were English nobles, all wearing costly chain-mail shirts and helmets decorated with badges of rank. Their horses were tall, strong-boned animals, not nearly as massive as the Norman destriers, but far superior to the smaller Norwegian horses in Harald's army.

I reined in my little pack pony and waited at a safe distance. I saw the group confer among themselves, and then half a dozen came forward at a trot. Among them a tall, heavily moustached man rode a particularly handsome chestnut stallion. There was something about his bearing, the way that he sat in the saddle, that told me at once that this was Harold Godwinsson himself, the king of England, though he was careful to remain among his companions as if he was just another rider.

'Tell King Harald that there is nothing of substance to discuss. But the King of England, grants him an audience. He may speak with the king's herald,' came a shout.

I was fairly sure that it was Godwinsson who had spoken. It was an old trick for a leader to pretend to be his own spokesman. Harald had often used it himself.

I turned and waved to Harald and his entourage, beckoning them forward.

The two groups, evenly matched in numbers, met midway between the two armies. They halted their horses, careful not to get within a sword's length of one another, and I thought to myself, as I watched them, how very similar they were. All were bearded and moustached, with hair that was mostly blond or light brown, and all of them seemed to be both haughty and suspicious as they eyed one another across the narrow gap. The main difference was in the shields they carried. Those of Harald's men who had wisely brought their armour carried round shields, brightly painted with war emblems, while several of the English riders held longer, narrow shields with a tapering lower edge. I had seen these same shields among Duke William's men and knew that on horseback they gave an advantage, for they protected a rider's lower leg as well as the vulnerable flank of his horse. It was another warning, I thought to myself, that I should give to Harald.

The exchange between the two groups was brief. The rider who purported to be the royal spokesman – more than ever I was sure that it was the English king himself – demanded to know with what purpose the Norwegian army was trespassing on England's soil. Styrkar, the royal marshal, replied for the Norwegians. 'King Harald has come to claim the throne of England which is his by right. His ally and companion, Tostig here, has come to claim what is also his by right – the earldom of Northumbria, of which he was unjustly deprived.'

'Tostig and his men may remain, provided they stay in peace,' came the answer. 'The King of England gives his word that he will be reinstated in his earldom. He will, in addition, grant Tostig one-third of the realm.'

Now I was sure that Godwinsson himself was speaking, for the speaker had made no attempt to confer with his colleagues. It also occurred to me that the parlay was no more than play-acting. Tostig must have recognised his half-brother, the English king, yet he was pretending that he did not know him. The entire meeting was a sham.

Tostig spoke up. 'And if I accept that offer, what lands will you give to Harald Sigurdsson, the King of Norway?'

Hard as a blow of a fist to the teeth came back the unrelenting reply, 'He will receive seven feet of English ground. Enough to bury him. Or more, as he is much taller than other men.'

The two groups of riders stiffened in their saddles. Their horses, sensing the sudden surge in tension, began to fidget. One of the English riders slapped his reins on his animal's neck to make the creature calm down.

To his credit, Tostig soothed the situation before it broke into open violence. 'Tell the King of England,' he called out, still keeping up the pretence that he did not recognise his own half-brother, 'that it will never be said that Tostig, the true Earl of Northumbria, brought King Harald of Norway across the sea in order to betray him.' Then he turned his horse and began to ride away down the hill. The parlay was over.

Kicking my pony into a trot, I hurried to rejoin Harald's group. I rode up behind Harald in time to hear him ask Tostig, 'Who was that who spoke for the English? He had a deft way with words.'

'That was Godwinsson,' Tostig replied. Harald was obviously taken aback by the answer. He had not intended to compliment his rival.

'Not a bad-looking man,' he acknowledged, then drew himself

to his full height so he sat very tall in the saddle, and added, 'but a little puny.'

On the threshold of a battle, Harald's vanity was dangerous, I thought to myself. Combined with his self-belief, it could lead us into disaster. It was unlikely that he would compromise his pride by ordering a strategic withdrawal to the fleet. In his eyes, that would seem too much like an abject retreat.

We came back down the hill to rejoin the Norwegian troops with Styrkar shouting to our men that they were to fall back across the bridge and take up a defensive position on the far slope. At least our marshal was not blind to our danger. If we remained where we were, the English would be attacking us downhill. Nevertheless, our withdrawal was a scrambled affair, the men gathering up their weapons and converging on the little bridge with no sense of order or discipline. They jostled their way across the loose planks of the bridge in an untidy torrent, and made their way up the far slope where they began to regroup.

Seeing the backs of their enemies, the English forces took their chance to try to turn the Norwegian withdrawal into a rout. A detachment of their cavalry came cantering down the hill and closed with our stragglers. It was not a concerted attack so much as a haphazard onslaught to take advantage of the moment. I had already crossed the bridge with Harald and his entourage, and looked back to see a chaotic engagement unfold. Isolated bands of Norwegian warriors or single individuals were ducking and dodging as they tried to evade the lances and swords of the English horsemen. There were occasional shouts of defiance and whoops of anger as our men turned and tried to fight back against their mounted opponents. I could see that the English forces were relishing the advantage of surprise. They knew that they had taken the Norwegians completely unawares, and this gave them a powerful advantage.

As I watched the confused fighting, my attention was caught by an extraordinary sight. Slowly making its way through the skirmish, as if nothing out of the ordinary was happening, was an ordinary farm cart. It was the sort of vehicle which might be found in any modest farmyard, a simple wooden platform on two solid wheels drawn by a single horse. On the back of the cart were several sacks of grain, some barrels, and, bizarrely, several chickens trussed up and hanging head down in batches. I could only suppose that the carter was one of those engaged to bring supplies to the Norwegian army as part of the tribute from the citizens of York, and he had blundered into the fight inadvertently. Now he was petrified by the danger in which he found himself and too scared to react, while his horse between the shafts was an ancient nag, half blind and deaf. Even as I watched, the cart reached the approaches to the bridge, and the elderly horse stopped in puzzlement, gazing at the press of struggling men which blocked its path.

The last of the Norwegians' rearguard – those who had not been cut down by the English – had reached the bridge. They were more disciplined than their fellows, and had formed up in a squad which turned to face the enemy; now the men were retreating step by step. As they passed the stationary cart, one of the Norwegian fighters reached up and pulled the driver from his seat, sending the poor wretch flying. Moments later, the cart horse disappeared, as the bewildered animal, its harness cut, galloped away. A dozen hands grabbed the cart and wheeled it to the middle of the bridge, where it was overturned to act as a barricade to delay the English advance. Moments later the Norwegian rearguard was running up the slope to rejoin the rest of Harald's troops.

The overturned cart did not block the bridge completely: there was a gap between the cart and the bridge's edge barely an arm's span in width, but sufficient to allow a man to pass. In this opening a single Norwegian warrior now took up his stance, facing the enemy. He had a fighting axe in one hand, a heavy sword in the other. Who he was I would never know, but he must have know that his position was suicidal. He was making it clear that, single-handed, he would hold the gap until his own side had taken up their battle formation. He challenged the English to come forward and fight him. For a bleak moment I wondered if that lone warrior was not like myself, a forlorn dreamer defying the inevitable.

Still, the English hesitated. Then one of their cavalrymen rode out on to the bridge, his spear poised. But the moment the horse stepped on the loose planks, the animal shied and would go no farther. With an angry wrench of his reins, the cavalryman turned his horse and rode back to solid ground. A second rider attempted the bridge, but his mount also baulked. So it was an English foot soldier who advanced to accept the Norwegian's challenge. Judging by his long coat of mail, the Englishman was one of Harold's professional soldiers, a royal huscarl, and he advanced with a confident step, sword in hand, scorning even to lift his shield. It was his fatal error. He was not yet within reach of the Norwegian when, without warning, his opponent flung his axe. The weapon whirled across the gap and struck the huscarl in the mouth, felling him instantly. With a satisfied whoop the Norwegian ran forward, bent down to retrieve his weapon and, moments later, was running back to take up his position once again. There he clashed his sword and axe together defiantly, daring the next to come forward and fight him.

Three more times an English huscarl accepted the challenge, and each time failed to clear the passage. The Norwegian champion was a master of hand-to-hand fighting. He killed one challenger with a sword thrust through the body, decapitated the second with a swiping back-handed axe blow that seemed to come from nowhere, and deftly tripped up the third attacker who had come close enough to grapple with him, then pushed him over the edge of the bridge into the river below. Each encounter was met with groans or cheers by the two armies watching the spectacle from each side of the river, and for a time it seemed that the Norwegian champion was invincible.

'He can't hold out for ever,' someone beside me muttered.

'Eventually the English will bring up their archers and shoot him down.'

'No,' countered another voice. 'The huscarls want to claim the victory for themselves. They won't let some common bowman take the credit. Look there, upstream.'

I glanced to my right. Drifting down the river on the gentle current was a small boat. Little bigger than a washtub, it was a humble punt that some farmer would use to paddle his way across the river rather than make a detour to reach the bridge. In the boat sat an armoured English huscarl, his weight almost swamping the little craft, and he was paddling with his hands to keep the boat in mid-river where it would pass directly under the Norwegian's position.

'Look out, beware to your right,' someone shouted, trying to warn the Norwegian. But our champion was too far away to hear, and the cluster of huscarls on the far end of the bridge had already begun to set up a deafening chant, beating rhythmically on their shields to drown out the sound of any warnings. As the little boat neared the bridge, two huscarls stepped out from their ranks and began to advance deliberately towards the barricade. This time they took no chances. Both carried long shields, and they crouched down behind them to protect themselves from another axe throw. The Norwegian had no choice but to wait until they were within sword range, and then he struck, hacking down with his axe and sword hoping to beat down their guard. But the two huscarls stayed behind their shields, knees bent and deflecting the blows, only occasionally making a stabbing thrust with their own swords in counter-threat.

Helplessly we watched from our vantage point, knowing what would happen. The Norwegian's stamina was extraordinary. He continued to rain down blows on the two huscarls until the moment came when his opponents judged that the man in the boat was directly under the bridge. Then they rose up and hurled themselves forward. The Norwegian retreated back a pace so that he stood in the narrowest part of the gap between the cart and the edge of the bridge, and there he traded blows with his attackers. But it was exactly where they wanted him. Even as the Norwegian concentrated on fending off the huscarls' frontal attack, we saw the boatman grab one of the timbers supporting the underside of the ancient bridge and bring his little craft to a stop. Then he stood up, and, still holding on to the bridge with one hand he brought his spear up vertically and slid it through a gap between the planks. There he waited, the spear pointing upwards, while his comrades gradually pushed the Norwegian champion back to the precise spot. Then, suddenly, the boatman thrust upwards with his spear, the iron point driving straight into the Norwegian's crutch, unprotected by his long shirt of chain mail. The surprise attack spitted the Norwegian. He doubled forward, clutching at his groin, and one of his opponents took the chance to step forward and chop down with his sword at the gap below the helmet, killing his foe with a blow to the back of the neck. The fight was over, and even as the Norwegian body splashed down into the river, a squad of huscarls was running forward to lay hold of the upturned cart, drag it to the edge of the bridge, and heave it over.

Moments later the advance guard of Harold's army began to clatter across the open bridge and advance towards us, led by a file of mounted huscarls. Watching their confident approach, I recalled Ulf Ospaksson's words when he had tried to dissuade Harald from invading England. Then he had said that one English huscarl was reputed to be worth two of the best of Norway's fighting men. Now we would learn the truth of the dead marshal's warning.

FIFTEEN

'FALL BACK, MY LORD, fall back.' Strykar was still pleading with Harald. 'Let us make a fighting retreat. It is best we make our stand near the ships when the rest of our men have joined us.'

'No!' retorted Harald sharply. 'We make our stand here. Let the rest of our forces come to join us. Send riders to summon them. They must come at once or they will miss our victory.'

The look on Styrkar's face made it clear that he disagreed profoundly with Harald's decision, but he was in no position to argue with his king. The marshal beckoned to three of our few horsemen.

'Ride to the ships. Spread out so that at least one of you gets through,' he ordered. 'Ask Prince Olaf to send up the rest of the army and not lose a moment, or they may arrive too late. They must get here before dusk.'

The marshal glanced up at the sky. The sun was past its zenith, still blazing from a clear blue sky. I saw the marshal's lips move, and I wondered to which God he was praying. He lacked Harald's utter conviction that our ill-prepared army would survive the English attack, and when I had watched the three riders kick their mounts into a gallop and ride back along the trail we had taken, I took a moment to count how many horsemen still remained. There were fewer than fifty.

Harald, by contrast, was behaving with as much swagger and self-assurance as if he, not the king of England, held the advantage. He cut a regal figure in a cloak of richly ornamented blue brocade and his customary browband of scarlet silk to hold back his shaggy blond hair. To complete the dashing effect he was mounted on a glossy black stallion with a white blaze, a trophy from his victory three days earlier and the only blood horse in our company. But he was not dressed in Emma, his famous full-length shirt of chain mail said to be impenetrable by any weapon. Emma, like so much of our body armour, had been left behind with the fleet.

'Form shield wall!' bellowed Strykar, and the cry was taken up and passed along by the veterans in our army. Our men began to shuffle into position, shoulder to shoulder, the rims of their round, leather-covered shields overlapping. 'Extend the line!'

The marshal rode out a little way in front of our troops and turned to face the men. He was mounted on a tough little Norwegian pony, and was gesturing to indicate that the shield wall should be as wide as possible.

Suddenly Harald shouted, 'Wait!' He rode forward and, turning to face his men, he called out, 'In honour of this battle, I have composed a poem.' Then, to my mingled astonishment and pride, he proceeded to declaim:

> 'We go forward
> into battle
> without armour
> against blue blades.
> Helmets glitter.
> My coat of mail
> And all our armour
> Are at the ships.'

I found a lump was gathering in my throat. Not for a generation had any war leader in the northern lands been sufficiently skilled in the old traditions to be able to compose a paean

on the eve of a battle. Harald was honouring a custom that had
almost passed from use. It was a mark of his deep-felt longing to
restore the glory of the Norse kingdoms, and for all his vanity
and arrogance I loved him for it. Yet even as I felt the tug of
admiration and remembered the oath which I had sworn to serve
him, I knew in my heart that it was all a show. Harald was
seeking to encourage his men, but the harsh truth would reveal
itself when the arrows began to fly and the two armies locked in
battle.

Harald was not finished. His horse was giving trouble, fidgeting and turning from side to side, so that there was a short pause
while Harald brought his mount back under control. Then he
shouted at his troops, 'That was a poor verse for such a momentous occasion! This one is better. Remember it as you fight!' and
he proceeded to declaim:

> 'We never kneel in battle
> Before the storm of weapons
> and crouch behind our shields;
> So the noble lady told me.
> She told me once to carry
> my head always high in battle
> where swords seek to shatter
> the skulls of doomed warriors.'

When his words died away, a strange silence fell. Some of our
men in the army, the older ones at least, had grasped the sombre
import of Harald's words. From them came a low murmur.
Others, I am sure, were not close enough to hear the king, while
still more would have lacked the knowledge to understand the
significance of his verse. Harald was warning us that we could be
facing our final battle. For a moment there was a brooding lull,
and from it emerged an eerie sound. A harp was being played
somewhere in our ranks. Whoever had brought the instrument
was a mystery. Probably it was one of those small light harps
favoured by the northern English, and the harpist had picked it

up on the earlier battlefield and brought it with him instead of his weapons. Whatever the reason, the first few clear notes hung in the air as a doleful lament. It was as if the harpist was playing a sorrowful tribute to our coming downfall.

As I and the army listened to the melancholy tune, it seemed as if the entire host was holding its collective breath. Not a sound came from the English lines. They too must have been listening. Then, cutting across the tune, came another sound, equally unexpected. In that hot, airless afternoon a single rooster crowed. The creature must have escaped from the toppled cart at the bridge, and now, for some unknown reason, it chose to let loose its raucous call, jarring across the plangent notes of the harp.

Once again Styrkar was bellowing at the top of his voice. 'Extend the line, extend the line. Wings fall back, form circle.' Slowly the flanks of our shield wall curved, the outer men stepping backward, glancing over their shoulders so that they did not trip, until our entire line had re-formed into a ring. In the first and second ranks stood those men who wore some of their armour, and all of our veterans. Behind them, within the circle, waited our archers and hundreds of our troops who were virtually defence-less. They wore no body armour, and some even lacked helmets. They clutched only their swords and daggers, and wore shirts and leggings, nothing more. When it came to a fight, they would be fatally vulnerable.

Harald and Strykar rode the perimeter, checking the shield wall. 'You are facing cavalry,' Styrkar called out. 'So remember, front rank direct the points of your spears at the riders. Second rank, plant the butts of your spears in the ground and hold them steady, aim lower, at the horses themselves. Above all, keep the line intact. Do not let the English break through. Should that happen, leave the king himself and our own horsemen to deal with the intruders. We will be waiting inside the ring behind you, ready to ride to any point where there is need.'

Harald and the marshal made the full circuit of our shield wall, and as they turned and began to ride in, preparing to take up their places, Harald's black stallion put its foot into a hole and stumbled. Harald lost his balance. He clutched at the animal's mane to steady himself, but too late. He lurched forward over the stallion's shoulder and tumbled to the ground while the startled horse danced away. Harald kept hold of the reins and pulled the stallion back to him, but the harm was done. The watching troops let out a groan, seeing the poor omen. But Harald laughed it off as he rose and dusted himself off. 'No matter,' he shouted, 'a fall means that fortune is on its way,' and rode into the shield ring. But many of his troops looked uneasy and afraid.

On my humble pack pony I found myself with the mounted force in the centre of our defensive circle. I glanced around nervously, looking for someone to lend me a weapon to carry. But everyone was preoccupied, watching the enemy. Harald, Tostig, Styrkar and two squadrons of perhaps twenty riders each were all we had to plug any breaches in the shield wall; all the rest of our army was on foot. By contrast the entire first wave of the English army now advancing against us was composed of mounted cavalry – huscarls armed with long spears and lances.

Perhaps the wild courage of the lone defender of the bridge had made the English cautious. Our battlefield was on an expanse of rough pasture sloping gently towards the river, open ground ideal for cavalry, yet the English horsemen appeared hesitant in their initial attack. Their riders came at us, cantering to within range, then thrusting tentatively with their spears at our shield wall before turning away and riding clear. There was no massed shock charge like that I had witnessed in Sicily when the Byzantine kataphract destroyed the Saracens, nor the crashing onslaught I had seen the Norman heavy horsemen rehearse. The English cavalry simply came, engaged, and then withdrew.

For a while I was puzzled. Why did the English not launch a mass attack? Harold Godwinsson must have seen that we had despatched riders to call up reinforcements from the fleet. As soon as the fresh troops arrived, the English would lose their advantage. The more I puzzled, the less I understood Godwinsson's tactics.

Only when the English cavalry had made their fifth or perhaps the sixth probing attack, did I begin to grasp what was happening. The English huscarls intended to wear us down. Each time they rode up and engaged our front ranks in combat, several score of our men were killed or badly wounded, while the English horsemen rode away virtually unscathed. Our shield wall was slowly weakening as more of our reserves had to step forward and fill the gaps. By forming a defensive ring, Harald and Styrkar had lost the initiative. The English controlled the battlefield. They were bleeding us to death.

As that long, cruel afternoon wore on, our circle slowly contracted and the men within it grew more hot and thirsty under the broiling sun. The English, by contrast, took water from the river to quench their thirst and launched their attacks whenever they wished. Soon they were riding right around the shield wall, almost casually, selecting the weakest points. Our army was like a wild ox in the forest surrounded by a pack of wolves. We could only stand and face our foes, and present our best defence.

'Can't put up with much more of this,' said a veteran Norwegian. He had been in the front rank and had fallen back after receiving a lance thrust in his shield arm. 'Just give m_ chance to get close enough to those English horsemen, a_ make sure that they leave their bones here.' He finished _ makeshift bandage around his bleeding arm, and befor_ away to take his place once again in the shield wall, _ at me. 'You haven't got a flagon of water to han_ man? Some of the lads with me are truly parche_

I shook my head. I was feeling tired and _ fight and burdened with the knowledge _ contributed to our predicament. Soon afterw_ war cry, and once again the mounted hu_ down towards us. This time, I noted, fa_ through the air to greet them. Our archers_ arrows.

Suddenly Harald was in front of me. _

half-crazed about his appearance. He was sweating heavily, the
perspiration running down his face, dark stains of sweat at his
armpits. His black stallion was equally distraught: foam dripped
from its mouth, and there was white sweat on its powerful neck
where the reins touched.

'Styrkar!' Harald snapped, 'we must do something. We have
to counter-attack!'

'No, my lord, no,' said the marshal. 'It is better we hold on,
wait for the reinforcements to arrive. Only a few hours more.'

'By then we'll all be dead of thirst if not from the English
spears,' said Harald, glancing towards the English huscarls. 'Just
one good charge will smash the enemy.'

As he was speaking, his horse put down its head and tried to
buck his rider off. In his frustration Harald snarled with anger
and rapped the stallion between the ears with the flat of his sword.
The horse only became more skittish, rearing and plunging, as
Harald, who had already fallen from the saddle once that day,
tried to control his mount. The members of his entourage
scattered out of the way to avoid the highly strung animal. Only
my small pack pony, still exhausted from our long ride, stood
firm. Harald's stallion careered into us, and I was almost knocked
from the saddle.

'Get out of my way,' Harald snarled at me. He was puce from
anger.

Looking up into his face as I scrambled to my feet, I saw the
wild gleam in his eyes. Harald was losing control of himself, just
as he had lost control of the battlefield.

Just then there arose a great cry from our troops, a swelling
of exultation. They were brandishing swords and axes above
heads as if in victory. Beyond them I could see the backs of
retreating English cavalry. Once again the huscarls' charge
on the shield wall had been rebuffed, and they were pulling
together at that moment it was Harald's anger, or a genuine
understanding by our men, or that their pent-up frustration
boiled over, I shall never know, but the sight of the

English cavalry falling back was seen as a full retreat, and our shield wall erupted. Our soldiers, both veterans as well as raw recruits, broke ranks. They abandoned all discipline and spontaneously charged forward in a broken mass, chasing after the retreating English cavalry, shouting at them to turn and fight, then veering off to run at the English infantry where they stood waiting to engage in the battle. It was a disastrous error.

Even then, I think, Harald could have saved the day. He could have ridden forward, shown himself ahead of his troops, ordered them to re-form the shield wall, and they would have obeyed him. But just at that critical moment Harald's black stallion bolted. The panicked horse galloped straight ahead of the Norwegian charge, and it seemed to every man there that Harald himself was leading the assault. From that moment forward, the battle was lost.

I watched, aghast. I had seen William's Norman knights rehearse how to defeat the shield wall by pretending to flee, then turning on their disorganised pursuers as they were drawn out of position. But that had been practice, and what I now witnessed was real. The English cavalry stayed clear of the pursuing Norwegian infantry, and then swerved aside, leaving their own foot soldiers to take the brunt of the Norwegian onslaught. Harald's men had already been run off their legs when the Norsemen's charge burst on to the English levies, and the impact was irregular and ineffective. The two sides mingled in a seething mass of violence, the men hacking and stabbing and slashing at one another. There was no sense of purpose, only that both infantries were desperate to inflict the greatest damage on one another.

Harald himself stood out like a beacon in a sea of turmoil. Seated high on his horse, whose frantic run had been halted by the mass of men, he could be seen fighting like a berserk warrior from the ancient days. He had neither shield nor armour, but held a long-shafted, single-bladed axe in each hand, his favoured weapons since his days in the Varangian guard. He was roaring out in anger. Each of his axes would normally have required a two-handed grip, but Harald was such a giant that he could wield them one in each hand. All around him the English foot soldiers were attempting to dodge his furious sweeping blows and, too slow, were falling to his attack. I tried to calculate where Harald was heading, and whether there was some purpose to his frantic advance, but I could see no selected target for his wrath. The English cavalry had withdrawn to one side and were regrouping, waiting for the right moment to ride to the rescue of their infantry. Among them I thought I recognised Harold Godwinsson, but he was too far away for me to be certain. Harald himself was oblivious to the gathering danger. His own battle flag, Land Ravager, was nowhere to be seen. His standard-bearer had been left far behind in the mad forward gallop.

Like hundreds of his own men, I looked towards Harald himself, waiting for a signal telling us what to do. Without his guidance we were lost. And as I did so, I saw the arrow fly. Perhaps it was my imagination, but I was sure I saw a dark blur skim over the heads of the struggling infantry, drawn fatally towards the tall figure on the black stallion. It remains a moment frozen in time for me: I saw the scarlet headband on Harald's brow, the blue cloak flung back over one shoulder so that his arms were free, and the two deadly axes rising and falling remorselessly as he hacked his way through the press of soldiers. His personal bodyguards had fallen back, hindered by the throng of men, but even if they had been close to him they could have done nothing to save their master. The arrow struck Harald in the windpipe. Later I heard it said that Harald's war cry was cut short into a single, choking gasp that turned to a bubbling grunt. All I saw from a distance was Harald suddenly sway in the saddle, stay upright for several heartbeats, and then slowly topple backwards, his tall figure disappearing into the chaos of the battle.

At that appalling moment, as those Norwegians close to the dying king halted in dismay, Harold Godwinsson unleashed his mounted huscarls at us. He sent them against our northern flank, even as word was spreading across the battlefield that Harald

Sigurdsson was struck down. The news, which elated the hard-pressed English infantry, shocked our own embattled men. Not one of them had dared imagine that Harald the Hard Ruler would ever be killed in battle. He had seemed invulnerable. From a dozen major battles and countless skirmishes he had emerged alive and as the victor. Now, suddenly, he was gone, and there was no one to take his place. Our troops faltered.

The mounted English troops smashed into the demoralised Norwegian foot soldiers and shattered what little was left of their formation. The riders tore great gaps through the disorganised mob of our men, cutting them down as if they were huddled sheep. At first the huscarls used their spears as lances, but then they abandoned these weapons and drew their swords or unslung their axes because the slaughter was so easy. Our men were confused and defenceless. They attempted to parry the attacks with whatever was to hand – staves, clubs, their daggers – but it was futile against an armed huscarl mounted on his horse and swinging a heavy sword or the deadly long-shafted fighting axe. It was a massacre. The huscarls rode back and forth through our men like reapers clearing a field of standing corn, and those they left on their feet were set upon by the triumphant English infantry who rushed in to increase the carnage.

Weaponless, and still wearing my monk's gown, I sat on the little pony watching the disaster unfold. Despite all my forebod-ings, I was still unprepared for the extent of the catastrophe. This, I knew, was a defeat from which there could be no recovery. Never again would my people muster such a large army nor follow a leader with so much to offer us. This was annihilation, the final calamity, and I grieved to see Harald killed. But even as I mourned, I found consolation in knowing that the man to whom I had sworn allegiance would have preferred to die with honour on the battlefield than fade away, old and pain-racked, in his bed, knowing that he had failed in his great ambition to restore the greatest kingdom of the north. The disappointment would have embittered Harald for the rest of his days. I told myself that even in defeat, he had earned himself exactly what he would have wished: an honourable reputation that would never fade.

With that thought in mind I nudged my pony in the ribs and rode down the hill to retrieve Harald's body.

All my life I have known moments when a strange sensation of physical invulnerability comes over me. It is as if I am no longer aware of what my limbs are doing. My mind goes numb and I feel that I am advancing down a long, brightly lit tunnel where nothing can do me harm. That was how I felt as I rode forward on a tired pack pony that hot afternoon through the shattered fragments of a defeated army. I was vaguely aware of the crumpled corpses of our men lying on the ground, their blood and urine darkening the dust around them. Occasionally I heard the groans of the wounded. Here and there was a slight movement as some poor wretch tried to drag himself upright or to crawl away and hide. In the distance small bands of Norwegians were still putting up some resistance, but they were surrounded and outnumbered by their opponents, who were moving in to finish them. Somehow I was ignored.

I rode towards the last place I had seen Harald, the spot where he had toppled from his horse. A small cluster of men was gathered around something on the ground. They were bending over it, pulling and tugging. As I approached, my pony stumbled. Looking down I saw that it had tripped on a broken wooden pole, its end splintered. The flag attached to it was Land Ravager, Harald's personal standard. Nearby lay the body of his standard-bearer, a great gaping wound in his chest. He, like the others, had worn no armour. I reined the pony to a halt, got down and picked up the banner. Only a few feet of the pole remained. With Land Ravager in my hand I walked towards the group of men, leading the pack pony. Irrationally I thought that somehow I would be able to load Harald's corpse on the pony and ride back to the fleet, unscathed.

The men were English foot soldiers. They were stripping Harald's body of valuables. His fine blue cloak was already gone, and someone was tugging at the heavy gold rings on his fingers. Another man was pulling off a shoe of soft leather. Harald's body lay face up, a great dusty bruise across his cheek. The arrow that killed him was clearly visible. It had passed right through his neck. But that I had already dreamed.

'Stop that!' I croaked. 'Stop! I have come to collect the body.'

The looters looked up in surprise and irritation. 'Clear off, father,' said one of them. 'Go say your prayers in another place.' He unsheathed his dagger and was about to saw off one of Harald's fingers. Something clicked inside my mind and I passed from my distant reverie into sheer rage.

'You bastards!' I shouted. 'You defile the dead.' Letting go of the pony's reins, I raised the broken shaft of Land Ravager and struck at the looter. But I was too old and slow. Contemptuously he knocked aside the pole and I almost overbalanced.

'Clear off,' he repeated.

'No!' I yelled back at him. 'He is my lord. I must have his corpse.'

The looter looked at me narrowly. 'Your lord?' he said. I did not answer but took another lunge at him with the pole. Again, he knocked aside the blow. 'How come he is your lord, old man?'

I realised that I made a strange sight: an elderly priest in a long black gown, his bald pate showing stubble, and wielding a broken wooden pole. The other looters had moved away from Harald's corpse and were forming up in a circle around me. I was trembling with anger and exhaustion.

'Let me have the body,' I shouted. My voice was thin and wavering.

'Come and get it,' jeered one of the men.

I ran at him, using the pole as a lance, but he dodged aside. I pulled up and turned to see that his comrades had again taken up their positions around me and were laughing. I lunged again. The pole was heavy in my hands, and the long skirts of my monkish gown hampered me. I tripped.

'Over here, grandad,' taunted another voice, and I spun round to see someone dangling Harald's scarlet headband from the tip of his dagger. 'You'll need this,' he jeered.

The sweat was running down into my eyes so that I could scarcely see. I lumbered towards him and tried to snatch the headband, but it was whisked out of reach. I felt a thump in my ribs. One of my tormentors had struck me with the flat of his sword. I reeled away, trying to approach Harald's body. A foot reached out and I tripped headlong into the dust. The blood pounding in my ears, I picked myself up, and not knowing who or where I was striking, I swung Land Ravager in a circle, trying to keep my tormentors back. I heard their scornful laughter, then someone must have come up behind me and hit me, because I felt a terrible pain in my head as I slumped forward on my knees and then down on to my face.

Slowly everything began to go dark, and in the last fading moments something came into my mind which had been troubling me since the opening moments of the great battle. The hair rose on the back of my neck, and an icy cold shiver prickled my skin as the certainty came to me that the Old Ways were finally gone. As I slipped away into darkness, I recalled the prophesy of my own God, Odinn the All-knowing. He had foretold that Ragnarok, the last great battle, would be heralded by the sound of a harp played by Eggther, watchman of the giants, and that Gullinkambe the rooster, perched in Yggdrasil, the World Tree, would cry his final warning. Since the beginning of the world Gullinkambe had been waiting in the branches to announce the time when the forces of evil were unleashed and on the march. Together the two sounds, the harp and the rooster's crow, would herald the last great battle and the final destruction of the ancient ways.

SIXTEEN

TOSTIG RALLIED THE remnants of our army, so I was told later. One of our men picked up Land Ravager from where I lay on the earth, apparently lifeless, and brought the banner to Tostig, who was grimly fighting a rearguard action. He set up the flag as a mustering point, and those of our men who were still on their feet – less than a fifth of our original force – gathered there and formed a final shield wall. Seeing their plight, Harold Godwinsson offered them quarter. Defiantly, they refused. The English closed in and cut down all but a handful. Soon afterwards the Norwegian reinforcements from the fleet arrived, too few and too late. Most had made the same mistake of leaving behind their armour so that they could run all the faster from the ships. They appeared on the battlefield in small groups, disordered and out of breath. There was no doubting their courage, for they flung themselves on the English troops. The lightly equipped archers, first on the scene, did such damage that Godwinsson's troops quailed under the arrow storm. But when the archers had exhausted their stock of arrows, they lacked armoured infantry to protect them and were overwhelmed by the huscarls' counter-attack. The remaining stragglers of the relief force met a similar fate, finding themselves outnumbered by an enemy already flushed with triumph. By the end of that catastrophic day, the Norwegian force was virtually wiped out. The mounted huscarls harried the survivors back to the landing beach, where a handful saved themselves by swimming out to those ships which had been warped out into the river for safety. The remaining vessels were set ablaze by the victorious English.

I heard the details of the calamity in dribs and drabs, for I was on the point of death for many weeks and not expected to survive. A priest from York found me on the battlefield where he had gone the day after the great battle to pray over the dead. Scarcely breathing, I lay where I had fallen in the English battle line, and he presumed I had been with Godwinsson's men. I was brought back to York on a cart, along with the badly wounded, and nursed to health by the monks of the minster.

It took almost a full year for me to regain my strength because I had been badly hurt. There was a gaping gash on my skull – how I acquired it, I do not know – and it led my healers to suppose that my wits were addled by the blow. I had the good sense to encourage their error by pretending that I was not yet sound of mind and speaking little. Naturally I used the interval to watch and listen and acquire the information which allowed me to present myself as an itinerant priest swept up in Harold Godwinsson's lightning advance to the battlefield at a place called Stamford Bridge. This deception was made easier by my advanced years, for all the world knows that old people mend more slowly than the young, and later, when I made mistakes in my pretended guise, the errors were ascribed to an approaching dotage.

This prolonged convalescence gave me ample time to marvel at the gullibility of the monks of York. Not only did they think I was a devout and maundering colleague, but they readily swallowed the pap of misinformation fed to them in the official accounts of what had happened in the struggle for the throne of England. Frequently my tonsured companions would assert that all good Christians should give their unstinting support to the new king, William, because Christ had clearly shown himself to be on his side. Apparently William of Normandy – no one called

him William the Bastard now – had disposed of Harold Godwinsson on the battlefield further south, in Hastings, just as effectively
as Godwinsson had crushed Harald Sigurdsson nineteen days
earlier. The proof of their God's favourable intervention, according to the monks, was that William's invasion fleet was held back
on the north coast of Frankia by a headwind until 'by the grace
of God' the wind changed to the south and allowed his barges to
cross the sea unscathed to a landing unopposed by Godwinsson. I
knew, of course, that 'the grace of God' had nothing to do with
it. William the Bastard stayed on the Frankish coast until he knew
his stratagem had succeeded and Harold had marched away to
face the Norwegian army. In short, King William was not a
virtuous believer rewarded for his piety, but a sly double-dealer
who betrayed his ally.

But then, history – as is well known – is written by the
victors, if it is written at all. It was with that commonplace in
mind that I began to pen this account of my life which is now
nearly at an end, and I suspect that Odinn himself had long
prepared me for this task. It cannot have been entirely coincidental
that I met the imperial chronicler, Constantine Psellus, when I
was in the Varangian guard and observed his passion for telling
an unvarnished history of the rulers of Miklagard. And I must
admit that I enjoyed posing as a royal chronicler when I was on
my way across Normandy to Duke William's court, even though
that imposture was brief before I was exposed as a fraud. Now it
amuses me that my deception is reversed: I find myself a genuine
reporter of events, but one who writes in secret and cloaks his
identity behind a monk's humility.

A question which has been puzzling me as I write my chronicle
was answered as I composed these final pages. I used to wonder
how the ways of the White Christ, apparently so meek, came to
overwhelm the more robust tenets of my Elder Faith. Then, only
yesterday, I was present when one of the local monks – it was the
junior almoner – was recounting with breathless wonder how he
had been in London and witnessed the court ceremony when a

local magnate swore allegiance to the new sovereign, our pious and amulet-wearing William. The monk mimed the ceremony for our benefit: the solemn entrance of the nobleman, the king seated on the throne, the approach between ranks of courtiers, the bending of the knee, and the kissing of the regal hand. As the monk went down on his knees to illustrate the moment of homage, I noted the easy familiarity of his action. It was a gesture he repeated each day before the altar, and I recalled my lord Harald prostrate in submission on the marble floor before the throne of the Basileus, a ruler also declared to be a chosen instrument of that same God. Then I knew: the worship of the White Christ suits men who seek to dominate others. It is not the belief of the humble, but of despots and tyrants. When a man claims he is specially selected by the White Christ, then all those who follow that religion must treat him as if they are revering the God himself. That is why they go down in obedience before him. Often they even clasp their hands together as if in prayer.

This is a contradiction of all that the God is meant to stand for, yet I have witnessed how, among rulers of men, it is the truly ruthless and the ambitious who adopt the Christian faith, then use it to suppress the dignity of their fellows. Naturally this opinion would horrify the inoffensive monks around me, and some of them are genuine and selfless men. But they are blind to the fact that even here, within the minster, they bow the head in obedience to their superiors, whatever their quality. How different it was for those who followed the Elder Faith. As a sworn follower of Harald of Norway, as his king's man, I never had to bend the knee to him, either in an act of submission or to acknowledge his leadership. I only knew that he was more suited to rule than me, and that I must serve him as best I could. And when I was a priest of the Elder Faith among the Old Believers of Vaster Gotland, I would have been shocked if those who came to me to ask for guidance or to intervene with the Gods had believed that I was divinely appointed. I was judged only for my knowledge of the ancient lore.

So this is the ultimate power of the White Christ faith: it is a belief suited to despots who would curb men's independence.

I will never abandon my devotion to Odinn, though some might say he has abandoned me, just as he and the Gods have forsaken all those who followed the Elder Faith. Our world may have come to an end, but we never expected our Gods to be all-powerful and eternal. That sort of arrogance is reserved for the Christians. We knew from the very start that one day the old order would collapse, and after Ragnarok all would be swept away. Our Gods did not control the future. That was ordained by the Norns, and no one can alter the final outcome. While we are on this earth, each individual can only live his life to the best of his ability, strive to mould daily existence to best advantage, and never, like the unhappy Mac Bethad of the Scots, be duped by outward signs and appearance.

Still, it grieves me that the body of my king Harald was taken back to Norway and placed in a Christian church. He should have received a true funeral in the old style, been burned on a pyre or interred within a barrow grave. That is what I had in mind when I tried vainly to rescue his body from the battlefield. I know that it was an old man's folly, but at the time I was sure that the Valkyries had already carried away his soul to Valhol, or that Freyja's servants had selected him and he was now in her golden hall, Sessrumnir, as befits the warrior whom some are already calling the last of the Vikings.

I myself do not expect to go to Valhol nor to Freyja's hall. Those palaces are reserved for those who fell in battle, and — truth be told — I have never been a warrior, although I did my military training with the brotherhood of the Jomsvikings and have been present at the great battles: in Clontarf when the Irish High King fell, when the great Greek general Maniakes smashed the Arabs in Sicily, and of course at the bridge in Stamford. But I was never really a fighting man. When I took up arms, it was usually for self-defence.

The thought of Sessrumnir has reminded me yet again of the

twins, Freyvid and Freygerd. What has happened to them, I wonder? The last report I had was when their uncle Folkmar took them and fled for safety into the fastnesses of Sweden. It is too late for me to go to seek them, but in my bones I feel sure that they have survived. Once again I believe this is Odinn's wish. He taught that after Ragnarok, when all has been consumed by fire and destruction, there will be two survivors, twins who have sheltered beneath the roots of the World Tree and survived unscathed. From them will spring a new race of men who will populate the happier world that emerges from the ruins. With that knowledge I can console myself that my line may again bring the return of the Elder Ways.

So, in these closing days of my life, I am content to set down on paper my gratitude to Odinn for the guidance he gave me. Odinn Gangradr, the journey adviser, was always at my shoulder. He showed me many marvels: the glittering reflection of the great ice cliffs in the still waters of a Greenland fjord, the endless sweet-smelling pine forests of Vinland in the west, the Golden Dome of the great Saracen temple in the Holy Land, the slow curl of the early morning mist rising from the surface of the broad river which leads eastward from Gardariki, the land of forts. And, more important, Odinn also brought me to the company of women I loved, and who loved me – a young girl in Ireland, a maiden among the ski-runners of the north, and – in the end – to the embrace of Runa. How can the monks around me compare their lives to that?

I am still restless, even at my advanced age. When I was at my weakest and sat feebly in the herb garden next to the small infirmary, I would notice the high-flying birds passing overhead on their distant journeys, and wanted to rise and follow them. Now that my body is mended and I have reached the conclusion of my chronicle, I will add these final pages to the cache of writing that I have concealed within a secret hiding place in the thick stone wall of the scriptorium. When the opportunity presents itself, as it surely will if I keep my allegiance to Odinn, I will slip away from this minster and make a new life somewhere in the outside world.

Where will I go? I cannot be precise. That is not a vision that has been given me. All I know is that my fate was decided long ago, at the time of my birth, and by the Norns. They were kind to me. I have enjoyed my life, and even if I had been able to change its course, I would not have done so.

So I will leave this minster with a sense of happy expectation and my twins in mind. I will find a place where, in my final duty as a devotee of Odinn, I shall preach, and instruct my listeners that there will be a second coming of the Old Ways.

My lord abbot, If you will forgive this final notation, I must report that two years past our monastery received occasional reports of an unidentified preacher known locally as the 'the black priest'. This man established himself at a remote spot on the moors, and the common folk flocked there to listen and pay their devotions. It seems that he was greatly revered, though what he preached is unknown. Now he is seen no more, and it is presumed that he has departed this life. His parishioners, if they may be called that, come almost weekly to us to importune that we build and consecrate a chapel at the place of his hermitage. They say he was some sort of saint. I tremble at the possibility that with such an act we may be serving the Antichrist. But the people are most insistent, and I fear that if we spurn their request, they will be deeply vexed, to the detriment of our own foundation.

In this, as in all things, I seek your blessed guidance.

Aethelred
Sacristan and Librarian